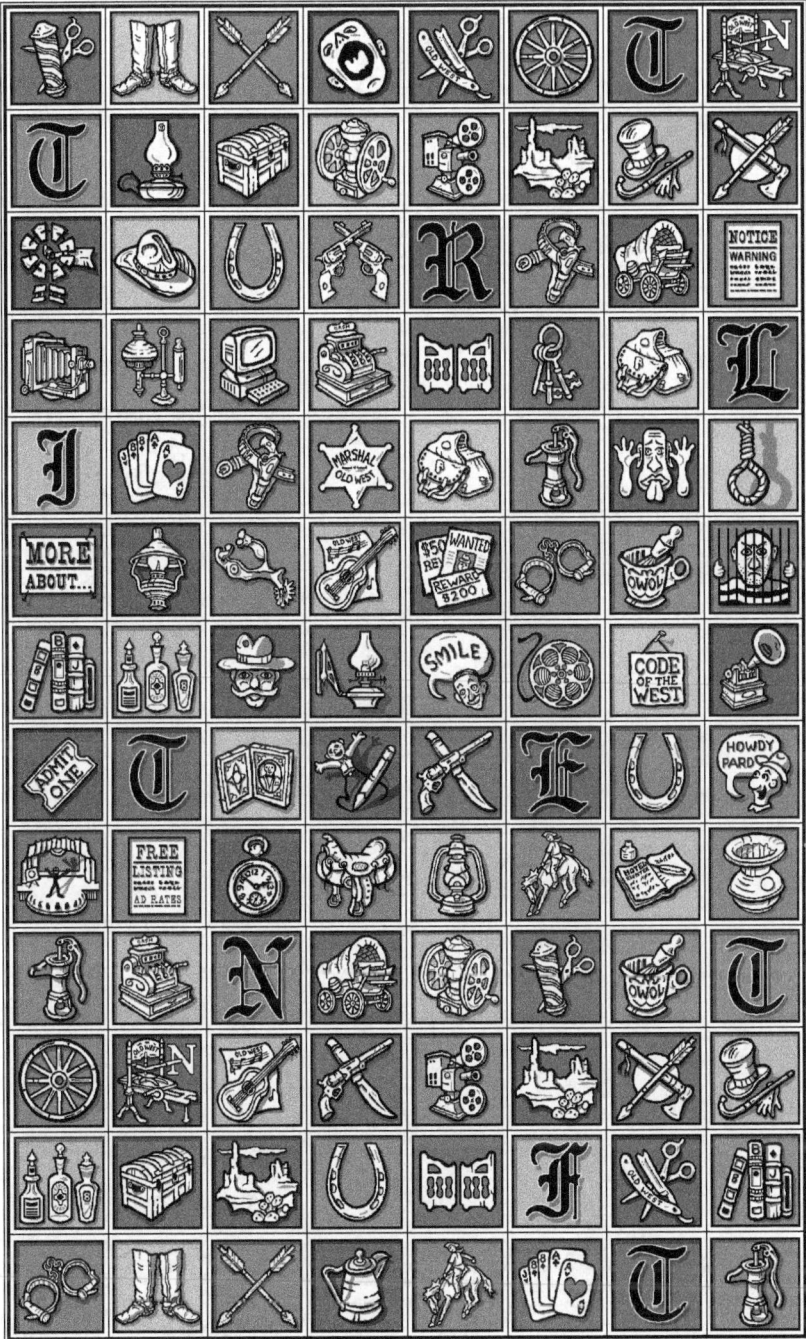

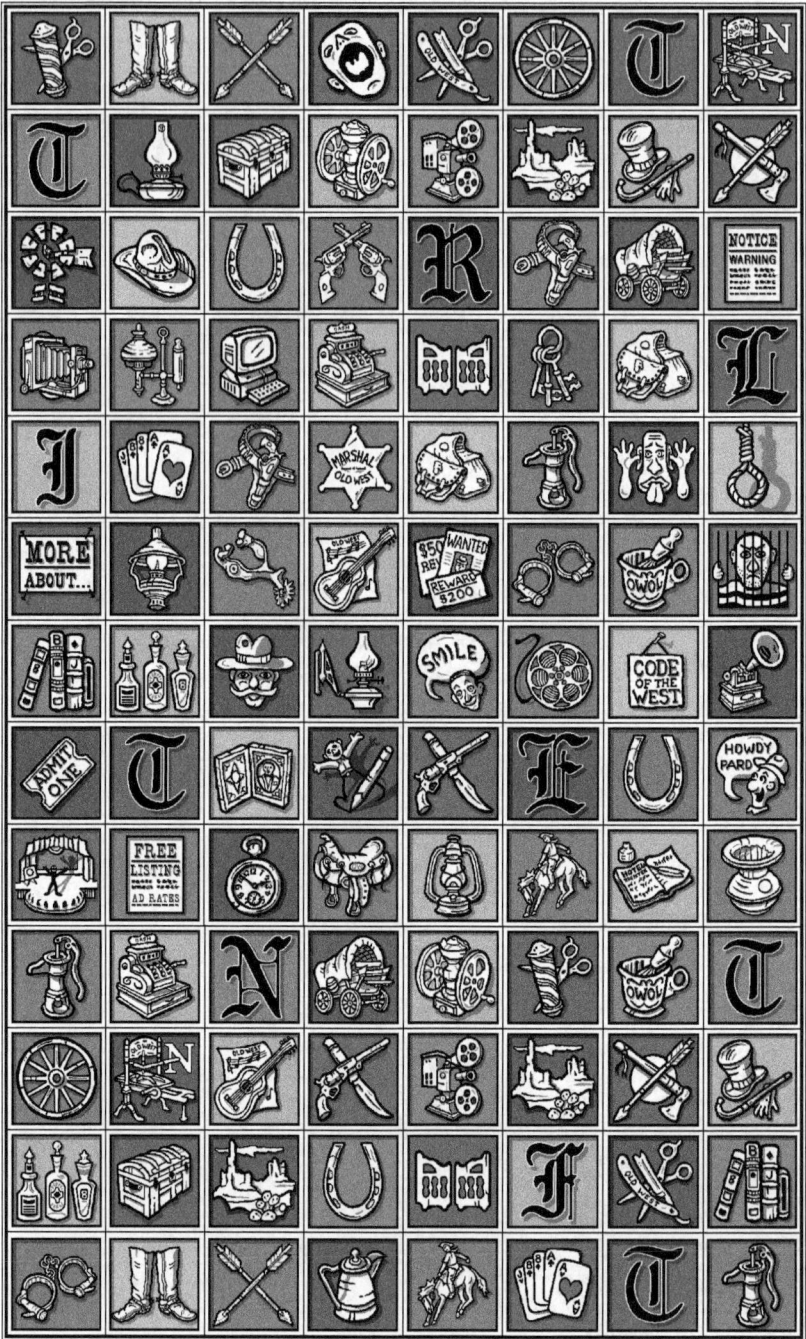

BARBED WIRE, WINDMILLS, & SIXGUNS

A Book of Trivia, Fact, and Folklore About Westerns & The American West

By

Donald K. Kirk

A CLASSIC BOOK OF LISTS
FOR THE OLD WEST FAN

WITHIN THESE PAGES YOU'LL FIND
EVERYTHING YOU NEED TO KNOW TO PASS
FOR A FAN OF THE WESTERN MOVIE GENRE.

BARBED WIRE, WINDMILLS, & SIXGUNS

A book of lists on subjects related to the Old West

All in one place.

"Everything you ever wanted to know about the Old West."

A fun read.

"I couldn't put it down once I had opened that first page."

TEST YOUR KNOWLEDGE
OF WESTERN LORE

Who shot Jesse James?
Where is Wyatt Earp buried?
What was John Wayne's last movie?
What were Black Jack Ketchum's last words before
he swung from the gallows?
Who first said, "When you call me that, smile?"
What was Roy Rogers' real name?
What year did Chief Crazy Horse defeat Custer at the
Battle of Little Big Horn?
How many westerns did John Wayne direct?
Who was "The Man With No Name?"
Why did the cowboy wear a bandanna?
Who died in the Gunfight at the O.K. Corral?
What three inventions aided in the settlement of the West?

A TRIVIA SOURCE BOOK
On The Western Motion Picture
And The American West Of The Nineteenth Century.

Sentinel of the Plains, 1906, oil on canvas by William Herbert Dunton (1878-1936) DECA

Therefore Trampas spoke, "You bet, you son-of-a-." The Virginian's pistol came out, and his hand lay on the table, holding it un-aimed. And with a voice as gentle as ever, the voice that sounded almost like a caress, but drawling a very little more than usual, so that there was almost a space between each word, he issued his orders to the man Trampas: "When you call me that, smile."

—Owen Wister, The Virginian, 1902

BARBED WIRE, WINDMILLS, & SIXGUNS

A Book of Trivia, Fact, and Folklore About Westerns & The American West

By

Donald K. Kirk

INCLUDES MANY NEVER-BEFORE-PUBLISHED
PHOTOS AND ILLUSTRATIONS BY THE AUTHOR

BARBED WIRE, WINDMILLS, & SIXGUNS
A Book of Trivia, Fact, and Folklore
About Westerns & The American West
Copyright © Donald K. Kirk 1997, 2007, 2010

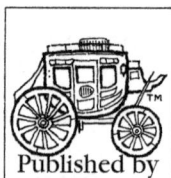

Published by

SWEETWATER STAGELINES™
an imprint of
THE OLD WEST COMPANY™
5118 Village Trail Drive, San Antonio, Texas 78218
sweetwaterstagelines.com   lulu.com/spotlight/sweetwater
kirkwest@sbcglobal.net

TRADEPAPER EDITION:
ISBN-13: 978-0-9801743-5-9
TRADECLOTH EDITION:
ISBN-13: 978-0-9654341-1-9
Library of Congress Control Number: 2010939864

All photos and illustrations by the author except where noted. The articles "Jinglebobs and Justins," The Cowboys of the Old West," "Custer's Last Stand," and "Gunfight at the O.K. Corral" were previously published in *Canyon Lake Week by* Morton Falls Publishing. The Ballads, "The Men of the Alamo," "Ridin' West on the Pacific Express," "Me and Ol' Sal," and "A Pine Box Will Do" were published in 2001 as *Western Ballads and Poetry by Don Kirk*.

This work not only includes photos and illustrations by the author, but also public domain photos from the Library of Congress, Wikimedia Commons, various motion picture companies, and photos by Michael Jay Smith, Jo M. Hames, Cris Ford, and Glynda Smith.

Book layout and design by Don Kirk
Additional editing by Michael Jay Smith and Art Burnett.
Flyleaf design by the author. Icons were from *oldwest.com* which was originally published on the Internet in 1993, also created by the author.

Printed and bound in The United States of America

This book is dedicated
to Berkley and Jeri Garrett
and all those western fans
who love—and live—the Old West.

Table Of
CONTENTS

*"For God's sake Earp, don't go
down there; these men are armed."*
—Sheriff John Behan, October 26, 1881

Freight Wagons in Death Valley, California (dk) — Room for a lot of collected things.

A Collection

INTRODUCTION

*"Americans know neither their country nor themselves
unless they know the story of the old Wild West."*
—Dee Brown

I love to collect things, especially those related to the American West: movie posters, antiques, handbills, books, music, films, costumes, etc. I have traveled the West taking photographs of Victorian architecture, western scenery, ghost towns, mines, homesteads, wagons, windmills, forts... But this book really began with an 1880's gunfight group in the mid-seventies called the "Salado Creek Gang" when I needed to know the language, historic names, and events of the Old West for writing humorous plays we could perform on the dusty streets of an Old West amusement attraction. Then in 1993, my scribbled notes on scraps of paper were turned into useful "content" for an Old West web site, and as more trivia piled up in cardboard boxes, I used it for writing a book on staging gunfights and a proposal for an Old West resort town. But the information was scattered and hard to refer to—it was time to turn it into a book. I added photos and sketches from my travels, and wa-lah, a book of lists for western movie buffs, fans, writers, re-enactors, and those who want to understand the link between the Hollywood Western and the American West, not only the folklore, but the real people, places, and things that have created the legend that has become a fabric of the American experience. The West, lasting less than 100 years, is part of our very being; we carry with it the values we cherish—like freedom, independence, self-worth, and self-reliance. Without that frontier experience, we would not be the nation we are today. My apologies: I have tried to include the humorous footnotes of history in preference to serious points of fact. If I've stepped on any toes, one's sensitivities, or riled the staunch historians, well, so be it. I leave it to historians to ferret out the truth, or re-write history as they see fit, but facts about the American West of the nineteenth century have become so intertwined with folklore that the truth may never be known, in part, because few desire it so. Remember the quote from *The Man Who Shot Liberty Valance:* "When legend becomes fact, print the legend."

Enjoy,   Don Kirk, June 1997.

Barbed Wire, Windmills and Sixguns
3 INVENTIONS THAT WON THE WEST

Would the Old West have existed or evolved as we know it without the invention of the REVOLVER (a rapid firing weapon that could be worn on the waistbelt) or the introduction of the WINDMILL to the plains (finding water where there was none) or BARBED WIRE that eventually fenced in the West and ended the frontier? These three inventions probably did more to settle the West than any other creation of man. They caused dramatic and even traumatic results that led to a revolution in independence and democracy.

1. The Revolver. The Colt "Peacemaker"—the gun that won the West—shaped the behavior of men. It led to violence and justice . . . and peace. Many manufacturers developed revolvers including *Smith and Wesson, Starr,* and *Remington,* but it was the Colt's—with their extensive national advertising—that catapulted into the minds and hearts of the westerner. The Colt Model 1873 "Peacemaker" was the first lightweight, well balanced revolver that allowed fast drawing and reliability, creating legendary stories about pistols... and men.

2. The Windmill. The Great American Desert, now known as the Great Plains—now with millions of acres of fertile farm land—would never have developed if there had not been a means of getting at the water hidden below ground. Windmills provided the power to bring the vital water to the surface. Many windmills were prefabricated kits shipped by rail to the well sites where they were then erected. This strange, squeaking contraption allowed the settlers to conquer and possess the land.

3. Barbed Wire. Timbers or stones were used to build fences in the East, but in the plains a substitute for wood had to be found to keep livestock from running off. Hundreds of patents and thousands of miles of wire—some of very strange designs—began to fence in the West starting in the mid 1860's. In 1874 a farmer named Joseph F. Glidden devised an efficient method of twisting two pieces of wire together to hold pointed barbs and "bobwar" quickly closed off the public lands of the West, drastically changing the economics and social structure of the westerner. Free-ranging cattle herds—and men—shared the land originally, but this came to an end along with the wild frontier we've come to know as the "Old West." By 1890, the open range was nearly all fenced in. The "thorny fence" kept the cows in, but it led to other less popular uses: the claiming of public land, the blocking of important access trails, and the fencing off of scarce water.

So, in the end, the West was really about conflict. Eventually though, fenced land helped ranchers control the breeding of their stock and the farmers also prospered, encouraging settlement, town after town. The railroad crisscrossed the West hauling cows and crops to eastern markets while carrying immigrants by the thousands to the new American West. The rest, they say is history.

Remains of the Frontier West settled by farming and ranching, Westcliff, Colorado (dk)

Kris Ford as cowboy Hoot "Britches" Washington, photo and costume by the author

Jinglebobs and Justins
COWBOYS AND THEIR COWPONIES

*"[The cowboy is] just a plain, everyday, bow-legged
human, carefree and courageous, fun-loving and
loyal, uncomplaining and doing his best to live
up to a tradition of which he is proud."*
—Ramon F. Adams, *Western Words*, 1944

The cowboy is legendary. He has become a symbol of the American West. He stood for the rugged individualist who took on a job with vigor and fortitude, fighting the harsh elements of an untamed frontier. His goal was simple: to raise cattle and drive them to market. He never complained—well, if he did, he did it without any intent of ever quitting, for that was not in his code of behavior. He worked for a hot meal at the end of the day and true friendship born by men who fought the hardships of the West together.

Where the name "cowboy" came from is unknown. Literature of the period usually hyphenated the word "cow-boy." But it is pretty clear to historians that it wasn't a word of affection. In the United States, the word has been traced to loyalist guerrillas in New York who stole cattle from the rebels. That was way back in the 1700's! In the early days of the cattle drives up from Texas, the word "cow-boy" applied to the young "green-behind-the-ears" kids who signed onto drives. And in the 1880's, the Clanton-McLowry faction of "O.K. Corral" fame were called "The Cowboys," referring to their rustling activities and general lawlessness. This was closer to the real meaning of the word during the heyday of the great cattle drives. Cow-boys were rough, uncouth, and lawless men, not the current romanticized figure of a brave and daring horseman with a high moral fiber. It was the pulp fiction written at the turn of the century that created the new cowboy myth of the honorable, free-spirited and independent cow wrangler, a son any mother would be proud of.

The Civil War halted cattle-raising in Texas, leaving the cows of the West to run free for over five years (with a 60% increase in numbers every year), with no "boys" to round them up. It was a visionary man named Joseph G. McCoy who established Abilene as the first railhead on the Union Pacific by building stock pens and railroad siding for cattle cars. After the war, men needed jobs and the East needed beef. The result was the great cattle drives north to the new cow towns that sprung up along the westward bound railroad. Towns like Abilene, Wichita, and Dodge City.

A drover watching over his heard, sketch by the author

THE COWBOY CODE

- IF A COWBOY PASSES SOMEONE ON THE DUSTY TRAIL, HE ALWAYS GIVES A "HOWDY."

- A COWBOY NEVER ASKS A MAN HIS FULL NAME IF IT'S NOT OFFERED. IT'S WHATEVER HE CHOOSES TO CALL HIMSELF, AND NOTHING MORE.

- A COWBOY NEVER MEDDLES IN ANOTHER'S AFFAIRS.

- A COWBOY NEVER WEARS ANOTHER MAN'S HAT.

- A COWBOY NEVER COMPLAINS; THAT'S WHAT QUITTERS DO, AND COWBOYS HATE QUITTERS.

- A COWBOY NEVER WAKES ANOTHER MAN BY SHAKING OR TOUCHING HIM. THE SLEEPING MAN MIGHT WAKE UP SUDDENLY AND SHOOT THE COWBOY.

- A COWBOY NEVER MISTREATS HIS HORSE. HE KNOWS HIS SURVIVAL DEPENDS ON IT. HE ALWAYS TENDS TO HIS HORSE'S NEEDS BEFORE HIS OWN.

- A COWBOY NEVER BOTHERS ANOTHER MAN'S HORSE. IT'S ALL RIGHT TO LIVE ON A HORSE, IF IT'S YOUR OWN HORSE!

- A COWBOY MAY CUSS ALL HE WANTS, BUT ONLY AROUND MEN, HORSES, AND COWS.

- A COWBOY NEVER WAVES AT A MAN ON A HORSE. THIS COULD SPOOK THE HORSE. A NOD IS THE PROPER GREETING.

- IF A COWBOY PASSES SOMEONE ON THE TRAIL, HE NEVER LOOKS BACK OVER HIS SHOULDER AT HIM. IT IMPLIES HE DOESN'T TRUST THE STRANGER.

- A COWBOY WILL ALWAYS HELP SOMEONE IN NEED, EVEN IF HE'S A STRANGER OR AN ENEMY.

- A COWBOY NEVER LETS A STRANGER LEAVE HIS CAMP COLD OR HUNGRY.

Humorous Similitude of Old West Broadside created by the author based on an unwritten value system in the new West

What'd he say?
38 COWBOY WORDS

"As long as there's one cowboy takin'
care o' one cow [ranching] ain't dead."
—Lee Marvin, *Monty Walsh*, 1970.

The era of the cattle drive lasted less than 30 years, but from it came the romance of the cowboy and his down to earth, no-nonsense way of expressing himself. The colorful language of the cowboy was descriptive, imaginative, and witty because it was practical and uncluttered by proper grammar. In other words, he simply said what he meant. *Ramon F. Adams, J. Frank Dobie, Peter Watts* and others have published works cataloging the language of the westerner. Here are just a few of the wonderfully imaginative words created by the cowboy:

1. Airtights. Such a wonderful and appropriate name: the cowboy's term for canned goods. There were few choices in the late nineteenth century, but they included canned peaches, tomatoes, beef, corn, and milk.

2. All horns and rattlers. A cowboy's reference to a man who has lost his temper.

3. Bushwhack. To attack suddenly and without warning, to ambush a man. Originally, the perpetrator would hide behind a bush and surprise the victim, hitting him over the head.

4. Button. A cowboy's name for a young boy. Charlton Heston used the word in *Will Penny* (1968).

5. Cahoots. When a westerner went into partnership with another, he "throwed in" with him or "went into cahoots."

6. Calico. A cowboy's name for a woman, because her dress was usually made of *calico*, a coarse cotton material originally imported from Calicut, India.

7. Cash in. To die, "kick the bucket," or in the game of poker, to hand in your chips in exchange for cash.

8. Caught short. Not prepared to deal with a situation that arises, for example, if one needs a gun and doesn't have one.

9. Cocklebur outfit. A small "one horse" outfit or shabby, run-down outfit.

10. Clouding the trail. Covering up or hindering someone from accomplishing a task; to deceive, "throw dust."

11. Coffin. A cowboy's term for a trunk.

12. Combed his hair. Hit someone over the head with a pistol.

13. Crack-a-Loo. A game that is played in a room where a coin is flipped to the ceiling and then falls to the floor. The person whose coin comes to rest on or nearest a predetermined crack in the floor wins the game.

14. Dofunnies. The useless little trinkets and baubles a cowboy carries with him.

15. Fish. A yellow oilskin slicker for wearing when it rains. It was kept rolled behind the cantle of the saddle until needed. It got its name from the trademark stamped on the coat: a fish.

16. Following the tongue. The tongue of a wagon is set to point to the North Star at night so the direction of travel can be determined the next day before sunrise. James Stewart does this in *Bend of the River* (1952).

17. Fumadiddle. Fancy dress. "Dressed to the nines."

18. Gully-washer. "A frog strangler," a very hard rain.

19. Hair in the butter. A cowboy's expression for a delicate situation.

Cowmen herding steers, sketch by author

20. Hell-bent-for-leather. To go in great haste, to move like a "bat outta hell."

21. Homeless as a poker chip. Said of a person who never stays in one place very long; a restless person.

22. Jinglebobs. Those little pear-shaped pendants hanging from the *rowels* of a spur. They were not just for decoration, but for the "music" they made. The term *jinglebobs* had already been used to describe a method of tagging a cow by slicing its ear so it hung downward.

23. Jingle your spurs. A cowboy's command to get with it; hurry up.

24. Justins. A good cowboy boot. Representing quality. *Joe Justin* made his first boots in 1879 at *Old Spanish Fort* in Texas. The factory is now in Fort Worth.

25. Ketch rope. The cowboy's name for his lariat to distinguish it from other ropes. A lariat was a rope made with a running noose for catching animals.

26. Kit and caboodle. A cowboy's word for the "the whole ball of wax," the entire sum, the whole lot.

27. Leavin' Cheyenne. Means going away. The expression came from the popular contemporary ballad: "Goodbye, Old Paint." (Lyrics on page 40.)

28. Levi's. A cowboy's trousers. The originals were first introduced in 1850 by *Levi Strauss* of San Francisco. He used copper rivets to reinforce the seams and pockets of a canvas ducking cloth that made the pants strong and rugged. Just what the California '49ers needed to pan for gold in those wet, rocky mountain streams. The cowboy quickly picked up on these rugged new trousers.

29. Makin's. The materials needed for making a cigarette: tobacco and papers.

30. Playin' with a string of spools. A reference to someone who is crazy or young and foolish.

31. Raised on sour milk. A reference to a person who is cranky or disagreeable.

32. Riding drag. The worst place to be when herding cattle—the junior drovers were left with the job of coming up the rear of the herd where they had to bring up stray and lagging animals, all the while swallowing the enormous cloud of dust created by thousands of heavy, four-footed creatures. The *point riders* rode in front of the herd, controlling its direction. The *swing riders* rode behind the point riders and the *flank riders* rode behind the swing riders.

33. Shadow Rider. Said of a cowboy who admired himself so much he'd ride along gazing at his own shadow.

34. Stetson. A brand name that became a popular term for a high-crowned, broad-brimmed cowboy hat of good quality. The *Stetson* was invented in 1865 by *John Batterson Stetson* of Philadelphia, Pennsylvania. During an earlier trip west, he had observed that no one was making a hat designed specifically for the needs of the cowboy. The wool hats the cowboys were using would quickly lose their shape in the rain. Stetson's improvement was the "Boss of the Plains," a durable hat with a high crown that could be easily shaped by hand so that a cowman could personalize his head gear. The name "10-gallon hat" didn't mean the hat could hold ten gallons of water; the phrase came from the numerous braids worn around the base of the crown by the early cowboys (*galón* is the Spanish word for "braid").

35. Some deck is shy a Joker. A cowboy, on seeing an outlandishly dressed person on the range, often used this explanation.

36. Take a look-see. To go and investigate something, to check it out.

37. Tenderfoot. Originally a cow from the East, or the great plains, who's tender feet were unaccustomed to walking long distances on the hard and rocky ground of the West. Later, ranch hands used the term to refer to a newcomer from the East who wanted to become a cowboy. He might also be called a *greenhorn* or *pilgrim*.

38. Waddy. A cowboy who is temporarily hired by an outfit during busy times. The name derives from the wadding used to "fill in" a gun barrel when loading it with ball and gunpowder.

Stock corrals , Colorado (dk)

An Essential Accessory

THE COWBOY BANDANNA

The cowboy's brightly-colored neckerchief or "wipe"—often folded diagonally into a triangle and tied at the front or back—wasn't just for looks, it had many practical uses as well. It was usually made of cotton, but silk was preferred because it was cooler in summer and warmer in winter.

- It protected his bare neck from the sun.

- It was worn over the mouth and nose to filter out a dusty trail when riding drag.

- He used it to tie the hat brim down around his ears during cold weather, or to filter out and warm a cold winter wind.

- The COWBOY used it to wipe the sweat from his brow.

- He used it to filter out muddy creek water for drinking.

- To keep his head cool, he would wet it down and fold it into his hat band.

- It could be used as a snakebite tourniquet, bandage, or sling for a broken arm.

- The COWBOY used it as a washcloth to clean up at the watering hole.

- It could be used to hold a hot branding iron or skillet.

- The BANDANNA could be used as a trail marker or signal flag.

- In a pinch, it could be used to hog-tie a troublesome calf.

- He could use it as a dish rag to wash his fry pan or coffee cup.

- He could use it to gag a noisy varmint or tie his hands.

- The COWBOY could use the bandanna as a bag to carry oats to his horse or cowchips to his campfire. He could use it to gather wild fruit or carry his lunch.

- He could use it to blindfold a wild bronco to calm him down before climbing on to break him.

- He could use it as a tablecloth or napkin.

- The BANDANNA could be used to tie down a hat in a brisk wind.

- A COWBOY could use it to disguise his identity if he wanted to rob a bank or stagecoach.

- And after a COWBOY'S death, his bandanna could be used to cover his face to keep the dirt off when he was buried.

The NECKERCHIEF was also used by railroad engineers to keep sparks, cinders, and soot from falling down their shirts. And the Gold Rush "forty-niners" would tie a bandanna around their arm when dancing the woman's part in an all-male Saturday night dance. †

Humorous Similitude of Old West Broadside created by the author

The Spanish Influence
ON THE AMERICAN COWBOY

*"That's what a wrangler is: a nobody on a horse—with
bad teeth, broken bones, a double hernia, and lice."*
—Jocasta Constantine,Tribute to a Badman, 1956.

The cowboy's language was a hybrid of many languages: European, Indian, and Spanish all rolled into one. The Anglo American ranchers worked side-by-side with the Mexicans in the Southwest and picked up what was to become the "technical language" of the cattle industry. Spanish words became corrupted because they were picked up by ear and repeated verbally, and new words were created. For example the Spanish *juzgado* became "hoosgow," *la reata* became "lariat." The first cowboys in the West were Mexican *vaqueros* who herded the hardy longhorn cattle that had descended from animals originally brought to America from Spain in the 16th century.

1. **Adiós.** Literally meaning "to God." Used in the Southwest as a "goodbye"—short for *Vaya con dios* meaning "Go with God."

2. **Amigó.** Spanish for friend.

3. **Arroyo.** A Spanish word for a small watercourse with steep sides that is usually dry as a bone except during *gully washers* (heavy rains).

4. **Bandido.** A bandit of Mexican origin.

5. **Calaboose.** From the Spanish *calabozo* meaning "to incarcerate," hence a jail.

6. **Cantina.** In Spain it meant "wine cellar," but evolved to mean "tavern" or "saloon" in America.

7. **Chaparajos.** Anglicized to *chaps* (prounounced "shaps") they were leather pants without a seat worn over ordinary trousers for protection from thorny brush, cacti and the cold.

8. **Chaparral.** A Spanish word for any place with a dense growth

of thorny bushes and scrub oak; a thicket. Because it is so common in Texas and New Mexico, chaps were probably invented there to navigate, without injury, through this dense tangle of briar. The *High Chaparral* ranch on the western TV series was named for the landscape on which it stood.

9. Comanchero. A Mexican who traded with the Comanche Indians and the whites, sometimes acting as a go between in releasing white captives.

10. Cimarron. From the Spanish word *cimarrón* meaning "wild, unruly, a solitary creature." In the 1840's in the English language, the word referred to big horn sheep which met that description. Cowboys used the word to refer to an abandoned animal that runs alone and has little to do with the rest of its kind. When referring to a man, a *cimarron* is a person who flees from civilization and becomes a fugitive or a wild person.

11. Compadre. From the Spanish word *compañero* meaning a close friend.

12. Frijoles. Kidney beans or any beans cultivated for food in Mexico and other South-American countries.

13. Gringo. A derogatory Mexican word for Yankees. The word comes from the Spanish word *griego* meaning Greek or foreigner.

14. Hacienda. Spanish literally translated as "landed estate." It is the homestead of a rancher who raises horses and cattle.

A Match Game
MEXICAN WORDS

Match the Spanish or Mexican word used commonly in the Old West with its English translation.

1.	Compadre	a.	dried Mexican beans
2.	Vamoose	b.	tomorrow
3.	Frijoles	c.	to clear out
4.	Dinero	d.	deep arroyo
5.	Mañana	e.	partner
6.	Hondo	f.	money
7.	Quien Sabe?	g.	Who knows?

1-e, 2-c, 3-a, 4-f, 5-b, 6-d, 7-g.

COWPOKES AND COWGIRLS

The word COWPOKE originated from the use by range hands of a long wooden pole to force cattle into railroad stockcars at the railhead. The term COWGIRL was coined by President Theodore Roosevelt in 1900 when he fondly referred to a young champion roper and rider named *Lucille Mulhall.*

15. Hoosegow. From *Juzgado* meaning "tribunal" or "Court of Justice." The American cowboy corrupted it to *hoosegow,* meaning a "jail."

16. Malpais. From the Spanish work *mal* meaning "bad" and *pais* meaning "country." It is worthless land, rugged, usually volcanic. Clint Eastwood named his movie production company *Malpais.* An example is the *Valley of Fires* lava beds at Carrizozo, New Mexico.

17. Mustang. A wild horse, from the Spanish word *mesteño* meaning "strays from the mesta." A *mesta* was a group of cattle and horse raisers, thus the early mustangs were horses that escaped from the *mestas* and ran wild.

18. Poncho. A wool blanket with a hole cut in the middle so it can be pulled over the head and worn for protection against the weather.

19. Pronto. Spanish word meaning at once, quickly, immediately.

20. Pueblo. A Mexican town or Indian village built of adobe or stone.

21. Ranchero. A rancher.

22. La Reata. Spanish for "rope to tie horses in a single file." It was corrupted into *lariat*, the rope thrown around the head or legs of a cow to catch him. Cowboys referred to it as the *ketch rope* to distinguish it from other kinds of rope. It was usually made of braided leather, horse hair, or rawhide. A grass rope had a much shorter life, but could take more strain without snapping.

23. Remuda. Extra mounts; a string of saddle horses from which the cowboys selected the best for the type of work to be done that day. From Spanish meaning "replacement." These horses are always *geldings.* Mares don't make good saddle horses and *stallions* are always rowdy and prone to fighting. There were about ten horses assigned to each cowman in the outfit.

24. Serape. A woolen blanket

or shawl, often brightly colored, worn as an outter garment in Spanish-American countries.

25. Sombrero. From the Spanish word *sombra* meaning "shade," thus a wide-brimmed hat worn in Spain and Latin America.

26. Texas Longhorn. A lean and self-sufficient cow originating from Spain—and brought up from Mexico—with very long horns (around eight feet) and found in a variety of colors. Long-horned cattle also came from England and eventually mingled with *Texas Longhorns* in Montana.

27. Tortilla. A large, round, thin cake prepared from a paste made of corn or flour and baked on a hot iron plate or stone slab. Used as a substitute for bread in Mexico.

28. Vaquero. From *vaca*, meaning "cow." A cowboy, a herder of cattle. Vaquero may have evolved to the word *Buckaroo.*

29. Wrangler. An American corruption of the Spanish *caverango.* The cowboy who's job it was to keep the horses together and ready for the cowmen. It was a beginner's job. Each ranchhand had his own string of horses: ones of different dispositions and training for different tasks like cutting, roping, circling, and night riding. See *Remuda.*

CHAPARAJOS

Chaps, pronounced "shaps," evolved from apron-like leather called *armas* that were fastened over the front of the saddle by early vaqueros and then lapped over their legs *after* mounting the horse. Today chaps come in three basic styles: The earliest kind was much like a pair of jeans without a seat; they looked like two leather stovepipes and were appropriately called *shotguns.* A cowboy had to remove his spurs and boots to put them on and take them off. To solve this problem, *batwing* chaps were developed around 1900. They were made of two wide leather flaps that could be quickly tied at the back of each leg. On the northern plains, the cowboys added much-needed warmth to their chaps by using goatskin or sheepskin with the fur retained and worn on the outside. They came to be called *woolies.* They were, of course, unusable in the brushy country of the southwest. Cowboys of the southwest usually referred to their chaps as *leggins.*

A COWBOY'S BOOTS

Boots were the most expensive part of a cowboy's *rigging* and they had to be *custom-mades* (hand-made to order) costing as much as $15. A cowboy originally wore high "stovepipe" (up to the knee) boots originally made for the cavalry to protect his legs from cacti, brush, and deep mud. Over time, the heels became higher to keep a cowboy's feet from slipping through the stirrups. Without the heels and thrown from his horse, he would be dragged, unable to eradicate himself from this dire situation. The cowboy boot gradually developed a pointed toe after the Civil War so that it would slip quicker and easier into the stirrup. The tops of boots were made of soft, lightweight, top quality leather and they were made loose to allow the air to circulate. And the soles were made thin so the cowboy would have the "feel of the stirrup." To be sure, cowboy boots weren't made for walking. The fancy tooling on the tops, so common today, did not appear until the mid-1880's. And it wasn't until the twentieth century that boots were cut shorter to half-thigh length as they are today. When this shortened design first came out, the cowboys called them *pee wees*.

A Cowboy Ballad
GIT ALONG LITTLE DOGIES

A cowboy herding cattle north to a railhead couldn't afford to have his cows spooked during the night—which was sure to cause a stampede—so he would sing to them in soothing tones to keep them calm. This old Texas cattle driving song was originally adapted from an Irish lullaby called "The Boy Who Was Taken." The cowboys were always adding their own verses to this ballad, so here is just a sampling. (A *dogie*, pronounced "doughgie," is an orphaned calf who is hungry; originally called *doughguts* because its belly was swollen from eating grass before digesting it).

1. As I was a-walkin' one morning for pleasure,
    I spied a cowpuncher a-ridin' along.
    His hat was throwed back and his spurs were a-jinglin'
    As he approached me a-singing this song:

2. **Whoopee ti yi yo, git along little dogies**
    It's your misfortune and none of my own.
    Whoopee ti yi yo, git along little dogies,
    For you know Wyoming will be your new home.

3. In the springtime we round up the dogies,
    Mark 'em and brand 'em, and bob off their tails;
    We round up the horses, load up the chuckwagon,
    And throw the little dogies out on the trail.

4. In the evening we bring in the dogies,
    As they are grazing from herd all around.
    You have no idea the trouble they give us
    As we are holding them on the bedground.

5. A whooping and yelling and driving them dogies,
    And wishing they would keep a moving along.
    If you think a-riding this range is a pleasure,
    Well that's where you've got it most awfully wrong.

Never Wear Another Man's Hat
A COWBOY'S HEADCOVER

It was the first thing he put on in the morning and the last thing he took off at night before going to bed. He had to have a good quality hat and was willing to pay the high price of a "John B." (a Stetson). It was worth the price in the long run. The hat had to be able to take a beating from weather and abuse. And it had uses other than just protecting the head from the sun:

1. THE WIDE BRIM SHADED THE COWBOY'S EYES FROM THE GLARE OF THE SUN, AND THE HIGH CROWN PROVIDED AN AIR SPACE TO KEEP THE HEAD COOL.

2. THE COWBOY COULD USE HIS HAT AS A SUBSTITUTE FOR A BUCKET TO WATER HIS HORSE OR PUT OUT A CAMPFIRE.

3. THE WIDE-BRIMMED HAT WORKED LIKE AN UMBRELLA WHEN IT RAINED, KEEPING WATER FROM GETTING DOWN IN THE COLLAR.

4. THE COWBOY COULD TIE THE BRIM DOWN AROUND THE EARS IN COLD WEATHER TO AVOID FROSTBITE.

5. THE HAT COULD BE USED TO FAN THE CAMPFIRE TO STIR THE EMBERS (though he risked burning his hat).

6. THE HAT COULD BE USED TO SIGNAL ANOTHER COWBOY, TO GET THE ATTENTION OF A LITTLE "DOGIE," OR TO WAVE ASIDE A CHARGING STEER.

7. THE HAT WOULD PROTECT THE COWBOY FROM LOW-HANGING BRANCHES THAT COULD SCRATCH HIS FACE.

8. AND THE COWBOY COULD USE HIS HAT AS A PILLOW WHEN SLEEPING ON THE GROUND, OR TO COVER HIS FACE TO PROTECT IT FROM FALLING LIMBS.

A COWBOY'S LARIAT

A cowboy and his horse can't get the job of roundin' up them "dogies" without a device to lasso them in for branding. *Vaqueros*—the first cowboys—made their *reatas* out of soft braided calf-leather to a length of about sixty feet. When the Anglo cowboy came on the scene, he wanted a cheaper, more rugged lariat that didn't snap so easily, so he twisted his rope out of tough bear grass. Other materials had been tried: cotton, manila hemp, maguey and even hair—but he found it could only be handled if it was shorter, around forty feet in length.

Throwing a loop. A tiny loop, called a *honda,* is tied or braided at one end of the rope. The other end of the rope is brought through the *honda* and pulled through until there's enough left to form a loop about four feet in diameter. The cowboy then takes his throwing hand and grasps the loop with an overlap of rope (about a quarter turn). The rest of the rope is coiled in his other hand which also holds the horse's reins. Using his thumb and index finger, the cowboy can feed rope as needed and use the last two fingers to hold the reins and steer the horse.

Come and Get It!
THE CHUCKWAGON

*"The Arbunkles' on the fire, boys. Throw your bedroll into
the wagon and hunker down to a fine mess a vittles.
We got sourdough biscuits, flapjacks and chuckwagon
chicken. Then boys, get out there and muster up a appetite
'cause we're gonna have son-of-a-bitch stew, corn dodges,
and a mess a frijoles for dinner."*
—the author, masquerading as a chuckwagon cook.

The chuckwagon was actually a plain old farm wagon with a large wooden box with shelves and drawers, secured on the tailgate of the wagon. The door to the box was hinged at the bottom allowing the door to become a work table. It is said that *Charles Goodnight* (who has a trail named after him) first came up with the idea in the 1860's by modifying an old army wagon (which had iron axles and larger wheels making it able to carry heavier loads). Before the chuckwagon, range riders carried their own grub. Companies such as *Studebaker* began making heavy duty wagons based on Goodnight's concept that could carry as much as two tons of goods; enough cooking equipment and provisions for "16 to 20 men for five or six weeks."

The chuckwagon was the central focus of activities for the range hand—the social center and meeting place for riders. The cowboys kept their bedrolls there. They could get first-aid, a fresh horse, dry clothes, and most importantly: companionship. Every evening they would sing songs and tell stories around a warm campfire. The chuckwagon was the cowboy's home away from the ranchhouse and it represented the "brand" they worked for. They were loyal to that brand. They were a family.

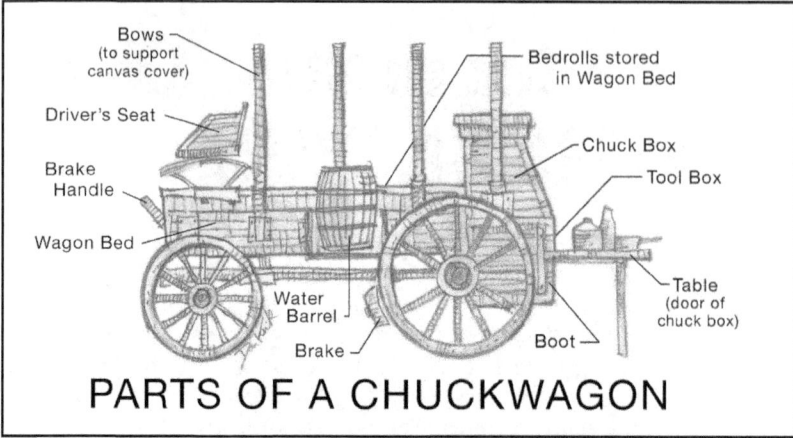

Bows (to support canvas cover)

Driver's Seat

Brake Handle

Wagon Bed

Bedrolls stored in Wagon Bed

Chuck Box

Tool Box

Water Barrel

Brake

Boot

Table (door of chuck box)

PARTS OF A CHUCKWAGON

A chuck box mounted to the rear of a covered farm wagon (dk)

Contents Of The Chuckwagon

1. Items to be found in the chuckbox. *Cooking Utensils:* a Dutch oven, several skillets, large pots, a coffeepot, tin plates, forks, knives, and spoons. *Foods And Condiments:* flour, brown sugar, corn meal, roasted coffee beans, salt, lard, vinegar, molasses, sourdough and dried fruit. *First-Aid:* whiskey, bandages, castor oil and baking soda. *Repairs And Hygiene:* a sewing kit, a straight razor and soap. *For Relaxation:* whiskey or rum, chewing tobacco, and tobacco for rolling cigarettes.

2. Items packed carefully into the wagon bed. Axle grease, firewood, a cook tent, the canvas wagon sheet, bedrolls, slickers, a cook stove, and *war bags* (each cowboy's sack of personal belongings). There was also extra rope, guns, ammunition, lanterns, and kerosene. Foods in bulk storage might include potatoes, green coffee beans, salt pork, beef jerky, flour, dried apples, bacon, beans, onions, sugar, and cornmeal.

3. Items in the toolbox. Iron rods and pot hooks for supporting pots and skillets over the cook fire. A shovel, saw, ax, hammer, nails, branding irons, iron stakes to hold the horses, and horse shoeing equipment. There would also be plenty of tallow to grease the wagon wheels.

4. Items strapped to the outside of the wagon box. A water barrel with a two-day supply of water and a five-gallon sourdough keg which the cook would set out in the sun at each stop so the dough could continue to ferment. At night the keg would be wrapped in blankets to keep the batter warm and active. The cook would take out just what he needed for each meal and add more flower, salt, and water. On the other side of the wagon was an extra wheel and a tool box which helped to balance the load. A cowhide was hung under the wagon (called a *coonie,* or *possum belly*) to carry firewood, buffalo chips, or cowchips to be used when the campsite was nowhere near a supply of wood. No wonder a heavy-duty army wagon was needed for use as a chuckwagon

Camp Cook's Troubles
1912 oil on canvas by Charles M. Russell (1864-1926) DECA

A Match Game
COWBOY LINGO

Match the cowboy phrase in the first column with its meaning in the second column.

1. *Oklahoma Rain*
2. *Woolies*
3. *Powder Burning Contest*
4. *Lizard Scorcher*
5. *Jerky*
6. *John Henry*
7. *Lamp Oil*
8. *Down to the Blanket*

  a. A gunfight.
  b. A signature.
  c. Almost out of money.
  d. Sheep.
  e. Whiskey
  f. A dust storm.
  g. A wagon without springs.
  h. A camp stove.

ANS: 1-f, 2-d, 3-a, 4-h, 5-g, 6-b, 7-e, 8-c.

The Value Of A Chuckwagon Cook

The movies usually cast him for comic relief and "color," but the cranky old white-haired, pot-bellied range cook (as portrayed by character actors like Dub Taylor, Gabby Hayes, Frank McGrath, and Paul Brinegar) was the most important and respected man on a cattle drive. He was paid as much as $70.00 a month, twice the average cowboy's wage—and he was well worth it. He greatly affected the morale of the whole outfit by providing three hot meals a day in all kinds of weather. But that was only one of his duties: he gave medical attention to the ill and injured, discussed personal problems, settled disagreements, did laundry, held a bet for him, or took care of his money if need be. The cook had to be able to repair his wagon, and every morning before sunrise he loaded the bedrolls and equipment and moved ahead of the herd to set up camp for lunch. He worked longer hours than the cowboy, and for just $70.00 a month.

14 SLANG NAMES FOR THE COOK:

Sourdough	Old Woman	Belly Cheater
Cookie	Grub Spoiler	Sallie
Grubworm	Hash Wrangler	Hash Slinger
Sop and 'Taters	Pot Hooks	Pot Rustler
Dough-Belly	Dough Puncher	Biscuit Shooter

SAYIN' GRACE

Cowboys said prayers such as these before they chowed down: *"Eat the meat and leave the skin. Turn up you plates and' let's begin."* Or this: *"Yes, we'll come to the table, as long as we're able; and eat every gal darn thing that seems sorta stable."*

A chuckwagon at Lyndon B. Johnson National Historical Park, Johnson City, Texas (dk)

5 Miscellaneous Terms Heard Around The Chuckwagon

1. Son-of-a-gun stew. A favorite dish of the cowboys, it was made from the brains, pancreas, tongue, kidney, liver, heart, and, well, all the meaty parts of a freshly killed calf. The unweaned calf was preferred. The parts were cut into little pieces, and ingredients like tomatoes, onions, chilies, and potatoes were added.

2. Corn dodgers. The favorite of "Festus" on the TV series Gunsmoke, it was a bread cake or biscuit baked on a skillet and made from milk and fried corn.

3. Dutch Oven. A heavy-duty cast iron pot with a tight-fitting lid that could be placed directly in a fire with the coals covering it so that food could be browned on all sides.

4. Gone bad pooch. You've heard the phrase "smells like gone bad pooch." Henry Fonda used the term in *The Cheyenne Social Club*. Well, *pooch* was a cowhand's name for a chuckwagon cook's dish made of tomatoes mixed with sugar and bread. It wasn't a favorite of the cowman.

5. The bedroll. A cowboy's "sleeping bag" consisted of a waterproofed seven-by-eighteen-foot canvas ducking "tarpaulin" in which was one or two wool quilts and a bag containing his personal belongs: toiletries, *pasteboards* (playing cards), extra cartridges, tobacco, cigarette papers, money, a change of clothes, and letters from home.

The GREAT SOUTH TEXAS CHUCKWAGON COOKOFFS AND COWBOY POETS GATHERING

COWBOY COFFEE RECIPE

The recipe for *cowboy coffee* went something like this depending on who told it. After a hard day riding the range, all a cowboy would have to do to make himself some good black coffee was to take a pound of *Arbunkles' Ariosa Coffee* beans, ground them up, wet them down good with water, boil them over a hot fire for a half-hour and then throw in a horseshoe. And if the shoe sank, he put in more coffee.

Keep the Pot Hot!
6 COWBOY NAMES FOR COFFEE:

1. Arbunkles'. The Old West's most famous brand of coffee. Developed by *John* and *Charles Arbunkle* in 1865. They patented a process for roasting and then coating coffee beans with a glaze of egg and sugar designed to seal in the flavor and aroma. Before this improvement, coffee was sold green and un-ground, requiring it to be roasted over a campfire before it could be ground and brewed. *Arbunkles* was sold in one-pound paper sacks which had printed on them a coupon (the trademark signature) redeemable for catalog merchandise such as straight razors, guns, wedding rings and handkerchiefs—just what the cowboy wanted. Every package also contained a trading card and a stick of peppermint candy, and this guaranteed *Arbunkles* to be a best seller.

2. Bellywash. A cowboy's word for very weak coffee.

3. Black water. A wagon freighter's term for weak coffee.

4. Indian coffee. Water added to old grounds in the pot, boiled and given to Indians who came into camp begging for food.

5. Jamoka. A cowboy's name for coffee. The word is a combination of *Java* (coffee from the island of Java) and *mocha* (coffee from Mocha, Arabia).

6. Six-shooter coffee. The way cowboys like it: strong enough to float a pistol.

A Match Game
10 GRUB WORDS

Cowboys had slang names for their favorite foods just like any tight-knit group—like the loggers, miners, or the cavalry. They referred to a meal as *bait, chuck, found* or just plain *grub*. For this game, try to match the cowboy's slang name to the food he's referring to.

1. *Axle Grease*	a. Beans
2. *Hen Fruit*	b. Pancakes
3. *Strawberries*	c. Light Bread
4. *Prairie Butter*	d. Donuts
5. *Hot Rocks*	e. Eggs
6. *Bear Sign*	f. Bacon Grease
7. *Calf Slobber*	g. Biscuits
8. *Gun-Wadding*	h. Butter
9. *Skunk Eggs*	i. Meringue Pie
10. *Splatter Dabs*	j. Onions

ANS: 1-h, 2-e, 3-a, 4-f, 5-g, 6-d, 7-i, 8-c, 9-j, 10-b.

TIDBIT: True or False: The history of the cowboy began after the Civil War during the great cattle drives north from Texas to the railheads.

The statement is false. Cowboying really began on January 2, 1492 when Christopher Columbus unloaded "24 stallions, ten mares, and an unknown number of cattle on the Caribbean island of Hispañiola." From then on, horses and cattle spread throughout South America, Mexico, and into North America, requiring someone to manage them.

Branding Calves on Roundup by John C.H. Grabill (Library of Congress)

CATTLE BRANDS

*"Stockman are now as proud of their brands as they
are of their wives, maybe even better, as a brand can
earn a feller a living when most wive's can't."*
—Edgar R. "Frosty" Potter, *Cowboy Slang*, 1986.

Brands have been around for thousands of years. As far back as 3000 B.C., the walls of Egyptian tombs show the branding of animals with a hot iron. The branding of cattle and horses was done in Europe throughout the Middle Ages, but it was Spain that first brought cattle brands to the Americas in the 1500's during the Spanish conquest of Mexico. The first major use of "trail brands" was by *Charles Goodnight* and *John Chisholm* in the 1860's, though *Richard H. Chisholm* used the brand "HC" as early as 1832. Brands were needed on the open range (before barbed wire turned the land into a bunch of feed lots) so that when a cattleman found another's animals in his stock, he could send him a check for the ones he sold.

Thievery by outlaw gangs was also a reason for brands. The brands were carefully registered and inspectors were trained to recognize altered brands. When unregistered brands were found on the range, they were suspect—probably rustled and branded by outlaws. But the outlaws quickly wised up to this and would register a brand similar to an existing rancher's brand, then steal his cattle and alter the brand to match their outlaw brand.

Numbers, letters, and simple shapes were used to form brands. They would be placed on the

Branding irons hand forged in steel (Wikimedia Commons)

hide at a variety of angles to identify the ranch. A design laying on its side was referred to as being "lazy" such as the "lazy bar M." A "crazy" brand is one that is burned into the cow's hide upside down. A "walking" brand is a letter with flanges on the bottom, and a letter with flanges on the top is said to be "flying." A "tumbling" brand is a letter tilted to one side or the other. A brand that looks like the letters overlap is called a "connected" brand. And finally, "running" brands are letters stretched out to eliminate sharp angles.

Branding Cattle by John C.H. Grabill (Library of Congress)

What's in a Name?
9 TYPES OF HORSES

*"A range horse is somewhere between a teddy
bear and good pocket knife."*
—Baxter Black

The original western cow horse was brought to America by Christopher Columbus and by Hernando Cortez in his conquest of Mexico in 1519. They had acquired the horse from Arabia or North Africa. The American Indian "acquired" the horse from the Spanish who left many behind in the American wilderness. It wasn't long before herds of wild horses roamed the West, eventually becoming a symbol of America's Wild Frontier.

1. Arabian. A breed of swift, graceful horses native to Egypt. They have no white coloring except possibly on the face and on the legs below the *hocks* and knees.

2. Bronc. Any wild or untamed western horse. From Spanish *bronco* meaning "rough one."

3. Dam. A horse's female parent.

4. Mustang. A stray horse gone wild on the southwestern plains. From the Spanish word *mesteño.*

5. Quarter Horse. Developed in the United States to run fast and turn quickly in order to cut out cattle from a herd. It came from the eastern colonies, a mixture of Spanish and English. It was short and stocky, but fast and maneuverable.

6. Shetland Pony. A breed of small, hardy, shaggy ponies originally bred in the Shetland Islands.

7. Sire. A horse's male parent.

8. Tarpan. A wild horse of Central Asia not larger than an ordinary mule. Tan or *dun* in color, with black mane and tail.

9. Thoroughbred. A horse who's ancestors can be traced through at least three generations; of pure or unmixed breed, bred from a *sire* and *dam* of official pedigree (bloodline).

Pinto or Paint?
THE COLOR OF A HORSE

*"There ain't a horse that can't be rode. There
ain't a man that can't be throwed."*
—Old cowboy adage

Horses come in many colors—color sometimes related to its breed. The following terms have been used in the Old West to classify a horse by its color.

1. **Albino.** Pure white to cream color with pink skin and dark eyes.

2. **Appaloosa.** A sturdy breed of western saddle horse distinguished by black-and-white round, or egg-shaped spots on the rump, and a lack of hair on the tail and inside the thigh. There is also pink on the nose. The horse was developed by the Nez Percé Indians who lived along the Palouse River in Northwest Idaho.

3. **Bay.** A horse of reddish-brown or reddish-yellow color and always has a black mane and tail. A *blood bay* is a darker shade of red.

4. **Black.** A black body with black eyes and hoofs.

5. **Buckskin.** A light reddish-yellow; the color of leather made from the skin of a buck antelope or deer.

6. **Chestnut.** Bright yellow-red or mahogany-red with mane and tail always the same chestnut color. Also called *sorrel*.

7. **Dun.** A dull grayish-brown with tail, skin, and hoofs white to almost black. A *coyote dun* has a dark stripe running down its back; a *zebra dun* has dark stripes on its legs and withers.

8. **Flea-Bitten.** Speckled; grayish in color with small black or blue specks or spots.

9. **Gray.** Actually white with pink skin, but is usually born blue or black and becomes white in later years.

10. **Paint.** Any horse with irregular patterns of white and colored areas, usually brown or black. A pretty horse, but not any

good as a cutting horse because it always *fights the bit*—throws its head around when reined. It was extremely popular among the American Indians.

11. Palomino. A light tan or golden-colored horse with light blond or silvery-white mane and tail. Called a *pumpkin skin* or *California sorrel* in some areas. In Old Spain, they were called *Isabellas,* named after the Queen.

12. Peanut. A soft brownish color with black markings.Horses with this coloring are known to have a tough disposition.

13. Piebald. Covered with patches or spots of two colors usually black and white.

14. Pinto. A popular term for *piebald* and *skew bald* horses. Any horse marked with spots of two or more colors, often white and brown with a dark mane. From the Spanish *pintar* meaning "to paint."The pinto horse is also

called a *calico*, and by many, the same as a *paint.*

15. Roan. A horse that is usually grayish-yellow or reddish-brown and uniformly mixed with gray or white hairs. If the darker color is *sorrel,* the horse is a *strawberry roan*.

16. Sabino. A horse with a pink *roan* upper body with a pure-white belly.

17. Skewbald. Irregularly marked with white and a color other than black.

18.Sorrel. Bright yellowish-red, or mahogany-red of the palomino type. Same as the *chestnut.*

19. Strawberry. Reddish with white hairs or dots.

Trivia Question: Which color described above is NOT a horse color?
ANS:The *Peanut.* It was made up by the author to see if the experienced horseman reading this is on his toes.

MOUNTING A HORSE

A horse is customarily mounted from the left side. In fact, to do otherwise may startle and confuse the horse, leaving the rider "biting the dust." Where did this custom come from? Probably from the mounted soldier who wore his long, heavy sword hanging down by his left leg. It was much easier to throw his right leg over the horse than his encumbered left leg. The American Indian, on the other hand, would mount his horse from the right side because he usually held his bow in his left hand, thus making it easier to pull himself up on the right side.

THE MAVERICK

A maverick is a stray horse, cow, or motherless calf without a brand, and thus of unknown ownership. Named for a Texas lawyer called *Samuel A. Maverick*, a signer of the *Texas Declaration of Independence*. The story goes that sometime before the Civil War he acquired 400 cattle in payment for a debt. Maverick left the cattle in the hands of a slave who failed to put his brand on the offspring. They wandered free on the range and were eventually sold in 1855 to a rancher by the name of *Toutant Beauregard* who put them in with his herd. The sale included any other unbranded cows found on Sam Maverick's range. When Beauregard's cowhands found an unbranded calf they called it a "Maverick" and branded it with Beauregard's iron. The territory was large and there were many calves without a brand. Some were probably never even owned by Sam Maverick. The name spread throughout the West and became associated with any range animal that was unbranded and therefore of unknown ownership.

Men who went out hunting for these unbranded calves without mothers and added them to their *own* herds came to be called *maverickers*. Originally these men had been sent out by the ranch owner, but the cowhands quickly learned they could create their *own* herds this way. As ranchers began to lose these "extra profits," they made sure laws were passed against the practice. *Mavericker* then became another word for "cow thief." Nowadays, the term also refers to any person who is not affiliated with any particular group or who acts independently.

The term rustler, now referring to a cow thief, also evolved in the 1860's from the word *hustle* (to energetically push to accomplish something) when ranchers told their cowhands to "get out and rustle a few mavericks." They did, often for themselves, hence the name *rustler* for men who were "careless with their branding iron."

A Glossary Of
EQUINE TERMINOLOGY

"There were only two things the old-time cowpunchers were afraid of: a decent woman and being set afoot."
— "Teddy Blue" Abbott

If you know your horses, you'll know these terms, if you don't know them, read on.

Amble. Moving at a slow, even pace. The horse raises both legs on one side, then both on the other.

Appointments. All the gear and clothing used in riding. a.k.a. *tack.*

Bit. The metal part of a *bridle* which is inserted in the mouth of a horse and is used to control the animal. See *Rein.*

Bite The Dust. To be thrown from a horse—"lost his hat and got off to look for it"—"he was taking up a homestead."

Brand. To burn a mark on an animal with a hot iron. The brand was a ranch's mark of ownership.

Bridle. The head harness used by a rider to guide the horse. It includes the *rein,* the *bit,* and the *headstall.*

Canter. A moderate, easy, collected *gallop.*

Cantle. The upward curving raised rear part of a saddle.

Chaps. Short for *chaparajos* (chapareros). Pronounced "shaps." Leather pants without a seat worn over ordinary trousers for protection from brush, cactus, barbed wire, rope burns, horse's teeth, cow horns and the cold of night.

Cinch. From the Spanish word *cincha.* A wide band of canvas or horsehair running across the belly of the horse with a metal ring on each end to which a strap running from the saddle is secured.

Coarse. An unrefined horse having a harsh appearance.

Colt. A young male horse.

Crowbait. A decrepit, worthless horse—"buzzard bait."

Dam. Female parent of a horse.

Eat Gravel. To be thrown from a horse.

Filly. A young female horse.

Foal. A *colt* or *filly* less than one year old.

Gait. A way of walking or running, either a *walk, trot, canter,* or *gallop*.

Gallop. A fast pace from 12 to 16 miles per hour.

Gelding. A castrated horse.

Girth. A leather, canvas, or corded strap used to fasten the saddle to a horse. Also, the circumference of a horse's body measured just behind the *withers*. A western saddle has a double girth (two straps)—as opposed to an English saddle's single girth—to hold the saddle securely against the pull of a roped calf tied to the saddle horn.

Hand. A unit of measurement equal to the breath of a hand, about four inches. The height of a horse is measured in "hands," 4-1/2 inches (A cowboy who is described as a "full sixteen hands high" is a man who is "worth his salt" or highly valued.)

Headstall. That part of the *bridle* which fits over the head, made of leather straps.

Hobble. To tie the front legs of a horse to keep it from running loose. Leather cuffs connected by a short swivel chain are buckled on each front leg. A wide piece of rawhide or gunnysack can also be used.

Hock. The joint bending backward on the hind leg of a horse corresponding to the human ankle.

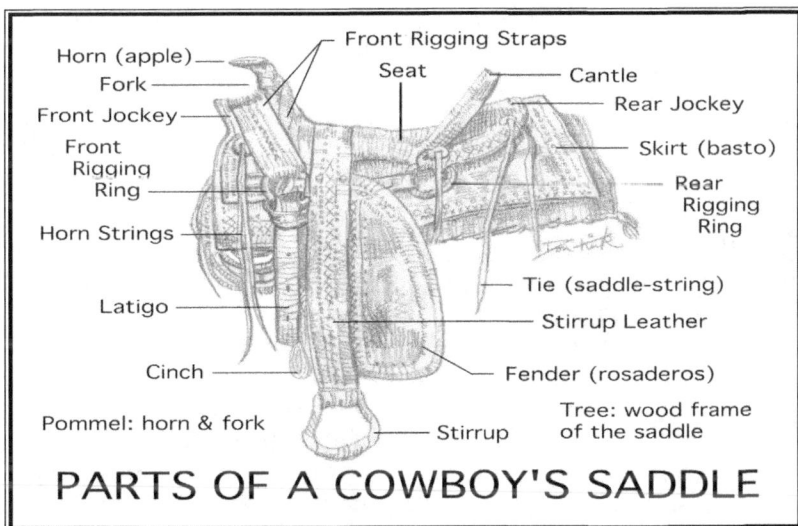

PARTS OF A COWBOY'S SADDLE

Horn (apple)
Fork
Front Jockey
Front Rigging Ring
Horn Strings
Latigo
Cinch
Pommel: horn & fork
Front Rigging Straps
Seat
Cantle
Rear Jockey
Skirt (basto)
Rear Rigging Ring
Tie (saddle-string)
Stirrup Leather
Fender (rosaderos)
Stirrup
Tree: wood frame of the saddle

Hoof. The foot of a horse; made of a horny substance.

Hogtie. To tie three legs with a narrow rope.

Jackass. A male donkey. The donkey resembles a horse, but with longer ears and shorter mane.

Jughead. A foolish horse.

Lariat. From the Spanish word *la reata* meaning "the rope."

Latigo. A long strap with which a saddle *girth* is adjusted. It passes through the cinch ring and the rigging ring.

Mare. A mature female horse.

Mule. The offspring of a *jackass* and a *mare*. Mules are usually sterile. It's trot makes it a little "jerky" to ride, but it was hardy and could handle hot climates better than a horse. The theme music used in *Two Mules for Sister Sara* (1970), fits the ride experience on a mule perfectly.

Near-side. The left side of the horse.

Off-side. The right side of a horse, the "Injun side."

Outfit. A cowboy's equipment used in his trade: his saddle, bedding, range clothing, horse tack, etc.

Plug. A broken down horse.

Outlaw. A horse so vicious that it can't be broken.

Quarter Horse. A saddle horse that is strong and quick and has great endurance. It got its name because of its ability to run a short distance—a quarter mile—at high speed.

Quirt. A riding whip with a short handle and a rawhide lash. Also, the first name of John Wayne's character in *Angle and the Badman* (1947).

Rein. A narrow strip of leather attached to each end of the *bit* in the mouth of a horse, and held by the rider or driver to control the animal.

Remuda. A bunch of saddle horses from which a cowhand could select the best horse for the day's work. From Spanish meaning "replacement." These horses are always *geldings*. Mares don't make good saddle horses and *stallions* are always rowdy and prone to fighting. There are about ten horses provided for every cowman in the outfit.

Rowels. The little wheel with sharp projecting points found on the end of a *spur*.

Saddle. A leather seat for a rider on a horse with a horn on the front for wrapping a lariat *after* lassoing an animal. This was called the *dally* method and was more dangerous (a potential loss of fingers) than first securing the rope to the saddle horn and *then* throwing the loop.

Saddlebags. A pair of leather bags attached together so they can be placed on the back of a horse just behind the *cantle*.

Sire. Male parent of a horse.

Spur. A device worn by horseman on the heel of a riding boot, having a *rowel* or toothed wheel of points to prick a horse's side to urge the animal forward. They were originally cut out of a solid piece of wood, later wood strips wrapped in leather.

Stallion. A male horse not castrated, especially one kept for breeding purposes. From the Old High German *stal*; literally "the horse kept in the stall."

Stirrup. A "U" shaped ring with a flat end on one side for receiving the foot of the rider and attached to a strap which is fastened to the saddle. It aids the rider in mounting the horse, supports part of the weight of the body, and enables the rider to sit steadily while riding.

Tenderfoot. One who is not accustomed to the hardships and deprivations of ranching in the West; a greenhorn.

Tree. The wooden or metal frame of a saddle.

Trot. The *gait* of a horse in which the legs are lifted in alternating diagonal pairs. Faster than a *walk* but slower than a *canter*; about nine miles per hour.

Walk. The slowest forward movement of a horse, a moderate pace; about 4 miles per hour. Two *hoofs* are firmly placed on the ground before lifting either of the others.

Withers. The juncture of the shoulder bones of a horse forming the highest part of the back.

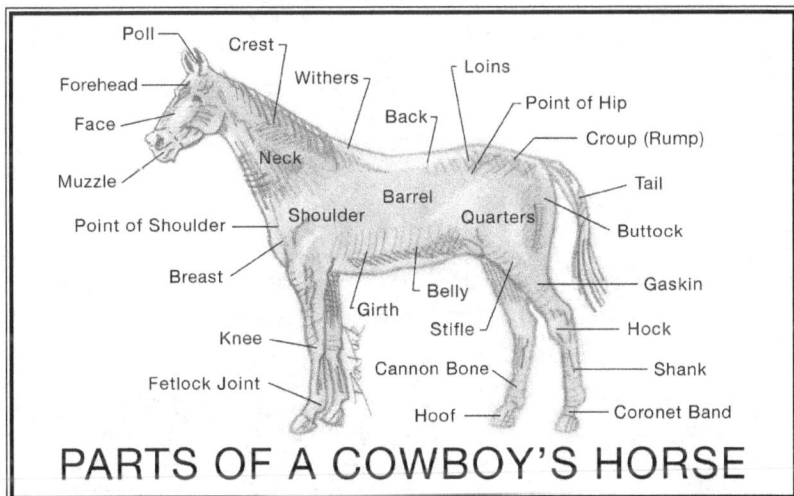

Poll — Crest
Forehead — Withers
Loins
Face — Point of Hip
Back
Muzzle — Neck — Croup (Rump)
Barrel — Tail
Point of Shoulder — Shoulder — Quarters — Buttock
Breast — Belly — Gaskin
Girth
Knee — Stifle — Hock
Cannon Bone — Shank
Fetlock Joint — Coronet Band
Hoof

PARTS OF A COWBOY'S HORSE

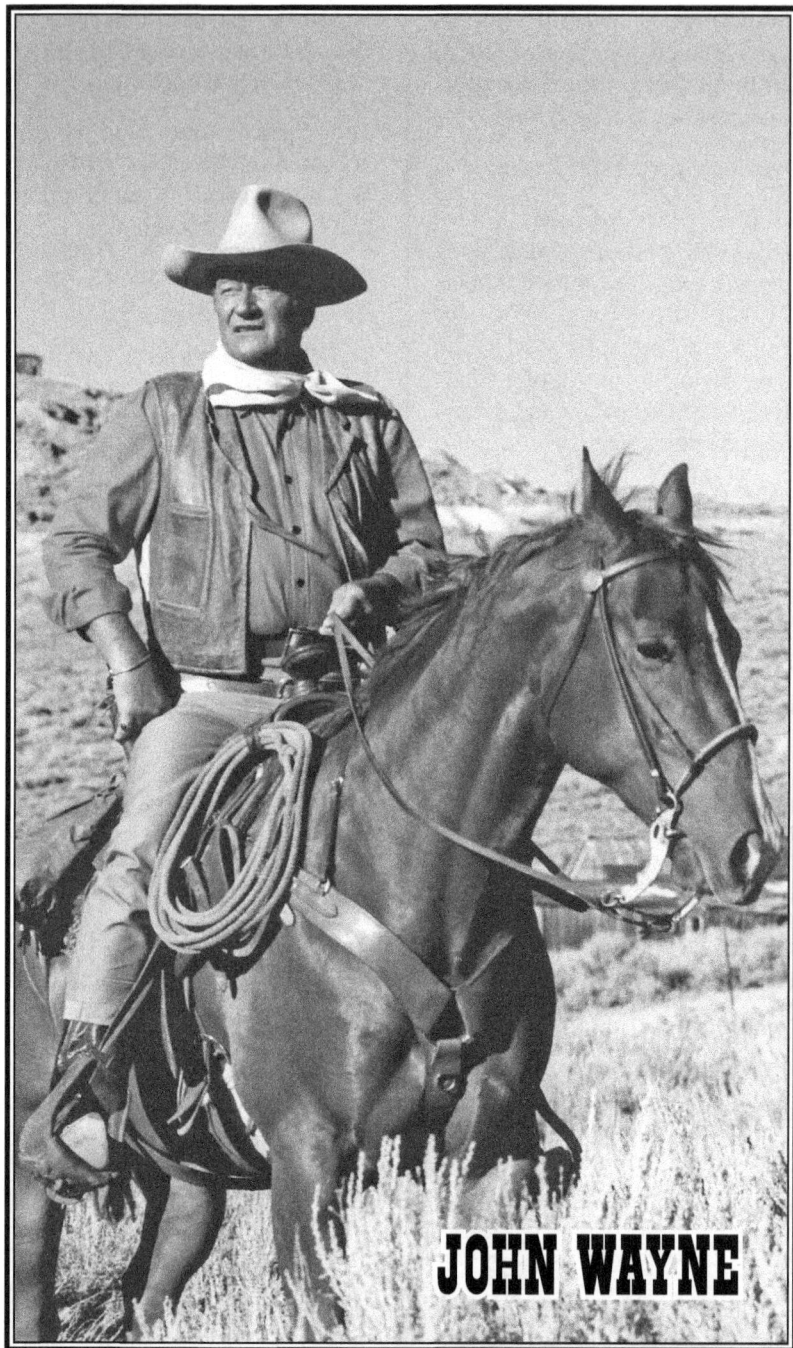

JOHN WAYNE

John Wayne as Will Andersen riding Ol' Dollor in *The Cowboys*, Sanford Productions (author's collection)

A Horse Is a Cowboy Star's Best Friend
MOVIE COWBOYS & THEIR HORSES

What's a cowboy without his horse? A man afoot! Here's a list of many of the early cowboy stars and their "pals" (their horses).

22 TELEVISION HORSES

THE ACTOR	HIS HORSE
1. Gene Autry	Champion
2. Victoria Barkley	Misty Girl
3. Vint Bonner	Scar
4. Ben Cartwright	Buck
5. Hoss Cartwright	Chub
6. Little Joe Cartwright	Cochise
7. Hopalong Cassidy	Topper
8. Matt Dillon	Marshal
9. Dale Evans	Buttermilk
10. Festus Hagen	Ruth (a mule)
11. Wild Bill Hickok	Buckshot
12. Wrangler Jane	Pecos
13. Jingles	Joker
14. Cisco Kid	Diablo
15. Annie Oakley	Buttercup
16. Pancho	Loco
17. Sergeant Preston	Rex
18. Lone Ranger	Silver
19. Roy Rogers	Trigger
20. Dirty Sally	Worthless (a mule)
21. Tonto	Scout
22. Zorro	Phantom, Tornado

33 MOTION PICTURE HORSES

THE ACTOR	HIS HORSE
1. Rex Allen	Ko-Ko
2. Johnny Mack Brown	Rebel, Reno
3. Smiley Burnette	Ring Eye
4. Harry Carey Sr.	Sonny
5. Sunset Carson	Cactus, Silver
6. Buster Crabbe	Falcon
7. Eddie Dean	Flash, White Cloud, Copper
8. Bill Elliott	Thunder, Sonny
9. Hoot Gibson	Mutt, Goldie
10. Monte Hale	Pardner
11. William S. Hart	Fritz
12. Tim Holt	Lightning
13. Buck Jones	King, White Eagle, Silver
14. Rocky Lane	Black Jack
15. Lash La Rue	Black Diamon, Rush
16. Ken Maynard	Tarzan
17. Tim McCoy	Starlight, Midnite
18. Tom Mix	Old Blue, Tony
19. Tex Ritter	White Flash
20. Reb Russell	Rebel
21. Fred Scott	White Dust
22. Randolph Scott	Stardust
23. Arkansas Slim	Josephine (a mule)
24. Charles Starrett	Raider
25. Bob Steele	Boy, Brownie
26. Jimmy Stewart	Pie
27. Fred Thompson	Silver King
28. Tom Tyler	Ace, Baron
29. Jimmy Wakely	Sunset
30. Wally Wales	Silver King
31. John Wayne	Ol' Dollor
32. Bob Wills	Black Diamond
33. Whip Wilson	Silver Bullet

A Match Game
COWBOY STARS AND THEIR HORSES

Many of the first movie-cowboy heroes galloped to stardom along with their trusty steeds. Around 1910, *William S. Hart* led the way with his horse "Fritz." Can you match these cowboy stars with the names of their horses. They are organized in groups of four to make your job easier.

1.	Lash LaRue	a.	Trigger
2.	Lone Ranger	b.	Rush
3.	Roy Rogers	c.	Diablo
4.	Cisco Kid	d.	Silver
5.	Tim McCoy	e.	Topper
6.	Dale Evans	f.	Midnight
7.	Hopalong Cassidy	g.	Ring Eye
8.	Smiley Burnette	h.	Buttermilk
9.	Hoot Gibson	i.	Ko-Ko
10.	Tonto	j.	Champion
11.	Rex Allen	k.	Scout
12.	Gene Autry	l.	Mutt

ANS: 1-b, 2-d, 3-a, 4-c. 5-f, 6-h, 7-e, 8-g. 9-l, 10-k, 11-i, 12-j.

TIDBIT: USING SPURS: Those little "U"-shaped things with a revolving pointed star strapped to the heel of a cowboy's boot, are used to help in controlling the horse. They are NOT used as punishment, but only to nudge the horse to turn, make quick stops, or do something he's hesitant about. A good *rowel* is large with dull points and does not sink into the horses hide. The cowboy only touches the horse lightly, he doesn't want to hurt him; that would only create a skittish, fearful horse.

A Ballad
GOODBYE OLD PAINT

Traditional Song

Goodbye Old Paint has an unknown history; it has many versions and is probably a conglomerate of other songs. There are hundreds of verses; cowboys wrote their own as they sung to their cattle herd on a dark night to keep them from stampeding.

1. My foot's in the stirrup, my pony won't stand,
Goodbye Old Paint, I'm off to Montan.'

**2. Old Paint, Old Paint, I'm a leavin' Cheyenne;
Goodbye Old Paint, I'm a leavin' Cheyenne.**

3. Old Paint's a good pony, he paces when he can,
Goodbye little doney, I'm off to Montan'.

4. Go hitch up your horses and feed 'em some hay,
An' set yourself by me as long as you'll stay.

5. We spread down the blanket on the green grassy ground,
While the horses and cattle were a-grazing around.

6. My horses ain't hungry they won't eat your hay,
My wagon is loaded and rollin' away.

7. They feed in the coulies, they water in the draw,
Their tails are all matted, their backs are all raw.

8. Oh, when I die, take my saddle from the wall,
Put it on my pony and lead him from the stall.

9. My foot's in the stirrup, my bridle's in hand,
Goodbye little Annie, my horses won't stand.

10. The last time I saw her was late in the fall,
She was ridin' Old Paint and a-leadin' Old Ball.

A Ballad
THE STRAWBERRY ROAN

By Curley W. Fletcher, 1915

Originally published as "The Outlaw Broncho" in the *Arizona Record* in 1915, Fletcher's poem was later published in his book *Rhymes of the Roundup*. He wrote it as the cowboy spoke it, in their "on-the-range" vernacular. (Great for those who want to "speak cowboy.")When various songwriters later put it to music, they "cleaned up" the language. Printed here is Fletcher's original poem. Gene Autry and Ken Maynard used it as the title song in their films. (A "strawberry roan" is a horse with a coat that is reddish in color and mixed with white hairs.)

1. I"m a-layin' around, just spendin' muh time,
Out of a job an' ain't holdin' a dime,
When a feller steps up, an' sez, "I suppose
That you're uh bronk* fighter by the looks uh yure clothes."

2. "Yuh figures me right—I'm a good one, I claim,
Do you happen tuh have any bad uns tuh tame?
He sez he's got one, uh bad un tuh buck,
An fur throwin' good riders, he's had lots uh luck.

3. He sez that his pony has never been rode,
That the boys that gets on 'im is bound tuh get throwed.
Well, I gets all excited an' asks what he pays,
Tuh ride that old pony uh couple uh days.

4. He offers uh ten spot. Sez I, "I'm yure man,
Cause the bronk never lived, that I could't fan;
The hoss never lived, he never drew breath,
That I couldn't ride 'till he starved plum tuh dath.

5. I don't like tuh brag, but I got this tuh say,
That I aint't been piled fur many uh day."
Sez he, "Get yure saddle, I'll give yuh a chance."
So I gets in his buckboard an' drifts tuh his ranch.

6. I stays until mornin', an right after chuck,
I steps out tuh see if that outlaw kin buck.
Down in the hoss corral, standin' alone,
Was this caballo, uh strawberry roan.

7. His laigs is all spavined an' he's got pigeon toes,
Little pig eyes an' uh big Roman nose,
Little pin ears that touch at the tip
An uh double square iron stamped on his hip.

8. Yew necked an' old, with uh long narrow jaw,
I kin see with one eye, he's uh reg'lar outlaw.
I put on muh spurs—I'm sure feelin' fine—
Turns up muh hat, and picks up some twine.

9. I throws that loop on 'im, an' well I knows then,
That before he gets rode, I'll sure earn that ten,
I gets muh blinds on him, an' it sure was a fight,
Next comes muh saddle—I screws it down tight.

The Cow Boy by John C.H. Grabill, 1888 (Library of Congress)

10. An then I piles on 'im, an' raises
   the blind,
   I'm right in his middle tuh see
   'im unwind.
   Well, he bows his old neck, an' I
   guess he unwound,
   Fur he seems tuh quit livin'
   down on the ground.

11. He goes up t'ward the East, an'
   comes down t'ward the West,
   Tuh stay in his middle, I'm doin'
   muh best,
   He sure is frog-walkin', he
   heaves uh big sigh,
   He only lacks wings, fur tuh be
   on the fly.

Bucking Bronco by John C.H. Grabill,
1888 (Library of Congress)

12. He turns his old belly right up toward the sun,
   He sure is uh sun-fishin' son-of-uh-gun,
   He is the worst bucker I seen on the range,
   He kin turn on uh nickle an' give yuh some change.

13. While he's uh-buckin' he squeals like uh shoat,
   I tell yuh, that pony has sure got muh goat.
   I claim that, no foolin', that bronk could sure step,
   I'm still in muh saddle, uh-buildin' uh rep.

14. He hits on all fours, an' suns up his side,
   I don't see how he keeps from sheddin' his hide.
   I loses muh stirrups an' also muh hat,
   I'm grabbin' the leather an' blind as uh bat.

15. With uh phenomenal jump, he goes up on high,
   An' I'm settin' on nothin', way up in the sky,
   An' then I turns over, I comes back tuh earth
   An' lights in tuh cussin' the day of his birth.

16. Then I knows that the hosses I ain't able tuh ride
   Is some of them livin'—they haven't all died,
   But I bets all muh money they ain't no man alive,
   Kin stay with that bronk when he makes that high dive.

Widowmaker Blackjack Slade (Photo of the author by Kris Ford)

Bullets, Beans, and Buscaderos
THE GUNFIGHTERS

*"A Gunfighter has to have guts, deliberation,
and a proficiency with firearms."*
—John Wayne, *The Shootist*, 1976

As soon as **Sam Colt** invented his "revolving pistol" and the Texas Rangers took to reining in the lawless, the legendary "gunfighter" was born. After the Civil War, many men, who knew only their guns, found themselves without a way to make a living. Out of desperation, they took to the "owlhoot trail," robbing banks, stagecoaches and "iron horses." As a result, the "gunfighter" became a part of American folklore. He was a man of no morals, able to kill unmercifully, to be judge, jury and executioner. Often called the "widowmaker," he was feared by all. But, contrary to the impression given by the movies, the gunfighter was a minority in the Old West. Even more rare, was the face-off on Front Street at high noon to prove who was the fastest draw. Most shootouts occurred when a skilled lawman tried to "bring in" a troublemaker, or when a couple of drunks fought over the results of a poker hand. If a man found he was at the business end of a six-shooter in a dingy, smoke-filled gambling hall, you can bet he was not just an innocent bystander.

The gunfighter evolved from that independent, self-reliant frontiersman who traveled west in search of a better life, who fought in the Mexican war, who used guerrilla tactics in the Civil War, and who was handed that new invention that became know as the "sixgun." He would never have become the gunfighter of lore with a single-shot flintlock musket. The wars produced a breed of men accustomed to violence and indifference to human life. They had to have nerves of steel to stand steady while bullets whizzed past them. They had to remain calm and carefully place their shots. Their life depended on it. We hope you too can remain calm as you "swap lead" with the pistoleers in this chapter who "wore their guns low" and backed down to no man or beast.

Reach For The Sky
9 SHOWDOWN
CALLIN-YOU-OUTS

It's high noon in a small, wind-swept town way out west. A notorious badman with a price on his head is confronted by the dutiful town Marshal. The wanted man refuses to throw down his sidearm and come in peaceably. He takes on a defiant posture in the center of the dusty street and pulls his long, black frock coat clear of his nickel-plated 45-caliber revolver. The situation is tense. There is a deathly silence. If no one makes the first move, one of the men will invariably say:

1. "Come a-smokin'!"
2. "Fill your hand!"
3. "I'm callin' yeh!"
4. "Grab your cutter!"
5. "Go for your iron!"
6. "Cut 'em loose."
7. "Show your hand!"
8. "Start your draw!"
9. "Pull your lead chucker!"

Like a flash of lighting, there's a blaze of blackpowder smoke that engulfs the street. We can't see who—if anyone—is still standing. More shots are fired. It becomes deathly quiet again. The smoke clears and both men are still standing, their pistols empty of cartridges. The old adage: "speed's fine, but accuracy's final" proves, once again, its weighty truth.

I'm Calling You Out!
8 CONFRONTATIONS

"Killing men is my specialty. I look at it as a business proposition."
—Tom Horn

Here are a few witty last lines from the movies—the last and final words spoken before the itchy-fingered gunfighters "slap leather" in their high-noon shootouts:

1. "It's your neck, Lockhart. If you want a Christian burial, better leave some money with the undertaker." —James Millican, *The Man From Laramie* (1955).

2. "Unless you want to see your own gravestone on your way to hell, you'll be on the next stage." —The Town Marshal, *The Badlanders* (1958).

3. "You ain't gettin' no older than tomorrow." —Slim Pickens, *One-Eyed Jacks* (1961).

4. "I'm just leaving town." "You're not leaving town until dead men can walk." —Gary Cooper, *The Plainsman* (1937).

5. "Sonny, I can see we ain't going to have you 'round long enough to get tired of your company." —Richard Widmark, *The Law and Jake Wade* (1958).

6. "Did you bring some gold with you?" "No." "Silver?" "Just lead." "You can't buy anything with lead. I guess I have to take your horses and kill you too." —A bandito and John Wayne, *Chisum* (1970).

7. "I've got you this time." "You're a daisy if you do!" —Frank McLaury confronting Doc Holliday (Val Kilmer) in *Tombstone* (1993).

8. "This town isn't big enough for the both of us!" —unknown.

REWARD

($5,000.00)

Reward for the capture, dead or alive, of one Wm. Wright, better known as

"BILLY THE KID"

Age, 18. Height, 5 feet, 3 inches. Weight, 125 lbs. Light hair, blue eyes and even features. He is the leader of the worst band of desperadoes the Territory has ever had to deal with. The above reward will be paid for his capture or positive proof of his death.

JIM DALTON, Sheriff.

DEAD OR ALIVE!
"BILLY THE KID"

Text from an actual Old West handbill

6 Verses About The Boy Bandit King
THE BALLAD OF BILLY THE KID

This is a story about **William Bonney,** shot to death by Sheriff Pat Garrett in a darkened room. He died on July 14, 1881 as a young 22-year-old cold-blooded killer. This song was written long after Billy was laid to rest at Fort Sumner. It was written by Reverend Andrew Jenkins and first recorded in 1927 by Vernon Dalhard. There are many versions of this song; this is but one.

Verse One I'll sing you a true song of Billy the Kid,
I'll sing of the desperate deeds that he did;
'Way out in New Mexico long, long ago,
When a man's only chance was his own forty four.

Verse Two When Billy the Kid was a very young lad,
In old Silver City, he went to the bad;
Way out in the West with a gun in his hand,
At the age of twelve years he killed his first man.

Verse Three Fair Mexican maidens play guitars and sing,
A song about Billy, their boy bandit king;
How, where his young manhood had reached its sad end,
Had a notch on his pistol for twenty-one men.

Verse Four 'Twas on the same night that poor Billy died,
He said to his friends, "I'm not satisfied;
There are twenty-one men I've put bullets through,
And Sheriff Pat Garrett must make twenty-two."

Verse Five Now this is how Billy the Kid met his fate,
The bright moon was shining, the hour was late;
Shot down by Pat Garrett who once was his friend,
The young outlaw's life had come to an end.

Verse Six There's many a man with face fine and fair,
Who starts out in life with a chance to be square;
But just like poor Billy, he wanders astray,
And loses his life the very same way.

A Match Game
14 FAMOUS MOTTOS

From the earliest days, the press created legendary figures simply through their sensationalized reporting of events in their prospering new towns. Of course, exaggeration and "hype" was the way to sell newspapers. For this quiz, match the famous phrase or fact with the person or group it is associated.

1.	"We Never Sleep"	a.	Colt Army Model 1873
2.	"The Buntline Special"	b.	Tom Horn
3.	"The dirty little coward"	c.	James Butler Hickok
4.	"Only man to capture Geronimo"	d.	The Pinkertons
5.	"The Ghost of Eldorado"	e.	George A. Custer
6.	"The Prince of Pistoleers"	f.	E.Z.C. Judson
7.	"The Peacemaker"	g.	The Wild Bunch
8.	"Yellow Hair"	h.	Joaquin Murietta
9.	"Robber's Roost"	i.	Charles E. Bolton
10.	"The Po8"	j.	Robert Ford
11.	"Little Sure Shot"	k.	Judge Roy Bean
12.	"The Lost Duchman"	l.	Sam Bass
13.	"The Robinhood of Texas"	m.	Annie Oakley
14.	"Law West of the Pecos"	n.	Jacob Waltz

ANSWERS:

1-d. "We Never Sleep" was the motto (along with the logo of a wide-awake eye) of the Pinkerton Detective Agency of Chicago.

2-f. The Buntline Special was a .45-colt revolver with 12-inch barrel given by Edward Zane Carroll Judson—dime novelist who used the pen name Ned Buntline—to several of his favorite lawmen, including Wyatt Earp, Bat Masterson, and Bill Tilghman. Trouble is, the story is a myth, created by biographer Stuart N. Lake, in his book *Wyatt Earp, Frontier Marshal,* 1931. Such a gun did not exist until 1977 when the Colt Company began manufacturing a "Buntline Special" to satisfy western fans.

3-j. "The dirty little coward" became the epithet applied to the man who shot Jesse James in the back. *The Assassination of Jesse James by the Coward Bob Ford* tells the sad story of Jesse's killer.

4-b. The only man to actually ever capture Geronimo was the scout and bounty hunter Tom Horn. At least that's what he said in his autobiography written while he awaited hanging in Cheyenne, Wyoming in 1903. He was the civilian Chief of Scouts in 1885 and was an important figure in the campaign which resulted in the final capture of Geronimo.

5-h. The "Ghost of Eldorado" was the sobriquet given to Joaquin Murietta, a southern California bandit who commanded over 100 terrifying men who murdered and pillaged unmercifully. Legend has it that the California Rangers, formed for the sole purpose of finding and capturing Joaquin, brought back his severed head in a pickle jar as proof of his death.

6-c. Hickok's accurate target shooting got him the name "Prince of Pistoleers" by dime novelists.

7-a. Samuel Colt's 1873 revolving pistol became the most popular handgun in the West. It was also known as the "Frontier Colt."

8-e. The Indians gave Custer the sobriquet "Yellow Hair" because of his long flowing blond hair.

9-g. The "Robbers Roost" was a hideout in Wyoming for the Wild Bunch gang led by Butch Cassidy and the Sundance Kid.

10-i. Charles E. Bolton was a gentleman bandit who robbed stagecoaches in California and on two occasions left behind a hand-written poem signed "Black Bart, the Po8 [poet]."

11-m. While Annie (Phoebe Anne Mozee) was working in Buffalo Bill Cody's Wild West show around 1885, Chief Sitting Bull called her *wantanya cicilia* meaning "Little Missy Sure Shot" and the name stuck.

12-n. Jacob Walz was an Arizona prospector who allegedly made a map where he claimed, while on his deathbed, to have discovered a rich vein of gold ore in the Superstition Mountains. To this day prospectors are still trying to find the Lost Duchman Mine.

13-l. Sam Bass was a Texas train and stagecoach robber who became known as the "Robinhood of Texas" because the public felt he was stealing only from the rich.

14-k Judge Roy Bean called himself this after establishing a court in a saloon in the small West Texas town of Langtry. He was legally appointed a Justice of the Peace at the insistence of the Texas Rangers in 1882 to help stem the tide of lawlessness in the area. He held the job for about 20 years (more about Bean on page 588.).

"You're the last man standing. You comin' in peaceable like?"
(Sketch by the author of a gunfight outside the Mexican cantina at Old Tucson Studios)

Never Ask A Man His Name Or Where He Comes From!
14 SLANG NAMES FOR THE GUNFIGHTER

In the nineteenth century many names were given to the men who made a living with their gun. The term "gunfighter" was not used much before the turn of the century, so here are some actual names used in the Old West before Hollywood got into the act:

1. Man Killer	6. Two-gun Man	11. Leather Slapper
2. Gunman	7. Tie-down Man	12. Quick-draw Artist
3. Pistoleer	8. Buscadero	13. Widow Maker
4. Gunny	9. Gun Popper	14. Shootist
5. Notcher	10. Gunslinger	15. Hired Gun

Oops! Which name was NOT used in the Old West? ANS: #9 Gun Popper.

Speeds Fine, But Accuracy's Final!
THE CODE OF THE GUNFIGHTER

*"Boys who play with guns have to be
ready to die like men."*
—Joan Crawford, *Johnny Guitar*, 1954.

The movies are full of advice for the young snot-nosed kid wantin' ta learn how to shoot a pistol. The old, past-his-prime gunfighter is, at first, hesitant to give advice to the youngin', but he always gives in, spoutin' out the things he learned to avoid lead poisoning and the watchful eye of the law. The following list is compiled from movies, dime novels, and autobiographies. It includes quotes from some real gunfighters.

1 **"The most important lesson I learned from those proficient gunfighters was that the winner of a gunplay usually was the man who took his time."** —Wyatt Earp, *Wyatt Earp: Frontier Marshall*, 1931.

2 "Don't waste your bullets. Four shots will kill four men." —unknown.

3 **"Whenever you get into a row, be sure not to shoot too quick. Take time. I've known many a feller to slip up for shootin' in a hurry."** —Wild Bill Hickok, 1865.

4 "Carry your six-shooter loaded with only five beans in the wheel and let the hammer rest on the empty chamber. And if you're expecting trouble fill that sixth chamber as a trump card." —unknown.

5 **"Any man who does not possess courage, proficiency in the use of firearms, and deliberation had better make up his mind at the beginning to settle his differences in some manner other than by appeal to the pistol."** —Bat Masterson, *Human Life*, 1907.

6   "Never tangle with a man who doesn't care whether he lives or not. He will always have an edge on you." —unknown.

7   **"Never holster an empty gun."** —Mike Henry, *More Dead Than Alive,* 1968.

8   "Never let them know how you're feeling or what you're thinking. If they know how you feel they know how to hurt you, and if they hurt you once, they will try again." —Louis L'Amour, *Flint,* 1960.

9   **"Shoot with both feet planted. Nothing fears a man more than to see a man standing still while he's being shot at."** —Willie Nelson in *Barbarosa,* 1982.

10   "Don't trust anybody, not even your closest friend. To trust is a weakness. It ain't necessarily that folks are bad, but they are weak or afraid." —Louis L'Amour, *Flint,* 1960.

11   **"I hope you're smart enough to know that 'Who hit John' [whiskey] don't go with guns."** —John Wayne in *The Shootist,* 1976.

12   "If you have to shoot a man, shoot him in the guts near the navel, you may not make a fatal shot, but he will get a shock that will paralyze his brain and arm so much that the fight is all over." —Wild Bill Hickok, 1871.

13   **"It isn't always being fast or even accurate that counts, it's being willing. I found out early that most men regardless of cause or need aren't willing. They blink an eye or draw a breath before they pull the trigger. I won't"** —John Wayne, *The Shootist,* 1976.

14   "Don't give up your pride, honor, or dignity." —unknown.

15   **"Look at the sweat on his shirt and shoot where you're looking."** —unknown.

16   "Be strong, be your own man. Go your own way, but whatever you do, don't go crossways of other folks' beliefs." —Louis L'Amour, *Flint,* 1960.

17   **"Why wear two guns? With one gun, a miss-fire can mean your life, with two guns the chance of a miss fire is almost cut in half. File off the front sight, it only gets in the way, and strap down your holster with a thong."** —unknown.

18   "There's some [gunfighters] who like two guns, but one's all you need if you can use it." —Alan Ladd, *Shane*, 1953.

19   **"Two guns will beat four aces anytime."** —Johnny Ringo.

20   "Did he mention that third eye you better have? It's usually some six-fingered buster that couldn't hit a cow on the tit with a tin cup that does you in." —John Wayne in *The Shootist,* 1976.

21   **"Study men. All your life there will be men who will try to keep you from getting where you're going, some out of hatred, some out of cussedness or inefficiency."** —Louis L'Amour, *Flint,* 1960.

22   "Come here to kill me? Let me give you some advice: if you have to shoot a man, you shoot him in the guts. Might not kill him, some times they die slow—or it'll paralyze his brain—his life's as good as over."
—Jeff Bridges, *Wild Bill*, 1995.

23   **"Never meet the enemy on his terms."** —Glenn Ford, *The Violent Men,* 1955.

Buckskin Joe, Cañon City, Colorado (dk)

24 "He'll come shooting. Have your gun cocked, but don't pull until you're certain what you're shooting at. Aim for his belly, low. The gun'll throw up a bit, but if you hold it tight and wait until he's close enough, you can't miss. Keep cool and take your time." —Wyatt Earp, *Wyatt Earp: Frontier Marshal, 1931*.

25 **"A gun is a tool, Marium, no better or no worse than any other tool, an ax, shovel, or anything. A gun is as good or as bad as the man using it. Remember that."** —Alan Ladd, *Shane*, 1953.

26 "Never have your holster at arms length . . . always have it here, where the grip is between the elbow and the wrist. When your hand comes up, your gun'll clear the holster without coming up too high." —Alan Ladd, *Shane*, 1953.

27 **"When two hunters go after the same prey, they usually end up shooting each other in the back."** —Clint Eastwood, *For a Few Dollars More*, 1967.

28 "Keep your knowledge to yourself. Never offer information to anybody. Don't let people realize how much you know." —Louis L'Amour, *Flint*, 1960.

29 **"When they get close enough so you want to scream, don't scream, shoot."** —Burt Lancaster, *The Unforgiven*, 1960.

30 "How many times have I told you; if you let your hate get the upper hand, it'll throw your timing off." —Richard Widmark, *The Law and Jake Wade*, 1958.

31 **"When you have to shoot, shoot, don't talk."** —Eli Wallach, *The Good, The Bad, and the Ugly*, 1966.

32 "You can't serve papers on a rat, baby sister. You gotta kill him or let him be." —John Wayne, *True Grit*, 1969.

33 **"Windage and elevation, Mrs. Langdon. Windage and elevation."** —John Wayne, *The Undefeated*, 1969.

34 I don't kill for amusement; man *or* rabbit!"
—Willie Nelson, *Barbarosa*, 1982.

35 **"You want to plan your moves, pick your place to fight; don't make any threats, and don't you ever walk away from one either."** —Brian Keith, *Nevada Smith*, 1966.

36 "All gunfighters are lonely. They live in fear; they die without a dime, a woman, or a friend." —Burt Lancaster, *Gunfight at the O.K. Corral*, 1957.

37 **"I gotta be goin' on. A man hasta be what he is Joey; can't break the mold. I tried it and it didn't work for me . . . Joey, there's no living with a killing. There's no going back for me. Right or wrong, it's a brand, a brand sticks. There's no goin' back."** —Alan Ladd, *Shane*, 1953.

38 "Your gun has got you everything. isn't that true?" "Yeah, everything. After a while you can call bartenders and faro dealers by their first name. Maybe two hundred of them. Rented rooms you live in, five hundred. Meals you eat in hash houses, a thousand. Home, none. Wife, none. Kids, none. Prospects, zero." —Steve McQueen, *The Magnificent Seven*, 1960.

39 **"In the end you end up dying all alone on a dirty street. And for what? For nothing!"** —Gary Cooper, *High Noon*.

Old Tucson Studios, Tucson, Arizona (dk)

A Match Game
5 BACKSHOOTERS

Gunfighters were killers; they had no code of conduct. Shooting a friend in the back for a few dollars wasn't immoral to these unscrupulous men. Match the famous outlaw or lawman with the man who took his life.

1.	Jesse James	**a.**	Jack McCall
2.	Bob Ford	**b.**	John Henry Selman
3.	Wild Bill Hickok	**c.**	Bob Ford
4.	John Wesley Hardin	**d.**	Pat Garrett
5.	Billy The Kid	**e.**	Ed O. Kelly

1-c. BOB FORD, a James Gang member, shot Jesse in the back while Jesse stood on a chair adjusting a picture in his home in Joseph, Missouri. Bad Bob did the "dirty deed" to collect the reward on Jesse's head.

2-e. ED O. KELLY murdered Bob Ford in Creede, Colorado with a sawed-off shotgun either because Ford accused Kelly in public of stealing his diamond ring or because he was allegedly offered $5,000 by the James family to track him down and kill him. Ed thought he would be famous if he killed the man who killed Jesse James.

3-a. JACK McCALL, a drifter, shot "Wild Bill" in the back while Bill was playing poker in Deadwood, D.T. He had lost $110 to Hickok in a poker game the previous day.

4-b. JOHN HENRY SELMAN, a peace officer, shot Hardin in the back of the head in a saloon in El Paso, Texas. Hardin had earlier threatened to kill Selman for arresting a prostitute Hardin had been seeing socially.

5-d. PAT GARRETT, an old friend of Billy's, shot him in an unlighted bedroom on Pete Maxwell's ranch in Fort Sumner, New Mexico where Billy was hiding out.

A Multiple-Choice Quiz
GUNFIGHT AT THE O.K. CORRAL

On one fine day in the Old West two groups of four men confronted each other to settle their differences with guns. It has become the most famous gunfight in the history of the American West. On one side of the fight were cowboys *Ike* and *Billy Clanton,* and *Frank* and *Tom McLaury.* On the other side were three of the four *Earp* brothers: *Virgil, Wyatt* and *Morgan,* and their friend *"Doc" Holliday.* It's a story that's been told over and over in movies and western fiction. For those fans of the Clanton-Earp legend, here's a quiz based on the testimony at the preliminary hearing of accused murderers Wyatt Earp and Doc Holliday in the court of Justice Wells Spicer, Tombstone, Arizona Territory as reported by the *Tombstone Epitaph.*

1. On what day did the fight occur?
A. June 25, 1876.
B. October 26, 1881.
C. February 14, 1886.
D. August 16, 1878.

1-B. October 26, 1881, in mid-afternoon.

2. Where did the gunfight occur?
A. On Fremont Street.
B. In the O.K. Corral.
C. Alleyway between Fly's Rooming House & Harwood House.
D. In Front of Fly's Photo Gallery.

WYATT EARP

"It's your neck, Lockhart. If you want a Christian burial, better leave some money with the undertaker!"
—James Millican,
The Man from Laramie, 1955.

2-C. *In the alleyway (actually a vacant lot between two buildings) facing Fremont street. The O.K. Corral was some distance away at the other end of the block on Allen Street.*

3. Who was the town marshal at the time of the shootout?
A. Ben Sippy.
B. Wyatt Earp.
C. John Behan.
D. Virgil Earp.

3-D. *Virgil Earp, at 35, was appointed Chief of Police (Marshal) after the retirement of Ben Sippy a year before the fight. Wyatt, 31, was the Deputy City Marshal at the time. Johnny Behan was the Sheriff of Cochise County and supported the dubious livestock dealings of "The Cowboys."*

4. Virgil Earp and three men walked down to where the Clantons and McLaurys were standing to do what?
A. They came to ask them to peaceably leave town.
B. They came to arrest and disarm them.
C. They came to tell them about the ordinance against carrying a lethal weapon in the city limits of Tombstone.
D. They came to invite them to a poker game at the Oriental Saloon.

4-B. *Virgil swore under oath that "I meant to disarm them."*

"Throw up your hands, I have come to disarm you."

"You ain't gettin' no older than tomorrow."
—Slim Pickens, *One-Eyed Jacks*, 1961

5. What were the first words said, and by whom, before the gunfire errupted?

A. "Throw up your hands; I have come to disarm you." by Virgil Earp.

B. "Are you heeled?" by Wyatt Earp.

C. "You've got a fight coming." by Doc Holliday.

D. "You [expletive], you have been looking for a fight, and now you have it." by Wyatt Earp.

5A&D. Virgil Earp (and others) testified in court that he was the first to speak and said something like "Boys, throw up your hands; I want your guns"(line A). But Sheriff Behan, Billy Claiborne and Ike testified that the first words they heard were those of Wyatt Earp (line D). Those who testified for the defense said one thing and those testifying for the prosecution said they heard Wyatt's insulting remark first.

6. Who said "Don't shoot me, I don't want to fight!"

A. Ike Clanton

B. Frank McLaury

C. William Claiborne

D. Billy Clanton

6-D. Wesley Fuller testified for the prosecution that Billy Clanton responded to someone saying "Throw up your hands!" by raising his hands in the air and saying "Don't shoot me, I don't want to fight!" Witnesses for the defense claimed no one threw up their hands to surrender.

DOC HOLLIDAY

7. How many men died in the Gunfight at the O.K. Corral?
A. One
B. Two
C. Three
D. Four

7-C. Three men were "hurled into eternity in the duration of a moment": Tom McLaury, Frank McLaury and Billy Clanton.

8. Of the eight men involved in the fight, who was NOT hit by a bullet?
A. Billy Clanton and Virgil Earp
B. Doc Holliday
C. Wyatt Earp and Ike Clanton
D. Morgan Earp, Ike Clanton and Frank McLaury

8-C. Wyatt Earp and Ike Clanton. Ike had run off, through Fly's photo studio and into a dance hall on Allen street. Virgil was shot in the calf of his leg, Morgan was shot through the shoulders (bullet chipping a vertebrae) and Holliday was hit in the left hip. Of the eight participants, three men died, three were wounded and two walked away without a scratch.

9. Who said "I won't be arrested today, I am right here and am not going away."
A. Ike Clanton
B. Wyatt Earp
C. Thomas Keefe
D. Frank McLaury

9-B. Gotcha, it was Wyatt Earp! Sheriff Behan attempted to arrest Wyatt immediately after the gunfight was over.

10. Which statement is NOT true?
A. Virgil Earp used a double-barreled shotgun in the fight.
B. Sheriff Behan asked Marshal Earp to disarm the Clantons and McLowerys just before the fight.
C. Ike Clanton had no weapon and broke and ran when the fight began.
D. William "The Kid" Claiborne was with the Clantons and McLaurys, but hit the dirt when firing began.

10-A. Is false. Virgil was seen carrying a shotgun before the shootout, but Doc Holliday, 28, had the shotgun during the fight. At some point before they arrived at the alley, Virgil must have handed the shotgun to Holliday who used it in the fight to kill Tom McLaury (wounds verified his death was by shotgun).

11. Which statement is NOT true?

A. Sheriff Behan tried to disarm the Clantons and McLaurys just before the fight.

B. Ike Clanton played poker the night before the fight with Tom McLaury, Sheriff Behan, Virgil Earp and an unknown man.

C. All witnesses at the trial agreed that Billy Clanton and Frank McLaury fired first.

D. When the fight began, Frank McLaury was holding the reins of a horse, on which hung a scabbard with a Winchester.

11-C. Is false. William Claiborne and Ike Clanton testified that Doc Holliday and Morgan Earp were the first to shoot. Other witnesses said it was Wyatt Earp and Billy Clanton that shot first. No two accounts agreed, only that the first two shots were fired almost simultaneously.

"The most important lesson I learned from those proficient gunfighters was that the winner of a gunplay usually was the man who took his time."

—Wyatt Earp, *Wyatt Earp: Frontier Marshall*, 1931.

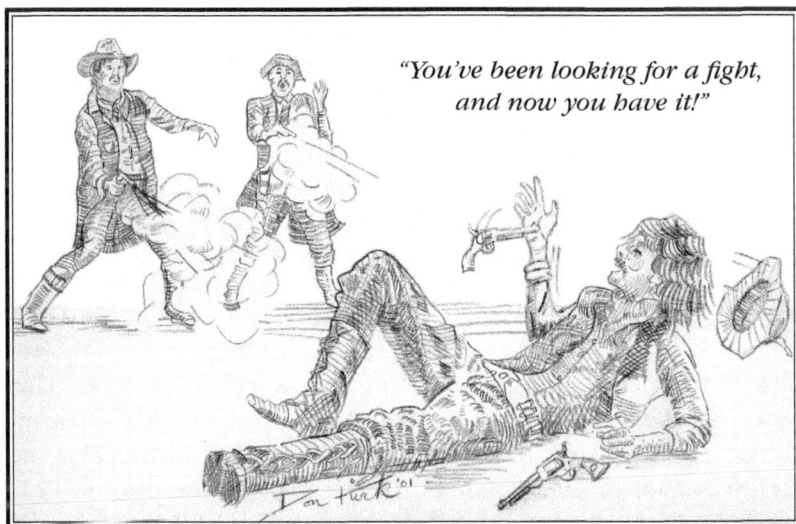

"You've been looking for a fight, and now you have it!"

THE VERDICT

Virgil and Wyatt testified at a preliminary hearing for the Murder of Tom McLaury, Frank McLaury and Billy Clanton. After a month long hearing the judge announced his decision. Here's an excerpt from Judge Wells Spicer's verdict in Justice's Court, Township No. 1, as reported by the Tombstone Epitaph:

> *In view of these controversies between Wyatt Earp and Isaac Clanton and Thos. McLaury, and in further view of the quarrel the night before between Isaac Clanton and J.H. Holliday, I am of the opinion that the defendant Virgil Earp, as chief of police, by subsequently calling upon Wyatt Earp and J.H. Holliday to assist him in arresting and disarming the Clantons and McLaurys, committed an injudicious and censurable act; and although in this he acted incautiously and without proper circumspection, yet, when we consider the condition of affairs incident to a frontier country; the lawlessness and disregard for human life; the existence of a law-defying element in our midst; the fear and feeling of insecurity that has existed; the supposed prevalence of bad, desperate and reckless men who have been a terror to the country, and kept away capital and enterprise, and considering the many threats that had been made against the Earps, I can attach no criminality to his unwise act. In fact, as the result plainly proves, he needed the assistance and support of staunch and true friends, upon whose courage, coolness and fidelity he could depend in case of an emergency.*
>
> *I conclude the performance of the duty imposed upon me by saying, in the language of the statute, "There being no sufficient cause to believe the within named" Wyatt S. Earp and John H. Holliday, "guilty of the offense mentioned within," I order them to be released.*

The verdict did not go well with the townspeople and "The Cowboys." An unknown assailant shot Virgil Earp with a shotgun, hitting him in his left side and causing him to loose an arm. Morgan Earp was shot in the back and killed while playing pool in Bob Hatch's Saloon.

A Match Game
6 O.K. CORRAL FILMS

Match the movies about the famous Gunfight at the O.K. Corral with the actors who played WYATT EARP.

1. *Tombstone* (1942)
2. *My Darling Clementine* (1946)
3. *Gunfight at the O.K. Corral* (1957)
4. *Hour of the Gun* (1967)
5. *Tombstone* (1993)
6. *Wyatt Earp* (1994)

a. James Garner
b. Richard Dix
c. Henry Fonda
d. Burt Lancaster
e. Kurt Russell
f. Kevin Costner

ANS: 1-b, 2-c, 3-d, 4-a, 5-e, 6-f.

Now match the same movies to the actors who played memorable roles as DOC HOLLIDAY.

1. *Tombstone* (1942)
2. *My Darling Clementine* (1946)
3. *Gunfight at the O.K. Corral* (1957)
4. *Hour of the Gun* (1967)
5. *Tombstone* (1993)
6. *Wyatt Earp* (1994)

f. Val Kilmer
g. Jason Robarts
h. Dennis Quaid
i. Victor Mature
j. Kirk Douglas
k. Kent Taylor

ANS: 1-k, 2-i, 3-j, 4-g, 5-f, 6-h.

"You aimin' to stay on here, Doc?"
"Yeah, the doctors tell me that the fine Arizona air you get in pool halls and saloons might do me some good."
"You stay in Tombstone, I guarantee you won't die in bed."

—Richard Dix as "Wyatt Earp" and Kent Taylor as "Doc Holliday" in *Tombstone,* 1942.

Saturday Morning Showdown
6 SIX-SHOOTER STUNTS

"Speed's fine, but accuracy's final."
—William Jordan, *No Final Place Winner,* 1965.

"I'll show you some fancy gun handling!"
"Hell, you couldn't hit a washtub tossed in the air at three-and-a-half feet." Maybe this clown couldn't hit the side of a barn at 25 feet, but many fast draw experts have proven that the legendary claims of famous gunfighters could indeed have been accomplished. One of those expert shooters, Ed McGivern, demonstrated what was possible in his 1938 book "Fast and Fancy Revolver Shooting." So here's a sampling of these legendary gun handling stunts actually accomplished with a single-action revolver. Remember, a single-action had to be cocked with the thumb, and then the trigger pulled each time it was to be fired.

1. The Quick Draw. The gun should be worn so that it is half way between the wrist and elbow. The right hand comes down well below the butt of the gun, then comes up grabbing the gun high on the butt with the thumb wrapped around the hammer. The index finger does not try to find the trigger guard, but stays outside it! As the gun comes forword, the index finger slips into the trigger guard and the thumb cocks the hammer in one easy motion. Both actions are completed *before* the gun comes level, where it can then be immediately fired.

6. The Single and Double Roll. The gun is spun forward on the index finger (in the trigger guard) and as it comes back around into firing position, the thumb cocks the hammer, ready to be fired. This can be done with two guns at the same time; they can be spun more than once and the direction of the spin can be reversed several times for some real flash. Numerous western movie actors have gone to the trouble of learning the "roll" for the part they are playing. You can see Kevin Costner do some fancy shootin' in the movie *Silverado,* 1985.

Photos by Michael Jay Smith

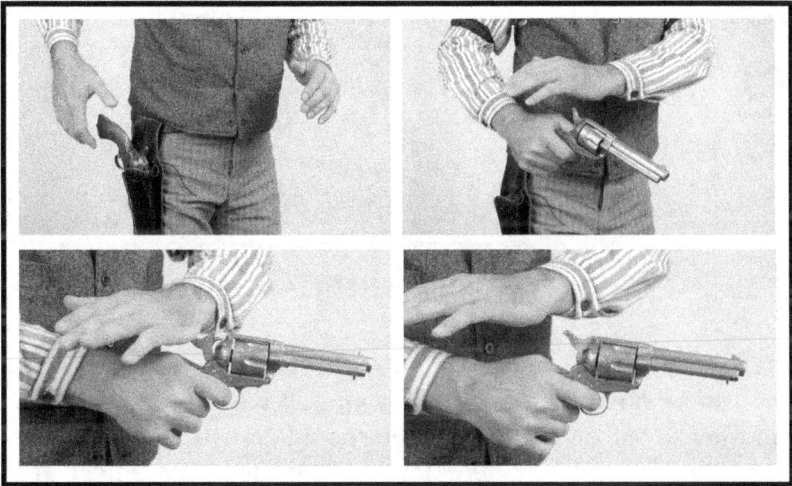

FANNING THE HAMMER

2. Fanning The Hammer. Even though fanning is fast, it's very inaccurate. The recoil of a large caliber pistol causes it to buck up into the air, making it hard to re-cock and even harder to hit anything. But if the black powder smoke is thick and you can't see your target anyway, why not? As you begin to draw the gun from your holster with your right hand, pull back on the trigger, and with the palm of the left hand force the hammer back. As the pistol comes level, release the hammer and a shot is fired. If the trigger continues to be held back, the palm of the left hand can repeatedly slap or "fan" the hammer back, firing the rest of the ammunition in rapid succession. Of course your aim leaves a lot to be desired. Remember, "speed's fine, but accuracy's final!"

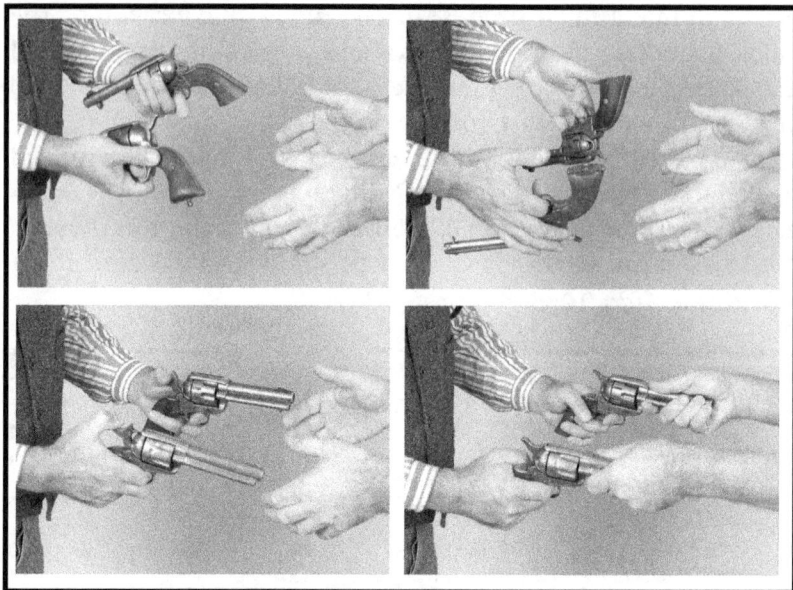

THE CURLY BILL SPIN

3. The Curly Bill, Road Agent's Spin, or Border Roll. This spin can be done with one or two guns. If a peace officer asks a gun toter to surrender his guns, he should draw them slowly and rotate them so that the butts face toward the peace officer as if to hand them to him (bottom of the butt faces outward). Then he should drop the pistols sideways so that the trigger guards slips over the fingers. He then spins the guns forward on the trigger fingers and cocks the hammers, so that the barrels of the guns flip over and into position to fire at the peace officer. *"Curly Bill" Brocius* may have been the first to use this trick using two guns against Marshal *Fred White* on October 22, 1880. After the spin, the Marshal grabbed the guns by the barrels and attempted to pull them from Curly Bill. The guns went off killing the Marshal. The scene was re-enacted by Powers Booth in the 1993 movie *Tombstone.* The famous outlaw *John Wesley Hardin* is said to have used this trick to embarrass Marshal *Bill Hickok* in Abilene.

4. Two-Gun Border Shift. A technique used to change shooting hands or shift an unloaded gun from the firing hand to the other

The author demonstrating his gun-handling skills (Photos by Michael Jay Smith)

TWO-GUN BORDER SHIFT

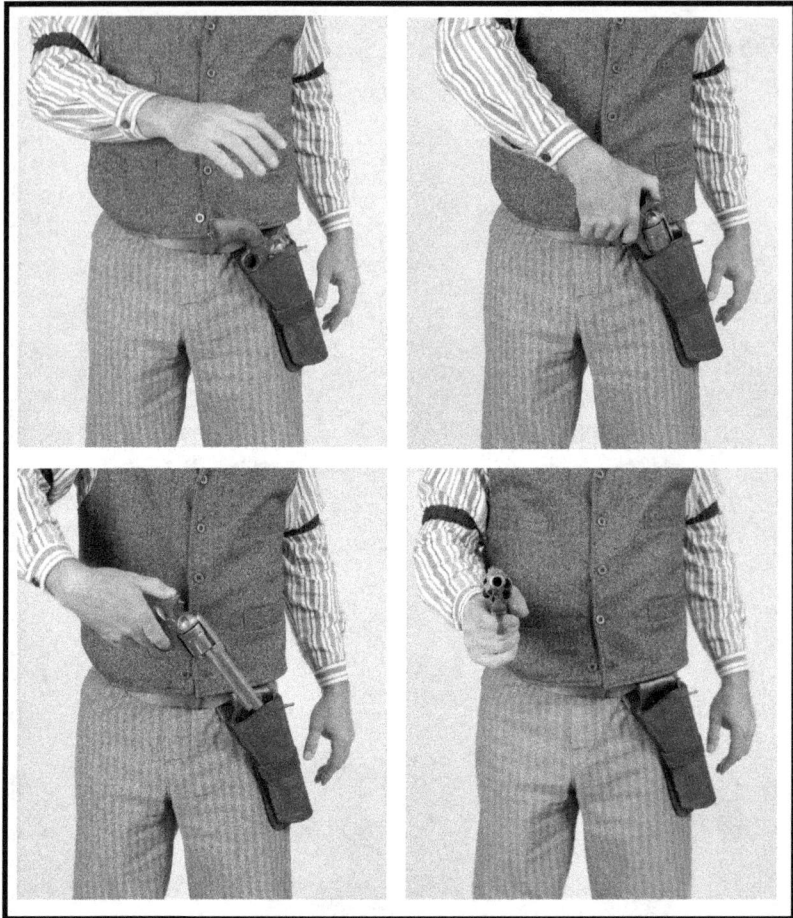

Photos by Michael Jay Smith

THE CROSS DRAW

hand with a minimum loss of time. This is done by tossing the empty gun (in this case, in the right hand) upward into the air and at the same time, passing the loaded gun held in the left hand over to the firing hand (right hand), and then continuing to shoot. The left hand catches the empty gun.

5. Two-Gun Cross Draw. The holsters are worn so that the butt of the guns face forward in military fashion. It's simple to just reach across the body with each hand and grab the pistols, pulling them into firing position. The thumbs cock the hammer as the

They Wore 'em High

In the Old West, gun holsters were normally worn high on the hip. A fast draw was not the objective. If trouble was expected, the gunfighter drew his gun before hand, or often moved his gun to a more accessible place, like in his waist or in a coat pocket. Gunfighters often found a favorite place to draw from, like sewing pockets into their vests so the pistol butts would be close at hand.

guns are drawn. To draw a butt-forward pistol with the *same* hand, the hand must be turned palm-out as it grabs the butt. The gun is cocked by the thumb simultaneously with the lifting of the gun from the holster.

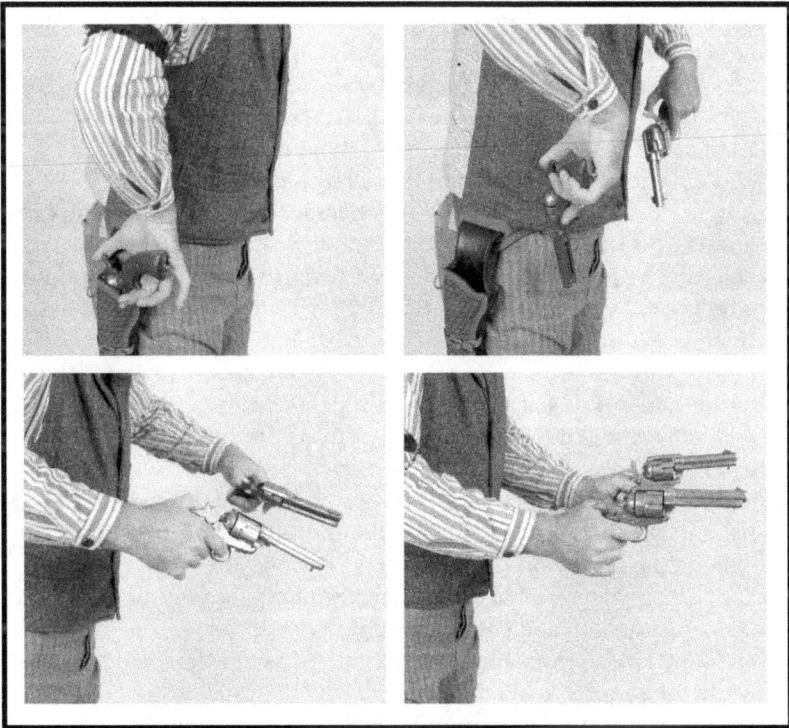

Photos by Michael Jay Smith

DRAWING TWO BUTT-FORWARD GUNS

I'll Bet Ya Two Bits
15 TRICK SHOTS

Fancy gun-handling stunts were often performed at Wild West shows around the turn of the century. Many of these legendary trick shots were used in various western films.

1. Cutting cards in half edgewise while in the air.
2. Shooting three shots into a can while in the air.
3. Hitting coins when thrown into the air. In the movie, *The Virginian* (1946) three whiskey glasses are thrown into the air and blown apart before hitting the ground.
4. Driving tacks and nails into a post with bullets fired at them. Westerners called the sport "driving the nail."
5. Shooting two guns at the same time in opposite directions and hitting targets! Kevin Costner's character did it in *Silverado*.
6. Shoot through a washer tossed into the air. A postage stamp is pasted over the hole as proof of the deed. James Garner did it in *Support Your Local Sheriff!* and James Stewart did it in *Winchester '73*.
7. Shooting aerial targets behind you using a mirror.
8. A bottle is thrown into the air, gun handler shoots through the cork and knocks out the bottom of the bottle without breaking the neck.
9. Shooting a profile picture, such as an Indian head, into the bottom of a tin plate. The stunt is simulated in *They Call Me Trinity*, 1971.
10. Hang target on a rope, cut the rope with first shot and hit the falling target with the second shot. In the 1998 TV movie, *Dollar For The Dead*, Emilio Estevez's character drops a shot glass full of whiskey and draws his gun to kill a man. He returns the gun to its holster and catches the glass before it hits the floor.
11. Shooting three targets with one bullet by shooting through one target behind which is an ax which splits the bullet into two fragments which then hit the other two targets.
12. Lay gun down on a table or chair, throw target into the air with same hand, pickup gun and shoot the target.
14. Shooting targets from a holder's mouth, hands, or the top of his head while the shooter is blindfolded.
15. Placing a large bottle on top of a smaller one and shooting the lower bottle with the first shot and before the top one hits the ground, breaking it with a second shot. Yes, these stunts have all been done.

The Man Killer!
JOHN WESLEY HARDIN

*"They say I killed six or seven men for snoring.Well, It
ain't true, I only killed one man for snoring."*
—John Wesley Hardin.

John Wesley Hardin, a violent man, killed 44 men by his
own count, all of them deserving what befell them, at least
according to Hardin.A merciless man, he's the killer famous
for shooting a sleeping man through a hotel room wall
because the man was snoring too loudly.This unstable man,
capable of senseless murdering, and feared by all, died by the
gun, just as he lived by it. So who was this man?

Well, he was a loner and the son of a Methodist preacher. Born
in Bonham,Texas in 1853, John Wesley Hardin killed his first man
when he was just 15 years of age.The Civil War had ended, but the
hatred for the freed blacks often spawned fights. In Moscow,Texas,
in 1868, Hardin found himself in a wrestling match with a black
man named Mage. During the tussle, Mage's nose was bloodied
and he declared to Hardin: "no white boy can draw my blood
and live." The next day Mage approached Hardin who was on
horseback, grabbed the horse's bridle, and dared Hardin to fight
him again.According to Hardin, as he wrote in his autobiography,
"I shot him loose. He kept coming back and every time we would
start, I would shoot him again and again until I shot him down."

At his fathers urging, Hardin went into hiding fearing he
wouldn't get a fair trial at a court run by carpetbaggers.Thus began
a long career of running from the law. Before he reached the age
of 16, he managed to kill three more men.At a creek crossing, he
bushwhacked Federal solders that had been tracking him. Two
years later he was brought in for a murder he *didn't* commit.
But, before he could be tried, he broke out of jail by buying a

gun from a prisoner in another cell. He killed a guard during his escape; this notch on his gun was victim number five. A few days later Hardin was hired on as a trail boss in Gonzales, Texas for a drive up the Chisolm Trail. During the trip, a Mexican herd of cattle approaching from behind came too close, and the cowboys were having trouble keeping the two herds apart. Hardin got into an argument with the boss of the Mexican herd. They were on horseback when the Mexican pulled his gun and fired at John Wesley. The bullet went through Hardin's hat, but didn't hit his head. Hardin drew his cap-and-ball revolver, and pulled the trigger. It didn't fire. The Mexican turned to run. Hardin jumped from his mount, steadied his pistol—which had a loose cylinder—and fired again. It went off this time and hit the Mexican in the thigh. The Mexican halted in truce, choosing to end the matter, but Hardin took a pistol from a fellow cowhand and ran after the Mexican. He succeeded in shooting the Mexican through the heart. A full gun battle then ensued among the two camps of drovers. In the end, the Mexicans got the short end of the stick, losing six vaqueros to lead poisoning. And it was Hardin who killed five of them. He could now boast about the 10 notches on his "peacemaker"—and he was just 18 years old!

It was at the American House Hotel in Abilene, Texas that John Wesley Hardin shot through a bedroom wall in order to stop the man next door from snoring. The first shot missed the sleeping man. The second hit its mark and killed him. At the time, Abilene was Wild Bill Hickok's town so Hardin chose not to stay around and confront Wild Bill; instead, he made his escape out the hotel window in his longjohns, never to return to Abilene.

TIDBIT: In the Old West, to PISTOL-WHIP someone meant to hit him over the head with the *barrel* of a sixgun. Some filmmakers and writers of western fiction have a character hitting an opponent with the *butt* of the gun. This would've been a stupid thing for a westerner to do—a good way to shoot himself. And, secondly, it would have taken him much longer to get his gun into action—having to turn the gun around so he could hold it by the barrel.

---

18 WORDS FOR THE HANDGUN

1. Equalizer
2. Lead Pusher
3. Persuader
4. Shooting Iron
5. Talking Iron
6. Hardware
7. Hog Leg
8. Manstopper
9. Pistol
10. Six Gun
11. Thumb Buster
12. Flame Thrower
13. Lead Chucker
14. Peacemaker
15. Iron
16. Skull Cracker
17. Forty Five
18. Blue Lightning

Hardin spend most of his notorious life in central Texas where family and friends repeatedly helped him skirt the law. He settled down for a time and had two children with Jane Bowen, a woman that remained faithful to him even though he often left her side for long periods of time. But the killings never stopped, and by age 21 John Wesley got into a fight that eventually landed him in prison. The count was already 38 killed (by his count), when on May 26, 1874 he confronted Deputy Sheriff Charles Webb in a saloon. Hardin invited the town sheriff for a drink. Wes had already heard that Webb was bent on ridding the state of his carcass. Webb politely accepted the drink, but as they moved toward the bar, someone yelled "Lookout, Hardin." John Wesley turned, saw Webb's gun drawn, and jumped aside as a bullet splintered the fine mahogany bar. Hardin was grazed in the shoulder, but he drew fast as lighting and shot Webb square in the face. Webb fell dead to the floor. With victim Number 39—a sheriff—Hardin high-tailed it out of town. He went for his wife Jane and they both traveled to Florida where he hid out for two years. During those years, living under the assumed name of J. H. Swain, he actually helped the local law round up some wanted men, and in their capture he shot and killed one of them "in the line of duty." This was his 40th man killed, and it was done legally!

Pinkerton detectives finally ferreted out his identity and caught up with him only to lose two more men to Hardin's smoking Forty-Five. He made his escape and hid out in Alabama where he shot two more men in a friendly card game. The body count was now 44, but would turn out to be the last notch on his gun. The Texas Rangers would corner him ten months later in a Pullman rail car. He was returning home after a gambling spree when Rangers approached him, guns drawn, from either end of the car. John Wesley Hardin went for his pistol only to have it catch in his suspenders.

Hardin was tried in Austin, Texas for the murder of Sheriff Webb, the one man you could argue he shot in self defense. He got off easy with a sentence of 25 years at Huntsville. He was just 25 years old.

Hardin served 15 years of his prison term, getting a pardon by the Governor of Texas. While in prison, he studied law and in 1894 he set up a law office in El Paso. Less than a year later, a man he had argued with the day previous, approached him from behind and shot him in the back. The killer, John Selman, was tried but acquitted of the murder. It seems the jurors were happy to be rid of the Texas menace, John Wesley Hardin. For a detailed description of the events of John Wesley's life, read *The Life of John Wesley Hardin as Written by Himself*, 1896.

A Match Game
4 SWEETHEARTS

Match the ladies of the wild Frontier West with the men for whom they had a special fondness.

1.	Etta Place	**a.**	Wild Bill Hickok
2.	Big Nose Kate	**b.**	Frank Butler
3.	Calamity Jane	**c.**	Doc Holliday
4.	Annie Oakley	**d.**	The Sundance Kid

ANS: 1-d, 2-c, 3-a, 4-b.

A Mental Case
CLAY ALLISON

"ROBERT CLAY ALLISON 1840-1887. He Never Killed A Man That Did Not Need Killing."
—Epitaph on his tombstone, Pecos, Texas.

This is a gruesome tale of a gruesome man. The weak of stomach need read no further. The man you will read about here had no regard for human life, none what-so-ever. He was one of the most vicious legendary outlaws on the American Frontier.

One evening when Clay Allison was downing a few thirst-quenching drinks at a saloon in Elizabethtown, New Mexico, a crazed rancher's wife approached him for help. She said her husband had gone berserk and killed several visiting strangers in their home and, in his wild rampage, he also killed their baby daughter. Incensed, Clay went with the woman to her ranch house where he found the husband saturated with liquor, inside and out, but there were no corpses, including the baby's, in evidence. A few days later, during a search of the property, a buried tangle of bones was found. Allison quickly assumed the drunken rancher was guilty and deserved appropriate punishment. While the town doctor was still trying to determine whether or not the bones were human or just animal, Clay Allison and a few drinking companions broke into the Elizabethtown jail where the rancher was being held and extracted him. They dragged him to a slaughter house and hanged him by the neck until dead. But this wasn't sufficient justice for Clay Allison and he proceeded to sever the head of the rancher's corpse, impale it on a stake, and ride to the town of Cimarron 30 miles away with the gruesome head held high as he rode. When he reached Cimarron, he took it to Henri Lambert's Saloon where he displayed the head next to the bar for all to see.

Source: Wikimedia Commons

CLAY ALLISON—AGE 45

It behooved no one to rile Clay Allison. If he felt anyone—including himself—had been wronged in the slightest, bear that man no fury as violent as Clay Allison's. Clay was born near Waynesboro, Tennessee on a small farm where he grew up as a "normal" sociable boy before turning to crime. When the Civil War began he enlisted in the Tennessee Light Infantry, but was quickly released with a medical discharge. The doctor's official report stated that he believed Clay was "incapable of performing the duties of a soldier because of a blow to the head received many years ago. Emotional or physical excitement produces paroxysmals of a mixed character, partly epileptic and partly maniacal." Whoa Flicka, it sounds like this man should have been locked up.

Paradoxically, Clay became a successful rancher in Colfax, New Mexico after a stint working as a cowpuncher in Texas where he moved with some relatives after the war. He was respected by some, feared by all. Men all over the West feared they might someday meet up with this man. He was like a wild serial killer on the loose, with not a soul daring to confront him. Clay had an obvious contempt for the law. He was a Southerner, and it was the "Yanks" who were the new lawmen of reconstruction. He felt men like Wyatt Earp and Bat Masterson were just trying to build up their reputation by going after the honest, hardworking cowmen. So Clay just ignored the law and took matters into his own hands when he felt justice needed to be done.

One such incident involved a neighboring rancher who had a disagreement over water rights. They eventually agreed on a way to solve their differences without interference from the law. Together, they would dig a good-sized grave, bring in an unmarked gravestone, and set it up at the end of the rectangular pit. They agreed to climb into the hole buck-naked, each with a bowie knife to defend himself. The one who survived the knife fight and was able to climb out would have the headstone engraved with the others name. Hours later, in the twilight of evening, a silhouetted man was seen shoveling dirt into the hole. It was Clay Allison. Such was the way he chose to solve his problems.

A legendary example of Clay's revengeful personality was the famous incident with the dentist. Allison had arrived in Cheyenne with a herd of cattle after a long trail drive. He had an inflamed, "festered up" tooth. He promptly found a dentist to relieve him of his pain. The dentist proceeded to drill, but it turned out to be on

---

TIDBIT: A gunbelt called the "Hollywood Rig" or "Buscadero rig" is what you'll see in most westerns made since the 1950's. In this design, the gun holster fits through a slit cut into a widened part of the belt. It was first built by Tio Sam Myres of El Paso, Texas at the turn of the century. The design had been suggested by Captain R. Hughes of the Texas Rangers. Before that time, the holster was looped over the top of a ordinary pants belt, with the belt worn high around the waist. So if you want to do an authentic nineteenth-century impression, please don't wear a "Hollywood Rig."

A HOLSTER BY ANY OTHER NAME

Early pistols before the 1850's were large and heavy (like the Colt Paterson), but were intended to be carried on the horse. To carry the pistol, a pocket was attached to the saddle called a "holster." When Samuel Colt and others invented lighter pistols, men found they could carry the pistol in a pocket on their pants belt. They called the pants pistol pocket a "scabbard." It wasn't until the late 1890's did "holster" come into common usage. "Scabbard" now refers to the sheath covering swords, knives and bayonets not pistols.

the wrong tooth, and cut to the quick. Clay jumped from the chair, said nothing, and left the Doc's office. He found another dentist in town and had him fix both teeth at a cost to him of $25. Clay then returned to the first dentist where he forced him into his own chair and began pulling a tooth with the dentist's own wretched forceps. After the first tooth was pulled from its bloody socket he started on another. The dentist's lip became clamped between the forceps and the tooth and a curdling yell came forth that brought help from the street. The surgery was brought to a halt by the crowd, so we'll never know how far Clay might have gone.

On one occasion, an outlaw by the name of Chuck Colbert went around claiming he had made seven kills, and that Clay Allison would be his eighth. Chuck invited Clay to dinner at a fine local Inn. Clay accepted. They ate a nice quiet meal together. To all observers they appeared to be becoming friends, but then things changed when the after-dinner coffee was delivered to the table. Chuck reached for his coffee cup with his left hand, at the same time quietly drawing his pistol from his gun holster with his right. But Allison went for *his* "equalizer." Panicked, Colbert fired before he had gotten his gun clear of the table and the bullet was deflected. Clay paused with a menacing grin, starred into Colbert's eyes, then calmly shot Chuck in the head, just above the right eye. Allison was later asked why he had conceded to dine with a man bent on killing him; his reply was: "I didn't want to send a man to hell on an empty stomach!"

Clay was a mad man free to roam the streets. He was often drunk and found riding through town naked, firing his gun at anyone who looked at him. On one occasion, a gunman with a reputation rode into town looking for Allison. Such incidents were common; the townspeople always headed for cover and waited for the outcome, powerless to do anything. In this case, a gunfighter named Mace Bowman got drunk with Clay and they decided to practice fast draws with each other. Mace proved to be the quicker man, so Clay suggested another test of their skill and Mace agreed. Both men undressed down to their underwear, and standing in their bare feet, each shot at the other's feet to determine who was the better dancer. The contest continued into the wee hours of night until both were exhausted. Neither lost a single toe, and after sleeping it off, Mace left town.

You would think such a man who lived by the gun, would die by it, and most outlaws of the west did indeed come to their end by hanging or violent gun battle, but Clay Allison was not to be so lucky. Clay was returning from Pecos, Texas on July 1, 1887 with a wagon load of supplies when one of the grain sacks began to fall from the wagon. Clay reached for it, lost his balance, and fell from the wagon. A rear wheel rolled over his neck, or his back, depending on who you talk to, and broke it smartly, killing Clay quietly without fanfare. During his time on earth, he lived as both a respectable cattleman and as a feared gunfighter.

Tidbit: FIVE BEANS IN THE WHEEL. If an old single-action six-shooter was inadvertently dropped, or while in its holster the hammer caught on a bush, a bullet could be accidentally discharged. To avoid this dreadful possibility, any self-respecting westerner would carry only five cartridges in the cylinder with the hammer sitting on the empty chamber. Cocking the gun would turn the cylinder and bring a loaded chamber into position ready for firing. "If you can't do the job in five shots, it's time to git ta hell outta there and hunt for a place to hole up." The westerner had respect for guns and knew how to use them safely. Anyone carrying six cartridges was considered a rank amateur.

A Ballad
EL PASO

By Marty Robbins, 1957 ©Acuff-Rose Music, Ltd.

A **wonderful and sad ballad**—though not written in the nineteenth century—it reflects the legend that is the Old West. Marty Robbins, born Martin David Robinson, always wanted to be a singing cowboy star. He did star in five westerns including *Ballad Of A Gunfighter* (1964). One of his greatest hit recordings was "El Paso," making him one of the great Country & Western Music stars of the time.

1. Out in the west Texas town of El Paso
I fell in love with a Mexican girl.
Night-time would find me in Rose's Cantina;
Music would play and Felina would whirl.

2. Blacker than night were the eyes of Felina,
Wicked and evil while casting a spell.
My love was deep for this Mexican maiden;
I was in love, but in vain, I could tell.

3. One night a wild young cowboy came in
Wild as the west Texas wind.
Dashing and daring a drink he was sharing
With wicked Felina the girl that I love.

4. So in anger, I challenged his right
For the love of this maiden.
Down went his hand
For the gun that he wore.

5. My challenge was answered in less than a heartbeat;
The handsome young stranger lay dead on the floor.
Out through the backdoor of Rose's I ran,
Out where the horses were tied.

6. I caught a good one it looked like it could run.
Up on its back and away I did ride
Just as fast as I could from the west Texas town of El Paso,
Out to the badlands of New Mexico.

7. Back in El Paso my life would be worthless.
Everything's good in life, nothing is left.
It's been so long since I've seen the young maiden.
My love is stronger than my fear of death.

8. I saddled up and away I did go,
Riding alone in the dark.
Maybe tomorrow a bullet may find me;
Tonight nothing's worse than this pain in my heart.

9. And at last here I am on the hill overlooking El Paso.
I can see Rose's Cantina below.
My love is strong and it pushes me onward;
Down off the hill to Felina I go.

10. Off to my right, I see five mounted cowboys;
Off to my left ride a dozen or more.
Shouting and shooting, I can't let them catch me.
I have to make it to Rose's back door.

11. Something is dreadful wrong for I feel
A deep burning pain in my side.
Though I am trying to stay in the saddle,
I'm getting weary, unable to ride.

12. But my love for Felina is strong and I rise where I've fallen.
Oh, I am weary; I can't stop to rest.
I see the white puff of smoke from the rifle.
I feel the bullet go deep in my chest.

13. From out of nowhere, Felina has found me,
Kissing my cheek as she kneels by my side.
Cradled by two loving arms that I'd die for;
One little kiss, and Felina, goodbye.

Wooden crosses, maybe the only evidence that a man once lived and died here in Artesia, New Mexico (dk)

Shovel, Top Hat, and Headstone
BADMEN ON BOOTHILL

"Have him meet me at Boothill. He'll have only
one direction to travel from there: down!"
—Kirk Douglas, *Gunfight at the OK Corral,* 1957

A wooden cross or a plank of lumber chiseled with a few departing words marked the graves of men who lived and died violently. Most of those original markers are gone now, but a few cemeteries in the American West still attract tourists—new markers replacing those that have been taken by the winds of time. "Boothill" cemeteries, in places like Virginia City, Nevada or Grafton, Utah, still look like those seen in your favorite western movie. Others like Glenwood Springs, Colorado (where there now sits a huge marble monument for the likes of Doc Holliday) bear little resemblance to the dusty, tumbleweed-choked boothill of the movies.

The legendary Boothill was a small cemetery of the Wild West where men who died in gunfights (with their boots on) were unceremoniously buried. It was usually near the town's cemetery, but not inside it where only decent God-fearing folks were laid to rest. Interring the victim *near* the cemetery was the townfolks way of showing at least some mercy (so the victim wouldn't be quite so lonesome for all of eternity). The cemetery was usually located high on a hill so that flooding wouldn't raise the coffins up out of the ground. The outlaws were often buried with their feet facing West allowing them a chance at a running start from the Devil, instead of facing Resurrection "which cometh from the East on Judgement Day." The Mount Moriah cemetery in Deadwood, South Dakota is said to be the first such "boot hill." Hope you enjoy the morbid facts that follow.

C & W
Mortuary Supply

EMBALMING
The Honored Dead

The undersigned will attend in all details to Preserving and Petrifying the Bodies of the Dead for those who give their lives in the Gallant Cause and who may be entrusted to His charge. Every embalment will be conducted under the supervision of a skilled surgeon; the process is the original of Doctor Holmes as performed upon

General Jackson

FUNERAL & MOURNING
items may be had at best prices.

Persons at a distance from the battlefields or campgrounds of the Army desiring to have the bodies of their deceased friends on the field of battle or elsewhere disinterred, embalmed, disinfected, or prepared and sent home, can have it PROMPTLY attended to by application to the undersigned, as may

Prudent Soldiers
for whom contracts for such services are available.

FINE COFFINS
Quality wooden construction Free from entry of VERMIN !

Doctor R.G. Williams   *Doctor B.J. Carmichael*
Embalming Surgeons

ENCAMPED AT ARMY MEDICAL DEPARTMENT HDQTRS

Text of actual Old West Broadside

Mortimer Peel's
WRITTEN GUARANTEE

"You plug 'em, I plant 'em."
—Claude Clay, Undertaker in the *Tumbleweeds* comic strip.

The Mortician, with black top hat and tails, is often portrayed as a comical character in the movies, but his job was a deadly serious business. The victim of consumption, gangrene, or lead poisoning, had to be put asunder before he could become a health problem (if he hadn't already been one while he was living). A bloated carcass would quickly attract opportunist buzzards and the stench, well, you "don't wanna be a-standin' downwind." The business of preparing a man for proper burial required a professional man with unique skills to build a suitable bonebox, make a respectable marker, and keep up with the latest embalming techniques. This sign found on a morticians's office attests to his professionalism and dedication to his craft:

MORTIMER PEEL'S WRITTEN GUARANTEE

ALL PINE BOXES ARE MADE TO ORDER;
NO BOXES TOO SHORT.

ALL BOXES MADE OF GOOD QUALITY LUMBER;
NO KNOTHOLES FOR BUGS TO ENTER.

WOOD PRESERVED WITH THE BEST TOBACCO JUICE.
BRASS HANDLES EXTRA.

CUSTOMER'S EFFECTS WILL BE SENT TO NEXT OF KIN.

FIVE MINUTE EULOGY GUARANTEED; NO BAD WORDS.

NOTICE OF DEATH PLACED IN NEWSPAPER AND
DULY RECORDED IN TOWN RECORDS.

(dk)

Swinging In The Wind
11 NAMES FOR A HANGING

A hanging was serious business—not to be taken lightly—
so why does a westerner's slang phrases for an "execution"
make us chuckle? As one vigilante said of a horse thief: "his
neck was too damned short so we took him out to stretch it."

Hung Out To Dry
Going To A Necktie Social
Decorating A Cottonwood
Wearing A California Collar
Guest Of Honor At A String Party
Stiff Rope And A Short Drop
Performing A Mid-Air Dance
Dying With Throat Trouble
Gurglin' On A Rope
A Lynching
Stretching Hemp

A Match Game
8 LAST WORDS

The last words spoken by some famous westerners before their untimely deaths have become legendary in the annals of Old West lore. Match the famous *last words* to those who said them.

1. "Hurry it up. I'm due in Hell for dinner."
2. "Quién es? Quién es?"
3. "This is the last game of pool I'll ever play."
4. "Hang on to the Matchless. It will make millions again."
5. "Bury me next to Bill."
6. "I will throw up my hands for no gringo dog."
7. "The Seventh can handle anything it meets."
8. "Center my heart boys. Don't mangle my body."

a. Calamity Jane
b. Gen. George Custer
c. Black Jack Ketchum
d. Billy the Kid

e. Three-Fingered Jack
f. Morgan Earp
g. Horace A.W. Tabor
h. John D. Lee

ANSWERS:

1-c. BLACK JACK KETCHUM said this to his hangman in 1901. He was hung for killing two miners in a saloon fight *and* the two officers who tried to apprehend him. The "fall" went badly and Jack's head was ripped from his torso and it rolled into the crowd.

2-d. BILLY THE KID asked in Spanish "Who is it [inside the house]?" of two men standing outside Pete Maxwell's house on July 14, 1881 at Fort Sumner, New Mexico. Billy, not expecting trouble, then entered the house where he was shot by Pat Garrett who was sitting their quietly in the dark.

3-f. MORGAN EARP was shot by unknown assassins while playing a Saturday night game of billiards in Tombstone, Arizona in 1882 after the famous O.K. Corral gunfight with the Clantons and McLaurys.

4-g. HORACE TABOR swore this to his wife Baby Doe in 1899. She returned to the Matchless mine and lived there in poverty until her death in 1935, the Matchless never living up to its promise.

5-a. CALAMITY JANE died in 1903 and wanted to be buried next to her love, "Wild Bill" Hickok, who was murdered in 1876 by Jack McCall and buried in Mount Moriah Cemetery, Deadwood, Dakota Territory. She got her last request.

6-e. THREE-FINGERED JACK GARCIA, a California bandit said these last words when refusing to be brought in 1853.

7-b. GENERAL GEORGE CUSTER on refusing to wait for reinforcements before the battle of Little Big Horn.

8-h. JOHN D. LEE, a devoted follower of Brigham Young, said these last words to his firing squad after he was tried and found guilty by his fellow Mormons of leading a band of Payote Indians and Mormon settlers to slaughter over 100 men, women, and children on a wagon train headed West. Lee was probably used as a scapegoat; the massacre was thought to have been authorized by Brigham Young himself.

Boothill, Virginia City, Nevada (dk)

FOR SALE: ONE HOME-MADE COFFIN
NEVER BEEN USED. FITS 6 FT 2 INCH.
REASON FOR SELLING: IMPROVED HEALTH
—Ron Kincade

A Tombstone For A Man Not Yet Dead:

PEDRO ARONDONDO

Born 1857 — Died 1889

From A Bullet Wound

Between The Eyes.

Fired By Red Ivan

This gravestone was written by a cowboy named Red Ivan *before* he shot down Pedro Arondondo in a high-noon shootout. Pedro, several days earlier, had accused Red Ivan—a gambler and card shark—of stacking the deck in a poker game. These were fighting words and the two men fumed for days. A showdown was inevitable, but Red Ivan had a plan. He would put the fear into his rival—thus giving himself an edge—by ordering a headstone chiseled with the above words. The headstone was finished by the stonecutter just hours before the final showdown, a showdown that sent Pedro Arondondo to a long life in hell!

TIDBIT: Were notorious owlhoots actually buried with their boots on? Not likely, boots where too valuable a commodity. If the grave digger's footcovers were not as good as the dead man's, you can bet a switch was made. Leather boots also made good brake shoes for wagons. The boots of the deceased were sometimes removed and placed under the head of the Corpus Delecti, presumably, for a more comfortable trip into hell for these badmen. As a corset salesmen said of Boothill in *The Magnificent Seven*: "There's nothing up there but murderers, cutthroats, and derelict old barflies."

The Hangman's Knot
6 DUTIES OF A HANGMAN

"Everyone of my hangings has been a scientific job. I have dropped as many as six through at one time, and twice have hanged five at one time, and there was no quiver in the entire sixteen—not even a foot moved."
—George Maledon, Hangman, Judge Parker's Court.

TECNIQUES FOR A BETTER JOB. A good hangman was dedicated to his job. It was a scientific endeavor requiring serious thought and study, and—to be sure—he didn't want to do a "messy" job in front of so many gawking onlookers.

1. New rope must be pre-stretched so it won't give any slack during a hanging.
2. The knot must be large enough to pull a man's head sideways, quickening the snap.
3. The rope must be well lubricated.
4. The length of the fall must be just right. A short drop won't kill a man instantly, and a drop that's too long could sever his head from his body. Look what happened to Black Jack!
5. A noose that's too loose around the victim's neck can also pull his head from his body.
6. The size of the rope must be matched to the weight of the man to be hanged.

A QUOTE: "You know something? Forty years from now, the weeds will grow as pretty on my grave as they will on yours. And nobody will even remember that I was yellow and that you died like a fool." —Walter Sande as corrupt Marshal Bartlett speaking to Kirk Douglas as Marshal Morgan in *Last Train From Gun Hill,* 1959.

Gallows inside the county jail, Jail Museum, Gonzales, Texas (dk)
They were placed *inside* so the inmates would behave during their tenure.

TRIVIA QUESTION: What movie did this quote come from:"Always uses top grade hemp, Schmidt does. Oils it so it slides real good. Snap your neck like a dried-out twig"?
ANS: *Hang 'Em High,* 1968.The prisoners were discussing their fate as they listen to Schmidt, the hangman, test his gallows outside.

NOTICE!

TO THIEVES, THUGS, FAKIRS AND BUNKO-STEERERS,

Among Whom Are

J.J. HARLIN, alias 'OFF WHEELER;' SAW DUST CHARLIE, WM. HEDGES, BILLY THE KID,

Billy Mullin, Little Jack, The Cuter, Pock-Marked Kid, and about Twenty Others:

If found within the Limits of this City after **TEN O'CLOCK P. M.**, this Night, you will be Invited to attend a **GRAND NECK-TIE PARTY,**

The Expense of which will be borne by

100 Substantial Citizens.

Las Vegas, March 24th, 1881.

Text of actual Old West Broadside

Gallows at Old Tucson Studios, Tucson, Arizona (dk)

THE PRINCE OF HANGMEN

GEORGE MALEDON, of Fort Smith Arkansas, was the official hangman for Judge Isaac Parker's court in Indian Territory. He carried out over 80 death sentences in his 20 year tenure as chief executioner for the Western District of Arkansas. Tall and slender, with deep-set eyes, dressed in a black tailcoat, and sporting a heavy white beard, he was the prototype of the western movie hangman. He seemed devoid of human feelings—children ran at the sight of him. He loved his trade, always working to perfect the goal of breaking a man's neck instantly so that his body "don't even twitch." He was paid $100 per hanging, and kept tintype photos of each victim until his wife made him throw them out. The local press tagged him the "Prince of Hangmen" and once when he was asked if he was haunted by the ghosts of his victims he replied, "No, because I reckon I hanged them too."

The haunt of the Plummer Gang, Bannack State Historic Park, Dillon, Montana (dk)

TRIVIA QUESTION: Name a western feature film with the word "hang" in the title?

ANSWER: *Hangman's Knot* (1952) Randolp Scott.
The Hangman (1959) Robert Taylor.
The Hanging Tree (1959) Gary Cooper.
Hang 'Em High (1968) Clint Eastwood.
The Hanged Man (1974) Michael Caffey.

HERE LIES
PETER TATE
1860-1881
HANGED BY MISTAKE
HE WAS RIGHT
WE WAS WRONG
BUT WE STRUNG HIM UP
AND NOW HE'S GONE.

(Gravestone on Boothill at Tombstone, Arizona)

VIGILANTISM

AND THE MAN WHO BUILT HIS OWN HANGING SCAFFOLD

The vigilante committee was a self-appointed group of citizens who felt they had to take the law into their own hands to maintain public order. They organized without legal authority and dispensed justice as they saw fit. The practice didn't originate in the West. There were "regulators" in South Carolina in the 1760's and in Pennsylvania in 1794 during the Whiskey Rebellion. Vigilantism was common in the Frontier West for many reasons. First, there existed a frontier psychology of self-reliance; if we don't do it no one else will. Second, the criminal element posed a threat to stability, hindering prosperity and security, and third, the legally constituted authority—if there was one—had failed to deal with the problem. The PLUMMER GANG of Bannack, Montana was one such group of men who felt the law wasn't doing its job. In this case, the law was part of the problem. One named Henry Plummer had been elected, on his charm and integrity, as Sheriff of Bannack in 1863. Little did the citizenry know that Plummer was doing a little moonlighting: he had hired a large gang of "road agents" to rob miners and travelers of their valuable possessions. The gang called themselves the "Innocents," committing over 100 murders and stealing at least $250,000 in gold before the good citizens of Bannack took up arms and organized themselves into a vigilance committee. It met regularly to determine the guilt or innocence of suspected thieves, road agents, and murderers. Over a period of 42 days the "hemp committee" hanged 23 men, including Sheriff Plummer (from scaffolds *he* had built) and sent many others packing. They were called "The Stranglers" by the local press, but peace, for a time, had indeed returned to the Wild West town of Bannack, Montana.

The Ox-Bow Incident

The classic western, *The Ox-Bow Incident* (1943) starring Henry Fonda and Dana Andrews was based on a real event that occurred in Nevada around 1885. In the film, Henry Fonda tried to stop a lynch mob hell-bent on hanging three men they believed murdered a rancher. One of the condemned men, before his hanging, wrote a letter to be delivered to his beloved wife after he had expired. Henry Fonda read the letter to the lynch mob in a barroom after they found out the three men were innocent. The movie was directed by William A. Wellman and scripted by Lamar Trotti. Here is the murdered man's letter:

My dear wife,

Mr. Davies will tell you what's happening here tonight. He's a good man and he's done everything he can for me. I suppose there's some other men here too, only they don't seem to realize what they're doin'. They're the ones I feel sorry for because it'll be over for me in a little while, but they'll have to go on rememberin' for the rest of their lives. Men just naturally can't take the law into his own hands and hang people without hurting everybody in the whole world, 'cause then he's just not breakin' one law but all laws. Laws are a lot morn' words you put in a book, or judges or lawyers, or sheriffs you hire to carry it out. It's everything people ever have found out about justice, what's right and wrong. It's the very conscience of humanity. There can't be any such thing as civilization unless people have a conscience. If people touch good anywhere, where is it except through their conscience, and what is anybody's conscience except a little piece of conscience of all men that ever lived. I guess that's all I got to say except kiss the babies for me and God bless you.

Your Husband,
Donald.

Pushing Up Daisies
27 PHRASES FOR DYING

The westerner had many slang phrases to describe the demise of someone, accidental or otherwise. Here are just a few:

1. He was done in.
2. He bit the dust.
3. He was dry gulched.
4. He played his last hand.
5. He kicked the bucket.
6. He was laid out cold.
7. He was bushwhacked.
8. He got lead poisoning.
9. He went belly up.
10. He played his last card.
11. He cashed in his chips.
12. His goose was cooked.
13. He's now meat for the wolves.
14. He's shaking hands with St. Peter.
15. He's hung up his saddle.
16. He's pushing up daisies.
17. He's gone to his last roundup.
18. Someone blew out his lamp.
19. They stopped his clock.
20. They put a window in his skull.
21. They put his lights out.
22. They wore him plumb down.
23. He was bed down for the last time.
24. He landed in a shallow grave.
25. He was kicked into a funeral procession.
26. He was tied to his horse, toes down.
27. The prairie grass is waving over him now.

The Cryptic Sign:
3-7-77

Painted on a door was "3-7-77." What did it mean? Early vigilantes in Montana used these numbers with a skull and crossbones as a warning to those suspected of violating the law. If these lawbreakers didn't "jingle their spurs" (leave town promptly), a "lynching bee" would see to it they left by another way not of their own choosing. But what do the numbers "3-7-77" mean? Could it be the size of a grave: three feet wide, seven feet long and 77 inches deep? No one but the vigillanties will ever know for sure. To this day, the badges of the Montana state police bear this cryptic sign.

CEMETERY, TERLINGUA, TEXAS (dk)

Graves in West Texas must be covered with rocks to keep away the coyotes and prevent the high winds from blowing away the grave.

Put To Bed With Pick And Shovel
42 TOMBSTONE EPITAPHS

*"For Sale: Second-Hand Tombstone.
Real Buy For Family Named Murphy."*
—old classified ad

The marble orchards of the Wild West are filled with legendary figures who died with their boots on and with colorful characters who were buried by morticians with a raw sense of humor. The graveyards of the American West have usually been ignored, but they are a part of our history and should be thought of as museums providing information and reflection on the people who populated the West. They should not be paved over and forgotten. These epitaphs are from the markers of actual "Boot Hill" residents, and some from the newspapers that reported the premature deaths. Here then, a little graveyard humor:

Here Lies
Lester Moore
Four Slugs From a .44
No Less, No More
(Boot Hill, Tombstone, Arizona)

Joseph B. Still
(Paris, Texas)

HERE IS
A. GRAVE
(Weimar, Texas)

HERE LIES
WILD BILL BRITT
Ran For Sheriff In '82
Ran For Sheriff In '83
Ran And Elected In '84
Died In '84
(Ruidoso, New Mexico)

It Was A Cough
That Carried Him Off
It Was A Coffin
They Carried Him Off In
(Greenwich, Massachusetts)

R. I. P.
JOHN HEMBLY
HE DIED AT A PUBLIC GATHERING
WHEN THE PLATFORM GAVE WAY
1858-1878

Murdered on the Streets Of Tombstone
Frank & Tom McLowery & Billie Clanton
(Boot Hill Cemetery, Tombstone, Arizona)

The First Man Killed Here Was
GEORGE MILLER
Member Of The Nevada
Assembly In The Sixties.
CORNELIUS BUCKLEY
Did It.
(Eurika, Nevada)

HERE IS WHERE HE
STOPPED LAST
J.S. Jacobs
Traveling Salesman
(Lincoln, Nebraska)

Here Lies Mary Street
She Was Hard To Beat

COPY ALL IN
Fuzzy Woodruff
Journalist

C O D
(Erie, Colorado)

Murdered By A Traitor
And Coward
Whose Name Is Not Worthy
To Appear Here.
Jesse James 1847-1882
(Kearney, Missouri)

Don't Hitch
Your Horse Here
(Redrock, Texas)

Here Lies An Athiest
All Dressed Up
And No Place To Go
(Thurmont, Maryland)

Goembel, Johnny E.
ATTORNEY AT LAW
1867-1946
"The Defense Rests"
(Rockford, Illinois)

JACK WAGNER
Killed Ed Masterson
April 9, 1878
Killed By Bat Masterson
April 9, 1878
He Argued With The
Wrong Man's Brother
(Boothill Cemetery, Dodge City Kansas)

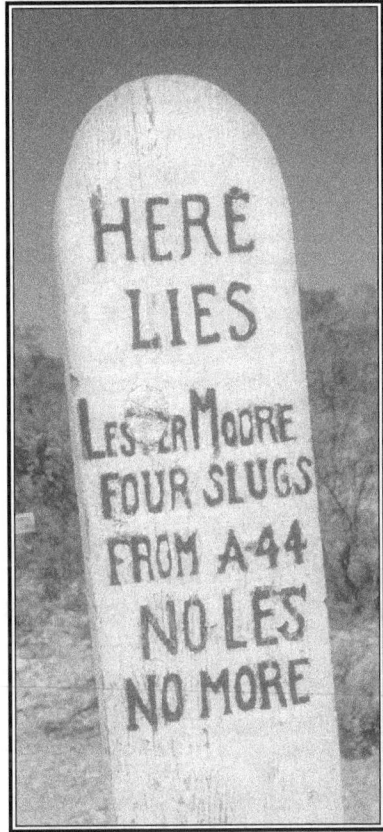

(dk)

I TOLD YOU I WAS SICK
-Harry Nomore

LIE HEAVY ON HIM EARTH
For He
LAID MANY HEAVY LOADS
On Thee
JOHN J. JOHNSON
Architect

BODY OF ZED SMITH
FOOD FOR THE WORMS

A Buffalo Hunter Named Mcgill
Who Amused Himself By Shooting
Into Every House He Passed.
He Won't Pass This Way Again.
DIED MARCH 1873
(Boothill Cemetery, Dodge City, Kansas)

WAITING FOR FURTHER ORDERS
Capt. James R. Rogan

Here Lies
JOHNNY YEAST
Pardon Me
For Not Rising
(Ruidoso, New Mexico)

J.M. ESSINGTON
November 1872
A Carpenter
And Part Owner
Of The Essington Hotel
SHOT BY THE COOK
(Boot Hill, Dodge City, Kansas)

DOCTOR
FRED ROBERTS
1807-1863
OFFICE UPSTAIRS
(Brookland, Arkansas)

JOHN HEATH
Taken From County Jail 8,
Lynched By Bisbee Mob
In Tombstone
Feb 22nd 1884
(Boot Hill, Tombstone, Arizona)

Here Lies
ALBERT FINNEY
Accidently Shot
As A Mark Of Affection
By His Brother

UNKNOWN
Found Hanging
From A Tree
West of Dodge City
(Boot Hill, Dodge City, Kansas)

(dk)

CORPORAL SAM REDFULL

1845-1871

The War Took His Leg
He Drank Dr. Kilmer's

SWAMP ROOT

It Took His Life
To Boot.
(Redrock, Texas)

Here Lie Five

BUFFALO HUNTERS

Whose Frozen Bodies
Were Found
North of Dodge City
On Feb 2, 1873
Following A Blizzard
(Boot Hill, Dodge City, Kansas)

Here Lies

LOTTA DUST

1863-1899

DR. M. MORTAL
BURIED IN HIS OWN
LIFE-TIME GUARANTEED COFFIN
(Redrock, Texas)

SOME MOTHER'S SON
(Unknown)

"Wild Bill" J.B. Hickok
Killed By Assasin
Jack McCall
In Deadwood, Black Hills,
August 2nd, 1876.

Here Rests Samuel Wells
BORN 1824 - DIED 1847
The Victim
Of A Dishonest Woman

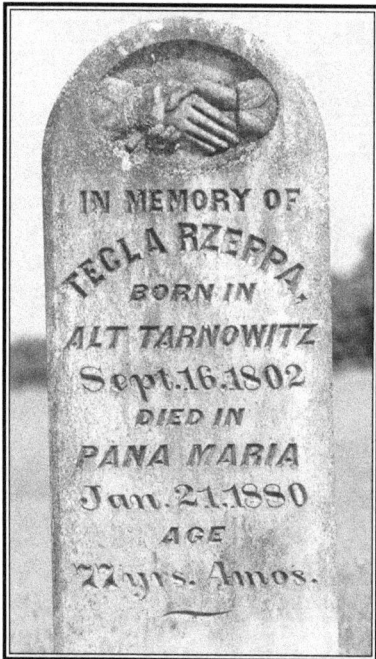

IN MEMORY OF
TECLA RZEPPA
BORN IN
ALT TARNOWITZ
Sept.16.1802
DIED IN
PANA MARIA
Jan.21.1880
AGE
77 yrs. Amos.

(dk)

IN MEMORY OF
ELLEN SHANNON
AGED 26
FATALLY BURNED
1870
BY THE EXPLOSION
OF A LAMP
FILLED WITH
DANFORTH'S
NON-EXPLOSIVE FLUID
(Girard, Pennsylvania)

Bad Men And Bad Whiskey
Are Said To Be Plentiful
And Measures Are Being Made
To Stop The Mingling Of The Two

JOHN HENRY
I'd Rather Be
In Montana
(Redrock, Texas)

RAB McBETH
WHO DIED FOR THE WANT
OF ANOTHER BREATH
HANGED 1876
(Larne, Ireland)

Never One To Quit

TIDBIT: One tough old man, before his death in Dangerfield, Texas, demanded that his family bury him standing upright with a shotgun in each hand so he could "go through Hell a-poppin'."

BILLY THE KID

Born   Died

Nov 23   July 14

1860   1881

The Boy

Bandit King

He Died As

He Had Lived

(Fort Sumner, New Mexico)

Pard, we will meet again
in the
Happy Hunting Ground
to part no more.

Back To Dust

(Jacksonville, Florida)

CHARLES DuPLESSIS

—DIED 1907—

NOW AIN'T

THAT TOO BAD!

(Chicago, Illinois)

Goodbye

(Mount Moriah Cemetery,
Deadwood, S. D.)

THAT IS ALL

(Unknown)

(dk)

Which one of the above epitaphs are fictional—completely fabricated by the author? Yes, that's right, a couple are fictional, you can't believe everything you read. Hint: the unfunny ones.
ANS: The four epigraphs listed as being in "Redrock, Texas."

TRIVIA QUESTION: In what movie did Clint Eastwood seek revenge on a group of men who tried to lynch him several years earlier? Hint: He was hired as a deputy by Judge Parker's court. **ANS:** *Hang 'Em High* (1967).

Jailor's Wagon, Hubbell Trading Post, Ganado, Arizona (dk)

A LYNCHING

Where did the word "lynching," meaning "to hang," come from? In the late 18th century, a Virginian by the name of *Captain William Lynch* organized a group of men to hunt down and hang a gang of troublemakers. The word "lynched" has been in our vocabulary ever since. Where the law couldn't keep up with the lawless, the vigilante committee became the solution to a problem.

The Hanging Judge
ISAAC CHARLES PARKER

It's the 1870's and the West is still wild and woolly and Indian Territory is filthy with rogues, bandits, and cutthroats. There are only Indian Police and courts which don't have jurisdiction over white men. Something has to be done. President Ulysses S. Grant appoints Ike Parker to the federal bench at Fort Smith, Arkansas to clean up the mess. At 36, already a successful congressman, attorney, and circuit court Judge, Parker turns out to be the man for the job. During his 21 year tenure he presides over 13,000 cases, convicting three-fourths of them, sentencing 172 to hang (only 88 actually have their neck stretched from a gallows). Parker keeps the Fort Smith jail full (and has to build a second one) by paying hundreds of deputy Marshals to go out and bring back these criminals. He pays the Marshals ten cents a mile. With a jailer's wagon and extra guards, they scoured the territory picking up prisoners from town jails. The jailer's wagon is for sick prisoners, the healthy have to walk. (See *Hang 'Em High* starring Clint Eastwood.) The "Hanging Judge" gets his reputation, not because of the number of men that go to the gallows, but because many men are often tried in a single session, the Judge giving out sentences like a sergeant barking work orders to his troops. This means that a multiple-hanging gallows is required, one that can hang twelve men at a time, though six is all that ever swing together. Thousands of people come from miles around to witness the mid-air dance. It is clear that the "heartless" hanging Judge Parker doesn't believe in rehabilitation of the wicked. Quick and final punishment is to be his recipe for a peaceful Territory. The appeals process comes into use near the end of Parker's reign and many of his hanging convictions are reversed on appeal. Judge Isaac Parker retires just two months before Indian Territory jurisdiction is removed from the *Court of the United States for the Eastern District of Arkansas* on September 1, 1896. Two months later he dies.

A Match Game
FAMOUS GRAVES OF GUNMEN

Match the famous gunfighter with the town where he was buried.

1. Buffalo Bill Cody	**a.** Fort Sumner, New Mexico.
2. Wyatt Earp	**b.** Deadwood, South Dakota.
3. Doc Holliday	**c.** Colma, California.
4. Billy the Kid	**d.** Golden, Colorado.
5. Wild Bill Hickok	**e.** Glenwood Springs, Colorado.
6. Sam Bass	**f.** El Paso, Texas.
7. John Wesley Hardin	**g.** Kearney, Missouri.
8. Jesse James	**h.** Round Rock, Texas.

ANS: 1-d, 2-c, 3-e, 4-a, 5-b, 6-h, 7-f, 8-g.

5 OTHER OUTLAW GRAVES:

1. Luke Short . . . . Fort Worth, TX.
2. Bill Doolin . . . . Guthrie, OK.
3. "Bloody Bill" Longley . . . . Giddings, TX.
4. "Captain Jack" Slade . . . . Salt Lake City, UT.
5. "Big Jim" Courtright . . . . Fort Worth, TX.

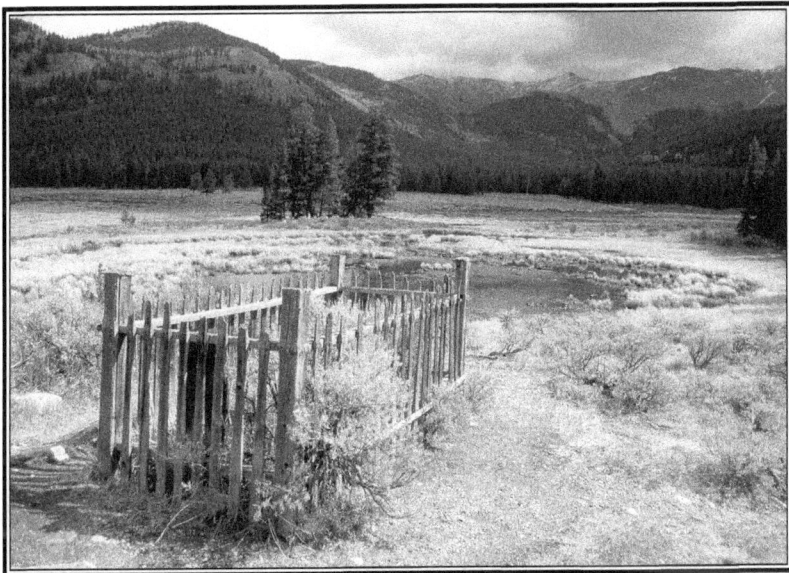

A cemetery high in the Rockies at Tincup, Colorado (dk)

ANOTHER MORTICIAN'S GUARANTEE

"AS THEY SAY IN OUR PROFESSION,
THE EARLY BIRD GETS THE WORM."

"I'm prepared to offer you,
Embalming by the most scientific methods,
A bronze coffin guaranteed good for a century,
regardless of the climatic or geological conditions.
My best hearse,
The minister of your choice,
And the presence of at least two mourners.
A headstone of the finest Carrara marble,
And a plot in size and location benefiting your status,
And perpetual care of the grounds."

—John Carradine, *The Shootist*, 1976.

AMAZING GRACE
By John Newton, 1779

So **many westerns** have mourners singing this song
that I had to include it in this western film trivia book.

1. Amazing grace, how sweet the sound,
   That saved a wretch like me.
   I once was lost, but now I'm found.
   Was blind, but now I see.

2. 'Twas grace that taught my heart to fear,
   And grace my fears relieved.
   How precious did that grace appear,
   The hour I first believed.

3. Through many dangers, toils and snares,
   I have already come.
   'Tis grace that brought me safe thus far,
   And grace will lead me home.

4. How sweet the name of Jesus sounds,
   In a believer's ear.
   It soothes his sorrow, heals his wounds,
   And drives away his fear.

5. When we've been there ten thousand years,
   Bright shining as the sun,
   We've no less days to sing God's praise,
   Then when we first begun.

THE LAST WORDS OF A DYING BOY:

"Pull off my boots, will ya?"
"Sure kid, sure."
"I promised my mother I wouldn't die with my boots on."
—Clem Bevans as "Tadpole" in *Tombstone,* 1942.

A Ballad
O BURY ME NOT ON THE LONE PRAIRIE
Traditional

A **world renowned cowboy classic,** this song was
originally from an 1839 poem by Edwin H. Chapin called
"The Ocean Burial." Someone, somewhere, adapted the song
to burials on the lonely western prairie.

1. "O bury me not on the lone prairie."
These words came low and mournfully,
From the pallid lips of a youth who lay
On his dying bed at the close of day.

2. He had wasted and pined till o'er his brow
Death's shades were slowly gathering now.
He thought of home and loved ones nigh,
As the cowboys gathered to see him die.

3. O bury me not on the lone prairie,
Where the coyotes howl and the wind blows free.
In a narrow grave just six by three,
O bury me not on the lone prairie.

4. It matters not, I've oft been told,
Where the body lies when the heart grows cold.
But grant, o grant, this wish to me:
O bury me not on the lone prairie.

5. I've always wished to be laid when I died,
In a little churchyard on the green hillside.
By my father's grave there let me be,
O bury me not on the lone prairie.

6. I wish to lie where a mother's prayer
And a sister's tear will mingle there.
Where friends can come and weep o're me.
O bury me not on the lone prairie.

7. "O bury me not ..." and his voice failed there,
But they took no heed to his dying prayer.
In a narrow grave, just six by three,
They buried him there on the lone prairie.

8. And the cowboys now as they roam the plain,
For they marked the spot where his bones were lain,
Fling a handful of roses o're his grave
With a prayer to God, his soul to save.

"They buried him there on the lone prairie." An Idaho valley (dk)

THIS TOMBSTONE MARKS THE LAST RESTING PLACE OF

_____

A PLAIN PINE BOX WILL DO

A Cowboy's Last Will And Testament

By Don Kirk, June 2002

This poem is the last words of a ranging cowboy and drifter. He led a simple life and wanted a simple burial.

1.   O' lay me not in a casket,
   With velvet lining and silk pillow.
O' lay me not in a basket,
   Of cherry, oak or willow.
   A plain pine box will do.

CHORUS:
A coupla pinewood planks, a loose knot or two;
A coupla rusty nails, and rope handles will do.

2.   O' lay me not in a bonebox,
   With handles made of gold.
No carvings and pretty peacocks,
   Or silvered bronze so cold.
   A plain pine box will do.

3.   Just keep your silver in your poke;
   Waste not on a dead man's crate.
No paint or hinges broke,
   For me, it's A's an' Eights.
   A plain pine box will do.

4.   And make my coffin wide and with
   A lot of elbow room;
Jus' like the wide an' open West,
   I wandered o'er 'til doom.
   A plain pine box will do.

5.   I never wore a necktie noose,
   So dress me not in Sunday's best—
A calico that's clean and loose,
   With Paw's pocket watch in my vest.
   A plain pine box will do.

6. And leave me not a-layin' in,
    An undertaker's lair,
Stuck with a gloomy mortician's,
    Ol' dark and sullen stare.
    A plain pine box will do.

7. Don't let 'em mess with my brains,
    And need I non o' that,
Embalmin' fluid in my veins,
    When layin' me out flat.
    A plain pine box will do.

8. O' haul me not to a meetin' house,
    I ain't a-been in one a-fore,
All outdoors is the Maker's House,
    With all the world to explore.
    A plain pine box will do.

9. And lay no flowers on my coffin,
    My hat can take their place.
Play over me no violin,
    Or sing Amazing Grace.
    A plain pine box will do.

10. Pallbearers wearin' ties and tails,
    I won't have none o' that—
Jus' what they wear a-ridin' trails:
    Their chaps and favorite hat.
    A plain pine box will do.

11. I need no special words a-said,
    Above my velvet bed;
Jus', "He was here and now he's gone,"
    'Tis all that need be said.
    A plain pine box will do.

12. And lay me not in a village,
    With crowds and walled-in streets;
Lay me instead on a mount'n ridge,
    Far from the lights of town.
    A plain pine box will do.

13. My marker needn't be of stone,
    Jus' planks with words thus cast:
"Here lies a drifter in grass overgrown,
    And here is where he stopped last."
    A plain pine box will do.

14. What's on my horse is all I own,
    So give my canvas ducks,
And my saddle and strawberry roan,
    To a cowhand down on his luck.
    A plain pine box will do.

15. Lay me with feet a-facing west,
    So iffen Satan comes,
A-chasing after me obsessed,
    I kin git a runnin' start!
    A plain pine box will do.

16. Then pull my boots a-from my feet,
    And place 'em 'neath my head,
So's I kin rest in comfee,
    As I wait for what's ahead.
    A plain pine box will do.

17. Now lower down my olden bones,
    To send me on my way,
And cover then the grave with stones,
    To keep the wolves away.
    A plain pine box will do.

18. Jus' tell my ma I did my best,
    And fair to all was I.
Tell her I dearly loved the West,
    Below that turquoise sky.
    A plain pine box will do.

19. Majestic mountains, boundless plains,
    Cool rain on windowpanes,
And tranquil deserts, forests cool,
    Below the sky, so true.
    I bid you all adieu.

James Kirkpatrick as Mortimer Peel, photo and costume by the author

Boothill Graveyard, Tombstone, Cochise County, Arizona
Tombstone Record of Deaths

Tombstone's Boothill cemetery lies on a rocky rise at the end of Allen Street and is dotted with prickly pear cacti and leaning wooden markers. It is said that the worst of them, the men who died with their boots on, lie here, but not all deaths were violent, some were accidents, and many were deaths due to disease at an early age. Much can be learned about life in the Frontier West from the markers in an old cemetery. Tombstone's Boothill is no exception.

1. Unknown man, well dressed, found in abandoned mine.
2. Two Chinese, died of leprosy.
3. Two unknown cowboys, drowned.
4. William Alexander, prospector, killed in a blast.
5. John Beather, killed by hanging.
6. Al Bennett, teamster, ambushed by Indians.
7. Johnnie Blair, died of smallpox. (A cowboy, to avoid touching the body, tied a rope around his feet and dragged him to his grave.)
8. Frank Bowles, 1880. As he was thrown from his horse his pistol went off, shooting himself in the leg. He didn't receive medical attention soon enough.
9. Mrs. R.B. Campbell, 1882, poisoned.
10. William Claibourne, 14 Nov 1882, shot by Frank Leslie.
11. Billy Clanton, 26 Oct 1881, killed in a gunfight at the O.K. Corral.
12. Thomas Cowan, 1881, died of diphtheria.
13. W.E. "Bill" Delaney, 1884, hanged for taking part in the grisly Bisbee Massacre perpetrated by five would-be payroll robbers.
14. J.D. Dernitt, 1881, fell into a mine shaft.
15. Freddy Foos, 1878, a young boy, died from drinking bad water.
16. John Gibson, 1881, fell off a wagon and a wheel crushed his head.
17. Gregory, 1882, died of meningitis.
18. Thomas Harper, 1881, hanged for shooting John Talliday.
19. John Heath, 1884, hanged by lynch mob.
20. Charles Helm, 1882, shot in dispute over how to drive cattle.
21. Mr. Huggins, 1882, burned to death in hotel fire.

Cemetery of the Mission San Gerónimo de Taos (1598), New Mexico (dk)

22. George Johnson, "Hanged by Mistake." He had bought a stolen horse, but was assumed to be the thief.

23. M.E. Kellogg, 1882, "Died a Natural Death."

24. John King, 1881, "Suicide" by strychnine.

25. Douglas Lilly, 1881, his tombstone is inscribed "Killed." He was thrown from his wagon, trampled by the horse, and then run over by the wheels.

26. "Happy Jack" McAllister, 1882, died of complications from a bullet lodged in one of his lungs.

27. J.D. McDermott, 1882, fractured his spine falling off his horse.

28. Robert "Frank" McLaury, 26 October 1881, killed in a gunfight at the O.K. Corral.

29. Thomas "Tom" McLaury, 26 October 1881, was also killed in a gunfight at the O.K. Corral. (Three men died that day.)

30. James Martin, 1881, died of consumption (tuberculosis).

31. Pat McMenomy, 1882, "Shot." He was a sheepman.

32. Lester Moore, on his marker: "Here Lies Lester Moore, Four Slugs From a .44, No Less, No More." As a Wells Fargo agent he had a dispute over a package. No record of what was in the package.

33. Alfred Packrel, 1882, English miner died from bowel inflammation.

34. J. Padden, 1884, fell down a mine shaft.

35. Rodriguez Petron, "Stabbed."

36. G. Renacco, 1882, fell off a cliff.

37. Jim Riley, 1881, "Murdered."

38. Rook, "Shot by a Chinaman."

39. Ben Scott, 1883, a teamster, shot by his own rifle when it fell over and discharged.

40. Frank Serroux, shot over a mining claim.

41. Charley Storms, 25 February1881, "Shot by Luke Short" in a duel.

42. Mrs. Stumpf, 1884, died in childbirth after being given chloroform.

43. Van Houten, 1879, "Murdered." Because of a dispute over a mining claim, he was beaten in the face with a rock until dead.

44. Ramon Vasquez, 1882, Knifed by Dan Allen.

45. Raymond Verra, 1882, "Stabbed."

46. Jasper, Von, 1882, "Shot."

47. Eva Waters, three-month-old baby, died of scarlet fever.

48. Tom Waters, father of Eva Waters, killed because of the color of his shirt.

49. Joseph Wetsell, 1882, stoned to death by Indians.

50. Fred White, first marshal of Tombstone, 30 October 1880, "Shot by Curly Bill Brocius."

51. John Wickstrum, 1882, a Swede who died after a well he was digging caved in.

Boothill Cemetery, Tombstone, Arizona (dk)

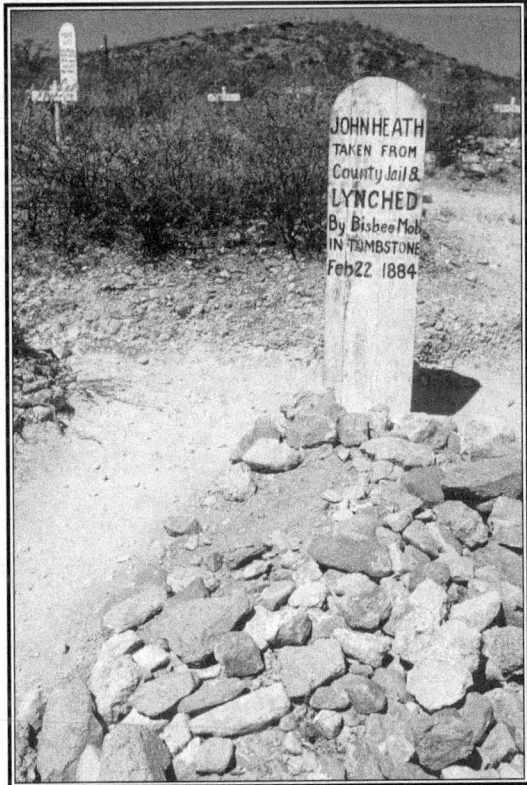

JOHN HEATH
TAKEN FROM
County Jail &
LYNCHED
By Bisbee Mob
IN TOMBSTONE
Feb 22 1884

52. Glenn Efrom Will, 1953, "His Ashes Arrived Collect on Delivery." He was cremated in Oakland, CA, and sent to Tombstone for internment.

53. Delilah, 1881, "Suicide" by arsenic.

53. Joseph Ziegler, 1882, "Murdered."

Source: From actual grave markers and Ben T. Traywick's book, *Tombstone's Boothill.*

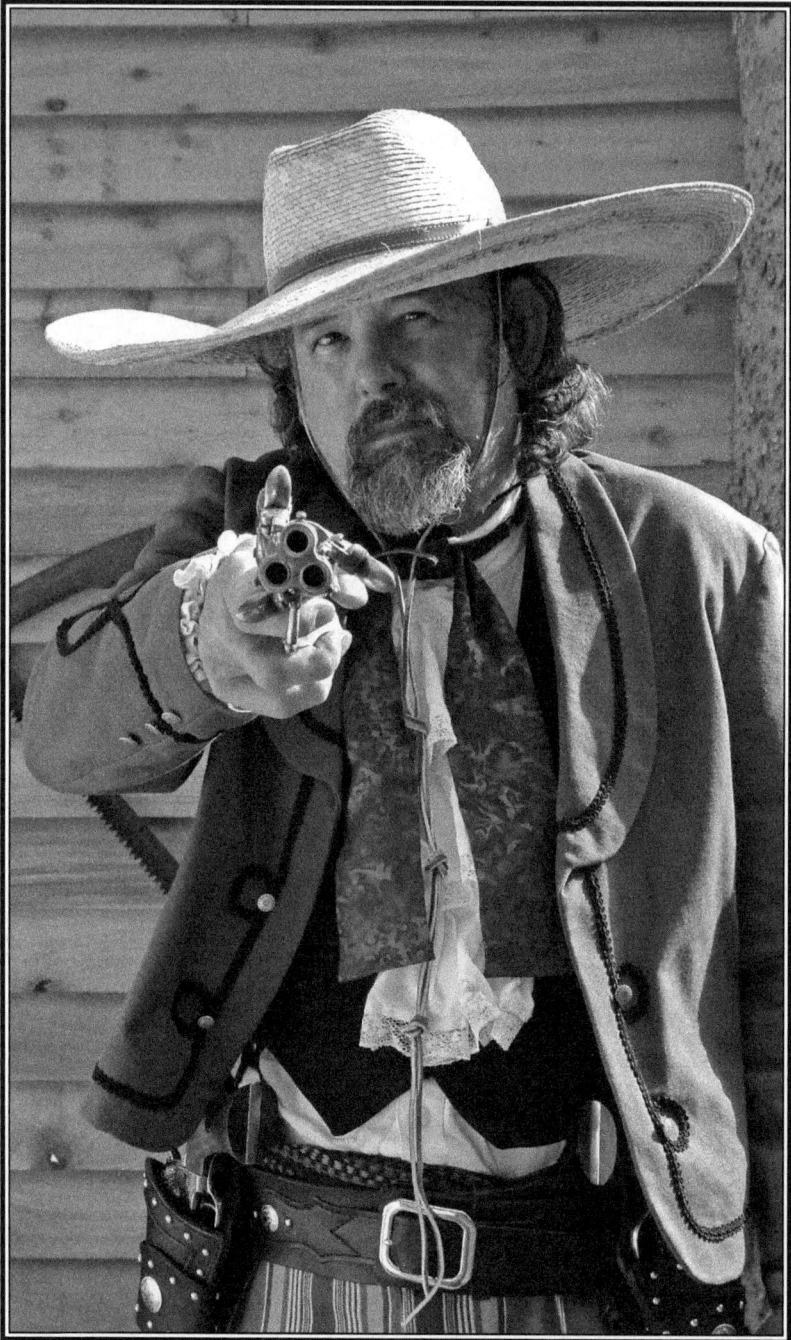

The author as Juaquine Medina Hernandez, Photo by C.R. Nowell

Lock, Stock, and Barrel

WEAPONS OF THE WEST

*"Anyone who knows the country and its people
will appreciate that underlying their apparent
preoccupation with guns, and their right to keep them,
is, on the one hand a fierce patriotism in defense of
National and individual freedom, and on the other an
inborn resistance to governmental interference."*
—Joseph G. Rosa, Guns of the American West, 1985

The Colt six-shooter is considered by some as one of the three inventions that helped to settle the American West—barbed wire and the windmill being the other two. But it was this revolving cartridge pistol that helped to create the legendary outlaws and lawmen that live on today. The role that firearms played in the American West cannot be underestimated.

The West was not as violent and bloody as novelists and filmmakers would have us believe. Industrialized cities like Chicago and New York had a lot more murders than the "wild" West. Everyone carried a weapon as defense against those who would use guns with criminal intent. Thus, a gun was an "instrument of justice and fair play," not one of violence and criminal behavior. High-noon shootouts, crack shots, and bloody range wars were dime novel fiction. Sure, there were a few incidents, but they were the exception and not the rule. The revolver was virtually useless except at point blank range. Its use as a defensive weapon helped to stem lawlessness and lead to settlement of the West.

A Glossary Of
32 FIREARMS TERMS

Every westerner worth his salt will know something about one of the inventions that greatly influenced the settlement of the West. Here's a beginner's glossary.

1. Army Model. A pistol meeting U.S. Army specifications which required a longer barrel and a larger caliber than that of the *Navy Model,* which because of its lightness, was more popular with the civilians.

2. caliber. The size of a bullet or shell measured by its diameter in hundredths of an inch. A .50 caliber barrel would be half an inch in its interior diameter. A .45-70 cartridge fits a .45 inch barrel and carries 70 grains of powder.

3. breech. The part of a cannon or other firearm at the rear end of a gun barrel.

4. breechloader. A *longarm* loaded at the rear of the barrel.

5. cannon. The earliest gun, fired by applying a flame, live coal, or a hot wire to an open "touchhole" at the rear of the barrel to ignite the powder charge.

6. cap & ball revolver. Usually refers to a *percussion* revolver which is loaded by packing gun powder and a lead ball into each *chamber* of the *cylinder* and then placing a priming cap on each nipple. See *percussion cap*.

7. carbine. A rifle or musket with a short barrel having good firepower, but little range; chiefly used by the Cavalry.

8. cartridge. A cylindrical case of paper, cardboard, or metal containing the powder charge and the projectile. The word "cartridge" is originally from the Latin *carta* meaning "paper."

9. centerfire. A brass cartridge with the primer installed in the center of the base. Compare with *rimfire*.

10. chamber. The cavity of a fire-arm which holds the powder charge or a *cartridge* to be fired through the barrel.

11. cylinder. The rotating part of a revolver—a cylindrical steel casting—containing *chambers* for holding *cartridges* until they are brought into firing position.

12. derringer. Any tiny short-barreled single or double-shot pocket pistol. Philadelphian gunsmith *Henry Deringer* (spelled with one "r") patented the first pocket pistol in 1835. It had a 1-1/2-inch barrel and .4 caliber bore. The name stuck for all small easily concealed large-caliber pistols made by many different manufacturers. No bigger than the palm of your hand, they were made popular among gamblers, ladies and businessmen as an "ace in the hole." *John Wilkes Booth* used one of these "pea shooters" made by *Deringer* to assassinate President Lincoln.

13. double-action. A revolver that can fire by simply pulling the trigger without having to pull back the hammer for each shot. Compare with *single-action*.

14. flintlock. In this early firearm of Spanish origin dating back to the seventeenth century, a spring-loaded *cock* (hammer) holding a piece of flint, when released, would scrape across a piece of roughened steel, knock open the lid of a priming pan containing explosive powder, and cause sparks to fall into the open pan, igniting the priming powder which then ignited the main powder charge in the barrel. A flintlock was very slow to load, requiring numerous steps: the lock is half-cocked, priming pan opened, primed,

lid closed, a measured powder charge poured into the muzzle, a lead ball rammed down the barrel with a rod, and the lock cocked. It was used until the 1820's when *percussion* weapons began to replace them.

15. fulminate. A chemical compound of fulminic acid which detonates by percussion, friction, or heat.

16. fulminate pill. A small ball of explosive compound used as a priming charge by placing it in the vent hole of a cylinder or barrel and holding it in place with a dab of wax which was weatherproof. A blow from the hammer detonated the pill. Predecessor to the *percussion cap*.

17. gauge. The "caliber" of a shotgun defined as the number of spherical balls required—if each is the inside diameter of the guns barrel—to add up to one pound of weight. The larger the weapon, the smaller it's gauge. A 12-gauge shotgun would be larger than a 20-gauge. Shot is also defined by its size: No.6 shot is smaller than the largest No.1 shot.

18. longarm. Any weapon fired from the shoulder. Rifles, shotguns, and carbines are longarms.

19. metallic cartridge. A major advancement in ammunition, it's a metal cylindrical casing containing explosive gunpowder which is sealed from moisture by the lead bullet pressed into one end. It has a primer installed in the base which when hit by the hammer explodes, setting off the gunpowder. It was the Sioux Nation who originally came up with the idea. After the Civil War they captured .50-caliber breechloading longarms from the Cavalry, but had no access to the metallic ammunition. They took empty shells found on the battlefield, punched a hole in the base, forced a percussion cap into it (from the old muzzleloaders), dropped a tiny rock into the cap to serve as a striking surface and added gunpowder and a bullet— and then shot them back at the enemy. See *paper cartridge*.

20. minié ball. An improvement over the standard round musket ball, it was a conical slug with a cavity in the base and fitted with a plug of wood which, by the force of explosion, was driven into and expanded the bullet to fill the rifling in the gun barrel, thus increasing pressure and extending the effective range of the bullet to about 1000 yards, compared to the 200 yard limit of the old round ball. It was invented by French military Captain *Claude-Etienne Minié*.

21. musket. A term used for early *smoothbore*, long-barreled fire-arms originally fired by a match (a length of cord) and later included the wheellock, *flintlock* and *percussion* cap designs.

22. muzzle. The front end of a barrel from which a projectile emerges on firing.

23. muzzleloader. A gun loaded through the front end of the barrel by first pouring in a measured amount of gunpowder, dropping in a round lead ball, and then packing the ball tightly

DETACHABLE STOCKS

Some pistols had a seperate stock that could be atached to the grip so they could be aimed like a rifle. Some of these stocks came with a cap or plug and could be used as a canteen to hold drinking water or a favorite beverage. A few of the *Sharps* carbines (model 1859) came with a coffee mill built into them. Coffee beans were poured into a hole in the bottom, and the detachable crank on the side of the butt would grind up the beans. The idea was not to provide one of these to each soldier, but to issue one to each troop company.

with a long wood or iron ramrod with a cup-shaped end. The rod was stored in a groove in the stock just under the barrel.

24. paper cartridge. Before the advent of metal cartridges, a measured amount of gunpowder was rolled into a piece of paper along with a lead ball and then inserted into the muzzle of the gun. Rolling "cartridges" before battle saved a lot of time while under fire; the soldier no longer having to pour in the powder and ram down the ball before shooting. Unfortunately the paper cartridge allowed moisture to wet the gunpowder rendering it useless if not used. See *metallic cartridge.*

25. percussion cap. A tiny copper cup is packed with a small amount of *fulminating mercury* and placed over a hollow nipple at the *breech* of the *barrel* or at the rear of the *cylinder.* A blow to the nipple with the hammer ignites this "primer" and sends a flame through a hole in the nipple, igniting the main powder charge. It was a major improvement over the *flintlock* because the puff of smoke from the power pan gave an enemy time to escape the shot. *Joshua Shaw* didn't patent the cap idea until 1822, but some give him credit for it dating back to 1814.

26. percussion lock. An early eighteenth-century invention whereby the *cock* or hammer

strikes a *fulminate* which explodes, and in turn ignites the gunpowder. It quickly replaced the 200-year-old *flintlock.*

27. pounder. Describes the size of a *cannon* based on the weight of a lead cannonball. A "six-pounder" fires a ball weighing six pounds. Other things besides iron balls could be shot from a cannon. Scrap metal, nails and the like were also used during war time.

28. powderhorn. A hollowed out animal's horn capped at both ends and used for holding gunpowder. The powder was first poured into a metal flask where a measured amount of powder could then be poured into the muzzle of a musket.

29. rifling. The system of grooves engraved on the inside of a gun barrel to improve distance and accuracy.

30. rimfire. A copper cartridge which has the *fulminating* material (primer) in the rim of its base. The firing pin of the weapon strikes the rim of the cartridge to set off the primer. Compare with *centerfire.*

31. single-action. Any repeating firearm whose hammer must be cocked by hand before each shot can be fired. Compare with *double-action.*

32. smoothbore. A gun barrel that has no *rifling.* Shotguns are always smoothbores.

A Western Chronology
18 GUNS THAT SETTLED THE WEST

"It is unknown by who or when gunpowder was invented—
what is sure, it had to be the work of the Devil."
—Unknown

It was over 700 years ago when the first firing of a gun took place. A metal tube, closed at one end, had a hole punched in it so that powder packed into the tube could be ignited with a hot piece of coal. The development of firearms during the nineteenth century greatly affected the outcome of western expansion. Some firearms invented during this period were significant improvements in technology and others became legendary in the wild American West. In the weapons chronology to follow, some weapons indicate the range. The first number is the effective range with accuracy, and the second, the range at which experts can achieve good results.

1525   **The "Brown Bess" Musket.** This "flintlock" was invented by the French around 1525 and adapted by the British in 1690. A piece of flint held by the weapon's hammer is brought down on the anvil, creating a shower of sparks above the priming charge. "Brown Bess" was the soldier's name for a series of muskets from the *Tower of London Armory* starting about 1730. The iron musket was an inaccurate weapon and took a long time to load. The only advantage: the cloud of black powder smoke created by a line of firing infantry enveloped the soldiers, creating cover for a bayonet charge. The *Brown Bess* would fail to fire at least 25% of the time; there was a flash in the pan without the lead ball being fired. ("Flash in the pan" later came to mean a person who talked big but did nothing.) Range: 50/100 yds.

1780   **The Kentucky Rifle.** The "Kentucky" was a muzzleloading flintlock made in Pennsylvania with a long, rifled barrel giving it an accurate range up to twice as far as a musket, up to 200 yards. It was nearly five feet long with a .45 caliber octagonal barrel. It was used to defeat the British troops during the Revolutionary War (1775-1782). The development of the percussion lock in 1810 allowed the Kentucky Rifle to be converted into the now famous "Plains Rifle" used by mountain men, fur trappers and Indian fighters including ol' *Dan'l Boone* himself. It had a shorter barrel (about three feet) with even larger calibers (up to .60) which could stop a buffalo or grizzly bear. The most famous "plains rifle" was the *Hawken* made in 1822 by *Jake* and *Sam Hawkens* of St. Louis. Range 200/400 yards.

1835   **The Colt Model 1835.** The American, *Samuel Colt* of Hartford, Connecticut patented a revolver in England in 1835 (1836 in the U.S.) that had a fixed barrel with a separate revolving cylinder containing several cartridges. Previously, pistols had five or six barrels *revolving around* a central shaft and were called "pepperboxes." But Colt couldn't sell his revolutionary design to the U.S. Army and went out of business in 1842. His pistol saw some use by the Texas Army during the war with Mexico in 1846.

1847   **The Colt Walker.** The Walker was a .44 caliber percussion cap & ball revolver made by *Samuel Colt* with design suggestions by *Captain Sam Walker* of the Texas Rangers. For the first time the Army bought some of Colt's pistols (1,000) for use in the Mexican War and Samuel was off and running with a new company in Whitneyville, New York. His pistol used a half-ounce conical bullet. Also new to the pistol was a trigger guard. The *Colt Walker* was manufactured for one year then evolved into subsequent designs.

1848   **The Colt Dragoon.** The Dragoons were a family of .44 caliber percussion pistols manufactured from 1848 to 1872 in Hartford, Connecticut. The *Walker-Whitneyville Dragoon* was a six-shot revolver weighing in at four pounds, 9 ounces. In the movie *True Grit,* Mattie Ross (Kim Darby) attempted to use this very large and heavy weapon. Ironically, this weapon had been designed for the cavalry, but it was unwieldy on horseback, and when the much lighter *Navy Colts* came out, the *Dragoon* was quickly left in the dust.

1848 **The Sharps Buffalo Gun.** This powerful rifle was invented by *Christian Sharps* in 1848. Available in several calibers, .40, .44, .45, and .50 (the *Big 50,* the ultimate in buffalo guns, came in 1875), it was an accurate, high-powered, long-range rifle (up to 800 yards) used by hunters to easily take down the bison on the plains with just one shot! This formidable weapon used the new paper cartridges inserted into a breech block which dropped open by pulling down on the hinged trigger guard. Closing the trigger guard closed the breech which cut off one end of the cartridge to make it ready for firing. Later versions of the *Sharps* were modified to take metallic cartridges. The heavy-barreled model of this single-shot longarm (developed in the 1870's), became known as "Old Reliable." The gun weighed 12-16 pounds and required the use of a forked stick to support the weight in long distance shooting. Range 500 yds/1200 yds.

1849 **The Jennings Rifle.** Michael Newton in his book *Armed and Dangerous* gives this description of the Jennings rifle: "a magazine atop the breech was loaded with percussion pills, while bullets with propellant charges packed inside their hollow bases filled a tube below the barrel. The shooter's index finger passed through a ring forming the end of a lever below the receiver; his thumb was on the hammer, and with the weapon's muzzle elevated slightly, gravity delivered a bullet to the carrier. As the hammer was drawn and the lever pushed forward, the breech block moved back and the carrier rose, placing the cartridge in line with the barrel. Pulling the lever back forced the breech block forward, driving the cartridge into the firing chamber; the same motion dropped a primer from the magazine by action of a revolving rack. The weapon fired by upward pressure of the shooter's index finger in the ring and there was no spent casings to eject. With a capacity of 24 rounds, the *Jennings* was indeed a formidable weapon."

1851 **The Colt 1851 Navy Revolver.** The "Colt Revolving Belt Pistol of Naval Caliber" was a .36 caliber percussion pistol with a 7-1/2 inch octagonal barrel that was smaller and lighter than the Army Model and so became popular among Army officers and civilians. It was used extensively by

both Union and Confederate officers in the Civil War. Colt alone sold 386,417 revolvers during the war. (The 1873 Colt single-action Army eventually replaced it.) The 1851 Navy became a favorite of *"Wild Bill" Hickok* and is popular with today's black powder shooters. It was manufactured from 1851-1872.

1853   **The Enfield.** Built by the *Royal Small Arms Factory* of England, the Enfield was a .577 caliber percussion-type muzzleloader with a 39-inch rifled barrel attached to the stock with three metal bands. It was heavily used in the American Civil War (700,000 were bought by the Union Army) even though repeaters like the *Spencer* and *Henry* had already been invented (*General Ripley*, Chief of the Federal Ordnance Department, was against the idea of breechloaders.) Range: 400 yds/1000 yds.

1860   **The Colt New Model Army.** A .44 caliber cap and ball pistol that became Colt's most successful percussion pistol. It was used by Union cavalry in the Civil War. Lighter and more efficient, it eventually replaced the unwieldy *Dragoon*. The New Model Army was manufactured from 1860 to 1872. This gun was used by Confederate raider *William Quantrill.*

1860   **The Spencer Repeating Rifle.** Developed by *Christopher Spencer,* this .52 caliber rifle had a range up to 600 yards. A tubular magazine built into the butt of the weapon held seven rim-fire cartridges (which could all go off at once if the rifle was dropped on its butt).An eighth cartridge could be loaded directly into the breech. It could be fired seven times in ten seconds (14 times a minute with reloading). Downward movement of the trigger guard ejected the spent cartridge and loaded the next round.The hammer had to then be cocked before the rifle could be fired. 100,000 *Spencers* were purchased by the Union Army after 1863 for use in the Civil War. The troopers nicknamed it "Load On Sunday—Shoot All Week," but tactics had not yet been developed to take advantage of higher rate of fire. (The company was bought out by *Winchester* in 1869). Range: 200 yds/400 yds.

1860   **The Henry Repeating Rifle.** Perfected by *B. Tyler Henry* at the *New Arms Company* using ideas from the *Jennings* rifle and the *Volcanic.* It was a 15-shot lever-action weapon using a .44 caliber rimfire cartridge that could fire 25 rounds per minute. By cocking the trigger guard, the spent cartridge was ejected, a fresh round chambered, and the hammer cocked all in one motion. Charges had to be loaded by dropping them one by one into a tubular magazine under the barrel, the opening being at the muzzle end of the gun. Range: 200 yds/400 yds.

1862 **The Gatling Gun.** A rapid fire "machine gun" invented by *Dr. Richard Jordan Gatling.* It had six rotating barrels fed with ammunition by means of a hopper and could fire 200 rounds per minute. A drum magazine of .45 caliber rim-fire cartridges would be mounted above a revolving carrier that received the cartridges which were then chambered with bolts moving forward in rapid succession. It was manually operated with a hand crank located at the right rear of the weapon. Because of its 380 pound weight, it was usually kept at the fort for defense. It was good for defending a position, like protecting a bridge, road, or fort. It had very little recoil, but was hard to keep on target. Rotating the crank automated all of the loading, firing, and extracting of cartridges; and it had the firepower of two companies of Infantry. The Federal army officially adopted the weapon in 1865, but never used it in the Civil War. The gun evolved into a ten-barrel version with a donut-shaped magazine made by the *Colt Company* in 1883. Dr. Gatling invented this deadly gun, he said, to reduce the horrors of war. Gatling had witnessed the enormous casualties of war caused by wounds and sickness and felt that a more efficient weapon would reduce the need of such large armies in battle and thus fewer casualties as a result.

1865 **The "trapdoor" Springfield Carbine.** This breechloader became the official weapon of the U.S. cavalry. It became a permanent part of the American West because of its extensive use by the cavalry in the fight with the Indians for the Great Plains. First used in the Spanish-American War, it lasted into the first decade of the twentieth century. It was a single-shot longarm designed to fire a .58 caliber metallic cartridge (changed to .50 caliber in 1868). But because of the cavalry's need for faster loading rifles, the *Springfield* muzzleloaders were converted to hinged breechloaders in 1865. The cartridges could now to be loaded

1873 "Trapdoor" Springfield Carbine (author's collection)

THE SHOTGUN

Great for the Marshal that had to defend his jail against a lynch mob, it was known as a "scattergun" or "Greener" after a manufacturer in London. It was usually a 12-gauge, single or double-barreled, smoothbore weapon. It fired a load of small shot; its wide dispersal meaning it was good only for a short distance. If the barrels were sawed off, it could stop a crowd, and if no ammunition was available, one could use scrap pieces of metal, nails and the like. Many manufacturers made this dangerous weapon including *Remington, Winchester* and *Whitney*.

---

one at a time through a trap door in the top of the receiver and then automatically ejected when the door was opened to load another cartridge. The carbine had a 20-inch barrel and a saddle ring to which a carbine sling could be attached so the weapon wouldn't be lost if dropped while fighting on horseback. After 1873, the *Spring-field* was modified to chamber a .45-70 cartridge. The rifle was patented by *Erskine S. Allin,* the Master Armorer at the *National Armory of Spring-field,* Massachusetts. The ideas for the *Springfield* were taken from other existing patents (the government eventually had to pay out $124,000 in claims to various inventors). The single-shot *Springfield Model 1873* was carried by General George Custer's troops at the Battle of the Little Bighorn, but the Indians had acquired the newer *repeating* rifles from traders giving the Indians a big advantage. During rapid fire the hot chamber of the *Springfield* would expand the copper shell casings preventing the extractor from removing them. A pocket knife had to then be used to remove each shell. (The government was always slow

---

to approve the latest weaponry and this hesitancy turned out to be a factor in the outcome of that battle.) Range: 350 yds/850 yds. The story of that battle starts on page 377.

1866   **Winchester Model 1866.** Known as the "Yellow Boy" for its distinctive bright brass receiver, it incorporated a side-loading gate so cartridges didn't have to be loaded into its tubular magazine at the muzzle end. It also had a lever-action mechanism for repeated firings before reloading. The *Model 1866* used the Henry's .44 caliber rimfire cartridge with 28 grains of powder.

1873   **The Winchester Model 1873 Repeating Rifle.** "The gun that won the West" was developed by the *Winchester Repeating Arms Company* owned by *Oliver Winchester.* In 1849, *Walter Hunt* patented a rifle that used a tubular magazine mounted below the barrel and fitted with a coil spring which pushed the rounds rearward and into the chamber. With the addition of a self-contained cartridge developed by *Benjamin Tyler Henry* and a loading gate invented by *Nelson King,* the legendary *Winchester 73* was born. Its medium length barrel was light and easy to handle and yet had enough accuracy for hunting game and Indians. The lever-action *carbine* model was by far the most popular in the West—the ideal rifle to holster on a saddle. The 1873 model used a .44-40 centerfire cartridge and Colt manufactured a Single Action Army revolver to chamber the same round. The gun had a 30-inch barrel and a solid-steel frame. The magazine held 15 cartridges. Its range: 200 to 400 yards. The 1876 model was sized to take advantage of the governments .45-70 caliber cartridge. In 1875, Winchester offered its "One of a Thousand" rifles as a promotion with the number engraved on the barrel. The 1873 Winchester was "Buffalo Bill" Cody's favorite arm and because of his accurate shooting with it on horseback in Wild West Shows, it became famous throughout the West. The 1873 Model was manufactured until 1898. The 1886 Model lasted until 1935 and the 1894 Model was produced by U.S. Repeating Arms until 2006.

1873 Winchester (author's collection)

A 1930's Spanish Colt (author's collection)

1873   **The Colt Model 1873 Single-action Army.** Known as the "Peacemaker" or "Frontier Colt," it became the most popular handgun ever made. Because of its balance, its fast draw, and thumb-slapping ability, it was used by Hollywood more than any other handgun—becoming a symbol of the American West. Originally introduced in 1873 as a military sidearm, the *Colt Single-action Army* revolver used a .45 caliber shell and had either a 4-3/4, 5-1/2, or 7-1/2-inch barrel. (It was an improved version of the 1860 New Model Army.) The hammer could be set at half-cock and cartridges loaded individually by spinning the cylinder instead of having to remove the whole cylinder to load it, as in the 1860 model. This was the first Colt handgun to have a metal strap above the cylinder tying the barrel to the frame, thus making it stronger and useful as a club. To be "buffaloed" was to be hit on the back of the head with the barrel of a gun. (P.S. Westerners were never so stupid as to use the *butt* of the gun as seen frequently in the movies. They'd shoot themselves if the gun went off.) Loved by outlaw and lawman alike, the *Colt Model 1873* was carried by *Wyatt Earp* and *"Wild Bill" Hickok* because it was the fastest shooting handgun of the day. Five shots could be fired in 1.5 seconds.

1881   **The Hotchkiss Gun.** The name usually refers to a 42mm (or 76mm) single-shot cannon that could be mounted on a light carriage or packed on a mule. It was designed to replace the twelve-pound Howitzer. It was used at Wounded Knee in 1890 to massacre hundreds of Sioux. (The 1872 *Hotchkiss Revolving Cannon* was a machine gun similar to the 1862 *Gatling Gun*, but with five barrels and capable of firing 43 rounds per minute.)

Corporal Paul Wernert and gunners of Battery "E", 1st Artillery
Photo by Grabill P.&V., Deadwood, S.D. (Library of Congress)
Seven Lakota scouts and four uniformed Euro-Americans pose behind a Hotchkiss gun, probably in the Pine Ridge Reservation near Wounded Knee.

A Match Game
LEGENDARY WEAPONS

Match the nickname for a legendary weapon of the Old West with its manufacturer.

1. "Trapdoor"
2. "Old Reliable"
3. "Plains Rifle"
4. "Peacemaker"
5. "Ace in the hole"
6. "Yellowboy"
7. "Brown Bess"
8. "Gun That Won the West"

a. Colt Single-action Army
b. Winchester Model 1873
c. Deringer
d. Sharps buffalo gun
e. Winchester 1866 carbine
f. 1822 Hawken
g. 1865 Springfield
h. Tower of London Armory

ANS: 1-g, 2-d, 3-f, 4-a, 5-c, 6-e, 7-h, 8-b.

An 1860 Colt .44 cap & ball revolver used in the Civil War and an 1872 open top .44 rimfire.

These Pistols are from the collection of James Pentecost.

A .44 caliber 1875 Remington revolver.

A 36 caliber, 1851 Colt percussion revolver with ivory grips.

An 1880 Colt S.A.A. of U.S. issue, and a Merwin & Hulbertn .44 caliber frontier revolver with mother of pearl grips, c1860's.

An 1860 Army converted to a Colt .44 cartridge, c.1860's-1870's, and an 1861 Colt converted from .36 percussion to .38 centerfire with ivory grips.

1880 Hampton pocket watch with c. 1890 Colt S.A., .44-40.

1890 U.S. Cavalry Issue .45.

Weapons are from the collection of James Pentecost.

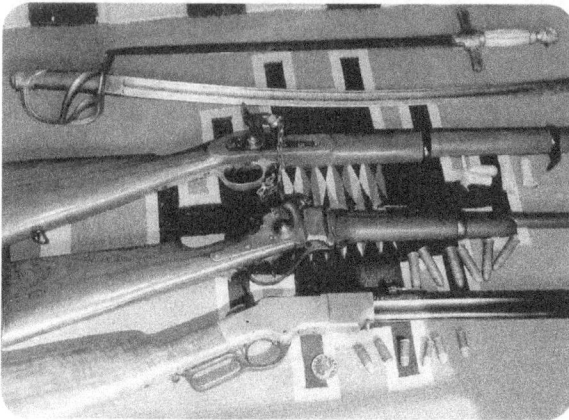

1830's military saber. 1860's English-made Confederate saber. .577 cal. English-made Civil War Musketoon, C.W. issue Sharps Carbine, .52 percussion converted to .50-70 during Indian Wars. Henry .44 Rimfire.

An Ace In The Hole
3 UNUSUAL GUNS

*"Derringer pistols were designed for effectiveness at
short range—across the poker table, for example."*
—William B. Edwards

A few unusual guns of the Old West became famous in the annals of western lore. The "penny dreadfuls" perpetuated the stories created around these fascinating guns.

1. THE PEPPERBOX: Also called a "coffee mill." It was developed in the 1830's by a number of companies. It was a small percussion

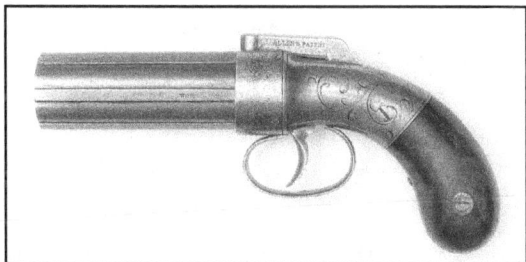

Allen & Thurber Pepperbox (author's collection)

pistol whereby four to six barrels revolved around a central shaft bringing each cartridge under a single hammer. It worked as a small pocket pistol, but when it was made into a larger caliber for the military (the *Dragoon*) it was far too heavy for practical use. Not until *Samuel Colt* devised a rotating cylinder to hold the cartridges that the six-shot cartridge pistol became practical.

2. THE LEMAT SPECIAL: The *LeMat* was a cap & ball percussion revolver that held *nine* balls in its revolving cylinder (.44 caliber) with an additional barrel (.66 caliber) attached to the bottom of the main barrel that could fire buckshot like a shotgun. Many a challenger died surprised by this "ace in the hole." To take down a number of men at once, all one had to do was fire the wide-spreading buckshot and then pick off those still standing with the nine balls from the upper barrel. The gun was

LeMat Revolver (Wikimedia Commons)

invented by a French doctor named *Jean-Alexandre-Francois LeMat* and was patented in the United States in 1856. Many confederate officers used the gun in the Civil War including *General J.E.B. Stewart.* Only 12,000 were ever delivered to the Confederacy. The gun was also carried by *Johnny Ringo,* famous gunfighter and the sheriff of Velardi, Arizona in the 1880's. A television western called *Johnny Ringo* was based on this lawman and aired in 1959-60.

3. THE BUNTLINE SPECIAL: This legendary weapon was a .45 caliber single-action Colt revolver with a very long 12" gun barrel. A real challenge to draw from a gun holster, but legend has it that *Ned Buntline* (real name *E.Z.C. Judson*), writer of dime novels, had five of them made up special to give to *Wyatt Earp, C.E. Bassett, Neil Brown, Bat Masterson,* and *Bill Tilghman,* men he had met in 1876 in Dodge City to swap stories. The story was first written by *Stewart N. Lake* in the *Saturday Evening Post* in 1930 and may have been that, just a story.

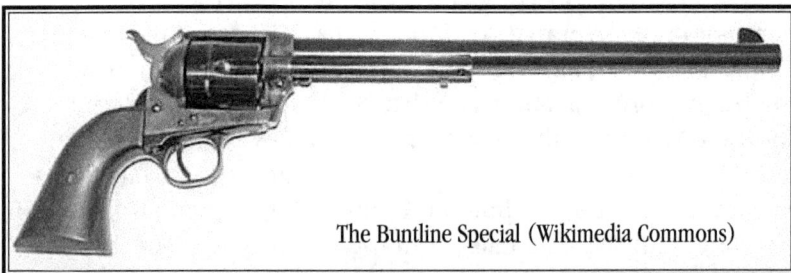

The Buntline Special (Wikimedia Commons)

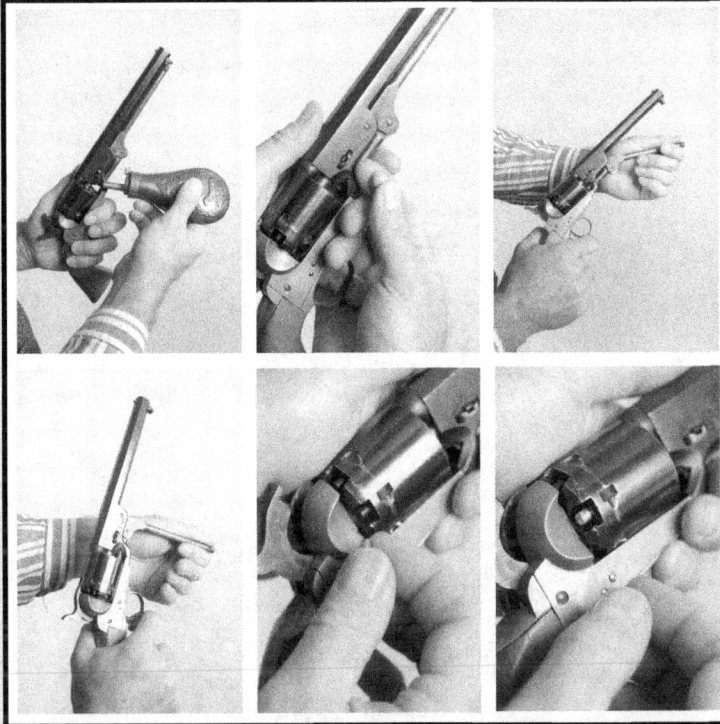

Photos by Michael Jay Smith

LOADING A CAP-AND-BALL REVOLVER

1. Pour the black powder from *flask* or *powder horn* into a *powder measure* first, to insure the proper size load. Then pour contents of the measure into the revolver's cylinder.

2. Drop a *lead ball* in the cylinder and seat the ball with the loading lever.

3. The hot gases from firing off a shot can ignite the powder in the other chambers. To prevent this, place a properly sized *felt wad* over the powder and use the loading lever to press it firmly in place. (If *grease* is used instead of a wad, the ball is placed *over* the powder, *then* the grease added.)

4. Repeat this process in each of the other cylinders, then point the revolver away from you and place a *percussion cap* on each nipple. The cap-and-ball is now ready for firing.

The author as Santiago "Frejole" Rodriguez, Photo by Kris Ford

Rustlers, Ruffians, and Road Agents
THE OUTLAWS

"We tried to rob the Three Rivers Flyer, but couldn't catch 'em. Passengers shot at us from windows for sport! Not easy being an outlaw in times like these."
—*The Life And Times of Judge Roy Bean*, 1972

The term "owlhoot" was a cowboy's name for a man who didn't walk the straight and narrow—straying off the trail because he was up to no good. Backshooters, desperadoes, bandits, and other men of bad character roamed the West when there was little or no law and few men to enforce what there was. These men—"who weren't on speaking terms with the law"—upset the law and order the immigrants and local businessmen were trying to establish so that they might live a prosperous and peaceful life. It was costly for land speculators and businessmen to have these lawbreakers running loose. It was men like Tom Horn (who said, "Killing is my specialty. I look at it as a business proposition") that had to be stopped even if it meant breaking the law to do it. And the "law" was often no more law abiding than the outlaw. If you were good with a gun you could get the job of Marshal and if you did a fair job of keeping the peace, you could have other jobs on the side that weren't entirely "on the up and up." You might run a sleazy gambling hall or secretly boss a gang of "road agents" (highwaymen) or men "handy with the running iron" (cattle rustlers). So here they are, some of the men of the Wild West who were just "two jumps ahead of the marshal."

The Author as Mean Joe Butter
(Photo by Michael Jay Smith)

REWARD!

WELLS, FARGO & CO'S

Express Was Robbed this Morning, between Ione Valley and Galt, by two men, described as follows:

One elderly, heavy set, and sandy complexion. The other tall, slim, and dark complexion.

$200 Each and one-fourth of the Treasure recovered, will be paid for the *arrest* and *conviction* of the robbers.

San Francisco, May 3rd, 1875.
JNO. J. Valentine, Gen. Supt.

Text from actual Old West handbill

Wanted Dead Or Alive
THE WEST'S 50 MOST WANTED

"That I killed men, I admit, but never unless in absolute self-defense, or in the performance of official duty. I never took mean advantage of an enemy, yet, understand, I never allowed a man to get the drop on me.
—Wild Bill Hickok

The most desperate and notorious gunfighters of the Wild West—made into folk heroes by the dime novel and the Hollywood western—actually led unromantic, violent careers that lasted only a few years and often ended in a violent death. Here then is list of historical figures that are now part of American West folklore. Note that some outlaws did indeed live to a ripe old age. Note too, that most of these outlaws were made famous by the pulp fiction of the time—the "dime novel" published by *Beadle* and *Adams* and others. We probably would not know of them otherwise.

TOP 10 MOST NOTORIOUS

Adopted Name:	Real Name:	Life Span:	Age:
Clay Allison	Robert A. Clay	1840-1887	47
Wes Hardin	John Wesley Hardin	1853-1895	42
Wild Bill Hickok	James Butler Hickok	1837-1876	39
Doc Holliday	John Henry Holliday	1852-1887	35
Jesse James	Jesse Woodson James	1847-1882	35
Black Jack Ketchum	Tom Ketchum	1866-1901	35
Billy the Kid	Henry McCarty	1859-1881	22
Bill Longley	William Preston Longley	1851-1878	27
John Selman	John Selman	1839-1896	57
Ben Thompson	Ben Thompson	1842-1884	42

5 BAD WOMEN

Adopted Name:	Real Name:	Life Span:	Age:
Poker Alice	Alice Ivers	1851-1930	79
Cattle Kate	Ella Watson	1862-1889	27
Calamity Jane	Martha Jane Cannary	1852-1903	51
Annie Oakley	Phoebe Anne Mozee	1860-1926	66
Belle Starr	Myra Belle Shirley	1848-1889	41

6 NOTORIOUS INDIANS

Adopted Name:	Real Name:	Life Span:	Age:
Sitting Bull	Tatanka Lyotake	1831-1889	58
Ned Christie	NeDe WaDe	1852-1892	40
Cochise	Cochise	c1805-1874	69
Geronimo	Goyathlay	1829-1909	80
Crazy Horse	Tashunka Witko	c1842-1877	35
Apache Kid	Sergeant Kidd	c1860-1894	34

7 "ABOVE THE LAW" LAWMEN

Adopted Name:	Real Name:	Life Span:	Age:
The Bearcat	Henry Starr	1873-1921	48
Wyatt Earp	Wyatt Berry Stapp Earp	1848-1929	81
Pat Garrett	Patrick Floyd Garrett	1850-1908	58
Charles Siringo	Charles Angelo Siringo	1855-1928	73
Texas John Slaughter	John Slaughter	1841-1922	81
Dallas Stoudenmire	Dallas Stoudenmire	1845-1882	37
Heck Thomas	Henry Andrew Thomas	1850-1912	62

21 MORE BAD HOMBRES

Adopted Name:	Real Name:	Life Span:	Age:
Black Bart	Charles E. Boles	1835-1917	82
Sam Bass	Samuel Bass	1851-1878	27
Kit Carson	Christopher Carson	1809-1868	59
Butch Cassidy	Robert Leroy Parker	1866-1937	71
Ike Clanton	Joseph Isaac Clanton	1847-1887	40

Buffallo Bill Cody	William Frederick Cody	1846-1917	71
Kid Curry	Harvey Logan	1865-1904	39
Tom Horn	Tom Horn	1860-1903	43
Frank James	Franklin James	1843-1915	72
Sundance Kid	Harry Longabaugh	1861-1908	47
Bat Masterson	William Bartholomew M.	1855-1921	66
Bitter Creek Newcomb	George Newcomb	1866-1895	29
Bill Quantrill	William Clarke Quantrill	1837-1865	30
Dirty Dave	Dave Rudabaugh	1841-1886	45
Luke Short	Luke L. Short	1854-1893	39
Jack Slade	Joseph Alfred Slade	1824-1864	40
Ben Thompson	Ben Thompson	1842-1884	42
Cole Younger	Thomas Coleman Younger	1844-1916	72
James Younger	James Younger	1848-1902	54
Bob Younger	Robert Younger	1853-1889	36
John Younger	John Younger	1851-1874	23

3 BLACK OUTLAWS

Isom Dart	Ned Huddleston	1849-1900	51
Ben Hodges	Ben Hodges	1856-1929	73
Cherokee Bill	Crawford Goldsby	1876-1896	20

A Match Game
THE LONG RIDERS

Real-life brothers were cast to play legendary outlaws in the 1980 western *The Long Riders*. Match the famous acting brothers to the infamous outlaw brothers.

1. The Younger Brothers   a. Dennis and Randy Quaid
2. The Ford Brothers   b. Nicholas and Christopher Guest
3. The James Brothers   c. David, Keith, and Robert Carradine
4. The Miller Brothers   d. Stacy and James Keach

ANS: 1-c, 2-b, 3-d, 4-a.

What's Your Handle?
21 WILD WEST NICKNAMES

"You're wanted aren't you?"
"Let's say I'm in public demand."
—Mel Fairmont, *Rancho Notorious*, 1952.

Names were not important in the early West. Many outlaws on the run left their name behind and were known only by a nickname. "The west don't care by what you call yourself, it's what you call others that lets you stay healthy." What's *your* moniker? Your friends—and your enemies—are the scoundrels that will harness you with a handle. Sometimes they're affectionate names, sometimes they're not, but in all cases you don't have a choice. In the Old West, it was no different.

1. **"Senator" Bassett.** He was never a state or U.S. Senator, instead, he operated the *Senate Saloon* in Kansas City.
2. **"Give-A-Damn" Jones.** It was his favorite byword.
3. **Dan "Dynamite Dick" Clifton.** A bank and train robber who used dynamite to crack his safes.
4. **Ed "Dirty-Face" Jones.** He had a powder-blackened face from working in the mines, and he washed infrequently.
5. **Thomas "Blackjack" Ketchum.** He may have acquired his handle because he had jet-black hair and a dark complexion.
6. **"Catacorners" Ketchum.** He once was overheard saying in a saloon full of patrons: "If I ever ketch that sneak he'll get a Bible crammed down his throat, catacorners"; it stuck.
7. **"Wrong Wheel" Jones.** It is said that on one occasion he got a might confused between a left and right-hand wagon wheel. A westerner with any smarts wouldn't make that mistake.
8. **Richard "Deadwood Dick" Clarke.** He was a man who made his living as an Indian fighter and express guard in the

Black Hills of Dakota Territory near the town of *Deadwood*. He was the real life character on which Edward L. Wheeler based his *Deadwood Dick* dime novels. (Some say black cowboy *Nat Love* was the basis for the books, Nat having got his name after winning a roping contest in Deadwood.)

9. **Jim "Fly-Specked Billy" Fowler.** He simply had a heavily freckled face.

10. **"Bat" Masterson.** His first name was actually "Bartholomew" and that wasn't a name to boast about, though some say he got his name in Dodge City for striking lawbreakers over the head with his silver-handled walking stick which he needed because of a pelvic gun-shot wound.

11. **"Prairie Dog Dave" Morrow.** He added to his buffalo-hunting income by catching prairie dogs and selling them to tourists at the railroad depot.

12. **"Hell And High Water" Jones.** From a phrase he was always shouting meaning "no way is it gonna' happen."

13. **"Rattlesnake" Pete.** Nothing dramatic, he just wore a snakeskin hatband.

14. **Jefferson Randolph "Soapy" Smith.** As a swindler, he was "slick as soap." He had a confidence game whereby he wrapped a few $100 bills in his packaged soap as an incentive to buy his product, and then easily sold these 5-cent bars for $5 a piece. He made sure those in the crowd that got the soap with the 100 dollar bills were confederates.

15. **Will "Black Jack" Christian.** He had a dark complexion.

16. **"Rowdy Joe" Lowe.** Often inebriated, he was always getting into saloon brawls.

17. **George "Bitter Creek" Newcomb.** On Saturday nights he went around strutting like a rooster and singing the words of a popular song of the period: "I'm a wild wolf from Bitter Creek, and it's my night to howl." The western phrase *"cut your wolf loose"* evolved from this song meaning "to raise hell because of strong drink"—in other words, to go on a bender.

18. **John "Johnny-Behind-the-Deuce" O'Rourke.** A professional gambler who was so good at bluffing that he could win a hand with a pair of deuces.

19. **Richard "Rattlesnake Dick" Barter.** His sobriquet was given to him because he refused to leave the played-out placer diggings at Rattlesnake Bar, California, believing he would find wealth there. He never did.

20. **"Off-wheeler" Harlan.** Harlan was a none-to-smart bullwhacker who got his nickname because the "wheelers" were the animals (bulls, horses or mules) hitched nearest the wagon (nearest the wheels) in a team. The "nigh-wheeler" stood on the teams left and the "off-wheeler" stood on the right. Drivers placed the smartest animal on the left, and well, Harlan was clearly lacking in smarts, thus his handle.

21. **"Captain John S. "Rip" Ford.** A Texas Ranger whose job it was to send death notices to the families of rangers killed in the war with Mexico. (R.I.P. means "Rest in Peace.")

A Match Game
6 BILLY THE KID PORTRAYALS

More than 40 films have been made about Billy since the first days of silent films, with actors like Johnny Mack Brown and Buster Crabbe playing the lead role. Match the actor who portrayed young Patrick "Billy the Kid" Henry McCarty with the motion picture. (Billy used many aliases during his Reign of Terror, the most famous being *Kid Atrim* and *William H. Bonney*. He was killed at age 21 by the gun of Pat Garrett.)

1.	Paul Newman	**a.**	*Son of Billy The Kid* (1949)
2.	Audie Murphy	**b.**	*Young Guns* (1988)
3.	Kris Kristofferson	**c.**	*The Left Handed Gun* (1958)
4.	Lash LaRue	**d.**	*Dirty Little Billy* (1972)
5.	Emilio Estevez	**e.**	*Pat Garrett & Billy the Kid* (1973)
6.	Michael J. Pollard	**f.**	*The Kid From Texas* (1950)

ANS: 1-c, 2-f, 3-e, 4-a, 5-b, 6-d.

Alias Smith and Jones
38 MORE WILD WEST NICKNAMES

*"Never ask a stranger his name or where he comes from. His
business is his own and you should not be too inquisitive
about his past. He could be on the dodge."*
— Unwritten Law of the Western Frontier

A westerner's **"handle"** might be derived from a
personality trait, an unusual physical characteristic,
their occupation, or their association with a
particular location. In the case of outlaws who were "always
on the dodge," they "changed their names more often than
they changed their socks." Here's some real aliases of real
westerners to ponder and chuckle over:

Bitter Creek Newcomb	Camp-Kettle Billy
Squirrel-Tooth Alice	Hog-Eyed Nellie
Canned Fruit Alex	Six-toed Pete
Dark Alley Jim	Cock-eyed Frank Loving
Diamond Annie	Pancake Fannie
Cripple Creek Cole	Jaybird Bob
Turkey Creek Jack Johnson	Gunny Sack Bill
Three-Shooter Smith	Shotgun Collins
Mysterious Dave Mather	Pegleg Annie Morrow
Pie Biter Baker	Happy Jack Morco
Three Mule Pete	Saw Dust Charley
Shoot-Em-Up Bill	Peckerwood Pete
Three-Fingered Dave	Pick-Handle Nan
Pack Saddle Jack	Rockin' Chair Emmy
Bones McCarty	Cemetery Sam
Ice Box Murphy	Soda Water Jimmy
Big-Nosed Kate Elder	Buckskin Frank Leslie
Frog-Mouth Annie	Flat Nose George Currie
Molly B' Damn	Broken Nose Jack McCall

14 Fictional Nicknames

Listed below are a few sobriquets by the author—I couldn't resist—in the same "western" vein as the real nicknames. Any resemblance to actual persons living or dead is purely coincidental.

Ant Hill Annie	Pussy Cat Pete
Last Thursday Flannigan	Three-Legged Henderson
Milk Money Mary	Ice Hole Charlie Wootin
Fart Face McFarley	Crack Shot Carson
Mary Ann "Butter" Bisquit	Buckshot Lame
Jawbreaker Mulligan	Washtub Willie
Dollar Short Dave Logan	Clarence "Cueball" Cutter

TIDBIT: *Pinkerton's National Detective Agency* was the most famous and celebrated law enforcement agency of the Wild West. Their motto "We Never Sleep" was spelled out under the illustration of a wide-awake eye (a familiar logo that eventually gave rise to the term "Private Eye"). Established in 1850 by Allan Pinkerton, a 31-year-old Scottish Emigrant and former detective of the *Chicago Police Department*, he wanted to run a respectable detective agency. He never took rewards for apprehending criminals and he turned down sleazy divorce cases and scandals, taking only clients like *Wells, Fargo & Co.* who hired him to hunt down bank, stage, and train robbers. He made a science of hunting criminals and business grew phenomenally with offices established throughout the West. He would interview witnesses, collect facts, and keep files about a wanted man's habits, apparel, favorite hangouts, and hideouts. After pursuing such notables as the James Gang and Butch Cassidy's "Hole in the Wall Gang," Allan Pinkerton died unceremoniously: he fell down on his way to the outhouse, bit his tongue, and died of gangrene.

A Trivia Question: What was the address of the original Pinkerton Detective Agency in Chicago?
ANS: 89 Washington Street. The office was later moved to 191-93 Fifth Avenue.

A Match Game
24 OUTLAW NICKNAMES

Match the alias or nickname of each outlaw with his real name. Choices are in groups of four to make the quiz easier.

1.	Big Foot Wallace	**a.**	Harvey Logan
2.	Buffalo Bill	**b.**	William Frederick Cody
3.	Kid Curry	**c.**	Manuel Garcia
4.	Three-Fingered Jack	**d.**	William Wallace
5.	Annie Oakley	**e.**	Ella Watson
6.	Calamity Jane	**f.**	Alice Ivers
7.	Cattle Kate	**g.**	Martha Jane Canary
8.	Poker Alice	**h.**	Phoebe Anne Mozee
9.	Black Bart	**i.**	Jacob Walz
10.	Butch Cassidy	**j.**	Charles E. Bolton
11.	Deadwood Dick	**k.**	Nate Love
12.	Lost Dutchman	**l.**	Robert Leroy Parker
13.	Billy the Kid	**m.**	Doroteo Arango
14.	Pancho Villa	**n.**	Henry McCarty
15.	The Sundance Kid	**o.**	William Graham
16.	Curley Bill Brocius	**p.**	Harry Longabaugh
17.	William Bonney	**q.**	John Wesley Hardin
18.	Little Arkansas	**r.**	Joe Horner
19.	Ben Wheeler	**s.**	Henry McCarty
20.	Frank Canton	**t.**	Ben F. Robertson
21.	Cherokee Bill	**u.**	Dan Clifton
22.	Dingus	**v.**	Jesse James
23.	Dynamite Dick	**w.**	John Holliday
24.	Doc	**x.**	Crawford Goldsby

ANS: 1-d, 2-b, 3-a, 4-c. 5-h, 6-g, 7-e, 8-f. 9-j, 10-l, 11-k, 12-i.
13-n, 14-m, 15-p, 16-o. 17-s, 18-q, 19-t, 20-r. 21-x, 22-v, 23-u, 24-w.

WILL BE

EXHIBITED

FOR ONE DAY ONLY!

AT THE STOCKTON HOUSE

THIS DAY, AUG 12, FROM 9 A.M. UNTIL 6 P.M.

THE HEAD

Of the renowned Bandit!

JOAQUIN!

— AND THE —

HAND OF THREE FINGERED JACK!

THE NOTORIOUS ROBBER AND MURDERER.

"JOAQUIN" and "THREE-FINGERED JACK" were captured by the State Rangers, under the command of Capt. Harry Love, at the Arreya Cantina, July 24th. No reasonable doubt can be entertained in regard to the identification of the head now on exhibition, as being that of the notorious robber, Joaquin Muri-atta, as it has been recognized by hundreds of persons who have formerly seen him.

Text from actual Old West handbill, see story next page

They Wore Their Guns Low
9 TALES OF OUTLAWRY

"Can't you put that gun away?"
"I can, but it helps quiet my nerves."
—Raymond Burr, *Station West*, 1948.

For some reason ruthless, murdering outlaws of the American West have been catapulted into legendary folk hero status—almost to a state of worship. And some of the incorrigible stunts by these outlaws have also made it into the history books of legend.

1. Clay Allison. Cheyenne, 1886. Clay Allison went to see a dentist about a toothache. The dentist began working on the wrong tooth. Clay stopped him and went to another dentist in town who fixed the correct chopper. Clay then returned to the first dentist and began extracting his teeth. He stopped pulling on the second tooth when the dentist's screams drew a crowd.

2. John Wesley Hardin. It was at the American House Hotel in Abilene, Texas that John Wesley Hardin shot through the bedroom wall in order to stop the man next door from snoring. The first shot missed the sleeping man, but the second killed him. At the time, Abilene was Wild Bill Hickok's town and Hardin chose not to stay around and confront Wild Bill, so he made his escape out the hotel window in his underwear, never to be seen in Abilene again.

3. Joaquin Murrieta. A California bandit—who was either a notorious outlaw or honored Mexican patriot depending on who you talked to—encountered a gross injustice after his wife was gang raped and he

"Joaquin the Mountain Robber." A drawing by Thomas Armstrong published in Sacramento's *Union Steamer*, April 22, 1853

himself whipped for complaining about it. As a result, he went on a rampage with a gang called "The Five Joaquins," stealing gold, horses, and cattle, and killing nineteen people (mostly Chinese mine workers) and three lawmen in the Sierra Nevadas during the gold rush. The California State Rangers were formed and a $5,000 reward placed on the bandits' heads. Finally, in July of 1853, after numerous posses failed to run down the gang, one Ranger came upon the gang and two of the members were successfully shot down. One of the men was apparently Murrieta, and as proof of their good deed— and to get their share of the reward—the California Rangers took his head and the hand of the other bandit, "Three-fingered Jack," a known sidekick, and displayed them in a large glass jar filled with brandy. The jar became a traveling exhibit around California and was displayed in such places as Stockton and San Francisco. The curious were charged a dollar each to view the remains of this notorious outlaw and hero. The Rangers got their reward after seventeen people, including a priest, identified the head as Murrieta's, though some believe it was not his and was just a scam to get the reward money.

4. Frank Leslie. The drunkard, but deadly-accurate pistol shot, "Buckskin Frank" Leslie—with twelve notches already on his matched pair of six-shooters— had taken as his companion, a pretty young woman by the name

A handbill advertising the display of the head of Murrieta in Stockton, CA, 1853.

of "Blonde Mollie" Bradshaw from the Bird Cage Theatre in Tombstone. Molly wasn't married, but Bradshaw was her "promoter" and after protesting, turned up dead in a back alley. Molly and Frank both got falling-down drunk on a regular basis and one evening during a quarrel with her, he pulled his gun and shot her between the eyes. One of Frank's hired hands witnessed the shooting (James "Six-Shooter" Neil) and was also promptly shot. But Neil survived the shooting and told all, and after killing thirteen men and one woman, Frank was sent to Yuma prison for twenty-five years—though he got off for good behavior in just six. He didn't have access to a pistol while in prison.

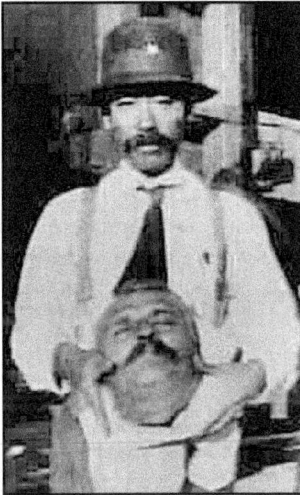

5. Dave Rudabaugh. "Dirty Dave" Rudabaugh was in a card game in a Mexican cantina in Parral, Mexico when the word "cheater" was heard. Everyone at the table drew their guns and Dave quickly shot one man between the eyes, another through the heart, and a third, he wounded in the arm. He calmly left the cantina without a scratch, but once outside, he found that his horse was no longer hitched there. Upset and ready to blame someone, he re-entered the cantina where several irate citizens hiding in the shadows shot him down in cold blood; they weren't going to wait for the constable to do his duty. They then, to make a point to any other American outlaw that might venture into their law-abiding village, chopped off his head with a machete, skewered it to a pole, placed his felt hat back on his severed head, and paraded it around the town plaza. Pictures were taken of the event. Nothing in the history books indicates whether any other outlaws dared to venture into Parral, Mexico.

6. Jules Beni. In the 1860's, a Frenchman named Jules Beni ran an Indian and immigrant trading post in Colorado Territory (near Lodgepole Creek on the Nebraska border) where he quietly carried on a fencing operation for stolen goods and other

Rudabaugh's head on a pole (Wikimedia Commons)

unlawful activities. An unknown gang would rob immigrants, many of whom had just bought from Jules, and bring the take back to Jules to resell or dispose of. The wagons that brought goods to his trading post also took "goods" away. Soon the Leavenworth & Pike's Peak Express Company came through town and built a stage station and the revered Jules Beni was appointed the manager. The town now began to grow and was named Julesburg in Beni's honor. But soon the stages were robbed all too frequently, and only when there was a large shipment of money or other valuables. Beni quickly became the prime suspect and the division superintendent, Jack Slade, a gunslinger of dubious character, was told to clean up the mess. Of course, that led to Beni as the ringleader—and several very personal altercations with him—until Beni got fed up and ambushed Slade, severely wounding him with a blast from a double-barreled shotgun. Beni was arrested and after three failed attempts to hang him, they released him after making him promise he would leave town for good. Slade survived his wounds and all was again quiet in Julesburg until about a year later when Beni returned and the vengeful Slade caught Beni unharmed and tied him to a fence post and used him for target practice. Beni, now looking a little worse for wear, was offered a chance to make out his Last Will and Testament *before* Slade continued with his target practice. Slade went into the cabin to get pen and paper, but when he returned, Beni was already dead—22 bullet holes at final count. Slade then pulled a knife and sliced off his ears. He kept the ears as souvenirs, using one as a watch fob—something he had promised to do years before—and used the other as payment for a drink at the Julesburg saloon.

7. Ned Christie. The outlaw who was not. On May 4, 1887 a deputy marshal by the name of Daniel Maples was shot to death in the Cherokee Nation (Oklahoma Territory). It so happened that this deputy worked for the infamous Judge Isaac Parker of Fort Smith, Arkansas and the judge wasn't going to let one of his men be gunned down without dispensing justice. He had sent five deputies into the Nation to capture a wanted man, but the posse was ambushed by unknown persons and Ned Christie, a Cherokee blacksmith and gunsmith, became a suspect when a known associate of Christie's, one named John Parris, was arrested for the murder and then swore to authorities that it was *Ned* "who done the killing." When Ned decided he would go tell Parker that he didn't do the dastardly deed, his Keetoowah father and his uncle told him he should lay low until they could find the real killer and then mount a defense. So Ned sent word to Judge Parker asking for bail to give him time to prove his innocence. Parker replied that he was not in a position to do this, and fearing a trial before a jury of white people, Ned barricaded himself in his home and turned it into a fort with a double layer of logs and a sand in-fill. Only tiny gun ports were left to shoot through. He surrounded himself with a small army of men and posted sentries for miles around. Ned had become a wanted man (dead-or-alive) for a crime he said he didn't commit. And he wasn't going to let Judge Parker in a U.S. District Court remove him from his beloved Nation and hang him from the courtyard gallows. For five long years, with the help of family and tribal members, he held off marshals and bounty hunters until December 14, 1892 when a posse decided to bring in a cannon to breach the fort. They were unable to get it up the hill

Ned Christi's Tombstone, Wauhilla, OK

to Christie's house so they went for a few sticks of dynamite. When the dynamite was lit, Ned Christie bolted from the house and was quickly shot down by a volley of fire. His body was tied to a door and taken by train to Fayetteville, Arkansas where he was photographed with lawmen and others who wanted their pictures taken with the "notorious outlaw." From there he was moved to Fort Smith for viewing and more photos. 26 years later, in 1918, a black man named Dick Humphreys finally came forward—having been afraid that he wouldn't be believed because he was a man of color—and said it was Bud Trainer, not Christie, that murdered Deputy Maples. Today Ned is considered a "brave, heroic man" and a plaque at the Cherokee Courthouse in Tahlequah, Oklahoma reads: "Ned Christie, assassinated by U.S. Marshals in 1892."

8. Dan Clifton. Known as "Dynamite Dan" Clifton, he was a member of the Doolin Gang and was wanted in Oklahoma Territory for robbery, safe cracking, and cattle rustling. In an 1893 shootout with law enforcement at Ingalls, three of his fingers were shot off, but he made his escape. This should have made him easily identifiable when a bounty of $3,500 was put on his head, but posse after posse would bring in a body claiming it was Clifton even though it still had ten fingers. In some cases, three fingers were cut off of a corpse to claim the reward money, but were seldom ever the correct three fingers. Clifton became known as the "most killed outlaw in America." In 1896, a US Deputy Marshal (Chris Madsen) killed a man who had the correct missing fingers. After that killing, "Dynamite Dan" never surfaced again, but no one knew for sure if even the man with the correct missing fingers was really him.

9. Billy the Kid, real name Henry McCarty, was caught and declared guilty of the murder of Sheriff Brady during the Lincoln County Cattle War and was sentenced to hang on May 13, 1881. He was moved to the Lincoln County courthouse to await his hanging and was kept under guard by two of Pat Garrett's deputies. Billy managed to make an escape, exactly how is not certain, but one theory has it that a sympathizer placed a pistol in a privy that Billy was permitted to use with an escort. Billy got the gun and shot deputy Bell while climbing the stairs to the second-story jail cell. Or maybe Billy, because of his small wrists, was able to slip off his cuffs, hit deputy Bell over the head, grab his pistol, and shoot him with it. Bell stumbled down the stairs and staggered into the street and died. Billy then took deputy Ollinger's 10-gauge double-barrel shotgun from the jail's office and waited at the upstairs window for Ollinger—he had been across the street with some other prisoners—to come to Bell's aid. As Ollinger came running into view, Billy called out "Hello Bob!" and fired both barrels that took Ollinger down. Billy then nonchalantly grabbed a pickaxe to free his leg irons while chatting with friends as other stunned townspeople looked on. He then, after about an hour, took a horse and with a complacent gate, rode out of town singing as he went. The horse sauntered back into Lincoln two days later.

Old Lincoln County Courthouse, Lincoln, New Mexico, now a museum (dk).

The Real Truth
5 HISTORIC QUOTES

Real Westerners left some famous lines behind, thanks to the chroniclers of American history. Here's a couple of outlaw quotes that have become famous. Do you know who said them?

1. **"For God's sake Earp, don't go down there, these men are unarmed."**
   ANS: Sheriff Behan said it to Wyatt Earp who was on his way to the OK Corral on October 26, 1881.

2. **"They say I killed six or seven men for snoring. Well, it ain't true, I only killed one man for snoring."**
   ANS: John Wesley Hardin said this in his autobiography: He indeed shot through a hotel room wall and killed a snoring man in Abilene in 1871.

3. **"I've labored long and hard for bread**
   For honor, and for riches.
   But on my corns, too long you've trod
   You fine-haired sons of bitches."
   ANS: Black Bart. He left this poem after his third stage holdup and signed it "The PO8" (Poet).

4. **"Killing men is my specialty. I look at it as a business proposition."**
   ANS: Tom Horn in his autobiography, *Life of Tom Horn: Government Scout and Interpreter*, 1904. He was hired by cattle barons in Wyoming to stop the rustling of their cattle by what ever means was necessary, but he was soon hung in 1903 for allegedly killing a 14-year-old boy in Wyoming.

5. **"This is a good day to die. Follow me."**
   ANS: Low Dog at Custer's last stand at the Little Big Horn, June 25, 1876.

REWARD

$10,000

IN GOLD COIN

Will be paid by the U.S. Government

for the apprehension

DEAD OR ALIVE

of

SAM and BELLE STARR

*Wanted for Robbery, Murder, Treason
and other acts against the peace
and dignity of the U.S.*

THOMAS CRAIL
Major, 8th Missouri Cavalry, Commanding

Text from actual Old West wanted poster

Wanted Dead Or Alive
8 REWARD POSTERS

*"May you be in heaven a half hour before the
devil knows your dead."*
—John Wayne, *The Undefeated*, 1969.

Here lies the text of eight actual wanted posters from America's Wild Wild West:

1. **Billy the Kid. $500 REWARD.** I will pay $500 reward to any person or persons who will capture William Bonny, alias the Kid and deliver him to any sheriff of New Mexico. Satisfactory proof of identity will be required. —*Lew. Wallace, Governor of New Mexico Dec. 1880.*

2. **REWARD $5,000.00.** Reward for the capture, dead or alive, of one Wm. Bonney, better known as "BILLY THE KID." Age, 18. Height, 5 feet, 3 inches. Weight, 125 lbs. Light hair, blue eyes and even features. He is the leader of the worst band of desperadoes the Territory has ever had to deal with. The above reward will be paid for his capture or positive proof of his death. —*Pat Garrett, Sheriff.*

3. **$2500 REWARD.** On Sunday night, 27th inst., the Stage from Colfax to Grass Valley was stopped by four highwaymen and our treasure box robbed of following amounts: $7,000 IN COIN in a leather pouch, and three packages of coin containing respectively $50, $18, and $10.

We will pay the above REWARD OF $2500 in Gold Coin for the capture of the robbers and the recovery of the Coin; or $1250 FOR THE CAPTURE of the Robbers, and $1250 FOR THE RECOVERY Of the Coin. —*L.F. ROWELL, Ass't. Supt. of Wells, Fargo & Co.*

4. **Proclamation of the Governor of Missouri.** Rewards for the Arrest of Express and Train Robbers Frank James and Jesse W. James, and each or either of them, to the sheriff of said Davis County, I hereby offer a reward of five thousand dollars, ($5,000.00). Done at the city of Jefferson on this 28th day of July, A.D. 1881. —*Thos. T. Crittenden.*

5. **FIVE HUNDRED DOLLARS REWARD!** Wells, Fargo & Co. will pay FIVE HUNDRED DOLLARS, for the arrest and conviction of the robber who stopped the Quincy Stage and demanded the Treasury Box, on Tuesday afternoon, August 17th, near the old Live Yankee Ranch, about 17 miles above Oroville. By order of J. J. VALENTINE, Gen'l Supt. Rideout, Smith & Co., Agents. Oroville, August 18, 1875.

6. **$5,000 REWARD** for capture DEAD OR ALIVE of BILL DOOLIN, Notorious Robber Of Trains And Banks. About 6 foot 2 inches tall, light brown hair, dangerous, always heavily armed. Immediately contact the U.S. Marshal's office, Guthrie, Oklahoma Territory.

7. **WARNING To Thieves, Thugs, Fakiers, and Bunko-Steerers.** Among whom are J. Harlin, alias 'Off Wheeler', Saw Dust Charlie, Wm. Hedges, Billy The Kid, Little Jack, Billy Mullin, The Cutter, Pock-Marked Kid, and about twenty others. If found within the limits of this city after TEN O'CLOCK P.M., this Night, you will be invited to attend a GRAND NECK-TIE PARTY, the expense of which will be borne by 100 Substantial Citizens. —*Las Vegas, New Mexico, March 24th, 1882."*

8. **$4000 REWARD.** The First National Bank of Winnemucca, Nevada was robbed of $32,640 at the noon hour September 19th, 1900. At least $31,000 was in $20 gold coin. It has been

positively determined that two of the men who committed this robbery were: 1. George Parker, alias 'Butch Cassidy' and 2. Harry Longbaugh, alias "The Sundance Kid" —*Jan. 24th, 1902."*

Road Agent!
DICK FELLOWS

This **notorious character,** a California stagecoach bandit in the 1870's, is the most comedic outlaw you'll ever have the opportunity to read about. He would have been a well known dime-novel outlaw hero if it hadn't been for his inability to understand horses. He might have remained completely unknown to history except for his prison records and the memoirs of the famous Wells Fargo detective J.B. Hume.

Dick Fellows became an unwrenchable burr under J.B.'s saddle because it was Hume's job to protect the Wells Fargo gold shipments carried by stagecoach in the California hills. It was Dick Fellows' job to rob the stagecoach line of its treasures. He thought himself a Robin Hood, bent on taking from the rich and giving to the poor, or so he said in an apologetic letter to J. B. Hume while sitting out his third prison term in Folsom Prison. A term to be for life. A comedic, bumbling, harmless "outlaw" destined to live out his life in a dark, damp prison. How did it happen?

It's a long story. Dick had many aliases, one of which was George Brett Lytle, another was Richard Perkins, but this story starts where the first real records were kept of him: the San Quentin penitentiary in the 1870's where he worked in the prison library and lectured convicts about the evils of crime and how it doesn't pay. He had set up a Sunday-school Bible class that eventually got him pardoned for good behavior, shaving five years off his sentence. He swore he was a prisoner that had seen the error of his ways, but after only two months of freedom, he was back to his old profession as a highwayman.

In 1877, Wells Fargo was planning a large shipment of gold coin and J.B. Hume was there to see that it was delivered. The gold first moved by train to Caliente and then was transferred to stagecoach for a rough overland ride to Los Angeles. In his memoirs, Hume says he thought he saw Dick Fellows there at the train depot when two large Wells Fargo express boxes were transferred to the stage. It turns out he was right: Dick saw the locked iron boxes, knew this had to be a special run, and proceeded to rent a horse at the livery stable. He had a partner at the time that agreed to meet him at a specific point on the road so they could do the dastardly deed. But Dick never made it there; his rented horse quickly surmised that Dick did not know how to handle a horse—and apparently threw him to the ground—because the horse came trotting back into town without his rider. In fact, it turned out Dick hit his head in the fall and was knocked unconscious for some time. After regaining consciousness, Dick felt he had let his companion down, that he didn't hold up his end of the bargain. He felt the word would get out that he was a coward, too chicken to rob a stage with J.B. Hume and several detectives riding shotgun. And he couldn't bear to tell his partner the truth either, so he had an idea. Another stage was scheduled to pass this way later that evening. If he robbed it all by himself—without help—he would regain the respect he desired. Dick Fellows, thus, returned to town, stole a horse hitched in front of a store, rode back out of town and waited for the stage. When the stage came, he brandished` his pistol, and told the driver to throw down the Wells Fargo box. The driver quickly complied and Dick sent the stage on its way. He felt better. He had done a good job. He could now face his partner.

But, upon looking at the strong box, Dick realized he had no way to open it—his pocket knife wouldn't do the job. Every good highwayman carried an ax to break open a lock. And even if he could open the box, he had no flour sacks or saddle bags in which to carry the loot. Picking up the heavy iron box, he tried to lift it onto the back of his horse, whereby the horse bolted and ran. Dick, once again, found himself on foot and he knew the posse would be after him in short order. He grabbed the box and dragged it into the woods, but it was late in the evening and the sun was approaching the horizon.

It so happened that the Southern Pacific Railroad was cutting a tunnel just over the hill. Dick, with that heavy iron box now

Mud Wagon, John C. H. Grabill photo (Library of Congress)

heaved up on his shoulder, stepped off an 18-foot drop and fell to the tracks below, first breaking his left leg followed by the box which crushed his left foot. But Dick Fellows was not a man to give up. He crawled, pushing the box ahead of him, out of sight of the railroad crews that would show up in the morning. During the night, he found an ax lying by a tent and was able to open the Wells Fargo box only to discover that it had a mere $1,800 in it. But, he thought, that was better than nothing. Dick buried the box, covered it with leaves, made a crude crutch from a willow branch and hobbled toward a farmstead in the valley where he hoped to find another horse. He was in luck. He found a saddle in the barn, cinched it to a horse and rode off into the woods.

Back in Los Angeles, J.B. Hume and the first Wells Fargo stage had arrived without incident, carrying nearly a quarter of a million dollars—no trouble on the road he said. But the telegrapher handed him a telegram with the news that the East bound stage had been hit on the same road. Hume immediately returned to Caliente with his men, ready to chase down the culprits. In their search through the woods, they came upon a boy on horseback who seemed to be looking for something. Upon inquiry, the boy said a horse was stolen from the family's farm. He said the thief had picked the easiest horse to track. The stolen horse had recently thrown a shoe and a mule shoe had been temporarily placed on the horse until a blacksmith could do a proper job. So there you have it, it was gonna be easy to track this varmint, just find the tracks of a horse with one mule shoe. Mr. Hume still had no idea the thief he was tracking was that irritating burr-under-his-saddle, Dick Fellows. Following the thief's trail, the posse eventually found the horse, but there was no sign of Dick Fellows. Had he been thrown again? Sure enough, further down the trail, was Dick himself, hobbling on his hand-hewn crutch, his left foot dragging and badly swollen.

'Tis a true story, and only the beginning of numerous trips to prison for Dick, and many confrontations with J.B. Hume, Wells Fargo Detective. You see, after Mr. Fellows spent six months in an infirmary he was sentenced to another 8 years in the state prison. Before he could be transported to San Quentin, Dick made an escape through the wooden floor of a temporary jail house. He left behind two new, finely-crafted crutches that were given him by the state.

After two days in the back country, Dick Fellows came upon another farm whereby he saw a splendid black horse staked in a corral. He hurried into the barn to find a saddle and headstall, and returned, saddle, stall, and crutches in hand. It must have been a frightening sight because the horse reared, broke the rope he was tied up with, jumped the corral, and ran off. It's the God's truth! But that ain't all, Dick proceeded to the main house and charmed the mistress for a meal. With a full stomach he went on his merry way, again on foot. To make a long story short: Dick was captured, sent to San Quentin for a second time and was released after several years for good behavior. He had preached to all the prisoners on the error of his ways, and apologized to Mr. Hume for his misdeeds. Once free, he began immediately robbing the Wells Fargo stage, and again he quickly got caught, and again he liberated himself from the local jail when they were transferring him to a prison wagon for the trip to Folsom Prison. In his attempt to steal a bare-backed horse he found staked near the jail, the horse went into a fit and threw Dick Fellows hard to the ground. It turns out the horse had been eating locoweed and was staked at this location to keep him from eating that vile hallucinogen.

Dick Fellows, road agent, was sent back to prison for life this time, but he quickly talked his way into being a teacher in the Department of Moral Instruction at Folsom Prison where he preached that "crime don't pay." This story is true, it was Dick's lack of understanding horses that kept him from becoming a dime novel hero.

REWARD!

—DEAD OR ALIVE—

$5,000⁰⁰ will be paid for the capture of the men who robbed the bank at

NORTHFIELD, MINN.

They are believed to be Jesse James and his Band, or the Youngers.

All officers are warned to use precaution in making arrest. These are the most desperate men in America.

Take no chances! Shoot to kill!!

—J. H. McDonald,
SHERIFF

Text from actual Old West handbill

The Po8
BLACK BART

"I've labored long and hard for bread,
For honor and for riches,
But on my corns too long you've trod
You fine-haired sons of bitches.
—Black Bart, the Po8"

A distinguished gentleman, Black Bart, he was. He robbed the *Wells, Fargo* stage, just because. While waiting for it to arrive, he jotted down a little ditty. Left it under a stone, he surely did, and the rest is history:

Black Bart, was a fanciful bandit who never shot anyone, never fired a shot. He was a California Stagecoach robber who wrote poetry and "dressed to the nines" in a Bowler hat, vested suit, and a long linen duster. His objective: the *Wells Fargo* strong box containing riches from the California goldfields. He did wield a double-barreled shotgun to convince the stage drivers that he meant business.

Black Bart would step out in front of the oncoming stage to stop it, and would stand in front of the lead horses to make it hard for someone to shoot at him. He wore socks on his boots to disguise his footprints and a white flour sack with eyeholes to hide his face. He would yell out in a deep commanding voice "Throw down the box!" If the driver questioned the authority of his shotgun, this daunting, debonair bandit would point out the rest of his gang in the bushes, all holding rifles pointed at the driver. The driver never wasted any time throwing the iron box to the ground. Black Bart would then tell the driver to move on, and then he would break open the box with an ax. When the driver returned to the scene of the crime, he would find the rifle barrels sitting in the bushes to be only sticks, and always there was a scrap of paper under a rock on which was scribbled a short poem signed the "Po8."

Black Bart robbed stagelines for eight years (1875-1883). Twenty eight holdups are accredited to him. In that time, he never fired a shot and always said "please" when asking for the cash box. And he never took anything from the passengers. In his first robbery on July 26, 1875, a lady passenger was reported to have thrown her purse out the window in fear, only to have it courteously returned to her by the gentleman robber. His actions made the newspaper, and he was soon to become a legend in his own time. After the robbery, he would leave behind a baffling clue: a short poem signed "Black Bart, the Po8." He would weigh it down with a stone at the spot where he held up the stage. The public loved this new, well-mannered bandit and other poems published in the local papers were attributed to him though only two actually were.

Wells, Fargo & Co. was doing a thriving business, not only moving millions of dollars in gold and silver from the gold fields of California to the nearest railheads, but hauling mail, passengers and even ice, doing it faster and cheaper than their competitors. *Wells Fargo* guaranteed their shipments, paying clients for any losses. This meant they had to hire a detective force to hunt down robbers in the hope of recovering at least some of the stolen gold. Profits would make up the rest. There was so much gold moving along the roads of California that holdups became an everyday occurrence. *Wells Fargo* eventually had to raise its reasonable prices to astronomical levels to offset the losses. The public didn't take kindly to this and began to look at the express company as just another crook, so when the polite, literary Black Bart turned up, he

Charles E. Bolles (Wikimedia Commons)

quickly became a cult hero. His exploits always made the paper, creating daily conversation among the hard working miners of California. This irked *Wells Fargo* and their Chief of Detectives James Hume, who made the poetic bandit his top priority.

Hume found Bart to be a man who always carefully planned his robberies, always choosing a site where the stage had to slow down at a hill or sharp turn in the road. He always followed the same pattern: the way he cut open mail sacks (a "T"-shaped cut), to the way he vanished quickly by escaping through the woods on foot, not using a horse, running for miles, and then returning to his former identity, what ever that might be. He also seemed to be toying with the detectives, thumbing his nose at the *Wells, Fargo Express Company.* He would wait many months between robberies and then hit several stages, far apart on different routes, in just a few weeks. Hume was fuming. He couldn't come up with a single clue to the highwayman's identity. Then on Black Bart's 21st robbery attempt—on a route he already hit twice before— the man riding shotgun, George Hackett—already fed up with this troublesome thief—quickly pulled his rifle and shot at Bart, creasing Bart's skull. Bart turned tail and, for the first time, left without any loot. Again, he managed to get away, but left a clear trail of blood . . . that led nowhere!

He continued to rob stages at irregular intervals until November 3, 1883 when he held up the same stage in the same exact spot as the first coach he had robbed in July 1875, near a small town named Funk Hill. On that stage was a passenger (young Jimmy

---

8 FAMOUS WOMAN OUTLAWS:

1. Dona Gertrudis

2. Virginia Slade

3. Bronco Moll

4. Pearl Black

5. Cattle Annie

6. Little Britches

7. Rose of the Cimmarron

8. Belle Starr, the "Bandit Queen"

Rolleri) who was going hunting and had dropped off the stage just down the hill from the holdup spot. Bart had seen the boy left behind, a Henry rifle over his shoulder, but it didn't deter the plans of such an arrogant outlaw. Bart brought the stage to a halt as usual, but on this occasion, instead of immediately commanding "throw down the box!" Bart The Poet asked the driver "Who was that man, the one who got off down below?" The driver, Reason McConnell, told him he was just a boy going hunting. Bart, visibly nervous, said, "Get down!" McConnell, confident he was gaining control of the situation delayed, "I can't, the brake won't hold on its own. If I get off the stage it'll roll back down hill." Bart then moved around the stage to chock the wheels and then presented the driver the business end of his double-barreled shotgun. Bart ordered the driver to climb down, unhitch the horses, and walk them up the road and over the hill. All of this activity taking time; very different from his usual plan. Black Bart then proceeded to chisel on the strong box which Hume had bolted to the floor of the coach, no longer traveling loose. Bart apparently knew of *Wells, Fargo's* new security procedure and brought the hammer and chisel. The stage driver, as soon as he was out of sight, circled through the woods and found Jimmy Rolleri. Taking his rifle from him, he returned to the stage and shot twice at Bart who was just climbing out of the coach, a sack full of gold in hand. But both shots missed their mark. Bart ran. The young hunter grabbed the gun from the driver and squeezed off a shot, hitting Bart in the hand that was holding the heavy booty. Bart, stumbled, switched the bag to the other hand and continued into the woods. He again disappeared mysteriously, but

17 WORDS FOR SHADY CHARACTERS

1. Gamblers	**7.** Prostitutes	**13.** Vigillanties
2. Drifters	**8.** Hardcases	**14.** Desperadoes
3. Malfactors	**9.** Horse Thieves	**15.** Highwaymen
4. Cutthroats	**10.** Scapawags	**16.** Rowdies
5. Shysters	**11.** Gunfighters	**17.** Scoundrels
6. Claim Jumpers	**12.** Whiskey Peddlers	

Wells Fargo Express Co. Deadwood Treasure Wagon and Guards with $250,000 gold
bullion from the Great Homestake Mine, Deadwood, S.D., 1890.
Photo by John C.H. Grabill. (Library of Congress)

this time when James Hume's assistant Detective Morse showed up to examine the crime scene he found a treasure-trove of clues: Bart had left behind a black derby, a leather case that might have held field glasses, a belt, a razor, a scented handkerchief filled with buckshot, three detachable linen shirt cuffs, two empty flour sacks, and a paper bag containing sugar and crackers. On the bag was stamped the name of a grocery store and on the handkerchief, a tell-tale laundry mark, "F.X.O.7." Great clues indeed!

The grocery store owner gave a description of the purchaser, and a search of laundries in San Francisco turned up the name Charles E. Bolton, a wealthy mining man. Hume brought him in, a fresh wound on one hand. They searched his hotel room and found clothes that matched those testified to by the stage driver, a letter matching the handwriting on the poetry, and handkerchiefs with the same laundry mark and the same perfume. Finally, after eight years, they believed they had their man. Even the black derby hat found at the holdup site, fit Bolton's head perfectly. And to "cap things off," Bart responded with "it fits very well doesn't it, perhaps you would be so kind as to allow me to buy it from you."

Probably based on a deal with Wells Fargo, Bart showed Morse where he could find his double-barreled shotgun and the $4,000 in gold taken by him in the last robbery—they were stashed in a hollow log near his last robbery. Charles E. Boles (once a First Sergeant in the Illinois Volunteer Infantry), alias, Bolton, alias Black Bart was sentenced to six years in San Quentin under the name "T.Z. Spaulding," the name he gave at his booking. He never admitted to being Black Bart, the Po8. Once in prison, he confessed to 28 of the hundreds of unsolved robberies on the books, and said that he never had any shells in his shotgun when he robbed a stage, said he wanted to make sure he didn't hurt anyone. In 1888, he was released, but disappeared, never to be heard from again, although a copycat robber began robbing stagecoaches after his release, causing a renewed flurry of stories about the Po8. The gentleman bandit never did say why he committed these robberies, or whether he chose to be caught on that last fateful day in 1883.

"Here I lay me down to sleep, To wait the coming morrow,
Perhaps success, perhaps defeat, And everlasting sorrow.
Let come what will I'll try it on, My condition can't be worse;
And if there's money in that box, 'Tis munny in my purse!
—Black Bart, the Po8"

Wells Fargo Concord stagecoach plastic model kit (author's collection)

A Ballad
JESSE JAMES

By Billy Gashade

Born in 1847, Jesse Woodson James violently shot his way through Kansas and Missouri robbing trains and banks— seven—until Bob Ford, a trusted friend, gunned him down in 1882 at the age of 35. Because of his notorious exploits, many songwriters wrote a ballad about Jesse. This is one of them.

1. Jesse James was a lad who killed many a man,
Once he robbed the Glendale train.
He would steal from the rich, he would give to the poor.
He'd a heart, and an hand and a brain.

2. Poor Jesse had a wife to mourn for his life,
Three children, they were brave.
But the dirty little coward who shot Jimmy Howard,
Has laid poor Jesse in his grave.

3. Jesse James was a friend and helped everyone out
With the loot he stole from the bank.
When a robbery occurred, no one had a doubt,
It was he and his dear brother, Frank.

4. Then one day, Robert Ford, for the sake of a reward,
His word to the Governor gave.
Oh, the dirty little coward who shot Jimmy Howard,
Has laid poor Jesse in his grave.

5. It was on a Wednesday night, the moon was shining bright,
They stopped the Glendale train,
He robbed from the rich and he gave to the poor,
He'd a heart, and an hand and a brain.

JESSE JAMES, 1864. age 17 (Library of Congress)

6. Jesse James took a name, "Jimmy Howard" and flew
To where he wasn't known.
But his friend, Robert Ford, neither faithful nor true,
Turned against him and caught him alone.

7. Poor Jesse, he was mourned, and his killer was scorned,
How can friendship so behave?
For he ate of Jesse's bread, and slept in Jesse's bed,
And then laid poor Jesse in his grave.

8. This song was made by Billy Gashade
As soon as the news did arrive,
He said there was no man with the law in his hand,
Who could take Jesse James when alive.

Alan Ladd as Shane in *Shane*, Paramount Pictures (author's collection)

ALAN LADD

Horse Operas and Oaters
WESTERN MOVIE TRIVIA

Billy Clanton (to Doc Holliday who's drawn
his gun):"Why, it's the drunk piano player!
You're so drunk, you can't hit nothin'. In fact,
you're probably seeing double."
Doc Holliday (drawing a second gun):"I
have two guns, one for each of ya."
—Tombstone (1993)

The Hollywood western has become an integral part of American history. Intertwined with the real events that occurred west of the Mississippi in the nineteenth century, is the story of that reality adjusted to entertain and fit an hour-an-a-half time slot. It's no surprise that "trivia" (small insignificant facts) about these movies has also become stuff of legend as we engross ourselves in all that is western. There's trivia about the outlaws and lawmen, about the actors who play the part of ordinary people taken to legendary status, and about the details and the facts of history as they contrast with their presentation on the big screen. Trivial facts are not just fun if you're a fan, but they can be educational as well. Included in this chapter are not only questions, quotations, and quizzes, but answers are provided that more fully explain the questions. So have fun, and may the western live long and prosper.

When you call me that, smile!
52 MOVIE TRIVIA QUESTIONS

"Badges? We ain't got no badges. We don't need no badges. I don't have to show you any stinking badges."
—Alfonzo Bedoya, *The Treasure of the Sierra Madre,* 1948.

Test your knowledge of western movie trivia with these questions, some very easy, some not so easy unless you've been replaying—over and over—the westerns in your video collection. Cover the page with a sheet of paper and pull it down slowly to reveal the answer to each question.

1. **Who said the most memorable line in Western fiction: "When you call me that, smile!"?**
ANS: It was first said by "The Virginian" in Owen Wister's 1902 novel *The Virginian* after he was challenged at a poker game by the losing villain "Trampas" who snarled: "Your bet, you son-of-a-bitch." Gary Cooper also said a similar line in the 1929 movie version of the novel, "If you want to call me that, smile."

2. **What character, in what movie, said the now famous line "When the legend becomes fact, print the legend."?**
ANS: The editor of the "Shinbone Star," Maxwell Scott in the 1962 movie *Who Shot Liberty Valance*, starring James Stewart.

3. **John Wayne won only one Oscar in his career. What film was it for?**
ANS: *True Grit* in 1969 for Best Actor, playing "Rooster Cogburn." He was nominated for an Oscar for the war movie *Sands of Iwa Jima* in 1949, but didn't win.

4. **How many sequels were there to the enormously successful western *The Magnificent Seven*, directed in 1960 by John Sturges and starring Yul Brynner? Can you name them?**

Promotion still from the movie *Stagecoach*, 1939 (United Artists)

ANS: Three: *Return Of The Seven* (1966), *Guns Of The Magnificent Seven* (1969), *The Magnificent Seven Ride!* (1972).

5. Who was the "Man With No Name"?

ANS: Clint Eastwood in Sergio Leone's "Spaghetti Westerns": *Fistful Of Dollars* (1964), *For A Few Dollars More* (1965), and *The Good, The Bad and The Ugly* (1966). His character was described as "unshaven, a serape draped over his shoulders, a flat-crowned hat shading his narrowed eyes and a half-smoked cigarillo drooping from the corner of his mouth."

6. Lee Marvin played two parts in the 1965 hit *Cat Ballou* and won the oscar for Best Actor that year. What were the names of the two characters he played?

ANS: He played twin brothers: an amiable drunk named "Kid Sheleen" and a sadistic killer with a silver nose who called himself "Tim Strawn."

7. What was John Wayne's real name?

ANS: The Duke was originally given the name Marion Robert Morrison, but when his younger brother "Robert" was born

> **TIDBIT:** Roy Rogers got his break in 1938 as a singing cowboy in *Under Western Stars*. He went on to star in 87 movies and 101 television shows. He died on July 6th, 1998 at the age of 86 in his home in Apple Valley, California. He rode his beloved horse "Trigger" from his first film onward, until Trigger's death in 1965 at the age of 33. Roy, who could not bare to bury Trigger, had him stuffed and placed in his museum in Victorville, California.

his middle name was changed to Michael. Wayne got the name "Duke" when, as a kid, he went everywhere with his large airedale terrior named "Duke," so everyone called the dog "Big Duke" and Marion "Little Duke."

8. In what movie does Dustin Hoffman play a 120-year-old man telling the story of his life in the Old West?

ANS: *Little Big Man* (1970).

9. What was Charles Bronson's real name?

ANS: Bronson was born "Charles Buchinsky."

10. What did Lt. Dunbar (Kevin Kostner), name the wolf he developed a relationship with in the 1990 epic western *Dances with Wolves?*

ANS: "Two Socks."

11. Henry Fonda only played one role as a villain. What western was it in?

ANS: Fonda played a hired killer in the classic spaghetti western *Once Upon A Time In The West,* directed by Sergio Leone in 1969. It also starred Claudia Cardinale, Charles Bronson and Jason Robarts. Remember that eerie harmonica music played by Bronson throughout the film?

12. Did John Wayne's character die in any of his westerns? If so which one(s)?

ANS: Yes, Wayne died in four of his movies: *The Shootist* in 1976, his last movie where he plays a famous gunfighter dying of cancer, *The Cowboys* in 1972 where he plays a rancher on a cattle drive dogged by a vengeful outlaw, *The Alamo* (1960) where he plays Davy Crocket at the battle of the Alamo, and

The Man Who Shot Liberty Valance (1962) when he played Tom Doniphon (don't fret if you missed this one; Wayne was killed *off* screen).

13. In what movie does Clint Eastwood wear a clerical collar and prefers to be called "Preacher"?

ANS: *Pale Rider* (1985). Eastwood shows up in a placer mining community to save the miners from a large mining company trying to take all the claims.

14. What classic western movie did this quote come from: "Kid, the next time I say, 'Lets go some place like Bolivia, lets GO some place like Bolivia!'"?

ANS: *Butch Cassidy And The Sundance Kid* (1969). It was said by Paul Newman to Robert Redford just before they jumped off a cliff into a raging river. They had been "dogged" by a relentless posse for days and had finally reached a canyon ledge with nowhere to go but down.

Once Upon a Time in the West, 1968, Henry Fonda as the baddest of the bad. (Paramount Pictures, author's collection)

15. **In what film did Clint Eastwood chew tobacco and spit at a mangy dog throughout the movie?**
    ANS: *The Outlaw Josey Wales* (1976).

16. **What was Roy Roger's real name?**
    ANS: Leonard Franklin Slye.

17. **How many westerns did John Wayne direct?**
    ANS: Just one. *The Alamo* in 1960. He co-directed, with Ray Kellogg, the war movie *The Green Berets* in 1968.

18. **Where was the stagecoach coming from, and going to, in the 1939 classic western *Stagecoach*?**
    ANS: From Tonto, New Mexico to Lordsburg, Arizona.

19. **Who shot Liberty Valance in the 1962 movie by the same name?**
    ANS: It was Tom Doniphon played by John Wayne. It was NOT the man given legendary credit for the killing, Ransom Stoddard, who was an Attorney at Law played by James Stewart. By the way, Lee Marvin played the outlaw "Liberty Valance."

Reel Oddballs
THE WESTERN MEETS THE HORROR FILM

The Beast of Hollow Mountain (1956)
Guy Madison takes on a prehistoric monster
that attacks a Mexican village.

Curse of the Undead (1959)
Cowboys fight off vampire zombies.

Billy the Kid vs. Dracula (1966)
Outlaw gets married and finds out his bride's
uncle is a vampire (played by John Carradine).

Jesse James meets Frankenstein's Daughter (1966)
The daughter of Frankenstein does brain
experiments on Jesse's partner.

> **TIDBIT:** Elvis Presley, the legendary Rock N' Roll idol, starred in 33 movies, four of which could be considered westerns: *Love Me Tender* (1956), *Frankie and Johnny* (1966), *Stay Away Joe* (1968), and *Charro!* (1969), the last, his most earnest attempt at becoming a serious actor, but the film was not very good and his hopes were dashed.

20. How many films did John Ford make in Monument Valley, Utah? Name three of them.

ANS: NINE. *Stagecoach* (1939), *My Darling Clementine* (1946), *Fort Apache* (1948), *She Wore a Yellow Ribbon* (1949), *Wagonmaster* (1950), *Rio Grande* (1950), *The Searchers* (1956), *Sergeant Rutledge* (1960), and *Cheyenne Autumn* (1964).

21. John Wayne's last film was *The Shootist* in 1976. What was the name of the character—a gunfighter—he played in that movie and how did he die?

ANS: John Bernard Books. He died of a gunshot wound perpetrated by a saloon keeper, not by his cancer. That had been his intent instead of suffering through his last days. Soon after this film was made, John Wayne died of cancer.

22. In what movies did Chuck Connors and Burt Lancaster play leading roles as Indian Chiefs?

ANS: Chuck Connors was an Indian in *Geronimo* (1962) and Burt Lancaster played an Indian in *Apache* (1954). Paul Newman played a half-breed Indian in *Hombre* (1967). Other actors like Charles Bronson (*Apache, Drumbeat, Run of the Arrow*) and Richardo Montalban (*Cheyenne Autumn*) often played Indians in the 1950's before Hollywood was willing to use real Indians as actors.

23. Who wrote the memorable theme song to the 1960 western, *The Magnificent Seven?*

ANS: Elmer Bernstein. He was the first composer to introduce jazz themes and instrumentation to film music. With a distinguished career spanning over 40 years as a Hollywood film composer, Bernstein scored over 100 films including several other westerns: *The Sons of Katie Elder* (1965),

Return of the Seven (1966), *True Grit* (1969) and *The Shootist* (1976). His non-westerns included *The Ten Commandments, The Great Escape, To Kill a Mockingbird, The Man with the Golden Gun,* and *Ghostbusters.*

24. **What was Clint Eastwood's first screen appearance?**
ANS: He was a lab assistant in *Revenge Of The Creature* (1955). His second part was as "Jonesy" in *Frances In The Navy* (1955).

25. **The first feature-length film shot in Cinerama was a western? What was it?**
ANS: *How The West Was Won* (1962). *Cinerama* was a widescreen process that used three cameras and three projectors to record and project a single expansive image. A vertical line can be seen on "pan & scan" TV versions of the film.

26. **In what movie did John Wayne say, "Don't apologize, it's a sign of weakness."?**
ANS: *She Wore A Yellow Ribbon* (1949). It was said by his character, Captain Nathan Brittles.

27. **What character did John Wayne play in John Ford's classic 1939 western *Stagecoach*?**
ANS: The Ringo Kid.

28. **What nickname did "The Ugly" (Eli Wallach) give "The Good" (Clint Eastwood) in the 1966 spaghetti western, *The Good, the Bad and the Ugly*? What nickname did he give "The Bad"?**
ANS: "Blondie." Eli Wallach's character "Tuco Ramirez" gave "The Bad" (Lee Van Cleef) the nickname "Angel Eyes."

29. **Eli Wallach of Polish decent played Mexican bandit "Tuco" in *The Good, the Bad and the Ugly*, but he was not the original actor selected for the part. What well know actor was?**
ANS: Charles Bronson of Lithuanian decent.

TIDBIT: In the old "B" westerns, the phrase "Dog Heavy" referred to the bad guy who revealed to the audience that he was the "baddie" by kicking a dog on screen. That was the only way for the audiences to know who was the bad guy, and thus, who to "boo."

*Once Upon a Time in the West.*1968, Charles Bronson and Henry Fonda
(Paramount Pictures, author's collection)

30. Name three of the seven actors who played "The Magnificent Seven" in the original movie of the same name?
> ANS:Yul Brynner (Chris), Steve McQueen (Vin), Horst Buchholz (Chico), Charles Bronson, Robert Vaughn, James Coburn and Brad Dexter. Eli Wallach played Calvera, leader of the pillaging band of bandits. Buchholz played psychiatrist "Ian Buchanan" on the daytime soap opera *The Bold and Beautiful.*

31. Who wrote the scores to Sergio Leone's spaghetti westerns: *A Fistful of Dollars, For a Few Dollars More, The Good, the Bad and the Ugly*, and *Once Upon a Time in the West?*
> ANS: Ennio Morricone. With over 400 films on his resume since his first film score in 1961 for *Il Federale,* he has not yet won an Oscar, but was nominated for *Days of Heaven* (1978), *The Mission* (1986), *The Untouchables* (1987) and *Bugsy* (1991). Born in 1928, he began his career arranging and conducting songs for Italian singers. It was the Sergio Leone westerns that catapulted him to fame.

32. **The spaghetti western,** *A Fistful of Dollars* **takes place in what town?**

ANS: San Miguel.

33. **What western movie star of the 1940's became the voice of "Mr. Ed," the talking horse, in the 1960's Television series of the same name?**

ANS: Allan "Rocky" Lane, star of the *Red Ryder* television series (1956-1957).

34. **What western movie opened with young children torturing scorpions on an ant hill?**

ANS: *The Wild Bunch* (1969) directed by Sam Peckinpah who wanted to say something profound about violence; what it was, I'm not sure.

35. **Who starred in the offbeat comedy western** *They Call Me Trinity* **(1971).**

ANS: A popular blond, blue-eyed Italian actor of German decent named Terence Hill played a laid-back anti-hero in several Italian westerns. He and his burly half-brother side-kick "Bambino" (Bud Spencer) also starred in *God Forgives, I Don't* (1967), *Boothill* (1969) and *Trinity is Still My Name* (1972).

36. **John Huston, director of** *The African Queen* **and** *The Maltese Falcon,* **directed several westerns and also acted in others. Name two of each.**

ANS: Huston directed *Treasure of the Sierra Madre* (1948), *The Unforgiven* (1960), and *The Life and Times of Judge Roy Bean* (1972) in which he had a cameo appearance as a medicine drummer with a bear. He also played a Cavalry General in *The Deserter* (1970), and a commander in *Man in the Wilderness* (1971).

37. **Name John Ford's trilogy of cavalry westerns starring John Wayne which was filmed in Monument Valley, Utah.**

ANS: *Fort Apache* (1948), *She Wore a Yellow Ribbon* (1949) and *Rio Grande* (1950). The trilogy was about the men of the U.S. 7th cavalry in the post-Civil War West. *Rio Grande*, the last of the trilogy to be released, takes place historically between the other two.

38. Name two westerns that began with the discovery of gold in a freshly dug grave?

ANS: *Paint Your Wagon* and *Support Your Local Sheriff*. Curiously, both were made in the same year (1969), both occuring at a funeral. As words are being said over the dearly departed, someone eyes the sparkle of gold in the freshly-dug hole and the disceased is quickly forgotten.

39. Name three westerns starring singer/comedian Dean Martin? There were seven.

ANS: *Rio Bravo* (1959) with John Wayne, *Four For Texas* (1963) a comedy with Frank Sinatra, *The Sons of Katie Elder* (1965) a John Wayne movie where four brothers are united after their mother's death, *Texas Across The River* (1966), a comedy with Joey Bishop, *Five Card Stud* (1968), a whodunit with Robert Mitchum as an avenging preacher, *Bandolero* (1968) with James Stewart and Raquel Welch, and *Something Big* (1971) with Brian Keith.

40. Who played Billy "The Kid" Claiborne in the 1993 movie *Tombstone*?

ANS: Wyatt Earp, the fifth cousin to the original Wyatt Earp.

The Wild Bunch, 1969, Ben Johnson, Warren Oats, William Holden, and Ernest Borgnine, © 1995 Warner Brothers (author's collection)

41. What actor, who starred with John Wayne in the war movie *The Green Berets*, played "The Man From Bodie" in the 1967 western *Welcome to Hard Times?*

ANS: Aldo Ray. In the movie he terrorizes a small town whose residents are too cowardly to stand up to him. Henry Fonda starred as the mayor who didn't want to get involved.

42. In the opening sequence of *Once Upon a Time in the West*, a scruffy cowboy sits at a train depot swatting a pestering fly which he eventually captures by trapping it in the end of a gun barrel. This actor, because of his performance, became a popular western character actor. Who was he?

ANS: Jack Elam. It took two days to shoot this scene and the fly cooperated only after the director, Sergio Leone, smeared watermelon juice on Elam's face.

43. Bob Hope starred in a successful comedy western in the late 1940's. What was it?

ANS: *The Paleface* (1948). It was a spoof of *The Virginian* and netted a sequel called *Son of Paleface* co-starring Roy Rogers and Trigger. Then in 1968, Don Knots did a remake of *The Paleface* called *The Shakiest Gun in the West.*

44. Remember Telly Savalas, famous for his "Kojak" portrayal in the 1970's television series? Before this success he had starring roles in several western movies. Name one.

ANS: *The Scalphunters* (1968), *Mackenna's Gold* (1969), *Land Raiders* (1970), *Pancho Villa* (1972), and *Massacre at Fort Holman* (1974). The best of the five films, *The Scalphunters*, cast Savalas as an outlaw leading a gang of cutthroats who find themselves battling with a fur trapper (Burt Lancaster) and a freed slave (Ossie Davis).

45. The female lead in John Wayne's *Rio Bravo* (1950) later co-starred in a successful 1970's cop show. Who was she?

ANS: Angie Dickinson starred as Sergeant Pepper Anderson in "Police Woman" (1974-1978), co-starring with Earl Holliman.

46. In what western did John Wayne first start calling greenhorns "pilgrim"?

ANS: *The Man Who Shot Liberty Valance* (1962). With the character of Tom Doniphon, Wayne also set in place his trademark walk which he worked on for years to perfect.

47. **Since 1929, the Academy of Motion Picture Arts and Sciences has given the Best Picture Oscar to only three westerns. Name them?**

ANS: *Unforgiven* (1992), *Dances with Wolves* (1990), and *Cimarron* (1931).

48. **What western featured an entire cast of midgets (Little People)?**

ANS: *The Terror of Tiny Town* (1983) starring Billy Curtis, Yvonne Moray and Little Billy. It had everything required to be a western, but it was a turkey; no one came to see it. It's still sold on video.

49. **Every western fan knows Sam Peckinpah directed the classic film *The Wild Bunch* (1969). Name two other successful westerns he directed?**

ANS: *Ride the High Country* (1962), *Major Dundee* (1965), *The Ballad of Cable Hogue* (1970), *Junior Bonner* (1972), and *Pat Garrett and Billy the Kid* (1973).

50. **Before his *Titanic* fame (1998) as a young immigrant on a ship destined for disaster, Leonardo Di Caprio co-starred in a western movie with Sharon Stone. What was the name of the movie?**

ANS: *The Quick and the Dead* (1995). DiCaprio plays a young gunfighter who competes in a "loser-dies" quick-draw competition.

51. **Irishman Richard Harris, who starred in the *A Man Called Horse* series of westerns, also starred in three other westerns? Name one.**

ANS: *Major Dundee* (1965), *Man in the Wilderness* (1971) and *The Deadly Trackers* (1973). He also played "English Bob" in 1992's *Unforgiven*. The other two "Horse" westerns were, *The Return of a Man Called Horse* (1976) and *Triumphs of a Man Called Horse* (1983).

52. **The 2007 remake of 3:10 to Yuma starred which two actors as the outlaw Ben Wade and Dan Evans, the man trying to take him to the train?**

ANS: Academy award winner, Russell Crow plays the outlaw and Christian Bail is the man who tries to bring him in. The movie was based on a short story published in *Dime Western Magazine* in 1953.

Who are those guys?
60 MOVIE QUOTATIONS

"A man's gotta do what a Man's gotta do."
—Alan Ladd, *Shane,* 1953

A lot of the classic western lines come from the same few western films. Why? Top-notch screenplays. This chapter is dedicated to those screenwriters who have written an entertaining western with original, believable—and oftentimes funny—dialog. Before you look at the answers (cover them with a sheet of paper), try to guess the name of the movie and the actor or character who said the line. Taken out of context, some great lines of dialog lose their meaning, so explanations have been added to the answers below.

1. **"Who are those guys?"**
   ANS: Paul Newman as Butch Cassidy in *Butch Cassidy and the Sundance Kid,* 1969. It was Butch's response when he saw that the large posse after them was not fooled by their trick of having both men ride one horse to split up the posse.

2. **"In my case, an accident at birth. But you sir, a self-made man."**
   ANS: Lee Marvin as "Rico Fardan" in *The Professionals,* 1966. Marvin's reply to Ralph Bellamy who has just called him a bastard.

3. **"Badges! We ain't got no badges. We don't need no badges. I don't have to show you any stinking badges."**
   ANS: Alfonzo Bedoya as a Mexican bandito in *The Treasure of the Sierra Madre,* 1948. Humphrey Bogart had challenged Alfonzo's claim that his band of outlaws are the "Federales" by asking: "If you're the police, where are your badges?" (The term "Federales" gained widespread usage because of films like *The Wild Bunch, The Treasure of the Sierra Madre* and *Machete.*)

4. **"Think you used enough dynamite, Butch?"**

ANS: Robert Redford as the Sundance Kid in *Butch Cassidy and the Sundance Kid*, 1969. This was said after Butch blows the entire mail car to smithereens in an effort to blow open the safe inside the car.

5. **"If you saw them sir, they weren't Apaches."**

ANS: John Wayne as "Captain Kirby York" in *Fort Apache*, 1948.

6. **"I'm lookin' at a tin star with a drunk pinned to it."**

ANS: John Wayne as Cole Thorton in *El Dorado* (1967) speaking to the drunken Marshal "J.P. Hara" played by Robert Mitchum.

7. **"I notice, when you get to *disliking* someone, *they* ain't around for long."**

ANS: Chief Dan George as Lone Watie in *The Outlaw Josey Wales*, 1976. Clint Eastwood has just said "I kinda liked her, but it's always like that ... When I get to liking someone, they ain't around for long."

8. **"When a man with a .45 meets a man with a rifle, you said that the man with a pistol is a dead man. Let's see if that's true."**

ANS: Clint Eastwood as "Joe" in *A Fistfull of Dollars*, 1964. Eastwood confronts his enemy at the end of the movie and reminds him of a previous statement his enemy had made. Eastwood, of course, out shoots his enemy with the rifle.

Tombstone, 1993, Cinergi Pictures Entertainment (author's collection)

9. **"Somebody back East is saying 'Why don't he write?'"**
     ANS: Robert Pasterelli as "Timmons" in *Dances with Wolves*, 1990.

10. **"I didn't surrender neither. They took my horse and made *him* surrender."**
     ANS: Chief Dan George as Lone Watie in *The Outlaw Josey Wales*, 1976. Dan George is an old Indian Chief "sidekick" to Clint Eastwood and he isn't quick to admit he can't do things as well as he used to when he was a young warrior.

11. **"If God didn't want them sheared, he would not have made them sheep."**
     ANS: Eli Wallach as the bandit leader "Calvera" in *The Magnificent Seven*, 1960. He was referring to the robbing of the peasant farmers of their grain; farmers he considered to be too cowardly to fight back.

12. **"I never stole a horse from someone I didn't like."**
     ANS: Emilio Estevez as Billy the Kid in *Young Guns II*, 1990.

13. **"Dying ain't much of a living, boy."**
     ANS: Clint Eastwood in *The Outlaw Josey Wales*, 1976. Eastwood asks a threatening man if he's a bounty hunter. The hunter responds with: "A man's got to do something these days," whereby Eastwood says the classic line.

14. **"Do you have anything to say before we find you guilty?"**
     ANS: Paul Newman as Judge Roy Bean in *The Life and Times of Judge Roy Bean*, 1972.

15. **"A man rides into town with two wives, wants to sell one at auction, nobody thinks twice about it. And if a town needs female companionship, hijacking them seems the natural thing to do. And if two partners want to share the same wife, why not!"**
     ANS: Lee Marvin as Ben Rumson in *Paint your Wagon*, 1969.

16. **"Duck, you sucker!"**
     ANS: James Coburn as an Irish mercenary in *A Fistful of Dynamite*, 1972.

17. **"Will you two beginners cut it out. Morons! I've got morons on my team. Nobody is going to rob us going *down* the mountain! We have got no money going *down* the mountain! When we have**

got the money, on the way back, then you can sweat. Bingo!"

ANS: Struther Martin as Percy Garris in *Butch Cassidy and the Sundance Kid,* 1969. Butch and Sundance, hired to protect the payroll, have been edgy, drawing their guns at every turn.

18. "How can you trust a man that wears both a belt and suspenders? The man can't even trust his own pants."

ANS: Henry Fonda as "Frank" in *Once Upon a Time in the West,* 1969.

19. "I don't think it's nice you laughin'. You see, my mule don't like people laughin'. He gets the crazy idea you're laughin' at him. Now, if you'll apologize like I know you're going to, I might convince him that you really didn't mean it."

ANS: Clint Eastwood in *A Fistful of Dollars,* 1964. Eastwood has just asked four troublemakers to apologize for shooting at the feet of his donkey. They laugh at his request and, as expected, they all end up dead.

20. "Now this is the way it's gonna be. I'm a man and you're boys, not cowmen, not by a damned sight. Nothin' but cow-boys, just like the word says, and I'm gonna remind you of it every single minute of every day and night."

ANS: John Wayne as Will Anderson in *The Cowboys,* 1972. Wayne gives the young boys he has hired onto a cattle drive a sobering speech as to who's the boss.

21. "Such ingratitude after all the times I've saved your life."

ANS: Clint Eastwood as "The Good" to Eli Wallach, "The Ugly," in *The Good, the Bad and the Ugly,* 1966. The two men had a scheme whereby Eastwood would take Wallach, who had a price on his head, to the Sheriff, get the reward and Eastwood would then rescue him from the hanging rope with a carefully placed rifle shot. The whole process would be done over again and again in other towns.

22. "Kid, the next time I say, 'Let's go some place like Bolivia', let's go some place like Bolivia!"

ANS: Paul Newman as Butch Cassidy in *Butch Cassidy and the Sundance Kid,* 1969, when a posse was hot on their tail.

23. "Fill your hands, you son-of-a-bitch."

ANS: John Wayne as Rooster Cogburn in *True Grit,* 1969.

Gary Cooper and Grace Kelly in *High Noon*, Stanley Cramer Productions (author's collection)

24. **"You don't remember me do ya . . . When you hang a man, you better look at him."**

ANS: Clint Eastwood as Marshall Jed Cooper in *Hang 'Em High*, 1967. In an attempt to arrest Reno (one of the men who tried to hang Cooper for rustling), Cooper pulls his scarf down to reveal the hanging scar on his neck.

25. **"I've been given command of the armies of Texas, but the fly in the buttermilk is there ain't no armies in Texas."**

ANS: Richard Boone as General Sam Houston in *The Alamo*, 1960. He was breaking the bad news to the men in the Alamo who had hoped he would bring reinforcements.

26. **"Keep your eyes open . . . we're running out of deputies."**

ANS: Brian Dennehy in *Silverado*, 1985. Dennehy is a corrupt sheriff who has seen most of his deputies killed by good guys.

27. **"Joey, don't get to liking Shane too much . . . He'll be moving on one day."**

ANS: Jean Authur as "Marium" in *Shane*, 1953. Shane is a gunfighter who has stayed over to help the boy's father on their farm.

28. **"Well, we had a seven man poker game here one night and it turned into a lynchin' party. Now three of us are dead. That's what we're here to talk about, those three and us four."**

ANS: Dean Martin as Van Morgan in *Five Card Stud*, 1968. Seven men who played at a poker game one night are being mysteriously killed one by one, and those still alive have congregated at the same table to figure out why.

29. **"Ordinarily I'd take you in my court and try you and hang you, but if you got money for whiskey, I guess we can dispense with those proceedings."**

ANS: Paul Newman as Judge Roy Bean in *The Life and Times of Judge Roy Bean*, 1972.

30. **"A band of hostile Comanche came through less than a week ago. I asked if there was a white girl with 'em—they got sullen and suspicious."**

ANS: John Wayne as Ethan Edwards in *The Searchers*, 1956. He was referring to a man at a trading post who told Wayne where to look for the girl.

31. **"Keep Santa Anna off the back of my neck until I can get in shape to fight him."**

ANS: Richard Boone as General Sam Houston in *The Alamo,* 1960. He was asking the men in the Alamo to hold the Alamo mission long enough for him to build an army to fight back.

32. **"If I find any cattle on our land after tomorrow, I'm going to start carving them into steaks."**

ANS: Danny Glover in *Silverado,* 1985. He says this to the rancher who is trying to take over his land by grazing his cattle on it.

33. **"I'm an Indian, all right. But here in the Nation they call us the civilized tribe. They call us civilized because we are easy to sneak up on."**

ANS: Chief Dan George as Lone Watie in *The Outlaw Josey Wales,* 1976.

34. **"Well, that might not be living, but it sure as hell ain't dying. And dying is what these white boys been doing going on three years now. Dying by the thousands. Dying for you, fool! I know 'cause I dug the graves."**

ANS: Morgan Freeman as Rawlins in *Glory,* 1989. A speech to his fellow black shoulders who want to quit the Civil War battalion they volunteered to join.

35. **"The hell with them fellas. Buzzards gotta eat same as worms."**

ANS: Clint Eastwood in *The Outlaw Josey Wales,* 1976. His partner wants to bury the two scoundrels that just tried, unsuccessfully, to take them in for the reward on their heads.

36. **"You just keep thinking, Butch. That's what you're good at."**

ANS: Robert Redford as the Sundance Kid in *Butch Cassidy and the Sundance Kid,* 1969.

37. **"If ever I meet one of you Texas waddies who ain't drunk water from a hoof print, I think I'll shake their hand or buy them a Daniel Webster cigar."**

ANS: John Wayne as Rooster Cogburn in *True Grit,* 1969. This was Wayne's response to Glen Campbell's incessant bragging.

38. **"A human rides a horse until he's dead and then goes on foot. An Indian rides another twenty miles and then eats him."**

   ANS: John Wayne as Ethan Edwards in *The Searchers* (1956).

39. **"Mam, I have the inclination, the maturity and the where-with-all, but unfortunately, I don't have the time."**

   ANS: Roscoe Lee Brown as Jedediah Nightlinger in *The Cowboys,* 1972. His answer when asked by a prostitute if he'd like to come in to her "crib" (whorehouse).

40. **"Ha, ha, ha, ha. Why, you crazy! The fall will probably kill you!"**

   ANS: Paul Newman as Butch Cassidy in *Butch Cassidy and the Sundance Kid,* 1969. Butch's response after Sundance refuses to jump off a cliff into a river because he says he can't swim.

41. **"The last time that bear ate a lawyer, he had the runs for thirty-three days."**

   ANS: Paul Newman as Judge Bean in *The Life and Times of Judge Roy Bean,* 1972. Bean was having second thoughts about feeding another lawyer to his bear.

42. **"I got this guy stealing our water . . . next time you try that, I'll let it out of you through little round holes."**

   ANS: Humphry Bogart as prospector "Fred Dobbs," in *Treasure of the Sierra Madre* (1948).

43. **"There are two kinds of spurs, my friend—those that come in by the door and those that come in by the window."**

   ANS: Eli Wallach as Tuco Ramirez in *The Good, the Bad and the Ugly, 1966.* Tuco gets the drop on "The Good" (Clint Eastwood) by coming in the window.

44. **"You see, in this world there's two kinds of people: those with loaded guns and those who dig."**

   ANS: Clint Eastwood as "The Good" in *The Good, the Bad and the Ugly.* In the cemetery scene at the end of the movie, Eastwood gets the upper hand on Tuco (The Ugly) when Tuco draws and fires on Eastwood only to discover that there are no cartridges in his gun. Eastwood had removed the cartridges the night before. The line was a reference to Tuco's maxim that he uttered earlier in the film (quote 43 above).

45. **"It's no good. I've got to go back Amy . . . they're making me run. I've never run from anybody before."**
    ANS: Gary Cooper in *High Noon* (1952). Just married, and headed out of town with his new wife, Will Kane (Cooper) brings his carriage to a halt, realizing he can't run from trouble. He decides to wait in town to face down the outlaws.

46. **"Your security isn't worth a damn; everybody's got a gun!"**
    ANS: James Coburn in *Maverick,* 1994. Coburn is speaking to the Marshal (James Garner) who's in charge of security on a riverboat during a big-stakes poker game. When several men pull guns and kill each other, Coburn says this to the Marshal.

47. **"As long as there's one cowboy takin' care o' one cow, ranching ain't dead."**
    ANS: Lee Marvin as Monte Walsh in *Monte Walsh,* 1970.

48. **"That one in the center, he had a flap holster and he was in no itching hurry. And the one second from the left, he had scared eyes; he wasn't gonna do anything. But the one on the far left, he had crazy eyes. I figured him to make the first move."**
    ANS: Clint Eastwood as Josey Wales in *The Outlaw Josey Wales,* 1976. Dan George, his Indian Chief sidekick had asked Eastwood, who just killed four soldiers in a flash, "How did you know which one was gonna shoot first?" And after answering, was asked by George, "How about the one on the right?" Josey replied, "I never paid him no mind. You were there."

49. **"Mister, I've been in a bad mood for a couple of years, so why don't you leave me alone."**
    ANS: Kevin Kostner in *Wyatt Earp,* 1994. A drifter tries to pick a fight with Kostner by insisting he drink with him, but Earp has just spent the last two years living in the streets as a drunk and is in no mood for games.

50. **"Pinkertons will be on you like buzzards on a dead mule."**
    ANS: Robert Ryan as a cattle baron in *The Tall Men,* 1955.

51. **"You think it's all made up don't you? You think it's all yarns and newspaper stories."**
    ANS: *The Assassination of Jesse James by the Coward Robert Ford* (2007). Charley Ford speaking about Jesse to his brother Robert, who thinks Jesse is not such a bad man.

The Man Who Shot Liberty Valance, 1962, John Ford Productions (author's collection)

52. "The law's slow and careless around here. We're here to see it speeded up."
ANS: *The Ox-Bow Incident,* 1943.

53. "I wouldn't a-said it right to his face, but wild horses couldn't drag me to Texas!"
ANS: Uncle Bannister in *The Cheyenne Social Club,* 1970. He said this after getting an invite to come to Texas from a Texan (Henry Fonda) after that Texan had ridden off.

54. "He's closed the eyes of many a man and opened the eyes of many a woman."

ANS: A telegraph operator in *The Angel and the Badman* (1947). He was referring to the handsome gunfighter "Quirt Evans" played by John Wayne.

55. "I mean to kill you in one minute, Ned, or see you hanged in Fort Smith at Judge Parker's convenience. Which'll it be?"

ANS: John Wayne as Rooster Cogburn in *True Grit* (1969) speaking to outlaw Ned Pepper (Robert Duvall). Pepper responds to Cogburn's threat with "I call that bold talk for a one-eyed fat man."

56. "Was Curly wearing checkered pants?"

ANS: John Wayne as "Thomas Dunsun" in *Red River* (1948). In the evening darkness, a tearful Wayne raises his lantern to reveal the remains of a missing cowhand killed in a cattle stampede.

57. "It's nice to have a conversation with a patient for a change."

ANS: "Doc Potter" in *3:10 to Yuma* (2007). It's the response to "Byron McElroy's (Peter Fonda) question "What the F*** kind of doctor are you anyway?" when he notices that all the anatomical drawings on the wall are those of various animals.

58. "Promise me one thing, Pete. If I die over here, carry me back to my family and bury me in my home town. I don't want to be buried on this side among all the f*ing billboards."**

ANS: Julio Cedillo as Melquiades Estrada in *The Three Burials of Melquiades Estrada (2005)*.

59. " Australia! What fresh hell is this?"

ANS: Ray Winstone as "Captain Stanley" in *The Proposition* (2005).

60. A mail clerk is hit over the head during a train robbery: "You didn't have to bop him, Charley!"
"Yeah I did, they need convincing. They got their company rules and I got my mean streak, and that's what gets things done around here."

ANS: Charley Ford (Sam Rockwell) in *The Assassination of Jesse James by the Coward Robert Ford, 2007*.

32—IS IT A WESTERN? QUIZ

Do you rent westerns from the video store? Do you watch every western on cable TV? This quiz will find out if you do or not. Which movies listed below are NOT westerns? Circle your best guess. Answers on the next page.

1. YES NO *Angel and the Badman* (1947)
2. YES NO *Streets of Laredo* (1949)
3. YES NO *Captain Lightfoot* (1955)
4. YES NO *Cat Ballou* (1965)
5. YES NO *Gun Crazy* (1949)
6. YES NO *Charro!* (1969)
7. YES NO *A Fistful of Dynamite* (1972)
8. YES NO *A Big Hand for a Little Lady* (1966)
9. YES NO *Bad Day At Black Rock* (1955)
10. YES NO *Riding High* (1950)
11. YES NO *No Name on the Bullet* (1959)
12. YES NO *The Redhead From Wyoming* (1953)
13. YES NO *The Kid From Texas* (1950)
14. YES NO *Night Passage* (1957)
15. YES NO *The Guns of Navarone* (1961)
16. YES NO *Dark Command* (1940)
17. YES NO *Union Pacific* (1939)
18. YES NO *Reap the Wild Wind* (1942)
19. YES NO *Star In the Dust* (1956)
20. YES NO *El Dorado* (1967)
21. YES NO *In Like Flint* (1967)
22. YES NO *Tennessee's Partner* (1955)
23. YES NO *Blaze Of Noon* (1947)
24. YES NO *Carson City Cyclone* (1943)
25. YES NO *Brimstone* (1949)
26. YES NO *Notorious* (1946)
27. YES NO *To Hell and Back* (1955)
28. YES NO *The Searchers* (1956)
29. YES NO *The Fastest Guitar Alive* (1968)
30. YES NO *Come On Tarzan* (1932)
31. YES NO *Escape From El Diablo* (1983)
32. YES NO *Heller in Pink Tights* (1960)

Answers to IS IT A WESTERN? quiz:

1. YES   **Angel and the Badman.** You bet, a John Wayne western where he plays "Quirt," a gunfighter who gives up his guns for a Quaker woman.

2. YES   **Streets of Laredo.** Three Buddies headed down the outlaw trail, two become Texas Rangers and have to bring in their lawless friend. Starring William Holden.

3. NO   **Captain Lightfoot.** Could it be a cavalry movie? No, it's a tale of nineteenth-century Irish patriots starring Rock Hudson.

4. YES   **Cat Ballou.** A Lee Marvin / Jane Fonda comedy western.

5. NO   **Gun Crazy.** The 1949 movie by this name was a gangster movie starring Peggy Cummins and John Dall. Maybe you were thinking of a movie made in 1969 called "A Talent For Loving" which was given the video title "Gun Crazy." It was a western starring Richard Widmark as a professional gambler trapped into marrying a lady from a rich Mexican family.

6. YES   **Charro!** A western starring an unshaven Elvis Presley in a serious roll. The movie didn't do well and dashed his hopes of becoming a western movie star.

7. YES   **A Fistful of Dynamite.** A Sergio Leone "spaghetti western" starring Rod Steiger and James Coburn as an Irish mercenary. The movie was also know as "Duck, You Sucker!"

8. YES   **A Big Hand for a Little Lady.** A comedy western played out around a high stakes poker game starring Henry Fonda and Joanne Woodward.

9. Y/N   **Bad Day At Black Rock.** An action film starring a one-armed Spencer Tracy as a stranger in town who discovers the townspeople have something to hide. The story takes place in 1945, but it is considered a western because the town is in the desolate west with a western theme, so either answer is correct. It certainly has a great title for a western.

10. NO   **Riding High.** A musical comedy starring Bing Crosby as a horse trainer. Directed by Frank Capra.

11. YES   **No Name on the Bullet.** An Audie Murphy western where he plays a gunman come to town to kill someone, but only he knows who his target is, and so paranoia engulfs the town.

12. YES   **The Redhead From Wyoming.** Maureen O'Hara falls in love with a sheriff while protecting a cattle rustler.

13. YES **The Kid From Texas.** This was war hero Audie Murphy's first western playing the legendary Billy the Kid.

14. YES **Night Passage.** Yes, this is a western starring James Stewart as a good and decent brother to Audie Murphy who has taken to the wrong side of the law.

15. NO **The Guns of Navarone.** A WWII movie about Allied commandos who must destroy huge German guns protecting the entrance to the Mediterranean sea, starring Gregory Peck, David Niven, and Anthony Quinn.

16. YES **Dark Command.** No, not a war movie, a John Wayne western directed by Raoul Walsh about Quantrill's Raiders. This serious film also starred Roy Rogers and Gabby Hayes!

17. YES **Union Pacific.** A story about the building of the first transcontinental railroad starring Barbara Stanwyck and Joel McCrea.

18. NO **Reap the Wild Wind.** A John Wayne movie, but it pits him against a 50-foot red squid in a sea adventure.

19. YES **Star In the Dust.** Sheriff (John Agar) has to fight the townspeople to keep law and order.

20. YES **El Dorado.** A John Wayne western directed by Howard Hawks, co-starring Robert Mitchum as they fight ranchers who want to take all the land for themselves.

21. NO **In Like Flint.** James Coburn, who did star in many westerns, plays a secret agent in this movie that parodies the James Bond films.

22. YES **Tennessee's Partner.** A Ronald Reagan western where he unknowingly befriends a bad guy.

23. NO **Blaze Of Noon.** William Holden plays a stunt pilot torn between his love for flying and his wife (Anne Baxter).

24. YES **Carson City Cyclone.** A good "B" western starring Don Barry playing a lawyer framed for murder.

25. YES **Brimstone.** No, not an Irish film, a Rod Cameron western where he plays an undercover lawman trying to break up a cattle rustling family.

26. NO **Notorious.** Nah, it's a classic Hitchcock thriller starring Ingred Bergman and Cary Grant as secret agents.

27. NO **To Hell and Back.** An Audie Murphy movie all right, but it's a war movie about Audie Murphy himself, the most decorated hero of WWII.

28. YES **The Searchers.** A western classic directed by John Ford and starring John Wayne as an ex-confederate soldier searching for his niece kidnapped by Indians.

29. YES   **The Fastest Guitar Alive.** A western starring Rock & Roll singer Roy Orbison as a confederate spy during the Civil War.

30. YES   **Come On Tarzan.** Believe it or not, this was an early Ken Maynard western where our hero must foil a plot to sell wild horses for dog food!

31. NO   **Escape From El Diablo.** California dirt bikers help surfers spring a buddy from a Mexican jail.

32. YES   **Heller in Pink Tights.** Starring Anthony Quinn and Sophia Loren, its about a traveling show troupe in 1880's Wyoming, a screenplay based on a Louis L'Amour novel! "Heller" is slang for a person who is wild and reckless.

How did you do? 25 or more correct and you've probably got every western in your video library, congratulations! 20-24 correct, you're a certified western fan, 10-19 correct, you need to get a subscription to cable TV, and less than 10 correct: you must prefer musicals to westerns.

17 COMEDY WESTERNS

1. *Paleface* (1948), Bob Hope, Jane Russell.
2. *Son of Paleface* (1952), Bob Hope, Jane Russel, Roy Rogers.
3. *Guns of Fort Petticoat* (1957), Audie Murphy, Kathryn Grant.
4. *4 For Texas* (1963), Frank Sinatra, Dean Martin.
5. *Cat Ballou* (1965), Jane Fonda, Lee Marvin.
6. *Shakiest Gun in the West* (1968), Don Knotts, Alan Rafkin.
7. *Support Your Local Sheriff* (1969), James Garner, Jack Elam.
8. *The Over-The-Hill Gang* (1969), Walter Brennan, Pat O'Brien.
9. *There Was a Crooked Man* (1970), Kirk Douglas.
10. *Support Your Local Gunfighter* (1971), James Garner, Jack Elam.
11. *Something Big* (1971), Dean Martin, Brian Keith.
12. *My Name is Nobody* (1974), Henry Fonda, Terrence Hill.
13. *The Apple Dumpling Gang* (1975) Tim Conway, Don Knotts, Bill Bixby.
14. *The Great Scout and Cathouse Thursday* (1976), Lee Marvin, Oliver Reed, Robert Culp.
15. *Apple Dumpling Gang Rides Again* (1979), Tim Conway, Don Knotts.
16. *The Villain* (1979), Kirk Douglas, Ann Margret.
17. *Draw!* (1984), Kirk Douglas, James Coburn.

With Just Three Clues
24 NAME THAT WESTERN

Can you identify a film if given just a one-word hint? In this quiz, three clues are provided to identify a well known western motion picture. Using a piece of paper to cover the page, see if you can name the film with just one clue. If you want to keep score, score three points if you get the correct answer with just the first clue, two points if it takes two clues, one point for three clues, and of course you get no points if you can't get the answer at all.

A. 3. Ta-tanka
2. Two Socks
1. Kevin Costner

ANS: *Dances With Wolves* (1990)

B. 3. Confederate cash box
2. Spaghetti western
1. Man With No Name

ANS: *The Good, The Bad and the Ugly* (1966)

C. 3. Glen Campbell
2. Lucky Ned Pepper
1. Rooster Cogburn

ANS: *True Grit* (1969)

D. 3. Three directors
2. Cinerama
1. Epic film

ANS: *How the West Was Won* (1963)

E. 3. Morgan Freeman
2. Gene Hackman
1. Clint Eastwood

ANS: *Unforgiven* (1992)

F. 3. Gold
2. Humphry Bogart
1. "stinking badges"

ANS: *The Treasure of the Sierra Madre* (1948)

G. 3. John Ford
2. Ringo Kid
1. Lordsburg

ANS: *Stagecoach* (1939)

H. 3. Dynamited mail car
2. "Raindrops keep falling on my head"
1. Bolivia

ANS: *Butch Cassidy and the Sundance Kid* (1969)

I. 3. Yul Brynner
2. Elmer Bernstein score
1. The Seven Samurai

ANS: *The Magnificent Seven* (1960)

J. 3. Jane Fonda
2. Lee Marvin
1. Kid Sheleen

ANS: *Cat Ballou* (1965)

K. 3. Clint Eastwood
2. Judge Isaac Parker
1. Innocent man hanged

ANS: *Hang 'Em High* (1968)

L. 3. Story told in "real time"
2. The hero's wedding day
1. Gary Cooper

ANS: *High Noon* (1952)

M. 3. Burt Lancaster
2. Kirk Douglas
1. Famous gunfight in Tombstone

ANS: *Gunfight at the O.K. Corral* (1957)

N. 3. A spaghetti western
2. Henry Fonda as a villain
1. Haunting harmonica music

ANS: *Once Upon a Time in the West* (1968)

O. 3. Black & white silent
2. Prospecting in the Yukon
1. Charlie Chaplin

ANS: *The Gold Rush* (1925)

P. 3. Sam Peckinpah
2. William Holden
1. Slow-motion violence

ANS: *The Wild Bunch* (1969)

Q. 3. Owen Wister novel
2. Gary Cooper
1. Smile when you call me that!

ANS: *The Virginian* (1929)

R. 3. General Santa Anna
2. San Antonio
1. John Wayne directing

ANS: *The Alamo* (1960)

S. 3. Burl Ives best supporting actor Oscar.
2. Classic Jerome Moross film score.
1. Gregory Peck stars as an ex-sea captain.

ANS: *The Big Country* (1958)

T. 3. John Ford
2. Cavalry
1. Second in Trilogy

ANS: *She Wore a Yellow Ribbon* (1949)

U. 3. Kevin Kline
2. Danny Glover
1. Kevin Costner

ANS: *Silverado* (1985)

V. 3. Aging Gunfighter
2. The Duke
1. Opie

ANS: *The Shootist* (1976)

W. 3. Custer's Last Stand
  2. 121-year-old storyteller
  1. Dustin Hoffman

  ANS: *Little Big Man* (1970)

X. 3. John Wayne's character dies.
  2. Jimmy Stewart stars
  1. Shinbone

  ANS: *The Man Who Shot Liberty Valance* (1962)

Y. 3. Russell Crow
  2. Ben Wade
  1. Waiting for a train

  ANS: *3:10 to Yuma* (2007)

Z. 3. Big Nose Kate
  2. Val Kilmer
  1. "I'm your huckleberry."

  ANS: *Tombstone* (1993)

WWII hero and Congressional Metal of Honor recipient, Audie Murphy (author's collection)

Like Fly Paper
9 IMAGES ETCHED IN MEMORY

Some scenes in a movie stick with you long after you've forgotten the rest of the film. Do you remember these?

1. *Cat Ballou* (1965). Lee Marvin as Kid Sheleen sitting inebriated atop his drunk horse which is leaning against the side of a building.

2. *High Plains Drifter* (1973). The opening scene as Clint Eastwood rides slowly through the town of Lago, the only sound you hear is the clopping of his horse's hooves.

3. *True Grit* (1969). John Wayne on horseback in an open field charges toward Lucky Ned Pepper's (Robert Duvall's) outlaw gang, and with the horses' reins in his teeth, he cocks his Winchester one-handed.

4. *The Good, the Bad and the Ugly* (1966). The last scene in the movie as Tuco Rameriz (Eli Wallach) hangs from a tree with his feet supported precariously by a grave marker as "The Man With No Name" (Clint Eastwood) rides off into the distance.

5. *The Wild Bunch* (1969). The bloody carnage in the last scene as the Wild Bunch fight to the death against a Mexican army, filmed in slow motion.

6. *Butch Cassidy and the Sundance Kid* (1969). A railway express car is blow to smithereens, debris flying all over Paul Newman and Robert Redford. The intent had been to blow just the safe inside with dynamite.

7. *The War Wagon* (1967). The opening scene as a team of horses pulls an iron-clad wagon across the landscape and is led by a massive army of security guards.

8. *The Wild Bunch* (1969). The opening scene of the movie as a group of children torment a scorpion on an ant hill.

9. *Butch Cassidy and the Sundance Kid* (1969). A romantic, frolicking scene as Paul Newman and Katherine Ross ride a bicycle around a barn yard and the song "Raindrops keep falling on my head" is heard.

John Wayne as Rooster Cogburn in *True Grit*, Paramount Pictures (author's collection)

JOHN WAYNE

The author as Marshal Clute Harrigan in Silverton, Colorado, photo by Jo M. Hames

Sagebrushers and Saddleriders
WESTERNS AND THEIR STARS

"The western is the best type of picture. It's action,
mostly true. You have horses, movement, background
scenery, and color. That's why it's interesting."
—John Ford.

O ne of the major mediums of entertainment, communication, and influence is the motion picture film. Hollywood has continued the pulp-fiction tradition by romanticizing the American West, creating a West of "larger than life" proportions. Westerns go beyond reality, but are true to our hopes and dreams of an America built on a high value system. The West was a period of democracy, independence and self-reliance, of heroes who stood for something—and died for it. C.L. Sonnichsen in his article "The West That Wasn't" (*American West Magazine Nov/Dec 1977*) said this about the western: "Everybody is aware that the western is responding to a basic need, but nobody tells us exactly what it is. I suggest that this basic need is a natural and normal hunger for a heroic past. We want to have roots in ancient times like other peoples, but we don't stay in one place long enough to grow them...Many of us know nothing about our own grandfathers. Pride of family is denied to all but a few of us. Pride of race has to be built. Any group with a thousand-year history has these things provided, but the American is a newcomer and not yet completely at home in his vast country; all he has is the mystical West, and he needs it desperately." The Western means many things to many people. The Europeans see it as an integral part of American art and culture. Children use it to define the hero: his image, his actions, how he should look. They, with their toy pistols, gunbelts, and dime store black hats, try to imitate that western "look" in the way they position themselves for their "high-noon gunfights." Western films come and go; they're feast or famine in the Hollywood Halls of Creation, but the western fan is never hot or cold; he waits patiently for the next wave of westerns, hoping for quality scripts that are true to the genre while adding a new cinematic style or perspective to the legend of the grand Old West.

John Wayne and Christopher George in *El Dorado*, 1967
Paramount Pictures (author's collection)
(Christopher George, who became a good friend of Wayne's, co-starred in the TV series "The Rat Patrol" from 1966-1968, and after playing with Wayne in *El Dorado*, he got a part in *Chisum* (1970), and *The Train Robbers* (1973).

Historically Significant
8 WESTERN FILM CLASSICS

Listed below are some of the "oaters" that have become historically important in the world of westerns. Film critics will argue which films should be on the list, so don't take this list as the final say. Included with the title are its director, date released, and its historical significance.

1. **STAGECOACH**, John Ford, **1939.** Rescued the genre from its dead-end decline of the 1930's, and helped bring John Wayne to stardom.

2. **SHANE**, George Stevens, **1953.** The film is a conscious retelling of the purest elements of the classic western legend. It codified the essence of the western.

3. **THE SEARCHERS**, John Ford, **1956.** A masterpiece pictorially, Ford's first wide-screen film, and considered by many to be Ford's masterpiece.

4. **FISTFULL OF DOLLARS**, Sergio Leone, **1964.** The first Italian "spaghetti western" defining a new brutal West with grittiness, offhand violence, extreme closeups and Ennio Morricone's "jangly" soundtrack. Clint Eastwood's portrayal of the "Man With No Name" made him a star.

5. **THE WILD BUNCH**, Sam Peckinpah, **1969.** Brought the element of graphic violence to the screen with its slow-motion bloodletting. Considered to be Peckinpah's greatest film.

6. **BUTCH CASSIDY AND THE SUNDANCE KID**, George Roy Hill, **1969.** Successfully combined action with comedy. Won Burt Bacharach and Hal David an Oscar for best score.

7. **DANCES WITH WOLVES**, Kevin Costner, **1990.** Reestablished the western's viability at the box office. Won "Best Picture" and six other Oscars.

8. **UNFORGIVEN**, Clint Eastwood, **1992.** A dark Western with an anti-hero; good and evil is no longer black and white. Revitalized the western as a pertinent genre. "Best Picture" and "Best Director" Oscars.

Westerns That Won Oscars
24 ACADEMY AWARD WINNERS

*"I can't act, I can't ride, I can't sing, and I've
got millions of dollars to prove it."*
—Gene Autry

The Academy of Motion Picture Arts and Sciences
has never paid much attention to the "lowly" western.
The "oater," was a "B" movie, a second film to add to the
feature presentation and it was a genre used to wean "greenhorn" actors. Some films ignored by audiences and critics at
their original release later became classics. Here then, are the
"horse operas" that *did* win an Oscar or two.

1928-29
Warner Baxter wins Best Actor for *Old Arizona*.

1930-31
Cimarron wins Best Picture, Best Writing, and
Best Interior Decorating.

1934
John Waters wins Best Assistant Director for *Viva Villa*.

1938
The Cowboy and the Lady wins Best Sound Recording.

1939
Thomas Mitchell wins Best Supporting Actor in *Stagecoach*.
Stagecoach also gets the Best Film Score Oscar.

1940
Walter Brennan wins Best Supporting Actor for his portrayal as
"Judge Roy Bean" in *The Westerner*.
Northwest Mounted Police wins Best Film Editing.

1948

The Treasure of the Sierra Madre wins three Oscars: Best Writing/Screenplay, Best Director (John Huston), Best Supporting Actor (Walter Huston). "Buttons and Bows" from *The Paleface* wins the Oscar for Best Music (Song).

1949

She Wore a Yellow Ribbon wins Best Color Cinematography.

1950

Annie Get Your Gun gets Best Music (Scoring of a Musical Picture).

1952

High Noon wins four Oscars: Gary Cooper for Best Actor, Best Film Editing, Best Scoring of a Dramatic or Comedy Picture, and Best Music (Song) for "Do Not Forsake Me, Oh My Darlin'."

1953

Best Color Cinematography Oscar goes to *Shane*. Best Music (Song) was for "Secret Love" in *Calamity Jane*.

1954

Broken Lance wins the Writing Oscar for Best Motion Picture Story.

1958

Burl Ives wins Best Supporting Actor for his work in *The Big Country.*

1960

The Alamo wins the Oscar for Best Sound.

1963

How The West Was Won wins three Oscars: Best Sound, Best Editing, and Best Writing (Story and Screenplay written directly for the Screen).

1965

Lee Marvin wins Best Actor for his duel role as "Kid Sheleen" and "Tim Strawn" in *Cat Ballou.*

1969

John Wayne wins Best Actor as "Rooster Cogburn" in *True Grit.*
Butch Cassidy and the Sundance Kid win four Oscars: Best
Cinematography, Best Music (Original Score), Best Music (Song)
"Raindrops Keep Fallin' on My Head," and Best Writing (Screenplay
based on material not previously published or produced).

1973

The Great American Cowboy wins Best Documentary (Feature).

1990

Dances With Wolves takes seven Oscars: Best Picture, Best Director (Kevin Costner), Best Screenplay, Best Original Score, Best
Cinematography, Best Editing, and Best Sound Recording.

1992

Unforgiven wins four Oscars: Best Picture, Best Director (Clint
Eastwood), Best Supporting Actor (Gene Hackman), Best Editing.

A Match Game
8 FEMALE STARS

Match the actress with the movie she was featured in:

1.	Anjelica Huston	**a.**	*Rio Bravo* (1959)
2.	Sharon Stone	**b.**	*Cat Ballou* (1965)
3.	Jane Fonda	**c.**	*Big Hand For the Little Lady* (1966)
4.	Raquel Welch	**d.**	*Hannie Caulder* (1971)
5.	Lauren Bacall	**e.**	*The Shootist* (1976)
6.	Angie Dickinson	**f.**	*Tom Horn* (1980)
7.	Joanne Woodward	**g.**	*The Quick and the Dead* (1995)
8.	Linda Evans	**h.**	*Buffalo Girls* (1996)

ANS: 1-h, 2-g, 3-b, 4-d, 5-e, 6-a, 7-c, 8-f.

Sitting In The Director's Chair
15 WESTERN MOVIE DIRECTORS

*"Westerns are closer to art than anything
else in the motion picture business."*
—John Wayne

Some western movie directors have become as famous as the outlaws portrayed in their movies. Listed are a few of the directors that were western-movie prolific along with some of their best known Western films.

1. JOHN FORD (1895-1973), is best known for his use of Utah's "Monument Valley" and for making John Wayne famous. His Western films include: *Drums Along the Mohawk* (1939), *Stagecoach* (1939), *My Darling Clementine* (1946), *Fort Apache* (1948), *She Wore a Yellow Ribbon* (1949), *Wagon Master* (1950), *The Searchers* (1956), *The Horse Soldiers* (1959), *The Man Who Shot Liberty Valance* (1962), and other successful westerns: *Straight Shooting* (1917), *The Iron Horse* (1924), *Three Bad Men* (1926), *3 Godfathers* (1949), *Rio Grande* (1950), *Two Ride Together* (1961), *How The West Was Won* (1963), and *Cheyenne Autumn* (1964). It was *Stagecoach* that established the "adult western" as viable and made John Wayne a star. He was the first person to receive the American Film Institute's Life Achievement Award.

2. SAM PECKINPAH (1925-1984), is remembered for his slow-motion bloody violence. His westerns included *Ride The High Country* (1962), *Wild Bunch* (1969), *The Ballad of Cable Hogue* (1970), and *Pat Garrett and Billy The Kid* (1973). Less successful westerns: *Major Dundee* (1965), and *Junior Bonner* (1972). Peckinpah constantly fought the studios for editing control because they often "butchered" his films. His most successful film was not a western: it was *The Getaway* (1972) with Steve McQueen and Ali MacGraw.

3. SERGIO LEONE (1921-1989), was the Italian director who invented the "spaghetti western" with a new stark, brutal West and "operatic" feel. He used extreme closeups and Ennio Morricone's new music style to make Clint Eastwood a star. His westerns: *Fistful Of Dollars* (1964), *For a Few Dollars More* (1965), *The Good, The Bad And The Ugly* (1966), *Once Upon a Time In The West* (1969), and *A Fistful of Dynamite* (1972). His last film was the epic Jewish crime-drama *Once Upon a Time in America* (1984) which had the same stylish feel as his westerns.

4. HOWARD HAWKS (1896-1977). His best westerns, most with John Wayne: *Red River* (1948), *Rio Bravo* (1959), *El Dorado* (1967), and lesser films: *The Barbary Coast, The Outlaws* (1943) *Rio Lobo (1970)* and *The Big Sky.* He is considered to be one of the greatest American directors of all time, in the same class as Ford, Hitchcock and Welles.

5. JOHN STURGES (1910-1992). His best westerns: *Bad Day At Black Rock* (1955), *Gunfight At The O.K. Corral* (1957), *The Magnificent Seven* (1960). Others: *Last Train From Gun Hill* (1959), *The Hallelujah Trail (1965)*, *The Law And Jake Wade* (1958), *Hour of the Gun* (1967), *Joe Kidd* (1972), and *Chino* (1973). He got a Best Director Oscar nomination for *Bad Day At Black Rock*" with his exceptional use of the new wide-screen Cinemascope format.

6. DELMAR DAVES (1904-1977), directed *Broken Arrow* (1950), *3.10 To Yuma* (1957) and *The Badlanders* (1958), *The Hanging Tree (1959)*, *Drum Beat* (1954), and *Jubal* (1956).

7. ANTHONY MANN (1906-1967). Best known for his westerns about violent, desperate men starring James Stewart: *Winchester '73* (1950), *The Naked Spur* (1953), *The Man From Laramie* (1955), *Bend Of The River* (1952), and *The Far Country* (1955). He also directed *The Tin Star* (1957), and *Man Of The West* (1958).

8. BUDD BOETTICHER (1916-2001). His off-beat men-of-action westerns were primarily Randolph Scott vehicles: *Seven Men From Now* (1956), *The Tall T* (1957), *Decision At Sundown* (1957), *Buchanan Rides Alone* (1958), *Ride Lonesome* (1959), and

Comanche Station (1960). He also directed *The Man From the Alamo* (1953) starring Glenn Ford.

9. HENRY HATHAWAY (1898-1985). His westerns: *To The Last Man* (1933), *Rawhide* (1951), *From Hell To Texas* (1958), *North To Alaska (1960), How The West Was Won* (1963), *Nevada Smith* (1965), *The Sons of Katie Elder*(1966), *Five Card Stud* (1968), and *True Grit* (1969). He began his career with Randolph Scott low-budget westerns.

10. BURT KENNEDY (1922-2001). His preference for light-hearted westerns produced: *The Rounders* (1965), *The War Wagon* (1967), *Support Your Local Sheriff* (1969), *Dirty Dingus Magee* (1970), and *Train Robbers* (1973). Other westerns included: *Hannie Caulder* (1972), *Return Of The Seven* (1966), and a grim tale of a run-down town victimized by a "bad man from Bodie" called *Welcome to Hard Times* (1967). He also wrote many westerns.

11. ROBERT N. BRADBURY (1886-1949), made many low-budget silent and sound horse operas starring Bob Steele, Jack Hoxie and John Wayne. He wrote many of his own scripts. His films include: *West of the Divide* (1934), *Riders of Destiny* (1933), *The Star Packer* (1934), *Trouble in Texas* (1937), *Texas Terror* (1935), *The Trail Beyond* (1934).

12. LESLEY SELANDER (1900-1979), directed: *Three Men From Texas* (1940), one of the best Hopalong Cassidy films ever made, *The Rustlers* (1949), *Buckskin Frontier* (1943), *Guns of Hate* (1948), *Brothers in the Saddle* (1949), *Rider from Tucson* (1950), *Road Agent* (1952), and dozens more.

13. HOWARD BRETHERTON (1896-1969), made mostly low-budget westerns including William Boyd and Buck Jones vehicles. *Riders of the Rio Grande* (1943), *Carson City Cyclone* (1943), *Ghost Town Law* (1942), *Hidden Valley Outlaws* (1944), *San Antonio Kid* (1944), *West of the Law* (1942).

14. RAOUL WALSH (1887-1980), Directed *In Old Arizona* (1929), Hollywood's first outdoor talkie. *The Big Trail* (1930), *Dark Command* (1940), *They Died With Their Boots On* (1941), and *Gun Fury* (1953).

15. GEORGE SHERMAN (1908-1991), directed low-budget westerns for Republic. He made many of the "Three Mesquiteers" films starring John Wayne. Films: *Colorado Sunset* (1939), *Kansas Cyclone* (1941), *Mexicali Rose* (1939), *Riders of the Black Hills* (1938), *Rocky Mountain Rangers* (1940), *Tulsa Kid* (1940), *Under Texas Skies* (1940).

10 OTHER PROLIFIC
WESTERN MOVIE DIRECTORS:

George Archainbaud, Spencer Gordon Bennet, Andrew McLaglen, Sam Newfield, D. Ross Lederman, Joseph Kane, William Wyler, Henry King, John English, William Witney.

James Garner as Captain Woodrow Call in "Streets of Laredo" (1995)

De Passe Entertainment (author's collection)

Boots and Saddles
99 WESTERN STARS

"I play John Wayne in every picture regardless of the character."
—John Wayne

In this section are some of the actors and actresses who made so many westerns that they became forever associated with the genre.

★ 6 — "A" WESTERN SUPERSTARS ★
(They shaped our image of the Western hero.)

1. Gary Cooper
2. Tom Mix
3. Clint Eastwood
4. Randolph Scott
5. Joel McCrea
6. John Wayne

★ 9 — "B" WESTERN STARS ★

1. Gene Autry
2. Buck Jones
3. Tex Ritter
4. Bronco Billy
5. Ken Maynard
6. Roy Rogers
7. William Boyd
8. Tim McCoy
9. Fred Thompson

Robert Redford, Katharine Ross, and Paul Newman (Campanile Productions)

★ 47 — POPULAR STARS ★

(Popular male stars that appeared successfully in
Westerns. Though they were not regarded as Western
stars, they were cast in numerous Westerns.)

1. Jean Arthur
2. Harry Carey
3. Joseph Cotten
4. Henry Fonda
5. James Garner
6. William S. Hart
7. William Holden
8. Katy Jurado
9. Lash LaRue
10. Steve McQueen
11. Audie Murphy
12. Maureen O'Hara
13. Anthony Quinn
14. Jane Russell
15. James Stewart
16. Richard Widmark

17. Charles Bronson
18. Jeff Chandler
19. Richard Dix
20. Glenn Ford
21. Hoot Gibson
22. Van Heflin
23. Rock Hudson
24. Alan Ladd
25. Dean Martin
26. Ray Milland
27. Paul Newman
28. Jack Palance
29. Robert Redford
30. Robert Ryan
31. Robert Taylor
32. Robert Young

33. Yul Brynner
34. James Coburn
35. Kirk Douglas
36. Clark Gable
37. Stewart Granger
38. Charlton Heston
39. Walter Huston
40. Burt Lancaster
41. Lee Marvin
42. Robert Mitchum
43. George O'Brien
44. Gregory Peck
45. Burt Reynolds
46. Barbara Stanwyck
47. Spencer Tracy

★ 37 — SUPPORTING PLAYERS ★

1. Claude Akins
2. James Best
3. Walter Brennan
4. Harry Carey, Jr.
5. Jim Davis
6. Gabby Hayes
7. Arthur Hunnicutt
8. Victor Jory
9. J. Carrol Naish
10. Michael Pate
11. Anthony Quinn
12. Bob Steele
13. Chill Wills

14. John Anderson
15. Ernest Borgnine
16. Edger Buchanan
17. Lee Van Cleef
18. Bruce Dern
19. Bo Hopkins
20. Ben Johnson
21. Strother Martin
22. Warren Oates
23. Slim Pickens
24. Roy Roberts
25. Dub Taylor

26. R. G. Armstrong
27. Henry Brandon
28. Rod Cameron
29. Ken Curtis
30. Jack Elam
31. Henry Hull
32. L. Q. Jones
33. Henry Morgan
34. Edmond O'Brien
35. Michael J. Pollard
36. Harry D. Stanton
37. Forrest Tucker

Western Filmographies
14 LEGENDARY SUPERSTARS

"Talk low, talk slow, and don't say too much."
—John Wayne on acting.

Here they are: the western films of fourteen legendary movie actors who shaped the image of the western hero. A few trivia questions have been added about these movies. The best films are printed in **bold** type.

⭐ JOHN WAYNE ⭐

(known as "The Duke") (1907-1979)
(This list does not include his early studio Westerns).

(1930) *The Big Trail*
(1939) ***Stagecoach***
(1940) *The Dark Command*
(1943) *In Old California*
(1944) *Tall in the Saddle*
(1945) *Dakota*
(1947) ***Angel and the Badman***
(1948) ***Fort Apache***
(1948) ***Red River***
(1949) ***3 Godfathers***
(1949) *The Fighting Kentuckian*
(1949) ***She Wore a Yellow Ribbon***
(1950) *Rio Grande*
(1953) ***Hondo***
(1956) ***The Searchers***
(1959) ***Rio Bravo***
(1959) ***The Horse Soldiers***
(1960) ***The Alamo***

North to Alaska (1960)
The Comancheros (1961)
The Man Who Shot Liberty Valance (1962)
How the West Was Won (1962)
McLintock! (1963)
The Sons of Katie Elder (1965)
The War Wagon (1967)
El Dorado (1967)
True Grit (1969)
The Undefeated (1969)
Chisum (1970)
Rio Lobo (1970)
Big Jake (1971)
The Cowboys (1972)
The Train Robbers (1973)
Cahill U.S. Marshal (1973)
Rooster Cogburn (1975)
The Shootist (1976)

1. **Which movie did John Wayne direct?**
    ANS: *The Alamo.* He also co-directed *The Comancheros.*

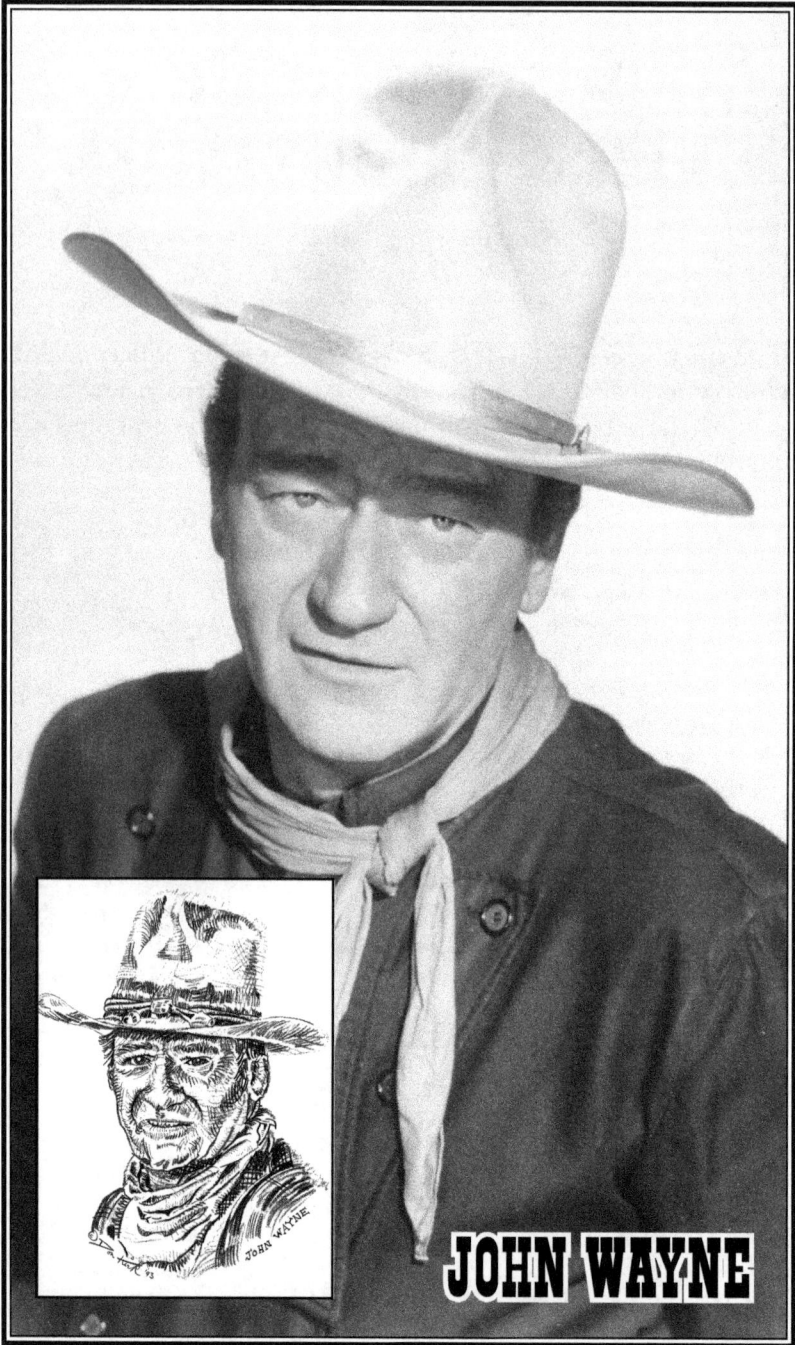

JOHN WAYNE

2. **Which movie won "The Duke" his only Oscar?**
   ANS: John Wayne won the Best Actor Oscar for *True Grit* playing the salty old "Rooster Cogburn."

3. **In which two movies did Dean Martin have a co-starring role?**
   ANS: In *The Sons of Katie Elder* he played "Tom," one of the four Elder brothers and in *Rio Bravo* he was an alcoholic deputy named "Dude." *Rio Bravo* also co-starred Ricky Nelson from the 1950's "Ozzie and Harriet" TV series.

4. **In which movies listed above did John Wayne's son Patrick play a part?**
   ANS: Patrick Wayne got his start acting in John Ford films and then got supporting roles alongside his father in *The Searchers, The Alamo, The Comancheros, McLintock!,* and *Big Jake.* He also had parts in several non-John Wayne westerns: *Cheyenne Autumn* (1964), *Shenandoah* (1965), *The Deserter* (1970), *The Gatling Gun* (1973), *Rustler's Rhapsody* (1985) and *Young Guns* (1988).

5. **Which movie was delayed four months while John Wayne recuperated from surgery due to lung cancer?**
   ANS: *The Sons of Katie Elder* (1965).

THE BADDEST OF THE BAD

Here are four consumate actors who played great villains:

1. **Jack Palance** as the hired gun "Jack Wilson" in *Shane*, 1953. He was nominated for an Oscar as best supporting player.

2. **Henry Fonda**—yeah really—as murdering psychopath "Frank" in *Once Upon a Time in the West*, 1969. You'll have to watch the movie to believe it, he's a real baddie. Fonda also played a villain in *Firecreek*.

3. **Bruce Dern,** a grungy rustler without scruples, as "Long Hair" in *The Cowboys*, 1972. He actually kills John Wayne's character! Such an evil man! The boys have to bury him.

4. **George Kennedy** is not his usual loveable self as bank robber, "Frasier" in *Cahill, United States Marshal*, 1973.

★ CLINT EASTWOOD ★
("The Man With No Name") (1930–)

(1958) *Ambush at Cimarron Pass*   *The Beguiled* (1971)
(1964) *A Fistful of Dollars*   *Joe Kidd* (1972)
(1966) *For a Few Dollars More*   **High Plains Drifter** (1973)
(1966) **The Good, Bad and Ugly**   *The Outlaw Josey Wales* (1975)
(1967) **Hang 'Em High**   *Pale Rider* (1985)
(1969) *Paint Your Wagon*   **Unforgiven** (1992)
(1970) *Two Mules for Sister Sara*

1. **Which of these movies did Eastwood direct?**
   ANS: The last four westerns listed.

2. **In what movie did Eastwood try his hand at singing?**
   ANS: *Paint Your Wagon.* In the mining town of Noname City, he sang songs like "I still see Elisa," "Gold Fever," and "I Talk to the Trees." So I guess you could say Clint starred in a musical!

3. **In what movie did Eastwood play the part of a preacher?**
   ANS: *Pale Rider.* He appeared out of nowhere to help struggling gold prospectors fight an unscrupulous company trying to take over their claims. Michael Moriarty, the Assistant District Attorney on the "Law and Order" TV series in the 1990's also co-starred.

4. **Clint Eastwood was paid a paltry $15,000 for his starring role in what movie?**
   ANS: *A Fistful of Dollars.* The film that turned the "Man with No Name" into a superstar had a budget of just $200,000; a low budget for a movie at that time.

5. **What was the first movie Eastwood made after forming his own film production company he dubbed "Malpaso"?**
   ANS: *Hang 'em High.* His company's second movie was *Coogan's Bluff* in 1968 about an Arizona Ranger sent to New York to bring back a fugitive. Malpaso means "bad land" in Spanish.

6. **Which movie was a tongue-in-cheek salute to spaghetti westerns, co-starring Shirley MacLaine?**
   ANS: *Two Mules for Sister Sara.*

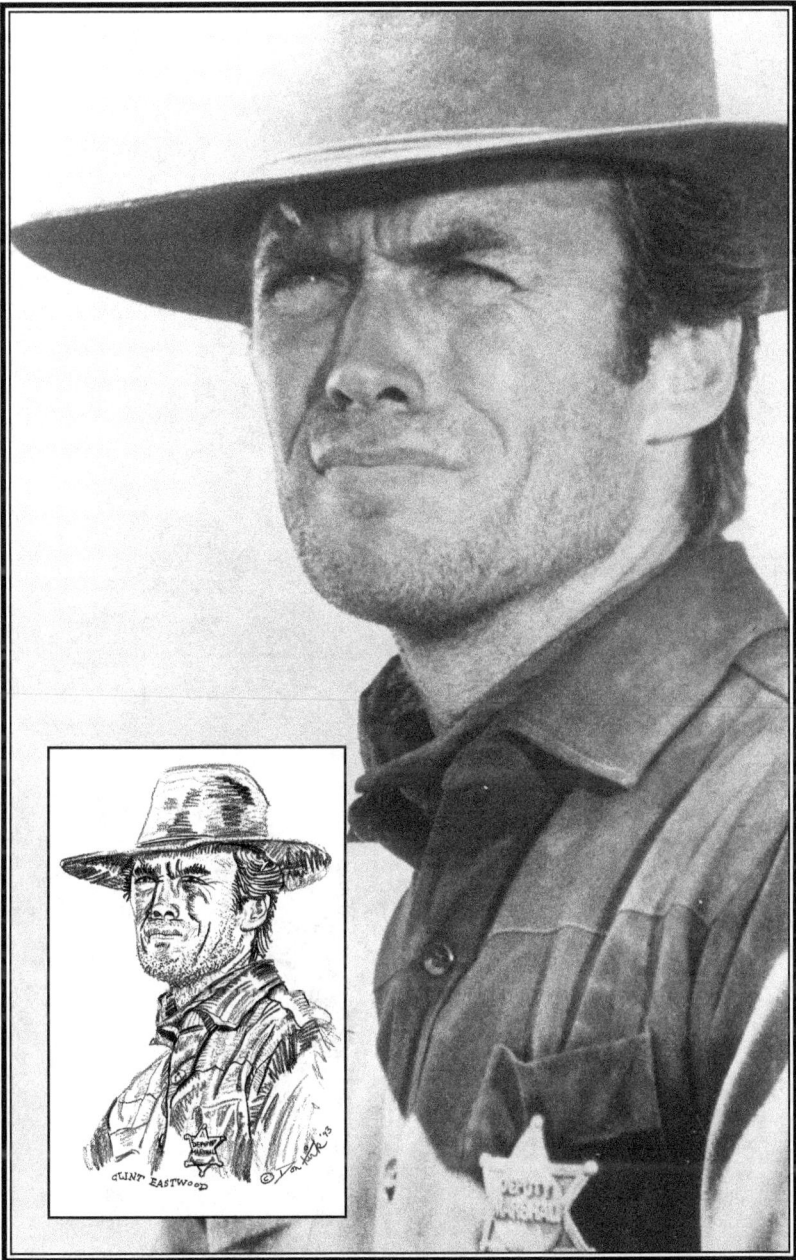

Clint Eastwood as Jed Cooper in *Hang 'em High*, a Leonard Freeman Production / Malpaso Company (author's collection)

CLINT EASTWOOD

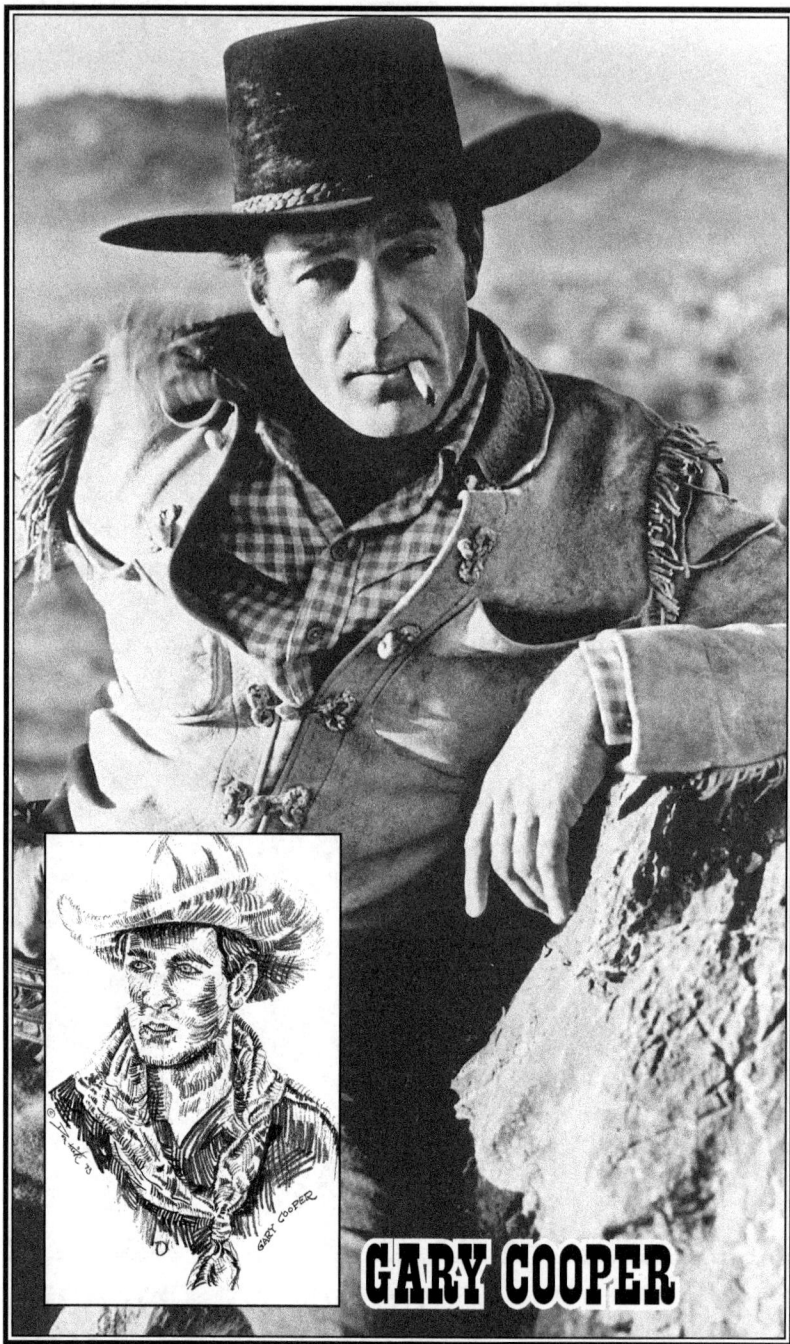

GARY COOPER

⋆ GARY COOPER ⋆
(known as "Coop") (1901-1961)
(This list does not include his many silent westerns)

(1929) *The Virginian*
(1936) *The Plainsman*
(1938) *The Cowboy and the Lady*
(1940) *The Westerner*
(1950) *Dallas*
(1951) *Distant Drums*

High Noon (1952)
Springfield Rifle (1952)
Vera Cruz (1954)
Man of the West (1958)
The Hanging Tree (1959)

1. **In what movie did Gary Cooper utter the now famous line: "When you call me that, smile!"?**
   ANS: *The Virginian.* Kids all over the country at the time were saying this line when playing "Cowboys and Indians" in their backyards.

2. **In what movie does Cooper play a newly-wed—having retired as town marshal—who chooses not to run from trouble when he hears an avenging gunman is coming after him?**
   ANS: *High Noon.* Cooper got the Best Actor Oscar for his portrayal as "Will Kane." The film won three other Oscars, including one for Best Song, the haunting, "Do Not Forsake Me, Oh My Darlin'."

3. **Which movie co-stars Walter Brennan as the legendary Judge Roy Bean?**
   ANS: *The Westerner.* Brennan won his third Oscar for this role as the Best Supporting Actor.

4. **What Cooper vehicle was George C. Scott's first movie?**
   ANS: *The Hanging Tree.* The screenplay was based on a short story by Dorothy M. Johnson.

TIDBIT: In 1938, Gary Cooper actually turned down the male lead role in the classic Civil-War-era movie *Gone with the Wind.* After he heard that a lead had finally been selected for the movie, Cooper said "I'm just glad it'll be Clark Gable who's falling flat on his face, and not Gary Cooper."

★ JAMES STEWART ★
(1908-1997)

(1939) **Destry Rides Again**	*How the West Was Won* (1962)
(1950) *Winchester '73*	*The Man Who Shot Liberty Valance* (1962)
(1950) *Broken Arrow*	*Cheyenne Autumn* (1964)
(1952) *Bend of the River*	*Shenandoah* (1965)
(1952) *Carbine Williams*	*Firecreek* (1968)
(1953) **The Naked Spur**	*Bandolero!* (1968)
(1955) *The Far Country*	*The Cheyenne Social Club* (1970)
(1955) *The Man From Laramie*	*The Shootist* (1976)
(1961) *Two Rode Together*	*An American Tail: Fievel Goes West,* voice (1991)

1. **In what movie did Stewart co-star with Dean Martin?**
   ANS: *Bandolero!* co-starring Raquel Welch and George Kennedy.

2. **In what movie did Lee Marvin play the bad guy?**
   ANS: *The Man Who Shot Liberty Valance.* Marvin was Liberty Valance.

3. **In what movie did Henry Fonda play the bad guy?**
   ANS: *Firecreek.* Fonda and his band of outlaws terrorize and plunder the town in which Stewart is Sheriff.

4. **In what western did Stewart inherit a bawdy house in Wyoming?**
   ANS: *The Cheyenne Social Club.* Henry Fonda tags along as the talkative sidekick as Stewart, playing "John O'Hanlan," discovers the joys and perils of owning a house of ill repute.

TIDBIT: Jimmy Stewart was so superstitious about his good luck in Hollywood that after the great success of *Winchester '73* in 1950, he insisted on wearing the same hat and riding the same horse (*Pie*) in every western he starred in for the next 20 years. *Winchester '73* was largely responsible for the renewed popularity of Westerns in the 1950's.

James Stewart as Lin McAdam in *Winchester '73*, Universal International Pictures (author's collection)

JAMES STEWART

★ RANDOLPH SCOTT ★
(1898-1987)

(1933) *Buffalo Stampede*
(1933) *Man of the Forest*
(1933) *To the Last Man*
(1934) *Wagon Wheels*
(1935) *The Fighting Westerner*
(1936) *Rocky Mountain Mystery*
(1936) *The Last of the Mohicans*
(1939) *Jesse James*
(1940) *Virginia City*
(1941) *Western Union*
(1942) *The Spoilers*
(1946) ***Abilene Town***
(1946) ***Badman's Territory***
(1947) *Trail Street*

Coroner Creek (1948)
Return of the Badman (1948)
Doolins of Oklahoma (1949)
Cariboo Trail (1950)
The Nevadan (1950)
Man in the Saddle (1951)
Sugarfoot (1951)
Hangman's Knot (1952)
Rage at Dawn (1955)
Ten Wanted Men (1955)
7th Cavalry (1956)
Decision At Sundown (1957)
Ride Lonesome (1959)
Ride the High Country (1962)

1. **What movie had Scott portraying the legendary Bat Masterson?**
   ANS: *Trail Street.* Robert Ryan also co-stars in this film.

2. **Which three movies were directed by Budd Boetticher?**
   ANS: *Decision At Sundown, Ride Lonesone,* and *The Tall T* (a classic).

3. **Which movie was directed by Sam Peckinpah of *Wild Bunch* fame?**
   ANS: Scott's last western, *Ride the High Country.*

4. **Name the western where Forrest Tucker of "F Troop" fame co-stars with Scott as an undercover government agent?**
   ANS: *The Nevadan.* Forrest Tucker also played an outlaw Reno brother in *Rage At Dawn.*

5. **What movie also co-stars John Wayne, Marlene Dietrich, and Harry Carey?**
   ANS: *The Spoilers.*

6. **What was the first film produced by a company formed by Randolph Scott and Harry Brown and which led to such hits as *Ride Lonesome* and *The Tall T?***
   ANS: *Coroner Creek.*

RANDOLPH SCOTT

★ HENRY FONDA ★
(1905-1982)

(1939) *Jesse James*   *Big Hand for the Little Lady* (1966)
(1940) *The Return of Frank James*   *Firecreek* (1968)
(1943) **The Ox-bow Incident**   *Once Upon a Time in the West* (1969)
(1946) **My Darling Clementine**   *There was a Crooked Man* (1970)
(1948) *Fort Apache*   *The Cheyenne Social Club* (1970)
(1957) *The Tin Star*   *My Name is Nobody* (1974)
(1963) *How the West was Won*

1. **Which film co-stars Anthony Perkins of *Psycho* fame as an inexperienced sheriff in a hard town?**
   ANS: *The Tin Star.*

2. **In which movie did Fonda play an Arizona prison warden out to get stolen money buried by a prison inmate?**
   ANS: *There Was a Crooked Man.*

3. **Which westerns were directed by John Ford?**
   ANS: *My Darling Clementine, Fort Apache,* and *How the West Was Won* (co-directed).

4. **Which movie has Fonda playing a compulsive gambler in a high-stakes poker game?**
   ANS: *Big Hand for the Little Lady.*

5. **Which movies were "spaghetti westerns"?**
   ANS: *Once Upon a Time in the West,* and *My Name is Nobody.*

6. **Which movie has Fonda teamed up with Jimmy Stewart, playing a chatty Texas cowhand named "Harley Sullivan"?**
   ANS: *The Cheyenne Social Club.*

7. **Which movie has Henry Fonda playing a drifter who tries to stop the lynching of three men?**
   ANS: *The Ox-bow Incident.*

8. **Which movie cast Henry Fonda as one of the coldest villains in screen history?**
   ANS: *Once Upon a Time in the West.*

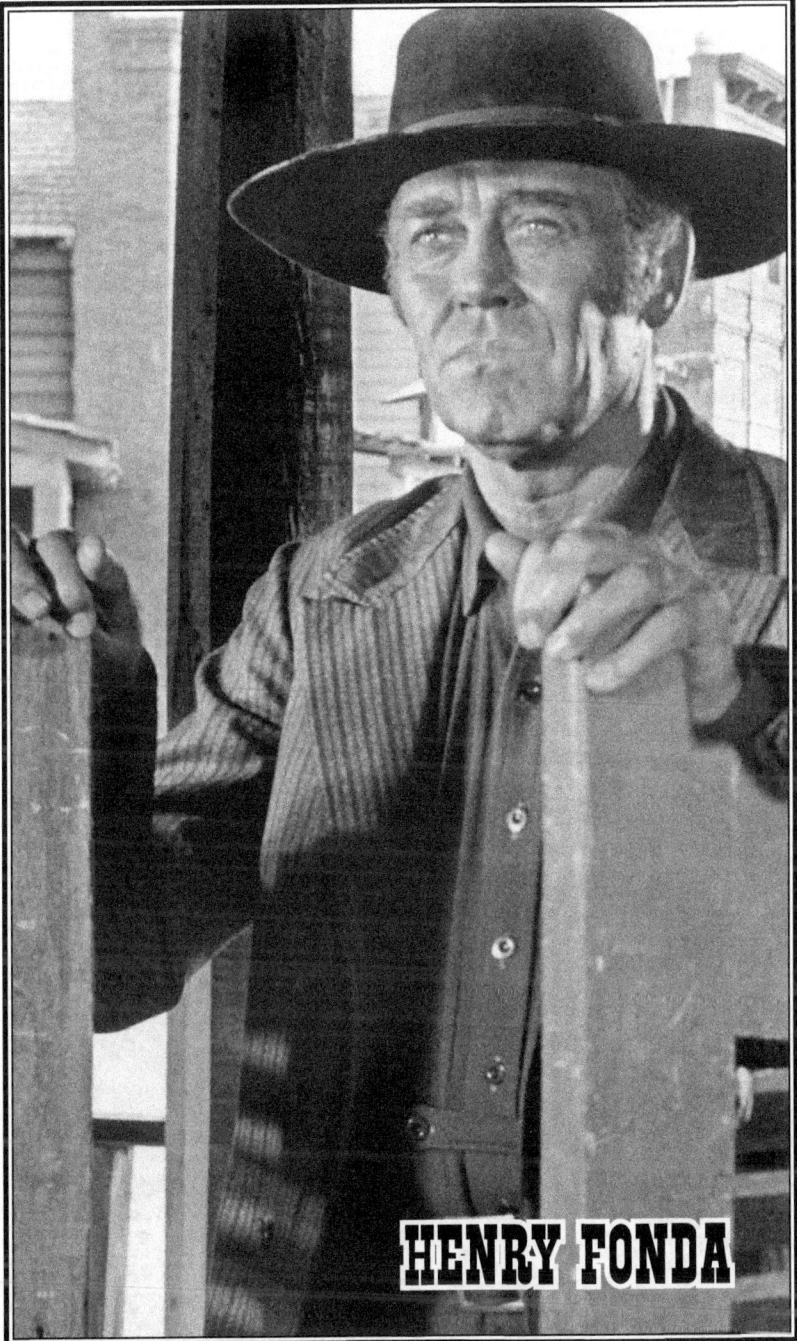

Henry Fonda as Frank in *Once Upon a Time in the West*, Paramount Pictures (author's collection)

HENRY FONDA

KIRK DOUGLAS

Kirk Douglas as Doc Holliday in *Gunfight at the OK Corral*, Paramount Pictures (author's collection)

★ KIRK DOUGLAS ★
(1916-)

(1951) *Along The Great Divide*   *The Way West* (1967)
(1952)*The Big Sky*   *The War Wagon* (1967)
(1952) *The Big Trees*   ***There Was a Crooked Man*** (1970)
(1955) *Man Without a Star*   *A Gunfight* (1971)
(1955) *The Indian Fighter*   *Posse* (1975)
(1957) ***Gunfight at the OK Corral***   *The Villain* (1979)
(1959) *Last Train From Gun Hill*   ***The Man From Snowy River*** (1982)
(1961) *The Last Sunset*   *Draw!* Cable TV movie (1984)

1. **Which three movies were comedies or satires on the Old West?**
   ANS: *There Was a Crooked Man, The Villain,* and *Draw!*

2. **In what movie did Kirk play the legendary Doc Holliday?**
   ANS: *Gunfight at the OK Corral.*

3. **In what movie does Kirk Douglas go in search of the man who raped and murdered his wife, only to find the man is the son of an old friend?**
   ANS: *Last Train From Gun Hill.*

4. **Which western was directed by Kirk Douglas?**
   ANS: *Posse.*

5. **Which movie co-starred Douglas' close friend, Burt Lancaster?**
   ANS: *Gunfight at the O.K. Corral.*

6. **Which movie is an Australian western?**
   ANS: *The Man From Snowy River.*

TIDBIT: A Hollywood agent told Kirk Douglas he couldn't use his real name so Karl Malden helped him come up with his stage name. Kirk was born *Issur Danielovitch Demsky* on December 9, 1916 in Amsterdam, New York and later changed his name to *Isidore Demsky*. His parents were Russian-Jewish peasant immigrants. Douglas got his big break in Hollywood with the leading role as a boxer in *Champion* (1949).

⭐ CHARLES BRONSON ⭐
(known as "Stoneface") (1921-2003)

(1954) *Vera Cruz*	*Villa Rides* (1968)
(1954) *Apache*	***Once Upon a Time in the West*** (1969)
(1954) ***Drumbeat***	*Chato's Land* (1972)
(1956) *Jubal*	*Red Sun* (1972)
(1957) *Run of the Arrow*	*Chino* (1973)
(1958) *Showdown at Boothill*	***Breakheart Pass*** (1976)
(1960) ***The Magnificent Seven***	*White Buffalo* (1977)
(1963) *4 For Texas*	

1. **In which movie does Bronson play a mysterious stranger who plays an eerie tune on his harmonica throughout the movie?**
   ANS: *Once Upon a Time in the West.* This film, made in Europe, brought him from supporting player parts into leading-man stardom.

2. **In which movies did Bronson play an Indian?**
   ANS: *Apache, Drum Beat, Run of the Arrow, Chato's Land, 4 for Texas,* and *Jubal.* He played a half-breed in *Chino.*

3. **In which westerns did Bronson's wife, Jill Ireland, have a role?**
ANS: *Villa Rides, Chato's Land, Chino,* and *Breakheart Pass.* Jill Ireland, his second wife, appeared in over fifteen films with her husband before her death at age 54 of cancer in 1990.

4. **In which movie does Bronson play a government agent on the trail of gunrunners; the story taking place on a train in winter?**
ANS: *Breakheart Pass.*

5. **Which movie has Bronson playing the legendary Wild Bill Hickock with an obsession?**
ANS: *White Buffalo.*

6. **Which film has Bronson playing a train robber who befriends a Japanese Samurai and helps him to retrieve a stolen sword?**
ANS: *Red Sun.*

★ JOEL McCREA ★
(1905-1990)

The 6"-3" blue-eyed McCrea initially got jobs in films as a wrangler, extra, and stuntman in 1922. By 1930 he was getting lead roles and starred in such films as Hitchcock's *Foreign Correspondent.* By 1946, he was making only westerns, something he preferred to do. He was the grandson of a stagecoach driver who had fought Indians and was considered one of the two best horsemen making westerns; Ben Johnson, a real cowboy, was the other.

(1939) *Union Pacific*   *Four Faces West* (1948)
(1944) *Buffalo Bill*   *The Tall Stranger* (1957)
(1946) *The Virginian*   ***Ride the High Country* (1962)**

1. **What movie put Joel in the same league with Gary Cooper?**
ANS: *Union Pacific* directed by Cecil B. DeMille.

2. **What film also starred Randolph Scott in the last film Scott would make?**
ANS: Sam Peckinpah's *Ride the High Country.*

3. **Which movie was from a novel by Owen Wister?**
ANS: *The Virginian.*

Photo from the author's collection

★ TOM MIX ★
(1880-1940)

Cowboy star of action-packed silent films and early talkies with 10-galón hat and horses "Old Blue" and "Tony." Said to have been a Texas Ranger. Got his start in films as a wrangler for the film *Ranch Life in the Great Southwest* (1910). He appeared in over 100 one- and two-reelers between 1911 and 1917. He rarely used stunt doubles in his films and as a result suffered frequent injuries. Mix created a successful formula for westerns that was imitated and followed to this day.

(1909) *Custer's Last Stand*   *Riders of the Purple Sage* (1925)
(1915) *On the Eagle Trail*   *Destry Rides Again* (1932)

1. **Which film was his first sound feature?**
   ANS: *Destry Rides Again.*

2. **Which film did he also direct?**
   ANS: *On the Eagle Trail.* Top Mix directed many of his own early silent westerns and always was heavily involved in their production and design.

★ LEE MARVIN ★
(1924-1987)

(1953) *Gun Fury*   *The Professionals* (1966)
(1953) *The Stranger Wore a Gun*   **Paint Your Wagon** (1969)
(1961) *The Comancheros*   *Monte Walsh* (1970)
(1962) *The Man Who Shot Liberty Valance*
(1965) **Cat Ballou**   *Great Scout & Cathouse Thursday* (1976)

1. **What movie won Marvin an Oscar playing two roles, a drunken gunslinger and a tin-nosed desperado?**
   ANS: *Cat Ballou.*

2. **Which movie also starred John Wayne and James Stewart?**
   ANS: *The Man Who Shot Liberty Valance.*

3. **Which melancholy western about a man caught up in a dying West, was from a novel by Jack Schaefer who also wrote Shane?**
   ANS: *Monte Walsh.*

Photo from the author's collection

★ LEE VAN CLEEF ★
(1925-1989)

(1952) **High Noon**	*The Good, the Bad and The Ugly* (1966)
(1952) *Untamed Frontier*	*Death Rides a Horse* (1967)
(1954) *Rails Into Laramie*	*The Big Gundown* (1968)
(1956) *Tribute to a Bad Man*	*Sabata* (1970)
(1957) *Gunfight at the O.K. Corral*	*Barquero* (1970)
(1957) *The Tin Star*	*El Condor* (1970)
(1958) *The Bravados*	*Captain Apache* (1971)
(1959) *Ride Lonesome*	*Return of Sabata* (1971)
(1961) *Posse From Hell*	*The Magnificent Seven Ride!* (1972)
(1962) **How the West Was Won**	*Take a Hard Ride* (1975)
(1962) *The Man Who Shot Liberty Valance*	
(1966) *For a Few Dollars More*	*The Stranger and Gunfighter* (1979)

1. **What movie was the first spaghetti western to catapult Van Cleef to European star status?**

   ANS: *For a Few Dollars More.*

★ JAMES COBURN ★
(1928-2002)

Originally cast in supporting roles as a gunslinger, the tall, lanky, lovable man from Nebraska, gained prominence playing a spy in the 1960's spoofs: *Our Man Flint* and *In Like Flint*.

(1959) *Ride Lonesome*
(1960) *The Magnificent Seven*
(1965) *Major Dundee*
(1966) *Waterhole No. 3*

Duck You Sucker! (1972)
Pat Garrett and Billy the Kid (1973)
Bite the Bullet (1975)
Young Guns II (1990)
Maverick (1994)

1. **What movie did Coburn co-star in with Rod Steiger?**
   ANS: *Duck You Sucker!* An Italian "spaghetti western,"—also released under the name *A Fistful of Dynamite*—where he played an explosives expert with an overcoat loaded down with sticks of dynamite.

2. **In what movie did Coburn play a lawman?**
   ANS: *Pat Garrett and Billy the Kid* as the man who killed Billy.

★ WARREN OATES ★
(1928-1982)

A wonderful character actor, he began his career in New York in live TV dramas in the 1950's. When parts became thin, he moved to Hollywood where he became a stock villain in TV westerns and the movies. He played the title role in the movie *Dillinger* in 1973. Sadly, in 1982, at age 53, he died of a sudden heart attack leaving a great emptiness in American cinema.

(1959) *Yellowstone Kelly*
(1960) *Ride the High Country*
(1964) *Mail Order Bride*
(1965) *Major Dundee*
(1966) *Return of the Seven*

The Shooting (1967)
Welcome to Hard Times (1967)
The Wild Bunch (1969)
There Was a Crooked Man (1970)
The Hired Hand (1971)

1. **In what movie did Oates play a good guy instead of a villain?**
   ANS: *Return of the Seven,* sequel to *The Magnificent Seven.*

JAMES COBURN

Photo from the author's collection

Scene Stealers
4 CHARACTER ACTORS

*"That's what you get when you've been living
in Bolivia for fifteen years; you get colorful."*
—Strother Martin, *Butch Cassidy and the Sundance Kid* (1969)

Many actors never "made it" with leading roles in films. They just didn't look like leading men or heroes, but they could act as well as any film superstar. They added "color and texture"—and often humor—to films that wouldn't have been the same without them.

★ STROTHER MARTIN ★
(1919-1980)

For thirty years he played low-life "prairie scum" in western films as a scraggly, white-haired, always-complaining, offbeat character with a whiny, nasal voice. His most famous line was not in a western, but as a prison farm warden in *Cool Hand Luke* (1967): "What we have here is failure to communicate."

(1954) *Drum Beat*	*The Wild Bunch* (1969)
(1959) *The Horse Soldiers*	*True Grit* (1969)
(1962) *The Man Who Shot Liberty Valance*	*The Ballad of Cable Hogue* (1970)
(1963) *McLintock!*	*Hannie Caulder* (1972)
(1964) *Invitation to a Gunfighter*	*Rooster Cogburn* (1975)
(1965) *The Sons of Katie Elder*	*The Great Scout and Cathouse Thursday* (1976)
(1965) *Shenandoah*	*The Villian* (1979)
(1969) *Butch Cassidy and the Sundance Kid*	

1. **In what movie did Martin play a Bolivian gold mine manager who had trouble delivering salaries to his employees because of "bandidos?"**
   ANS: *Butch Cassidy and the Sundance Kid.*

2. **In what movie did Martin and L.Q. Jones play scavenging members of a posse who was chasing an outlaw gang?**
   ANS: *The Wild Bunch.*

Photos from the author's collection

STROTHER MARTIN

JACK ELAM

GABBY HAYES

DUB TAYLOR

★ JACK ELAM ★
(1920-2003)

Jack Elam was once described as "the man with the face that wrecked a thousand stagecoaches." Tall and lanky with one eye turned outward giving the appearance of an evil leer—and a voice that would rub anyone raw—he stole every scene he was ever in. He once said that with his cockeyed eyeball he never had to worry about screen direction; it didn't matter which way he looked. He began his career playing low-down sidewinders and ended up playing lovable old coots. Without a doubt, he's up there with the top western character actors of all time.

(1950) *High Lonesome*

(1950) *The Sundowners*

(1951) *Rawhide*

(1952) ***High Noon***

(1952) ***Rancho Notorious***

(1953) *Ride Vaquero!*

(1954) *Vera Cruz*

(1954) *Cattle Queen of Montana*

(1955) *The Far Country*

(1955) *The Man From Laramie*

(1956) *Jubal*

(1957) ***Gunfight at the O.K. Corral***

(1957) *Night Passage*

(1961) ***The Comancheros***

(1963) *4 for Texas*

The Rare Breed (1966)

The Way West (1967)

Firecreek (1968)

Once Upon a Time in the West (1968)

Support Your Local Sheriff! (1969)

Dirty Dingus Magee (1970)

Rio Lobo (1970)

Support Your Local Gunfighter (1971)

Hannie Caulder (1972)

Pat Garrett and Billy the Kid (1973)

Pony Express Rider (1976)

The Apple Dumpling Gang Rides Again (1979)

The Villian (1979)

Once Upon a Texas Train TV Movie (1988)

Where the Hell's That Gold? TV Movie (1988)

1. **Elam began his career playing a moronic thug. What was the first film in which he played a major comedic role?**
   ANS: *Support Your Local Sheriff.*

2. **In what movie did he play a thug sitting at a railroad station swatting a pesky fly?**
   ANS: *Once Upon a Time in the West.*

3. **Which film also featured Strother Martin and Ernest Borgnine as fellow bandits?**
   ANS: *Hannie Caulder.*

★ GEORGE HAYES ★

("Gabby")(1885-1969)

The crusty, but lovable and toothless, bearded old-timer with ragged prospector's hat, played in more than 200 westerns. In the 20's he played villains in John Wayne "B" westerns and in the 30's he began playing comic sidekicks to Hopalong Cassidy, Wild Bill Elliott, and Roy Rogers. The following films don't include his serials.

(1936) *The Texas Rangers*	*The Big Bonanza* (1945)
(1936) *The Plainsman*	*Badman's Territory* (1946)
(1940) *Dark Command*	*Wyoming* (1947)
(1943) *In Old Oklahoma*	*El Paso* (1949)
(1944) *Tall in the Saddle*	*The Carboo Trail* (1950)

1. **Which movie starred Gary Cooper as Wild Bill Hickok?**
   ANS: *The Plainsman*, DeMille's first full-scale western epic.

2. **Gabby plays Judge Jim Hawkins in what movie starring Fred MacMurray of "My Three Sons" fame?**
   ANS: *The Texas Rangers*.

3. **What Civil-War-era story starred both John Wayne *and* Roy Rogers, with Gabby playing "Doc Grunch?"**
   ANS: *Dark Command*.

4. **In what movie did Gabby first learn to ride a horse?**
   ANS: I have no idea, but I understand that it was in 1934 after he had already been in forty westerns and was nearly fifty years old. He made his first film in 1929.

TIDBIT: Gabby Hayes, born George Francis Hayes,—after retiring in New York and then losing all his money in the 1929 stock-market crash—went to Hollywood and got the job as Hopalong Cassidy's sidekick "Windy Halliday." But, after three hit years, a salary dispute sent him packing without his "Windy" handle and he had to come up with a new one: "Gabby." He continued to stay on the top-ten list of western box office stars, working with Roy Rogers, Randolph Scott, and John Wayne.

★ DUB TAYLOR ★
("Cannonball")(1907-1994)

Dub Taylor earned his nickname as a sidekick in 1940's and 50's westerns before he got parts in the "A" westerns. He had a grizzled, unkempt appearance, was short and squatty, and had a Southern drawl. He co-starred with Allan Hale Jr. in "Casey Jones" and had many guest appearances on "Gunsmoke" and "Little House on the Prairie." His son is Buck Taylor who played "Newly" on "Gunsmoke." The only movie they were together in was the 1991 TV movie "Connagher."

(1962) ***How the West Was Won***   *A Man Called Horse* (1970)
(1965) ***Major Dundee***   *Back to the Future Part III* (1990)
(1968) *Bandolero!*   *My Heroes Have Always Been Cowboys* (1992)
(1969) *The Undefeated*   *Maverick* (1994)
(1969) ***The Wild Bunch***

1. **What movie was Dub Taylor in that also starred character actors Strother Martin and L.Q. Jones?**
   ANS: *The Wild Bunch*.

A Match Game
MOVIE STARS REAL NAMES

Match the "B" western movie stars with their screen names.

1. Smiley Burnette	**a.** George Francis Hayes
2. Roy Rogers	**b.** Francis Smith
3. Hoot Gibson	**c.** Lester Burnette
4. Hopalong Cassidy	**d.** Gilbert M. Anderson
5. Dale Evans	**e.** William Boyd
6. Gabby Hayes	**f.** Leonard Franklin Slye
7. Bronco Billy	**g.** Edmund Richard Gibson
8. Buck Jones	**h.** Charles Frederick Gebhard

ANS: 1-c, 2-f, 3-g, 4-e, 5-b, 6-a, 7-d, 8-h.

Smile When You Call Me That!
15 HUMOROUS DIALOGS

*"People like westerns because they always
know who's gonna win."*
—Hoot Gibson

Every western needs a little humor. Here are a few funnybone ticklers from western movies. Our ten-galón hats off to the writers.

1. **"What brought you into town?"**
"A real tired horse."
—James Stewart in *Bend Of
The River,* 1952.

2. You want me to tell Joe Danby [a gunfighter] he's under arrest for murder! . . .What're you gonna do after he kills me?"
"Then I'll arrest him for both murders."
—James Garner and Jack Elam in *Support Your Local Sheriff,* 1969.

3. **"Why did you kill him?"**
"He had my horse!"
**"Is your horse worth the life of this
man?"**
"I couldn't say; I didn't know him."
—Katherine Ross and Willie Nelson in
Redheaded Stranger, 1986.

4. "I *have* read the Bible, Mrs. Fenty."
"Didn't that discourage you about drinking?"
"No, but it sure cured my appetite for readin'."
—Lee Marvin in *Paint Your Wagon,* 1969.

Trivia Question: Who played the white girl kidnapped by Indians in John Ford's western *The Searchers?*
ANS: Natalie Wood, who's husband was Robert Wagner.

Lee Marvin and John Wayne in *The Man Who Shot Liberty Valance,* 1962
(In the background are future western stars Lee Van Cleef and Strother Martin)

5. **"Look at your eyes!"**
   "What's wrong with my eyes?"
   "Well, they're red, blood shot."
   "You otta see 'em from *my* side!"
   —Lee Marvin as the drunk "Kid Sheleen" in *Cat Ballou,* 1965.

6. "They [the Indians] outnumber us three to one!"
"Well, if it makes you nervous, don't count 'em."
—Errol Flynn and Ronald Reagan, *Santa Fe Trail,* 1940.

7. **"Well, see, we had to buy these knickknacks
'cause we've sort of got a girl in Santa Fe."
"What do you mean 'we'? *I'm* engaged to her."
"Well, who ain't?"**
— "Big Boy"Williams and Alan
Hale in *Santa Fe Trail,* 1940.

8. "If you ain't outta town here in five minutes, I'm
gonna open court in earnest!"
"I haven't even got a horse."
"Steal one, a fast one! Remember we hang horse
thieves around here."
—Paul Newman in *The Life And Times of
Judge Roy Bean,* 1972.

9. **"We'll make our stand here, Sergeant . . . Circle the wagons."
"We ain't got enough, sir."
"Well, make a half moon!"**
—John Dehner in *Dirty Dingus Magee,* 1970.

10. "Honey, you were smelling bad enough
to gag a dog on a gut wagon."
—Stella Stevens, *The Ballad of Cable
Hogue,* 1970.

11. **"Mr. Hickok, there's a man in the street gonna
give me a dollar to come in here and tell you
that you're a coward and a wife stealer. Can't
say the rest, but was much worse."
"What'd he say?"
"He said that you were a horse molester."
"Did he say what horse?**
—Jeff Bridges, *Wild Bill,* 1995.

> **Tidbit:** The slapstick team known as *The Three Stooges* (Moe, Larry, and Curly) had a starring role with George O'Brien in a 1951 western called *Gold Raiders* where they managed to fool the bad guys and save the day.

12. "How is he Doc?"

"Well, he suffered lacerations, contusions, and a concussion. His jugular vein was severed in three places. I counted four broken ribs and a compound fracture of the skull. To put it briefly, he's real dead."
—A doctor in *Rancho Notorious,* 1952.

13. Safe! Who knows what's safe? I know a man dropped dead from looking at his wife. My own grandmother fought the Indians for sixty years, then choked to death on lemon pie!"
—Ford Rainey in *3:10 to Yuma,* 1957.

14. "No matter where, there's nothing sweeter than the scent of lavender."
"Yeah, until it turns sour."
"Whoever it was and whatever she did, it wasn't good for you, Amigo."
—William Holden in *Streets of Laredo,* 1949.

15. "What about your [dead] friend there, wanna bury him?"

"Na, maybe somethin' 'el come out of the hills and drag him off."
—Albert Salmi and Brian Keith in *Something Big,* 1971.

> **Tidbit:** *Blazing Saddles* (1973) was directed by Mel Brooks. It was his first and best hit movie. Richard Pryor was one of the screenwriters. A host of comedians made up the cast of this western spoof including Cleavon Little, Gene Wilder, Harvey Korman, Madeline Kahn, and Slim Pickens. You know they had fun making this movie.

A Match Game
5 Western Film Composers

*"In the beginning, when I began to write scores for films,
I felt as if I were a traitor to an art form, but then I
realized that the same integrity, the same talent
is put to use when writing for films."*
—Ennio Morricone, Hollywood Reporter, 1989.

The **Film composer plays an important part** in the success of a western movie. Their stirring and descriptive theme music often completes the wide-screen view of the West's panoramic landscape. Watch one of these westerns without the music track and see if it has the same impact. Match these westerns with memorable theme songs to their composers/writers:

1. Bonanza   **a.** Ennio Morricone
2. *The Magnificent Seven*   **b.** Dimitri Tiomkin / Ned Washington
3. Rawhide   **c.** John Barry
4. *Dances with Wolves*   **d.** Jay Livingston & Ray Evans
5. *The Good, Bad, and Ugly*   **e.** Elmer Bernstein

ANSWERS:

1-d. LIVINGSTON & EVANS scored the opening theme music for the popular *Bonanza* series which ran for 440 episodes from 1959 to 1973. As a team, they scored over 100 films for the silver screen garnishing three Oscars and seven Academy Award nominations.

2-e. ELMER BERNSTEIN, born in New York in 1922, became a concert pianist, and was the first to introduce jazz themes and instrumentation to his film scores. He went on to score all three *"Seven"* films. Other western film credits include: John Wayne's *The Comancheros, The Sons of Katie Elder,* and *The Scalphunters* which starred Burt Lancaster. Bernstein also scored non-westerns including *Sudden Fear* (his first film score), *The Man With the Golden Arm, Walk on the Wild Side* and *The Sweet Smell of Success.*

3-b. DIMITRI TIOMKIN, a Russian born composer educated in Berlin, began writing music for the movies in the 1930's and it wasn't long before he was scoring westerns like *The Westerner, Duel in the Sun, Red River, Gunfight at the O.K. Corral, Rio Bravo, The Unforgiven, The Alamo, Giant,* and *High Noon* (with Ned Washington). Non-westerns scored by Tiomkin include *The Guns of Navarone, 55 Days at Peking,* and *Old Man and the Sea.*

4-c. JOHN BARRY, most famous for scoring the James Bond films, was born in 1933 in York, England. He studied piano and eventually formed an instrumental group until the 1960's when he began scoring film music. He got his break with *Dr. No* and the now world famous "James Bond Theme." Barry scored over 35 films, winning Oscars for *Born Free, The Lion in Winter, Out of Africa* and *Dances with Wolves.* The theme to *Midnight Cowboy* was also his.

5-a. ENNIO MORRICONE, born in Rome in 1928, played a trumpet in nightclub jazz bands before an Italian western made him famous throughout the world. He had already scored *A Fistful of Dollars* and *For a Few Dollars More* before he scored *The Good, the Bad and the Ugly* which introduced him to American audiences. He went on to score many more westerns including *Once Upon a Time in the West, Duck You Sucker, Navajo Joe, The Big Gundown* and *Guns for San Sebastian.* Morricone received Oscar nominations for *The Mission, The Untouchables, Days of Heaven, and Bugsy.* Other films include *Once Upon a Time in America, Body Heat* and *Cinema Paradiso.* With over 400 films to his credit, he is, so far, the most prolific film composer of all time.

Mood Enhancing Notes
20 CLASSIC FILM SCORES

*"Most important, the score [for The Wild Bunch]
communicates the essence of the film: the vibrant love of
the West and regret for the loss of the West and regret for the
loss of the wild freedom of the American frontier."*
—Jay Alan Quantrill, 1980.

Some western film scores have become classics, defining the music for America's western films. The large, swelling scores evoking the grandeur and majesty of the American West or the rhythmic sounds mimicking the clop of horse's hooves, have made composers famous and their music forever associated with westerns. Music is critical to the success of a "horse opera;" it makes the West bigger than reality and the myth larger than life. In fact, Clint Eastwood was catapulted to legendary status with the help of a music score.

1. *The Big Country* ....Jerome Moross
2. *Cheyenne Autumn* ....Alex North
3. *Duel at Diablo* ....Neal Hefti
4. *Far and Away* ....John Williams
5. *A Fistful of Dollars* ....Ennio Morricone
6. *The Good, the Bad and the Ugly*.Ennio Morricone
7. *Hang 'Em High* ....Dominic Frontiere
8. *High Noon* ....Ned Washington / Dimitri Tiomkin
9. *High Plains Drifter* ....Dee Barton
10. *How the West Was Won* ....Alfred Newman
11. *The Magnificent Seven* ....Elmer Bernstein
12. *Once Upon a Time in the West* ....Ennio Morricone
13. *The Outlaw Josey Wales* ....Jerry Fielding / Jerome Moross
14. *The Professionals* ....Maurice Jarre
15. *The Scalphunters* ....Elmer Bernstein
16. *The Wild Bunch*...........................Jerry Fielding
17. *Wild Rovers* ....Jerry Goldsmith
18. *Bonanza* (TV Theme) ....Jay Livingston / Ray Evans
19. *Rawhide* (TV Theme)..................Ned Washington / Dimitri Tiomkin
20. *Wagon Train* (TV Theme)............Jerome Moross

Do Not Forsake Me
45 Best Western Theme Songs

I wish you could hear these tunes, some are elating, grandiose, as big as the western skies, like *The Big Country*. Some make me shed a dusty tear for these long-ago westerns. It was the music that defined the westerns and became an essential part of the experience—an American West that may have never been—but is real in our hearts and souls. Some are tearjerkers like "The Call Of The Faraway Hills" and soulful like "Jill's Theme," or haunting like "The Harmonica Man," and "Do Not Forsake Me," but they all speak of the Old West.

1. *The Alamo*: Overture—Dimitri Tiomkin.
2. *The Alamo*: The Green Leaves Of Summer—Dimitri Tiomkin & Paul Francis Webster, sung by The Brothers Four.
3. *The Alamo*: Davy Crockett—Dimitri Tiomkin.
4. *The Big Country*: The Welcoming—Jerome Moross.
5. *The Big Country*: Main Title—Jerome Moross.
6. *Butch Cassidy And The Sundance Kid*: Raindrops Keep Falling On My Head—Burt Bacharach, Hal David, sung by B.J. Thomas.
7. *The Comancheros*: Main Title—Elmer Bernstein.
8. *The Cowboys*: Main Theme—John Williams.
9. *Dances with Wolves*: John Dunbar Theme—John Barry.
10. *A Fistful of Dollars*: Theme—Ennio Morricone.
11. *A Fistful of Dynamite*: Duck, You Sucker—Ennio Morricone.
12. *For a Few Dollars More*: Main Titles—Ennio Morricone.
13. *The Good, the Bad and the Ugly*: Main Title—Ennio Morricone.
14. *The Good, The Bad And The Ugly*: Ecstasy Of Gold—Ennio Morricone.
15. *Gunfight at the O.K. Corral*: Suite—Dimitri Tiomkin & Ned Washington, sung by Frankie Laine.
16. *The Hallelujah Trail*: Overture—Elmer Bernstein.
17. *Hang 'Em High*: Main Theme—Dominic Frontiere.
18. *The Hanging Tree*: Main Title—Max Steiner, Jerry Livingston.
19. *High Noon*: Do Not Forsake Me—Dimitri Tiomkin & Ned Washington, sung by Tex Ritter.

Columbia Pictures (author's collection)

The Professionals (1966) with Burt Lancaster, Lee Marvin, Robert Ryan, Woody Strode.

20. *High Plains Drifter*: Main Theme—Dee Barton.

21. *How the West Was Won*: Finale—Alfred Newman.

22. *The Magnificent Seven*: Overture—Elmer Bernstein.

23. *Monte Walsh*: Main Theme—John Barry.

24. *My Name is Nobody*: Main Theme—Ennio Morricone.

25. *Once Upon a Time in the West*: Jill's Theme—Jill Washington.

26. *Once Upon a Time in the West*: Man With A Harmonica—Ennio Morricone.

27. *Once Upon a Time in the West*: Farewell to Cheyenne—Ennio Morricone.

28. *The Scalphunters*: Main Title—Elmer Bernstein.

29. *Shane*: Main Theme:The Call of the Faraway Hills—Victor Young.

30. *The Sons of Katie Elder*: Main Theme—Elmer Bernstein.

Music Trivia Question: Burt Bacharach composed and conducted the music for *Butch Cassidy and the Sundance Kid* (1969). Bacharach won the Oscar for Best Original Score. He and Hal David won the Oscar for what song in the same movie?

ANS: "Raindrops Keep Fallin' On My Head," sung by B. J. Thomas.

Trivia Question: Who was the first singing cowboy of the movies?

ANS: Ken Maynard sang "The Lone Star Trail" and the "Cowboy's Lament" in the western, *The Wagon Master* (1929). Other singing cowboys soon followed: Gene Autry, Tex Ritter, Roy Rogers, and the Sons of the Pioneers.

15 More Western Movie Themes

1. *The Assassination Of Jesse James By Coward Robert Ford*—Nick Cave, Warren Ellis.
2. *How the West Was Won:* Main Theme—Alfred Newman.
3. *Johnny Guitar*—Peggy Lee, Victor Young.
4. *The Last of the Mohicans*—Randy Edelman, Trevor Jones.
5. *Paint Your Wagon:* Wand'rin' Star—Alan J. Lerner & Frederick Loewe, Nelson Riddle, sung by Lee Marvin.
6. *The Professionals*—Maurice Jarre.
7. *Ride the High Country*—George Bassman.
8. *Rio Bravo:* Main Theme—Dimitri Tiomkin.
9. *The Searchers:* Opening Theme—Max Steiner.
10. *She Wore a Yellow Ribbon:* She Wore a Yellow Ribbon —Richard Hageman.
11. *Silverado:* Main Theme—Bruce Broughton.
12. *Tombstone:* Main Theme— Bruce Broughton.
13. *Unforgiven:* Claudia's Theme—Lennie Niehaus & Clint Eastwood.
14. *Wild Rovers:* The Bronc—Jerry Goldsmith.
15. *Wyatt Earp*—James Newton Howard.

Music Trivia : Because of delays in starting principal photography on *The Good, the Bad and the Ugly,* Ennio Morricone's musical score for the film was actually completed before shooting began, (which is not the usual procedure). The director, Sergio Leone, and the actors were able to listen to the music on the set and choreograph their actions and camera movements to the music. The technique was so successful that Morricone composed other film music projects before a film was shot instead of writing the score to match the already cut film.

Cowboy Classics
18 FAMOUS WESTERN BALLADS

Before **Ennio Morricone** re-defined western film music with his haunting, quirky scores, vocal ballads were often used as theme songs to western films. Frankie Laine, Marty Robbins, and Sons of the Pioneers, were highly successful at recording numerous "hit" ballads for westerns. The movie, the song, the singer, and writer (in brackets) of some of the most popular ballads from theatrical films are listed here.

1. *The Alamo (1960),* Marty Robbins (Francis Webster/Dimitri Tiomkin).
2. *The Alamo (1950),* The Brothers Four (Paul Francis Webster).
3. *Butch Cassidy and the Sundance Kid (1969),* B.J. Thomas (Hal David).
4. *Cat Ballou (1965),* Nat King Cole & Stubby Kaye (Mack David/Jerry Livingston).
5. *Gunfight at the O.K. Corral (1957),* Frankie Laine (Ned Washington/ Dimitri Tiomkin).
6. *The Hanging Tree (1959),* Marty Robbins (Max Steiner).

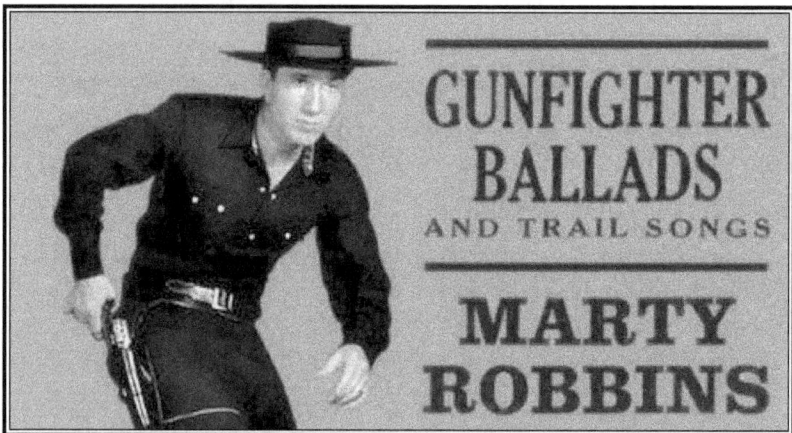

GUNFIGHTER BALLADS AND TRAIL SONGS MARTY ROBBINS

Album cover (author's collection)

Roy Rogers and the Sons of the Pioneers (author's collection)

7. *High Noon (1952)*, Tex Ritter (Ned Washington/Dimitri Tiomkin).

8. *Hollywood Canteen (1944)*, Roy Rogers (Cole Porter).

9. *The Man Who Shot Liberty Valance (1962)*, Gene Pitney (Burt Bacharach/Hal David).

10. *Paint Your Wagon (1969)*, Rotten Luck Willie (Alan Jay Lerner).

11. *Pat Garrett and Billy the Kid (1973)*, Bob Dylan (Bob Dylan).

12. *Rovin' Tumbleweeds (1939)*, Gene Autry (Rat Whitley).

13. *The Searchers (1956)*, Sons of the Pioneers (Stan Jones).

14. *The Sons of Katie Elder (1965)*, Johnny Cash (Elmer Bernstein).

15. *Strawberry Roan (1948)*, Roy Rogers (Curley Fletcher).

16. *True Grit (1969)*, Glen Campbell (Elmer Bernstein).

17. *Tumblin' Tumbleweeds (1935)*, Sons of the Pioneers (Bob Nolan).

18. *Under Western Stars (1938)*, Sons of the Pioneers (Johnny Marvin/ Gene Autry).

Music Trivia Question: Name the John Wayne movie that inspired Buddy Holly to write a hit song.

ANS: *The Searchers* (1956). The song was "That'l Be the Day," a phrase Wayne used several times in the movie.

Gail Davis, Flying 'A' Productions (author's collection)

GAIL DAVIS

Gail Davis was the star of *Annie Oakley*, the first television western to star a woman. A children's program from 1952 to 1956, it was produced by Gene Autry's Flying A Productions.

Kicking Up Their Heels in Wild West Saloons
10 WOMEN IN WESTERNS

"You know, there are only two things more
beautiful than a good gun: a Swiss watch or
a woman from anywhere."
—John Ireland, Red River, 1948.

In the early westerns, in fact, all the way into the 1990's, a woman's only value in a western was as the hero's love interest. They were usually relegated to playing prostitutes or the wife or daughter of a settler. It wasn't until the 1990's—with few exceptions—did a woman have the starring role as the "hero." Barbara Stanwyck was the only actress I can think of that got leading roles in westerns as the strong independent hero. To honor the women's importance in westerns, here's a few female western stars and their westerns, plus a few tidbits for trivia questions of your own:

1. BARBARA STANWYCK
Annie Oakley (1935)
Union Pacific (1939)
Cattle Queen of Montana (1954)
The Maverick Queen (1955)
The Violent Men (1955)
Forty Guns (1957)
"The Big Valley" (1965-1969)

Born as "Ruby Stevens," she garnered four Oscar nominations and won two Emmys (one for "The Big Valley").

2. MAUREEN O'HARA
Buffalo Bill (1944)
Comanche Territory (1950)
Rio Grande (1950)

War Arrow (1953)
The Deadly Companions (1961)
McLintock! (1963)
The Rare Breed (1966)
Big Jake (1971)

O'Hara first worked with John Wayne in John Ford's film *Rio Grande*.

3. KATY JURADO
High Noon (1952)
Broken Lance (1954)
The Badlanders (1958)
One-Eyed Jacks (1961)
Pat Garrett and Billy the Kid (1973)

Jurado was nominated for best supporting actress in *Broken*

Lance. She was once married to Ernest Borgnine.

4. MARLENE DIETRICH
Destry Rides Again (1939)
Western Union (1941)
Rancho Notorious (1952)

In her portrayal as saloon girl "Frenchy" in *Destry,* she made a hit of the song "See What the Boys in the Back Room Will Have."

5. JANE RUSSELL
The Outlaw (1943)
The Paleface (1948)
Son of Paleface (1952)
The Tall Men (1955)
Johnny Reno (1966)
Waco (1966)

Howard Hughes, producer of *The Outlaw,* designed a brassiere for her to use in that film.

6. YVONNE DE CARLO
This Gun For Hire (1942)
Frontier Gal (1945)
Black Bart (1948)
Calamity Jane and Sam Bass (1949)
The Gal Who Took the West (1949)
Tomahawk (1951)
Raw Edge (1956)
McClintock! (1963)
Hostile Guns (1967)
Arizona Bushwackers (1968)

Typecast by Hollywood as an exotic temptress, she played a heroine and dancehall girl in westerns. Don't remember her? She was "Lily" on the half-hour sitcom "The Munsters," 1964-66.

7. JEAN ARTHUR
The Plainsman (1936)
Arizona (1940)

A Lady Takes A Chance (1943)
Shane (1953)

Her real name was Gladys Georgianna Greene. She began her film career doing westerns in the 20's. John Ford first cast her in *Cameo Kirby* in 1923.

8. CLAUDIA CARDINALE
The Professionals (1966)
Once Upon A Time In the West (1969)

Claudia was discovered in 1957 when she, at 19, won a contest for the Most Beautiful Italian Girl in Tunis. Her first American film was *The Pink Panther* in 1964. This Italian actress was never able to attain the same fame in America as Sophia Loren and Gina Lollobrigida, possibly because she never mastered English as well as the other two.

9. INGER STEVENS
Fire Creek (1968)
Hang 'Em High (1968)
Five Card Stud (1968)

With such great performances, what happened to Swedish actress Inger Stevens? She killed herself in 1970 with a sleeping pill overdose.

10. SHELLY WINTERS
Winchester '73 (1950)
Untamed Frontier (1952)
Treasure of Pancho Villa (1955)
The Scalphunters (1968)

Winter's starred with Michael Caine in *Alfie* and was nominated for best Supporting Actress in *The Poseidon Adventure.* She won oscars for *A Patch of Blue* (1965) and *The Diary of Ann Frank* (1959).

On The Silver Screen
126 TOP WESTERN MOVIES

*"The western is a haunting form. It's useful dramatically
because it's so simple: good and evil, men and nature,
earth and sky. But there's more to it than that. Westerns
have a lot to do with the myth that is still America, and so
long as that myth survives, so will the western."*
—James Monaco

126 **of the best western movies** ever made are listed below. They are in alphabetical order and are listed by title first, then director, date, and lead actor. Critics and western fans will have different opinions as to how many "stars" these westerns should be honored with, but most will agree that those listed below stand out among the thousands of "A" and "B" westerns that were produced. The list includes not only the classics but also the better "B" westerns.

10 FIVE-STAR WESTERNS

The Grey Fox, Philip Borsos, 1982, Richard Farnsworth.
The Gunfighter, Henry King, 1950, Gregory Peck.
High Noon, Fred Zinnemann, 1952, Gary Cooper.
The Man Who Shot Liberty Valance, John Ford, 1962, John Wayne.
Once Upon a Time in the West, Sergio Leone, 1969, Cardinale.
The Searchers, John Ford, 1950, John Wayne.
Shane, George Stevens, 1953, Alan Ladd.
She Wore a Yellow Ribbon, John Ford, 1949, John Wayne.
Stagecoach, John Ford, 1939, John Wayne.
The Tall T, Budd Boetticher, 1957, Randolph Scott.

28 FOUR-STAR WESTERNS

The Ballad of Cable Hogue, Sam Peckinpah, 1970, Jason Robards, Jr.
Bite the Bullit, Richard Brooks, 1975, Gene Hackman.
Butch Cassidy and the Sundance Kid, George Roy Hill, 1969.
The Cheyenne Social Club, Gene Kelly, 1970, James Stewart.
The Cowboys, Mark Rydell, 1972, John Wayne.
Dances With Wolves, Kevin Costner, 1990, Kevin Costner.
El Dorado, Howard Hawks, 1967, John Wayne.
Fort Apache, John Ford, 1948, John Wayne.
The Last Outlaw, Christy Cabanne, 1936, Harry Carey.
The Magnificent Seven, John Sturges, 1960, Yul Brynner.
The Man From Laramie, Anthony Mann, 1955, James Stewart.
McCabe & Mrs. Miller, Robert Altman, 1971, Warren Beatty.
My Darling Clementine, John Ford, 1946, Henry Fonda.
The Naked Spur, Anthony Mann, 1953, James Stewart.
The Outlaw Josey Wales, Clint Eastwood, 1976, Clint Eastwood.
The Ox-Bow Incident, William Wellman, 1943, Henry Fonda.
Pat Garrett and Billy The Kid, Sam Peckinpah, 1973, James Coburn.
Red River, Howard Hawks, 1948, John Wayne.
Ride Lonesome, Bud Boetticher, 1959, Randolph Scott.
Ride The High Country, Sam Peckinpah, 1962, Joel McCrea.
Rio Bravo, Howard Hawks, 1959, John Wayne.
The Shootist, Don Siegel, 1976, John Wayne.
Silverado, Lawrence Kasdan, 1985, Kevin Kline.
Support Your Local Sheriff, Burt Kennedy, 1969, James Garner.
Unforgiven, Clint Eastwood, 1992, Clint Eastwood.
Wagonmaster, John Ford, 1950, Ben Johnson.
The Wild Bunch, Sam Peckinpah, 1969, William Holden.
Will Penny, Tom Gries, 1968, Charlton Heston.

92 THREE-STAR WESTERNS

The Alamo, John Wayne, 1960, John Wayne.
Along Came Jones, Stuart Heisler, 1945, Gary Cooper.
Angel and the Badman, James Edward Grant, 1947, John Wayne.
Bend Of The River, Anthony Mann, 1952, James Stewart.
Arizona Legion, David Howard, 1939, George O'Brien.
Bad Company, Robert Benton, 1972, Jeff Bridges.
The Ballad of Gregorio Cortez, Robert M. Young, 1982, E. J. Olmos.

Barbarosa, Fred Schepisi, 1982, Willie Nelson.
Brimstone, Joseph Kane, 1949, Rod Cameron.
Broken Lance, Edward Dmytryk, 1954, Spencer Tracy.
Caravan Trail, Robert Emmett Tansey, 1946, Eddie Dean.
Cariboo Trail, Edwin L. Marin, 1950, Randolph Scott.
Carson City Cyclone, Howard Bretherton, 1943, Don Berry.
Cat Ballou, Elliot Silverstein, 1965, Jane Fonda.
The Comancheros, Michael Curtiz, 1961, John Wayne.
Come On Tarzan, Alan James, 1932, Ken Maynard.
Comes a Horseman, Alan J. Pakula, 1978, Jane Fonda.
Coroner Creek, Ray Enright, 1948, Randolph Scott.
Daniel Boone, David Howard, 1936, George O'Brien.
Dark Command, Raoul Walsh, 1940, John Wayne.
Days of Old Cheyenne, Elmer Clifton, 1943, Don Barry.
Destry Rides Again, George Marshal, 1939, James Stewart.
Dodge City, Michael Curtiz, 1939, Errol Flynn.
Doolins Of Oklahoma, Gordon Douglas, 1949, Randolph Scott.
End of the Trail, D. Ross Lederman, 1932, Tim McCoy.
Enemy of the Law, Harry Fraser, 1945, Tex Ritter.
Flaming Star, Don Siegel, 1960, Elvis Presley.
The Good, the Bad and the Ugly, Sergio Leone, 1966, Eastwood.
Gunfight at the O.K. Corral, John Sturges, 1957, Burt Lancaster.
Heart of the Rockies, Joseph Kane, 1937, Robert Livingston.
Heartland, Richard Pearce, 1979, Con Chata Ferrell.
Hombre, Martin Ritt, 1967, Paul Newman.
Hondo, John Farrow, 1953, John Wayne.
The Horse Soldiers, John Ford, 1959, John Wayne.
Jeremiah Johnson, Sydney Pollack, 1972, Robert Redford.
The Last of the Mohicans, George B. Seitz, 1936, Randolph Scott.
Law and Order, Edward L. Cahn, 1932, Walter Huston.
Lawless Valley, Bert Gilroy, 1938, George O'Brien.
Lightnin' Crandall, Sam Newfield, 1937, Bob Steele.
Little Big Horn, Charles Marquis Warren, 1951, Lloyd Bridges.
Little Big Man, Arthur Penn, 1970, Dustin Hoffman.
Loney Are the Brave, David Miller, 1962, Kirk Douglas.
The Lusty Men, Nicholas Ray, 1952, Robert Mitchum.
The Man From Snowy River, George Miller, 1982, Tom Burlinson.
Man in the Saddle, Andre de Toth, 1951, Randolph Scott.
Man of the Forest, Henry Hathaway, 1933, Randolph Scott.
Man of the West, Anthony Mann, 1958, Gary Cooper.
Marshal of Cripple Creek, R.G. Springsteen, 1947, "Rocky" Lane.
Marshall of Mesa City, David Howard, 1939, George O'Brien.

Mexicali Rose, George Sherman, 1939, Gene Autry.
The Missourians, George Blair, 1950, Monte Hale.
North to Alaska, Henry Hathaway, 1960, John Wayne.
One-Eyed Jacks, Marlon Brando, 1961, Marlon Brando.
Pony Express Rider, Hal Harrison, 1976, Stewart Peterson.
Quigley Down Under, Simon Wincer, 1990, Tom Selleck.
Rage at Dawn, Tim Whelan, 1955, Randolph Scott.
Range Feud, D. Ross Lederman, 1931, Buck Jones.
Renegade Ranger, David Howard, 1938, George O'Brien.
Riders of the Rio Grande, Howard Bretherton, 1943, Bob Steele.
Rio Grande, John Ford, 1950, John Wayne.
The Rustlers, Lesley Selander, 1949, Tim Holt.
Santa Fe Saddlemates, Thomas Carr, 1945, Sunset Carson.
Santa Fe Uprising, R.G. Springsteen, 1946, Allan "Rocky" Lane.
Shenandoah, Andrew V. McLaglen, 1965, James Stewart.
Short Grass, Lesley Selander, 1950, Rod Cameron.
Skin Game, Paul Bogart, 1971, James Garner.
South of St. Louis, Ray Enright, 1949, Merlene Dietrich.
The Spoilers, Ray Enright, 1942, Marlene Dietrich.
Stampede, Lesley Selander, 1949, Rod Cameron.
Stone of Silver Creek, Nick Grinde, 1935, Buck Jones.
The Sundown Rider, Lambert Hillyer, 1933, Buck Jones.
Tall in the Saddle, Edwin L. Marlin, 1944, John Wayne.
Texas Cyclone, D. Ross Lederman, 1932, Tim McCoy.
Texas Masquerade, George Archain Baud, 1944, William Boyd.
The Texas Rangers, Phil Karlson, 1951, George Nelson.
Thousand Pieces of Gold, Nancy Kelly, 1991, Rosalind Chao.
Three Men From Texas, Lesley Selander, 1940, William Boyd.
3:10 to Yuma, Delmer Daves, 1957, Glenn Ford.
The Tin Star, Anthony Mann, 1957, Henry Fonda.
To the Last Man, Henry Hathaway, 1933, Randolph Scott.
Trail Drive, Alan James, 1933, Ken Maynard.
True Grit, Henry Hathaway, 1969, John Wayne.
Two-Fisted Law, D. Ross Lederman, 1932, Tim McCoy.
Ulzana's Raid, Robert Aldrich, 1972, Burt Lancaster.
The Virginian, Victor Fleming, 1929, Gary Cooper.
The Westerner, William Wyler, 1940, Gary Cooper.
When a Man Sees Red, Alan James, 1934, Buck Jones.
Wild Frontier, Phillip Ford, 1947, Allan "Rocky" Lane.
The Wild Rovers, Blake Edwards, 1971, William Holden.
Wild West, Robert Emmett Tansey, 1946, Eddie Dean.
Windwalker, Keith Merrill, 1980, Trevor Howard.

20 TWO-STAR WESTERNS

The Big Country, William Wyler, 1958, Gregory Peck.
Big Jake, George Sherman, 1971, John Wayne.
The Bravados, Henry King, 1958, Gregory Peck.
Broken Arrow, Delmer Daves, 1950, James Stewart.
Cheyenne Autumn, John Ford, 1964, Richard Widmark.
Duel in the Sun, King Vidor, 1946, Gregory Peck.
Hang 'Em High, Ted Post, 1968, Clint Eastwood.
The Hanging Tree, Delmer Daves, 1959, Gary Cooper.
How the West Was Won, Hathaway, Marshal & Ford, 1963.
Johnny Guitar, Nicholas Ray, 1954, Joan Crawford.
A Man Called Horse, Elliot Silverstein, 1970, Richard Harris.
Monte Walsh, William Fraker, 1970, Lee Marvin.
Nevada Smith, Henry Hathaway, 1966, Steve McQueen.
River of No Return, Otto Preminger, 1954, Robert Mitchum.
The Sons of Katie Elder, Henry Hathaway, 1965, John Wayne.
There Was a Crooked Man, Joseph L. Mankiewicz, 1970, K. Douglas.
The Three Godfathers, John Ford, 1949, John Wayne.
The Treasure of the Sierra Madre, John Huston, 1948, H. Bogart.
The Unforgiven, John Huston, 1960, Burt Lancaster.
Winchester '73, Anthony Mann, 1950, James Stewart.

A bank robbery, *Rio Diablo*, Alamo Village, Bracketville, Texas (dk)

The Man With No Name
25 Best Spaghetti Westerns

It all started in 1964 with a little-known Italian director named Sergio Leone when he was given $200,000, thousands of feet of "short ends" of film stock, a script based on Akira Kurosawa's samurai epic *Yojimbo* (1961), an American TV actor named Clint Eastwood from a western TV series called "Rawhide," and a music composer named Ennio Morricone, who liked to recreate the sounds of birds in his music. With this unlikely combination, Leone made a western that changed the style of American westerns. The film: *A Fistful of Dollars*. It was a gritty, stylized, and violent approach to the western (completely different than a John Wayne western) with tough, crude, take-no-prisoners protagonists, extreme theatre-filling close-ups, badly dubbed dialogue, a new sound with Ennio Morricone's sonically bizarre music, and lensed in areas of Spain that resembled the American Southwest. It became an instant success in Europe. It wasn't until *The Good, the Bad and the Ugly* hit American Theatres did fans discover Sergio Leone and knockoffs of his film style went quickly into production. Listed here are the top twenty-five "Spaghettis" with director and a couple of the stars:

1. *Once Upon a Time in the West* (1968)—Sergio Leone—Henry Fonda, Jason Robards, Charles Bronson, Claudia Cardinale.
2. *The Good, the Bad and the Ugly* (1966)—Sergio Leone—Clint Eastwood, Eli Wallach, Lee Van Cleef.
3. *For a Few Dollars More* (1965)—Sergio Leone—Clint Eastwood, Lee Van Cleef.
4. *A Fistful of Dynamite*, a.k.a. *Duck, You Sucker!* (1971)—Sergio Leone—Rod Steiger, James Coburn.
5. *A Fistful of Dollars* (1964)—Sergio Leone—Clint Eastwood.
6. *The Great Silence* (1968)—Sergio Corbucci—Jean-Louis Trintignant & Klaus Kinski.
7. *Campaneros* (1970)—Sergio Corbucci—Franco Nero, Tomas Milian, Jack Palance.
8. *My Name is Nobody* (1973)—Tonino Valerii—H. Fonda, Trance Hill.

9. *Django* (1966)—Sergio Corbucci—Franco Nero, José Bódalo.
10. *They Call Me Trinity* (1970)—Enzo Barboni—Terence Hill, Bud Spencer.
11. *Trinity is STILL My Name* (1971)—Enzo Barboni—Terence Hill, Bud Spencer.
12. *Keoma* (1976)—Enzo G. Castellari—Franco Nero.
13. *Death Rides a Horse* (1967) Giulio Petroni—Lee Van Cleef, John Phillip Law.
14. *The Big Gundown* (1966)—Sergio Sollima—Lee Van Cleef, Tomas Milian, Walter Barnes.
15. *The Grand Duel* (1972)—Giancarlo Santi—Lee Van Cleef.
16. *Red Sun* (1971)—Terence Young—Charles Bronson, Ursula Andress, Toshirô Mifune.
17. *A Bullet for the General* (1966)—Damiano Damiani—Gian Maria Volonté, Klaus Kinski.
18. *The Mercenary* (1968) a.k.a. *Revenge of a Gunfighter*—Sergio Corbucci—Franko Nero, Jack Palance.
19. *Ace High* (1968)—Giuseppe Colizzi—Eli Wallach, Terence Hill, Bud Spencer.
20. *Day of Anger* (1968)—Tonino Valerii—Lee Van Cleef.
21. *Face to Face* (1967)—Sergio Sollima—Gian Maria Volonte, Thomas Milian.
22. *Sabata* (1969)—Gianfranco Parolini—Lee Van Cleef.
23. *Navajo Joe* (1966)—Sergio Corbucci—Burt Reynolds.
24. *Cemetery Without Crosses* (1968)—Robert Hossein—Michele Mercier, Robert Hossein.
25. *Run Man, Run* (1968)—Sergio Sollima—Tomas Milian, Donald O'Brien.

Spaghetti Trivia Question: Name a Spaghetti western directed by Burt Kennedy that starred a heroic female as the lead, a rare thing in Italian westerns?
ANS: *Hannie Caulder* (1970) starring Raquel Welch, Robert Culp, and Ernest Borgnine.

Another Spaghetti Trivia Question: Which film listed above was directed by a French director?
ANS: *Cemetery Without Crosses* (1968).

A tough Spaghetti Trivia Question: What movie listed above was remade by a Korean director with Korean actors in 2007?
ANS: *Django.* It was called *Sukivaki Western Django.*

Turkeys, Bombs, and Dogs
25 OF THE WORST WESTERNS

Here is a list of bad westerns that even a western fan will skip...or will he? To make up this list may be sacrilegious to a western fan who loves all westerns, but a book like this can't go without such a list of films that may be embarrassing to their director and star—films you don't want to take a friend to if you want to introduce him to the western film genre. (The list is in this order: title, director, year released, and one starring actor.)

Bandits, Robert Conrad, 1967, Robert Conrad.
Cry Blood Apache, Jack Starrett, 1970.
Duchess and the Dirtwater Fox, Melvin Frank, 1976, George Segal.
Four Rode Out, John Peyser, 1968, Pernell Roberts.
Great Gundown, Paul Hunt, 1976, Robert Padilla.
The Hellbenders, Sergio Corbucci, 1967, Joseph Cotton.
Jonah Hex, Jimmy Hayward, 2010, Josh Brolin.
Land Raiders, Nathan Juran, 1970, Telly Savalas.
Last of the Pony Riders, George Archainbaud, 1953, Gene Autry.
The Legend of Frenchie King, Christian Jaque, 1971, Brigitte Bardot.
The Legend of the Lone Ranger, William Fraker, 1981, K. Spilsbury.
Little Moon & Jud McGraw, Bernard Girard, 1978, James Cann.
Lonesome Cowboys, Andy Warhol, 1968.
The Mountain Men, Richard Lang, 1980, Charlton Heston.
Quick and the Dead, Sam Raimi, 1995, Sharon Stone.
Ride in the Whirlwind, Monte Hellman, 1965, Jack Nicholson.
Rootin' Tootin' Rhythm, Mack V. Wright, 1938, Gene Autry.
Rough Justice, Mario Costa, 1987, Klaus Kinski.
Slaughter Trail, Irving Allen, 1951, Brian Don Levy.
Something Big, Andrew V. McLaglen, 1971, Dean Martin.
Texas Rangers, Steve Miner, 2001, Ashton Kutcher.
The Terror of Tiny Town, Sam Newfield, 1938, Billy Curtis.
Triumphs of a Man Called Horse, John Hough, 1983, Richard Harris.
White Buffalo, J. Lee Thompson, 1977, Charles Bronson.
The Wild Wild West, Barry Sonnenfeld, 1999, Will Smith.

Western Movie Sets
14 MOVIE RANCHES

O**ver the years**, Hollywood filmmakers have built entire western towns in which to shoot their movies. Most were torn down at the completion of the movie (they are usually just fronts made of plywood and plaster), but others of wood have been kept up by the owner (often a rancher) to be used in future movies, television shows, and commercials. Below is a list of some of those that are still being used to shoot westerns.

1. Mescal, near Benson, Arizona (Private ranch), *Young Riders* TV series.
2. Bittercreek, Bradshaw Ranch, Sedona, Arizona (Private ranch), *The Rounders, The Wild Rovers*.
3. Alamo Village, Happy Shahan Angus Ranch, Bracketville, TX (Open to public), *The Alamo, Two Rode Together, Bandolero, Barbarosa*.
4. Buckskin Joe, Canon City, Colorado (Open to public), *Cat Ballou, The Cowboys, True Grit*, "The Sacketts."

Alamo Village, Bracketville, Texas (dk)

J. W. Eaves Ranch, Santa Fe, New Mexico (dk)

4. **Old Tucson**, Tucson, Arizona (Open to public), *Arizona, The Last Outpost, Gunfight At The O.K. Corral, 3:10 to Yuma. Rio Bravo, El Dordo, Joe Kidd, Posse, The Outlaw Josey Wales.*

5. **Rancho Alegre**, J. W. Eaves Ranch, Santa Fe, New Mexico (Open to Public), *The Cheyenne Social Club, The Cowboys, Gambler III.*

6. **Cook Ranch**, Santa Fe, New Mexico (Private ranch), *Silverado, Gambler Part III, Desperado, Lonesome Dove, The Lazarus Man, Appaloosa, 3:10 to Yuma.*

7. **Disney's Golden Oak Ranch**, Placertia Canyon, Newhall, California (Backlot), *Shenandoah, The Apple Dumpling Gang, Bonanza, Little House On The Prairie, Zorro, Paradise, North and South.*

8. **Western Six Points**, Universal Studios, Hollywood, California (Backlot), *Destry Rides Again, Winchester '73, Bend of the River, The Far Country, Invitation to a Gunfighter, The War Wagon.*

9. **Columbia Ranch**, Columbia Pictures, Burbank, California (Backlot), *Arizona, High Noon, 3:10 to Yuma, The Man from Laramie, Jubal.*

10. **Bordertown**, Maple Ridge, B. C. Canada (Private ranch) *Bordertown.*

11. **Bonanza Creek Ranch,** Glen Hughes Ranch, Santa Fe, New Mexico (Private ranch), *The Man From Laramie, The Cowboys, Silverado, Lonesome Dove* (TV mini series), *Cheyenne Social Club, The Lazarus Man* (TV series), *All the Pretty Horses, 3:10 to Yuma.*

12. **Red Hills Ranch**, Sedona, Arizona (Private Ranch).

13. **Apacheland**, Apache Junction, Arizona. (Private Ranch).

14. **RHS Studios**, Spicewood, TX (Private Ranch), *Red Headed Stranger.*

Where was it lensed?
13 WESTERN MOVIE LOCATIONS

"It's a shame to take this country [California]
away from the rattlesnakes."
—D. W. Griffith

Where in the American West are the westerns filmed? A western has to look like it is taking place in the nineteenth century in a barren landscape far from civilization, but a movie company with dozens of semi-trucks and crews numbering in the hundreds have to live, eat, work and sleep for months in a wilderness that appears void of modern life on film. So, the producers have to find attractive landscapes without telephone wires and contrails, but still have paved highways and hotels nearby. As a result, there are a few locations in America that are

Big Bend National Park, Texas (dk)

used over and over again because the needed services are available, including access to an airport for receiving actors and sending raw film for processing. Some of Hollywood's favorite western locals:

1. Monument Valley, Arizona/Utah. This most unusual western location is on a Navajo Reservation, and was made famous by John Ford who shot nine westerns there. The towering red sandstone buttes scattered like stalagmites on a sandy floor stretching to the horizon make for the perfect western locale for a big, wide-screen movie. It's located in the northeastern corner of Arizona and reaches into the canyonlands of southern Utah. It was Harry Goulding who first brought attention to this area by building a trading post in the 1920's and bringing John Ford out to see the location. Some of the Westerns lensed at Monument Valley include *Stagecoach* (1938), *My Darling Clementine* (1946), *She Wore a Yellow Ribbon* (1949), *Fort Apache* (1948), *The Searchers* (1956), *Sergeant Rutledge* (1960), *How the West Was Won* (1962), *Cheyenne Autumn* (1964), and the *Legend of the Lone Ranger* (1980). *Back to the Future III* (1988) starring Michael J. Fox was also shot in Monument Valley.

Monument Valley, Arizona (dk)

Canyonlands National Park, Moab, Utah (dk)

2. Moab, Utah. This little town has hosted hundreds of production companies since 1949 when John Ford's *Wagon Master* was shot here. Its a very small summer tourist town in Southern Utah on the Colorado border, the only town in the area. It's surrounded by several National Parks that protect the beautiful and colorful canyonlands—ideal for western moviescapes. Arches National Park and the Canyonlands National Park are a stone's throw from Moab, and crews don't have to be on National Park land to find good places to shoot because civilization still hasn't reached this "god-forsaken land." The weather is mild because of its low elcvation. Butch Cassidy's Wild Bunch hung out here and Zane Grey wrote many novels set at this locale. Today the town is a jumping off point for white-water rafting on the Colorado River, hiking, and jeep safaris. Western films lensed here include *Rio Grande* (1950), *The Comancheros* (1961), *Cheyenne Autumn* (1963), *Rio Conchos* (1964), and *Against a Crooked Sky* (1975).

3. Santa Fe, New Mexico. A location where actors can enjoy themselves when not on the set. Film companies have built several western town sets within just a few miles of the town center (see Movie Ranch listing). A company can shoot their entire western

Old Tucson Studios, Old Tucson, Arizona (dk)

without moving the company, having a variety of landscapes and towns to choose from.

4. Tucson, Arizona. Old Tucson Studios, built in 1939 for the motion picture *Arizona* starring Jean Arthur and William Holden, has hosted hundreds of movies, more than any other western town set. It was becoming a historic tribute to western filmmaking until it burned to the ground in 1994. It has since been rebuilt, though nowhere near its former grandeur—and won't likely be used as a western movie set again. You can always identify the movies shot in this area by the saguaro cactus found only in this area of the Sonoran Desert. Westerns lensed here include John Wayne films like *McClintock* (1963), *El Dorado* (1967), and *Rio Lobo* (1970). Clint Eastwood shot *Joe Kidd* (1972) and parts of *The Outlaw Josey Wales* (1976) here. *Posse* (1975) and *Gunfight at the O.K. Corral* (1957) starred Kirk Douglas and Burt Lancaster. The television western *High Chaparral* (1967-71) shot its entire series at these studios.

5. Sedona, Arizona. This was an early location for the first westerns to leave the Hollywood studios. Now it's a popular resort area with shopping and golf courses so good uncluttered views without telephone poles is now hard to find. Towering red-rock outcroppings define this area. *The Rounders* (1965) and the *Wild Rovers* (1971) were shot here.

6. West Texas along the Rio Grande. This area along the "El Camino del Rio" river road is part of the Chihuahaun desert and has become a popular film location in recent years. Film crews with their 18-wheelers can work just off the paved road. Lying just west of Big Bend National Park, it's a rugged, dry, deserted locale that makes for a great western setting. The muddy Rio Grande River cut a swath through this landscape creating canyons and vistas, and volcanoes once erupted here creating a pumice-covered desolate wonderland. East of here at Brackettville, Texas is the western movie set "Alamo Village" originally built for John Wayne's 1960 epic movie *The Alamo*. It sits on a flat plain with one hill on which sits the Alamo compound with a view of the town of "San Antonio" in the valley. Movies shot here and along the Rio Grande include: *Two Rode Together* (1961), *Barbarosa* (1982), *Up Hill All The Way* (1984) , and *Bad Girls* (1994).

The Rio Grande River, Boquillas Canyon, Texas (dk)

Joshua Tree National Park, Twentynine Palms, California (dk)

Locations Around Los Angeles, California

Many locations in the hills and deserts around Hollywood were used for the early westerns before urban sprawl covered them over with asphalt and concrete. Western town sets were build by ranchers to host the new Hollywood westerns. Some of them are listed here:

7. The San Juaquin Valley. This desert area sits just over the hills from Los Angeles and was used by the makers of early westerns for their exteriors, just a few miles from the Hollywood studios where all the interior sets were built. Roy Rogers made so many movies in the valley that he built his home and the Roy Rogers–Dale Evans Museum in Victorville (Now closed, sadly).

8. Lone Pine. About 200 miles north of Los Angeles is the town of Lone Pine situated in the Owens Valley just east of the Sierras. It is a rugged, rock-strewn land with a backdrop of snow capped mountains. The *Alabama Hills* area was used for early "B'" westerns like those starring Hopalong Cassidy, Gene Autry, Ken Manard and Hoot Gibson. In the 1940's and 50's, a western street called "Anchorville" was used just south of town. Movies shot at Lone Pine include *Springfield Rifle* (1952), *Bad Day at Black Rock* (1955), *Comanche Station* (1960), *How the West Was Won* (1962), *Nevada Smith* (1966), *Waterhole #3* (1967), and *Joe Kid* (1972).

9. Corriganville. This movie ranch in Chatsworth, California—with its desert location and rock outcroppings—was developed by Ray "Crash" Corrigan in the late 1930's. The great-looking fort for the movie *Fort Apache* (1948) was built there and was later used for the "Rin Tin Tin" TV series. The western street was called "Silvertown." "The Cisco Kid" and most of the 50's TV westerns also shot episodes there. Corriganville was turned into a popular western town amusement park in 1949 and in 1965 was bought by Bob Hope, but then in 1970, fire burned down the town.

10.   Iverson's Movie Location Ranch. Chatsworth, California. Rugged rock outcroppings and one area that came to be called the "Garden of the Gods," was named after the park in Colorado Springs, Colorado. From the 1930's to the 50's, thousands of westerns were shot here including many John Wayne "B" westerns, *Stagecoach* in 1939, and 1950's television westerns. In 1987, a developer by the name of Robert Sherman subdivided the property and sold off building lots, turning the land into acres of high-priced homes and apartment complexes.

11. Vasquez Rocks County Park. You've seen it in hundreds of low-budget westerns and television episodes: a unique rock formation jutting out of the ground at an angle along with acres of huge boulders. It's in a county park in Agu Dulce, California about 40 miles north of Los Angeles. The rocks were named after the notorious bandito, Tiburcio Vasquez. Movies shot there include *Along the Oregon Trail* (1947) and *The Conquest of Cochise* (1953).

12. Pioneertown. East of Palm Springs in the Yucca Valley of California. This real town, with real residents, stands in an arid, desert environment with scattered Joshua Trees. Nearby is Joshua Tree National Monument. The town had a dirt street and was used in the 1950's, but has become a virtual ghost town today.

13. Melody Ranch. In Newhall, California, just north of Los Angeles, it had a western street built by Monogram Pictures. It was bought by Gene Autry in 1952 and used for his "B" westerns and TV shows like "Gunsmoke" and "Wyatt Earp." It burned down in 1962. The fate of movie towns is, sadly, too often, the same as many real Old West communities.

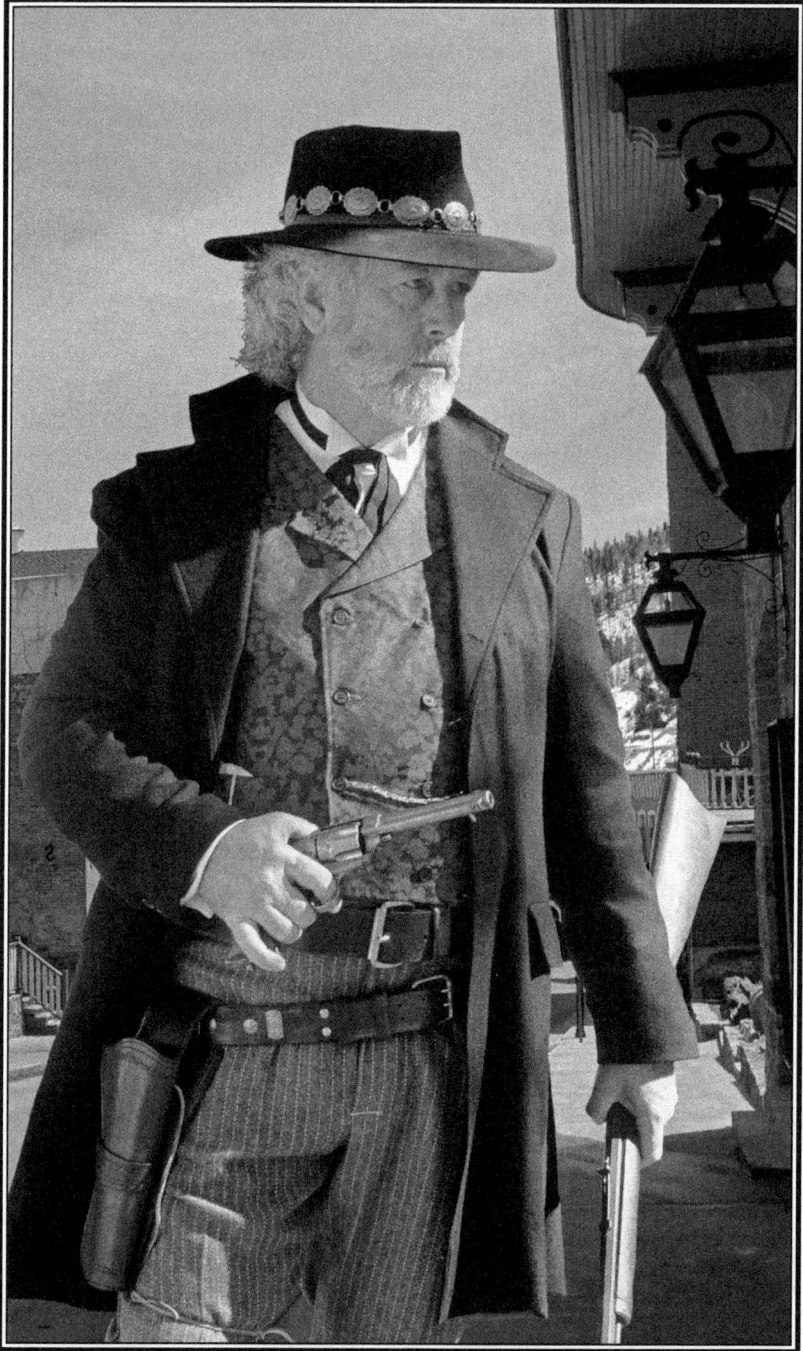

C.R. Nowell as Bret Law, photo and costume by the author

Western Words of Wisdom
THE CODE OF THE WEST

"Never give salt nor advice until it's asked for."
—old frontier adage

A man caught with a stolen horse was sure to hang from the nearest cottonwood. No questions asked. A horse was a man's most important possession; his saddle a close second. It made sense; a man left without a horse in the wild arid lands of the West had little chance of surviving so a "stiff rope and a short drop" was not unreasonable punishment. And who had time for a judge and jury. It was doubtful they could be had anyway in a territory of thousands of wilderness miles linked only by a few dusty trails. A person's word in this new frontier West was also sacred. So was his property. You didn't mess with his belongings, you didn't tell a lie. You were hospitable to anyone that came across your path. If a stranger came to your door needing a meal, you didn't charge him for it, nor did the stranger offer to pay you for it, for that was an insult, suggesting you couldn't afford to have him as his guest. This was the unwritten Code of the West, sometimes contradictory and inconsistent, but always evolving to meet the needs of a wide variety of nationalities attempting to make a new life in a land with no rules of etiquette or standing law. The standards they brought with them from their varied homelands often didn't work. Here you had to trust a man; your life might depend on it. Your real enemy was the land itself.

The words of wisdom in this chapter came from the media that has done so much to create and preserve the lore of the American West. It began with the dime novels and Wild West Shows and as soon as the moving picture came along, it too, had to do its duty and preserve our unique frontier heritage, even if it meant obscuring the truth with folklore. But who are we to quibble? It's our past and we'll make it what we want.

☞ **Unwritten Law Of The Western Frontier** ☜

THE CODE OF THE WEST

One should not ask a stranger his name or where he comes from; his business is his own and you should not be too inquisitive about his past. He could be on the dodge.

One should be hospitable to a stranger come to town, for tomorrow he could be your neighbor.

Always give your enemy a fighting chance. Never shoot him in the back. A bushwacker is the lowest of cowards.

A man's word must be good, for there is no other contract. And calling another man a liar will surely have you leaning against a bullet!

Under no circumstances should you shoot an unarmed man, even if he is your bitter enemy. To do so is fair call for a hanging.

One should not make threats or insult a man without expecting dire consequences. And to be insulted is just cause for defending your honor.

It is an insult to offer to pay a host for your room and board. To make such an offer is to imply that he can't afford to have you as his guest.

To steal a man's horse is to ask for a stiff rope with a short drop. A man left stranded in an untamed wilderness without a means of conveyance is a man left for dead.

It is to your good name to honor and revere all women, be they farmer's wives or saloon girls, and never think of harming one hair of a woman.

One should always look out for himself, for it is no one else's duty but his own.

Humorous Similitude of Old West Broadside created by the author

Humorous Similitude of Old West Broadside created by the author

BUTTERFIELD STAGE LINES

NOTICE TO PASSENGERS

ADHERENCE TO THE FOLLOWING RULES WILL INSURE A PLEASANT TRIP FOR ALL

☞ SPIRITS ☜
Abstinence From Liquor Is Requested, But If You Must Drink, Share The Bottle.
To Do Otherwise Makes You Appear Selfish And Un-neighborly.

☞ SMOKING & CHEWING ☜
If Ladies Are Present, Gentlemen Are Urged To Forego Smoking Cigars And Pipes As The Odor Of Same Is
Repugnant To The Gentle Sex. Chewing Tobacco Is Permitted, But Spit With The Wind, Not Against It!

MEN MUST REFRAIN FROM USING ROUGH LANGUAGE IN THE PRESENCE OF LADIES AND CHILDREN.

☞ WINTER TRAVEL ☜
Buffalo Robes Are Provided For Your Comfort During Cold Weather. Hogging Robes Will Not Be
Tolerated And The Offenders Will Be Made To Ride With The Driver.

☞ SLEEPING ☜
Don't Snore Loudly While Sleeping. Don't Use Your Fellow Passenger's Shoulder For A Pillow;
He (Or She) May Not Understand And Friction May Result.

☞ USE OF FIREARMS ☜
Guns May Be Kept On Your Person For Use In Emergencies.
Do Not Fire Them For Pleasure Or Shoot At Wild Animals As The Sound Riles The Horses!

☞ EMERGENCIES ☜
In The Event Of Runaway Horses, Remain Calm. Leaping From The Coach In Panic Will Leave You
Injured, At The Mercy Of The Elements, Hostile Indians And Hungary Coyotes.

FORBIDDEN TOPICS OF DISCUSSION: STAGECOACH ROBBERIES AND INDIAN UPRISINGS!

☞ CONDUCT ☜
Gents Guilty Of Un-chivalrous Behavior Toward Lady Passengers Will Be Put Off The Stage.
It's A Long Way Back. A Word To The Wise Is Sufficient.

– B.S.L., District Manager, San Antonio 1868

Hopalong Cassidy's
8 RULES FOR BOYS & GIRLS

1. Be kind to birds and animals.

2. Always be faithful and fair.

3. Keep thyself neat and clean.

4. Always be courteous.

5. Be careful when crossing streets.

6. Avoid bad habits.

7. Study and always learn your lessons.

8. Obey your parents.

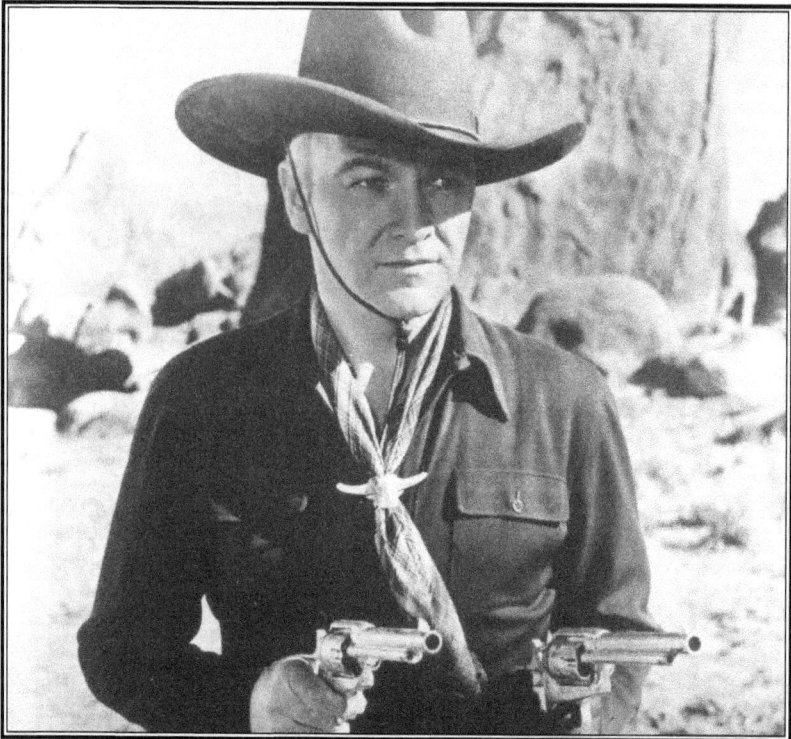

William Boyd (Hopalong Cassidy Productions)

Gene Autry (Flying 'A' Productions)

Gene Autry's
10 COMMANDMENTS OF A COWBOY

1. He Must Not Take Unfair Advantage Of An Enemy.
2. He Must Never Go Back On His Word.
3. He Must Always Tell The Truth.
4. He Must Be Gentle With Children, Elderly People, And Animals.
5. He Must Not Possess Racially Or Religiously Intolerant Ideas.
6. He Must Help People In Distress.
7. He Must Be A Good Worker.
8. He Must Respect Women, Parents, And His Nation's Laws.
9. He Must Neither Drink Nor Smoke.
10. He Must Be A Patriot.

10 COMMANDMENTS OF THE FRONTIER
by Clarence S. Paine
(Wild Bill Hickok and Calamity Jane)

1. Thieves and robbers will be driven out of camp for first offense—hung for the second.

2. The man who picks a quarrel had better pick up his traps.

3. Men convicted of murder will be hung on the same day.

4. Passing bogus money will entitle a chap to pass out of town, everybody taking a kick at him as he goes.

5. Don't covet your neighbor's wife.

6. Lying should be discouraged.

7. Whack up even on all "finds."

8. No shirking in an Indian fight.

9. All notes of hand must be paid when due, or down goes the maker.

10. Rebellion against the legal authority of the town shoves the rebel out and confiscates his claim.

COURTESY: *The Black Hills*, Roderick Peattie, editor, New York: Vanguard Press, 1952.

MAKIN' A HAND

TIDBIT: Ramon F. Adams, in his book *Western Words* (1968), gave the following definition for the cowboy phrase *makin' a hand:* "A cowboy expression meaning that someone is living up to the exacting code of the calling—a high compliment. This code calls for courage and loyalty, uncomplaining cheerfulness and laughter at dangers and hardships, lack of curiosity about another's past, and respect for womanhood."

COWBOY CODE

By Eugene C. Vories

The old-time cowboy lived by a code of honesty, integrity, honor, and loyalty. The rancher he rode for lived by those same values.

1. When a cowboy rides for an outfit, he is completely loyal to that outfit and anyone who harms anything representing that brand automatically becomes his enemy.

2. A cowboy always treats the boss's family with complete trust and respect, especially the wife.

3. A cowboy never lies to his employer about the condition or number of cattle under his care.

4. If a cowboy says he can do something, he does it, and if the task becomes impossible, he never gives up until he's given it his best effort.

5. A cowboy never sleeps in, no matter how late he was out the night before.

6. A cowboy never steals from an outfit, nor lets anyone else steal from the brand he rides for.

7. A rancher never uses, or allows anyone to ride, a cowboy's personal horse without that cowboy's permission.

8. A ranch owner never asks his cowhands to do anything he has not done himself.

9. When a cowboy felt he could no longer be loyal to the brand, he would quit honorably and drift to another job.

COURTESY: *Cowboy Magazine*, La Veta, Colorado;
Darrell Arnold, editor, spring 1997.

Native Indian Law
THE TEN INDIAN COMMANDMENTS

The American Indian also had a code to direct them in their pursuits. This list was found in a cabin at the Hat Creek Ranch in British Columbia, Canada.

Treat the earth and all that dwell thereon with respect.
Remain close to the Great Spirit.
Show great respect for your fellow beings.
Work together for the benefit of all mankind.
Give assistance and kindness wherever needed.
Do what you know to be right.
Look after the well being of mind and body.
Dedicate a share of your efforts to the greater good.
Be truthful and honest at all times.
Take full responsibility for your actions.

Old schoolhouse, Old Tucson Studios, Tucson, Arizona (dk)

A Western Code Of Conduct
19 WORDS OF ADVICE

"If movies could be a religion, I think you'd get more
out of westerns than any other genre."
—Bud Boetticher

Dave Marinaccio once wrote a book about the lessons of life he learned from the *Star Trek* television series. Well, from time to time, western movies have also thrown out a little guidance in dealing with your fellow man, even if that man was toting a pair of sixguns.

1. "Those who live by the gun die by the neck." —Pappy Maverick (James Garner), *Maverick* TV series, 1957-1962.

2. "When it looks like you're not gonna make it, then you gotta get mean. I mean plumb, mad dog mean!" —Josey Wales (Clint Eastwood), *The Outlaw Josey Wales*, 1976.

3. "I won't be wronged, I won't be insulted, I won't be laid a hand on. I don't do these things to other people and I require the same of them." —J.B. Books (John Wayne), *The Shootist*, 1976.

4. "Quantity is never a worthy substitute for quality, whether it is in the choice of a book, a play, a friend, or a gun." —Paladin (Richard Boone), *Have Gun Will Travel*, 1957-1963.

5. "A man has to be what he is, Joey. Can't break the mold ...There's no living with a killing. There's no going back from it. Right or wrong, it's a brand. A brand sticks." —Shane (Allan Ladd), *Shane*, 1953.

6. "Man just naturally can't take the law into his own hands and hang people without hurting everybody in the world, 'cause then he's just not breaking one law but all laws." —Gil Carter (Henry Fonda), *The Ox-Bow Incident*, 1943.

7. "The West don't care by what you call yourself, it's what you call others that lets you stay healthy." —John Wayne.

8. "Water's precious, sometimes more precious than gold." —Walter Huston, *The Treasure of the Sierra Madre*, 1948.

9. "There is a whole world waitin' for you out there. Good places and bad places. Nice people and some not so nice. Look 'em all over, Arthur. Bide your time, and maybe somewhere, someplace, you'll find a real woman. A good woman. A woman that'll love honor and obey you, Arthur, in sickness and health. Find one that'll comfort ya'." —Jason Robarts, *A Big Hand For A Little Lady*, 1966.

10. "We're all gonna die someday. It's better to die fightin' than lying with your face in the dirt." —Audie Murphy, *40 Guns To Apache Pass*, 1966.

11. "When you start killing for a dream you usually end up killing the dream too. And that's what Hell is: watchin' your dreams die." —*Last Train From Gun Hill*, 1959.

12. "It's better to follow a star, than have a man with a star following you." —Arthur Kennedy, *Bend Of The River*, 1952.

13. "There ain't never a horse that couldn't be rode; there ain't never a rider that couldn't be throwd." —Gary Cooper.

14. "There's a time for running wild. There's a time for bucking against a saddle on your back, but there comes a time you do the work you're cut out for." —*Heaven With A Gun*, 1969.

15. "When an apple's rotten there's nuttin' you can do except throw it away or it'll spoil the whole barrel." —Jay G. Flippen, *Bend Of The River*, 1952.

16. "When a woman's talkin' to ya, you can be pretty sure she thinks she's in control. When she's not talking to ya, you can be pretty certain you're in control." —Henry Fonda, *The Cheyenne Social Club*, 1970.

17. "A man's gotta do his own growin' no matter how tall his father was." —Rock Hudson, *Gun Fury*, 1953.

18. "You gotta look like you're somebody and act like you're somebody. Like you can take care of yourself no matter what happens. You do that, pretty soon you *are* somebody." —Gary Cooper, *Along Came Jones*, 1945.

19. "I'm not responsible for what people think—only for what I am." —Gregory Peck, *The Big Country* (1958).

Rules For Teachers

1. Teachers each day will fill lamps and clean chimneys.

2. Each teacher will bring a bucket of water and a scuttle of coal for the day's session.

3. Make your pens carefully. You may whittle nibs to the individual taste of the pupil.

4. Men teachers may take one evening each week for courting purposes or two evenings if they go to church regularly.

5. After ten hours of school, the teacher may spend the remaining time reading the Bible or other good books.

6. Women teachers who marry or engage in unseemly conduct will be dismissed.

7. Every teacher should lay aside from each pay a goodly sum of his earnings for his benefit during his declining years so that he will not become a burden on society.

8. Any teacher who smokes, uses liquor in any form, frequents pool or public dance halls, or is shaved in a barber shop will give good reason to suspect his worth, intention, integrity, and honesty.

9. The teacher who performs his labor faithfully and without fault for five years will be given an increase of 25¢ per week in his pay providing the Board of Education approves.

— Superintendent of Schools, September 7, 1872

Humorous Similitude of Old West Broadside created by the author

Victorian Etiquette
10 RULES FOR GOOD MANNERS

1. Never neglect to call upon your friends.
2. Never leave home with unkind words.
3. Never exaggerate.
4. Never betray a confidence.
5. Never laugh at the misfortunes of others.
6. Never point at anyone.
7. Never give a gift, hoping for one in return.
8. Never pick your teeth in public.
9. Never wantonly frighten others.
10. Never will a gentleman allude to a conquest he may have made with a lady.

Victorian Etiquette
8 RULES FOR THE STREET

1. The gentleman gives the lady the inside of the walk.
2. Ladies should not walk rapidly. It is ungraceful.
3. No gentleman should stand on the corner, making remarks about the ladies passing by.
4. A gentleman should give his seat to a lady who may be standing in a public conveyance.
5. It is customary to give silent respectful attention to a passing funeral procession.
6. Swinging the arms, eating upon the street, sucking the parasol handles, and loud and boisterous talking and laughing are all signs of ill-breeding.
7. A gentleman should accommodate his pace to a lady, and not be ahead of her.
8. Staring at people or spitting are evidence of poor breeding.

1887 ETIQUETTE OF THE TABLE

E ase, savoir-faire and good breeding are nowhere more indispens-
able than at the dinner-table, and the absence of them is nowhere
more apparent. How to eat soup and what to do with cherry-
stones are weighty considerations when taken as the index of social
status. Dinner table etiquette should be mastered by all who aspire
to become members of polite society.

RULES OF CONDUCT

Seat yourself in an upright position
not too close to nor yet too far from the table.

1. Take your napkin, partially unfold it and lay it across your lap. It is not the correct thing to fasten it in your button-hole or spread it over your breast.

2. Do not trifle with your knife or fork, or drum on the table, or fidget in any way, while waiting to be served.

3. Keep your hands quietly in you lap, your mind composed and pleasantly fixed upon the conversation. Let all your movements be easy and deliberate. Undue haste indicates a nervous lack of ease.

4. Should grace be said, you will give the most reverent attention in respectful silence during the ceremony.

5. Exhibit no impatience to be served. During the intervals between the courses is your opportunity for displaying your conversational abilities to those sitting near you. Pleasant chat and witty remarks compose the best possible sauce to a good dinner.

6. Eat slowly; it will contribute to your good health as well as your good manners. Thorough mastication of your food is necessary to digestion. An ordinary meal should occupy from thirty minutes to an hour.

7. You may not desire the soup, which is usually the first course, but you should not refuse to take it. You can eat as much or little as you please, but you would look awkward sitting with nothing before you while the others are eating.

8. When eating soup, take it from the side of the spoon, and avoid making any noise.

9. Should you be asked by the host what part of the fowl you prefer, always have a choice, and mention promptly which you prefer. Nothing is more annoying than to have to serve two or three people who have no preferences and will take "anything."

10. Never place waste matter on the table-cloth. The side of your plate, or side-dishes that have contained sauces or vegetables, will answer as a receptacle for bones, potato skins, etc.

11. You will use your fork to convey all your food to your mouth, except it may be certain sauces that would be more conveniently eaten with a spoon. For instance, you should not attempt to eat peas with a fork. If you are not provided with a spoon, ask for one.

12. The knife is used only for cutting meat and other articles of food, for spreading butter upon the bread, etc.

HABITS TO BE AVOIDED

1. Do not eat fast.

2. Do not make noise with mouth or throat.

3. Do not fill the mouth too full.

4. Do not open the mouth in masticating.

5. Do not leave the table with food in your mouth.

6. Be careful to avoid soiling the cloth.

7. Never carry anything like food with you from the table.

8. Never apologize to the waiters, for making them trouble; it is their business to serve you. It is proper, however, to treat them with courtesy, and say "No, I thank you," or "If you please," in answer to their inquiries.

9. Do not introduce disgusting or unpleasant topics of conversation.

10. Do not pick your teeth or put your finger in your mouth at the table.

11. Do not come to table in your shirt-sleeves, or with soiled hands or tousled hair.

12. Do not cut your bread; break it.

13. Do not refuse to take the last piece of bread or cake; it looks as though you imagined there might be no more.

CARING FOR YOURSELF
8 Rules For The Ladies

A. Retire early to get your necessary rest.

B. Make sure there is plenty of fresh air admitted to your bedroom.

C. Upon rising, take a complete bath.

D. Meals should be partaken of with regularity, with more or less of fruit, oatmeal, graham bread, etc. to keep the skin clear.

E. A remedy for foul breath is powered charcoal, half a teaspoon spread on bread.

F. For greasy skin, mix one half-pint of distilled water, 18 grains of bicarbonate of soda, and 6 drops of essence of Portugal, and bathe the face with it.

G. A broad heel, half an inch in height, is all that comfort for the feet will allow.

H. For removing dandruff, glycerin diluted with a little rosewater is very cleansing.

ETIQUETTE OF
RIDING AND DRIVING

Victorian America published rules for proper etiquette for every activity and every place except the bath and bedroom. These rules are excerpted from an 1887 book on etiquette.

19 RULES FOR HORSEBACK RIDING

Riding is an accomplishment in which all ladies and gentlemen should be proficient. Riding, like swimming, cannot be taught by precept; it must be taught early and practiced constantly—as little in the school and as much upon the road as possible.

1. A lady's riding-habit should be simple, close-fitting, and made by a first-rate tailor. The later habit is much shorter and narrower than the old style, and is always worn with pantaloons of the same material underneath.

2. A lady can indulge her love of luxury only in her riding-whip. This may be jewelled, and as elegant as she may wish. Her gloves must always be unexceptionable.

3. The art of mounting must be properly acquired, since in riding, as in other things, it is proficiency in trifles that proclaims the artist.

4. The lady, having mounted the riding-steps, places her left foot in the stirrup, rises into her seat and lifts the right leg into its place taking care to let the habit fall properly.

5. If no riding-steps are at hand, her escort or groom must assist her to mount. Hence she must learn to mount in both ways. In the latter case she places her left foot in the right hand of the gentleman or servant; he lifts it vigorously but gently, and she springs lightly into the saddle.

6. A lady who rides much and wishes to keep her figure straight should have two saddles and change from one to the other.

7. The great point in riding is to sit straight in the middle of your saddle, to know the temper of your horse, and to be able to enjoy a good gallop in moderation.

8. Ladies should not lean forward in riding.

9. They should not rise in the saddle in trotting.

10. They should know how to hold the reins and different uses of each.

11. A gentleman, in riding, as in walking, gives the lady the wall.

12. In assisting a lady to mount, hold your hand at a convenient distance from the ground, that she may place her foot in it. As she springs, assist her with the impetus of your arm. Only practice will enable you to do this properly.

13. A gentleman should be able to mount on either side of his horse. He places his left foot in the stirrup, his left hand on the saddle, and swings himself up, throwing his right leg over the horse's back. Nothing is more awkward than to see a man climb into a saddle with both hands.

14. The correct position is to sit upright and well back in the saddle; to keep the knees pressed well in against the sides of the saddle; and the feet parallel to the horse's body; to turn the toes in rather than out. The foot should be about half-way in the stirrup.

15. The great desideratum in the art of riding is plenty of confidence. A timid person can never be a good rider.

16. When escorting a lady be sure that her horse is quite safe, every part of its harness in perfect condition, and keep on the alert to assist her on the slightest sign of danger.

17. A gentleman riding with two ladies will keep to the right of both, unless it be necessary for him to ride between them in order to render some assistance.

18. In dismounting, the gentleman will take the lady's left hand in his right, remove the stirrup and place her foot in his left hand, lowering her gently to the ground.

19. Keep on the right or off side, and never presume to touch her mount any more than you would that of a gentleman friend.

7 RULES FOR DRIVING A CARRIAGE

The art of driving is simple enough, but requires practice. No one should pretend who does not understand every part of the harness and be able to harness or unharness a horse himself.

1. A good driver will use his horse well, whether it be his own or another's. He will turn corners gently, and know when to drive fast and when to ease up.

2. In the carriage, a gentleman places himself with his back to the horses, leaving the best seat for the ladies. Only very elderly gentlemen are privileged to take the back seat to the exclusion of young ladies. NO gentleman driving alone with a lady should sit beside her, unless he is her husband, father, son, or brother. Even an affianced lover should remember this rule of etiquette.

3. To get in and out of a carriage gracefully is quite an accomplishment. If there is but one step, and you are going to face the horses, put your left foot on the step and the other in the carriage, so that you can drop at once into your seat. If you are to sit the other way, reverse the process. Be careful to turn your back the way you intend sitting, so as to avoid turning around.

4. A gentleman should be careful to avoid stepping on the lady's dress in getting into the carriage. He should be careful also not to catch it in the door as he closes it.

5. A gentleman should always get out of a carriage first, in order to assist the lady in alighting.

6. When a gentleman intends taking a lady driving in a one-seated vehicle, he should always be sure his horse is a safe one before trusting himself with it, as he is obliged to get out to assist the lady in and out of the vehicle. When helping her in, he should be careful always to hold the reins so that he can check the animal in case it should start suddenly.

7. The dress should never be lifted in alighting from a carriage, but left to trail upon the ground.

The author as Monte "Five Aces" Bartholomew, photo by Glynda Smith

Pocket Pistols and Pasteboards
GAMBLERS AND THEIR GAMES

*An easterner who walked into a western saloon was amazed
to see a dog sitting at a table playing poker with three men:
"Can that dog really read cards?" he asked. "Yeah, but he
ain't much of a player," said one of the men, "Whenever he
gets a good hand he wags his tail."*
—Anonymous

Everyone gambled in the Frontier West. Why? There wasn't much else to do and there were always those who wanted to make a quick buck by cheating others and opening a gambling hall was the way to do that. Gold miners, working all day in the hard-rock mines or panning for flakes of gold in ice-cold creek waters, needed some good rest and relaxation, comradeship, and a good game of poker. The gambling hall satisfied those needs. But, card sharps came from all over the West to ply their trade in the mining camps. They found they could make a big stake in the Old West without getting their hands dirty.

This chapter covers the basics of what any man out West in the nineteenth century should know about gambling before making a Saturday night trip into town—all gussied up, his horse groomed and watered—ready for a little comradeship, a few hands of poker, and a spin of the Wheel of Fortune.

Aces & Eights,
The dead man's hand

Keep Your Back To The Wall!
THE DEAD MAN'S HAND

*"Oh, dyin' was easy, for livin' was hard. You died for a
word or the turn of a card."*
—Ballad from the movie *Bronco Billy*, 1980.

J **ames Butler Hickok** always made it a point to sit with his
back to the wall when playing a game of poker. On August 2,
1876 in the *No. 10* saloon, Deadwood, Dakota Territory, Hickok
was playing with three friends* and failed to sit with his back to
the wall.** A drifter, *"Broken Nose" Jack McCall,* quietly entered
the saloon and shot Wild Bill in the back. Bill was 39. The poker
hand he was holding at his demise has become legendary. It's
know as the *Dead Man's Hand.* Woe to the person who draws
"Aces and Eights."

Ace of Clubs	Ace of Spades
8 of Clubs	8 of Spades
Jack of Diamonds***	

* Bill's friends Charley Rich, Carl Mann and Captain Frank Massey.

** On several occasions, Hickok had asked his poker buddy, Frank Massey,
who was sitting against the wall, if he would kindly exchange places
with him. On this day, Massey declined, saying he wasn't giving anyone a
chance to shoot him in the back.

***There is no consensus in the history books as to the identity of the fifth
card. Some witnessess disagreed, saying it was a queen of diamonds. The
mortician who buried Hickok said he saw the Jack of Diamonds.

McCall was hired by outlaws *Tim Brady* and *Johnny Varnes* to kill
Hickock for $300 and all the whiskey he could drink. They feared Hickok
might be given the job of town Marshall in the upcoming election. McCall
was tried in Deadwood, but was found not guilty by the jury. A year later
he was retried in a "legal" federal court, found guilty, and hanged.

Ya Got To Know When Ta Hold 'Em.
19 POKER IDIOMS

"I wouldn't play poker with Henry Drummond
if his back was to a mirror!"
—Noah Keen, *A Big Hand for the Little Lady,* 1966.

A lot of expressions used during the play of a card game have developed their own unique meanings different from the original literal understanding. Some of those still used today include:

1. **Holding all the cards:** to have complete control over the situation.

2. **Play your hand:** to deal or act in a calculated manner to gain an end.

3. **Put all your cards on the table:** to show what you have or can do, to be perfectly frank about your plans, resources, etc.

4. **Poker face:** a face that does not show one's thoughts or feelings.

5. **Ace in the hole:** anything decisive or conclusive held in reserve to use at a critical time; a secret advantage. The phrase comes from the game of *stud poker* where the first card dealt is laid face down and called the "hole card." An ace in the hole was, of course, an advantage. In the Old West, the phrase also came to mean a concealed weapon carried in a pocket, sleeve, or boot.

6. **Ready to cash in your chips:** to close or sell a business, retire, or die. In cowboy parlance, "Ready to hang up his saddle."

7. **Card up one's sleeve:** a plan in reserve; extra help kept back until needed.

8. **When the chips are down:** when the moment of decision or definite action arrives in a crisis.

9. **Chip in:** to join with others in giving.

10. **Show your hand:** reveal your real intentions.

11. **Stack the deck:** to prepare for circumstances in advance.

12. **Not playing with a full deck:** meams a person doesn't have what's needed to play the game; he's not all there in mental capacity.

13. **Working against a stacked deck:** trying to succeed when circumstances have been prearranged secretly and unfairly.

14. **Dealing from the bottom:** not playing fair, cheating.

15. **Ante up:** To pay up or hand over.

16. **A square deal:** A fair and honest deal. Cards dealt using a pack of cards with squared edges as opposed to tapered ones (called *strippers*), thus reducing the chances of a crooked deal.

17. **On a shoestring:** working with limited funds. In *faro*, "playing on a shoestring," meant the player started the game with only a few dollars, but because of numerous lucky bets, he made a princely sum.

18. **In hock:** run up a debt, out of money. "Up to your armpits in debt," "Up against the wall." In *faro*, the last card in the box was called the *hock*, thus it was the last chance to win a bet and get "out of hock."

19. **Playing both ends against the middle:** Selected cards in a deck are trimmed secretly—usually the aces—so they can be found in the middle of the deck simply by running the thumb and forefinger along the edge of the deck. A dealer who used such a deck was said to be "playing both ends against the middle."

AN ACE IN THE HOLE

If President Lincoln had never been shot, there might never have been a Remington DERRINGER—the gun associated with the western gambler as his favorite "hole card." The nickel-plated "over-and-under" (referring to the placement of the two barrels) pocket pistol was first made by *E. Remington & Sons* in 1866 and labeled the "Derringer" as a marketing gimmick. A pocket pistol had been found on the floor of Ford's Theatre after President Abraham Lincoln was shot in 1865. The obscure pistol that killed the President had the maker's name engraved on it: "H. Deringer Phil'a." *Henry Deringer* (spelled with one "r") of Philadelphia made high-priced custom rifles and matched pairs of belt and vest-pocket pistols. He sued Remington for using his name, and eventually won after a 10 year court battle, but he died before he could collect damages. The name "Derringer" became generic for all pocket pistols.

Three Of A Kind Beats Two Pair
11 OLD WEST GAMES OF CHANCE

*"The quickest way to double your money is to fold it
over and put it back in your pocket."*
—Old cowboy saying

Games of chance were a major pastime for miners, cowboys, and professional gamblers on the western frontier. Hours of comradeship would be spent in smoke-filled rooms punctuated with the sound of a player piano. Patrons played against the house where the odds gave them no chance of walking away happy, or against strangers who played with an ace up their sleeve. Here then is a cursory description of the games of chance that cleaned out the pockets of so many a hard-working westerners.

1. FARO. The most popular casino game of the Old West, known by westerners as "Bucking the Tiger" because there was an illustration of a Bengal tiger on the playing board. It was a simple game that came to America from France by way of New Orleans, traveling northwest with the Mississippi Riverboat. It was called "Pharaoh" by the French because the cards bore the likeness of an Egyptian ruler. The game is played on a green oilcloth painted with images of the 13 cards of one suit (usually spades). In each round, two cards are dealt by the dealer from a standard 52-card deck. Players wager on the cards they think will be drawn in each round by placing their chips (called *checks*) on the appropriate image of the card. Players play against the house. The first card drawn in a turn is a "loser," and wins for the house any bets placed on that card. The second card drawn is a "winner" and wins for any player who has chips on that particular card. If a pair is drawn (called a *split*) the house takes half of any bet on that card. This was the house's only advantage in the game, that is, if the game was run fairly, which it usually wasn't. Players can also choose to bet that a card will NOT be drawn by placing a *copper* (a hexagonal token) on top of their bet chips, and groups of cards (called *figures, pots* and *squares*) could also be bet (a little like today's roulette). The entire deck is played to the last card before shuffling. In fact, players can bet on the order of the last three cards drawn, the house paying four to one. Based on statistical odds, this game could give the players a fair chance to win against the house, but in the Frontier West, the dealer could—and often did—try to improve the house's winnings by stacking pairs of cards together while shuffling the cards, or by using a rigged faro box that contained extra cards. Originally the dealer dealt from his hands. Later, to discourage slight-of-hand cheating by the dealer, the cards were shuffled and dropped in a box with a slot at the bottom. Cards were then drawn from that slot. Then, someone thought to rig the box so dealers could predict or manipulate the order and number of cards played. And then, to stop *those* shenanigans, a dealer's assistant (called the *casekeeper*) was given an abacus-like device for keeping a record of the cards dealt. Of course, the *casekeeper* worked for the house! Special cards were also made (like "strippers" and "sanded" cards) to make it easier to cheat. Not only did

An Old West saloon, South Park City Museum, Fairplay Colorado (dk)

the house try to gain an unfair advantage, but so did the players, resulting in a crooked game on both sides. For example, a *copper* with a horse hair attached could be yanked by a player from a winning card. The game isn't played today in the casinos because there never was a way, legally, for the house to make money!

2. CRAPS. Blacks developed "rolling the bones" or "clickin' the ivories" from a European dice game called *Hazard*. Craps is played with two cube-shaped die, each with six sides numbered 1 through 6. The two numbers that land face up—after being thrown on a table—are added together for the deciding number. If a player throws a "7" or a "11" it is called a "natural" and wins. If a 2, 3, or 12 is rolled, it's called "craps" and the player loses. If a player throws a 4, 5, 6, 8, 9, or 10, the number becomes his "point" and he must throw this number again *before* the "7" is thrown to win his bet. As with all Old West games of chance, everyone on both sides of the table tried to improve their odds with crooked dice:

> **MIS-SPOTTED DICE:** The crooked gambler could bring to the table—with a little slight-of-hand—dice with a different number of spots. Common was a die with two aces, two fives, and two sixes, and a second die with two threes, two fours, and two fives. With that pair of dice, a "7" cannot be rolled, assuring the player of repeating his number before the "7" comes up again! Even though the duplicate numbers were placed on opposite sides of the die so they couldn't be seen at once (a player can only see three sides of a cube at once), no one else could be allowed to pick them up and discover the con.

> **SHAVED DICE:** Corners and edges could easily be shaved off ivory die to increase the chances of a number landing upward.

> **LOADED DICE:** These were simply weighted to fall more often on a chosen number by drilling out spots on the opposite side of the die and filling them with a heavy metal like lead or mercury. The technique was known as "plumbing the bones."

> **ELECTRIC DICE:** A thin disk of iron was imbedded in each die (the extra weight on one side was counterbalanced with lead on the other) that would be drawn to a magnetized table; a battery operated electromagnet under the table was turned on and

off at will by the game operator. The operator had to remember to turn off the magnet before the dice were picked up, for it would be revealed that the dice were stuck to the table. Some players, savvy to this trick, began to carry small compasses on their watch chains! It turns out, the gambling games of the Old West were also a game of outsmarting the crooks.

Such devices did not have to be custom made, as many "sporting emporiums" sold crooked equipment to the trade. Far more rigged dice were sold in the Old West than legitimate "fair" dice.

3. TWENTY ONE. Originating from France where it was called *Vingt-et-un,* it is played with a full 52-card deck. Players play against the house dealer who gives each player and himself two cards, placing one up and one down. Each player, in turn, decides if he wants one or more cards added to the first two, with the hope of making twenty-one points or as close to that number as possible. An ace counts as one *or* eleven, the picture cards (king, queen, and jack) count as "10" and the other cards count according to their *spots* (numbers). All the players who draw a number higher than the dealer's draw, but not more than "21" (called a *bust*) also wins. If the dealer draws more than "21" *all* the players win. A player whose first two cards are an ace and face card has a *blackjack* or *natural* and wins.

4. ROULETTE. A steel or wooden ball is thrown onto a horizontally rotating wheel with randomly-placed numerals along its perimeter. The wheel will eventually come to a stop, the ball falling in a hole next to the winning number. The odds are heavily stacked against the player, making the game a loser in the long run. The earliest American roulette wheels had 28 numbered slots and *three* unnumbered ones with the house paying only 26 to 1. Later, as European wheels were brought to the United States in the 1890's, the odds improved a bit: these wheels had 36 numbers and *two* unnumbered slots ("0" and "00"). Roulette wheels could be easily tilted, or magnets added, to influence the outcome, toward the "0's" of course, the house's take.

Faro board and Roulette felt, South Park City Museum, Fairplay Colorado (dk)

5. POKER. This game of skill and luck didn't become popular in the West until the 1870's, but quickly developed many variations including *seven-card stud, 5-card draw,* and *lowball.* Poker first appeared on Mississippi steamboats in the 1830's where it first garnered the name "poker"—a mispronunciation of the French *pogue*—and was played with only 20 cards. The game came from France, but may date back as far as 2,000 years to Iran where they played the game of "A's." In this game, bluffing, bargaining, and stealing other players coins on the table was part of the game. Today's game is played with a 52-card deck containing four suits of 13 cards each. The four suits (hearts, spades, clubs, and diamonds) have no intrinsic value; one suit is not more valuable than another. The highest ranking card is the ace followed by the King, Queen and Jack (known as "face cards" because they have pictures of people on them instead of spots). The rest of the cards in each suit are numbered 2 through 10. In the nineteenth century, cards were not numbered in the corners as they are today, but were identified by counting the number of "spots" on a card. In *draw poker,* introduced about 1860, each player is dealt five cards face down, and players bet on this hand. In the next round of betting, they can choose to discard one or more cards, replacing those with an equal number from the top of the deck. Several rounds of betting can take place before the "showdown." Highest hand wins the pot.

In *stud poker,* each player is given his first card face down and the rest face up. No extra cards are drawn. In *five-card stud,* the dealer gives each player five cards, but the first card is placed *face down.* This "hole card" cannot be seen by the other players and bets are made. The rest of the cards are dealt face up.

The Ranking of Poker Hands, listed from best to worst:

Royal Flush: An ace high straight flush; the A-K-Q-J-10 all in one suit. It must include the Ace.

Straight Flush: Five consecutive cards in one suit, but with the top ranking card lower than an ace. For example: K-Q-J-10-9 of spades or 7-6-5-4-3 all hearts.

Four of a Kind: Four cards of the same rank, the fifth odd card doesn't matter. Examples: Q-Q-Q-Q-3 or 4-4-4-4-7.

Full House: Three of a kind, and a pair. Examples: 8-8-8-Q-Q or J-J-J-3-3. The suits don't matter.

Flush: A hand with all cards in the same suit. Example: J-10-7-5-2 all diamonds.

Straight: Five cards in sequence but not of the same suit. Example: J-10-9-8-7 in mixed suits. An ace-high straight is the highest of the straights.

Three of a Kind: Three cards of the same rank and two odd-ball cards. Example: 7-7-7-A-4.

Two Pair: Two separate pairs of identically ranked cards and an odd card. Example: Q-Q-6-6-2 or A-A-8-8-Q.

One Pair: Two cards of the same rank and three odd cards. Example: 3-3-7-Q-10.

No Pair: Five odd cards not of the same suit and not in any sequence. When two or more players hold this hand, the one with the highest ranked card wins the pot.

TIDBIT: Some slang for certain poker hands: the "Jewelry Store" is a diamond flush, the "Dallas To Fort Worth" is three tens (because 30 miles separated the two cities), an "Arkansas Straight" is a hand containing every other card, such as 2-4-6-8-10, which is a totally worthless hand, and the "Dead Man's Hand" is two aces and two eights. It was named for the hand Wild Bill Hickok had when he was shot in the back at a poker table. Gamblers have called the queen of spades the "Calamity Jane" and the four of clubs the "Devil's bedposts." "Elk River" was also used to mean a hand with three tens.

Cheating at poker can be done with "cold decks." Cards are previously stacked by the crooked gambler to give the *other* players great poker hands, but with the "card sharp" getting the best hand, thus causing the other players to bid the pot up. "Holdouts" are good cards kept from a previous hand, collected until they can be used to make a winning hand. The extra cards are "put in the dirt": secretly returned to the discard pile by pushing the pile away as if it's bothering the crooked gambler because it's too close. Sometimes the "tinhorn" works with a "confederate" across the table, the two working together and splitting their winnings after the game. In the "stripped deck," certain cards such as the Aces have the edges trimmed slightly at an angle so when they are reversed in the deck, they can be pulled out of the stack with the thumb and first finger and put on top of the deck while shuffling. The cowboys called these decks "high-belly strippers." "Reflectors" were cards with small indentations on their backs, so they could be identified by the card sharp. The glare of kerosene lanterns made the dents show up.

Poker odds. Here are the odds of drawing a given poker hand with the first five cards dealt. (The opportunity to draw additional cards in draw poker improves these odd depending on how many cards are drawn.

ROYAL FLUSH	1 in 649,740.00
STRAIGHT FLUSH	1 in 72,193.33
FOUR OF A KIND	1 in 4,165.00
FULL HOUSE	1 in 694.16
FLUSH	1 in 508.80
STRAIGHT	1 in 254.80
THREE OF A KIND	1 in 47.32
TWO PAIR	1 in 21.03
ONE PAIR	1 in 2.36
NO PAIR	1 in 1.99

TIDBIT: Dealing from the bottom of the deck. Slight-of-hand techniques by an accomplished gambler of the Old West would always give him control of the game of poker. Such card manipulation as *palming*, the *double-lift*, the *pass*, and *false shuffles*, gave the professional gambler the edge. *Palming* allowed the card sharp to hide a card in the palm or on the back of his hand; the *double-lift* allowed him to show you what appears to be the top card of a deck, when it was really the second card down; the *pass* allowed him to place a selected card on the top or bottom of the deck; and *false shuffles*, are just that, they looked like the dealer was shuffling the cards when he was doing no such thing, keeping important cards in the same place in the deck. So poker players beware!

---

6. MONTE. A game popular in the Southwest, it traces its history back to Spain. A Spanish deck of 40 cards is used—the eights, nines, and tens are removed from a standard 52-card deck. With the dealer holding the deck face down, he draws the two bottom cards and places them on the table face up; this is the *bottom layout.* He then draws two more cards from the top of the deck; this is the *top layout.* The deck is then turned face up to reveal the bottom card (called the *gate*). If it matches in denomination, a card in either *layout,* the dealer pays any bets placed on those cards. If the card isn't a match, but is of the same suit, it still might payoff a small return. The odds in this game heavily favored the dealer, and since dealers of the Old West were usually crooked as a snake's back anyway, the chances of a player walking away from the table with any money in his pocket was slim indeed. Because of this, the game developed bad favor and fell into disuse.

7. THREE-CARD-MONTE. In this game (which has no relation to *monte*), sometimes know as "Tossin' The Broad," the monte dealer (the *thrower*) shows the player three cards: two black aces and one red ace, for example, or two red kings and one black queen. The dealer throws the three cards face down on a table, shift-

---

Ttivia Question: When does a pair of sixes beat four aces?
ANS: When they're six-guns!

The White Elephant Saloon, Fredericksburg, Texas (dk)

ing their position several times until they come to lie neatly in a row. The dealer asks the player to pick out the black ace (or the queen—"the lady"). If the player picks it, he wins back his money two to one. The cards are bent slightly lengthwise to make it easier to shuffle the three cards (called *rickets*); it also allows the monte dealer to use a little slight-of-hand to put the black ace on the table anywhere he wants to, while creating the illusion that that card is somewhere else. The player is a sucker and can't win at this game. The con man often has a confederate (an associate) in the crowd who plays the game, and wins, to get skeptical onlookers enticed to try their luck. The dealer usually lets a player try out the game without placing a bet—and amazingly he wins, "why the odds are just 3 to 1!" he says. The player is hooked, he puts his money on the table. And from then on the poor sucker loses.

> **Monte Dealer Banter.** *"Here you are gentlemen; this Ace of Hearts is the winning card. Watch it closely. Follow it with your eye as I shuffle. Here it is, and now here, now here and now (laying the three cards on the table face down) where? If you point it out the first time, you win, but if you miss, you lose. Here it*

is, you see (turning it up); now watch it again (shuffling). This ace of hearts, gentlemen, is the winning card. I take no bets from paupers, cripples or orphan children! The ace of hearts. It is my regular trade, gentlemen—to move my hands quicker than your eyes. I always have two chances to your one. The ace of hearts. If your sight is quick enough, you beat me and I pay; if not, I beat you and take your money. The ace of hearts; who will go me twenty?"

—source unknown

8. THE SHELL GAME. Three walnut shells and a pea, that's all that's needed to con a man out of his hard-earned money. In this game, played the same as *three-card-monte,* the unsuspecting victim is invited to keep his eye on the shuffled shells and bet which one contains the pea. Slight-of-hand by the dealer allows him to control the movement of the pea.

9. KENO. This game was much like today's game of *bingo* and is still played in some casinos. In large gambling halls with long tables, sat hundreds of players who waited for "the roller" at each table to release a numbered ivory ball from the neck of the "goose," a container that could be spun to shake up the 90 balls. Players bought Keno cards—each with random numbers on them—from the house, and placed buttons on the cards over the drawn numbers. The first person with five numbers in a row yells out "keno" and is the winner. The game originally evolved from the English game of *lotto.* The "goose" could, of course, be rigged by the house

---

TIDBIT: Today, a TINHORN is anyone who makes a "flashy appearance on a cheap scale." The phrase began during the 49er gold rush in California, and was applied to gamblers who could not afford to play the more aristocratic and costly game of *Faro* and were relegated to playing the less pretentious game of *Chuck-A-Luck.* The game of *Chuck-A-Luck* used a cone-shaped container called a "tin horn" to shake up the dice. Those without a lot of money, or didn't want to spend a lot, would play the game. These players were "cheap," and came to be called "tinhorns," a word that evolved into today's use of the term.

A south-of-the-border saloon, Old Tucson Studios, Tucson, Arizona (dk)

TIDBIT: The term PASSING THE BUCK began in the 1860's with the introduction of *draw poker,* where it became customary to pass the deal to the left after each hand. To keep track of who had the deal, some object—usually a knife—was passed around; placed in front of the dealer. And in those days most knives had Buckhorn handles. Any player who did not want to deal would ante up and then pass the buck. It naturally followed that the term would come to mean "letting someone else perform a task originally imposed upon one or letting someone else take the blame."

to drop prearranged numbers which would allow a house "confederate" to win (and thus everyone else lose). Cowboys picked up the word "keno" and used it as an exclamation meaning "fantastic." Kids were still using the word in the 1960's.

10. THE WHEEL OF FORTUNE. A large spoked wheel mounted on a post, and having randomly placed numbers painted around the rim, is spun after bets are placed. A clapper mounted at the top of the wheel chatters as it hits small dowels protruding from the perimeter of the wheel. Eventually—agonizingly—the wheel would gradually come to a stop, the winning number to be found under the clapper.

11. CHUCK-A-LUCK. This game of English origin came to America about 1800. It is played with three dice, the gamblers betting the house that a) all three will turn up with the same number (called a *raffle*), or (b) that the sum of the three die will equal a certain number, or (c) that at least one of the three die will appear with a specific number on its face. The three die were thrown into a cone-shaped container made of tin that looked much like a horn, then shaken, and the horn laid down on the table so the dice could not be seen. Players would then place their bets on which numbers were showing on the dice. Bets were placed on a layout stenciled with the numbers 1 through 6 called the *baffling board.* The man who tumbled the dice was know as the "tinhorn gambler," a name which later came to be used as a derogatory term for anyone with low stature.

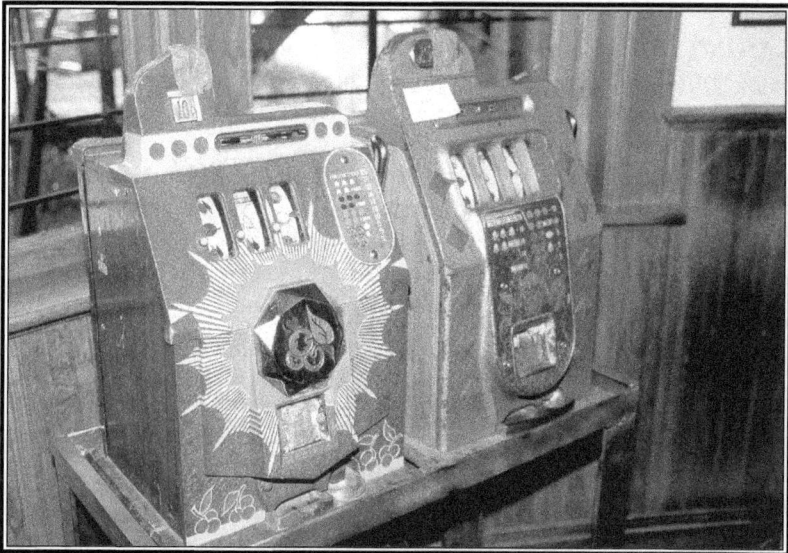

Early one-armed bandits at the South Park City Museum, Fairplay, Colorado (dk)

TIDBIT: A famous woman gambler was the legendary POKER ALICE—her real name "Alice Ivers"—who learned gambling from her mining engineer husband who took to gambling establishments for amusement. She picked up the trade, began carrying a pistol and smoking cigars, and for the next forty years—in six states—operated gambling halls and whorehouses. In her career, she shot two men, killing one of them. She died in 1930 at the age of 79, quite old for a lady in her line of work.

A Match Game
GAMBLING LINGO

Match the Old West gambling terms to their meaning. The words are grouped in fours to make the task easier.

1. Hearse driver
2. Card mechanic
3. Pigeon
4. Saddle-blanket gambler

a. crooked faro dealer.
b. cowboy addicted to gambling.
c. case keeper.
d. victim of professional gambler.

5. Box cars
6. Big Joe from Boston
7. Snake eyes
8. Ada Ross, the stable hoss

e. in dice, eight as a point.
f. in dice, ten as a point.
g. in dice, a pair of sixes.
h. in dice, a pair of *aces* (ones).

9. Load the Doctor
10. Cold deck
11. Brace box
12. Strippers

i. a stacked deck.
j. faro box.
k. trimmed cards.
l. weighted dice.

13. Deadfall
14. Monkey flush
15. Lincoln skins
16. Kitty

m. greenbacks.
n. shady gambling establishment.
o. a fund for refreshments.
p. three cards of a flush.

ANS: 1-c, 2-a, 3-d, 4-b. 5-g, 6-f, 7-h, 8-e. 9-l, 10-i, 11-j, 12-k. 13-n, 14-p, 15-m, 16-o.

2 POKER MOVIE TRIVIA QUESTIONS

1. Name the murder-mystery western that centered around a poker game and starred Dean Martin and Robert Mitchum.
ANS: *5 Card Stud*, (1968).

2. Name the western based on a play about a poker playing con-game starring Henry Fonda and Joanne Woodward.
ANS: *A Big Hand for the Little Lady*, (1966).

Oatman, Arizona (dk)

Cuspidors and Card Tables

Cuspidors and Card Tables
THE WESTERN SALOON

"No shooting, cutting, fighting, or loud cussing allowed,
and absolutely no spitting on floor. —R. Bean, Prop."
(Sign in Judge Roy Bean Saloon, Langtry, Texas)

The saloon of the Frontier West was a long narrow room with a couple of wood planks thrown over a pair of whiskey barrels. It usually had a dirt floor, and not a single place to sit—just standing room at the bar. The spittoon was a plain wood box filled with sawdust. Contrast that with the large city saloon during its heyday: a long hand-carved, imported mahogany bar with gold-leaf trim and a shiny brass rail running along the bottom, red flocked wall paper, a kerosene-lantern chandelier, and brass "gaboons" scattered about the solid oak floor. Either way, there was plenty of liquor and a good time to be had by all. Ballads from an old upright player piano, the tinkling of shot glasses, the shuffling of cards, and the clatter of poker chips made the saloon a bright and boisterous place on any night of the week.

"The saloon has become an icon of the America's Wild West. Through those swinging doors was the center of a man's universe after a hard days work. It was the focal point of all his free-time activities, not just drinking and gambling, but socializing. It was the center of the community. And the saloon was, for all practical purposes, the "first public building" in every frontier town. It was up and running long before the churches and long before the bordellos. It is said that most of western history was made inside these boisterous saloons. Democracy was built in these saloons with heated debates on the slavery issue, the next territorial governor, or the pros and cons of admission to the Union. Sometimes the saloon served as a courthouse with jury trials held on short notice with half-drunk customers as jurists. The saloon keeper might have also been the judge, he just wore a different hat. And there was frequent entertainment that included a barroom brawl or a little gunplay or both." —Don Kirk, "Redrock Canyon Territory" (1996).

RULES FOR PATRONS
Of The

BRASS RAIL SALOON

♥ SHOTGUNS WILL BE DEPOSITED WITH THE BARKEEP ♥

SADDLE TRAMPS AND DROVERS MUST CHECK ALL HARDWARE.

►♦ THAT INCLUDES KNIVES! ◄♦

ALL PATRONS WILL KINDLY USE THE SPITTOONS

THROWING CHAIRS AT THE BAR MIRROR

☞ WILL NOT BE TOLERATED! ☜

Barroom Brawlers Will Pay For All Damages To Chairs, Tables,
Glassware, Chandeliers, And Balustrades.

NO MORE THAN FIVE PLAYERS ALLOWED AT EACH POKER TABLE.

CARD CHEATS WILL HANG IF NOT SHOT FIRST

►♦ ALL FACE-OFFS WILL BE MOVED OUT TO THE STREET. ◄♦

NO DRINKS ON THE HOUSE UNLESS PAID FOR IN ADVANCE

MULESKINNERS AND FUR TRAPPERS

♥ NOT ALLOWED UPSTAIRS WITHOUT A BATH ♥

Obscene Language Will Not Be Tolerated.

❖ SHEEPHERDERS ❖
NOT WELCOME

Humorous Similitude of Old West broadside created by the author

Keepin' The Doors A-swingin'
27 DUST CUTTERS OF THE OLD WEST

"Name your poison gentlemen,
if we haven't got it, we'll make it."
—barkeep in "Gunsmoke," 1953

isted here are actual **"dust cutters"** sold in the saloons of the Old West. If these drinking parlors had kept a "Bill of Fare" posted behind the bar, it might have looked something like this. This list is based on actual slang names for concoctions of the period with popular phrases that were used to describe them. And a pinch of actual recipes for these drinks are sprinkled throughout.

1. **Apache Tears.** Guaranteed to make the roughest customer weep. Shipped direct from Tombstone.
2. **Block And Tackle.** One swig is enough to make a man walk a block and tackle anything.
3. **Blue Ruin.** A Torchlight whiskey imported from Leadville. A favorite of Buffalo Bill Cody.
4. **Brave-Maker.** For all you brave souls, it's potent enough to make a hummingbird spit in a rattlesnake's eye!
5. **Bumblebee.** The whiskey with a sting. Drink with caution, it will make your ears buzz! Plenty kept in stock.
6. **Corn Licker.** Dare you try it? One swig will have all the sensations of having swallowed a lighted kerosene lamp. A sudden violent jolt of this burning beast has been known to stop the victim's watch, snap his suspenders, and crack his glass eye right across!
7. **Creepin' Whiskey.** Careful. It will creep up behind you and knock you down.
8. **Forty Rod.** A genuine forty-niner drink, the smell of which will fell a man at that distance, even around a corner. Because of this, we require that you drink it out back.

Rio Diablo saloon set, Alamo Village, Brackettville, Texas (dk)

9. **Green Whiskey.** Davy Crockett once said of this drink that it was so hot you didn't need your food cooked for at least two months.

10. **Irish Whiskey.** We make it to your satisfaction by starting with a barrel of New Orleans wine and adding a pint of creosote, a pound of burned sugar in grape juice, and a plug of chewing tobacco to give it bead. Satisfaction guaranteed or second drink free.

11. **Joy Juice.** One stout shot will tempt one to steal his own clothes, two shots will make him bite off his own ears, while three slugs will instill in him the desire to save his drowning mother-in-law. We're not responsible for any brawls you might get into.

12. **Lake Whiskey.** Shipped from Chicago. Fine as silk.

13. **Lamp Oil Licker.** One shot will keep a man well lit. Don't smoke after a slug of this firewater.

14. **Red Dynamite.** The Miner's Friend. This, our most powerful gut warmer, will blow your head clean off! Do you dare try it? Guaranteed to out blast any other explosive or your money back.

15. **Red Disturbance.** Potent enough to raise a blood blister on a rawhide boot. Don't spill a drop; we've already got too many holes in the floor.

16. **Red Dog.** Tucson's finest phlegm cutter. The stuff legends are made of.

17. **Red Eye.** The "King of Lickers." So strong it'll eat rifling from a gun barrel.

18. **Sheepherder's Delight.** Made from clear alcohol, plug tobacco, prune juice (for color and taste), and strychnine to enhance the jolt.

19. **Skull Bender.** Deadlier than an Indian tomahawk. It makes sane men walk into walls. A specialty of Custer City.

20. **Stone Fence.** So potent that one swig is like running into one. Made of a shot of rye and a twist of lemon in a glass of cider.

21. **Taos Lighting.** Imported from Old Towse, New Mexico. A favorite of trappers and Indians. One shot will strike a man down on the spot. A baked apple is included in every glass.

22. **Tanglelegs.** This drink will tie your toes in knots. A gripping concoction of tobacco, molasses, red pepper and our best raw alcohol.

23. **Tarantula Juice.** A most powerful poison. Just the thing after a day in the mines. It will have you reeling around like a pup trying to find a soft spot to lie down in.

24. **Tequila Twister.** This rotgut will put a man into a spin and have him swinging from the nearest chandelier.

25. **Tom And Jerry.** A specialty for the Dudes and Dandies. Contains whiskey with hen fruit, saccharine substance, and lacteal fluid [eggs, sugar, and milk]. Drink up!

26. **White Mule.** Corn whiskey with a most powerful kick. Satisfaction guaranteed.

27. **Who Shot John.** This drink will fell a man instantly. A second shot free if you can stand up to the first. Guaranteed 100 proof or better!

Some More Old West names for Whiskeys and Ales:

Ginger Pop	Coffin Varnish	Stump-Puller	Apple Dam
Skull Popper	Kickapoo Jubilee	Widow-Maker	Pop Skull
Old Pepper	Rooster Tail	Spanish Sack	DoLittle
Tiger Spit	Holland Gin	Lucky Lady	Valley Tan

RULES OF THIS TAVERN

I

No gambling allowed in dining room or elsewhere on premises.

II

No gambling allowed in bedrooms.

III

No credit extended except to those with proper credentials and in proper standing. Bills payable on demand in current specie.

IV

Gentlemen imbibing foreign and alien spirits other than Bourbon whiskey may be requested to pay in cash.

V

Gentlemen must not leave their horses beyond three months, otherwise they will be sold at auction and poundage charged.

VI

No Gentlemen will wear or display firearms on the premises. Upon arrival, all pieces must be laid at the entrance to the tavern.

VII

No Gentlemen showing the ill temper of having consumed beyond his capacity will be served at bar or table.

VIII

No cock-fighting within hearing distance.

— By Order of Jim Porter, Proprietor
Froggy Grog Inn, Louisville, Kentucky, 1857

Humorous Similitude of Old West Broadside created by the author

Step Up To The Bar
58 WESTERN SALOON NAMES

*"Sepin' some woman o'course, they ain't
nothin' 'prettiern' a full bottle."*
—a town drunk in a "Gunsmoke" episode.

Here are some **actual saloon names** from towns of the Wild West and from Hollywood films. And naming saloons sounds like fun, so I added a few of my own.

ACTUAL SALOONS:

Bucket Of Blood
Red Onion
Long Branch
The Stockman
Soapy Smith
Double Eagle
Bale Of Hay
Buckhorn Exchange
Pioneer Club
Copper Dollar
Chicago Saloon
The Cosmopolitan
The El Dorado
Bull's Head
Bob's Place
Frenchy's Place
The Office Bar
St. Louis House
Kelly's
Last Chance
Blue Front
Rio Grande
No. 10
The Winchester

The California Bar
The Horse Shoe
The Senate
The San Francisco
The Jersey Lilly
Sheehan's
The San Francisco
First Chance
Holy Moses

FROM MOVIES:

Silver Dollar
Red Dog
Golden Eagle

> **Tidbit:** Tom Mix, star of westerns from 1909 to 1935, was a bartender at the Blue Bell Saloon in Guthrie, Oklahoma.

THE AUTHOR'S:

(any similiarity to actual saloons is purely coincidental)

Marty Muldoon's
The Blood-Shot Eyeball
The Brass Rail
Golden Nugget
Crippled Dog
Pick & Shovel
Prospector Pete's
The Buzzard's Roost
Dry Gulch
Red Garter
Crystal Palace
The Pocket Pistol
The Gargle & Spit
Crow Bait
Shorty's Sawdust
The Nickel Spitoon
The Capitol
Donkey Dan's
The Nighcrawler
The Grubworm
The President's Palace

A Match Game
4 MOVIE SALOONS

Okay, here's a tough one. Match the western saloon with the movie or television series it was in!

1. The Long Branch	**a.** Bonanza
2. The Last Chance	**b.** Union Pacific
3. The Silver Dollar	**c.** The Rifleman
4. The Golden Nugget	**d.** Gunsmoke

ANS: 1-d, 2-c, 3-a, 4-b.

Movie still from "Gunsmoke." James Arness sits in the Long Branch Saloon with Amanda Blake, Buck Taylor, Ken Curtis and Milburn Stone (Arness Productions & CBS Television)

Trivia Question: Who played the bartender (barkeep, bardog) of the Long Branch Saloon in television's longest running western? **ANS:** Glen Strange as *Sam* on "Gunsmoke" (1955-1975).

Advertising
14 SALOON SIGNS

"All Nations Welcome Except Carrie"
—sign on saloon in South Pass City, Wyoming.

Here are a sampling of signs that were actually posted in the frontier saloons of the American West:

Thirst Comes First, Drink Till You
Burst! Everything Else Can Wait.

Dust Cutters For Those Dry Enough To Spit Cotton!

ALL BOTTLE LABELS GENUINE

We Have A Good Supply Of Apache Cactus Beer
SO POWERFUL IT CANNOT BE CORKED!

DRIFTER & ROVERS
We Have Your Favorite To Cut That Trail Dust!

Freighters And Miners Welcome
Fur Trappers Would Be Obliged To Take A Bath Before Entering

We Got On Hand The Best Dust Cutters In Town!
All Drinks Served With The Snakes Strained Out First.

BEER   WHISKEY
15 Cents A Glass   Two Bits A Shot

It Was Outside This Saloon
That Wild Bill First Demonstrated His Skill
At Driving A Cork Into A Whiskey Bottle
Without Breaking The Neck.
He Used A .36 Caliber Bullet. One Shot.

NO SUBSTITUTES SOLD HERE.

No Fusel Oil, Oil Of Turpentine, Or Varnish Solvent

California Champagne

50¢ A Quart. Imported $1.00
Some Cocktails Available.
(Egg Nog Made For Special Customers)

All Barrelhouse Whiskey $3.00 A Gallon

NO SNAKE HEAD WHISKEY SOLD HERE!

BIGGEST 5 CENT BEER IN TOWN

In God We Trust
All Others Pay Cash

Tidbit: Whether it was called a *gaboon, cuspidor* or *spittoon*, it was an essential fixture in every saloon and place of entertainment. A bowl made of brass, nickel or tin—or just a wooden box filled with sawdust—it sat on the wooden floor ready to receive the sputum of the tobacce chewin' westerner.

Tidbit: When a cowboy *hears the owl hoot*, it means he has gotten drunk.

In Without Knocking, 1909, oil on canvas by Charles M. Russell (1864-1926) DECA
(A cowman in the Old West did indeed, on occasion, ride his horse into a saloon.)

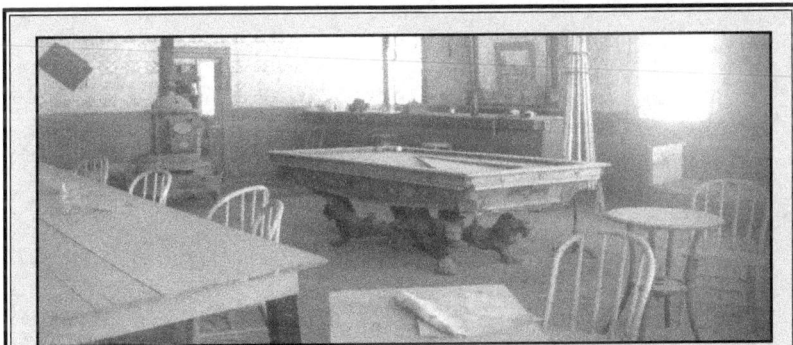

Ghosts are still drinking in this saloon, Bodie State Historic Park, Bodie, California

9 NAMES FOR THE WESTERN SALOON

"Don't spill that liquor, son. It eats right through the bar."
—Walter Brennan, *The Westerner,*1940.

1. Watering Hole
2. Bucket of Blood
3. Hurdy-Gurdy House
4. Whiskey Mill
5. Honkey Tonk
6. Cantina
7. Dive
8. Gin Mill
9. Saloon

Michael Jay Smith as Doc W.T. "Wrong Tooth" Hennessey, photo and costume by the author

Nomadic Hustler, Peddler, and Quack
PATENT-MEDICINE SALESMEN

*"Step right up folks. You've heard about it, you've read about it,
and for years you've looked forward to it."*
—salesman's banter

Before the Pure Food and Drug Act of 1906, the traveling patent medicine salesman stood on the back of his colorfully-decorated wagon, pitching his cure-all nostrums, most of which were nothing more than sugar water or alcohol he bottled the night before. To sell his miracle concoctions, he would add a little exotic entertainment to rally the crowd.

13 WAGON ENTERTAINMENTS

1. Tumblers
2. Minstrels
3. Fortune tellers
4. Ventriloquism acts
5. An alligator on a leash
6. Sword swallowers
7. Jugglers
8. Singing quartets
9. Monkey shenanigans
10. Jokes or magic tricks
11. Brass band or banjo music
12. Fire-eaters
13. Witness a free tooth extraction by a "painless" dentist!

36 ACTUAL PATENT MEDICINES

Narcotics use was common in the Old West. Narcotics could be found in the patent medicines of the day and in doctor prescribed medications like Laudanum and Paregoric. Opiates were used during the Civil War to treat diarrhea, malaria and dysentery, and later used just for pleasure, available through your favorite wish book: the *Sears & Roebuck* catalog. *Coca-Cola,* patented in 1886, contained some cocaine. *Bayer* sold a cough suppressant made with heroin. Cocaine was touted as a

Apothecary's display window, Nevada City, Montana (dk)

cure for morphine and alcohol addiction. The nineteenth century was an era when chemists experimented with the new drug technologies hoping to cure all ills, but had no knowledge of potential side effects. With that serious note, here then are some names of ACTUAL patent medicines.

Ayer's Extract of Sarsaparilla
Dr. Dickey's Old Reliable Eye Water
Kickapoo Indian Prairie Plant & Worm Killer
Hoffland's Entirely Vegetable German Bitters
Dr. Thomson's Celebrated Eye Water Tiger Fat
Dr. Radway's Sarsaparillian Renovating Resolvent

Sanford's Invigorater
Hamlin's Wizard Oil
Dr. Acker's English Elixir
Black-Draught
Kickapoo Indian Salve
Burnett's Cocane
Dr. Kilmer's Swamp Root
Boker's Stomach Bitters
California Waters of Life
Oregon Kidney Tea
Cram's Fluid Lighting
Hooker's Wigwam Tonic
Mexican Mustang
Prickly Ash Bitters

Dr. King's Indian Worm Eradicator
Mulford's Laxative Salts of Fruit
Dr. Raphael's Galvanic Love Powders
Dr. Simm's Arsenic Complexion Wafers
Lydia Pinkham's Vegetable Compound
Dr. Miles Rheumatic Blood Purifyer
Dr. Seth Arnold's Cough Killer.
Hostetter's Celebrated Stomach Bitters
Gilbert & Parsons Hygienic Whiskey
Dr. McMunn's Elixer of Opium
Barker's Nerve & Bone Linament
Thayer's Slippery Elm Lozenges
Dr. Haswell's Witch Hazel Creme
Gold's Liquid Beef Tonic

18 DISEASES PATENT
MEDICINES CAN CURE

("...cures instantly with lasting relief.")

1. Hair Loss	7. Rheumatism	13. Consumption
2. Diphtheria	8. Nervous Disease	14. Hysterics
3. Corns	9. Ringworm	15. Drunkeness
4. Epileptic Fits	10. Female Weakness	16. Insanity
5. Syphilis	11. Heart Palpitations	17. Lost Vigor
6. Paralysis	12. Tobacco Habits	18. Back Spasms

4 GADGET CURES

1. Magnetic Rings   2. Electric Belts   3. Trusses   4. Vaporizors

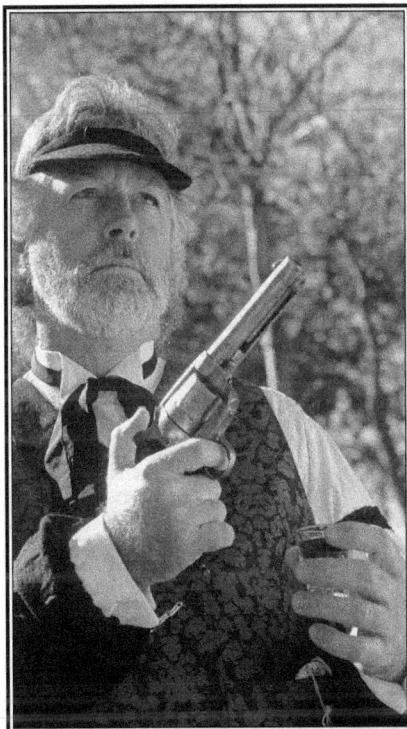

C.R. Nowell as "Cap": "Don't shoot in the direction of my bar mirror!" (dk)

Pharmacy bottles, Nevada City, Montana (dk)

MEDICINE SHOW BALLYHOO

"...and now for the first time in Cheyenne: Dr. Foy's Bull Nectar, cures warts, opens the bowels, prolongs life ... [aside] *Now don't smile Mister* [looking back at crowd] *because I have here today the living proof of what I tell ya': Mr. C.Y. Yatze. Now at the tender age of eight, Mr. Yatze contracted the most horrible and incurable disease, the name of which I can't mention to Christian people. He began taking this potent Elixir ... and now ladies and gentlemen Mr. Yanatze is one hundred and eleven years old, thanks to the preservative* [old man takes a drink] *and health rendering powers of Blue Nectar!* [Music starts, old man dances, when music stops the old man stops dancing, sits down and the crowd cheers. The barker continues.] *The good people of New Orleans, stood in line, in the rain, for the rare opportunity of paying one dollar, for a bottle of this Miracle Magic. Today, I'm letting it go for 50 cents a bottle or $3.00 a case! ..."*

—*Cheyenne Social Club,* 1970

MORE MEDICINE SHOW BANTOR

"Allright, thank you my friends, thank you. Now we're gonna have some more entertainment here in just a minute neighbors, but right now my friends, I've got a message for you—listen friends, let me tell you something—long before the hand of man set foot in this country, it was uninhabited, yeah, only Indians lived here—and sickness among those Indians—my friends and neighbors—was absolutely unknown, because—that's what I wanted you to ask me friends—why? I'll tell you why, because they had the secret, they had the secret of good health, they had a compound my friend. A compound made of loose herbs, barks, and bitters—and that compound is known as Dr. Carter's Famous Indian Remedy. Listen friends, I wanna tell ya something. Fifteen years ago, I was given up by the doctor, yes, they told me that. I couldn't live for a week, but I fooled 'em—yes sir—and I got well, and let me tell you something, if you've got the proper amount of determination, listen, you can overcome any kind of a physical handicap with the proper amount of determination. Why listen, I once knew a man that didn't have a tooth in his head, yet that man learned to play a base drum better than anybody I ever listened to. Now that's an absolute fact friends. I only deal in facts. I'm telling you the truth. I went out in the country; I went out in the open spaces and I lived with the Indians and I was cured by those Indians. I was cured by taking that secret compound of theirs, and let me tell you something that those Indians, my friends—for generations—have been laughing up their sleeves, uh—at least laughing up their blankets—at the doctors, and that's an absolute fact and I've brought back with me to civilization, the secret of that marvelous compound know today as Dr. Carter's Indian Remedy. And now friends, I'm gonna give you an opportunity to buy a bottle of that remedy for the advertised price of one dollar—one dollar is all she'll ask—right now I'm goin' on with the entertainment."

—*Paradise Canyon*, 1935

The author as Buck "Flea Bite" Skinner, photo by Michael Jay Smith

Land, Loot, and Larceny
OLD WEST HISTORICAL EVENTS

*"All men were made by the same great spirit. They
are all brothers. The earth is the mother of all people,
and all people should have equal rights upon it."*
—Chief Joseph, Nez Percé Indian Nation

This chapter is intended to give an overall structure to the settlement of the American West. It's a chronology of events from the real American West so you can compare them with the incidents portrayed in movies and novels. It's always interesting to see famous people represented in movies at the wrong age, in the wrong period, in the wrong place, with weapons that hadn't even been invented yet. This and other chapters will help you ferret out the truth and provide another layer of depth to the westerns you watch, many of which are very shallow and bear little resemblance to actual historical reality.

When did the Old West begin and when did it end? The opinion of historians varies greatly on this subject. The most popular era by western fans is the 1860 to 1890 wild west period when western expansion was exploding by leaps and bounds—with cattle drives, Indian wars, booming mining towns, and railroads connecting to all points west. But that time frame leaves out the mountain men and fur trade era, the California gold rush, the Mormon trek west, the Battle of the Alamo, and the Mexican War. But if you start the western era with the 1803 Louisiana Purchase—when we acquired a large part of the West—and then end with the publication of Owen Wister's 1902 novel *The Virginian*—the first western novel, because that was the beginning of the myth of the West—well, you have about one hundred fascinating years of the Old West (1803-1902); and that's a nice round number and a more true picture of the whole story of the people that settled the American west. (For a fictional condensation of western expansion, see the blockbuster, originally-awseomely-presented-three-projector Cinerama epic, *How the West Was Won* (1962). Unfortunately—sorrowfully—the reader will likely never have the opportunity to see it as originally presented.)

LARGE DISCOUNTS FOR CASH.

BETTER TERMS THAN EVER!

THE BEST

PRAIRIE LANDS

IN

IOWA AND NEBRASKA

ARE FOR SALE BY THE

BURLINGTON & MISSOURI RIVER RAILROAD CO.

10 Years Credit LOW PRICES 6 PER CENT INTEREST
ONLY THE INTEREST PAYMENT DOWN.
PAYMENTS OF PRINCIPAL BEGIN THE FOURTH YEAR.

PROSPECTS will PAY FOR LAND and IMPROVEMENTS
BUY BEFORE JULY 1st, 1875, and Secure these Terms.

BUY LAND EXPLORING TICKETS

And the Cost of Same will be Allowed on First Payment made
on Land bought within 90 Days from Date of Ticket.

HALF FARE to Families of Purchasers.
LOW FREIGHTS on Household Goods and Farm Stock.

— LAND COMMISSIONER B. & M. R. R.

PREMIUMS FOR IMPROVEMENTS.

Text from an actual Old West handbill

Bargain Basement Prices
6 U.S. LAND ACQUISITIONS

"The country itself is the best I have ever seen for producing all the products of Spain. But what I am sure of is that there is not any gold or any other metal in all of that country."
—Juan Vásquez de Coronado.

The U.S. government fought and bargained its way west to the Pacific Ocean, to the Rio Grande, to the 49th Parallel—millions of acres of land with infinite possibilities, all acquired in just 50 years.

1. Louisiana Purchase (1803). (Montana, Wyoming, Eastern Colorado, Oklahoma, Kansas, Nebraska, North and South Dakota, Minnesota, Iowa, Missouri, Arkansas and Louisiana.) Purchased from France for 15 million dollars; 828,000 square miles. In one acquisition, the size of the United States was doubled. Napoleon's plans for a colonial empire were dashed.

2. Ceded by Britain (1818). (Eastern half of North Dakota and western Minnesota.)

3. Texas Annexation. (1845). (Texas, eastern half of New Mexico and part of Colorado.) Texas is annexed to the U.S. as the 28th state.

4. Oregon Country (1846). (Washington, Oregon, Idaho, and the western part of Montana.) A treaty with the British sets Oregon's northern border at the 49th parallel.

5. Ceded by Mexico (1848). (California, Nevada, Utah, Arizona, and the western part of New Mexico and Colorado.) The *Treaty of Guadalupe Hidalgo* promises all benefits of U.S. citizenship to Mexican Americans and $15 million dollars goes to Mexico for all of the land north of the Rio Grande, which amounted to 1,193,061 square miles.

6. Gadsden Purchase (1853). (Southern part of Arizona and a piece of New Mexico.) U.S. paid Mexico $10 million for 300,000 square miles. The U.S. wanted it for constructing a southern transcontinental railroad route. The *Southern Pacific* railroad was completed in 1881 and a bonanza of gold and silver was soon discovered on the purchase.

16 PRESIDENTS OF THE U. S.

Government **politics,** often the main topic of discussion in the smoke-filled western saloon, started many a raucous saloon brawl. Debates over becoming a territory or inviting federal troops to fight the Indians always led the "presidential debates." It behooves a western fan to know when the presidents were in office so he can participate in any saloon brawl. (Interestingly, as the Frontier came to an end with its freedom and self-reliance, Progressivism was taking hold under Roosevelt.)

3. **1801-1809** Thomas Jefferson
4. **1809-1817** James Madison
5. **1817-1825** James Monroe
6. **1825-1829** John Quincy Adams
7. **1829-1837** Andrew Jackson
8. **1837-1841** Martin Van Buren
9. **1841** William H. Harrison
10. **1841-1845** John Tyler
11. **1845-1849** James K. Polk
12. **1849-1850** Zachary Taylor
13. **1850-1853** Millard Fillmore
14. **1853-1857** Franklin Pierce
15. **1857-1861** James Buchanan
16. **1861-1865** Abraham Lincoln
17. **1865-1869** Andrew Johnson
18. **1869-1877** Ulysses S. Grant
19. **1877-1881** Rutherford Hayes
20. **1881-1881** James A. Garfield
21. **1881-1885** Chester A. Arthu
22. **1885-1889** Grover Cleveland
23. **1889-1893** Benjamin Harrison
24. **1893-1897** Grover Cleveland
25. **1897-1901** William McKinley
26. **1901-1909** Theodore Roosevelt

WHEN 21 STATES JOINED THE UNION

In less that a century the wild American West—dry, barren, and wind swept—went from colonial rule to self-government. When the population of a territory reached "5,000 free male voters," it could send a non-voting representative to Congress. When it reached 60,000 it could petition for admission to the Union. But it was politics in Washington that usually determined when approval was made. The slave issue in the 1850's held back several states.

1812 Louisiana	**1859** Oregon	**1889** Washington
1821 Missouri	**1861** Kansas	**1889** Montana
1836 Arkansas	**1864** Nevada	**1890** Idaho
1845 Texas	**1867** Nebraska	**1890** Wyoming
1846 Iowa	**1876** Colorado	**1896** Utah
1850 California	**1889** North Dakota	**1907** Oklahoma
1858 Minnesota	**1889** South Dakota	**1912** Arizona

When Did It All Happen?
AN OLD WEST CHRONOLOGY

"Do not misunderstand me, but understand me fully and my affection for the land. I never said the land was mine to do with as I chose. The one who has the right to dispose of it is the one who has created it. I claim a right to live on my land and accord you the privilege to live on yours."
—Chief Joseph, Nez Percé Indian Nation

The West was (and still is) mostly about conflict. It was a fight for either land or water. It was the ranchers versus the "sodbusters," laws versus individual freedoms, and Indian Nations versus the white man's Manifest Destiny. Men went "West" to acquire land, or convert the Indians to Christianity, or to collect furs for the ladies of England who thought beaver hats were "all the rage." The French came from the North, the Spanish from the South, the Chinese from the West and the English from the East. And the fact that this new frontier was dubbed "the West" and not "the North," etc., attests to the fact that the peoples from the East won the battle for this very special land.

Anyone professing to be a westerner should have some idea as to when historic and legendary events occurred in the American West, so here's a very brief and concise chronology of the inventions, transportation developments, battles, literature, federal laws and legendary figures that "settled" the American West. It's far from complete, but if you can remember all these places, names, and dates, you'll even impress a historian. It's also a great source for lots of trivia. I think you'll find it quite interesting.

1767 After hearing that Russian traders are building outposts along the Pacific Coast, the Spanish establish 21 missions in California as a way to protect their interests. Cities founded include San Diego, San Jose, San Francisco (1776), and Los Angeles (1781). The Christianized Indians die by the thousands from the white man's diseases.

1769 Indian fighter DANIEL BOONE, with his coonskin cap atop his head, crosses the Cumberland Gap (a pass through the Allegheny Ridge) and builds the Wilderness Road in 1775 which opens a floodgate to Kentucky and the West. With an amendment to the constitution, the Federal Government creates a commission to collect taxes by making the route a toll road.

1794 ELI WHITNEY'S cotton gin (gin was short for "engine") which separated the cotton from the seeds, made growing Upland Cotton a profitable enterprise, quickly spreading it—and slavery—throughout the West.

1804 MERIWETHER LEWIS AND WILLIAM CLARK go on a long camping trip to explore the Louisiana Purchase of 1803. They are gone for two years, four months and ten days, having crossed 7,689 miles of wilderness. Their report of a rich beaver supply in Washington and Oregon set off a rush of fur trappers West—the beginning of the legendary "Mountain Man."

1808 The *Missouri Gazette* of St. Louis is the first newspaper published west of the Mississippi. The *American Fur Company* is established by John Jacob Aster.

1821 STEPHEN F. AUSTIN establishes the first Anglo-American settlement in Texas at Columbus and Washington-On-The-Brazos. Mexico wins its independence from Spain (May 5th) and then welcomes Americans to Texas hoping settlement will discourage raids by Apache and Comanche Indians.

1824 JEDEDIAH SMITH, trail blazer, finds the South Pass in Wyoming route across the Rocky Mountains to Oregon and California. Congress creates the *Bureau of Indian Affairs.*

1825 The U. S. Government, which has decided to move all Indian tribes to the west of the Mississippi River, makes Kansas an Indian Territory. Thirty tribes are moved. The land is granted to them for "as long as grass grows and rivers run." The Republic of Mexico invites American colonization in the state of Texas-Coahuila and declares California to be a Territory of Mexico.

1826 Fur trapper JEDEDIAH STRONG SMITH leads a party of explorers west across the Great Salt Lake and the Mohave desert to Southern California. JAMES FENIMORE COOPER writes the

Bodie State Historic Park, Bodie, California (dk)
A genuine gold-mining ghost town preserved in "arrested decay." Founded about 1877,
the interiors remain as they were left, and are still stocked with goods.

Last of the Mohicans, one of many books he will write about frontier life.

1828 A rebellion breaks out in California against Mexican rule.

1829 The US Government offers to purchase "Texas" from Mexico. They decline to sell, but Americans continue to flood into the Mexican territory.

1830 The first steam locomotive, the "Tom Thumb," is built by PETER COOPER. Two engines are bought by the Baltimore and Ohio to replace the horses used to pull passenger coaches on rails. The legend of the West begins when MORGAN NEVILLE writes about the exploits of Mike Fink, the King of the keelboat men in *The Last of the Boatmen* (remember Walt Disney's Davy Crockett series?) The Mormon Church is founded at Fayette, New York by JOSEPH SMITH and 30 followers. The *Book of Mormon* is published later in the year. 200 steamboats move passengers and goods up the Ohio and Mississippi Rivers at the astounding rate of 25 mph downstream and 16 mph upstream. The *Indian Removal Act* is passed expediting forced resettlement of Tribes.

1831 CYRUS McCORMICK invents a gadget that will revolutionize farming on the prairie: the mechanical reaper, but it won't be until 1841 that he can sell his first two machines. 1950's school children will build little wooden models of his invention.

1832 Sioux Chief, BLACK HAWK refuses to recognize an 1804 treaty which ceded all their lands east of the Mississippi. His nation is massacred at Bad Axe River in Wisconsin. For the first time, Congress sends mounted troops West to protect travelers on the Santa Fe Trail; they become known as "Dragoons."

1833	SAMUEL COLT begins manufacturing a percussion pistol with a revolving cylinder at *Patent Arms Manufacturing Company* of Paterson, New Jersey. He gets a U.S. patent in 1836.
1834	In existence since 1822, *The American Fur Company* buys out the *Rocky Mountain Fur Co.* because there's no longer enough beaver left alive for the both of them to trap. It's a sign that the end of the fur trade and the Mountain Man is near. Indian Territory is created in present-day Oklahoma.
1835	GENERAL ANTONIO LOPEZ DE SANTA ANNA is elected President of Mexico and then declares himself a dictator. Lesson to be learned: be careful who you vote for.
1836	President SANTA ANNA tries to enforce Mexican law on Anglo settlers in Texas. They defy him and declare Texas' independence. On March 6, after six days of fighting, 189 defenders of the Alamo, including DAVY CROCKETT, JIM BOWIE and WILLIAM B. TRAVIS, are killed by General Santa Anna's 4,000 (more or less) Mexican troops. Santa Anna massacres 371 Texas prisoners at Goliad. "Remember the Alamo, remember Goliad" becomes the rallying cry and on April 21, SAM HOUSTON defeats Santa Anna's Army at San Jacinto. Santa Anna is forced to sign a treaty granting Texas' independence from Mexico. On November 3, the Provisional Government of Texas formally organizes the *Texas Rangers.*
1837	JOHN DEERE, a blacksmith, invents a steel plow that can cut through the tough grass roots of the plains (previously plows were made of wood or cast iron). It revolutionizes prairie farming. To discourage Apache Indian attacks along the Santa Fe Trail, the citizens of Chihuahua, Mexico offer rewards for Indian scalps: $100 male, $50 squaw, and $25 for a papoose. ALFRED JACOB MILLER makes the first pictorial representation (in the form of paintings) of the natural wonders of the West such as the Grand Tetons, Chimney Rock, Devil's Gate and the Wind River Mountains.
1839	Cherokee, Choctaw, Chickasaw, Creek, and Seminole Indians are driven into concentration camps by the federal government and then led on a forced march from their homelands (Alabama, Georgia, Florida, and Tennessee) to present-day Oklahoma. 4000 (give or take a few) die from lack of food and water. It becomes known to the Indians as the "Trail of Tears."
1841	The first large wagon train, with a whopping 48 wagons, reaches Sacramento, California, via the Oregon Trail. After that, no wagonmaster ever again tries to lead that many settlers in a single train. JAMES FENIMORE COOPER publishes "The Deerslayer."

1842   The Great Pathfinder, COLONEL JOHN C. FRÉMONT, leads an expedition West to find the best route over the Continental Divide to Oregon. His guide is KIT CARSON. He publishes maps and journals which send settlers scurrying to Oregon. San Antonio, in the Republic of Texas, is captured by Mexican soldiers.After months of fighting, a truce is declared in 1843.

1844   An American painter, SAMUEL MORSE, with his 1837 patent, inaugurates the first telegraph link betweenWashington D.C.and Baltimore with the words "What hath God wrought!" Business communications can now span the entire country and the railroad puts this newfangled device to good use.That same year, the first soap powder is invented: *Babbitt's Best Soap.* Invented by BenjaminT. Babbitt, it becomes nationally known.Westerners would now smell sweeter.JOSEPH SMITH (Mormon leader) and his brother are killed by an angry mob in Carthage, Illinois.

1845   Texas is annexed to the U. S. as the 28th state. Mexico is angered by this development to say the least.President Polk quickly sends U. S. troops to the Texas-Mexican border. The term "Manifest Destiny" is first used in an article in the "United States Magazine and Democratic Review" in reference to foreign governments trying to prevent the U.S. from acquiring new lands. It is used to justify all continental expansion becoming "the right of our manifest destiny to overspread and to possess the whole of the continent which Providence has given us."

1846   Mexican armies move north across the Rio Grande, Texas' declared border. The U. S. eventually declares war on Mexico because Mexico declines to sell California and New Mexico to the U.S. and refuses to make payments to Texans for lost land.A treaty with the British sets Oregon's northern border at the 49th parallel. The *Donner Party,* caught by an early October snow, is stranded in the Sierra Nevada mountains and half of the wagon train dies, others resort to cannibalism to survive. *Mince Pie for the Millions* is published: stories about DAVY CROCKETT attract Easterners to the frontier. With design suggestions from Texas Ranger Sam Walker, SAMUEL COLT develops the large caliber revolver, revolutionizing handguns and their use.

1847   In their attempt to escape religious persecution, the Mormons, led by BRIGHAM YOUNG, settle in Utah near the Great Salt Lake. *Nitroglycerin* is developed in Italy by Ascanio Sobrero.

1848   On the 24th of January, gold is inadvertently discovered by JAMES MARSHALL, a mechanic working on a sawmill for JOHN SUTTER in the Sacramento Valley of Northern California. But as luck would have it, JOHN SUTTER is driven into bankruptcy when his Mexican land grant is overrun with crazed men with "gold fever." Cheyenne and Sioux populations are cut in half in a year's time, dying from the diseases carried by white men. Chinese immigrants land at San Francisco (more trouble on the horizon!). The Mexican War ends in 1848 with the signing of *The Treaty of Guadalupe Hidalgo* whereby the U.S. gives Mexico a meager 15 million dollars for all the land north of the Rio Grande including parts of Utah, New Mexico, Colorado, Nevada, Arizona and California (a total of 1,193,061 square miles). The treaty promises all benefits of U.S. citizenship to Mexican Americans, except they are NOT allowed to vote or hold land. The national topic of discussion: who has the right to decide if slaves can be held, the States or the Federal Government? Oregon Territory is created (today's Oregon, Washington and Idaho).

1849 *The California and Oregon Trail* is published by FRANCIS PARKMAN about his trip west. It becomes a classic. In order to reduce labor competition, the California legislature charges a $20.00 per month tax on all miners who are not U.S. citizens. Chinese are denied citizenship, Mexicans are sent home, and a California law declares any jobless Indian a vagrant whos services can be auctioned off for up to four months. Even children under 18 can be legally used as slaves.

1850 The Compromise of 1850 admits California to the U.S. as a free state. Mexico Territory is divided into New Mexico and Utah with the residents being allowed to decide on the slave issue. Gold is discovered in Oregon along the Rogue River, drawing thousands of miners and leaving the Indians powerless as the wild game disappears. The original single-shot "Deringer" is invented by HENRY DERINGER, JR. Sailors in the thousands desert their ships in San Francisco bay to hunt for gold.

1851 JOHN B.L. SOULE, editor of the *Terre Haute Express,* says in an editorial "Go West, young man, go West!" (HORACE GREELEY, who is usually attributed with the phrase, had only reprinted Soule's editorial in his paper, the *New York Tribune,* but because Greeley was better known, he got the credit.)

1852 The Mormons officially sanction "plural marriage" as a means of increasing their population. Brigham Young takes 27 wives. *Wells, Fargo & Company* is founded in California by HENRY WELLS and WILLIAM FARGO to transport gold and mail for the 49ers. This provides highwaymen a new source of income; some of them like Black Bart and Dick Fellows become legendary "road agents." (read about these two scoundrels in Chapter V.) HARRIET BEECHER STOWE'S "Uncle Tom's Cabin" is published.

1853   Hoop skirts come into fashion. The Gadsden Purchase deal (29,640 square miles for 10 million dollars) buys southern New Mexico and Arizona from Mexico so the U. S. can build a southern transcontinental railroad. Just three years later, large fields of gold and silver are discovered! Bad luck for Mexico.

1854   The *Kansas-Nebraska Act* opens western lands previously reserved for Indians by U. S. treaties to white settlers.

1855   Secretary of War JEFFERSON DAVIS sells Congress on the idea of introducing camels into the Southwestern desert as mounts for the cavalry. Thirty-three camels are ordered from Egypt. The experiment is considered a failure and abandoned. (See the comedy western *Hawmps* which was based on this event.)

1856   Borax is discovered in California by D. JOHN VEATCH. 20-mule-team freight wagons haul it out of this very hot and dry valley. Kansans fight over the slavery issue. The *Western Union Telegraph Company* is formed and wires quickly crisscross the country.`

1857   The *Dred Scott Decision* by the Supreme Court of the United States rules that Congress has no right to deprive persons of their property without due process according to the Fifth amendment, and since slaves are property and not citizens, they cannot be taken away.

Fort Union National Monument, New Mexico (dk)

1858   Gold is found in Montana at Gold Creek and in western Kansas Territory around Pike's Peak (now in Colorado). *The Butterfield Overland Mail Company* wins the federal contract to provide mail and passenger service from St. Louis and Memphis, Tennessee to Los Angeles and San Francisco by way of Arkansas and Texas. The complete trip is about 3000 miles, one way, and takes about 25 days.

1859   "Pikes Peak or Bust" is the cry of '59ers rushing blindly to the gold discoveries, but it's a bust and many farmers and laborers return home. All the good mining claims are already staked. But in May, JOHN H. GREGORY hits it big at Gregory's Gulch on Clear Creek west of present day Denver and the gold seekers return. In June, PETER O'RILEY and PATRICK McLAUGHLIN discover the first major U.S. silver deposit, the Comstock Lode, in the Washoe Mountains of western Utah creating the boom town of Virginia City, Nevada. *The Harper's Ferry Raid* on a federal arsenal by JOHN BROWN and a band of abolitionists leads to his, and six other men's, hanging by federal troops. Anti-slavery sympathy grows. CHRISTIAN SHARPS patents the four-barrel pepperbox pistol. CLARINA NICHOLS pushes for women to get the right to vote, threatening with "If men don't give us our right, we will revolt! We won't marry! What a row that will make!" DAN EMMETT publishes "Dixie."

Silver Plume, Colorado (dk)

1860   *Pony Express* mail service begins on April 3rd with scores of young riders, mostly orphans, relaying mail between St. Joseph, Missouri and San Francisco in about 12 days. The service is organized by WILLIAM H. RUSSELL and ALEXANDER MAJORS, owners of a freight and passenger service. It lasts only 18 months, until October 1861, when a transcontinental telegraph is completed from Washington DC, via Salt Lake City, to San Francisco. Abraham Lincoln is elected President of United States.

1861   Seven states secede from the Union, the Confederacy is formed, and a South Carolina artillary fires on Fort Sumter on the 12th of April, beginning *The War Between the States*. The South makes alliances with five Indian tribes in Indian Territory (now Oklahoma). The Union army is defeated at Bull Run. In the West, CHIEF COCHISE, leader of the Chiricahua Apache tribe, begins a twelve year reign of terror in Arizona and New Mexico. MARK TWAIN (Samuel Longhorn Clemens) is hired as a reporter by the *Territorial Enterprise* in Virginia City, Nevada.

1862   The battle between the Union's ironclad "Monitor" and the Confederate's "Merrimack" was a draw. The *Gatling Gun* is developed; a modified version is adopted by the U.S. Army in 1865. Congress passes a law against bigamous marriages in order to dilute the growing power of the Mormon Church. The *Transcontinental Railroad Act* grants railroads wide strips of land on each side of the track they lay. The *Pacific Railroad Act* authorizes the building of a transcontinental railroad and charters two companies to do it: the *Central Pacific* and the *Union Pacific*. For every mile of track laid, the railroads would receive a grant of 10 square miles of land in alternate sections on either side of its right of way (the deal doubled to twenty square miles in 1864).

1863   The Alder Gulch gold strike in Montana Territory creates Virginia City, and to the chagrin of the Mormons, silver is discovered in Bingham Canyon, Utah, attracting more outsiders. The Bozeman Trail (running from Fort Laramie, Wyoming, to Virginia City, Montana) is opened to the gold fields. The Homestead Act is passed which gives 160 acres to any 21-year-old with a family if he can build a house on the land and occupy it for five years. The "Emancipation Proclamation" declares the slaves of the *Confederate States of America* to be free (This did not include 800,000 in five slave-holding states of the Union). Confederate irregulars led by WILLIAM CLARKE QUANTRILL raid the town of Lawrence, Kansas, burn the town, and kill 150 citizens.

1864   GENERAL WILLIAM TECUMSEH SHERMAN captures Atlanta, Georgia. A gold strike at Last Chance Gulch creates the boom town of Helena, Montana. COLONEL CHIVINGTON, with his 1st Colordo Volunteers, massacres an Arapaho village at Sand Creek just two months after ordering them to move there to reduce hostilities. BLACK KETTLE, a southern Cheyenne chief, escapes. COLONEL KIT CARSON'S army of volunteers enters Canyon de Chelly, destroys homes and crops and captures 3,000 Navajo Indians, then force marches them to a reservation at Ft. Sumner, N.M.—300 die. (Anyone see a trend developing here?) Because of the shortage of labor due to the large losses of young men in the Civil War, Congress passes The *Immigration Act* to import contract labor to build the transcontinental railroad. Chinese from Shanghai build the *Central Pacific* while Irish immigrants work the *Union Pacific*. WILLIAM "BLOODY BILL" ANDERSON leads a guerrilla band of Confederates that loots, kills, and burns towns in Missouri. He is chased down and killed by Union troops near Richmond on October 26th. The *Plummer Gang* robs and murders miners near Bannack and Virginia City (in present day Montana). A vigilante committee takes the law into its own hands and hangs more than two dozen of these outlaws. It was a bloody year.

1865   ROBERT E. LEE surrenders to ULYSSES S. GRANT at Appomattox, Virginia. The war officially ends, but isolated fighting continues in the West and federal troops (freed from Civil War duty) are moved west to fight the Indians. President ABRAHAM LINCOLN is assassinated on April 14th by JOHN WILKES BOOTH (lone assassin or a conspiracy?). The *Battle of Palmito Ranch* in Texas on the 12th of May is the last battle of the Civil War. The 13th amendment to the United States Constitution abolishes slavery. In the West, JESSE CHISHOLM, an Indian, forges a trail from Oklahoma to Wichita, Kansas; big cattle drives soon follow. RED CLOUD fights white settlement in Montana. *Remington* makes the double-barreled "derringer" which becomes the most popular pocket pistol of all time. After many delays due to a lack of money, the *Central Pacific* railroad begins building eastward over the Sierras from Sacramento as the *Union Pacific* heads West from Omaha with the intention of creating the first transcontinental railroad. The federal government offers great incentives to the railroad builders (congressmen are bribed): bonds, loans, and land grants eventually totaling 116 million acres. GEORGE MORTIMER PULLMAN builds the first comfortable railroad sleeping car with carpet, ventilated clerestory windows, candle lighting, heated air from under-floor furnaces, and fold-away sleeping berths. JESSE and FRANK JAMES form an outlaw gang of ex-Confederates.

1866   NELSON STORY bosses the first cattle drive from Texas to Montana. The RENO BROTHERS (Frank, Simeon, and William) are the first to rob a train on October 6th near Seymour, Indiana. The government tries to build a chain of forts along the Bozeman Trail on Indian lands to protect miners. Sioux leader RED CLOUD protests by attacking forts in what becomes *The First Sioux War.* The Indians massacre WILLIAM J. FETTERMAN and eighty troops near Fort Kearney, Wyoming. CHARLES GOODNIGHT and OLIVER LOVING establish a trail for cattle drives running from Belknap, Texas to Fort Sumner, N.M. and then on to Denver.

1867   Reconstruction of the South begins, but Congress "gives no quarter" and sets harsh policies; among other restrictions, voters are required to take an oath of loyalty to the Union. Naturally this doesn't sit well with the Southerners. JOSEPH G. McCOY takes the first herd of Texas longhorns to Abilene, Kansas. A shortage of beef in the East because of the Civil War fuels this new industry. *The Great Powder Company* of San Francisco makes dynamite from the ALFRED NOBEL patents which greatly aids railroad building and mining. WILLIAM F. CODY is hired to kill

Once a quiet town, legalized gambling has taken over. Central City, Colorado (dk)

Buckskin Joe, Cañon City, Colorado (dk)

buffalo along the planned route of the Kansas Pacific Railroad in order to starve the Indians (Is that fair?). He kills 4,000 buffalo in eight months and is nicknamed "Buffalo Bill." OLIVER HUDSON KELLEY forms the "Grangers" to protect the rights of farmers. They eventually fight exorbitant railroad and grain elevator rates by taking over state legislatures and enacting regulations. The U.S. buys Alaska from Russia for two cents an acre.

1868 The Sioux war with RED CLOUD ends with a treaty that calls for the abandonment of several forts on the Bozeman Trail and creates the Great Sioux Reservation in western South Dakota. The 14th amendment to the U.S. Constitution grants citizenship to blacks naturalized or born in the US. Native North Americans are specifically denied citizenship. At the *Battle of Beecher's Island,* ROMAN NOSE, a Northern Cheyenne chief noted for skill and invincibility in battle, is killed. BRET HARTE becomes the editor of the *Overland Monthly* which leads to his classic fiction novels about the West. The *United States Commissioner of Indian Affairs* estimates that the Indian Wars in the West are costing the government one million dollars per Indian killed.

1869 Central Pacific's *Juniper* and Union Pacific's *No. 119* meet at Promontory, Utah on the 10th of May to complete the first transcontinental railroad. Average travel time from coast to coast is now just eight to ten days. The steam-powered brake (air brake) is patented by GEORGE WESTINGHOUSE which eliminates the need for a brakeman on each railway car and makes travel safer. MAJOR JOHN WESLEY POWELL is the first to explore the Grand Canyon. Only five of his nine men survive the ordeal down the Colorado River. The U.S. Fifth Cavalry attacks the renegade Cheyenne Dog Soldiers in *The Battle of Summit Springs* in northeast Colorado Territory and ends their reign as warriors. Wyoming is the first territory to give women the right to vote, hold office, and serve on juries. High-grade silver ore is discovered near Denver, Colorado.

1870   The 15th amendment to the constitution gives blacks the right to vote (women don't get that right until 1920). A treaty is signed between the Sioux and the U.S. at Fort Abercrombie.

1871   The *Indian Appropriation Act* declares that Indian tribes will no longer be recognized as sovereign powers with which the federal government must make treaties. They will now be subject to all the laws of Congress (Is *that* fair?). Apache leader GERONIMO begins his war in New Mexico and Arizona Territories. Mobs riot against the Chinese on the West Coast because they are willing to work long hours for low wages.

1872   MARK TWAIN (Samuel Clemens) publishes a humorous book about his western experiences. It's called *Roughing It* and becomes an instant classic of western Americana. Apache Chief COCHISE surrenders to General O. Howard and is sent to a reservation. Dodge City, Kansas is founded. The JAMES GANG robs its first passenger train near Council Bluffs, Iowa.

1873   A Modoc band (60-90 warriors) led by CAPTAIN JACK is defeated after holding off 3,000 U.S. troops for a month at California's Lava Beds. The tribal leaders are sent to Oklahoma. SAMUEL COLT introduces the "Peacemaker" which chambers a .45 long Colt cartridge. OLIVER F. WINCHESTER develops the .44-40 Winchester Model '73 rifle that becomes known as "the gun that won the West." JOSEPH F. GLIDDEN starts the manufacture of barbed wire in De Kalb, Illinois—much needed on the plains where wood is not available for fences. (Glidden did not invent barbed wire—there were many patents before him—but he organized, advertised, and mass produced this new invention.)

1874   29 buffalo hunters fight off 700 Indians at *The Second Battle of Adobe Walls* in Texas by using breech-loading Sharps .50-caliber rifles. Over the next few months the Indians voluntarily surrender at Fort Sill and 72 chiefs are taken in irons to a prison in St. Augustine, Florida. This finally ends fighting on the north Texas plains. The worst grasshopper plague in U.S. history devastates the Great Plains. Thousands of families leave. *Levi Strauss* adds copper rivets to his denim blue jeans (a David Jacobs idea).

1875 With a military expedition, LT. COL. GEORGE CUSTER, confirms reports of gold in the Black Hills of Dakota Territory even though very little had been found by this time. This causes miners to flood into Dakota gold fields. The U.S. government offers to buy the Black Hills for six million dolllars, but SITTING BULL and CRAZY HORSE turn down the offer. The lawless town of Deadwood is founded. The U.S. government gives up trying to stop the influx of miners and orders the Sioux to move to reservations (That's right, if you won't sell, we'll take).

1876 In a half-hour fight (*The Battle of the Little Big Horn*), Sioux and Cheyenne wipe out GEORGE CUSTER and 1/3 of his 7th Cavalry Regiment of 700 soldiers. The bodies are stripped of all possessions and mutilated. The telephone is invented by ALEXANDER GRAHAM BELL. WILD BILL HICKOK is shot in the back by JACK McCALL while playing poker in Deadwood, Dakota Territory. He is holding a pair of aces and a pair of eights which comes to be known as "the dead man's hand." The *Northfield, Minnesota Raid* by the JAMES-YOUNGER GANG turns into a blood bath as the townspeople surprise them with an ambush, ending their "reign of terror;" only Jesse and Frank James escape.

1877 The Nez Percé, under CHIEF JOSEPH, surrender after 12 battles and 1,300 miles of running, the chase ending just 30 miles short of the Canadian border. They are exiled to Oklahoma (sound familiar?). Sioux chief CRAZY HORSE is arrested and killed under mysterious circumstances at Fort Robinson, Nebraska. BRIGHAM YOUNG, leader of the Mormon church dies. JACK McCALL is hanged for killing "WILD BILL" HICKOK. *Swift and Company* begins shipping meat from Chicago in ice-cooled railway cars designed by owner GUSTAVUS SWIFT. The *Desert Land Act* offers 640 acre plots for $1.25 per acre to anyone willing to irrigate part of it.

1878 The town of Leadville is founded after the discovery of silver in central Colorado. A Nebraska war between settlers and cattlemen begins when ranch hands of G.P. OLIVE hang and burn two settlers. The notorious outlaw SAM BASS is killed in Texas. The murder of JOHN TUNSTALL, an English rancher, ignites *The Lincoln County War* which rages on for five months among cattlemen and political rivals in New Mexico Territory; many die as gunmen and desperadoes join sides. In that war, WILLIAM BONNEY (later know as Billy the Kid) kills two posse men to avenge his boss's (John Tunstall's) murder.

1879   THOMAS ALVA EDISON invents the electric light bulb. *The Wyoming Stock Growers Association* is formed to deal with the growing cattle industry; they become a political powerhouse. The Ute Indians in north-western Colorado are relocated to Utah after the Utes battle to save their reservation. Their 12 million acre reservation is then opened for white settlement (so what else is new). BUFFALO BILL CODY publishes his autobiography, *The Life of Buffalo Bill.*

1880   JAMES J. HILL builds the *Great Northern Railway*, spurring development in North Dakota and Montana. In San Francisco, the Anglo war against the Chinese continues as mills fire hundreds of the "Chinese pest" (Hardworking employees are "pests"?). The *Atchison, Topeka & Santa Fe Railroad* reaches Santa Fe in New Mexico Territory. Alaska's first major gold strike is in Juneau.

1881   A gunfight at the OK Corral (Tombstone, Arizona, October, 26th) among the Earps, Clantons and McLowrys results in three men dead. MARSHAL VIRGIL EARP and his two deputized brothers, Morgan and Wyatt, attack these ranchers (know as The Cowboys) in order to cover up a stagecoach robbery involving their friend "Doc" Holliday. CHIEF VICTORIO is killed at Chihuahua, Mexico. The famous Indian scout JIM BRIDGER dies in his bed in Missouri. Sentenced to hang for the murder of Sheriff Brady, BILLY THE KID escapes jail by killing two guards, and then

The Wal-Mart of the 19th century: the General Store, Nevada City, Montana (dk)

on the 14 of July is killed by friend SHERIFF PAT GARRETT at Fort Sumner, New Mexico Territory. SITTING BULL surrenders. HELEN HUNT JACKSON publishes *A Century of Dishonor,* describing the atrocities committed against the Indians by the government (About time!).The second transcontinental railroad is completed when the Southern Pacific meets the *Atchison, Topeka and Santa Fe* at Deming, New Mexico Territory.The third transcontinental railroad along the southern route is opened; the last spike is pounded in at Sierra Blanca, Texas joining the *Southern Pacific* and the *Texas and Pacific* tracks.

1882 In St. Joseph, Missouri, April 3rd, BOB FORD, a James Gang member, shoots JESSE JAMES in the head in Jesse's own home and claims the reward. He has previously made a deal for immunity from prosecution of past crimes if he does this dirty deed. Under the *Edmunds Act* used to break the power of the Mormon Church, 1300 Mormons are found guilty of polygamy and sent to prison. Hundreds more flee the territory to escape prosecution. The *Chinese Exclusion Act* suspends immigration of Chinese labor for 10 years. China is angered by this, to say the least. A. J. PRITCHARD makes a lead and silver strike near Coeur d'Alene Lake in northern Idaho. It becomes the largest lead-silver mining district in the nation. The worthless copper ore found in the Anaconda silver mine at Butte, Montana becomes very valuable in the new electricial power industry, but *The War of the Copper Kings* results when there is a shortage of water to process the copper.The allusive California stagecoach robber, BLACK BART, is caught. JUDGE ROY BEAN opens the *Jersey Lily* saloon in Langtry, Texas.

1883 The northern transcontinental railroad (*Northern Pacific*) is completed between Duluth, Minnesota and Portland, Oregon. The golden spike is driven at Independence Creek near Helena, Montana. The *Southern Pacific* railroad, by absorbing other railroads, completes a line to New Orleans creating the "Sunset Route." In order to standardize schedules, the railroads adopt four standard time zones (see page 491). "BUFFALO BILL" CODY exhibits his first Wild West Show on the 4th of July in North Platte, Nebraska. GERONIMO is captured in Mexico by GENERAL GEORGE CROOK and brought back to the reservation.

1884 Smokeless gunpowder is developed in France.

1885 JOHN TAYLOR (president of the Mormon Church) and his administration is forced into hiding by pressure from the federal government. GERONIMO, with 100 Apaches—tired of playing

A mining ghost at Bannack State Historic Park, Dillon, Montana (dk)

farmer in the desert—leaves the reservation in Arizona Territory and heads for Mexico, killing 73 civilians and soldiers along the way. Thousands of federal troops (3/4 of the U.S. Army) are dispatched, again lead by GENERAL GEORGE CROOK. His lack of understanding of the Apache leads him to fail at bringing in GERONIMO. Troops are also sent to Washington Territory to quell violence against the Chinese. CHIEF SITTING BULL and sharpshooter ANNIE OAKLEY join Buffalo Bill's Wild West Show. MARK TWAIN publishes the *Adventures of Huckleberry Finn.*

1886 GERONIMO—having never been captured—and his warriors voluntarily surrender to GENERAL NELSON MILES and are carted off to Fort Marion, Florida where they will sit until 1894. Severe blizzards on the northern plains wipe out large herds of cattle (barbed wire is a significant factor in the deaths of the cattle as they bunch up on fence lines, preventing them from escaping). That tragedy, new laws restricting interstate commerce, and fencing of the open range by settlers, bring the era of cattle drives and huge stock raising corporations to an end (the era of the cowboy has lasted just 25 years). BUTCH CASSIDY robs his first bank in Telluride, Colorado. *Sears, Roebuck & Co.* produces its first mail order catalog—a "wish book" and a useful item for the outhouse.

1887 The *Dawes General Allotment Act* gives citizenship and ownership of small pieces of land to Native Americans if they give up their tribal ways and become farmers. The Act is a failure. The *Interstate Commerce Commission* is formed by Act of Congress to regulate railroads. It is the first regulatory commission in U.S. history. The railroads soon gain control of the commission (surprise, surprise!). Congress amends the *Edmunds Anti-Polygamy Act* of 1882 in further efforts to destroy the Mormon Church by abolishing woman suffrage in the Territory and requiring those who want to vote or hold office sign an oath to support anti-polygamy laws. (1,300 are imprisoned under the *Edmunds Act!*) The Federal Government un-incorporates the Mormon Church and impounds its property. It also dissolves the *Mormon Perpetual Emigrating Fund Company* which was being used to bring foreign converts to the Zion.

1888   The first rodeo competition is held in Prescott, Arizona Territory, with medals given to winners. FREDERIC REMINGTON'S illustrations turn up in a book by Theodore Roosevelt, *Ranch Life and Hunting Trails*. He becomes famous for his accurate look at the American West of the nineteenth century with over 2,700 images.

1889   After Indian claims are settled, two million acres in Oklahoma Territory is opened to white settlement. On April 22, thousands of settlers race across the plains to claim a piece of the West. Those who get an early jump by claiming land before the race officially began are called "sooners."

1890   SITTING BULL is killed by the Indian Police in South Dakota; tempers flare and the Indians are ordered to surrender their weapons. A shot goes off and the Cavalry returns fire resulting in the *Wounded Knee Massacre* of CHIEF BIG FOOT'S band of 350 Sioux. Hotchkiss machine guns, firing one shell per second, are used to fire on the encampment. For this action, eighteen soldiers of the seventh cavalry are awarded the congressional metal of honor! The Liberal Party replaces all Mormons in elective offices, including the mayor of Salt Lake City. Half of the 22-million-acre Sioux reservation is opened for settlement (Who said life was fair?). The Buffalo (*Ta Tanka*) have been reduced from 60 million to less than 1,000 head. The Indians are growing quite hungry; federal policy is a success.

1892   *The Johnson County War* between homesteaders and cattlemen erupts in Wyoming after the cattlemen compile a "death list" of over 70 "squatters" and suspected rustlers, then hire 25 gunfighters from Texas to execute it. After only two killings federal troops put a stop to the war. The *Dalton Gang* attempts to rob two banks at the same time in *Coffeyville, Kansas;* four gang members and four townspeople die. Only EMMETT DALTON survives to serve 15 years in prison. BOB FORD, the man who shot Jesse James ten years earlier, is killed in his own saloon in Creede, Colorado.

1893 The Greatest Oklahoma Land Rush begins when the United States opens the Cherokee Strip for settlement (6.5 million acres). On the 16th of September, 100,000 homesteaders try to claim a piece of America. (See *Far and Away,* 1992.)

1894 GERONIMO is transferred from Florida to a guard house at Fort Sill, Oklahoma; he is converted to Christianity and succeeds as a farmer until his death in 1909.

1895 JOHN WESLEY HARDIN is gunned down by JOHN SELMAN at the Acme Saloon in El Paso.

1896 Gold is discovered near Klondike Creek in northwestern Canada luring over 100,000 miners. JUDGE ROY BEAN, "Law West of the Pecos," promotes a world heavyweight championship fight between MAHER and FITZSIMMONS at Langtry, Texas.

1897 Jell-O is invented. Oil is discovered in Bartlesville, Oklahoma gushering in a new era. The horse of the nineteenth century is replaced by an automobile that will change the landscape of the West in the twentieth century.

1898 "TEDDY" ROOSEVELT'S "Rough Riders" is formed for the Spanish-American War in Cuba. Spain has been asked to remove its armed forces from Cuba. In Skagway, Alaska, SOAPY SMITH is killed in a gunfight by FRANK REID who also dies. Soapy was practicing his usual scam of selling soap claiming there are $100-dollar bills in some of them, but confederates always get the winning bars of soap. THOMAS EDISON makes a short film with his new movie-making equipment: it's the first western film and is called "Cripple Creek Ballroom." Lasting only a few minutes, it shows a group of cowboys playing cards at a saloon table.

1899 The Wild Bunch led by BUTCH CASSIDY and THE SUNDANCE KID rob a train at Wilcox, Wisconsin. In trying to blow open the safe, they also blow up the railway car (see the movie!). CARRIE NATION holds a temperance meeting in front of an unlicensed saloon in Medicine Lodge, Kansas. Her name becomes "Carry A. Nation" as a billboard slogan.

1900 The Cripple Creek, Colorado gold boom peaks at $20 million.

1902 OWEN WISTER publishes *The Virginian* about cowboys in Wyoming. The most memorable line in western fiction comes from that novel: "When you call me that, smile!"

1903   On November 20th, TOM HORN, the last of the Old West bounty hunters, is hanged at Cheyenne, Wyoming for allegedly killing a 14-year-old boy. The first movie to tell a story is also a western: "The Great Train Robbery." In it, bandits hold up a train and after a chase are captured—all in just eleven minutes. It's filmed by EDWIN S. PORTER and one of the players is GILBERT "BRONCO BILLY" ANDERSON. The film is shot in New Jersey!

1907   EMMETT DALTON (a survivor of the Coffeyville bank robbery), after getting out of jail, goes to California to make movies about the gang's exploits. In Winterset, Iowa JOHN WAYNE is born.

1908   "The Bank Robbery" is the first film shot "on location" (Cash, Oklahoma Territory). It's shot by Al Gennings, a convicted bank robber and creates the first movie cowboy hero: BRONCO BILLY, who eventually makes over 500 films.

1911   BUTCH CASSIDY and THE SUNDANCE KID are reportedly gunned down by Mexican police in San Vicente, Bolivia.

1917   BUFFALO BILL CODY dies on the 10th of January and is buried on Lookout Mountain just west of Denver.

1914   A Hollywood motion picture company pays Pancho Villa $25,000 to shoot a movie *during* Villa's revolution in Mexico. The director, watchful of light conditions and meal breaks, tells Pancho Villa when he can fight. Great action footage was shot, but never used because it was too unbelievable (A movie based on these events: *And Staring Pancho Villa as Himself,* 2004.) The making of Westerns becomes a part of Old West history.

1929   GARY COOPER stars as *The Virginian* in the movie version of Owen Wister's novel, and WYATT EARP dies peacefully in Los Angeles, and so ends the wild Frontier West.

THE MOUNTAIN MAN

TIDBIT: The Lewis and Clark Expedition of 1804 opened the way for a new breed of independent "Mountain Men" who were the first to forge west and make the country profitable. Companies like the *Hudson's Bay Company* and the *American Fur Company* were set up to collect and ship fur pelts to the East and to Europe. In just a few years, the beaver were almost trapped out of existence which increased their cost to a point where no one could afford them and silk hats quickly replaced beaver. The era of the legendary, tough, independent mountain man lasted less than 40 years.

Trailblazing
22 FAMOUS TRAILS & EXPEDITIONS

*"What do we want with this region of savages and wild beasts, of
deserts, of shifting sands and whirlwinds of dust, of cacti and
prairie dogs? . . . What could we do with the western coast line
three thousand miles away, rockbound, cheerless and uninviting?"*
—Daniel Webster

Expeditions into the uncharted West began at
the beginning of the nineteenth century mapping
out the first trails and writing of the wonderments
of the land west of the Mississippi River. Soon wagons full
of homesteaders trekked west and stagecoach routes began
to cross the "Great American Desert" to California. The need
for beef in the East after the Civil War spawned the cattle
trails north from Texas to the railheads popping up along
the Union Pacific Railroad as it beat a frantic dash to the
west coast. Free government grants spurred the building of
railroads west. Railroad handbills pitching bountiful, rich land
brought the immigrants west in droves. And by 1893, 70,000
miles of railroad covered the Wild West in a web of track that
ended the reign of the stagecoach, the pony express, and the
pathfinder.

3 EXPEDITIONS

1. Lewis & Clark. (1804-1806). St. Louis, Missouri to Astoria, Oregon.
President Thomas Jefferson convinced Congress to buy the "Louisiana
Purchase" from France for 15 million dollars even though many thought
it was a worthless wasteland. In the first official exploration of the Far
West, Jefferson sent U.S. Army officers *Meriwether Lewis* and *William
Clark* on what would be a two year, four month, and ten day trip, crossing
7,689 miles of uncharted wilderness. They followed the Missouri River

Fort Clatsop National Memorial, Astoria, Oregon (dk)

west looking for its headwaters. An Indian woman named *Sacajawea* joined the expedition in what is today North Dakota and led the men over the Rockies (Lemhi Pass) and down along the Columbia River to the Pacific Coast. They set up Fort Clatsop at Astoria and weathered the cold, wet winter, and near starvation, until they could make the return trip. Lewis and Clark returned with a map showing a route to the Pacific and reported the large supply of beaver in the Northwest. This set off a stampede of fur trappers who blazed new trails West.

2. Pike. (1806–1807). St. Louis to Nacogdoches, Texas. *Zebulon Montgomery Pike* (1779-1813), explorer and military leader, was sent by the Governor of Louisiana Territory to lead expedition parties to the headwaters of the Mississippi in Northern Minnesota. Leaving St. Louis in 1806 and passing through Bent's Fort—and while tracing the Arkansas and Red Rivers—Pike discovered a 14,110 foot mountain he dubbed Pike's Peak. His expedition could not climb the peak and he went south through Santa Fe, Albuquerque and El Paso, only to be captured by the Spanish who thought he was trespassing on Spanish Territory. Eventually freed, he returned East to report on potential money-making trade with Mexico. It was his glowing reports that led to U.S. expansion into Texas.

3. Frémont. (1842–1847). St. Louis to Fort Vancouver, Oregon. *John Charles Frémont* (1813-1890), U.S. soldier and politician, led three expeditions (1842, 1843-44 and 1845-47) through the Northwest to document and map out new trails. One route went along the South Platte River to South Pass and then down the Snake River to the Pacific Coast. Another route worked its way south to southern California and then north across Nevada to Oregon. *Christopher "Kit" Carson* was his guide on all three expeditions.

4 CATTLE TRAILS
(Ran generally South to North)

1. Shawnee Trail. (1840's–1850's). Brownsville through Dallas to St. Louis, Sedalia, and Kansas City, Missouri. It was the first cattle trail, covering about 800 miles, but Missouri's quarantine on fever-bearing longhorns shut it down even before the Civil War began.

2. Goodnight-Loving Trail. (1866–1880's). San Angelo, Texas, to Fort Sumner, New Mexico then on to Colorado. *Charles Goodnight* and *Oliver Loving* opened the trail in 1866 when they began selling livestock to ranchers in Colorado and New Mexico because they couldn't get enough for their beef in Texas during Reconstruction after the Civil War. The route began in West Texas and followed the Pecos River north through New Mexico and then to Pueblo, Denver, and Cheyenne up what is now Intestate 25 along the eastern edge of the Rocky Mountains. Oliver Loving was killed in 1867 by Indians on their third cattle drive north.

3. Chisholm Trail. (1867–1882). Brownsville, Texas, through San Antonio and Fort Worth, to Abilene, Kansas and later Ellsworth, "The Wickedest Cattletown in Kansas." Fed by tributary trails, the *Chisholm* handled half the beef herded from Texas. The trail was named after *Jesse Chisholm* (c1806-c1868) a Cherokee half-breed trader and military scout who traveled along this route from the Mexican border to Abilene from 1864 to 1866 hauling goods from San Antonio to Wichita, Kansas. The huge Texas cattle drives that took place *after* his death made the trail famous.

4. Western Trail. (1876-1884). Bandera, Texas to Dodge City, Kansas a distance of 900 miles. Also called the *Dodge City Trail* after its original terminus. The trail eventually extended all the way to Fort Buford in Dakota Territory passing through Ogallala, Nebraska. A branch also went west from Ogallala to Cheyenne, Wyoming and then north to Miles City, Montana.

National Historic Oregon Trail Interpretive Center, Baker City, Oregon (dk)

10 WAGON TRAILS
(Ran generally East to West)

1. Santa Fe Trail. (1820's–1880's). Independence, Missouri to Santa Fe, New Mexico, about 780 miles. The Santa Fe Trail was an early trade route to a small adobe town in Mexico called Santa Fe. It snaked across the plains of Kansas and along the Arkansas River into Colorado, turning southward at the Rockies and passing over Raton Pass to Santa Fe. The *Cimarron Cut-off,* turning south at Fort Atkinson just west of Dodge City, crossed 60 miles of desert and then followed the Cimarron River into New Mexico. It was a shorter route, but had less access to water and far more Indian attacks. *Captain William Becknell* was the first to traverse the route in 1821 after the Mexican Independence from Spain improved relations. For 10 years Becknell outfitted his pack trains in Franklin, Missouri, then moved his operation 100 miles west to Independence. Moving about 12 miles a day, or less if pulled by oxen, the huge Conestoga wagons—each carrying 2,000 pounds of trade goods—made the trip in about three months.

2. Oregon Trail. (1832–1890's). Independence, Westport Landing (now Kansas City) and St. Joseph, Missouri to Ft. Vancouver, Washington. This

2,000 mile wagon road ran west along the North Platte River in Nebraska and Wyoming, crossed through the South Pass into Idaho following the Snake River and then into Oregon and Washington along the Columbia River. In 1834 a Boston businessman named *Nathaniel Wyeth* lead the first emigrants over the Oregon Trail in hopes of starting a fur trapping business on the Pacific coast. Wyeth took along 24 men and a famous scout named *William Sublette.* In 1836, missionary *Marcus Whitman* and *Rev. Henry Spalding* were the first to attempt to move wagons— and their wives *Narcissa* and *Prentiss*—over the long trail. Their wives became the first white women to make the journey. The wagons didn't finish the trip, but the wives did "in fine shape." It took determined travelers heading west four to six months to get to Oregon, working 18 hours a day. They would leave the Missouri River in the spring as soon as the Prairie greened up. If they delayed too long, the fall snows would trap them in the mountains. In 1850, during the peak years of travel, 55,000 settlers rode (or walked alongside) their wagons west. In total, a half-million hardy souls took this route west.

3. Overland Trail. (1862-1866). Also known as the *Cherokee Trail,* it was a shortcut off the *Oregon Trail* to Fort Bridger, Wyoming following the south bank of the South Platte River into Colorado and then up the Oashe La Poudre River into Wyoming. The route was first used by a fur trader named *W.H. Ashley* in 1824.

A stop for provisions on the Santa Fe Trail: Bent's Old Fort NHS, La Junta, Colorado (dk)

4. The Bozeman Road. (1863-1868). Fort Laramie, Wyoming to Virginia City, Montana. The route ran along the Powder River east of the Bighorn Mountains to Virginia City. *John Bozeman* and *John Jacobs* blazed the trail in 1863 as a short cut to the newly-discovered gold fields in Montana. Fort Reno, Fort Phil Kearny, and Fort C.F. Smith were built by the army to protect the gold seekers from Indian attack. The Cheyenne, Arapaho, and Sioux didn't think much of the invasion of whites on their land and began an active and violent campaign to run them off. The *Red Cloud War* ended in 1868 with a treaty that closed the three forts and sent the army packing.

5. Butterfield Overland Stage Route. (1858-1860). St. Louis to San Francisco. "The longest stage run in the world" was founded September 15, 1858 by *John Butterfield,* an ex-stage driver (with controlling interest by *Wells, Fargo*). The trip took 24 days with a maximum load of 750 pounds. No longer did mail and express have to go by sea through Panama to California. By 1860, Butterfield had 160 stagecoaches, 250 coaches, and 1,800 horses. The fare was $200 westward and $150 eastward. The 2,800 mile route went from central Missouri across Arkansas (Fort Smith) and Texas (Fort Belknap and El Paso) and along the Mexican border (Tucson and Yuma) and up the California coast to San Francisco. Other stage lines included the *San Antonio & San Diego Mail* which followed the same route to California and the *Central Overland* which traveled along the Oregon Trail.

Fort Laramie National Historic Site, Fort Laramie, Wyoming (dk)

6. California Trail. (1841-1865). South Pass to Sacramento. Leaving the Oregon Trail west of South Pass, and passing through Salt Lake City to Sacramento and the Pacific Coast. It followed the Humbolt River to Reno, Nevada, then from Truckee, California across the Sierra Nevada and along the Sacramento River to the Pacific Coast. Fur trapper, *Joseph R. Walker* is credited with blazing the trail in 1833. The trail served thousands of gold seekers in the 49er gold rush.

7. Pony Express Route. (1860-1861). St. Joseph, Missouri to Sacramento, California. The *Central Overland Express Company* began hauling mail on horseback between St. Joseph, Missouri, and Sacramento, California, on April 3, 1860. The venture was organized by a private company called *Russell, Majors and Waddell Kansas Freight Masters.* Riders rode the 1,966 mile trip in 7 days and 17 hours galloping at full speed, changing horses every 12 to 15 miles, and using a fresh rider every 5 or 6 horses. In his youth, the infamous *"Buffalo Bill" Cody* was one of these heroic riders. But after only 18 months, on October 26, 1861, a new invention called the "singing wire" (the telegraph) put the company out of business, ending this legendary accomplishment.

8. Old Spanish Trail. (1829-1855). Running through mountains, desserts, and canyons, it ran from Santa Fe northwest into Utah, and then turned southwest across southern Nevada to Los Angeles via the Mohave River and Cajun Pass, about 1,200 miles. It was pioneered by *Antonio Armijo. John C. Frémont* gave the route its name in an 1844 report on a trip guided by *Kit Carson.* It was used to trade slaves and wool from New Mexico for horses from California. As freight wagons came into use in the mid 1850's, the trail became obsolete.

9. Mormon Trail. (1847-1857). Nauvoo, Illinois, passing through Fort Laramie and South Pass, Wyoming to Salt Lake City, a total of 1,300 miles. In 1847, *Brigham Young* led a westward migration of church members to the "Valley of the Great Salt Lake." *The Church of Jesus Christ of Latter-Day Saints* was founded by *Joseph Smith* in the 1830's in upper state New York, but continual prosecution forced him, and his growing number of followers, to move from place to place until they landed in Nauvoo, Illinois where Smith was jailed for his beliefs and shot by a crazed mob of citizens. *Brigham Young* was named the new leader of the flock, whereby he immediately packed up the church and headed west looking for a permanent home. They found it in the Salt Lake Valley in July of 1847. Young died in 1877 with over 100,000 followers living, and prospering, in the dry desert of the Great Basin.

10. Gila River Trail. (1846–1854). Santa Fe, New Mexico, through southern Arizona, to San Diego, California. The Gila River rises in Sierra Madre in Southwest New Mexico and crosses Arizona to the Colorado River. The river—the southern boundry of the fur trade—marked the line between the U.S. and Mexico before the Gadsten Purchase in 1854. Because the Gila valley was too rough for a transcontinental railroad, the U.S. Government bought the land south of the river from Santa Anna for ten-million dollars and this became the primary route west to California.

Promontory Summit, Golden Spike National Historic Site, Utah (dk)
Steam locomotives Jupiter and No.119 meet head to head for the ceremony.

5 TRANSCONTINENTAL RAILROADS
(Ran east and west)

1. The Union Pacific/Central Pacific Route. (1869). Omaha, Nebraska to Sacramento, California. This middle route was approximately 2,000 miles long, passing through Cheyenne (Wyoming), Ogden (Utah), and Virginia City (Nevada). On this, the first transcontinental route, *Theordore Judah* was the architect of the Union Pacific, and chief engineer *Grenville Dodge* made the Central Pacific a reality. With millions in federal loans and land grants, the two railroads finally met at Promontory Summit, Utah on May 10, 1869.

2. The Southern Pacific. (1881). New Orleans to Los Angeles. The southern route ran just inside the Mexican border from New Orleans through San Antonio, El Paso, Tucson and Yuma, to Los Angeles. The second transcontinental route began as a charter to build a line from San Francisco to San Diego, but *C.P.Huntington* took it on to Los Angeles and then east to Demming, New Mexico where it met up with the *Santa Fe*. It then scampered through Texas to Sierra Blanca where it merged with the *Texas & Pacific* (Today, *Amtrak* calls it the Sunset Route).

3. The Northern Pacific. (1883). Duluth, Minnesota, through Fargo, N.D., along the Yellowstone River in Montana to Tacoma, Washington. *Henry Villard* became President of the railroad in 1878 after the railroad went into receivership, having begun by *Joseph Perham* with a charter (and 40 million acres) from Congress in 1864.

4. The Atchison, Topeka and Santa Fe. (1885). Atchison and Topeka, Kansas to Santa Fe and Los Angeles. It followed the *Pony Express* route to Santa Fe.

5. The Great Northern. (1893). Minneapolis, Minnesota to Fargo, then Seattle, running just below the Canadian border. Created by *James Jerome Hill,* it originally began in 1879 to access the grain growing areas of the Red River Valley between St. Paul and Winnipeg. Westward expansion sent the line to Puget Sound in 1893, making it the fifth and last transcontinental railroad to tie the Pacific Coast to the East.

Durango & Silverton Narrow Gauge Railroad, Silverton, Colorado (dk)

Fort Union National Monument on the old Santa Fe Trail, New Mexico (dk)

Boots, Beans, and Bridals

Boots, Beans, and Bridals
XII. THE CAVALRY

"On her knee she wore a yellow garter. She wore it for her lover who was far far away. And when they asked her why she wore the garter, she wore it for her lover in the U.S. Cavalry."
— Old Cavalry marching song.

The allure of the Wild West—a new life and new riches—caused a wild stampede of immigrants to come face to face, pistol to arrow, with the hundreds of thousands of Native Americans who populated the continent. Settlers and gold seekers tried to send them packing, but continued confrontation required Washington to send federal troops to the West after the Civil War. The result was another war: *The Indian Wars,* a war that lasted for nearly 40 years from 1862 to 1898.

Military outposts were set up along the major trails west and the federal troops were charged with protecting those emigrants who ventured west. On fifty cents a day and beans, they lived in tents or drafty wooden barracks, and drilled and labored at chores from dawn to dusk with no entertainment except gambling and "red eye" whiskey. In just 30 years, and "countless skirmishes and dozens of pitched battles throughout the Great Plains," a whole way of life was destroyed. Washington had a simple policy of "removal" to deal with the "Indian question": put them on reservations far from the "white man's" trade routes.

It should be noted that fighting with the Native Americans was only a small part of cavalry troop duties in the West, even though Hollywood would have you believe otherwise. They were also charged with exploring and mapping their districts, keeping records on the weather, building roads, delivering mail and setting up telegraphs and communication lines. They built schools, hospitals, and churches, and helped local officials enforce the law. The cavalry was more often trying to keep the peace between the interlopers and the Indians than make war with them.

ATTENTION!

INDIAN

FIGHTERS

Having been authorized by the Governor to raise a Company of 100 men

U. S. VOL CAVALRY!

For immediate service against hostile Indians. I call upon all who wish to engage in such service to call at my office and enroll their names immediately.

Pay and rations the same as other U. S. Volunteer Cavalry.

Parties furnishing their own horses will receive 40c per day, and rations for the same, while in the service.

The Company will also be entitled to all horses and other plunder taken from the Indians.

Office first floor East of Recorder's Office.

HAL SAYR.

Central City, Aug. 13, '64

Text from an actual Old West handbill

Troop B, 10th Cavalry
10 INSTRUCTIONS FOR SENTINELS

General Orders for the US Cavalry, 1882
From the collection of Captain Robert G. Smither,
Troop B, 10th Cavalry

Those troops pulling guard duty, usually a 24 hour shift, were required to know these general orders by heart and follow them to a "T" or face a court martial. Each day new guard's uniforms were inspected, passwords issued, and special instructions passed on. Those guarding prisoners or protecting buildings usually had a two-hours-on, two-hour-off shift during those 24 hours. Similar orders are still being used today.

A Sentinel when ordered to turn over his instructions will reply *My general orders are:*

1. To walk my post, carrying my piece at "support," or on either shoulder, muzzle elevated. In wet weather, I carry my piece at "secure." I keep myself on the alert, observing everything that takes place in sight or hearing of my post.
2. I do not take orders from, or allow myself to be relieved by, anyone, except officers of the guard, non-commissioned officers of the guard, the commanding officer, and the officer of the day.
3. I report all violations of orders which I am required to enforce.
4. I cannot leave my post; nor can I hold any conversation, except in the proper discharge of my duties.
5. I repeat all calls made by sentinels more distant from the guardhouse than myself.
6. In case of a disturbance in the vicinity of my post, I cry, "The guard, No.___." In case of a fire, I cry, "Fire, No.___." Whether it be a fire or disturbance, if the danger be great, I discharge my piece before calling out.
7. During the day, from reveille to retreat, I salute all officers according to rank: The commanding officer and officer of the day

(whatever the rank) and all officers above the rank of captain I salute with "present." Captains, and all officers of lower rank, I salute with a "sergeant's salute."

8. From retreat until taps I stand "at attention" to officers, but do not salute.

9. After taps I stand "at attention" to officers only after they have given the countersign, or have been passed by a non-commissioned officer of the guard.

10. During the night, from taps to reveille, I challenge all persons who approach me, taking, at the same time, the position of "ready" and do not allow any person to come within reach of my piece until he has given the countersign, or been passed by a non-commissioned officer of the guard.

My special orders* are: [the sentinel then gives all the special orders of his post.]

—Troop B, 10th Cavalry, Fort Davis, Texas 1882.

* Specific orders issued by headquarters pertaining to or concerning certain individuals or elements within the command.

Fort Davis National Historic Site, Fort Davis, Texas

TIDBIT: The name BUFFALO SOLDIERS was given to black cavalry soldiers by the Indians who compared them to the buffalo, an animal with a tough curly hide similar to their short curly hair.

The Last Stand by Frederic Remington, c1907 (Library of Congress)

A Multiple-Choice Quiz
CUSTER'S LAST STAND

*"The Indians have long opposed all efforts of white men
to enter the Black Hills, but I have a well-equipped
force, strong enough to take care of itself."*
—George Armstrong Custer

Pondered, analyzed, discussed, re-enacted. The single most important engagement—and the greatest debacle— of the Indian Wars has come to be known as *Custer's Last Stand*. On the Great Plains of North America camped the greatest concentration of Indians ever assembled. Maybe 12,000 strong. At least 1,500 warriors. All of them ready to do battle with the white man. Washington kept pushing and pushing. The Sioux were infuriated by the hordes of miners and settlers moving onto their reservation in the Black Hills of Dakota Territory. The Indians of the Northern Plains had run out of patience. Washington was fed up. *General Philip Sheridan* was intent on crushing the Indians. He knew they were building in numbers for the annual *Sun Dance* near the Valley of the Little Big Horn River. It was time to mount a three-pronged offensive on the encampment that would trap the Indians and prevent their escape. *General George Crook* led 1,300 men north to Montana from Fort Fetterman, Wyoming. *Colonel John Gibbon* brought a column of 400 men east from Fort Ellis in Montana, and *General Alfred Terry* led the 7th Cavalry, with a little over 600 men, westward from Fort Abraham Lincoln, in Dakota Territory. The Indians would surely be caught by one column or another. At one point Gibbon's column met briefly with Terry's command and Terry decided to stay with Gibbon and leave the 7th to Custer, ordering him up the Rosebud River to approach the Big Horn River from the south. Gibbon's last words to Custer were "Now, Custer, don't be greedy. You wait for us." Custer replied "I won't." The rest is history—to be analyzed over and over again. The battle ended an era in American History. The winners of the battle actually lost the war and a lot of factors influenced the outcome. What really happened that day? Many movies have been made about this tragic battle. Here's a multiple-choice quiz to challenge Custer buffs.

The movement of troops in the valley of the Little Big Horn River

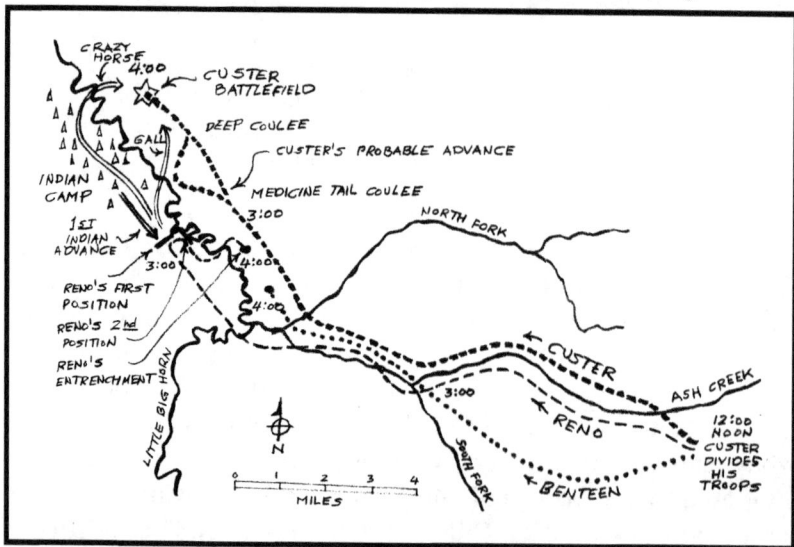

MAJOR GENERAL GEORGE ARMSTRONG CUSTER
Officer of the Federal Army, c1863 (Library of Congress)

1. On what day did the battle occur?

A. October 26, 1881.
B. June 25, 1876.
C. May 12, 1865.
D. March 3, 1871.

1-B. *June 25, 1876, at about 4:00 p.m. Estimates put the duration of the fight from about 3o minutes to two hours. October 26, 1881 was the famous gunfight at the*

O.K. Corral. May 12, 1865 was the Battle of Palmetto Ranch, the last battle of the Civil War, and March 3, 1871 was the date the Indian Appropriation Act declared that Indian tribes would no longer be recognized as a sovereign power and thus the U.S. would not be required to make treaties with them.

2. Where did the battle occur?
A. Rosebud Creek.
B. The Yellowstone River in Southeastern Montana.
C. The Little Bighorn River in Southeastern Montana.
D. The Bighorn River in Wyoming.

2-C. *The Little Bighorn River in Southeastern Montana. The Indian encampment was situated just to the west of the river. The Last Stand occurred on the bluffs on the east side of the river.*

3. Which Indian Nation was NOT a participant in the battle?
A. Sioux
B. Apache
C. Cheyenne
D. Aarapahoe

3-B. *Apache Indians lived in the Southwestern United States.*

4. Who led the Indian Nations to a victory over the 7th Cavalry at Little Big Horn?
A. Cochise.
B. Black Kettle.
C. Crazy Horse and Gall.
D. Geronimo.

4-C. *Crazy Horse first hit Custer from the north and west and Gall attacked from the south and east. Sitting Bull, a medicine man, was in the camp, but did not participate in the battle.*

5. What was George Armstrong Custer's military rank at the time of the battle?
A. Captain.
B. Lieutenant Colonel.
C. Colonel.
D. Major General.

5.-B. *Lt. Colonel Custer had a field promotion to Major General in the Civil War, but as was the usual practice, his rank was reduced after the war.*

6. General Philip Sheridan's plan of attack was predicated on the belief that:
A. The Indian force was smaller than their own.
B. The Indians would flee when attacked.

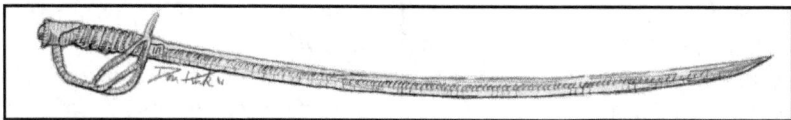

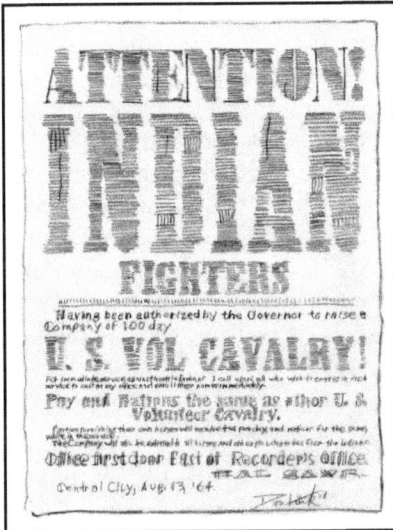

C. The 7th Cavalry could handle anything it confronted.

D. Chief Sitting Bull was suffering a "mental instability" making tactical errors on his part likely.

6-B. *The Indians had previously used guerilla warfare and always avoided direct confrontation with cavalry units.*

7. Which event is NOT true?

A. Because of lack of a liaison, General Alfred Terry's force did not know General Crook's column—coming up from Fort Fetterman—had been turned back by the Indians.

B. The cavalry never made a serious attempt to determine how many Indians were in the area.

C. Custer surrounded himself with officers who would challenge his ideas and make better decisions by consensus.

D. Custer refused an extra battalion of cavalry and a battery of Gatling guns just before the campaign began.

E. As many as 40% of the 7th cavalry were raw recruits or had never fought Indians before.

7-C. *Custer actually surrounded himself with family members and those who agreed with his tactics. At the Little Big Horn were two brothers, Boston and Thomas, Henry Armstrong Reed (a nephew), and Lt. James Calhoun, a brother-in-law. Custer left behind three Gatling guns because he felt they would slow down his march; these rapid-fire weapons might have changed the result of the battle.*

8. Believing the Indians would turn and run when attacked, General Terry sent Custer's column around to the south to:

A. Block the escape route of the Indians.

B. Meet up with Crook coming from the South.

C. Find water to refill supply wagon water barrels.

D. All of the above.

8-A. *Block the escape route of the Indians. He believed the Indians would turn and run when his column attacked them from the north and he didn't*

Gatling Gun, Fort Concho, Texas (dk)

want them to get away. The entire attack was predicated on the belief that the Indians would flee when attacked as they had done in the past, usually using guerrilla tactics: running, striking, and running again.

9. Which personal weakness contributed to Custer's downfall at Little Big Horn?

A. Custer was unable to command the respect and loyalty of his officers after the Washita River incident where he abandoned Major Joel Elliott and

19 men eight years earlier (1868).
B. He had an immense ego that kept him from listening to his subordinates. He believed he was always correct.
C. He believed that success always lay in striking the enemy unmercifully and without delay.
D. He never learned from his mistakes.
E. Custer believed the Indians, when attacked, would never stand and fight.
F. All of the above.

9-F. *All of the above. Its any wonder he had a command at all. In fact, Sheridan originally did not want him on this campaign. Without some new military accomplishment, Custer felt his career was over. It was now or never. He had to have a major victory. To be sure, Custer had proven himself courageous in a fight, never taking the easy way out.*

SITTING BULL c1888 (Library of Congress)

10. What was considered by military historians to be Custer's most fatal error?

A. Not developing a close personal relationship with Captain Benteen.

B. Ignoring the orders of General Terry to block the Indian's escape.

C. Dividing his command of 600 men into three columns.

D. Wearing his hair so long, the wind would blow it in his eyes, disturbing his aim.

10-C. *Dividing his command was his single most important mistake. A mistake he had made before. He might have had a chance with the Indians if he hadn't broken and scattered his strength. Custer sent Benteen with three companies (180 men) to swing left and stop any*

GEORGE A. CUSTER - 1865

fleeing Indians, a big mistake because Benteen was his senior. Benteen was a captain and a most effective combat officer— now taken out of the fight. After seeing a few Indians, Custer then sent Major Reno (180 more men) after them, giving the order to "charge after them and you will be supported by the whole outfit." Reno assumed that meant Custer would come behind him—which he didn't.

11. Which statement is true?

A. Three men actually survived at Custer's Last Stand.

B. Reno and Benteen heard the gunfire of Custer's battle (just two miles away) and elected not to go to his aid.

C. On Custer's last day, General George Crook was fly fishing.

D. General Terry sighted the smoke and dust from Custer's fighting and pushed his column at a gallop to join the fight.

11-C. *Crook was fly fishing on the 17th of June, eight days before the battle of Little Big Horn. Crook encountered a Sioux and Cheyenne force led by Crazy Horse at Rosebud Creek, and after hand-to-hand combat, Crook was forced to retreat. The next day Crook gave his men the day off. Crook had no idea what was happening just 100 miles north of him; he had no communication with the other two columns. That also meant Terry didn't know*

Crook's 1,300 men were out of the upcoming fight. Choice "B" is only speculation and has not yet been proven, though audio tests at the site suggest Reno and Benteen could very well have heard the shots. But they felt no sense of urgency. The last communication from Custer's messenger had indicated no need for additional troops. The message from Custer's adjutant said "Benteen. Come on. Big village. Be quick. Bring packs. —W.W. Cooke P.S. Bring Pacs," meaning bring the pack trains of supplies which would take a lot longer to move than just troops. Benteen did not like Custer; he frequently questioned Custer's orders and accused him of cowardice in an article to the "Missouri Democrat" shortly after the Washita River incident. Curly, a scout for Custer, was the sole survivor of the massacre. The sole surviving animal of Custer's command was "Comanche," Captain Miles Keogh's mount. The wounded horse survived until 1891, was "stuffed," and now sits in the Natural History Museum on the Kansas University campus.

12. What warning did Custer get that there was a very large concentration of Indians in the valley ahead?
A. The Indian trail running toward the valley was wide and clearly defined (at places it was more than a half-mile wide, and the earth turned up as if by a cattle drive).
B. The column passed many deserted Indian campsites only a mile or two apart suggesting a large encampment.
C. Custer's Crow and Arikara scouts believed a freak snowstorm and high water in the streams were bad omens.
D. Lonesome Charley Reynolds informed Custer that the Indians had been gathering guns for months and had every intention of fighting.
E. All of the above.

12-E. *All of the above. The news of a large concentration of Indians made Custer all the more eager to fight. He considered it his good luck. The more Indians he killed the greater would be his fame.*

SITTING BULL

Cavalry First Sergeant, Ft. Concho, Texas (dk)

13. Custer chose not to wait around to block the retreating Indians as ordered and instead advanced westward to attack the Indians himself. Which TWO were probably his reasons for doing so?

A. Custer, impatient, wanted to get home before the July 4th celebration.

B. He didn't want to share victory with Terry and Gibbon who intended to attack from the North.

C. His scouts told him Sitting Bull had left camp to receive a vision and his warriors wouldn't fight until he returned.

D. He didn't want to continue south and meet up with General Crook's column, thus making him a subordinate, and the victory then Crook's.

13-B&D. *Both reasons would have followed his desire to make himself a hero again. His decision to turn west—rather than continue south—was the crucial move that led to battle. And of course, that's what he wanted.*

14. Terry sent Reno to block any Indian retreat from the South. Which statement is NOT true?

A. Reno had previously commanded several fights against the Indians.

B. Reno started an aggressive attack against the village only to halt his men and dismount before any fighting actually occurred.

C. In his hasty retreat he abandoned his wounded.

D. He made no attempt to cover his rear during retreat up the bluffs, allowing Indian warriors to ride up and shoot his men from behind like fish in a barrel.

14-A. *A is False. Reno had never before led a fight against Indians.*

15. What name did the Indians give to George Armstrong Custer after the battle?

A. Yellow Hair.

B. Long Hair.

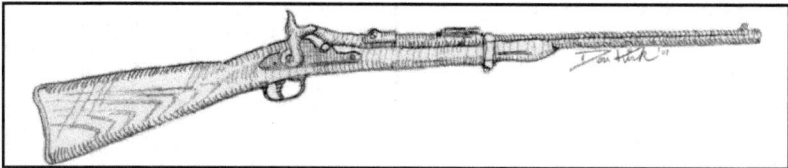

C. Yellow Legs.
D. Long Legs.

15-B. *Long Hair. Sitting Bull called him that a year after the battle when he said, "I tell no lies about dead men. These men who came with the 'Long Hair' were as good men as ever fought."*

16. Was George Armstrong Custer wearing a buckskin shirt and red neckerchief at his last battle as is so often seen in paintings depicting "Custer's Last Stand"?
A. Yes.   **B.** No.

16-B. *No. Custer was dressed in a Civil War general's navy-blue uniform.*

17. What age was George Custer when he died?
A. 23   **C.** 36
B. 32   **D.** 52

17-C. *He was 36, (1839-1876). Custer was a Civil War general at 23 and was dubbed "The Boy General" by the press.*

IN SUMMATION:

Custer's Last Stand was the U.S. Army's most decisive defeat of the Indian Wars and it destroyed any chance of making peace with the Indians. They would have to be completely subdued. Military forces were strengthened on the plains to make sure they stayed on reservations. Never again could the Native Americans fight with the strength they had amassed at the Little Big Horn.

No one knows exactly what happened to Custer in his final battle that eventually brought him more fame than if he had won the battle. Messenger *Giovanni Martini* was the last to see him alive. Because the Indians had no organized structure of command, interviews with Indians only revealed what each had done, not any tactical maneuvers. The Indians were not even aware, until after the battle, that Custer was there.

Custer apparently led his command to *Medicine Tail Coulee* and moved toward the

central ford on the Little Bighorn. The huge Indian encampment was directly across the river. Maybe 1,000 warriors facing 200 men! Custer would have considered it his good luck, and probably would have attacked, but the Indians charged across the river pushing Custer's men back into the gullies and arroyos of the hills. Custer would seek high ground and then stand and fight. Custer's 7th expired while Reno and Benteen's columns stood just two miles away!

From the Indian Nations' point of view, Crazy Horse was in camp and he was a tactician having had great success at Fort Phil Kearny where he destroyed William Fetterman. Sioux Chief

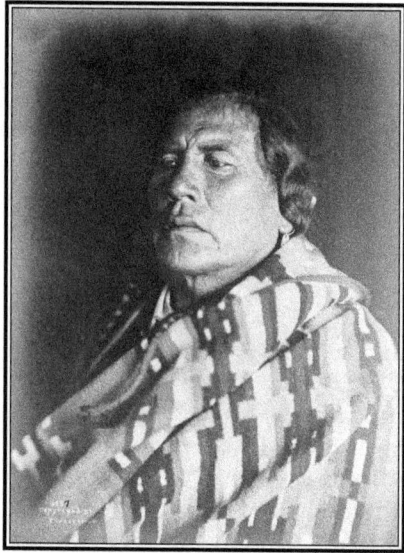

Curly, a scout for Custer, was the sole survivor of the massacre. (Richard Throssel, photographer, c1907, Library of Congress)

Gall, who had been fighting Reno upriver, heard the fighting and brought hundreds of warriors to attack Custer's rear while Crazy Horse came around to the other side of the very hill Custer was retreating to, climbed the hill, and hit him head on. Custer's men were now standing back to back as Gall's braves dismounted and crawled toward Custer, killing them by shooting arrows into the air. The cavalry troopers couldn't see nor hear the approaching Indians, making it virtually impossible to return fire. A note should be made that the Cavalry's antique Springfield carbines overheated in battle and caused the copper cartridges to jam requiring a knife to extract them (The officer's trapdoor carbines had a ramrod and extraction tool). The Indians actually had some of the newer Winchester repeating rifles which the quartermaster in Washington had chosen not to adopt for the Army.

The next day the Indians again attacked Reno and Benteen, and by mid-afternoon they suddenly retreated, pulled up camp, and left the valley. General Terry's troops finally arrived from the north only to find 197 naked bodies strewn all over the ground. Three years later, Major Marcus Reno, the senior surviving officer, requested a court of inquiry which, after 26 days of testimony, exonerated him of any wrongdoing. But did Reno and Benteen hear gunshots from Custer's position? Did their dislike of Custer lead to his death? And even if they had been able to reach Custer in time, could they have done any good? We will probably never know.

A Match Game
5 CUSTER MOVIES

Match the movies about Custer's Last Stand with the actor who played GEORGE ARMSTRONG CUSTER.

1. *Little Big Man* (1970)
2. *Son of the Morning Star* (1990)
3. *Tonka* (1958)
4. *Little Big Horn* (1951)
5. *They Died With Their Boots On* (1941)
6. *Custer of the West* (1968)

a. Robert Shaw
b. Richard Mulligan
c. Errol Flynn
d. Gary Cole
e. No Custer in film
f. Britt Lomond

ANS: 1-b, 2-d, 3-f, 4-e, 5-c, 6-a.

A well-appointed officer's office, Fort Davis National Historic Site, Texas (dk)

TIDBIT: Forts were ramshackle affairs, built in desolate places to protect settlers and supply routes. They were constructed with whatever materials were handy—logs, stone, adobe—and were kept minimal and without defensible walls with the belief held by many generals that "it is better for troop morale to depend on vigilance and breechloaders for protection than to hide behind palisades."

Publicity still for *Fort Apache,* 1948, Argosy Pictures (author's collection)

Dismounted: The Fourth Trooper Moving the Lead Horses, 1890
Oil on Canvas by Frederick Remington (1861-1909) DECA

A Glossary
CAVALRY TERMINOLOGY

*"As we say in the cavalry,
a man without a horse is a man afoot."*
—Waterhole #3, (1967)

Get out your best cavalry impression, trot down to the local elementary school, and these definitions will come in handy.

1. **accoutrements.** The troopers accessories like his pistol belt and saber, but not his firearms and clothing.

2. **ambush.** The place where troops are hidden in advance of the approach of an enemy in order to spring an unexpected surprise attack on them.

3. **ammunition.** Everything required to charge a weapon: balls, powder, shells, etc.

4. **avant-garde.** The advance troops traveling in front of the main force. The word later came to apply to the leaders of a new movement, especially in the arts.

5. **appointments.** An officer's clothing accessories such as his sash, belt, hat plumes, etc.

6. **artillery.** One of the three main branches of the military whose responsibility it is to haul and fire large caliber guns too heavy to carry on foot: cannons, *mortars, howitzers,* and the ammunition for them. One two-wheeled gun carriage would carry the cannon. Hooked to the front was a second two-wheeled carriage called the *limber* which carried an ammunition chest containing black powder, balls, ramming rods, ignition cord, cleaning supplies, etc.

7. **barricade.** A hastily-constructed fortification built for protection from an impending enemy attack. It might be built of anything handy such as earth, logs, wagons, or crates.

8. **battalion.** A force of infantry consisting of two to ten companies, one of which is a headquarters company. Three battalions form a regiment.

9. **battery.** The cannon placements (of one or more cannon) strategically stationed around a

fortification for maximum coverage of the area to be defended. Also the lowest administrative unit of the artillery, equivalent to an army *company*.

10. **bayonet.** A sharp pike-like steel weapon that can be attached to the barrel of a rifle for use in hand-to-hand combat.

11. **bivouac.** A temporary encampment of soldiers in the open with campfires, but usually without tents. Without protection, guards must keep a close watch.

12. **blockhouse.** A building for defense constructed of heavy timbers containing only small openings through which guns can be fired.

13. **bomb.** A hollow iron ball filled with explosive powder, ignited with a fuse, and used in *mortars* and *howitzers*. The fuse is timed to explode the ball in the air showering shrapnel down on the enemy.

14. **breastwork.** A low, quickly constructed, barrier of earth and timbers behind which a man can stand and fire at the enemy. It would be as high as the breast of a man.

15. **caisson.** An ammunition chest, in artillery; the two-wheeled wagon carrying the chest that follows the gun.

16. **campaign.** A series of military operations with a particular objective.

17. **Captain.** Company commander.

18. **carbine.** A relatively light-weight rifle with a short barrel used by mounted troops because a musket would be unwieldy to fire from horseback.

19. **cavalry.** The branch of the army where troops are trained and equipped to fight on horseback with swords, *carbines* and pistols.

20. **Colonel.** Regimental commander.

HARDTACK

TIDBIT: Hardtack was the staple of the nineteenth-century soldier. It was a standard issue ration both in the Civil War and in the Cavalry during the Indian wars. Officially called "hard bread," it was a plain water and flour biscuit that had not risen. It was extremely hard and almost impossible to eat, but it would last forever. To make this biscuit more edible, the soldier would soak it in coffee or crumble it into soup. A decent pastry could be make from hardtack by soaking it in cold water, frying it in pork fat, and then sprinkling it with sugar.

21. **colors.** The flags of a unit to act as a rallying point for troops and to mark the location of the commander.

22. **company.** Lowest administrative unit in the cavalry; 50 to 100 men commanded by a captain, with one lieutenant, sergeant, and corporal. Equivalent to an artillery's *battery*.

23. **deadline.** The line in a military prison beyond which a prisoner would be shot by a guard.

24. **depot.** The building where military provisions are warehoused.

25. **detachment.** A small body of army troops broken off from the main unit to perform a specific duty.

26. **equipage.** All the furnishings, accessories, tentage, kitchen, etc. necessary for a body of troops to survive in the field.

27. **dragoon.** A name first given to blunderbusses in the 17th century. Also a soldier armed with a short musket and trained to fight either on foot or on horseback; a mounted infantryman.

28. **file.** A single line of soldiers, one behind the other, see *rank*.

29. **grape-shot.** Small iron balls put into a lead canister and fired from a cannon.

30. **haversack.** A cloth bag with a shoulder strap carried by foot soldiers for rations.

31. **howitzer.** A short light-weight cannon with a low muzzle velocity used to fire hollow-shot, canister-shot, etc. in a relatively high trajectory.

32. **knapsack.** A leather or canvas bag carried on the back by an infantry soldier containing his clothes, rain gear, eating utensils, etc.

33. **Lieutenant.** Second officer of a company. Lowest officer who receives a commission.

34. **Light Colonel.** Second officer of a regiment.

35. **Lincoln shingles.** A hard bread approximately 3"x3"x1/2" in size that the troopers often ate with molasses and gave it appropriate names like: *sheet-iron crackers* and *teeth-dullers*.

36. **magazine.** A heavy fortified storehouse for provisions, munitions, arms, explosives, etc.

37. **Major.** Third officer in command of a battalion.

38. **Major General.** Commands a division.

39. **mortar.** A short cannon with a large bore used to throw *bombs* into an enemy.

40. **muster.** To assemble the troops for a roll-call, inspection, exercise, parade, etc.

41. **non-commissioned officer.** All officers below the grade of a company lieutenant.

TIDBIT: The TWENTY-ONE-GUN SALUTE used by the military at funerals was derived from the number **1776**, the year of American independence from Britain. By adding up the individual numbers in the date, they came up with 21.

---

42. **ordnance.** A term applied to all the weapons and ammunition used in warfare.

43. **outpost.** The troops (or the place) outside of a camp or fort where they are stationed to guard or protect an area, or provide an early warning of enemy attack.

44. **park.** An area set aside in an encampment for the temporary storage of animals, wagons, artillery, etc.

45. **parley.** To confer with the enemy under a temporary flag of truce.

46. **parole.** A word of honor, a promise given by a military prisoner that if he is turned loose (released from captivity) or given certain privileges, he will meet the requirements made by his captors such as a promise to take no further part in the fighting.

47. **party.** A small group of soldiers "detailed" to perform a task.

48. **rank.** A line of soldiers standing or marching shoulder to shoulder, see *file*. Also the official grade of a soldier on which authority and the pay scale is based.

49. **ration.** The daily allotment of food, drink and provisions for each soldier. They were issued three days rations when going into the field.

Enlisted barracks, Fort Davis National Historic Site, Fort Davis, Texas (dk)

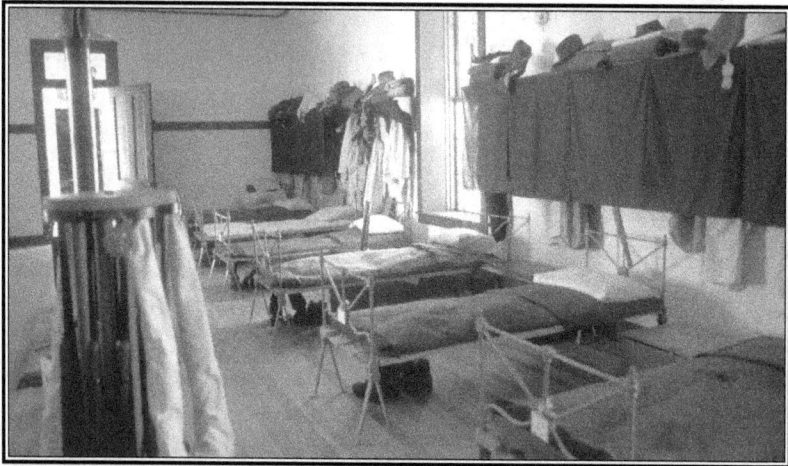

Ready, Aim, Fire!
33 MAJOR INDIAN-WAR BATTLES

"Keep the last bullet for yourself."
—advice to new cavalry recruits when fighting the Indians.

Here's a list of the major battles fought with the Indians from 1862 to 1898. During that period 423 Medals of Honor were awarded. 24 at Little Big Horn alone. The entries are listed by date with the white man's name for the battle, then the territory where it took place, date of the battle, the Indian's name for the battle, the tribes and Indian chiefs that participated, the cavalry unit and cavalry commanders, numbers of men, and the "victor" of the confrontation.

1857 **Spirit Lake Massacre**—Iowa—March 8th—Wahpekute Dakota: Chief Inkpaduta—Sioux Indians attacked settlers for being on their sacred land—32 white settlers are killed.

1862 **Wood Lake**—Minnesota—Sept. 23rd—Santee Sioux: Chief Little Crow & Chief Mankato (700-1200 men)—6th & 7th Minnesota Infantry: Col. Henry Sibley & Col. William Marshall (1619 men)—A part of the Dakota War—U.S. victory. Chief Mankato was killed and Sibly was promoted to Brigadier General.

1862 **Birch Coulee**—Minnesota—Sept. 2nd—Santee Sioux: Chiefs Gray Bird, Red Legs, Big Eagle, and Mankato (200 men)—Major Joseph Brown (170 men)—a part of the Dakota War—Indian victory. Most deadly for the U.S. in the Dakota Wars: 13 soldiers and 90 horses killed, 47 wounded. The Indians lost just two.

1863 **Big Mound**—Dakota Territory—July 24-25—Santee and Teton Sioux: Chief Inkpaduta (unknown number of men)—Henry Hastings Sibley (3,000 men)—U.S. victory. Sibling attacked entrenched Indian positions and they scattered. A few days later the two forces met at Dead Buffalo Lake.

1863 **Whitestone Hill**—Dakota Territory—Sept. 3-5—Chief Inkpaduta, Santee, Chief Yankton, Cut-Head, and Hunkpapa of the Teton Sioux (1,200-1,500 men)—Brig. Gen. Alfred Sully, 6th Iowa Cavalry and

Phil Sheridan and Staff, c1862 (Library of Congress)
Left to Right: Major Gen. Sheridan, Col. Jos Forsythe, Chief of Staff Merritt,
Brig. Gen. Thos. C. Devins, and Major Gen. Geo. A. Custer.

2nd Nebraska Cavalry (600-700 men)—U.S. victory, 72 U.S. soldiers and 750 Indians killed. Even though Sibley completely overran the Sioux encampment, burned their tents and equipment, and captured women and children, the Sioux were not destroyed.

1864 **Battle of Kildeer Mountain** (aka Battle of Tahkahokuty Mountain)—Dakota Territory—July 28th—Santee & Teton Sioux: Inkpaduta (5,000-6,000)—U.S. Army: Alfred Sully (2,500)—Sully attacked camp, and after heavy fighting, sent them running without their belongings—U.S.: 15 dead, Sioux: 31. U.S. victory. The loss broke the spirit of the Sioux.

1864 **Canyon de Chelly**—Arizona—Sept. 1863-Jan 1864—Navajo: Barboncito, Armijo, Manuelit—U.S: Gen. James Carlton, "Kit" Carson—With a "scorched earth" policy, Carson chased, killed, captured, stole stock, and destroyed crops and hogans. Without food or shelter the Navajo were gradually forced to surrender and marched on *The Long Walk* across New Mexico to the Bosque Redondo prison camp at Fort Sumner.

1864 **Sand Creek Massacre**—Colorado Territory—Nov, 29th—Cheyenne and Arapaho: Chief Black Kettle (500 men)—Col. John Chivington (800 men)—U.S. victory. Chivington's battle cry was *"Kill them all, big and tall, nits make lice."* 15 soldiers killed, mostly due to friendly fire, and over fifty wounded; 200 Indians killed, but they were mostly elderly men, women, and children. Because the U.S. Government had promised peace with Black Kettle and told him if he flew an American flag over his camp they would not attack. All but 60 of his men were gone hunting when Chivington's drunken men attacked, ignoring a white flag of surrender. Most of the elderly men and boys were unarmed. The soldiers plundered the teepees, took the horses, scalped the dead, and made some body parts into tobacco pouches.

1864 **First Battle of Adobe Walls**—Texas—Nov. 26th—Dohãsan & Satanta, Kiowa & Comanche (5,000 men)—Kit Carson (321 soldiers, 75 Indian scouts)—U.S. victory. The Indians, heavily outnumbering Carson, forced him to retreat, but Carson set backfires and used twin howitzers that prevented the Indians from overrunning his position. Just three soldiers dead, 15 wounded to the Indians 50 to 60 killed.

1865 **Battle of the Tongue River (aka Connor Battle)**—Wyoming Territory—August 29th—Arapaho: Chief Black Bear and Chief Medicine Man (500 men)—Brigadier General Patrick Edward Connor (400 men). This battle was the major engagement of the Powder River Expedition which was directed against the Southern Cheyenne, Arapaho, and Lakota Sioux with the purpose of stopping the raids on the Bozeman Trail. Connor attacked Black Bear's Village, 63 Indians killed or wounded. U.S. victory.

1865 **Sawyer Expedition Ambush**—Wyoming Territory—August 31th—Arapaho—Expedition surveying route for Bozeman Trail led by Col. James Sawyer, attacked by Arapaho in retaliation for Connor's attack on Black Bear's Village. Lasted 13 days until rescued by General Conner's Powder River Expedition Force.

1866 **Crazy Woman Battle**—Wyoming Territory—July 20th—Sioux & Cheyenne—Lt. George M. Templeton (18th U.S. Infantry)—U.S. victory. A small party of wagons was ambushed in the middle of Crazy Woman Creek. There were 37 in the wagon train, but nine were woman and children, and only 10 of the enlisted men had weapons. Templeton was able to hold off the Indians until help

Officers of the 9th Cavalry, John C.H. Grabill, photographer (Library of Congress)

arrived from a nearby supply train dispatched from Fort Phil Kearny. Two soldiers died, most of the men wounded. A U.S. victory, but it signaled the beginning of hostilities on the Bozeman.

1866 **Fetterman Massacre—***Battle of a Hundred Slain*—Wyoming Territory—Dec. 21st—Sioux, Cheyenne & Arapaho: Red Cloud & Crazy Horse (2,000 warriors)—U.S: Capt. William Fetterman, Capt. Frederick Brown, and 2nd Lt. George Grummond (80 soldiers)—Indian victory. Fetterman ignored orders to stay in support distance from the fort and pursued a small band of Sioux, but found himself surrounded and completely wiped out in under twenty minutes. The Fetterman Massacre was second only to Custer's defeat in 1876. The trail became know as the "Bloody Bozeman."

1867 **The Hayfield Fight—**Montana Territory near Fort Smith—Aug. 1st—Cheyenne & Sioux (500-800 warriors)—Lt. Sigismund Sternberg & Al Colvin (27 men)—U.S. victory. Three soldiers died, four wounded, 60-300 Indians killed, 300 wounded. While cutting hay, the men were attacked and retreated to a log stockade where they were able to defend against repeated attacks. Their success was due to a recent issue of the .50-caliber Model 1866 "trapdoor" Springfield, a breechloading rifle. It had been supplied as the direct result of the Fetterman Massacre. Unfortunately for the Indians, their attack strategy was based on the slow reloading time of the muzzleloaders.

1867 **Wagon Box Fight**—Wyoming Territory—Aug. 2nd—Cheyenne and Arapaho: Red Cloud, Crazy Horse, American Horse (1,000-2,000)—Capt. James Powell (31 men)—U.S. victory. Five soldiers killed, two wounded, 50-150 Indians killed, 100 plus wounded. Soldiers assigned to protect a wood-cutting detail used fourteen upended wagons as a defensive position and successfully turned away repeated attacks. This U.S. victory was also attributed to the recent issuance of the "trapdoor" Springfield.

1867 **Mountain Meadows Massacre**—Utah Territory—September 11th—Arkansas immigrants traveling to California were attacked by a Mormon militia disguised as Indians. Paiute tribesman were also involved in the fight. After a long battle, the surviving men were coaxed to surrender and were then summarily executed, including many women and children.

1868 **Battle of Becher Island**—Colorado Territory—*The Fight Where Roman Nose Was Killed*—Sioux, Cheyenne and Arapaho: Tall Bull, Pawnee Killer and Roman Nose—U.S. 9th Cavalry: Major Forsyth—U.S. victory after a nine-day battle.

1868 **Battle of the Washita**—Oklahoma Indian Territory—Nov. 27th—Cheyenne: Black Kettle (150 warriors)—7th Cavalry: George Custer (full regiment)—U.S. victory. Custer led a surprise attack on Black Kettle's village on the Washita River.

A PROBLEM WITH THE WIND

TIDBIT: George Custer once solved a pesky problem that women encountered on the military posts of the windy plains. A sudden gust of wind would often sweep a woman's skirts up over her head, revealing those bare ankles and bloomers. To save the ladies this repeated embarrassment, he ordered buckshot to be sewn into the hem of their skirts.

1872 **Salt River Canyon**—New Mexico Territory—December 28th—Kwevkepaya (110 men)—Capt. William Brown (220 men)—U.S. Victory. 76 Indians killed. Brown's men trapped the Indians in a cave and pushed boulders down on them until they surrendered.

1873 **Massacre Canyon Battle**—Nebraska Territory—August 5th—Sioux: Spotted Tail, Little Wound, Two Strikes (1000 warriors); Pawnee: Sky Chief, Sun Chief, Fighting Bear (250 warriors)—The Pawnee, allied with the whites against

Mounted cavalry soldier, c1865
(Libraey of Congress)

their hated enemy the Brule and Oglala Sioux, headed off the reservation on their authorized summer buffalo hunt with 250 men and 150 women and children. John Williamson was trail agent. The Sioux attacked the Pawnee believing that their sub-agent, Janis, didn't say they *couldn't* fight their enemy if off the reservation. Approx. 6 Sioux killed, 69 Pawnee killed. It was the last battle between the Sioux and Pawnee. The Pawnee eventually traded their Nebraska lands for the Indian Territory of Oklahoma.

1873 **Lava Beds War,** First and Second Battle of the Stronghold (aka Captain Jack's Stronghold) (The Modoc War)—Oregon & California—January 17th—Modoc: Captain Jack, Hooker Jim (53 warriors)—Lt. Col. Frank Wheaton, Col. Alvin C. Gillem (400-500 men)—In an attempt to move the Modocs to their own reservation after trouble with the Klamaths, a soldier was killed and the band of Indians retreated to the lava beds to set up a defensive position. Several battles ensued before Captain Jack was finally captured. 17 warriors killed, 73 army and civilians. This was the last of the Indian wars to occur in Oregon and California.

1874 **Second Battle of Adobe Walls**—Texas—June 27th—Comanche: Isa-tai and Quanah Parker (300 warriors) versus American hunters (28 men)—U.S. victory, four hunters killed versus 16 Indians. The hunters defended an adobe ruin for four days until reinforcements came and the Indians retreated. The battle led to the Red River War that resulted in the relocation of the Southern Plains Indians to reservations in present-day Oklahoma.

1874 **Battle of Palo Duro Canyon**—Texas—Sept. 28th—Cheyenne, Comanche and Kiowa: Iron Shirt, Poor Buffalo, and Lone Wolf—4th Cavalry: Ronald S. Mackenzie—U.S. victory. 1 soldier killed, 3 Indians. Mackenzie routed the Indians from their Palo Duro safe haven and their stash of winter supplies, effectively ending the Red River War.

1876 **Battle of the Rosebud**—*Battle Where the Girl Saved Her Brother*—Montana Territory—June 17th—Lakota & Cheyenne: Crazy Horse (1,500)—U.S.: General George Crook, Shoshone, and Crow (1,300)—A military effort to get the Lakota and Cheyenne to return to their reservation led to a ferocious six-hour battle on the Rosebud River—The Sioux and Cheyenne eventually retreated. An Army victory, but Crook returned to base camp which prevented him from meeting up with Custer's 7th cavalry—Lakota: 21 dead, 63 wounded, U.S. Army: 32 dead, 21 wounded.

INDIAN SCOUT TRACKING

Indian scouts were superior to U.S. soldiers at tracking the enemy whether on foot or horseback. They could determine the number of Indians, animals, and number of days ahead,

1. by examining dead campfires,
2. by examining the droppings of animals,
3. by examining the condition and color of beat down grass,
4. by examining moccasin footprints to determine the tribe,
5. by examining anything left behind such as clothing, shoes, and hair locks,
6. by noting the size of the trail to determine how many had passed,
7. by noting the kinds of grasses in the horse dung which would reveal from where they had come,
8. and by noting the position of urine puddles in relation to hoof prints which revealed the sex of the horse, and as mares were usually ridden by women, the purpose of the party was determined.

1876 **Battle of the Little Bighorn**—*The Battle of the Greasy Grass*—
June 25th—Lakota, Northern Cheyenne, Arapaho: Sitting Bull and
Crazy Horse (900-1,800 men)—7th cavalry: Lt. Col. George Custer,
Marcus Reno, Frederick Benteen, and James Calhoun—Indian
victory. The Indian forces lost 36 to 136 with about 160 wounded
and the 7th lost 268 men and 55 wounded. Investigations were
conducted after the battle questioning the tactics, strategy, and
conduct of the officers.

1876 **The Dull Knife Fight** (a.k.a. Battle of Bates Creek)—Wyoming
Territory—November 25th—Northern Cheyenne: Dull Knife,
Little Wolf (400 warriors)—Colonel Ranald S. Mackenzie, 2nd, 3rd,
4th, and 5th cavalry regiments (1,000 Men). Mackenzie attacked
their camp on the North Fork of the Powder River and destroyed
173 lodges. After hard fighting, the Indians retreated without their
blankets and robes—9 U.S. killed, 25 warriors, and eventually most
of Dull Knife's followers froze to death.

DUTIES ON THE FRONTIER

When the soldiers of a fort weren't on a campaign against
Indians they might be:

1. protecting a stage or supply wagons,
2. detailed as a woodcutting party in search of fuel,
3. building roads and bridges,
4. repairing telegraph lines,
5. escorting new recruits, paymasters, mail carriers, or emigrant
   trains,
6. on water details to haul and fill post water barrels,
7. on guard duty,
8. performing cavalry drills and target practice, and preparing for
   inspections,
9. or they might be assigned police details such as the disposal
   of garbage, cleaning the stables, digging latrines, caring for the
   post garden, KP (kitchen police) duty, painting and repairing
   post buildings, or weeding the parade ground.

Nothing much has changed for the military soldier in the last 150
years!

1877 **The Battle of White Bird Canyon**—Idaho Territory—June 17th—The opening battle of the war with the Nez Percé (60-70 warriors)—Gen. Oliver O. Howard, Captain David Perry (117 men)—Gold discoveries on their reservation caused the U.S. to insist that the peaceful Nez Percé give up 90% of their land. Attack on settlers and a failed truce led to the battle—34 U.S. Army volunteers killed, 3 warriors wounded. Indian victory.

1877 **Battle of the Big Hole**—Montana—August 9th—Nez Percé: Chief Joseph, Chief Looking Glass (200)—U.S. Army: John Gibbon, Oliver O. Howard (206)—Gibbon attacked encampment at Big Hole Basin, the Indians were not expecting an attack—U.S.: 32 killed, 37 wounded, Nez Percé: 42 killed. Indian victory, but it put Joseph's band on the run toward Canada.

1877 **The Battle of Canyon Creek**—Montana—Summer—Nez Percé: Chief Joseph, Chief Looking Glass (unknown number of warriors)— U.S. and Crow: Samuel D. Sturgis, Lewis Merrill, Frederick Beenteen (350)—Indians take tourists captive at Yellowstone National Park, several killed, 7th Cavalry fight at Canyon Creek sending them packing—U.S.: 3 killed, 11 wounded, Nez Percé: 1 killed, 3 wounded.

1877 **The Battle of Bear Paw Mountain**—Montana—Sept.30-Oct. 5th—Nez Percé: Chief Joseph, Chief Looking Glass (900)—U.S. Army 7th Cavalry: Nelson A. Miles, Oliver O. Howard (520)—Chief Joseph tries to escape to Canada, but Miles finds his camp just 40 miles from the Canadian border. After a first attack, Joseph asked for a truce, but was kept as a prisoner. Nez Percé took a lieutenant as their own and Howard fought on until Chief Joseph agreed to surrender, but White Bird escaped with 50 warriors. U.S.: 36 dead, 47 wounded, Nez Percé: 25 dead, 46 wounded, 500 surrendered. U.S. victory.

1879 **The Meeker & Thornburg Massacre**—Colorado—White River Utes: Chief Captain Jack and Chief Johnson—U.S. Army: Major T. Thornburg (200)—Agent Meeker, who had been trying to make farmers of them, threatened to plow up a Ute racetrack and kill half the ponies, and then claimed he had been assaulted by an Indian and wired for military assistance. The Utes ambushed and killed Thornburg and his men when they continued into Ute land for peace talks, after being told to keep his troops 50 miles away. They then attacked the Indian Agency killing Meeker. Congress immediately passed the *Ute Removal Act of 1880*, which denied to Utes twelve million acres of land that had been guaranteed to them in perpetuity.They were then to be removed to the arid lands of eastern Utah Territory.

1886 **Gerónimo Pursuit and Surrender**—Arizona—Sept. 4th— Apache: Gerónimo—4th Cavalry: Capt. Henry Lawton, Charles B. Gatewood. Geronimo officially surrendered to General Miles at Skeleton Canyon. Gerónimo and the Apache scouts who helped track him down were sent to Pensacola, Florida, then to Alabama and finally to Fort Sill Oklahoma, but Gerónimo was never allowed to return to Arizona.

1890 **Wounded Knee Massacre**—South Dakota—December 29th— Lakota—7th cavalry: Major Samuel M. Whitside, James Forsyth— The military went into camp to disarm the Lakota, but Black Coyote refused and the army opened up with four Hotchkiss guns, killing men, woman, and children. Some Lakoata fired back and then fled, only be pursued and shot down—Lakota: 150 dead, 50 injured, U.S.: 31 soldiers dead, 33 injured, some probably caused by friendly fire.

And in the end Congress repeatedly failed to keep its treaty promises: protecting Indian lands from white encroachment and feeding, clothing, and housing them on the reservations..

The author on the set of *North & South, Book III* (1994), San Antonio, Texas (dk)

THIS STONE MARKS THE BURIAL PLACE

—OF—

SIX TRACK LABORERS

WHO WERE IN THE EMPLOY OF THE UNION PACIFIC RAILWAY, EASTERN DIVISION, AND WHILE ON DUTY, ABOUT ONE MILE WEST OF HERE, WERE MASSACRED BY A BAND OF CHEYENNE INDIANS.

—OCTOBER, 1867.—

ERECTED BY THE UNION PACIFIC RAILROAD COMPANY

Text from an actual stone marker at the site

This attack on track laborers occurred in Victoria, Kansas as a retaliation by the Indians after the Sand Creek Massacre, an unprovoked attack on a Cheyenne Village led by Colonel J. M. Chivington in November 1864.

Indian Wars
18 FEDERAL MILITARY LEADERS

Some of the important military leaders in the Frontier West during the Indian Wars.

Frederick Beecher
Frederick Benteen
Christopher "Kit" Carson
John Chivington
George Crook
George Armstrong Custer
William Fetterman
George Forsyth
James Forsyth

Benjamin Grierson
George Grummond
Ranald Mackenzie
Nelson Miles
Philip Sheridan
William Tecumseh Sherman
Henry Sibley
Alfred Terry
Henry Carrington

TIDBIT: Most of the military units placed in outposts scattered about the west were company-sized. Two or three companies to a post, each commanded by a captain and first and second lieutenant. The NCO's (non-commissioned officers) handled the day-to-day operations of the company. Many were well experienced, having come from fighting in the Union and Confederate armies in the sixties.

Mansker's Station, Goodlettsville, Tennessee

NELSON MILES   GEORGE CUSTER

(Photos: Library of Congress Prints and Photographs Division)

WILLIAM SHERMAN   GEORGE CROOK

A Match Game
FAMOUS PHRASES

Match the legendary military general with the phrase attributed to (or in reference to) him.

1. "War is Hell"
2. The Gray Fox
3. Took credit for bringing in Gerónimo
4. Iron Butt

a. George Crook
b. Nelson Miles
c. George Custer
d. William Sherman

ANS: 1-d, 2-a, 3-b, 4-c.

1-d. In 1880, General William Tecumseh Sherman said this in a speech at the Ohio State Fair: "It is only those who have neither fired a shot nor heard the shrieks and groans of the wounded who cry aloud for blood, more vengeance, more desolation. War is Hell." But the exact wording of the speech is unknown as the press left the room when the general got up to pontificate.

2-a. The name "The Gray Fox" was given to George Crook by the Apaches as a mark of respect, not just because of his huge grey beard, but because he made every effort to understand and learn from his opponents.

3-b. Replacing General Crook in 1886 after Crook was unable to round up Gerónimo, Nelson A. Miles dogged Gerónimo in Arizona and Mexico for 3,000 miles with white troops—instead of Crook's choice to use Apache scouts—until Gerónimo surrendered with his followers. He took credit for this "capture," but it was actually General Charles B. Gatewood who succeeded in negotiating the surrender, though Miles would deny this. He and his band were exiled to a reservation in Florida, but Gerónimo could still say he was never actually captured.

4-c. George Custer's troops called him "Iron Butt" because he pushed his Cavalry columns at a brutal pace, himself never seeming to tire of riding.

Kris Ford as Corporal Akers (dk)

The Buffalo Soldier

The Army established six separate regiments exclusively for black enlisted men: two cavalry (the 9th and 10th) and four infantry (the 38th through 41st), but the units were commanded by white officers. They fought chiefly in the southwest (West Texas, New Mexico and Arizona) with Apache Chief Victorio being one of their worst combatants (1879-1880). (Contrary to the 1997 TNT movie "Buffalo Soldiers," it was Mexican troops that eventually attacked and killed Victorio.) In 1890, the 9th cavalry rescued the 7th from a Sioux attack at Drexel Mission in South Dakota. The Buffalo Soldiers got their name from the Indians who thought their hair was a lot like that of a buffalo's wooly fur. It became a name of pride to them and a buffalo was used on the regimental crest. These men took their duties seriously and had the lowest desertion rate and highest reenlistment of all units in the army. Even with their exemplary record, racial prejudice continued, their units not getting equal consideration in quality and quantity of supplies. Separate black units in the U.S. army were not abolished until 1950.

Officer's quarters, Fort Davis National Historic Site, Fort Davis, Texas (dk)

A Ballad
OH MY DARLING CLEMENTINE
By Percy Montrose (1884)

Here are the lyrics to a couple of cavalry songs made famous by John Ford, the director who used them repeatedly in his cavalry movies filmed in Monument Valley. You can see why the troopers would have liked these songs. "Clementine" is probably based on another song penned in 1863: *Down by the River Liv'd a Maiden* by H.S. Thompson. This one is about a miner's daughter during the '49 California Gold Rush.

In a cavern, in a canyon,
Excavating for a mine,
Lived a miner, forty niner,
And his daughter Clementine.

Chorus:
Oh my darling, oh my darling,
Oh my darling, Clementine.
You are lost and gone forever,
Dreadfull sorry, Clementine.

Light she was and like a fairy,
And her shoes were number nine,
Herring boxes, without topses,
Sandals were for Clementine.

Drove she ducklings to the water,
Ev'ry morning just at nine,
Stubbed her toe upon a splinter,
Fell into the foaming brine.

Ruby lips above the water,
Blowing bubbles soft and fine,
But, alas, I was no swimmer,
So I lost my Clementine.

How I missed her! How I missed her,
How I missed my Clementine,
So I kissed her little sister,
And forgot my Clementine.

The author as Sergeant Jack Honest, Photo by Glynda Smith

Movie still, *The Horse Soldiers,* 1959, John Ford's only Civil War feature. The story is based on Grierson's Raid of April-May 1863, United Artists (author's collection).

SHE WORE A YELLOW RIBBON

'Round her neck she wore a yellow ribbon.
She wore it in the spring-time and in the month of May,
And if you asked her why the heck she wore it,
She says, "It's for my lover who is far, far away."

Far away, far away.
She wore it for her lover far away.
Round her neck she wore a yellow ribbon,
She wore it for her lover who is far, far away.

QUOTE from *The Horse Soldiers*: Major Kendall to Marlowe:
"As usual, I'm just presenting the grim facts. Colonel Secord doesn't seem to understand that the coffee tastes better when the latrines are dug downstream instead of upstream. How do you like *your* coffee, Colonel?"

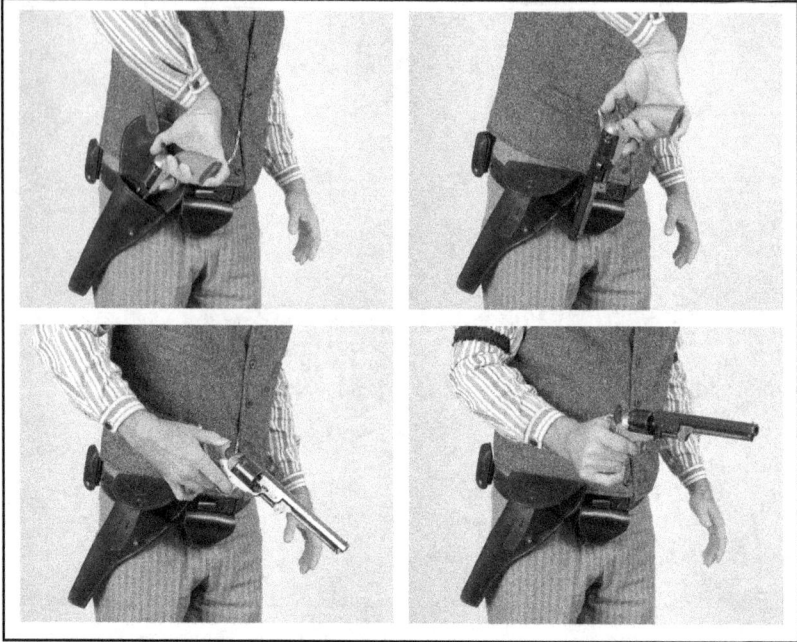

Photos by Michael Jay Smith

THE MILITARY HOLSTER

The pistol holder, worn on the right with only the cap box in front, had a flap that covered the butt of the gun to protect it from rain and loss while on horseback. The pistol fit in the holster butt-forward for added security while on horseback, greatly reducing the chance of loss while mounting, dismounting, or the ocassional bucking horse. It had to be drawn by twisting the wrist to turn the palm out and cocking the hammer with the thumb as the gun is pulled from the holster.

> **A TIDBIT:** As opposed to men in the infantry, a cavalryman needed to be the smallest of the bunch, what with all the equipment the horse had to carry (saddle, bedroll, food, clothes, weapons and ammunition). According to regulations, a cavalryman should be no more than 165 pounds, with 130 to 150 being ideal.
> **ANOTHER TIDBIT:** All of the enlisted men were volunteers. Many were recent immigrants, most having come from England, Germany, and Ireland. Young boys from farming families, looking for adventure, also joined the military out west.

Promotional still from *Rio Grande*, 1950, the last of Ford's Cavalry trilogy, Argosy Pictures (author's collection).

A QUOTE by Lt. Colonel York, from *Rio Grande*:

"I don't want you men to be fooled about what's coming up for you. Torture, at least that. The War Department promised me 180 men. They sent me eighteen. You are the eighteen... so each of you will have to do the work of ten men. If you fail, I'll have you spread-eagled on a wagon wheel. If you desert, you'll be found, tracked down, and broken into bits. That is all."

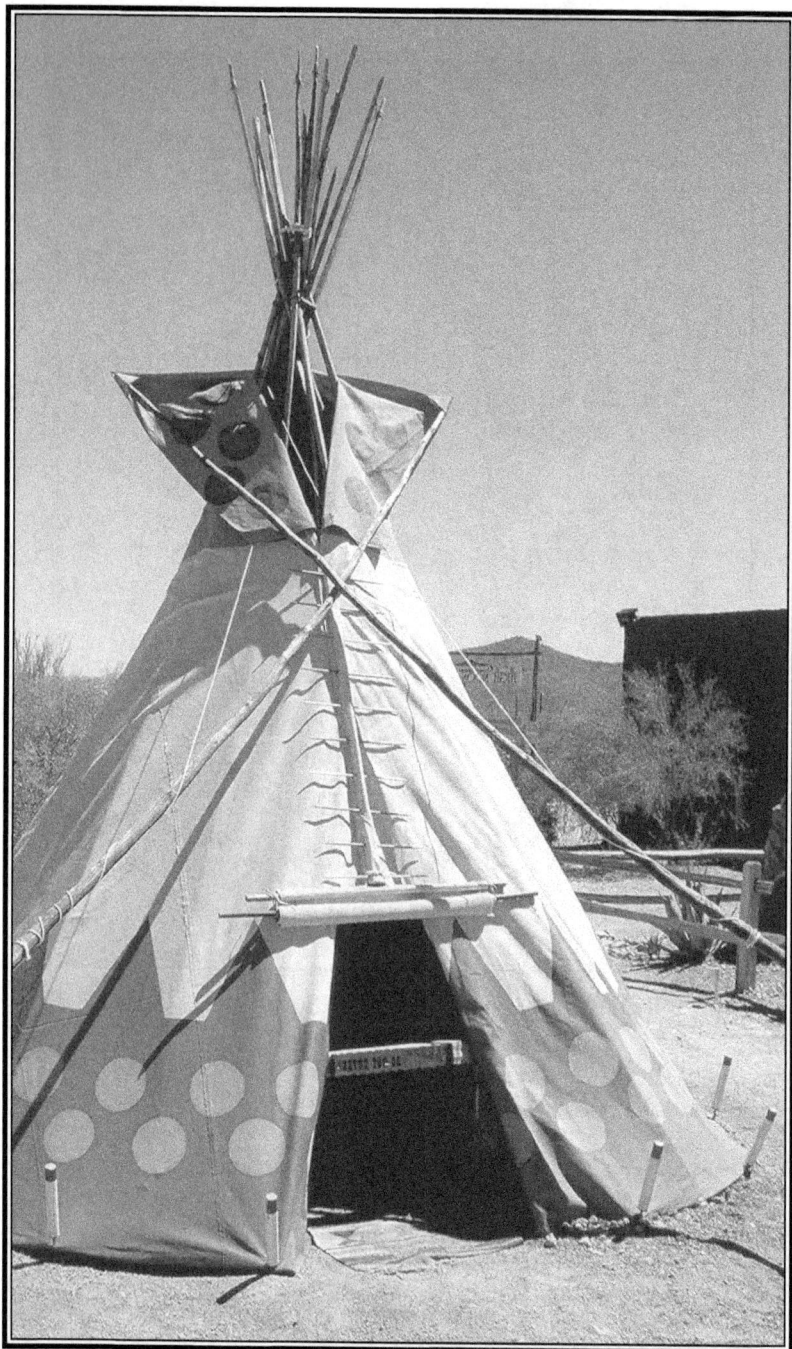

Indian Teepee, Old Tucson Studios, Tucson, Arizona (dk)

Eagle Feathers and Silver Sabers
THE INDIAN NATIONS

*"Little Wolf, what happened today changes nothing. The Indian Bureau
is still pledged to provide you with adequate clothing and rations.
You're still pledged to abide by the law. Remember that." "We are
asked to remember much. The white man remembers nothing."*
—Richard Widmark & Ricardo Montalban, *Cheyenne Autumn,* 1964

The much maligned "hostile" Indians of the American West were anything but until the Spanish, Mexicans, and whites encroached upon their lands. Many tribes were farmers, planting rice, corn, and wheat. Others were nomadic, traveling on foot in search of small game animals for food. As the horse from Spain gradually found itself farther and farther north, the Indians captured it and became more mobile, now able to hunt buffalo and large game. They then encountered other tribes, some of them vicious warriors who routinely stole from the peaceful tribes. Most tribes were initially peaceful to whites, but as the number of whites increased—drawn west by discoveries of gold—the Indians could no longer tolerate the overrunning of their sacred grounds and the deliberate destruction of their food sources, which was in fact their whole livelihood. The Federal government encouraged the killing of buffalo, believing that was the only way to eradicate the "hostile" Indians.

The great Indian Wars of the West spanned the years 1861 to 1885 as the Federal government attempted to quell the clash of cultures by forcing tribes to abandon their hunting grounds by sending them to reservations far from Anglo trade routes where they then tried to teach them agriculture. The reservations were often in barren, arid territory run by greedy Indian agents and politicians who had no regard for the Native American, and who often sold the goods earmarked for the Indians (agreed to by treaty), on the black market. This gradually eroded the Indian's pride and dignity and they would leave the reservation, disgruntled and starving, only to be chased down and dragged back.

THE GHOST DANCE

The Ghost Dance derived from the Mexican culture of the Southwest where a dancing ritual allowed participants a glimpse of their honored dead. The dance was done by both men and women who held hands and walked in a circle. In 1869 at a California harvest festival, "Fish Lake Joe" had a dream that prophesied that the dead would return—and the *Ghost Dance* was born. They came to believe that a "flood or fire would wipe the world clean of white people and their polluting culture." In the 1880's, the Paviotso Indians of present day Nevada started a resurgence of the dance. A Paiute medicine man from Nevada named *Wovoka* founded the practice among the plains Indians after he had a spiritual revelation that said the Indians would enjoy a restoration of traditional tribal ways if they practiced the Ghost Dance. When the Sioux (still very hostile to whites in the 1890's) adopted the ceremony, they added ornamented "ghost shirts" (a hunting shirt patterned after early nineteenth-century shirts) which they believed were impervious to a white man's bullet. The *Ghost Dance* spread like a prairie fire across the West with each tribe modifying the ceremony to fit with its own beliefs and hopes. The Indians came to believe all Indians, both living and dead, would soon be resurrected on a regenerated Earth, with plenty of game and no sickness or death. *Sitting Bull*, believed to be the *Ghost Dance* leader, was shot in the back of the head on December 15, 1890 by an Army soldier. That led to the Wounded Knee Massacre.

TIDBIT: People living east of the Rocky Mountains today call the warm dry winds from the West the *Chinook Winds*. The name was originally given by early inland settlers to sultry sea breezes blowing in from the Oregon-Washington coast because that was the direction in which the Chinook (shi-NOOK) Indians lived.

160 Indian Nations Of
THE AMERICAN WEST

*"Every foot of what you call America not very long
ago belonged to the Red Man."*
—Chief Washakie

This list will give the reader some idea as to where some of the American Indian tribes resided in the West of the nineteenth century. Because today's U. S. states are political divisions, the location of the original Indian Nations (a group of related tribes) had no relationship to today's state boundaries and so there are overlaps. (Apologies to those tribes who didn't make the list.)

1. **Arkansas:** *Quapaw, Caddo, Chakchiuma.*
2. **Arizona:** *Hopi, Yuma, Navajo, Pima, Apache, Maricopa, Walapai, Zuni, Chiricahua, Havasupai, Yayapai, Coyotero, Arivaipi.*
3. **California:** *Modoc, Pomo, Hupa, Shasta, Serrano, Yokuts, Mono, Yurok, Wiyot, Yuki, Wintun, Pomo, Maidu, Cosatano, Chumash, Luiseno, Patwin, Miwok, Panamint, Chemehuen, Cahuilla, Diegueno, Esselen, Salinan, Gabriellno.*
4. **Colorado:** *Arapaho, Cheyenne, Comanche, Kiowa.*
5. **Idaho:** *Shoshone, Bannock, Nez-Percé, Flathead, Coeur d'Alene, Lemni.*
6. **Iowa:** *Yankton.*
7. **Kansas:** *Kansas, Kiowa, Osage.*
8. **Louisiana:** *Atakapa, Chitimacha, Washa, Chawasha, Natchez, Tunica.*
9. **Minnesota:** *Ojibwa, Santee Dakota, Wahpeton, Iowa Saukcfox.*
10. **Missouri:** *Missouri, Osage.*
11. **Montana:** *Crow, Flathead, Blackfeet, Kootenay, Piegan, Atsina.*
12. **Nebraska:** *Pawnee, Arapaho, Oto, Omaha, Ponca.*

13. **Nevada:** *Paiute, Washo, Shoshone.*

14. **New Mexico:** *Navajo, Zuni, Mescalero, Apache, Taos, Faraon, Peublo, Gileno, Mimbreno, Coyotero, Jicarilla Apache.*

15. **North Dakota:** *Assiniboin, Yanktonai, Mandan, Hidatsa, Arikara.*

16. **Oklahoma:** *Kiowa, Osage, Wichita, Caddo.*

17. **Oregon:** *Cayuse, Klamath, Paiute, Nez Percé, Modoc, Karok, Walpapi, Till-amook, Siletz, Yaquina, Kalapuica, Siusiaw, Kusa, Tutunti, Kalapuya, Kusa, Umatilla.*

18. **South Dakota:** *Sioux, Teton, Dakota, Santee Dakota, Brule, Hunkpapa, Ponca, Ogala Sioux.*

19. **Texas:** *Comanche, Wichita. Lipan Apache, Tonkawa, Apache, Mescalero, U-anero, Waco, Tonkawa, Kichai, Tawakoni, Alabama Coushatta, Atakawa, Karankawa, Coahuiltec.*

20. **Utah:** *Ute, Paiute, Navajo, Gosiute.*

21. **Washington:** *Chinook, Yakima, Spokane, Nez Percé, Squamish, Nesqually, Walla Walla, Palus, Cowutz, Quinault, Chehalis, Methow.*

22. **Wyoming:** *Cheyenne, Wind River Shoshone.*

Photo of Indian Encampment, Fort Hall Replica, Pocatello, Idaho (dk). In a sheltered bend of the Snake River known as "The Bottoms," —a favorite camping site for the Shoshone-Bannock Indians—Nathan Wyeth, a New England businessman, built a log trading post in 1834 he called Fort Hall. Rendezvous re-enactments are held their annually.

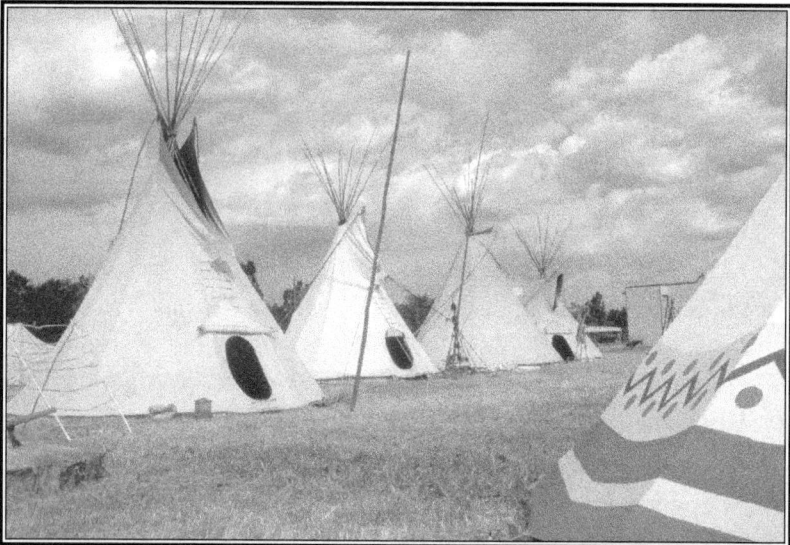

Oklahoma or Bust!
10 AMERICAN INDIAN NATIONS

*"Once I moved about like the wind. Now,
I surrender to you, and that is all."*
—Geronimo, 1886.

Briefly described here are the Indian Nations that played a significant part in the nineteenth-century settlement of the American West—chiefly during the Indian Wars with the United States—tribes that have become a part of western fiction.

1. Apache. An *Athapascan* tribe that lived in the mountains of New Mexico and west Texas. They were made up of many separate clans that raided whites, Mexicans, and other tribes. Their given names were taken from natural features, never from animals. Tribal leaders included *Cochise, Gerónimo, Victorio* and *Nana*. Originally living on the plains, they were forced into the Southwest by the *Comanches* and *Utes* around 1400 A.D. There, they successfully defended their territory waging a constant battle against the Spanish and later the Mexicans, and then the Anglo Americans when the U.S. acquired the region after the Mexican War. From 1861 until 1886, the U.S. Cavalry was unable to crush the Apaches until *Gerónimo's* final surrender, when 36 tired and hungry men gave in to 5,000 troops led by *General George H. Crook.*

2. Arapaho. A plains tribe of the *Algonquian* family closely associated with the *Cheyenne*. Originally farmers in the Red River Valley of Minnesota, they moved to the plains in the late eighteenth century, becoming buffalo hunters. The Arapaho attempted to live in peace with the whites until *Colonel John M. Chivington* led the *Sand Creek Massacre* against the *Cheyenne* and *Arapaho* in 1864, sending the *Arapaho* on a path of revenge until hostilities came to a quick end after the *Battle of the Little Big Horn.*

3. Cheyenne. Part of the *Algonquian* family of tribes, they lived on the plains along the Missouri River in Minnesota and the headwaters of the Mississippi, following the bison herds wherever it led them. Forced out of Minnesota in the eighteenth century by *Chippenas* and *Sioux,* they became buffalo hunters and eventually split into two groups: The *Northern Cheyenne* which stayed in Minnesota, and the *Southern Cheyenne* which migrated to the southwest where they were confronted with the stampeding California gold seekers. After the *Sand Creek Massacre* and the *Fetterman Fight,* the *Medicine Lodge Treaty of 1867* moved them to a reservation in Indian Territory, but fighting with the whites didn't subside until 1875. The Cheyenne Nation fought with the *Sioux* in the 1876 battle against George Custer.

4. Comanche. The southern branch of the *Shoshonean* groups, they lived entirely on the plains—in what is now Kansas—after migrating from as far north as Wyoming. Their first treaty with the Anglo Americans was in 1835. The fiercest warriors on the plains, the *Comanche* fought what became their worst enemy: the Texan settlers who were taking their best hunting grounds. *Comanche* leader *Quanah Parker* led a failed attack on buffalo hunters at

Interior Indian Teepee, Fort Hall Rendezvous, Pocatello, Idaho (dk)

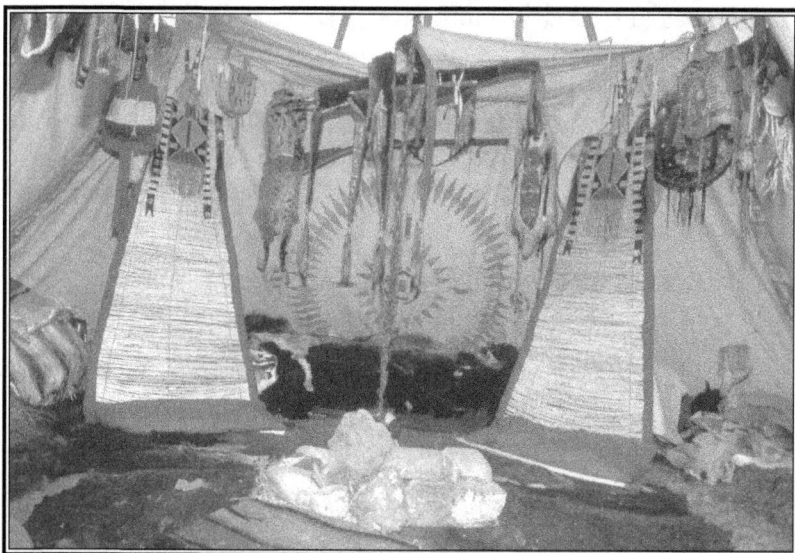

Adobe Walls, Texas but it led to the *Red River War* of 1874-75. The U.S. Government eventually moved the Indians to reservations in Oklahoma where they farmed and raised cattle.

5. Modoc. A *Penútian* tribe, the *Modoc* homeland was in Northern California and Oregon. In 1864, the *Modoc* and *Klamath* ceded their land to the U.S. in the *Council Grove Treaty of 1864* and moved to a reservation. The *Modocs*, led by *Chief Kintpuash* (Captain Jack), left the reservation in 1870 which led to the *Modoc War* (1872-73). 100 warriors defended themselves against 1,000 Federal troops in the Lava Beds of northern California (the only major Indian battle fought in California). They eventually succumbed, Captain Jack was hanged, and the rest of the tribe was sent to Indian Territory.

6. Navajo. An *Athapascan* tribe that lived in Arizona and New Mexico as farmers and ranchers. They were a peaceful tribe until raided by the Spanish, Mexicans, and other tribes, chiefly the *Comanche* and *Utes.* They retaliated against the whites, attacking *Fort Defiance* in 1860, an act that infuriated the U.S. resulting in severe retaliation in an 1863 campaign led by *Colonel Kit Carson* where he attempted to starve them out by destroying their crops and killing their sheep. Thousands of Navajo were forced to surrender and were marched on "The Long Walk" to Fort Sumner, New Mexico where they were put into prisons until a treaty with the U.S. in 1868 created a reservation for them at Canyon de Chelly, Arizona.

7. Nez Percé. One of the *Penutian* tribes of Idaho and Oregon. They lived in small bands, each with its own leadership. Friendly with the whites, they actually asked for books and teachers to help them learn. Mission schools were set up and the *Nez Percé* eventually became Christians—until around 1840 as whites poured into the territory by the thousands. When The Pacific Railway crossed their land and they were forced into a treaty that made them surrender their land, *Chief Joseph* led his tribe on a 1,300 mile retreat to Canada, skirmishing with the cavalry all the way—but just 30 miles short of the Canadian border, Chief Joseph's tribe was captured and herded to a reservation in Indian Territory.

8. Pawnee. A *Caddoan* tribe found in eastern Wyoming, Nebraska, and Kansas. As corn raisers, the *Pawnee* fought with the *Sioux* and *Cheyenne,* but never warred against the United States. They did, on occasion, raid wagon trains on the Santa Fe Trail. During the Indian Wars, the *Pawnees* served as scouts for the U.S. Army, but even their tribes were moved to reservations in Indian Territory in 1876.

9. Pima. An *Uzo-aztecan* tribe living in central and southern Arizona—a peaceful tribe fighting only the Apache—were farmers who actually sold food to the United States to feed Federal troops and European immigrants. They had an ethics code that said "Do not steal, get up early and go to work, help everyone who needs anything, and always kill Apaches."

10. Sioux. Originally, the *Eastern Sioux* (Santees) hunted animals, fished, and harvested wild rice in what is now Minnesota. Migrating southwest into the plains—as far as the Black Hills—looking for better hunting grounds, they acquired Spanish horses (coming up from Mexico) and began to hunt buffalo. They became the *Western Sioux* calling themselves *Lakotas.* With the introduction of firearms—from French and American traders—warfare among enemy tribes on the plains intensified in the early nineteenth century. Treaties with the United States in the 1840's and 1850's forced the Sioux to give up their hunting grounds and move to a reservation. The usual starvation conditions and greedy agents resulted in Indian uprisings led by *Little Crow* in 1862. *Red Cloud* won the Bozeman Trail in 1868 and *Sitting Bull* and *Crazy Horse* won the *Battle of Little Bighorn* in 1876, but by 1881 all the Sioux were confined to reservations.

TIDBIT: The practice of SCALPING did not originate with the American Indian. They learned the practice from the earliest whites who came to America. The scalp was used as proof they had killed an Indian in order to collect the bounty being paid for dead Indians by governments and individuals.

The People
18 TRIBAL NAME ORIGINS

"I love to roam over the prairies. There I feel free and happy,
but when we settle down, we grow pale and die.
—Satanta

The Etymology, or derivation, of Indian tribal names can be a fascinating subject of study. More often than not, the names we use today for Indian tribes usually were given to them by other tribes or by early European explorers; the names they called *themselves* usually didn't make it into the history books. Native American languages were not originally written down; they used only verbal speech. Early missionaries were the first to translate Indian speech to a written alphabet. Before that, Indian history was recorded by passing along songs and stories orally from generation to generation. When different tribes or races met each other, what was heard was interpreted; when the Europeans tried to write down what they heard, the words became corrupted.

1. **Apache** (uh-PATCH-ee). A Zuni word *apachu* meaning "enemy." To themselves, they are the *Nidé*, "the people."
2. **Arapaho** (uh-RAP-uh-ho) Probably from the Pawnee word *tirapihu* meaning "trader" or the Kiowa's name for the tribe: *Ahyato*. (Arapahos originally called themselves *Inuna-ina* meaning "our people," but other tribes called them "dog-eaters." They called themselves *Hinonoeino*, "big-sky people."
3. **Cherokee** (CHAIR-uh-key) The name was give to them by a neighboring tribe, the Creeks, who called them the *tciloki* meaning "people of a different speech."
4. **Cheyenne** (SHY-ann). Sioux name for the tribe, *shahiyena*, meaning "Red Talkers" or "people who speak another language than ours." The Cheyenne called themselves *Tsistsisstas*, "Beautiful People."

5. **Coeur d'Alene** (kur-duh-LANE). A French word meaning "heart of awl" or "pointed heart," referring to their astuteness in trading, their "sharpness." It was probably first used as an insult to a trader who mistook it for the tribe's name.

6. **Comanche** (cu-MAN-chee). Evolved from the Ute word *Komantcia* meaning "Anyone who wants to fight me all the time."

7. **Crow.** They called themselves *Absaroka* meaning "Bird People." Seeing the bird sign given, the white's gave them the name "Crow."

8. **Flathead.** French fur trappers gave this name to Indians who deformed their heads by strapping a board to their heads at birth to create a tapered, ovehanging look to their foreheads.

9. **Hopi** (HO-pee). A contraction of their own word *Hopituh* meaning "Peaceful Ones" as they were a tribe who believed in peace and cooperation in their dealings with others.

10. **Kickapoo** (KICK-a-poo). A white corruption of the Indian word *Kiwegapaw* meaning "he moves about, standing now here, now there." It turns out, the Kickapoo did live in many areas of the West, probably starting around the Great Lakes and migrating all the way to Mexico.

11. **Kiowa** (Ki-uh-wuh). In this case, they actually got their *own* name put in the white man's history books: *Kaigwa,* meaning "Main People."

12. **Lakota** (La-KOH-ta). Sioux word *dah-kota* meaning "friends" or "allies."

13. **Navajo** (nah-vuh-ho). A Pueblo Indian word referring to an area of land in the Southwest, and later given to the people who resided on this land. Spanish explorers called the Indians *Apaches de Navahu* to distinguish them from the Apaches in the area. (The Navajo had called themselves *Dine*, "The People.")

14. **Nez Percé** (nes-PURSE). Means "pierced noses." They were given that name by French Canadian voyageurs because of the tribe's practice of piercing their noses to insert ornaments. (The French pronounced the name as "NAY-per-say" BUT the English won the West.)

15. **Omaha** (o-mu-haw). Living along the Missouri River, but eventually settling upriver from the other tribes of the same Siouan language, their name appropriately became "those going against the current."

16. **Pima** (PEE-mah). From the word *pi-nyi-match* meaning "I don't know." It was the tribe's response to the questions of Spanish explorers, but the explorers thought it was the name of their tribe.

17. **Sioux** (SUE). A French corruption of the Chippewas' word for their enemy, *nadowe-is-iw,* meaning "adder," a type of snake.

18. **Ute** (yoot). Means "higher up," as opposed to the Navajo Indians who lived further down the mountains. The White Mountain Apache distinguished the two tribal groups by the name *yuthahih*—it stuck.

Heap Big Medicine
13 GREAT INDIAN CHIEFS

"I never said the land was mine to do with as I chose. The one who has the right to dispose of it is the one who created it."
—Chief Joseph

They fought to save their way of life on the plains. They never thought the lands (or sky and air) was theirs, for they didn't believe it could be owned by anyone, only used for a time. Here are some of the legendary Indian Chiefs of the American West that fought the great battle against white man's Manifest Destiny, when they lived, and what Indian Nations they led to greatness.

1. **Black Kettle** (??-1868). A chief of the *Southern Cheyenne,* he continually strived for peace. He escaped from the *Battle of Sand Creek* (1864), a bloody massacre of Indian women and children at a lodge the tribes believed to be under the guardianship of the government. *Colonel John M. Chivington,* who led the massacre—even though a white flag and the American flag flew over the village, and who ordered his troops to take no prisoners—was allowed to resign his commission without being punished. In 1868, *George A. Custer* led a surprise attack on Black Kettle's band which was camping near today's Cheyenne, Oklahoma. Black Kettle and his wife were shot and killed while fleeing; his tribe dug in and Custer retreated leaving some of his men behind. A black mark on Custer's career, it became known as the *Battle of the Washita.*

2. **Captain Jack** (??-1873). Chief of the *Modoc.* Indian name: *Kintpuash.* When the Modoc tribe of California was removed to an Oregon reservation in 1864, Captain Jack led his people back home and there he was arrested, starting the Modoc War. Tribal members killed several peace commissioners and blamed it on Captain Jack. He was given to the authorities in 1873, and hanged.

3. Cochise (c1812-1874). Chief of the *Chiricahua Apache.* In 1861 Cochise and his band were accused of taking the young son of an Anglo rancher. Under a flag of truce, Cochise and his chiefs went to the U.S. government to deny the charge only to be jailed. All were hanged, except Cochise, for refusing to confess to the crime. Cochise escaped and organized the Apache of Arizona to fight a battle of vengeance that lasted 10 years. His band terrorized Mexican, and later Arizonian citizens, with guerrilla-style raids with murdering, raping and kidnapping that gave Indians a bad name. An agreement with Cochise to stop the raids was finally made by giving Cochise a reservation of his choosing. After Cochise's death in 1874, the kidnapped boy turned up and said he had been taken by renegade Apaches, not by Cochise.

4. Crazy Horse (c1842-1877). Indian name, *Iashunka Witko,* Chief of the *Oglala Sioux.* Along with Sitting Bull, he led the fight against the encroachment of gold miners in the Black Hills of South Dakota (1876-77). *General George Crook* with 1,300 troops attacked Crazy Horse on the Rosebud River in 1876, only to be repelled with severe losses. Custer's troops were then defeated at Little Big Horn. *General Mackenzie* then defeated Crazy Horse in the spring of 1877. In that same year Crazy Horse was killed by soldiers who were attempting to arrest him for leaving the reservation without permission. It turns out, he had just wanted to visit his ailing wife.

5. Dull Knife (1810-1883). Chief of the *Cheyenne.* Also known as Morning Star. He took part in the *Cheyenne-Arapaho War* (1864-65) and was the signer of the *Fort Laramie Treaty of 1868.* After 20 years on a reservation in Indian Territory, he and *Little Wolf* took 300 of his people on a 1,500 mile trek back to their homeland only to surrender at Ft. Robinson, Nebraska. When they were told they would be taken back to Indian Territory, they escaped, but lost one third of their number in a winter pursuit by the cavalry. Dull Knife escaped and stayed with Red Cloud's Sioux until his death in 1883.

6. Gerónimo (c1829-1909). Medicine man of the Chiricahua Apache. Born in what is today Clinton, Oklahoma, he was given the name *Gokhlayeh* meaning "one who yawns." In 1858 at a peace conference, Mexican soldiers in a surprise attack, killed his wife, mother, and three children which turned him into the most dangerous Apache raider of all time. Arrested and sent to a reservation in Arizona, Gerónimo became disillusioned and escaped with some of his followers. He twice surrendered to *General Crook* only to escape and return to the warpath. After a manhunt involving 5,000 troops chasing only three dozen Apache, Gerónimo surrendered to *General Nelson Miles* in 1886 and was exiled to Florida. In his old age, he appeared in numerous Wild West expositions. Gerónimo may have gotten his name from Mexican soldiers who screamed when attacked: *"Cuidado! Watch out Gerónimo!"* which was a corruption of his given name. His fellow warriors picked up the name and it stuck. He died at Fort Sill, Indian Territory in 1909. The name became the jumping call of U.S. Paratroopers.

Gerónimo c1886 (Library of Congress)

Joseph c1900 (Library of Congress)

7. Joseph (1840-1904). Chief of the Nez Percé. His Indian name *Heimot Tooyalaket.* Given his name by Spanish missionaries who had raised him near Lewiston, Idaho, he was committed to peace with the whites until the treaty of

> **TIDBIT:** Arrowheads were usually made of flint when available, but also bone, wood, shells, deer antler and copper were used. It wasn't until the coming of the whites, did the Indians make their arrowheads out of iron.

1863 forced him to northeastern Oregon, a dry desert-like region east of the Cascade mountains. In an attempt to escape American troops and avoid a fight, he led a 1,300 mile trek toward Canada with skirmishing all along the way until he was caught just 30 miles from Canada by *General Nelson Miles* on September 30, 1877. His tribe was then herded to Kansas. Chief Joseph's final surrender words became legend: "*Hear me, my Chiefs. I am tired; my heart is sick and sad. From where the sun now stands, I will fight no more forever.*" In 1904, he died on a reservation in Washington, and according to the doctor's diagnosis, of a broken heart.

8. Quanah Parker (1845-1911). Chief of *Quohada* band of *Comanches.* The son of white captive *Cynthia Ann Parker* and *Chief Peta Nocoma,* he tried to keep both his tribe and the U.S. Army happy. He was constantly negotiating terms for continued peace with the hope of protecting reservation lands. After an unfruitful meeting at Medicine Lodge in 1867, *Quanah Parker* led a failed attack on buffalo hunters at *Adobe Walls, Texas,* but that led to the *Red River War* of 1874-75. Parker eventually surrendered to *Colonel MacKenzie* of the 4th U. S. Cavalry at Fort Sill Oklahoma. He came to be a good friend of President Theodore Roosevelt.

9. Red Cloud (1822-1909). Indian name, *Mock-Peah-lu-tah,* Chief of *Oglala Teton Sioux.* He led *Sioux* and *Cheyenne* against immigrants and military forts on the Bozeman Road in Montana to stop white settlement. Red Cloud was a leader in the 1865-66 *Powder River War,* taking *Fort Phil Kearny* and trapping the cavalry in a battle called the *Fetterman Massacre.* After three years of fighting, Red Cloud made his point and the Government signed a treaty at Fort Laramie in 1868 requiring U.S. troops to withdraw and close the forts. They did, leaving with their tails between their legs. In 1877, Red Cloud and the Sioux were moved to the Pine Ridge reservation in South Dakota. He has the honor of being the only western Chief to win a war with the United States.

10. Roman Nose (??-1868). Chief of the *Northern Cheyenne*. Born along the Platte River in Nebraska, Roman Nose was give the name *Woqini*, meaning "hooked nose," because of the shape of his nose. A leader in the Cheyenne-Arapaho War of 1864-65, he destroyed a cavalry unit at *Prairie Dog Creek* in Kansas in 1867. Along with *Tall Bull*, he led a band of warriors called the "Dog Soldiers." He fought, and died, fighting *Major Forsyth's* cavalry command at the *Battle of Beecher's Island* in eastern Colorado, September 1868. The Cheyenne say he died because he ate food with metal utensils without first performing a war bonnet purification ceremony.

11. Santanta (Set-t'ante, White Bear, ??-1878). A chief of the *Kiowas*, also know as *White Bear.* When Santanta observed the white man's wasteful method of cutting trees for lumber and the commercial destruction of the buffalo he said "*When I see that, my heart feels like bursting.*" He agreed to sign the *Medicine Lodge Treaty of 1867,* and was sent to a reservation to grow corn, but he continued to attack buffalo hunters and raid white settlements. On an invitation to council at Fort Sill, Santanta was deceived by *General William Sherman* and was put in irons. In dire despair as a prisoner in Huntsville, Santanta committed suicide in 1878 by throwing himself out the upper-story window of the prison hospital. When Santanta was a young Cheyenne medicine man, *White Bull* gave him a war bonnet he said would protect him in battle. Throughout his life Santanta would challenge soldiers in battle to shoot him at close range—and they would indeed always miss.

Portrait of Sitting Bull, 1885
by David Frances Barry
(Library of Congress)

12. Sitting Bull (1831-1889). Indian name, *Tatanka Yatanka*, Chief of *Hunkpapa Teton Sioux.*

Born in South Dakota, son of warrior *Returns-Again,* his father named him "Slow" because of his "careful and deliberate ways." By the age of 25 he became leader of the "Strong Hearts," an elite military group. He became a Sioux chief in the 1860's and ignored treaties with the U.S. that took his ancestral lands. In 1872, during a battle, he walked to the center of the fighting, sat down, and smoked his pipe while bullets and arrows whizzed by. But he was most famous for winning the *Battle of the Little Big Horn* in 1876 (he predicted the defeat of General Custer and Cook, but did not actually take part in the battle). *Sitting Bull* and *Crazy Horse* led 4,000 Sioux, Cheyenne, and Arapaho against the influx of gold seekers to the Black Hills of Dakota after having been promised by the Government that the land was theirs. The *Battle of the Little Big Horn* led to the end of the Indian Wars. In the 1880's, Sitting Bull toured with *Buffalo Bill Cody's Wild West Show.* He was killed by Indian police at the age of 59 when some of his people tried to rescue him from prison.

13. Victorio 1809-1880. Apache Chief, succeeding *Mangas Coloradas* and *Cochise.* In 1877, his band of Apaches were moved from Ojo Caliente in New Mexico to the *San Carlos* reservation in Arizona. He escaped with his band and raided settlements in Mexico and the southwest for over a year until Mexican soldiers led by *Colonel Joaquín Terrazas* trapped him in the *Tres Castillos Mountains* of Mexico where he committed suicide rather than surrender.

The author as Apache warrior Sitting Duck, a.k.a. "Dung Between Toes," photo by Michael Jay Smith

Tribal Leaders
58 INDIAN WARRIORS & CHIEFS

Significant Indian leaders who fought in the battle against the United States for the West. The **Chiefs** are in bold type.

Big Eagle	**Kamiakan**	Pawnee Killer
Black Bear	**Kicking Bird**	Peaches
Black Dog	**Lame Deer**	Rain in the Face
Black Kettle	Little Big Mouth	**Red Cloud**
Bull Head	Little Crow the Younger	**Roman Nose**
Chato	Little Wolf	**Santanta**
Cochise	**Loco**	Satank
Conquering Bear	Lone Wolf	Short Bull
Crazy Horse	**Looking Glass**	Sitting Bull, M.M.
Diablo	Low Dog	**Spotted Tail**
Dull Knife	Mangas Coloradas	Steep Wind
Gall	Mamonti, M.M.	Stumbling Bear
Gerónimo	**Manuelito**	Tall Bull
Horse	**Nachez**	**Victorio**
Hump	Nakaidoklini, M.M.	**Washakie**
Inkpaduta	**Nana**	**White Bird**
Iron Jacket	**Numaga**	**Yellow Hand**
Isatai	**Old John**	**Benito**
Josanie	Owhi	
Joseph	**Quanah Parker**	M.M. = Medicine Man

18 Fictional Indian Identities

In a way, Indian names are like nicknames because babies are given their names based on an event or observation that happened at birth or later. Here are a few FICTIONAL names by the author:

Bent Knife	Tail Between Legs	Kicking Fit
Twisted Fork	Hole In Head	Pretty Shoes
Sitting Duck	Crying Sissy	Laughing Cow
Bad Weather	Three-Legged Dog	Well Hung Bull
Hair In Nose	Nits In His Hair	Big Toe
Prairie Dog	Dung Between Toes	Two Left Feet

Jo Hames wearing a warbonnet

THE INDIAN WARBONNET

The warbonnet we usually see in westerns evolved over a period of several hundred years and most tribes have now adopted some form of this regalia. The bonnet probably started in the 1700's with just an eagle feather stuck in a headband. Decoration was gradually added over the years with fancy trim, medallions, and ermine (a weasel with white fur in winter). The flared bonnet was first developed by the plains Indians and was used to "count coup." Coup was an act of bravery that would get a warrior another feather added to his bonnet. Bravery would include such things as touching an enemy without killing him, capturing the horse or weapon of an enemy, taking his scalp, or killing him. Some tribes didn't allow the warrior to make his own bonnet, instead it had to be made by his friends at a feast while he recounted each deed that gave him the right to wear that feather.

Native American Actors
21 INDIANS IN THE MOVIES

*"I think you had better put the Indians on wheels. Then you
can run them about whenever you wish."*
—Red Dog, speaking to government agents in 1876.

Before the 1960's, Hollywood typically used non-Indians to play the part of Native Americans, actors like Burt Lancaster, Ricardo Montalban, and Charles Bronson, but some Native American actors *did* get the opportunity to work in Hollywood over the years.

ACTOR	TRIBE	DATE	WESTERN FILMS
1. Michael Ansara	no tribe	1922-	*The Lawless Breed, Brave Warrior, The Comancheros,* "Broken Arrow," over 30 films.
2. John Big Tree	Seneca	1875-1967	*She Wore a Yellow Ribbon, Western Union, Custer's Last Stand.*
3. Monte Blue	Cherokee	1890-1963	*Gesert Gold, Thunder Trail, Born to the West.*
4. Chief Dan George	Sioux	1899-1981	"Caribou Country," *Harry and Tonto, Little Big Man, Outlaw Josey Wales.*
5. Iron Eyes Cody	no tribe	1907-1999	*Custer's Last Stand, Code of the Redman, Son of Paleface, Gray Eagle.*
6. Graham Green	Oneida	1952-	*Dances With Wolves, Thunder Heart, Medicine River.*
7. Clu Gulager	Cherokee	1928-	*Ballad of a Gunfighter, The Gunfighter, Kenny Rodgers as the Gambler.*
8. Chief Many Treaties	Blackfoot	1875-1948	*Code of the Redman.*

ACTOR	TRIBE	DATE	WESTERN FILMS
9. Rodd Redwing	Chickasaw	1905-1971	*Shalako,Charro!,Apache Uprising, Johnny Reno.*
10. Will Sampson	Creek	1935-1987	*The Whiste Buffalo, Standing Tall, Fish Hawk. Firewalker.*
11. Charles Stevens	Apache	1893-1964	*The California Trail, Drumbeats, Call of the Coyote, Trackers.*
12. Jay Silverheels	Mohawk	1919-1980	*Brave Warrior, Walk the Proud land, The Lone Ranger, Indian Paint,* "The Lone Ranger"TV series.
13. Woody Strode	no tribe	1914-1994	*Sergeant Rutledge, Boothill, The Last Rebel, The Quick and The Dead.*
14. Nipo Strongheart	Yakima	1884-1966	*Pony Soldier, Charge at Feather River.*
15. Wes Studi	Cherokee	1947-	*Dances With Wolves, Last of the Mohicans (1992), Geronimo:An American Legend, Crazy Horse.*
16. Jim Thorpe	Sac & Fox	1889-1953	*Code of The Mounted.*
17. Chief Thundercloud (Victor Daniels)	Cherokee	1899-1955	*The Big Trail, Geronimo (1939), Western Union, Buffalo Bill, Ambush, Colt .45,* "Lone Ranger" serials, over 70 films.
18. Chief Thundercloud (Scott Williams)		1901-1967	*Annie Oakley, Heroes of The West.*
19. John War Eagle (William Hazlett)	Sioux	1901-1991	*Tomahawk.*
20. Dennis Weaver	Cherokee	1924-2006	*The Lawless Breed, War Arow, Duel at Diablo, A Man Called Sledge.*
21. Chief Yowlachie	Yakima	1890-1966	*Buffalo Bill in Tomahawk Territory.*

Michael Ansara.

Born in Syria in 1922, Michael Ansara has been in over 175 films. While studying medicine at the Los Angeles City College, he acted at the Pasadena Playhouse with students like Charles Bronson, Carolyn Jones, and Aaron Spelling. He got his big break in 1956 as Cochise on the television series "Broken Arrow."

(Author's collection)

Graham Greene.

Born in 1952 at the Six Nations Reserve in Ontario, Canada, Graham Greene has won or been nominated for 12 awards for film and television work. In 1991, he was nominated for Best Actor in a Supporting Role for *Dances with Wolves*. He also played "Conquering Bear" in the 2005 mini-series "Into the West," and "Walter Crow Horse" in *Thunderheart*.

Dances with Wolves, TIG Productions (Author's collection)

Navajo Reservation, Canyon de Chelly National Monument, Chinle, Arizona (dk)

TRIVIA: Which actor co-starred in the television western series "Gunsmoke" playing, for nine years, the deputy Chester Goode? ANS: Dennis Weaver. He gave his character a limp for fear he wouldn't be noticed playing next to the 6-foot-6 James Arness.

A Match Game
5 WHITE MEN AS INDIANS

Match the famous actor with the western movie in which he played a leading role as an Indian.

1.	Burt Lancaster	**a.**	*Chato's Land* (1972)
2.	Chuck Connors	**b.**	*Cheyenne Autumn* (1964)
3.	Charles Bronson	**c.**	*Apache* (1954)
4.	Ricardo Montalban	**d.**	*Geronimo* (1962)
5.	Jack Palance	**e.**	*Arrowhead* (1958)

ANS: 1-c, 2-d, 3-a, 4-b, 5-e.

Bow First
TIPI ETIQUETTE

Proper behavior among Plains Indians—as in most societies—was governed by extensive, strict, and often subtle rules. The principles below are a sampling of various points of etiquette that Indians knew and heeded when paying a social call at a friend's teepee.

If the door is open, a friend may enter the teepee directly. But if it is closed, he should announce his presence and wait for the owner to invite him to come in.

When a male visitor enters the teepee he goes to the right and waits for the host to invite him to sit in the guest place to the left of the owner at the rear. A woman enters after the man and goes to the left.

When invited to a feast, guests are expected to bring their own bowls and spoons and to eat all they are given. No visitor should ever walk between the fire and another person, but instead should pass behind the sitters, who for their part, lean forward to make room.

Woman should never sit cross-legged like men. They can sit on their heels or on their legs to one side.

(dk)

In a group of men, only the older ones should initiate conversation. The younger men should politely remain silent unless they're invited to speak by an elder.

When the host cleans his pipe everyone should leave.

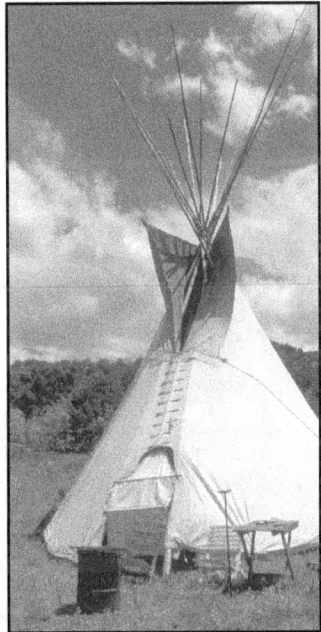

(Courtesy of the Old West series of Time Life Books, "The Indians," 1973)

A Match Game
INDIAN V.S. CAVALRY

Match the Indian chief with the famous battle or war he fought in.

1.	Red Cloud	**a.**	*Battle of Beecher's Island*
2.	Captain Jack	**b.**	*War of the Lava Beds*
3.	Sitting Bull	**c.**	*Battle for Bozeman Trail*
4.	Black Kettle	**d.**	*Battle of Little Big Horn*
5.	Roman Nose	**e.**	*Battle of Sand Creek*
6.	Quanah Parker	**f.**	*Battle of Adobe Wall*

ANS: 1-c, 2-b, 3-d, 4-e, 5-a, 6-f.

Match the US Federal Troop Commander with the famous Indian battle.

1.	Col. J. M. Chivington	**a.**	*Battle of Little Big Horn*
2.	Gen. George Crook	**b.**	*Red River War*
3.	Col. George Custer	**c.**	*Wounded Knee*
4.	Col. James Forsyth	**d.**	*Battle of Rosebud Creek*
5.	Major George Forsyth	**e.**	*Battle of Sand Creek*
6.	Col. Randal Mackenzie	**f.**	*Battle of Beecher's Island*

ANS: 1-e, 2-d, 3-a, 4-c, 5-f, 6-b.

A MOVIE QUOTE: "Only thing they're feared of is the white man's sickness." "What's that?" "Grabs. White men don't see nothin' pretty unless they want to grab it. The more they grab, the more they want to grab. It's like a fever and they can't get cured. Only thing for them to do is keep on grabbing 'till everything belongs to white men, and then they start grabbing from each other."
— Arthur Hunnicut as "Uncle Jeb" in *The Big Sky*, 1952.

Charge!
10 INDIAN WARS

"The life my people want is a life of freedom, I have seen nothing that a white man has—houses or railways or clothing or food—that is as good as the right to move in the open country, and live in our fashion."
—Sitting Bull

Ten of the major Indian wars are listed here with their location and tribes involved.

1855-56 **Yakima War** (Washington). *Yakima, Walla Walla, Umatilla, Cayuse.*

1858   **Coeur d' Alene War** (Washington). *Spokan, Palouse, Yakima, Northern Paiute.*

1863-66 **Navajo War** (New Mexico, Arizona). *Navajo.* Led by Chief Manoelito.

1864-65 **Cheyenne-Arapaho War** (Colorado, Kansas). *Cheyenne* and *Arapaho.*

1866-68 **War for the Bozeman Trail** (Wyoming, Montana). *Cheyenne, Sioux, Arapaho.* Led by Chief Red Cloud. This was the only full-scale war officially declared won by the Indians.

1872-73 **Modoc War** (California, Oregon). *Kintpuash.* Led by Captain Jack.

1874-75 **Red River War** (Southern Plains*). Comanche, Kiowa, Cheyenne.* Led by Quanah Parker, Santana, and others.

1876-77 **Sioux War for the Black Hills** (Dakota Territory). *Sioux, Cheyenne, Arapaho.* Led by Sitting Bull and Crazy Horse.

1878   **Bannock War** (Idaho and Oregon). *Bannock, Northern Paiute, Cayuse.*

1868-69 **Southern Plains War.** *Cheyenne, Sioux, Arapaho, Kiowa, Comanche.*

Put On the War Paint!
24 Indian Wars of the West

"There is no use talking to these Americans.
They are all liars."
—Sitting Bull, 1877

The Indian Wars were a series of smaller wars and battles fought by individual tribes who made their own decisions and were not controlled by a central "government" or "council." Whether the wars were a conscious effort at genocide is still being debated, but what is undisputed is that brutal savagery and massacres of woman and children ran rampant on both sides. This, a more detailed list of wars, comes from Wikipedia, the Free Encyclopedia.

1. **Comanche Wars** (1836-1875). On the southern plains, primarily Texas Republic and the state.
2. **Cayuse War** (1848-1855). Oregon and Washington Territories.
3. **Rogue River Wars** (1855-1856). Oregon Territory.
4. **Yakima War** (1855-1858). Washington Territory.
5. **Spokane-Coeur d'Alene-Paloos War** (1858). Washington Territory.
6. **Fraser Canyon War** (1858). British Columbia (U.S. irregulars on British territory).
7. **California Indian Wars** (1860-65). War against *Hupa, Wiyot, Yurok, Tolowa, Nomlaki, Chimariko, Tsnungwe, Whilkut, Karuk, Wintun* and others.
8. **Navajo Wars** (1861-1864). Ended with Long Walk of the Navajo—Arizona Territory and New Mexico Territory.
9. **Walapais War** (1864-1869). Arizona Territory.
10. **Apache Wars** (1864-1886). Careleton put *Mescelero* on reservation with *Navajos* at Sumner and continued until 1886 when Gerónimo surrendered.
11. **Dakota War of 1862**. Skirmishes in the southwestern quadrant of Minnesota result in hundreds dead. In the largest mass execution in U.S. history, 38 Dakota were hanged. About 1,600 others were sent to a reservation in present-day South Dakota.

For Supremacy, 1895, oil on canvas by Charles M. Russell (1864-1926) DECA.
Known as "the cowboy artist," Russell created more than 2,000 paintings of cowboys,
Indians, and landscapes set in the Western United States.

12. **Red Cloud's War** (1866-1868). *Lakota* Chief Makhpyia Luta (Red Cloud) conducts the most successful attacks against the U.S. Army during the Indian Wars. By the *Treaty of Fort Laramie* (1868), the U.S. granted a large reservation to the *Lakota*, without military presence or oversight, no settlements, and no reserved road building rights. The reservation included the entire Black Hills.

13. **Colorado War** (1864-1865). Clashes centered on the Colorado Eastern Plains between the U.S. Army and an alliance consisting largely of the *Cheyenne* and *Arapaho*.

14. **Comanche Campaign** (1867-1875). Maj. Gen. Philip Sheridan, in command of the Department of the Missouri, instituted winter campaigning in 1868-69 as a means of rooting out the elusive Indian tribes scattered throughout the border regions of Colorado, Kansas, New Mexico, and Texas.

15. **Modoc War** (1872-1873). 53 *Modoc* warriors under Captain Jack held off 1,000 men of the U.S. Army for 7 months. Major General Edward Canby was killed during a peace conference—the only general to be killed during the Indian Wars.

16. **Red River War** (1874-1875). Between *Comanche* and U.S. forces under the command of William Sherman and Lt. General Phillip Sheridan.

> **TIDBIT:** Audrey Hepburn portrayed an Indian girl raised by whites in *The Unforgiven* (1960), which starred Burt Lancaster.

17. **Black Hills War, or Little Big Horn Campaign** (1876-1877). *Lakota* under Sitting Bull and Crazy Horse fought the U.S. after repeated violations of the Treaty of Fort Laramie (1868).

18. **Nez Percé War** (1877). *Nez Percé* under Chief Joseph retreated from the 1st U.S. Cavalry through Idaho, Yellowstone Park, and Montana after a group of *Nez Percé* attacked and killed a group of Anglo settlers in early 1877.

19. **Bannock War** (1878). Elements of the 21st U.S. Infantry, 4th U.S. Artillery, and 1st U.S. Cavalry engaged the natives of southern Idaho including the *Bannock* and *Paiute* when the tribes threatened rebellion in 1878, dissatisfied with their land allotments.

20. **Cheyenne War** (1878-1879). A conflict between the United States' armed forces and a small group of Cheyenne families.

21. **Sheepeater War** (May-August 1879). On May 1, 1879, three detachments of soldiers pursued the *Idaho Western Shoshone* throughout central Idaho during the last campaign in the Pacific Northwest.

22. **Ute War** (September 1879-November 1880). On September 29, 1879, some 200 men, elements of the 4th U.S. Infantry, the 3rd U.S. Cavalry, and 5th U.S. Cavalry under the command of Maj. T. T. Thornburgh, were attacked and besieged in Red Canyon by 300 to 400 *Ute* warriors. Thornburgh's group was rescued by forces of the 5th and U.S. 9th Cavalry Regiment in early October, but not before significant loss of life had occurred. The *Utes* were finally pacified in November 1880.

23. **Pine Ridge Campaign** (November 1890 -January 1891). Numerous unresolved grievances led to the last major conflict with the *Sioux*. A lopsided engagement that involved almost half the infantry and cavalry of the regular army caused the surviving warriors to lay down their arms and retreat to their reservations in January 1891.

24. **Wounded Knee Massacre** (December 29, 1890). Sitting Bull's half-brother, Big Foot, and 152 other *Sioux* were killed. 25 U.S. cavalrymen also died in the engagement. 7th Cavalry. Only fourteen days before, Sitting Bull had been killed with his son Crow Foot at Standing Rock Agency in a gun battle with a group of Indian police that had been sent by the American government to arrest him.

Me Wantum Firewater
1 RECIPE FOR INDIAN WHISKEY

Do not try to make this stuff. It was a cheap whiskey made by early Missouri River traders to sell to the Indians. The prescription is reported by E.C. Abbott and Helena Huntington Smith in their 1939 book *We Pointed Them North*. Henry Fonda recites this recipe for "drunk water" in the western movie *Cheyenne Social Club* as he and James Stewart ride north from Texas to claim Stewart's inheritance.

> *Take one barrel of Missouri River water, and two gallons of alcohol. Then you add two ounces of strychnine to make them crazy because strychnine is the greatest stimulant in the world; add three bars of tobacco to make them sick because an Indian wouldn't figure it was whiskey unless it made him sick; add five bars of soap to give it a bead, a half-pound of red pepper, and then you put in some sage brush and boil it until it's brown. Strain this into a barrel and you've got your Indian whiskey.*

"The Only Good Indian is a Dead Indian"

It was *General Philip H. Sheridan* who is credited (or derided) for saying "The only good Indian is a dead Indian."—A phrase which became the philosophy of the U.S. Cavalry in the war for the American plains. When the first Comanches surrendered to Sheridan at Fort Cobb in an 1868 campaign after the *Battle of Washita*, Sheridan had asked a captured warrior his name, and his reply "Tosawi, good Indian," prompted Sheridan to shake his head and reply: "The only good Indian I ever saw was a dead Indian."

Don't Stare
14 NAVAJO BELIEFS

"The love of possessions is a disease among [white men].
—Sitting Bull

Navajos teach their younguns right from wrong from the day they're born—beliefs that go back thousands of years. Some have a logical basis, some are part of the deeply religious culture that allows the American Indian to exist with Mother Earth. A number of Navajo taboos were selected here for their humorous element, but are not meant to be taken lightly. Reflect on why they might be good advice.

Four things that'll make you go crazy:
1) Wearing your blanket with the stripes crossways.
2) Putting your shoes on the wrong feet.
3) Putting your clothes on inside out or backwards.
4) Throwing your hat around in the house.

Five things that'll make you go blind:
1) Staring at someone for a long time.
2) Turning the pages of a book backward.
3) Looking at an eclipse of the sun.
4) Looking at a couple sleeping together.
5) Looking at your mother-in-law, or even speaking to her.

Five do's and don'ts:
1) Don't count your sheep too often, your flock will decrease in number.
2) Don't laugh at bears; they will come after you.
3) Don't do a rain dance during a rainstorm; you'll surely be struck by lightning.
4) Don't use a rock for a pillow, it will cause bad dreams.
5) Don't talk to animals, they might talk back to you.

How!
Glossary of Indian Words

"[The Indians] are as thick as hops about the mountains in this vicinity, and occasionally they knock over a poor fellow and take his hair."
—anonymous (1840's)

These are actually English words referring to American Indian activities and clothing.

1. **allotment.** In effect from 1887 until 1934, a federal government policy to take lands held by Indian tribes, break them up, and distribute them to individual Indians.

2. **band.** A subdivision of an Indian tribe often made up of an extended family.

3. **beadwork.** Colored beads stitched together to decorate clothing, bags, etc. Their use replaced *quillwork* when the Europeans brought glass beads to the Americas.

4. **bison.** Also know as buffalo, they once roamed the central plains of the Americas in the millions. They are large, hoofed animals with a rust-colored mane, shaggy front legs, humped back, and short black horns that curve upward.

5. **bola.** A hunting weapon made from a long leather thong with a stone at each end. Throwing it entangles the legs of mammals or the wings of birds.

6. **breechclout.** A cloth of deerskin or wool worn to cover the loins, leaving the thighs bare. Also called "breechcloth" or "loincloth."

7. **Bureau of Indian Affairs.** Formed in 1824, an agency of the federal government assigned to deal with Indian issues.

8. **calendar stick.** Used by the Papago tribe to keep track of important events by cutting notches in a wood stick.

9. **confederacy.** A political union of several tribes.

10. **coup.** Plains Indians would "count coup,"—keep a record of how many times they had physically touched an enemy during battle as proof of bravery.

11. **cradleboard.** A wooden or leather rack worn on the back to carry a baby.

12. **deadfall.** A small animal trap built by setting up a trip wire that releases a stone or log to crush the game.

13. **flint.** A type of quartz rock that can be shaped into tools and points for arrows and spears.

14. **hogan.** An eight-sided dwelling used by the Navajos made out of a frame of logs and sticks and covered with mud.

15. **Indian Territory.** A large section of territory west of the Mississippi set aside as a permanent homeland for the Indian tribes that were pushed West in the 1830's, but its size was gradually reduced until it became the state of Oklahoma in 1907.

16. **jerky.** Sun-dried strips of meat.

17. **maize.** Indian corn.

18. **medicine man.** A member of the tribe who keeps tribal lore and rituals and attempts to cure disease, bring success in food gathering and warfare, and control the supernatural by using magic spells.

19. **medicine pouch.** A leather pouch often worn around the neck and filled with a collection of charms or remedies to ward off bad spirits.

20. **mission Indians.** Those Indians that gave up their tribal ways to live at Spanish missions and grow crops.

21. **mortar and pestle.** A bowl-shaped stone and club-shaped stone used in food preparation to pulverize plants and animal parts. Can also be made of wood.

22. **papoose.** The Algonquian word for "baby" used by North American Indians.

23. **parfleche.** A rawhide bag worn over the shoulder for carrying personal belongings, clothes, ceremonial objects and food.

24. **peyote.** A mescal cacti found in the Southwest with button-like tops which, if eaten, produce an intoxicating trance-like effect. Considered a sacrament by the Native American church.

25. **powwow.** A ceremony or festival to conjure up the cure for a disease, success in war, etc., usually accompanied by magic, dancing, and feasting.

MOVIE TRIVIA QUESTION:
In what starring role did *Paul Newman* play a white man raised by Indians?
ANS: *Hombre* (1967). As a passenger of a stagecoach that has been robbed, he finds himself having to save the lives of the white men who are prejudiced against him because he was raised by Indians.

BOW AND ARROW

The bow and arrow wasn't the American Indian's only instrument of war (they also used spears, blowguns, clubs, etc.), but it is the weapon most often associated with them. It was a weapon far more accurate than the early single-shot firearms and a brave could shoot as many as 20 arrows in the time it took a white man to reload and fire one shot.

26. **quillwork.** Decorative work on clothing and bags made from porcupine quills dyed with vegetable colors.

27. **relocation.** The forced removal of a tribe from one location to another. A common U.S. government practice in the nineteenth century.

28. **sacred pipe.** A smoking pipe with a special meaning to a tribe and used in ceremonies. It was usually an intricately carved bowl in stone with a long wooden stem which was then decorated with beads, quills, and feathers.

29. **soapstone.** A soft talc in rock form having a soapy texture used to make pipes, pots, & sculptures.

30. **Sun Dance.** Worship of the sun at the summer solstice performed by many plains Indian tribes. Many rituals are involved in the ceremony but the most dramatic involved self-torture by warriors.

31. **teepee** (tepee, tipi). A conical tent used by the Plains Indians with a pole frame and usually covered with buffalo hides.

32. **tomahawk.** An ax-like weapon and tool with a metal head. Originally it had a stone or bone head. An Algonquian word, it was made by the Europeans and traded to the Indians.

33. **travois.** A wooden frame shaped like a "V" with planking or rope webbing in the middle; used to carry possessions or people behind horses or dogs.

34. **tribe.** Any of a number of different kinds of Indian social organizations composed of a number of bands or villages. The tribe will have something in common such as territory, culture, descendants, or history.

35. **Vision Quest.** A rite of passage, usually from childhood to adulthood, accomplished by creating visions or dreams through self-deprivation, exposure to the elements, or hallucinogenic drugs.

36. **warbonnet.** A headdress with each feather representing acts of bravery. Common among the plains Indians.

37. **wickiup.** An oval-shaped, stick-frame dwelling covered with brush, grass, or reeds; typical of the nomadic Apaches of the Southwest.

Buffalo Robes
23 USES OF THE BUFFALO

It is clear that the buffalo was far more important to the Plains Indians than just for food. They depended on it for their very survival. Because of this, the tribes were forced to follow the buffalo herds wherever they went across the Great Plains of America. Listed here are some of those uses. —Courtesy: Michael F. Steltenkamp, author of *Black Elk: Holy Man of the Oglala*, 1993.

1. **beard.** For ornamentation.
2. **bladder.** Pouches, medicine bags.
3. **blood**. Soup, pudding, paint.
4. **bones**. Fleshing tools, pipes, knives, arrow points, shovels, splints, sleds, war clubs, scrapers, quirts, awls, paintbrushes, game dice, tableware, toys, hoes, and jewelry.
5. **brain.** Used as food and for hide preparation.
6. **buckskin.** Cradles, moccasins, winter robes, bedding, shirts, belts, vessels, leggings, dresses, bags, quivers, teepee covers, teepee liners, bridles, backrests, sweat lodge covers, dolls, mittens, and tapestries.
7. **chips (dung).** Used for fuel and diaper powder.
8. **fat.** Tallow, soap, hair grease, cosmetic aids.
9. **gall.** Tallow paints.
10. **hair.** Ropes, hairpieces, halters, bracelets, medicine balls, moccasin lining, doll stuffing, pillows, pad fillers, and headdresses.
11. **hind-leg skin.** Pre-shaped moccasins.
12. **hoofs, feet, dewclaws.** Glue, rattles, spoons.
13. **horns.** Arrow points, fire carriers, spoons, headdresses, cups and ladles, toys, powder horns, signals, medications.
14. **liver.** Tanning agents.
15. **meat.** Requiring immediate preparation: sausages, caches, jerky (dehydrated).
16. **muscles.** Glue preparation, bows, thread, arrow ties, cinches.
17. **paunch liner.** Meat wrappings, buckets, collapsible cups, basins, canteens.
18. **rawhide.** Containers, shields, buckets, moccasin soles, drums, splints, mortars, ropes, sheaths, saddles, blankets, stirrups, bull boats, masks, lariats, straps, caps, and snowshoes.

19. **scrotum.** Uesd for rattles and containers.
20. **skull.** Used in the Sun Dance and medicine prayers.
21. **stomach liner and contents.** Medicines, paints, water containers, cooking.
22. **tail, teeth, tongue.** Whips, switches, brushes, ornaments, combs, choice meat.
23. **tendons.** Sewing thread, and bow strings.

BAD MEDICINE

To the Indians of the Old West, "bad medicine" meant that for some reason a man's spirits were guiding him wrongly. An Indian's "medicine" depended on whether the dreams and the spirits were working for or against him. His body and soul, reputation, character, and potential—all rolled into one—affected his luck in life. Indians would quit a battle anytime they felt their medicine had gone bad for them. To a white man, anyone with "bad medicine" was a dangerous man to be avoided at all costs.

A wooden cigar store Indian, originally used to identify a store as a place that sold tobacco for people who couldn't read (dk)

TRIVIA: What Indian actor co-starred with Jack Nicholson in *One Flew Over the Cuckoo's Nest?*
ANS: Will Sampson (1935-1987).

PRINCIPAL DOGS

Plains Indian tribes often organized into military societies, one of which was the Kiowas' *Principal Dogs,* a group limited to just ten outstanding braves. During a battle the leader of the *Dogs,* wearing a long colorful sash, would dismount and jab his spear into the earth and fight the entire battle from that spot. If he became injured or surrounded by the enemy, he could not leave his place until another *Dog* came to remove the spear.

Monument Valley Navajo Tribal Park with its world famous red buttes and mesas surrounded by a flat sandy desert on the Utah-Arizona border (dk).

A MOVIE TRIVIA QUESTION:
In what movie did Paul Fix (Marshal "Micah Torrance" on *The Rifleman* TV series) play an Indian chief?
ANS: *Dirty Dingus Magee* (1970). He played "Chief Crazy Blanket" in this comedy western spoof starring Frank Sinatra and George Kennedy.

Buffalo Hunt, 1861, Charles Wimar (1828-1862), oil on canvas. DECA

THE SUN DANCE

With the introduction of horses to the Plains Indians, making the tribes far more mobile, this religious festival spread quickly from tribe to tribe. Tribal encampments congregated into a large circle for sacred ceremonial dancing and singing. Each tribe interpreted the *Sun Dance* ritual differently; for some it was a renewal of their tribal race, others to strengthen their war making powers, but for all, it was the uniting of tribes behind a common supernatural force.

A MOVIE QUOTE: "Injuns give their lives to dreams, and when an Injun dreams—no matter how far fetched—he'l wait'll he dies for it to come true. White men, they're different, the only time they dream is when things are goin' their way. I'm no expert on the subject, but it seems to me that what Sittin' Bull does is a hell of a lot cheaper than mountin' a Wild West Show—which is just dreamin' out loud. Just put yourself in that Injun's place: you sit in your teepee and you dream, and then you go to wherever the dream might take place— might come true—and you wait for real life to catch up."
—Burt Lancaster, *Buffalo Bill and the Indians*, 1976

THE DOG SOLDIERS

The "Dog Soldiers" is a group of elite Cheyenne warriors led by *Roman Nose* who refused to abide by the *Fort Laramie Treaty of 1868* made with the United States concerning the Bozeman Trail. The treaty stated that the U.S. troops would abandon the forts along the trail if the Indians would stay peacefully on reservations established by the U.S., but Roman Nose refused to stay on a reservation and continued to fight. The Dog Soldiers were given privileges and duties such as presiding over ceremonies, hunts, and leading raids.

Sioux War Council, c. 1848, oil on canvas by George Catlin (1796-1872). DECA

The Scout, c1922, oil on canvas by William Robinson Leigh (1866-1955) DECA

QUOTE: "We will not have the wagons which make a noise in the hunting grounds of the buffalo. If the palefaces come farther into our land, there will be scalps of your brethren in the wigwams of the Cheyennes. I have spoken."
—Roman Nose of the Cheyenne speaking to General Palmer

Buffalo Bill Fighting Indians, c.1885, oil on canvas by Louis Maurer (1832-1932)DECA

> "The earth is the Mother of all people, and all people
> should have equal rights upon it."
> —Chief Joseph, 1879.

Paint on canvas teepee, Fort Hall Rendezvous, Pocatello, Idaho (dk)

Sitting Bull and Buffalo Bill, Montreal, QC, 1885.
(Library of Congress Prints and Photographs Division)

SITTING BULL'S EPIGRAPH
"One does not sell the earth on which the people walk."

THE LONE RANGER AND SILVER

The Legend of the Lone Ranger starring Clayton Moore and Jay Silverheels (author's collection)

Coonskin Caps and Cap Guns
TELEVISION WESTERNS

"Yer dern tootin'!"
—Gabby Hayes

T he earliest television westerns began on radio: *Death Valley Days* aired in 1933 as the first western drama and *The Lone Ranger* and *Tom Mix* followed. Gene Autry and Roy Rogers got into the act with *Red Ryder* and *The Cisco Kid*. Gene Autry was the first to recognize that the western would translate well to television—catering to kids with shows like *Annie Oakley* and *Buffalo Bill, Jr.* In 1952 *Gunsmoke* was the first western on radio aimed at adults, with William Conrad as the voice of Matt Dillon. Television aired the first adult western in 1955 with a thirty-minute anthology series called *Frontier.* Other adult westerns quickly followed: *The Life and Legend of Wyatt Earp, Have Gun Will Travel, The Rifleman* and of course *Gunsmoke,* the longest running western television series lasting 20 years.

Fess Parker in *Davy Crockett: King of the Wild Frontier*, Walt Disney Productions

Hey Wild Bill, Wait For Me!
51 TV TRIVIA QUESTIONS

*"A firey horse with the speed of light,
a cloud of dust, and a hearty Hi-Yo Silver."*
—opening line to TV's Lone Ranger, 1949-1965

TV Western trivia will surely evoke nostalgia—
and maybe a few tears—among the baby
boomers who were weaned on the 1950's
western heroes that flickered across that newfangled gadget
called a *television.* Characters like Matt Dillon, Davy Crockett,
and Lucas McCain made an indelible impression on young
minds, influencing their view of the world, and leaving them
forever fond of the western. You can test your knowledge of
TV western trivia by placing a piece of paper on this page
to cover the answers and then pulling it down to see if you
got it right.

**1. In the popular early TV western, *Wild Bill Hickok*, who starred
as Guy Madison's sidekick "Jingles"?**
> ANS: Andy Devine. He was always heard saying in a high-
> pitched gravel-voice: "Hey, Wild Bill, wait for me!"

**2. What western detective had this slogan on his business card:
"Have Gun, Will Travel"?**
> ANS: Paladin, played by Richard Boone in the TV western *Have
> Gun, Will Travel* in 1957 through 1963. His business card bore
> the image of a chess knight and read: "Have Gun, Will Travel.
> Wire Paladin, San Francisco."

**3. The longest running weekly prime-time television series was a
western. What was it?**
> ANS: Gunsmoke. CBS aired the series from 1955 to 1975, total-
> ing 635 episodes. 409 were in black and white and 226 were
> in color.

4. Return to the thrilling days of yesteryear. Who played the Lone Ranger's (Clayton Moore's) faithful Indian companion "Tonto" in the *Lone Ranger* television series in the 1950's?

ANS: Tonto was played by Jay Silverheels. He was also in several movies: He was in two Lone Ranger movies, in 1956 and 1958, and in *Broken Arrow* (1950), and *Santee* (1973).

5. Who played Bret, Bart and Beau Maverick in the original *Maverick* television series (1957-1962)?

ANS: James Garner (Bret), Jack Kelly (Bart), and Roger Moore (Beau). Maverick was an adult western full of humor and shenanigans by a well-dressed gambler and his brother who just wanted to make a peaceful living by playing cards, but instead got roped into trouble that required a clever con to get out of.

6. Who played Marshal Dillon's (James Arnez's) deputy on the long running television series *Gunsmoke?*

ANS: There were two. Starting in 1955 Dennis Weaver played the gimpy-legged "Chester Good" and in 1964 Ken Curtis took over the part as "Festus Hagen." In 1958 Dennis Weaver won the Emmy for Best Supporting Actor in a Dramatic Series.

The Stars of *Gunsmoke*, Arness Production Company & CBS (author's collection)

7. *Little House On The Prairie* **(1972-1982) was based on a series of novels by what author?**

ANS: Laura Ingalls Wilder. The series was told from the point of view of young Laura played by Melissa Gilbert.

8. What President of the United States hosted a long running anthology series called *Death Valley Days***?**

ANS: Ronald Reagan, our 40th United States president (1980-1988), hosted the show during the 1965-1966 season. Stanley Andrews was the original host (1952-1965) and after Reagan, it was hosted by Robert Taylor (1966-1969) and Dale Robertson (1969-1972). The 20 Mule Team Borax Company sponsored all 532 episodes of the show.

9. In *Alias Smith & Jones***, two bank robbers were offered full pardons if they could go straight for a year. To stay "incognito," they went by aliases Joshua Smith and Thaddeus Jones. What were their real character names?**

ANS: Smith was Hannibal Hayes played by Peter Devel and Jones was Jed "Kid" Curry played by Ben Murphy. Sally Field of "Flying Nun" fame also co-starred in the series as Clementine Hale.

A Match Game
8 CHILD ACTORS

Match the western television series to the child actor:

1. Rin Tin Tin	**a.**	Jimmy Hawkins as "Tagg"
2. Fury	**b.**	Johnny Washbrook as "Ken"
3. Annie Oakley	**c.**	Mickey Braddock as "Corky"
4. The Rifleman	**d.**	Bobby Diamond as "Joey"
5. My Friend Flicka	**e.**	Lee Aaker as "Rusty"
6. Buckskin	**f.**	Kurt Russell as "Jamie"
7. Circus Boy	**g.**	Tommy Nolan as "Jody"
8. Jamie McPheeters	**h.**	Johnny Crawford as "Mark"

ANS: 1-e, 2-d, 3-a, 4-h, 5-b, 6-g, 7-c, 8-f.

---

10. What classical music was used as the theme song to introduce *The Lone Ranger* TV series?

ANS: The fast-tempoed "William Tell Overture" by Italian composer Gioachino Rossini (1792-1868). Written in 1829 as the overture to the opera "Guillaume Tell."

11. Who was the first black actor to be a featured regular on a western TV series? What was the series?

ANS: Raymond St. Jacques played "Simon Blake" on *Rawhide* (1959-1966).

12. In what TV western did actor Walter Brennan always say "No brag, just fact" when his skill at gun handling was questioned?

ANS: *The Guns Of Will Sonnett* (1967-1969). Brennan played Will Sonnett and Dack Rambo played Jeff Sonnett, his grandson. They searched the West for Jeff's father, a wanted gunman.

13. Who played the part of Davy Crockett, The King of the Wild Frontier, on Walt Disney's popular five-part adventure series that aired in 1955?

ANS: Fess Parker. The series resulted in the sale of coonskin caps to millions of children. The first three episodes were made into a successful feature film, which led to the making of yet another feature using the last two episodes. Because of the boxoffice success of the two films, Disney made other westerns for television like *Zorro* and *Elfego Bacca*.

14. What star in the 1960's TV series *Gilligan's Island* also starred in a 1950's western, and what was the name of that western?

ANS: Alan Hale, the "Skipper" marooned on a deserted island with his crew, also played a famous railroad engineer running the Cannonball Express in *Casey Jones*, 1957-1959.

15. Who starred as Lucas McCain's son in *The Rifleman* (1958-1963)?

ANS: McCain's son "Mark" was played by Johnny Crawford.

16. Who played the gullible Tom Brewster in the western series *Sugarfoot* (1957-1961)?

ANS: Will Hutchins. Brewster was an Easterner who had gone west to become a lawyer, but found himself involved in other people's problems.

17. A film star who played "007" in several James Bond movies also played one of the Mavericks in the original *Maverick* TV series (1957-1962). Who was he?

ANS: Roger Moore played cousin Beauregard Maverick (Beau) when James Garner left the series in 1960 over a contract dispute. Moore also starred in a short-lived series *The Alaskans* in 1960.

18. In what state was Ben Cartwright's Ponderosa ranch located in the TV series *Bonanza* (1959-1973)?

ANS: Western Nevada, near Virginia City. A reproduction of the ranchhouse is located at Incline Village on the Eastern shore of Lake Tahoe where it was used as a set for some episodes.

19. What were the names of Ben Cartright's (Lorne Greene's) three sons in the long running TV western *Bonanza*?

ANS: Hoss (Dan Blocker), Little Joe (Michael Landon), and Adam (Pernell Roberts). Each son was a half-brother to the other two, Ben Cartright having been married (and divorced) three times—and this was a family western!

The Stars of *Bonanza,* left to right: Dan Blocker as Hoss, Lorne Greene as Ben, Pernell Roberts as Adam, and Michael Landon as Little Joe.
National Broadcasting Company (author's collection)

TIDBIT. JOHNNY CRAWFORD, who starred as Mark—Lucas McCain's son—in *The Rifleman* TV series, landed a couple of parts in westerns after the series ended. He was shot by John Wayne in *El Dorado* (1967), had a part in *The Great Texas Dynamite Chase* (1977) and the TV western *The Gambler: The Adventure Continues*. He and Chuck Connors were reunited in a 1990 episode of *Paradise*.

---

20. What was the name of the town where "The Rifleman" (Lucas McCain) often had to quell trouble with his .44-40 Winchester rifle?

ANS: North Fork, New Mexico. The ineffective Marshal of North Fork was Micah Torrance (played by Paul Fix) who always seemed to need McCain's help.

21. Several years before Robert Culp starred with Bill Cosby in the secret agent series *I Spy*, he also was the lead in a television western. What was it?

ANS: *Trackdown.* Culp played a Texas Ranger named Hoby Gilman for two seasons, 1957-1959.

22. What character did Clint Eastwood play in the western TV series *Rawhide?*

ANS: A cowboy named Rowdy Yates. The series aired from 1959 to 1966. In 1964 Sergio Leone invited him to star in a Spaghetti western called *A Fistful of Dollars,* playing an anti-hero called *The Man With No Name.* Eastwood took the job. The rest is history.

23. William Shatner of *Star Trek* fame starred in a short-lived western in the 1970's. What was it?

ANS: *The Barbary Coast.* Only 13 episodes were aired in 1975. Shatner played "Jeff Cable, Special Agent."

24. What were Bat Masterson's trademark clothing accoutrements?

ANS: A gold-tipped walking cane and a black derby hat. William Barclay Masterson, played by Gene Barry, was always "dressed to the nines" as a gentleman gambler who dispensed justice in the Wild West.

A Match Game
7 WESTERN MINI-SERIES

Match the mini-series, or two-hour movies, with one of the lead stars.

1. *How the West Was Won* (1978)	**a.** Alex Karras
2. *Centennial* (1978)	**b.** Patrick Swayze
3. *The Gambler* (1980)	**c.** Alex McArthur
4. *North and South* (1985)	**d.** Robert Duvall
5. *Desperado* (1988)	**e.** James Arness
6. *Lonesome Dove* (1989)	**f.** Kenny Rogers

ANS: 1-e, 2-a, 3-f, 4-b, 5-c, 6-d.

---

25. In *Little House On The Prairie* (1972-1982) starring Michael Landon of *Bonanza* fame, what state was the town of Walnut Grove in?
ANS: Minnesota.

26. Who played Johnny Yuma in the series *The Rebel* (1959-1961)?
ANS: Nick Adams played an ex-confederate soldier roaming the West. He used a sawed-off double-barreled shotgun to help other people with their problems.

27. Who played the lovable, but contrary, chuckwagon cook Charlie Wooster in the TV western *Wagon Train* (1957-1965)?
ANS: Frank McGrath. Ward Bond played Major Seth Adams, the wagonmaster, until his death in 1960. He was replaced by Chris Hale as John McIntire.

28. Was Jay Silverheels, the man who played Tonto on the *The Lone Ranger* TV series (1949-1957), an Indian?
ANS: Yes. He was a Mohawk who grew up on a reservation in Canada.

---

29. What TV western opened with a scene showing a twenty-mule team pulling a train of freight wagons hauling Borax?

ANS: *Death Valley Days* (1952-1975).

30. What western starred David Carradine as a half-breed Chinaman wandering the West?

ANS: *Kung Fu* (1972-1975). Carradine played "Kwai Chang Caine," a quiet drifter who abhorred violence, using his martial arts skills only when necessary. Carradine had previously starred in the short-lived *Shane* in 1966, based on the 1953 movie of the same name. In 1979, Carradine starred in a four hour TV mini-series called *Mr. Horn*.

31. Who wrote the immortal theme song to *Bonanza* which played over a burning map of the Ponderosa?

ANS: Jay Livingston and Ray Evans. Jay was the composer and Ray the lyricist. Of note, the first episode of Bonanza (aired 12 Sept. 1959) had the four Cartwrights riding toward the camera actually *singing* the song! They never sang again. A 60-year partnership netted Livingston and Evans three Oscars and seven academy award nominations.

32. Everyone knows the Lone Ranger's horse was named "Silver," but what did Tonto call *his* horse?

ANS: Scout.

33. Believe it or not, James Arness was not the producer's first choice for the part of Matt Dillon in the television western *Gunsmoke*. What famous western actor was?

ANS: John Wayne. He graciously turned down the job because of a prior movie commitment, but he recommended a young friend of his. James Arness. The rest is history.

TIDBIT: KURT RUSSELL made his acting debut at the age of 12 in the 1964 TV western *Guns of Diablo* with Charles Bronson. It was edited from two episodes of *The Travels of Jamie McPheeters* where he played a doctor's son in a TV series that lasted only one season. In 1976, Russell co-starred with Tim Matheson in *The Quest* as a boy raised by Indians who is re-united with his brother. They then go on a quest for their sister, also a captive which lead to its quick demise. In 1993, he starred as Wyatt Earp in *Tombstone*.

---

34. Which one of these was not an actual comedy western aired on American television: *Gun Shy, Rango, F Troop, The Nine Lives of Gunny McCoy* or *Pistols 'N' Petticoats*?

ANS: *The Nine Lives of Gunny McCoy* never existed. *Gun Shy* (1983) was based on the Disney movie *Apple Dumpling Gang*, where Barry Van Dyke (son of Dick Van Dyke) plays a gambler saddled with raising two orphan kids. *Rango* (1967) starred Tim Conway as an inept Texas Ranger with an Indian Scout named "Pink Cloud." *F Troop* (1965-1967) starred a scheming Sergeant O-Rourke and his bumbling partner-in-crime, Corporal Agarn. *Pistols 'N' Petticoats* (1966-67) starred "Henrietta," a gun-totin' widow who fights outlaws in Wretched, Colorado.

35. What was the first television western to be aired in color?

ANS: *Bonanza.* Other westerns like *The Cisco Kid* and *The Lone Ranger* had been shot in color, but were aired in black and white. When Bonanza was shown in color it brought a quick end to the sale of black & white television sets. The show lasted from 1959 to 1972 when Dan Blocker (Hoss) died unexpectedly and the show was moved from Sundays to Tuesdays, leading to loss of viewership and cancellation of series.

36. Dan Blocker's "Hoss" Cartwright character in *Bonanza* had a first name besides his nickname. What was it?

ANS: His name was Eric. "Hoss" was Norwegian for "good luck."

37. What fantasy western teamed two special agents of the federal government—traveling in a railroad car—to ferret out criminals who used high-tech devices in their mischievous deeds?

ANS: *The Wild, Wild West* (1965-1969). Robert Conrad played "James T. West" and Ross Martin played "Artemus Gordon," secret service investigators working directly for President Ulysses S. Grant. West and Gordon fought maniacal villains who were often bent on destroying the world or getting rich using their own high-tech schemes. A popular villain in the series was the dwarf Dr. Miguelito Loveless played by Michael Dunn. A very bad movie based on the series was made in 1999.

38. In the series *Rin Tin Tin*, what were the cavalry ranks of "Rusty" and his German-shepard dog?

ANS: Rusty (Lee Aaker) was commissioned a corporal and Rin Tin Tin was made a private. The 101st cavalry troop had taken them in after an Indian raid left them the only survivors.

39. What character in *The Big Valley* went on to star in the popular evening soap opera *Dynasty?*

ANS: Linda Evans, as "Audra" in *The Big Valley* (1965-1969), played "Krystle Jennings" in *Dynasty* (1981-1989).

40. In the 1960's comedy western series, *F Troop*, what was the name of the military fort?

ANS: Fort Courage, Kansas. The scheming Sergeant O'Rourke was played by Forrest Tucker; the incompetent Captain Parmenter by Ken Berry, and bumbling Corporal Agarn was played by Larry Storch.

41. What western actor in the TV series *Yancy Derringer* played the famous ape man in *Tarzan Goes to India* (1962) and *Tarzan's Three Challenges* (1963)?

ANS: Jock Mahoney. He became the thirteenth actor to play Tarzan. He played heavies in low-budget westerns before he starred in the TV western *The Range Rider* in 1951 and then *Yancy Derringer* in 1958. He was the stepfather of actress Sally Field after his marriage to actress Margaret Field.

Hugh O'Brian as *Wyatt Earp*
(Wyatt Earp Enterprises)

Guy Williams as *Zorro*
(Walt Disney Productions)

> **TIDBIT:** BRUCE BOXLEITNER, co-star of *How the West Was Won* with James Arness (1978-1979) playing Luke Machan, and co-star in "The Gambler" series of Kenny Rogers TV movies (1980-1990) playing Billy Montana, also played McCloud, the young man who sold Clint Eastwood someone else's cows in *Hang 'em High* (1968). He had his face on screen for only three-seconds because a black hood was placed over his head just before he was hanged!

42. What two TV westerns did handsome Burt Reynolds of *Smokey and the Bandit* fame play key rolls in?

ANS: *Gunsmoke* as Quint Asper, a half-breed blacksmith (1962-1965), and *Riverboat* as Ben Frazer, a riverboat pilot (1959). *Riverboat* was Reynold's first continuous TV role.

43. In *Paradise* (1988-1991), how many children did Ethan Allen Cord inherit?

ANS: Cord (Lee Horsley) is an ex-gunfighter living in Paradise, California who inherits FOUR young children from his deceased sister: Claire, Joseph, Benjamin, and George.

44. What was the name of Hondo's traveling companion and best friend?

ANS: He was a dog named "Sam." Hondo Lane, played by Ralph Taeger, said *"He's not my dog, he belongs to himself."* Noah Beery, Jr. as Buffalo Baker, also "sidekicked" with Hondo.

45. In *The Roy Rogers Show* (1951-1957) Roy's sidekick Pat Brady rode around in a jeep. What was the name of the jeep?

ANS: "Nellybelle." The show starred Roy Rogers, Roy's real wife Dale Evans, sidekick Pat Brady, and the *Sons of the Pioneers*. Roy's horse was named "Trigger" and Dale rode "Buttermilk." The German shepherd's name was "Bullet."

46. What character disguised in a black mask and cape won his battles with expert swordsmanship?

ANS: Zorro, the defender of the people, was really Don Diego de la Vega, a nobleman from Spain who came to California at his father's request to rid the area of a commandant bent on ruling the region and taking over every ranch he could get his hands on.

47. Anthoney Zerbe played what character in the series *The Young Riders* (1989-1992)?

ANS:Teaspoon Hunter, a way-station manager for Express riders.

48. What was Miss Kitty's last name on the TV western *Gunsmoke*?

ANS: Kitty Russell, owner of the Long Branch Saloon. The character was played by Amanda Blake.

49. In what TV western was the lead character always saying "My pappy always said"?

ANS: *Maverick* starring James Garner.

50. What television series starred Steve McQueen and a sawed-off Winchester carbine?

ANS: *Wanted: Dead Or Alive*. This series, lasting 94 episodes (1959-1961), made Steve McQueen a star.

51. In the eight years *Wagon Train* was on the air, there where only two wagonmasters. Name them?

ANS: Ward Bond (1957-1961) and John McIntire (1961-1965). They played the character "Chris Hale."

McQueen in *Wanted: Dead or Alive* Duncan Renaldo as *The Cisco Kid*
(Frontier Productions)   (ZIV Television Productions)

Head 'Em Up, Move 'Em Out
38 TELEVISION WESTERNS

"Who was that masked man?"
—The closing line to TV's *Lone Ranger,* 1949-1965

Westerns were once regular TV fare. Do you remember these westerns and their stars? Some of the longest running series are listed below.

1. **Bat Masterson**, 1958-1961, Gene Barry (*Bat Masterson*).

2. **The Big Valley**, 1965-1969, Barbara Stanwyck (*Victoria Barkley*), Richard Long (*Jarrod*), Peter Breck (*Nick*), Lee Majors (*Heath*).

3. **Bonanza,** 1959-1973, Lorne Greene (*Ben Cartwright*), Michael Landon (*Little Joe*), Dan Blocker (*Hoss*), Pernell Roberts (*Adam*).The first TV western to air in color and second longest running western series.

4. **Cheyenne**, 1955-1963, Clint Walker (*Cheyenne Bodie*).Television's first hour-long western.

5. **Death Valley Days**, 1952-1970, hosted by Stanley Andrews, Ronald Reagan, Robert Taylor, and Dale Robertson.

6. **Gunsmoke,** 1955-1975, James Arness (*Matt Dillon*), Amanda Blake (*Kitty Russell*), Dennis Weaver (*Chester B. Goode*), Milburn Stone (*Doc Adams*), Ken Curtis (*Festus Haggen*).The longest running western on television.

7. **Have Gun, Will Travel**, 1957-1963, Richard Boone (*Paladin*).

8. **The High Chaparral**, 1967-1971, Leif Erickson (*John Cannon*), Linda Cristal (*Victoria Cannon*), Cameron Mitchell (*Buck Cannon*), Mark Slade (*Blue Cannon*).

9. **Hopalong Cassidy**, 1949-1954, William Boyd (*Hopalong Cassidy*).

10. **Kung Fu**, 1972-1975, David Carradine (*Kwai Chang Caine*), Keye Luke (*Master Po*), Philip Ahn (*Master Kan*), Radames Pera (*Grasshopper*, the young Caine).

11. **The Lawman**, 1958-1962, John Russell (*Marshal Dan Troop*), Peter Brown (*Johnny McKay*), Bek Nelson (*Dru Lemp*), Barbara Long (*Julie Tate*), Peggie Castle (*Lily Merrill*).

12. **Little House on the Prairie**, 1974-1983, Michael Landon (*Charles Ingalls*), Karen Grassle (*Caroline Ingalls*), Melissa Sue Anderson (*Mary*), Melissa Gilbert (*Laura*), Richard Bull (*Nels Oleson*), Katherine MacGregor (*Harriet Oleson*).

13. **The Lone Ranger**, 1949-1957, Clayton Moore (*Lone Ranger*), Jay Silverheels (*Tonto*).

14. **Maverick**, 1957-1962, James Garner (*Bret Maverick*), Jack Kelly (*Bart Maverick*).

15. **Rawhide**, 1959-1966, Eric Fleming (*Gil Favor*), Clint Eastwood (*Rowdy Yates*), Jim Murdock (*Mushy*), Paul Brinegar (*Wishbone*), Steve Raines (*Quince*).

16. **The Rifleman**, 1958-1963, Chuck Connors (*Lucas McCain*), Johnny Crawford (*Mark*).

17. **Rin Tin Tin**, 1954-1959, Lee Aaker (*Rusty*), Jim L. Brown (*Lt. Ripley "Rip" Masters*).

18. **The Roy Rogers Show**, 1951-1957, Roy Rogers, Dale Evans, Pat Brady, and Sons of the Pioneers.

19. **Sugarfoot**, 1957-1960, Will Hutchins (*Tom Brewster*).

20. **Wagon Train**, 1957-1965, Ward Bond (*Major Seth Adams*), John McIntire (*Chris Hale*), Robert Horton (*Flint McCullough*), Frank McGrath (*Charlie Wooster*), Terry Wilson (*Bill Hawks*).

21. **Wanted—Dead or Alive**, 1958-1961, Steve McQueen (*Josh Randall*).

22. **Wells Fargo**, 1957-1962, Dale Robertson (*Jim Hardie*), Jack Ging (*Beau McCloud*), Virginia Christine (*Ovie*), Lory Patrick (*Tina*), Mary Jane Saunders (*Mary Gee*), William Demarest (*Jeb*).

23. **Wild Bill Hickok**, 1951-1958, Guy Madison (*U.S. Marshal James Butler*), Andy Devine (*Jingles B. Jones*).

24. **The Wild, Wild West**, 1965-1969, Roberet Conrad (*James West*), Ross Martin (*Artemus Gordon*).

25. **The Virginian**, 1962-1970, James Drury (*The Virginian*), Doug McClure (*Trampas*), Lee J. Cobb (*Judge Henry Garth*), Roberta Shore (*Betsy Garth*), L.Q. Jones (*Belden*), Harlan Warde (*Sheriff Brannon*). What's name of the town in Wyoming where the Shiloh Ranch is located? ANS: Medicine Bow.

26. **Wyatt Earp**, 1955-1961, Hugh O'Brian (*Wyatt Earp*), Douglas Fowley (*Myron Healey*), Morgan Woodward (*Shotgun Gibbs*).

27. **The Young Riders**, 1989-1992, Anthony Zerbe (*Teaspoon Hunter*), Ty Miller (*The Kid*), Stephen Baldwin (*Billy Cody*), Josh Brolin (*Jimmy Hickok*), Travis Fine (*Ike McSwain*), Gregg Rainwater (*Buck Cross*), Yvonne Suhor (*Lou McCloud*).

A FEW OTHERS WITH SHORTER RUNS:

28. **Branded,** 1965-1966, Chuck Connors (*Jason McCord*).

29. **Cisco Kid**, 1951-1953, Duncan Renaldo (*Cisco Kid*), Leo Carillo (*Pancho*).

30. **Davy Crockett**, 1954-1955, Fess Parker (*Davy Crockett*).

31. **F Troop**, 1965-1967, Ken Berry (*Capt. Wilton Parmenter*), Forrest Tucker (*Sgt. Morgan O'Rourke*), Larry Storch (*Corporal Randolph Agarn*), Melody Patterson (*Wrangler Jane*), Edward Everett Horton (*Roaring Chicken*), Frank Dekova (*Wild Eagle*).

32. **The Guns Of Will Sonnett**, 1967-1969, Walter Brennen (*Will Sonnett*), Dack Rambo (*Jeff Sonnett*), Jason Evers (*Jim Sonnett*).

33. **Hondo**, 1967, Ralph Taeger (*Hondo Lane*), Noah Beery, Jr. (*Buffalo Baker*), Gary Clarke (*Captain Richards*).

34. **How The West Was Won**, 1978-1979, James Arness (*Zeb Macahan*), Bruce Boxleitner (*Luke*), Kathryn Holcomb (*Laura*), Fionnula Flanagan (*Molly Culhane*), William Kirby Cullen (*Jed Macahan*), Vicki Schreck (*Jessie*).

35. **Iron Horse**, 1966-1968, Dale Robertson (*Ben Calhoun*), Gary Collins (*Dave Tarrant*), Bob Random (*Barnabas Rogers*), Roger Torrey (*Nils Torvald*), Ellen McRae (*Julie Parsons*).

36. **Laramie**, 1959-1963, John Smith (*Slim Sherman*), Robert Fuller (*Jess Harper*), Hoagy Carmichael (*Jonesy*), Bobby Crawford, Jr. (*Andy Sherman*), Don Durant (*Gandy*), Arch Johnson (*Wellman*), Dennis Holms (*Mike*), Spring Byington (*Daisy Cooper*).

37. **Paradise**, 1988-1991, Lee Horsley (*Ethan Allen Cord*), Jenny Beck (*Claire Carroll*).

38. **Riverboat**, 1959-1961, Darren McGavin (*Grey Holden*), Burt Reynolds (*Ben Frazer*), Noah Beery (*Bill Blake*), Dick Wessel (*Carney*), Jack Lambert (*Joshua*), Mike McGreevey (*Chip*), John Mitchum (*Pickalong*), Bart Patton (*Terry*).

Saddle Up With Saddle Sores
86 WESTERN TV STARS

Listed here are a handful of stars from the most memorable TV westerns. Can you name the character they played or the show they were in? Cover the second and third column with a piece of paper and pull down to reveal the answer. Check off the ones you get right.

TV STAR	CHARACTER	SHOW
1. Nick Adams	*Johnny Yuma*	The Rebel
2. Rex Allen	*Dr. Bill Baxter*	Frontier Doctor
3. Michael Ansara	*Cochise*	Broken Arrow
4. Michael Ansara	*Marshal Sam Buckhart*	Law of the Plainsman
5. James Arness	*Marshal Matt Dillon*	Gunsmoke
6. James Arness	*Zeb Macahan*	HowTheWestWasWon
7. Stephen Baldwin	*Cody*	The Young Riders
8. Gene Barry	*Bat Masterson*	Bat Masterson
9. William Bendix	*Frederick Kelly*	The Overland Trail
10. Ken Berry	*Capt. Wilton Parameter*	F Troop
11. Amanda Blake	*Miss Kitty*	Gunsmoke
12. Dan Blocker	*Hoss Cartwright*	Bonanza
13. Ward Bond	*Seth Adams*	Wagon Train
14. Richard Boone	*Paladin*	Have Gun, Will Travel
15. Richard Boone	*Hec Ramsey*	Hec Ramsey
16. Neville Brand	*Reese Bennett*	Larado
17. Walter Brennan	*Will Sonnett*	Guns of Will Sonnett
18. Edger Buchanan	*Judge Roy Bean*	Judge Roy Bean
19. Rory Calhoun	*Wild Bill Longley*	The Texan
20. Richard Comar	*Jack Craddock*	Bordertown

Trivia Question: What comic sidekick of "B" westerns was always saying "Durned persnickety females!"?
Answer: George "Gabby" Hayes.

THE YOUNG RIDERS
Stephen Baldwin, Ty Miller, Josh Brolin, Travis Fine, Gregg Rainwater, Anthony Zerbe, and Yvonne Suhor. (MGM Television)

THE WILD, WILD WEST
Ross Martin and Robert Conrad

(Bruce Landsbury Productions and CBS)

THE LAWMAN
John Russell and Peter Brown

(Warner Brothers Television)

TV STAR	CHARACTER	SHOW
21.David Carradine	*Kwai Chang Caine*	Kung Fu
22.Leo Carrillo	*Pancho*	The Cisco Kid
23.Chuck Connors	*Lucas McCain*	The Rifleman
24.Chuck Connors	*Jason McCord*	Branded
25.Robert Conrad	*James T. West*	The Wild, Wild West
26. Ken Curtis	*Festus Haggen*	Gunsmoke
27.Robert Culp	*Ranger Hoby Gilman*	Trackdown
28.Gail Davis	*Annie Oakley*	Annie Oakley
29.Andy Devine	*Jingles*	Advs.of Wild Bill Hickok
30.James Drury	*The Virginian*	The Virginian
31.Clint Eastwood	*Rowdy Yates*	Rawhide
32.Leif Erickson	*Big John Cannon*	The High Chaparral
33.Linda Evans	*Audra Barkley*	The Big Valley
34.Eric Fleming	*Gil Favor*	Rawhide
35.Henry Fonda	*Marshal Simon Fry*	The Deputy
36.Glenn Ford	*Sheriff Sam Cade*	Cade's County
37.Robert Fuller	*Jess Harper*	Laramie
38.James Garner	*Bret Maverick*	Maverick
39.Melissa Gilbert	*Laura Ingalls*	LittleHouseOnThePrairie
40.Kirby Grant	*Sky King*	Sky King
41.Lorne Greene	*Ben Cartwright*	Bonanza
42.Dan Haggerty	*Grizzly Adams*	Grizzly Adams
43.Alan Hale	*Casey Jones*	Casey Jones
44.Ty Hardin	*Bronco Lane*	Bronco
45.Lee Horsley	*Ethan Allen Cord*	Paradise
46.Will Hutchins	*Tom Brewster*	Sugarfoot
47.Jack Kelly	*Bart Maverick*	Maverick
48.Michael Landon	*Little Joe Cartwright*	Bonanza
49.Michael Landon	*Charles Ingalls*	LittleHouseOnThePrairie
50.Keith Larson	*Brave Eagle*	Brave Eagle
51.Robert Loggia	*Elfego Baca*	Nine Lives of ...
52.Richard Long	*Jarrod Barkley*	The Big Valley
53.Guy Madison	*Wild Bill Hickok*	Adventures of ...

TIDBIT: Leslie Nielson of *Naked Gun* fame starred in a *Disney* series called *The Swamp Fox* way back in 1960 where he played Colonel Francis Marion, a Revolutionary War hero.

TV STAR	CHARACTER	SHOW
54. Jock Mahoney	*The Range Rider*	The Range Rider
55. Lee Majors	*Heath Barkley*	The Big Valley
56. Ross Martin	*Artemus Gordon*	The Wild, Wild West
57. Doug McClure	*Trampas*	The Virginian
58. Darren McGavin	*Captain Grey Holden*	Riverboat
59. Frank McGrath	*Charlie Wooster*	Wagon Train
60. Steve McQueen	*Josh Randall*	Wanted Dead or Alive
61. Cameron Mitchell	*Buck Cannon*	The High Chaparral
62. George Montgomery	*Matt Rockford*	Cimmaron City
63. Clayton Moore	*The Lone Ranger*	The Lone Ranger
64. Ben Murphy	*Jed "Kid" Curry*	Alias Smith and Jones
65. Hugh O'Brian	*Wyatt Earp*	Life and Legend of ...
66. Merlin Olsen	*Father Murphy*	Father Murphy
67. Fess Parker	*Davy Crockett*	Davy Crockett
68. Duncan Renaldo	*The Cisco Kid*	The Cisco Kid
69. Burt Reynolds	*Ben Frazer*	Riverboat
70. Dale Robertson	*Jim Hardie*	Tales of Wells Fargo
71. Dale Robertson	*Ben Calhoun*	Iron Horse
72. John Russell	*Marshall Dan Troop*	Lawman
73. Kurt Russell	*Jamie McPheeters*	The Travels of ...
74. William Shatner	*Special Agent Jeff Cable*	The Barbary Coast
75. Jay Silverheels	*Tonto*	The Lone Ranger
76. Barbara Stanwyck	*Victoria Barkley*	The Big Valley
77. Melburn Stone	*Doc Adams*	Gunsmoke
78. Larry Storch	*Corporal Agarn*	F Troop
79. Ralph Taeger	*Hondo Lane*	Hondo
80. Tom Tryon	*Texas John Slaughter*	Texas John Slaughter
81. Forrest Tucker	*Sergeant O'Rourke*	F Troop
82. Clint Walker	*Cheyenne Bodie*	Cheyenne
83. Dennis Weaver	*Chester Goode*	Gunsmoke
84. Bill Williams	*Kit Carson*	Adventures of Kit Carson
85. Guy Williams	*Zorro*	Zorro
86. Anthony Zerbe	*Teaspoon Hunter*	The Young Riders

TIDBIT: Alan Hale, the skipper on Gilligan's Island, starred in the TV western *Casey Jones* where he played the famous engineer who ran the Cannonball Express. Airing in 1958, it ran for 78 episodes.

Long Live The Western
24 TNT WESTERNS

Turner Network Television has consistently added new western fare to their MGM library. They are the only network that has made making quality westerns a profitable and routine enterprise when Hollywood has been ignoring the genre. Here's a list of westerns made by Ted Turner:

Gore Vidal's Billy the Kid (1989)
Conagher (1991)
The Borrowers (1993)
Geronimo (1993)
Broken Chain (1993)
Cisco Kid (1994)
Lakota Woman (1994)
The Avenging Angel (1995)
The Good Old Boys (1995)
Tecumseh: The Last Warrior (95)
The Desperate Trail (1995)
Riders of the Purple Sage (1996)

Crazy Horse (1996)
Last Stand at Saber River (1997)
Rough Riders (1997)
Buffalo Soldiers (1997)
Two for Texas (1998)
Everything That Rises (1998)
Dollar for the Dead (1998)
Purgatory (1999)
You Know My Name (1999)
King of Texas (2002)
Monte Walsh (2003)
Into the West (2005) miniseries

A Match Game
6 COMIC SIDEKICKS

Match the "B" Western hero with his comic sidekick.

1. Gene Autry
2. Roy Rogers
3. Lash LaRue
4. Wild Bill Hickok
5. Johnny Mack Brown
6. The Cisco Kid

a. "Fuzzy" St. John
b. "Fuzzy" Knight
c. Smiley Burnett & Pat Buttram
d. Leo Carrillo (Pancho)
e. Andy "Jingles" Devine
f. "Gabby" Hayes & Pat Brady

ANS: 1-c, 2-f, 3-a, 4-e, 5-b, 6-d.

Top left: Robert Fuller as Cooper Smith and John McIntire as Christopher Hale from the television series "Wagon Train," Revue Studios (Author's collection)

***Wagon Train* Trivia: 1.** The series was inspired by the 1950 film *Wagon Master* directed by John Ford and starring Ben Johnson, Harry Carey Jr., and Ward Bond. Bond was also in the 1930 *The Big Trail* with John Wayne. **2.** *Wagon Train* was sponsored by the Edsel Division of the Ford Motor Company during its first season. **3.** The wagonmaster, Ward Bond, died in 1961 and was replaced by John McIntire, then Robert Horton left in 1962 and was replaced by Robert Fuller.

King of the Wild Frontier
18 Western Television Themes

"Supposin' I was to go to work and learn how to... to read writin'. Well, how'd I know that the feller that... that wrote the writin' was a writin' the writin' right? See, it could be that he wrote the writin' all wrong. Here I'd be just a readin' wrong writin', don't ya see? You probably been doin' it your whole life, just a readin' wrong writin' and not even knowin' it."
—Ken Curtis as Festus Haggen in "The Devil's Outpost."

Here are eighteen of the most memorable songs of the baby boomers back when entire families gathered around a small black & white television to watch *Gunsmoke*, the longest running of them all, at 20 years, from 1966 until 1975.

1. "The Big Valley"—George Duning.
2. "Bonanza"—Jay Livingston & Ray Evans.
3. "Davy Crockett, King of the Wild Frontier"—George Bruns.
4. "Gene Autry Show": Back in the Saddle Again—Gene Autry
5. "Gunsmoke": Old Trails—Rex Koury.
6. "The High Chaparral"—David Rose.
7. "The Life and Legend of Wyatt Earp"—Herman Stein.
8. "Lonesome Dove": Main Theme—Basil Poledouris.
9. "The Lone Ranger": William Tell Overture—Rossini.
10. "Maverick"—David Buttolph, Paul Francis Webber.
11. "Paladin: Have Gun Will Travel"—Bernard Herrman, sung by Johnny Western.
12. "Rawhide"—Dimitri Tiomkin, Ned Washington, sung by Frankie Laine.
13. "The Rebel": The Ballad of Johnny Yuma—Richard Markowitz, Andrew J. Fenady.
14. "Roy Rogers Show": Happy Trails—Roy Rogers, Dale Evans.
15. "The Rifleman"—Herschel Burke Gilbert.
16. "The Virginian": Lonesome Tree—Percy Faith.
17. "Wagon Train"—Henri Rene, Bob Russell.
18. "The Wild, Wild West"— Richard Markowitz.

#191 2-8-0 Burnham, Parry, Willimas & Co., Colorado Railroad Museum, Golden, Colorado (dk).

Oil Cans and Monkey Wrenches

Oil Cans and Monkey Wrenches
THE WESTERN RAILROAD

*"The railroads had an incomparably romantic appeal, far
beyond mere transportation. Railroad travel exercised a
charm upon the human spirit."*
—Phyllis Zauner, "The Train Whistle's Echo"

A shrill whistle cracks the silence of the desert. In the
distance rises a puff of white smoke, and then another,
and another, like Indian smoke signals. Something black
and ominous shivers through waves of heat rising from
the desert sand. The image looms larger at the end of glinting
silver rails. Another long whistle echoes off the canyon walls. It's
the northbound train, arriving only two hours late. The huge iron
horse chugs up to, and past, the tiny one-room depot and stops
at a leaking wooden water tower. The windmill that draws water
from deep within the desert floor squeaks an eerie rhythmic tune.
A soot-covered fireman jumps to the tender and jerks down the
water spout. The fresh invigorating water rushes into a tender that
also carries tons of cord wood for the firebox. Pressurized steam is
released from the side of the powerful beast as it waits patiently for
passengers to board. A slender, mustached man dressed in a blue
suit with brass buttons, steps down the ladder of the passenger car
and yells "Allll Ahhh-board!"

This visually dramatic scene is played out in many a western
film just as it happened in the real American West, immigrants
moving westward to settle in a huge untamed frontier. After the
Civil War, the railroad trekked westward, spur lines jutting off in
every conceivable direction like cancerous tentacles. Farmers
could now grow crops and ranchers raise cattle because their
products could be shipped back East by railroad and sold for a
decent profit. The West would never be the same again.

THE SHORTEST AND QUICKEST ROUTE
BETWEEN THE

MOUNTAINS AND THE EAST
IS VIA THE

UNION PACIFIC R.R
NOW OPEN FROM

OMAHA TO NORTH PLATTE
300 Miles West of the Missouri River, and 200 Miles nearer Denver and Salt Lake than any other Railroad Line.

All Passenger Trains of this Road Connect Direct
CHICAGO & NORTH-WESTERN R'Y, WHICH IS NOW COMPLETED FROM

CHICAGO TO OMAHA
Making 500 Miles of Railroad directly West of Chicago with but "One Change of Cars."

PASSENGERS CROSSING THE PLAINS
Will save 200 Miles Stage Travel and 48 Hours Time by taking this Route.

PULLMAN'S PALACE SLEEPING CARS ON ALL NIGHT TRAINS
Equipment all new. and Roadbed in perfect order. Good Eating Houses at convenient points on line.

DIRECT CONNECTIONS MADE AT NORTH PLATTE WITH WELLS, FARGO & CO'S DAILY LINES OF

OVERLAND MAIL AND EXPRESS COACHES
To and from Denver, Central City, Salt Lake, and ALL POINTS in Colorado, Utah,, Idaho, Montana, Nevada and California.

PASSENGERS TO AVAIL THEMSELVES OF THE QUICK TIME AND SURE CONNECTIONS OF THIS ROUTE, MUST

Ask for Tickets via Omaha.
THE ATTENTION OF SHIPPERS OF FREIGHT FOR THE MOUNTAINS

Be particularly called for the opening of the great Platte Valley Route to NORTH PLATTE, and its connections. 200 Miles of Wagon Transportation is saved in sending Goods via OMAHA. Reliable Freight Lines are at all times prepared to transport Goods from the Western terminus of this Road to all points in the Mountains. Careful handling and quick time guaranteed. ***RATES ALWAYS AS LOW AND CHANGES FEWER THAT BY ANY OTHER ROUTE.***

W. SNYDER, Genl Frit and Ticket Agent   SAMiL B. REED, Genll Superintendent.

Text from an actual Old West handbill

A Match Game
18 RAILROAD SLANG WORDS

Humor can be found in the language of any profession. The hardworking railroad men of the nineteenth century created many colorful words and phrases for the equipment and activities of their budding industry. Printed here are a couple of "match the names" quizzes relating to the slang terminology used by these early railroaders.

Match the ROLLING STOCK (right column) with the railroader's loving slang names for them (left column).

1. snoozer		a. caboose
2. hotcake		b. boxcar
3. crate		c. tank car
4. crummy		d. stock car
5. skeleton car		e. pullman
6. steam wagon		f. passenger car
7. oil can		g. refrigerator
8. cow crate		h. flatcar
9. cushions		i. logcar
10. reefer		j. locomotive

ANS: 1-e, 2-h, 3-b, 4-a, 5-i, 6-j, 7-c, 8-d, 9-f, 10-g.

Match the RAILROAD EMPLOYEE'S affectionate slang names for their fellow workers.

11. brass button		k. car inspector
12. ash eater		l. telegrapher
13. hog jockey		m. brakeman
14. wheel man		n. conductor
15. car knocker		o. switchman
16. bug		p. engineer
17. cinder crusher		q. yardmaster
18. the general		r. fireman

ANS: 11-n, 12-r, 13-p, 14-m, 15-k, 16-l, 17-o, 18-q.

A Railroad Ballad
WRECK OF THE OLD 97

"I hate to hear that lonesome whistle blow."
—from old railroad ballad

Dozens of ballads were originally composed about the wreck of the locomotive numbered "97." Witnesses to the crash and photographs distributed around the country made it a well known disaster. Many versions of the song led to a hit parade song in the 1920's. David Graves George, who was there after the wreck, may have been the original author, but over the years many have laid claim to it. The wreck occurred on a high trestle on September 27, 1903 on the Southern Railway near Danville, Virginia. Engine 97, a 4-6-0 locomotive, pulled a high-priority mail train, and young engineer Joseph A. "Steve" Broady, who took over at Monroe, was trying to make up lost time when he hit the 325-foot-long curved wooden *Stillhouse Trestle* at too fast a speed. New to this line, Broady underestimated his slowing distance and began breaking late. Going 90 mph, he locked wheels, and blew his whistle in warning. Engineer Broady hung on and rode the engine and five wooden mail cars off the 75-foot-high trestle. Men groaned in the splintered mess and a load of yellow canaries hovered overhead. Broady, two firemen, the conductor, and four postal clerks died in the wreck. Engineer Broady was heard to say before his run "I'll get this train on time or I'll sink this thing into Hell." That he did, and it became the most famous wreck next to Casey Jones' last ride, thanks to the ballads written about it. One version follows on the next page.

WRECK OF THE OLD 97

(September 27, 1903—Danville, Virginia)

1. On a cold frosty morning in the month of September
When the clouds were hanging low,
Ninety-seven pulled out of the Washington station
Like an arrow shot from a bow.

2. Old Ninety-seven was the fastest mail train
That was ever on the Southern line,
But when she got to Monroe, Virginia
She was forty-seven minutes behind.

3. Well, they handed him his orders at Monroe, Virginia,
Saying: "Steve, you're away behind time.
This is not Thirty-Eight, but it's old Ninety-Seven.
You must put 'er in Spencer on time."

4. He looked around and said to his black greasy fireman,
"Just shovel in a little more coal,
And when we cross the White Oak Mountain
You can watch ol' Ninety-Seven roll."

5. It's a mighty rough road from Lynchburg to Danville,
And the line's on a three mile grade.
It was on that grade that he lost his air brakes,
And you see what a jump he made.

6. He was going down hill at ninety miles an hour,
When the whistle broke into a scream,
He was found in the wreck with his hand on the throttle,
He was scalded to death by the steam.

7. Now ladies you must all take fair warning,
From this time now on learn:
Never speak harsh words to your true loving husbands,
They may leave you and never return.

Sketch of scene at Colorado Railroad Museum, Golden, Colorado, 1980.

ASLEEP AT THE SWITCH

Today the term refers to anyone who is inattentive or unprepared. During steam railroading's heyday, switches and turnouts onto sidings had to be moved over by hand with a lever. It was the duty of the brakeman to operate the switch at the right time and in the right direction or a train of cars would go down the wrong track, derail, or crash into another train. Any brakeman who was distracted or inattentive was literally said to be "asleep at the switch."

NOTICE TO RAILROAD PASSENGERS

THE SUBJECT OF TRAIN ROBBERIES
WILL NOT BE DISCUSSED.

PLEASE, NO OBSCENE LANGUAGE,
OR BEHAVIOR UNBECOMING TO GENTLEMEN
IN THE PRESENCE OF LADIES.

NO SHOOTING FROM WINDOWS
EXCEPT IN CASE OF INDIAN ATTACK.

NO THROWING OF PASSENGERS OR INDIGENTS
OFF TRAIN WHILE IT IS IN MOTION.

IN THE EVENT OF A TRAIN ROBBERY,
THE RAILROAD IS NOT RESPONSIBLE FOR ACTS OF HEROISM
OR BODILY INJURY DUE TO SUDDEN STOPS.

NO HORSES OR OTHER ANIMALS
ALLOWED IN PASSENGER CARS.
THIS INCLUDES MULESKINNERS AND FUR TRAPPERS.

IF ANY RAILS ARE FOUND
TORN UP, ALL PASSENGERS
WILL BE OBLIGED TO HELP
MAKE REPAIRS.

—*Wayne Hodges*

District Agent, W.W.G., T.& D. Railroad

Humorous Similitude of Old West Broadside created by the Author

A Railroad Ballad
THE LAST RIDE OF CASEY JONES

Probably **the most famous railroad song** was that of Casey Jones' last ride. Casey was an engineer who had a reputation for speed, but was known for being on time. His real name was Jonathan Luther Jones. His nickname came from the town in which he lived: Cayce, Kentucky. In 1900, Casey was working for the Illinois Central Railroad piloting trains between Memphis, Tennessee and Canton, Mississippi. On that fateful day of April 30th, another engineer, scheduled to take over the soon-to-arrive southbound "Cannonball" passenger train, called in sick. Casey, who had just finished his northbound run and was do for a rest, agreed to take the run that night. He hopped onto No. 282, a McQueen 4-6-0 locomotive, and pulled out of the station determined to make up a ninety minute late start (the train had arrived in Memphis late). Pushing her to over 100 miles per hour, he made up most of the time and with only fourteen miles to go, he saw the back end of a waiting freight train on a siding sticking out onto the main line. Casey saw the lights of the caboose and told Simeon Webb, his fireman, to jump. Casey applied the brakes, pulled the reverse lever, and hung on. The train slowed to 35 miles per hour, but collided anyway, hitting wooden cars loaded with hay and shelled corn. The engine left the track and rolled over, crushing Casey. The rest of the train stayed on the track and no one else was hurt. A black engine wiper named Wallace Saunders composed a ballad about his friend Casey Jones and thus, the legend was born. To this day corn still grows every year where the accident took place in Vaughn, Mississippi. One version of the ballad follows.

THE LAST RIDE OF CASEY JONES
Traditional
April 30, 1900

Come, all you rounders, If you want to hear
A story 'bout a brave engineer.
Casey Jones was the rounder's name;
On a six-eight wheeler boys, he won his fame.

Early one mornin', 'bout four o'clock,
Told his fireman, "Get the boiler hot."
He mounted the cabin with his orders in hand,
And he took his farewell trip to that Promised Land.

Put in your water and shovel your coal,
Look out the window, see them drivers roll!
I'll run her 'till she leaves the rail,
'Cause I'm two hours late with that Western mail.

He looked at his watch and his watch was slow;
He looked at the water and water was low.
The switchman knew by the whistle's moan,
That the man at the throttle was Casey Jones.

When he come within a mile of the place,
Old Number Four stared him right in the face.
He turned to the fireman and said: "Boy, you better jump
'Cause there's two trains that's a-goin' to bump.

You ought to have been there to see the sight,
Screamin' an cryin', both colored and white.
And I was a witness for the fact,
They flagged Mr. Casey, but he never looked back.

The Klackity Klack
15 RAILROAD NICKNAMES

Apopular pastime for the riders of early American railroads was to give their favorite, but slow and rickety, dilapidated, nerve-racking, or never-on-time rail line a nickname based on the railroad's initials. Some of those nicknames stuck to the chagrin of the railroad owners.

RAILROAD	NICKNAME
Texas Pacific & Western	Take your Parcels & Walk
Delaware, Lackawanna & Western	Delay, Linger & Wait
Colorado & Southern	Cough & Snort
Toronto, Hamilton & Buffalo	To Hell & Back
Newburgh, Dutchess & Connecticut	Never Did & Couldn't
Baltimore & Ohio	Beefsteak & Onions
Hosac Tunnel & Wilmington	Hoot, Toot & Whistle
Bellaire, Zanesville & Cincinnati	Bent, Zigzagging & Crooked
Houston, East & West Texas	Hell Either Way you Take it
Carolina & Northwestern	Can't and Never Will
Houston & Texas Central	Hoboes & Tin Cans
Georgia, Florida & Alabama	Gophers, Frogs & Alligators
Buffalo, Rochester & Pittsburgh	Bumpy, Rocky & Peculiar
Chicago, Bluffton & Cincinnati	Corned Beef & Cabbage
Waco, Beaumont, Trinity & Sabine	Wobblety, Bobblety, Turnover & Stop

Ever wonder how the term "HELL ON WHEELS" originated? During the building of the transcontinental railroad, little honky-tonk towns teaming with gambling and prostitution would "appear" at the end of the line to take the hard-earned pay of the railroad workers. As track was laid westward, the town buildings, tents, prostitutes, everything, would be moved to the new terminus. The town's "hell" was then "on wheels!"

November 18, 1883
STANDARD TIME

Before November 18, 1883, there was only local time. Each city, town, village, and province had to set their own time. They used "sun time" which was based on the movement of the sun over the meridian. When the sun crossed it, it was noon. Of course "noon" was different in every city in the U. S. and it varied from month to month throughout the year. Thanks to railroads, commerce was advancing across America at breakneck speed. But each railroad set up their own time schedules based on various cities along their route and passengers found they had to continually change their timepieces every time they came into a station. Chaos was the result when two (or more) different railroads came into the same station. Stations had to have separate clocks on the wall for each railroad! In other words, there were several different clock times in the same location. It was Einsteinian time. A passenger's "frame of reference" was the train he was on, or about to get on! It was crazy. Confusion ran rampant. Something had to be done. The federal government had done nothing up to this point, so the railroads took it on themselves to solve the problem and they developed "Standard Time" with four time zones across the U.S. It is also fascinating to note that "Standard Time" was put into effect *without* any federal legislation! And all the competing railroads actually *got together* to agree on a standard. The states and the federal government quickly adopted the plan and the concept spread around the world creating 24 time zones.

Scene Stealers
6 MOVIE RAILROADS

What's a good western without a train puffing across a rugged landscape or pulling into a tiny railroad depot sitting at the edge of a frontier town. *The Great Train Robbery,* shot in 1903 in Paterson, New Jersey, showed that the steam train was by its very nature a dramatic and exciting element to add to any film. In the early days of filmmaking, a few original nineteenth-century steam engines were bought and preserved by the Hollywood motion picture studios for use in their westerns. And the best engines to use in westerns were the wonderfully proportioned 4-4-0's. They were colorfully painted, covered with bright brass and sometimes had a wood cab, and of course they were correct for the time period. On several working railroads, only the oil-burning 1920's engines were available so art directors would "camouflage" them to appear as wood-burning nineteenth-century locos. They added diamond smokestacks, box type headlights, and cord wood to the top of the oil tenders. In the 1970's, when westerns waned, Hollywood studios tore down their western backlots and sold their steam engines to museums and private individuals. Today, the Virginia and Truckee 4-4-0's can be seen at the Nevada State Railroad Museum in Carson City and the California State Railroad Museum in Sacramento.

> *NOTE: When you see three numbers used to define an engine, the first number is the number of leading pilot wheels it has, the second number, the driver wheels, and the last number, the trailing wheels. If you looked at one side of the engine and saw two small wheels at the front and two large wheels in the middle, and none at the rear, that would be a 4-4-0.*

Working railroads that were frequently used by Hollywood when not shooting on their own backlot are listed on the next page along with a few of the westerns that were shot on these railroads.

(Oakdale, California)
(1891 Rogers 4-6-0 No.3, 1888 Cooke 4-4-0 No.8, and 1906 Baldwin 2-8-0 No.18)

The Virginian (1929)
Union Pacific (1939)
Dodge City (1939)
The Return of Frank James (1940)
Duel in the Sun (1946)
Wyoming Mail (1950)
The Great Misouri Raid (1950)
High Noon (1952)
The Cimarron Kid (1952)
Man of the West (1958)
The Great Northfield Minnesota Raid (1972)

The Apple Dumpling Gang (1975)
The Long Riders (1980)
"Petticoat Junction" (1963-1970)
"Casey Jones" (1957-1958)
"Tales of Wells Fargo" (1957-1962)
"Death Valley Days" (1952-1970)
"The Wild Wild West" (1965-1969)
"The Iron Horse" (1966-1968)

(Chama, New Mexico)
(1925 "Mikado" 2-8-2 locomotives, No. 483, 484 and 487)

The Good Guys and Bad Guys (1969)
Shootout (1970)
Showdown (1973)
Bite the Bullet (1974)
The Misouri Breaks (1976)
The White Buffalo (1977)
Butch and Sundance: The Early Years (1979)
The Lone Ranger
Wyatt Earp (1994)

(Durango, Colorado)
(1923 K-28 Class 2-8-2 locomotives, No. 473, 476 and 478)

A Ticket to Tomahawk (1950)
Denver & Rio Grande (1952)
The Maverick Queen (1956)
Night Passage (1957)
Butch Cassidy and the Sundance Kid (1969)
Support Your Local Gunfighter (1971)
"The Tracker" (1987)

(Phoenix, Arizona)
(1917 Baldwin Mikado 2-8-2 No.7 and 1922 Alco 2-8-0 No.5)

How the West Was Won (1963)
Cheyenne Autumn (1964)
Young Billy Young (1969)
The Life and Times of Judge Roy Bean (1972)

(Durango, Mexico)
(Baldwin 2-6-0 No.650)

The Sons of Katie Elder (1965)
The Wild Bunch (1969)
Rio Lobo (1970)
Big Jake (1971)
The Train Robbers (1973)
Cahill, U.S. Marshal (1973)
The Great Scout and Cathouse Thursday (1976)
Cattle Annie and Little Britches (1980)

(Durango, Mexico)
(1907 Baldwin 2-8-0 No.75)

The Professionals (1966)
The Devil's Brigade (1968)
Breakheart Pass (1976)
Heavens Gate (1980)
"Alias Smith and Jones" (1971-1973)
"Centennial" (1978)

5 STUDIO BACKLOT ENGINES
(Los Angeles, California)

1. **Metro-Goldwyn-Mayer Studios** (1872 Baldwin 4-4-0 No.11, sold in 1970.)
2. **RKO-Radio Studios** (1905 Baldwin 4-6-0 No.25 sold 1971.)
3. **Twentieth Century Fox Studios** (1888 Cooke 4-4-0 NO.8, sold in 1972.)
4. **Paramount Studios** (1873 Central Pacific 4-4-0 No.18, 1875 Baldwin 4-4-0 No.22, sold 1974.)
5. **Warner Brothers Studios** (1875 Baldwin 4-4-0 No.5, sold in 1979.)

Cinders And Smoke
46 WORDS OF THE RAILROADER

As in any profession, the railroad industry has its own colorful language to describe the people, things, and activities of the trade. Listed here is a sampling of terms and slang phrases to whet your appetite to the life of the railroader. Many more words can be found in *"The Language of the Railroader"* by Ramon F. Adams.

1. Angel's Seat. Also called the *crow's nest* or *penthouse*. The cupola or observation tower of a caboose. From that vantage point it was possible for the brakeman to spot hot journals, brake beams that had dropped down, and other dangers.

2. Ballast. The slag or gravel used to hold the crossties in place after the rails have been spiked to them.

3. Beanery. A railroad eating establishment.

4. Bedbug. Slang for the *Pullman* porter.

5. Boxcar Tourist. A hobo *riding the rods* (the tensioning bars under a car).

6. Brakeman. The crewman who's job it is to take care of the brakes and couplings, to signal and flag trains, and generally to oversee the cars under the direction of the conductor. In the early days of railroading, he had to climb on top of cars and jump on and off the moving train. He had to run ahead of an engine, throw a switch, and stand there until the train had passed. He had to work in the rain, snow, and sleet. If he was a rear brakeman, he had to go back some distance behind the train and flag a following train, no matter how bad the weather. *And* he was the lowest-paid crewman!

7. Brass Buttons. A passenger train conductor.

8. Brass Hat. A rail official or executive.

9. Bug. The sending instrument of the telegrapher. Many operators carried their own personal "key" adjusted to their touch.

10. Buzzard's Roost. Slang for the yardmaster's office which was up on a tower so he could see the whole yard.

11. Cinder Trail. The hobo's term for the railroad right-of-way. *Cinders* are partly burned pieces of coal capable of further burning without flame. Cinder dust is seen flying from the smoke stack and getting into passenger's eyes.

12. Consist. The conductor's report, sent by telegraph to the next station up the line telling the yardmaster the *makeup of the train:* types of cars, destinations of the freight, etc. so he can plan switching operations.

13. Cowcatcher. The projecting, wrought-iron bars on the front of the engine designed to push cattle off the track. Before

it's invention, cattle would get caught under the engine and cause it to derail.

14. Crummy. Slang name for the *caboose.* There were many other names for the car at the end of the train where the conductor took care of his paperwork, the train crew prepared their meals, the stockman rode when traveling with a shipment of cattle, and the brakeman rode to protect the rear of the train. Some other names: *angel's seat, ape wagon, crow's nest, penthouse,* and *skunk speeder.*

15. Cushions. Slang for a passenger car.

16. Dinky. A switch engine with a tender used around the shops and roundhouse to shuffle cars.

Wooden Passenger Car, Nevada State Railroad Museum, Carson City, NV (dk)

17. Dispatcher. The railroad employee who has the critical job of controlling the movement of the trains. He must keep track of where each train is, where trains are to meet in order to pass, and how much time one or the other has lost.

18. Doubleheader. A train hauled by two engines, usually needed in the mountains and during heavy snows.

19. End-Of-Track. The terminus of the line. It was a celebrated status because it meant growth for the city, until the line was built beyond it to another city.

20. Firebox. The locomotive fire chamber into which is thrown wood or coal to keep up steam.

21. Fireman. The crewman whose job it was to keep up steam by shoveling coal into the firebox and placing the coal evenly to prevent smoke. He sat on the left side of the cab, and it was also his duty to watch that side of the track, ring the bell, keep the cab clean, wash the windows, and keep coal close to the firebox. He had to stoke the fire and maintain the water level in the boiler. His was the job of hopeful apprenticeship to becoming an engineer.

22. Fishplate. Not a plate of fish, but a flat steel plate with bolt holes used to fasten the ends of the rails together.

23. Frog. An X-shaped metal plate that permits flanged wheels riding on one rail to cross an intersecting rail.

24. Gandy Dancer. A right-of-way laborer; so called because many of the tools used by the section gangs were made by the *Gandy Manufacturing Company of Chicago*.

25. Handcar. A platform with four flanged wheels propelled by a two-handled pump. It was used in the early days to carry section crews along the right of way to make repairs. It was light enough to be lifted off the track to avoid a collision with a passing train. Later, gas driven cars called *speeders* were used.

26. Highball. A signal given by the conductor or brakeman by waving a hand or lantern in a high, wide semicircle, meaning "leave town" or "full speed ahead."

27. Hoghead. One of many slang names for the engineer, since he was the pilot of the *hog* or *pig*.

28. Homestead. To jump off a run-away train.

29. Jerkwater. A small town, because stopping for water was the only reason for stopping. In refilling the tender, the fireman would pull down on the tank's spout and "jerk water."

Pullman Car Interior, Texas Transportation Museum, San Antonio, Texas (dk)

30. King Snipe. The foreman of a section gang. The workers under him were called *snipes.*

31. News Butch. The peddler on early-day passenger trains who walked up and down the aisles selling candy, newspapers, fruit, peanuts, racy magazines, coffee, cigars, and soap—the necessities for surviving those long, arduous trips. The *butch* was a business man: he would go through the train selling salted peanuts and then return with cold, bottled drinks. At the end of a run, he would gather up all the used newspapers and resell them to the newly boarded passengers!

32. Old Girl. A steam loco, a term of affection. A locomotive is referred to as "she" not "it."

33. Orders. Train orders telegraphed by the dispatcher and delivered to the conductor, who then certifies them. They instruct him about stops, waits, meets, and any other train movements.

TIDBIT: The beautiful No.22, Virginia & Truckee, 4-4-0—an 1875 Baldwin woodburner—was used in these movies:
The Last Train From Gun Hill (1959)
Carson City (1952)
"The Great Locomotive Chase" (1956)
"The Wild Wild West"TV series (1965-1969)

34. Pullman. A railway passenger car invented and manufactured by *George M. Pullman.* More comfortable for day travel than the ordinary passenger car, it could be converted into bed sections for night travel. Later Pullmans were divided into roomettes, bedrooms, and compartments.

35. Reefer. A refrigerator car.

36. Rolling Stock. The wheeled cars owned by a railroad.

37. Roundhouse. A semi-circular building housing idle locos and those needing repair. On the outside, in front, is a *turntable* to move them in and out on the proper track.

38. Section Gang. A crew of track workers employed to keep a certain section of track in good condition. They also weed the right-of-way, replace rotted ties, re-ballast, and raise sagging track.

39. Semaphore. A mechanical arm with colored lights, used for visually signaling the engineer. The position of the arm during the day gave the signal: horizontal (red) for "stop", and vertical (green) for "clear, permission to proceed."

40. Tank Town. A town so unimportant that trains stopped there only to refill the engine tender with water.

41. Teakettle. Slang for a small locomotive, especially an old leaky one.

42. Tender. A vehicle attached behind the locomotive for carrying fuel (wood, oil, or coal) and water for the engine.

43. Turntable. A rotating platform with a section of track long enough to hold a locomotive. It is used to reverse the direction of the engine or send it down another radiating track.

44. Varnish. Wooden passenger cars, so called because they were lacquered to a shine.

45. Whistle Stop. A small station or town.

46. Wye. A method of turning an engine around if there was no turntable. It was a turnout in the shape of the letter "Y" that by driving onto it, then backing up, got the engine running in the opposite direction on the main line.

An Old Semaphore (dk)

THE BIG FOUR

A TRIVIA QUESTION: In 1861, Theodore Judah, along with four men, incorporated the *Central Pacific Railroad Company* in California for the purpose of crossing the Sierra Nevada mountains and connecting to the Eastern railroads. Who were **The Big Four**?

ANS: Collis P. Huntington (a partner in a hardware store).

Mark Hopkins (the other partner in the hardware store).

Leland Stanford (a wholesale grocer).

Charles Crocker (a dry-goods dealer).

1925 Baldwin 2-8-2 on the Cumbres & Toltec Scenic Railroad, Chama, New Mexico (dk)

Sketch made at Old Tucson Studios, 1990

A Match Game
18 MORE RAILROAD WORDS

Match the RAILROAD SLANG with their meanings.

1.	Cripple	**a.**	a wooden passenger car
2.	Pasteboard	**b.**	a narrow-gauge car
3.	Varnish Wagon	**c.**	the dining car chef
4.	Peanut Roaster	**d.**	a car in bad condition
5.	Chippy	**e.**	the yard office
6.	Lizard Scorcher	**f.**	the cupola of a caboose
7.	Buzzard's Roost	**g.**	a railroad ticket
8.	Pliers	**h.**	a small steam engine
9.	Angel's Seat	**i.**	conductor's ticket punch
10.	Candy Run	**j.**	old hands at railroading
11.	Cinder Trail	**k.**	throw a switch
12.	Broken Rails	**l.**	to jump off a runaway train
13.	Flimsy	**m.**	a fast run of perishable freight
14.	Homestead	**n.**	a local passenger train
15.	Bend the Iron	**o.**	a short, easy haul
16.	Butter-and-Egg Run	**p.**	record of trainman's workday
17.	Meat Run	**q.**	the railroad right-of-way
18.	Bean Sheet	**r.**	a train order

ANS: 1-d, 2-g, 3-a, 4-h, 5-b, 6-c, 7-e, 8-i, 9-f, 10-o, 11-q, 12-j, 13-r, 14-l, 15-k, 16-n, 17-m, 18-p.

A Ballad In 54 Verses (and counting)
RIDIN' WEST
ON THE PACIFIC EXPRESS
BY DON KIRK
September 2000

In 1869, a **Golden Spike** was driven at Promontory Summit (Utah) and families could finally come West without traveling for six months in a prairie schooner. A ride on the rails from Omaha to Sacramento now took less than a week. The second-class passengers rode in "day coaches" for the transcontinental trip. Called "way passengers," they did not usually travel the entire length of the line; instead, they would ride from one station to another, maybe just a few miles down the line.

This poem is a four-line ballad of rhymed couplets commonly used by poets of the nineteenth century. Any number of verses can be added to the ballad; verses about people met on the train and incidents that occurred during the long arduous trip. Try your hand at adding a verse or two to this already unusually long ballad.

1. My story begins in Omaha City,
Where I embarked upon a journey,
Across the Great Ol' Desert Plateau,
And o'er the Sierras to Sacramento.

2. Hissin' and gurglin', and darin' ta roar.
Belchin' hot steam from every pore.
The 4-4-0, she will never retire,
Pullin' and pullin'—that's her desire.

3. Her knowin' this wern't the terminus,
She wern't a-happy a-waitin' for us.
She idled calmly, a-standin' fast instead,
A-waitin' for the word to go ahead.

4. Shun-shun, shun-shun,
Steam a-racin' for a-freedom won.
Click-click, click-click,
Air compressors with a quirky tick.

5. The bell clanged and the whistle did blow,
'Twas "all-aboard" for Sacramento.
So on my back with canteen an' gunnysack,
I boarded the train, 'twas better'n ridin' horseback.

6. Down the aisle I looked for a seat;
Faces stared, eyes glared, they all looked beat.
Beards and 'staches on their faces,
Rugged men from many a-places.

7. They was gunmen with long bandoliers,
And cowpunchers a-travelin' with steers.
They was Injuns in top hats and tails,
And gold seekers all ridin' the rails.

8. They was fur trappers with beaver pelts,
And cowmen with big guns in their belts.
They was miners with tin pans and rock picks,
All a-totin' revolvers with six.

9. Rugged men who lived along the line,
Way riders, they was, all with a carbine.
From Grand Isle, North Platte and Laramie,
To Julesburg, Rawlings, and Cheyenne City.

10. The ol' coach was as dirty as a hobo's bed,
And clouds o' tobaccie smoke lingered o'er head.
And rough women they uttered aloud,
Their rough language could scatter a crowd.

11. I tried to jawbone with a Cherokee,
The leather-faced stranger next to me.
But he pulled his ten-galón o'er his face,
And slumped quietly into his place.

12. The engine's whistle let loose a shriek;
The wooden coaches, they begun to creak.
Smoke bellowed from the old girl's stack;
The coach jerked forward, then jerked back.

Cumbres & Toltic Scenic Railroad, Chama, New Mexico (dk)

13. The big iron beast took a deep breath,
A fever roared in 'lizabeth.
On the rails, she poured some gritty sand,
And the drivers took hold, it was grand.

14. Chug-chug, wench-wench,
The girl struggled for every inch.
Her breathing quickened, her check valve bled,
Her bright lantern a-shinin' ahead.

15. Off we went into the wilderness,
Ridin' West on the Pacific Express.
From Hangtown, Twin Buttes, and Lone Pine,
To Mule Creek, Bone Hill, and Palestine.

16. The door swung open, there stood the news butch,
There to sell candy, fruit, cigars, and such.
There to sell newspapers already sold,
To earlier passengers, truth be told.

17. He was sellin' tin cups and sugar and coffee,
To brew your own on the potbelly.
He was sellin' towels and soap to wash up,
To smell a might less like a wolf pup.

18. He was sellin' the racy "Velvet Vice,"
And the "Police Gazette"—for a price.
He would sell salted peanuts at every stop,
And then return with cold sodie pop.

19. SUDDENLY, the screech of steel, the squeal of wheels,
The shudder of varnish so unreal.
The noise would wake a sleepin' cat,
I braced myself and grabbed my hat.

20. Bang-bang, bang-bang,
Cars a-comin' together with a clang.
Couplers hittin' each other as they closed,
Like a row of falling dominos.

21. Then became all very still and quiet,
Out the window, oh what a riot!
Standin' squarely on the track ahead,
Was a big blusterin' longhorn stead.

22. The crew jumped off and butchered the beast,
A few words said they o'er the deceased:
For the section gang and roundhouse crew,
Tonight won't be no prairie-dog stew.

23. It wern't long a-'fore we was off again,
Ridin' the rails to the town of Buckskin.
"How 'bout a hand o' three-card monte?"
Barked a tall man who sat down beside me.

24. "Care to toss the ol' broad?" he did ask,
"Win a grubstake, it ain't a hard task.
Ya can't go wrong with this game my son,
The odds o' losin' just three to one!"

25. "My pa said ne'er to gamble, you see."
"Why, its not a gamble, son," said he.
"My hands are fast, but your eyes is quicker,
"They'll move fastern' a candle flicker!"

26. "I'll bet my last ten agin your rig,
Play this game and you'll dance a jig.
All's you do is throw down a ten,
And see if you kin muster a win."

27. Well, I peeled my grubstake outta my boot,
And I threw on the table the last of my loot.
I then skinned my eyes to the calico,
But she was fast as San Francisco.

28. I picked a card, but it wern't the queen;
I'd put my head in a guillotine.
My knurly neck in a nasty noose,
I had picked the ol' poor-man's deuce!

29. Suffocatin' smoke, white as sourdough,
Bellowed through the open window.
Then a hot cinder fell in my collar,
And I stood up and threw a big holler.

30. 'Twas talk of Injun trouble up ahead—
On the warpath—the settlers they fled.
A homestead was burned to the ground,
And the telegraph line, it was downed.

31. All our Winchesters they were made ready,
And our pistols were loaded and steady.
We sat alert, our eyes were keen,
But no Sioux—or Crow—were ever seen.

32. Soon 'twas nightfall that came upon us,
And there wern't nothin' else to discuss.
Oil lamps flickered and shadows they danced,
Men snored and wheezed, women talked and pranced.

33. Clickety, clickety, clickety-clack,
Nighttime passin' so slow on this track.
No room for lanky legs, and no shoes undone,
And not a sole a-playin' twenty-one.

34. Clickety, clickety, clickety-clack,
Ridin' the rails on a ribbon of track.
The coach a-swayin' to and fro,
A rock and roll that calmed the soul.

35. When the night was a-finally done,
A ray of sun, a new day had begun.
Prairie grass was a-blowin' in the breeze,
Like waves a-dancin' on the high seas.

No. 40, 1921 Baldwin 2-8-0 on the Georgetown Loop Railroad,
Georgetown, Colorado (dk)

36. A loud voice, I sat up in my seat,
My gizzard was sure 'twas time to eat.
"Milk, fresh cow milk, fresh eggs and warm bread."
'Twas a farmer a-hawkin' his spread.

37. A lonely thought fur a solitary grave;
From a soddy, a little girl's wave.
In the windows was blowin' a breeze;
We all played five-card stud on our knees.

38. A dust devil in the distant dawn?
A band o' Injuns, we did come upon!
They slung their arrows at the Iron Horse,
Hopin' to steer it from its ordained course.

39. The old girl would not throw in the towel,
Black smoke bellowed forth from her bowel.
Twenty cars in tow, ka-choo, ka-choo.
Pullin' up a grade to Kalamazoo.

40. A puffin' smoke with every stroke,
The runnin' gear as strong as oak.
A-steady an' strong, a-singin' a song,
She kept pullin'-pullin', pullin' along.

41. Firebox burning, the drivers turning,
Pistons pounding, the whistle sounding.
Pulling with plenty of horsepower,
Fast and sure at thirty miles an hour.

42. The horizon was movin' this morn,
And "BUFFALO!" was yellin' a greenhorn.
So grabbin' his rifle, he drew a bead,
A-taking pleasure a-startin' a stampede.

43. To jerk water the Express did stop;
'Twas a quick meal at a whistle-stop.
And we ordered some beefsteak and 'tatoes,
But the whistle blows, and off we gos.

44. A loony climbed a-top our car,
And turned the brake wheel much too far.
The train came to a jolting halt.
And did we all a somersault.

45. 'Twas a Hobo with frayed apparel,
He was three pickles shy a barrel.
They threw a straight jacket on the louse,
And carried him off to a madhouse.

46. A mounted gang of desperadoes,
A-wavin' pistols and sombreros,
Boarded the train with apparent distain,
And asked the fireman not to complain.

47. They got the drop on the engineer,
And threw the conductor off the rear.
They brought the train to a standstill,
On board—they hoped—no Buff'lo Bill.

48. They took the cashbox from the express car,
Then took from a young boy, his guitar.
With the trav'lers, this didn't set so well,
They told the outlaws, to go to hell!

49. With enough guts to fill a smokehouse,
These men a-headin' west, they did delouse.
They ganged' up on the outlaws a-raisin' Cain,
Threw them all—short and tall—from the train.

50. Heavy rains had now begun to fall,
And approachin' a trestle much too tall,
The engineer, he feared it wouldn't hold,
And so he made us all unload.

51. He pushed the cars across there empty,
The trestle's long walk, we made in agony,
Step by step across the ties so per'lous,
A-watchin' the river a-ragin' below us.

52. Smoke a-billowin' past my window,
A young man a-strummin' his banjo.
A lone windmill a-turnin' a tune,
And us singin' a song about Dan'l Boone.

53. And the wail of the whistle so grand,
Through the valley and across this land.
4-4-0, runnin' steady and strong,
Trav'lin' on westward a-singin' a song.

54. From Granite, Green River, and Reno,
To Sandy Hill and Sacramento.
Off we go to a brand new address,
A-ridin' west on the Pacific Express.

No. 2248, 1896 Cooke 4-6-0, Grapevine Vintage Railroad, Fort Worth, Texas (dk)

Cabin in the canyonlands of southern Utah—maybe a hangout for Butch Cassidy's Wild Bunch (dk)

Towns, Creeks, and Rivers
WESTERN PLACE NAMES

*"I have fallen in love with American names. The sharp
names that never get flat. The snakeskin titles of
mining towns. The plumed war-bonnet of Medicine
Hat. Tucson and Deadwood and Lost Mule Flat."*
—Stephen Vincent Benet, *American Names,* 1931.

The names of the towns of the American West are fun and so very western. Practical names, to-the-point names—a need addressed simply and elegantly by using the immediate environment as the inspiration for the name. A man stops to pan for gold. He sets up his tent in a canyon where he has just passed a dead horse. He goes to the nearest town to stake a claim. "Where is it, you say?" The canyon—one of thousands—needs a name so the claim can be entered in a log. The prospector replies, "Why, its in Dead Horse Canyon." His claim is registered, and other tents soon pop up in the canyon. They too register a claim in the canyon that now has a name. Soon, a name for the settlement is needed to distinguish it from other encampments in the area so the mail from back East can find its addressee. The mining town of Dead Horse is the result.

The sign reads: The Kirby Cattle Company, (New Mexico). See any cows? (dk)

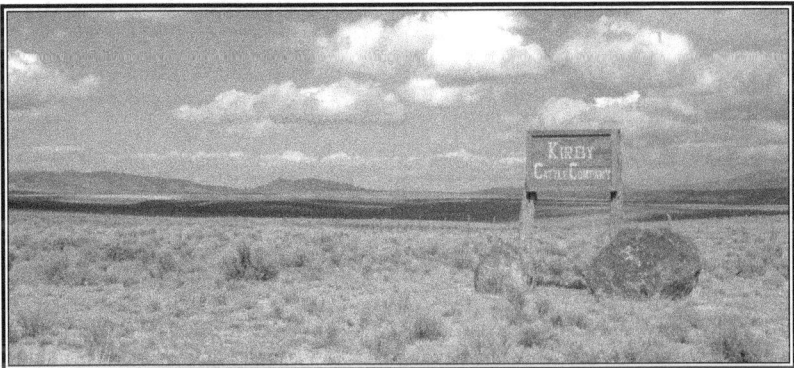

Prairie Dog Towns
12 PLACE NAMES

"This town [Deadwood], I really think it's like
something out of the Bible."
"What part of the Bible?"
"The part right before God gets angry."
—John Hurt, *Wild Bill*, 1995.

The names given to places—towns, creeks, rivers, and mountains—is an interesting subject in itself. Land features were often named by the first Indians and explorers using their first impression of the feature, or because of a sighting or event that took place at the site. Names for towns became official when a U.S. Post Office was established. Practically every state in the Union has a book published about the origins of the state's place names. Many fascinating stories are found behind these names and thus these books make interesting reading.

1. Cherry Creek. Located near Denver, Colorado, the creek flows into the South Platte River. The area vegetation consists of scraggly cottonwood trees and chokecherry shrubs whose delicious fruit gave the creek it's name.

2. Cripple Creek. In Colorado. So named because the large rocks in the river bed would lame cattle trying to cross it.

3. Woman Hollering Creek. Near San Antonio, Texas. At night you could hear what sounded like a woman hollering. It was leopards whining in the night.

4. Bone Hill. A mountain summit in Ellis County, Texas was given its name after a herd of cattle was left there by Don Torbellino, a cattle baron from Mexico. The cattle starved while waiting for the return of the baron, their bones bleached by the sun and scattered about the summit, and so followed the name.

5. Bug Tussle. One of Texas' most famous place names. Road signs are no longer put up because college kids use them to decorate their dorm rooms. The story goes that the site was a popular place for Sunday school picnics—even if ruined by swarms of bugs! Another story says that there was not much to do in this dry panhandle town except watch the "tumblebugs tussle."

6. Mule Creek. A tributary in Wyoming known to have a quicksand bottom in various places. The story goes that one day some cowboys came along to find a man with his head and torso sticking out of the muddy water. "Here, we'll throw you a rope," the cowboys shouted. "Don't bother about me," came the reply, "just save my mule!" "Where is your mule, mister?" shouted the cowboys. "I'm a sittin' on him!" You can believe the story—or not.

7. Buggy Whip Creek. The buggy teams fording a swift creek in Texas required special inducements to get them to cross. It so happened that a strong, flexible switch cane grew along the creek and made an excellent buggy whip.

8. Calamity Creek. Brewster County, Texas. Named after a man and his wife who drowned because they made camp in a dry creek. A distant cloudburst washed them away during the night. A word to the wise: don't ever camp in a dry creek.

9. Maggie's Nipples. Carbon County, Wyoming. Two sharp-pointed hills were named by cowboys for the well-endowed Maggie Baggs. Many hills have similar designations, coined by men who saw two lone hills in that light: Nipple Mountain, Twin Peaks, Tit Butte, Squaw Tits, and even Wyoming's Grand Tetons!

10. Goose Egg Ranch. Natrona County, Wyoming. The ranch was named for the wild goose eggs that were found by a cowhand and brought to the cook. This incident gave the owners the idea for a brand and a ranch name. It turned out that the next owner of the ranch got the "goose egg" when he bought the 20,000 plus cattle just *before* the big cattle "die-out" of 1886. Having sold out "just in the nick of time," the original owners, two brothers from Texas, got the goose that laid the *golden* egg!

11. Dead Man's Well. A community in Burnet County, Texas carries this name. To this day, a gruesome tale is told of its naming: In the 1860's, an elm tree growing over the well opening was used as a hanging tree; the bodies were conveniently disposed of by simply cutting loose the victim. Later cattlemen also used this disposal system for rustlers they captured.

12. Lone Pine. Located in a barren, rocky valley between Death Valley and the Sierras in central California. Named by the 49ers for a single pine tree growing beside a creek—the only tree visible for miles.

Friend or Foe?
21 STATE NAME ORIGINS

*"'Hell' ain't cussing! It's geography, the name of a place,
like you might say Abilene or Salt Lake City."*
—Harry Carey, Jr., *Wagon Master,* 1950.

S o how did the western states of the U.S. get their name? What does the name mean? Many state names trace their origin to native American Indian languages (Is it any wonder since they were here first?). Some of the answers are only speculation, with historians arguing over others. With that disclaimer, here are the western states, including the date when each one joined the union.

18	1812	**Louisiana**	Named in honor of Louis XIV of France.
24	1821	**Missouri**	Named after the Missouri Indian tribe which meant *"town of the large canoes."*
25	1836	**Arkansas**	A French interpretation of the Sioux word meaning *"downstream place."*
28	1845	**Texas**	*Tejas,* Caddo Indian for *"friends"* or *"allies."* It was applied to the Indian tribes who organized together to fight the Apache.
31	1850	**California**	Either Catalan for *"hot oven,"* or it was from a woman named "Calafia" in an old Spanish Romance novel.
32	1858	**Minnesota**	From a Dakota Sioux Indian word meaning *"sky-tinted water."*
33	1859	**Oregon**	Possibly from the Spanish *Oregones* meaning *"big-eared men,"* referring to the Indians that lived in Oregon, or an Indian word for the Columbia River, *Wauregan,* meaning *"beautiful water."* Or, maybe it was derived from a 1715 French map which referred to the Wisconsin River as "Ouaricon-sint."

34	1861	**Kansas**	A Sioux Indian word meaning *"land of the South Wind People."*
36	1864	**Nevada**	Spanish for *"snowed upon."*
37	1867	**Nebraska**	From the Omaha Indian word *Ni-bthaska* referring to the Platte River and meaning *"river in the flatness."*
38	1876	**Colorado**	Spanish meaning *"Red Land"* or *"colored red"* because of the red sandstone seen during the Pike's Peak gold rush.
39	1889	**North Dakota**	Named for the Dakota Indian tribes in the region, from the Sioux name for themselves, *Lakota,* meaning *"to think of as friends (allies)."*
40	1889	**South Dakota**	Same meaning as North Dakota.
41	1889	**Montana**	A Spanish word for *"mountainous."*
42	1889	**Washington**	Named after our first President, George Washington. The only state named for a president.
43	1890	**Idaho**	A Shoshone word meaning *"light on the mountain,"* or possibly it was completely fabricated by mining lobbyist George M. Willing when he presented the new territory to congress.
44	1890	**Wyoming**	An Algonquin Indian word, *macheweaming,* meaning *"big flats,"* or *"large prairie place."*
45	1896	**Utah**	From a Navajo word meaning *"hill dwellers,"* or Europeans gave the name to the Ute Indian tribe living on the *"Upper Land,"* or it evolved from the Apache Indian word *yuttahih* meaning *"one that is higher up."*
46	1907	**Oklahoma**	Choctaw Indian word meaning *"red people"* referring to the Indians who inhabited the area.
47	1912	**New Mexico**	*Nuevo Mexico,* named by Spanish explorers in 1562 for lands north of the Rio Grande.
48	1912	**Arizona**	The Papago Indian word *arizonac* meaning *"place of few springs,"* or possibly the Spanish interpretation of Aztec word *arizonac* meaning *"silver bearing."*

What's In A Name?
OLD WEST TOWN NAMES

"Most of the old settlers told it like it was, rough and rocky. They named their towns Rimrock, Rough Rock, Round Rock and Wide Ruins, Skull Valley, Bitter Springs, Wolf Hole, Tombstone. It's a tough country. The names of Arizona towns tell you all you need to know."
— Charles Kuralt, "Dateline America," 1979.

A **few western towns** have been selected for this entry because they were either historically famous, made famous by the movies, or just because they have a phonetic beauty that speaks "Old West." These old-west-sounding towns still exist, even though their name often no longer reflects how they look. Some common towns found in nearly every western state, such as *Sweetwater, Eldorado* and *Eureka,* were eliminated in all but one entry. Also a trivia question is asked at the beginning of each state's listing with one of the cities as the answer (Answers are at the end of this section).

A ghost town 10 miles from Aspen: Ashcroft, Colorado (dk)

377 TOWNS STILL ON THE MAP

1. ALASKA

The first gold discovered in Alaska was at the site of what city?

Beaver Creek
Coldfoot
Crooked Creek
Deadhorse
Fort Yukon
Hope
Juneau
McClintock
Moose Pass
Placerville
Poorman
Red Devil
Skagway
Sourdough
Stony River
12 Mile House
Willow Creek

2. ARIZONA

In what town was the Territorial Prison built in 1876?

Apache Junction
Bisbee
Bitter Springs
Cottonwood
Dirty Sock
Fort Apache
Fort Defiance
Fort McDowell
Grasshopper
Jackrabbit
Mexican Water
Palo Verde
Red Rock
Skull Valley
Sweetwater
Tombstone
Tortilla Flat
Tucson
Twin Buttes
Two Guns
Yuma

3. CALIFORNIA

Site of the first Wells–Fargo stagecoach robbery in 1861.

Angels Camp
Bakersfield
Big River
Bodie
Bonnie Doon
Boulder Creek
Calico
Chinese Camp
Coyote
Diablo
Diamond Bar
Dinkey Creek
Eagle Rock
Fort Bragg
Furnace Creek
Grizzly Flats
Hallelujah Junction
Hat Creek
Indian Wells
Jamestown
Joshua Tree
Lone Pine
Mad River
Ocotillo
Paradise
Red Rock
Rough And Ready
North Fork
Placerville
     (Hangtown)
Sacramento
San Francisco
San Jose
Sierra Madre
Sleepy Hollow
Squaw Valley
Stovepipe Wells
Sulfur Springs
Sutter Creek
Silverado
Three Rivers
Tres Piños
Truckee
Twin Peaks
Two Rocks
Walnut Grove
West Patch
Whiskeytown
Willow Creek

4. COLORADO

Bob Ford, the man who shot Jesse James, was killed here in 1892.

Bedrock
Black Hawk
Bonanza City
Buffalo Creek
Central City

Cheyenne Wells
Clear Creek
Climax
Creede
Crested Butte
Cripple Creek
Denver
Durango
Fort Collins
Franktown
Frisco
Georgetown
Gold Hill
Hasty
Leadville
Knob Hill
Ophir
Placerville
Rio Blanco
Silver Plume
Silverton
Slick Rock
Telluride
Trinidad
Two Buttes
Wagon Wheel Gap
Squaw Point
Paradox

5. IDAHO
One of the first permanent settlements in Idaho, established as a trading post in 1834.

Blackfoot
Bonanza
Clearwater
Coeur d'-Alene
Cottonwood
Elk City
Fort Hall
Horseshoe Bend

Idaho City
Lewistown
Placerville
Silver City

6. KANSAS
In what town was the last ride of the Dalton Gang?

Abilene
Black Wolf
Buttermilk
Coffeyville
Coldwater
Dodge City
El Dorado
Fort Dodge
Fort Scott
Kansas City
Lancaster
Medicine Lodge
Modoc
Pawnee Rock
Rock Creek
Shady Bend
Shallow Water
Topeka
Trading Post
Wichita
Wheeler
White Cloud
Winchester

7. MONTANA
What town harbored the Plummer Gang of road agents?

Alder Gulch
Arrow Creek
Bannack
Beaver Creek
Big Sandy

Billings
Bozeman
Bridger
Butte
Checkerboard
Elkhorn
Ft. Belknap
Four Buttes
Goldcreek
Helena
Nevada City
Hungry Horse
Lewistown
Silver Star
Three Forks
Trading Post
Virginia City

8. NEBRASKA
Marlon Brando's mother gave Henry Fonda acting lessons at the Community Playhouse of what city?

Big Springs
Broken Bow
Hazard
Lincoln
Lone Pine
Omaha
Red Cloud
Silver Creek
Table Rock

9. NEVADA
In what town did Mark Twain and Bret Harte work as reporters on the "Territorial Enterprise"?

Boulder City
Cactus Springs

Carson City
Cherry Creek
Cold Springs
Elko
Eureka
Goldfield
North Fork
Reno
Stillwater
Tonopah
Virginia City

10. NEW MEXICO
Where did Pat Garrett kill Billy the Kid?

Albuquerque
Apache Creek
Black Rock
Coyote Canyon
Elephant Butte
Five Points
Fort Stanton
Fort Sumner
Hondo
Las Cruces
Lincoln
Mesquite
Mexican Springs

Mosquero
Mule Creek
Road Forks
Santa Cruz
Santa Fe
Silver City
Taos
Three Rivers
Wagon Mound

11. NORTH DAKOTA
Town named for a partner in a famous express Company.

Cooperstown
Dawson
Fargo
Grand Forks
Hillsboro

12. OKLAHOMA
Home of the National Cowboy Hall of Fame and Western Heritage Center.

Broken Arrow
Cimarron City
Comanche

Custer City
Deer Creek
Eldorado
Fort Coffee
Geronimo
Ketchum
Oklahoma City
Paradise Hill
Pawnee
Pumpkin Center
Redrock
Sand Creek
Shady Point
Shawnee
Slick
Stillwater
Stonypoint
Sweetwater
White Eagle

13. OREGON
The Lewis and Clark expedition camped here before the return trip east in 1806.

Alder Creek
Astoria
Beavercreek
Bonanza

This gost town was saved from looters: Bodie State Historic Site, Bodie, California (dk)

Echo
Gold Hill
Harmony
Homestead
Independence
Jacksonville
Jasper
North Bend
Paradise
Pleasant Hill
Quartzville
Rock Creek
Willow Creek
Wolf Creek

14. SOUTH DAKOTA
The town where Wild Bill Hickok played his last game of poker.

Big Springs
Buffalo Gap
Cactus Flat
Cherry Creek
Deadwood
Eagle Butte
Hill City
Junction City
Lone Tree
Porcupine
Pumpkin Center
Red Shirt
Silver City
Virgil
Wounded Knee

15. TEXAS
In what town did Judge Roy Bean dispense justice?

Abilene
Amarillo
Aransas Pass

Big Sandy
Big Spring
Buffalo Gap
Camp Verde
Carrizo Springs
Cherokee
Cisco
Crystal City
Cut And Shoot
Deadwood
Dripping Springs
El Paso
Fort Davis
Fort McKavett
Fort Stockton
Goodnight
Grit
Hidalgo
Independence
Indian Gap
Joshua
Junction
Lajitas
Langtry
Laredo
Mesquite
Muldoon
Muleshoe
Needmore
Oatmeal
Pecos
Piedras Negras
Point Blank
Presidio
Rio Hondo
Round Rock
Shallowwater
Sierra Blanca
Smiley
Study Butte
Sundown
Telegraph

Terlingua
Three Rivers
Twin Sisters
Van Horn
Uvalde
Waco

16. UTAH
The ceremonial location where the Union Pacific and Central Pacific met.

Bear River City
Black Rock
Bonanza
Cisco
Granite
Green River
Jericho
Junction
Mexican Hat
Paradise
Promontory
Salt Lake City
Sandy
Spanish Fork

17. WASHINGTON
Town named for an Indian chieftain who was paid $16,000 for the use of his name.

Four Corners
Lakota
Lost Creek
Mill Creek
Rimrock
Seattle
Seven Mile
Snake River
Spokane
Spring Valley

Union Gap
Walla Walla
Wiley City

18. WYOMING
Harry Longabaugh chose his nickname while spending 18 months in this town's jail.

Arapahoe
Badwater

Bittercreek
Centennial
Cheyenne
Crazy Woman Creek
Fort Bridger
Fort Laramie
Fort Steele
Four Corners
Horse Creek
Iron Mountain
Lost Springs
Medicine Bow

Muddy Gap
Paradise Valley
Pine Bluffs
Point Of Rock
Powder River
Reliance
Sand Draw
Shawnee
South Pass City
Spotted Horse
Sundance
Ten Sleep

ANSWERS TO TOWN NAMES QUIZ:
1. Alaska: *Juneau,* **2.** Arizona: *Yuma,* **3.** California: *Placerville,* **4.** Colorado: *Creede,* **5.** Idaho: *Fort Hall,* **6.** Kansas: *Coffeyville,* **7.** Montana: *Bannack,* **8.** Nebraska: *Omaha,* **9.** Nevada: *Virginia City,* **10.** New Mexico: *Fort Sumner,* **11.** North Dakota: *Fargo,* **12.** Oklahoma: *Oklahoma City,* **13.** Oregon: *Astoria,* **14.** South Dakota: *Deadwood,* **15.** Texas: *Langtry,* **16.** Utah: *Promontory,* **17.** Washington: *Seattle,* **18.** Wyoming: *Sundance.*

The privately-owned ghost town of Shakespeare in New Mexico (dk)

19 More Name That City?

More **Trivia questions:** name the city in which the event occurred. The answer will be one of the towns listed under the appropriate state in the previous section. Answers on next page.

1. The town in NEVADA named after a legendary frontiersman, scout and soldier.
2. The town in NEW MEXICO where Billy the Kid revenged the death of his boss John Henry Tunstall.
3. A town in KANSAS made famous on television because it had the Long Branch Saloon.
4. In NEVADA, what town was know as the "Pittsburgh of the West?"
5. In OREGON, name the historical town that was preserved because the railroad passed it by?
6. The town in TEXAS where the Golden spike was pounded home, linking the East and West on the *second* transcontinental railroad.
7. The town in WYOMING named for French trapper Jacques LaRamie.
8. Name the last resting place in TEXAS of the infamous outlaw Sam Bass who was killed by Texas Rangers in 1878.
9. In what town in ARIZONA did the gunfight at the OK Corral occur?
10. The WYOMING home of the Buffalo Bill Historical Center.
11. Where in NEW MEXICO is Billy the Kid's grave?
12. The town in WYOMING named after a famous mountain man.
13. What town in NEVADA once had a United States mint?
14. Where in WYOMING was Tom Horn legally hanged for allegedly killing a fourteen-year-old boy?
15. In 1885, Owen Wister spent his first night sleeping on the counter of this town's general store; the town was in WYOMING.
16. Which town in ALASKA was the final resting place of confidence man "Soapy" Smith in 1898?
17. What town in WASHINGTON was named after an Indian tribe that inhabited a valley with "a small rapid stream?"
18. The town in SOUTH DAKOTA where the U.S. Cavalry shot down 350 Sioux with Hotchkiss machine guns in 1890.
19. In what town in KANSAS did Carrie Nation hold a temperance meeting in front of a saloon in 1899 that made history?

NAME THAT CITY ANSWERS:

1. Carson City (Kit Carson), 2. Lincoln, 3. Dodge City, 4. Eureka,
5. Jacksonville, 6. Sierra Blanca, 7. Laramie, 8. Round Rock, 9. Tombstone,
10. Cody, 11. Fort Sumner, 12. Fort Bridger (Jim Bridger),
13. Carson City, 14. Cheyenne, 15. Medicine Bow, 16. Skagway,
17. Walla Walla, 18. Wounded Knee, 19. Medicine Lodge.

17 TOWN NAMES FROM WESTERNS

1. Apache Wells (*Stagecoach*, 1939)
2. Black Rock (*Bad Day at Black Rock*, 1955)
3. Bottleneck (*Destry Rides Again*, 1939)
4. Crooked Tongue (*Comanche Territory*, 1950)
5. Dry Fork (*Stagecoach*, 1939)
6. Sand Hill (*The Good, the Bad and the Ugly*, 1966)
7. Yerkes Hole (*Dirty Dingus Magee*, 1970)
8. Medicine Bow (*The Virginian*, 1946)
9. Rock Springs (*Escape from Fort Bravo*, 1953)
10. Prairie Dog Creek (*The Tall Men*, 1955)
11. Clearwater (*The Sons of Katie Elder*, 1965)
12. Poker Flat (*The Outcasts of Poker Flat*, 1919)
13. Silver Spur (*The Desperado*, 1943)
14. Quake City (*The Apple Dumpling Gang*, 1975)
15. Dead Dog (*The Ballad of Cable Hogue*, 1970)
16. Black Creek (*A Big Hand for the Little Lady*, 1966)
17. Hard Times (*Welcome to Hard Times*, 1967)

Book Quote from Welcome to Hard Times: "I come West to farm, but soon I learn, I see farmers starve, only people who sell farmers their land, their fence, their seed, their tools—only these people are rich. And is that way with everything, not miners have gold, but salesmen of burros and picks and pans; not cowboys have money, but saloons who sell to them their drinks, and gamblers who play with them Faro; not those who look for money, but those who supply those who look." —Zar.

93 FICTIONAL TOWN NAMES

Here's a few western-sounding and humorous town names created by the author for use in comedy westerns. (Any similarity to actual towns or names already used in westerns is purely coincidental.) If you don't crack a smile reading some of these, something is seriously wrong with you.

Dead Mule	Royal Flush	Peckerwood
Corn Cob	Prairie Dog	Broken Bottle
Lizard Tongue	Grizzly Flats	Mud Dobber
Blistered Foot	Dry Rot	Outhouse Hill
Twisted Ankle	Sixgun	Horn Toad
Wagon Rut	Snake Hole	Scattergun
Bonebox	Crooked Tree	Bent Fork
Tin Plate	Spunk	Rusty Iron
Bug Scuffle	Five Card	Scorpion Sting
Dog Bite	Busted Spur	Worthless Claim
Buzzard Bait	Toady Frog	Aunt Hill
Coffinville	Tweety And Sylvester	Beaver Tracks
Point Blank	Bustagut	Down And Out
Cash And Luck	Gravestone	Two Cents
Thistlebloom	Two-Legged Dog	Heavens To Betsy
Old Woman Springs	Mealy Bug	Skunk Hollow
Snowflake	Vulture's Diner	Jelly Biscuit
Dry Spell	Knot Hole	Dirt Clod
Tumblin' Weed	Wagon Tongue	Bitterroot
Flapjacks	Bad Day	Last Dollar
Grubworm	Hard Knocks	Banjo
Highweeds	Sourdough	Cabin Fever
Jackrabbit Flats	Sick Mule	Stubby Toes
Knothole	Ten Mile Walk	Wormy Apple
Saddle Sore	Prickly Pear	Snake Stump
Mud Puddle	Thorny Flats	Falling Rock
Contrary	Yeller Dog	Buck Knife
Pesky Fly	Last Drink	Whiskey Flats
Pine Box	Two Pair	Blowing Dust
Sarsaparilla	Pork And Beans	ShangriLa
Poker Flats	Pig Wallow	No Water

Always cold, wet, or muddy: St. Elmo, Colorado (dk)

The "ghost town" of St. Elmo, Colorado, originally named Forrest City in 1878, now has only eight year-round residents, but at its peak had over 2,000. All the buildings in this snow-covered, high-altitude town of 10,054 feet are well preserved, but not restored, just aging gracefully.

A Match Game
7 TOWN NAMES FROM MOVIES

Can you name the movies these towns were in?

1. Shinbone	a. *Support Your Local Gunfighter* (1971)
2. Purgatory	b. *The Quick And The Dead* (1995)
3. Hadleyville	c. *Paint Your Wagon* (1969)
4. Redemption	d. *High Noon* (1952)
5. Noname City	e. *The Man Who Shot Liberty Valance* (1962)
6. Lago	f. *Unforgiven* (1992)
7. Big Whiskey	g. *High Plains Drifter* (1973)

ANS: 1-e, 2-a, 3-d, 4-b, 5-c, 6-g, 7-f.

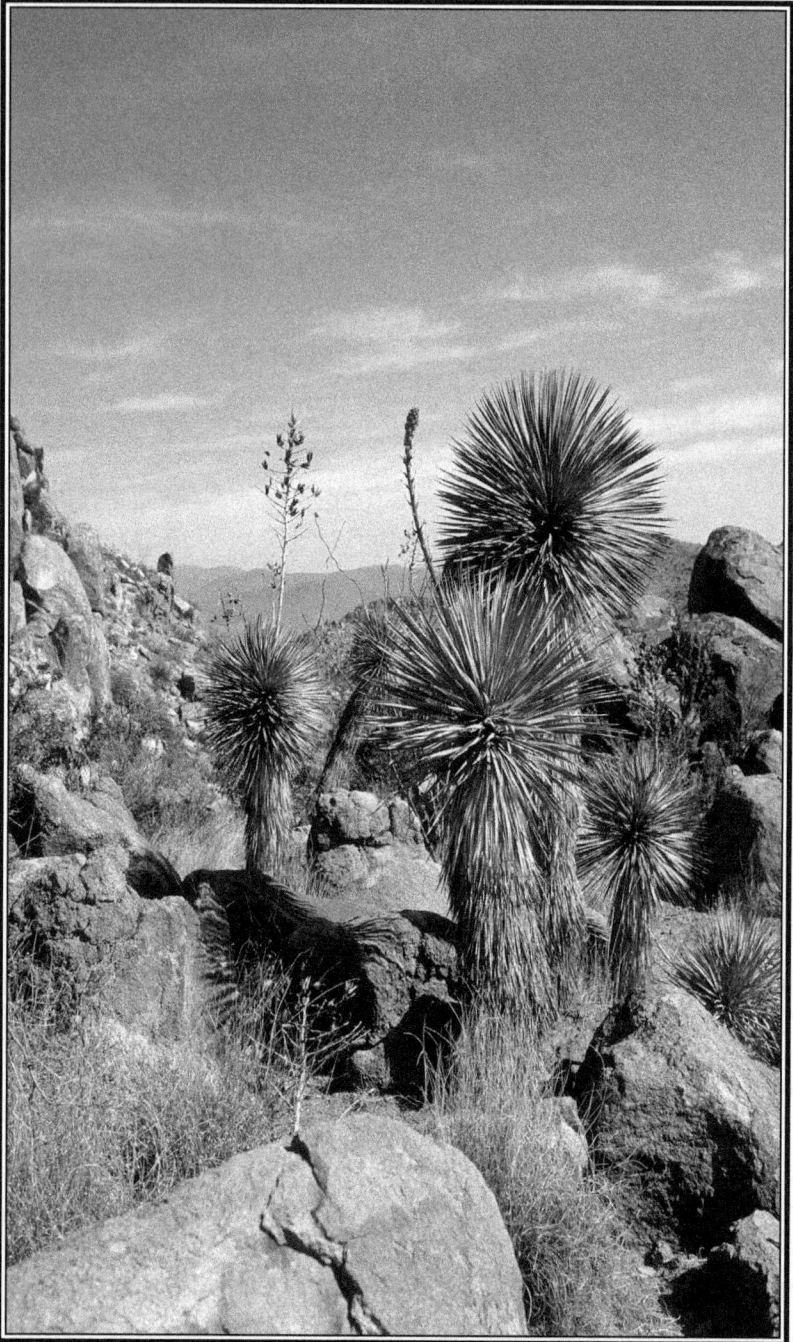

Yucca and red limestone rocks at Big Bend National Park. (dk).

Lizards, Cacti, and Mesquite
THE WESTERN LANDSCAPES

"What do we want with this vast, worthless area? This region of savages and wild beasts, of deserts, shifting sands and whirlwinds of dust, of cactus and prairie dogs?"
—Daniel Webster, 1838

The vast western landscape, with its huge skies draped to the horizon, became an integral part of the legend of the Old West. Rugged rock formations, dry creeks, small canyons and arroyos, blowing sand, and tumbling tumbleweeds, all provided a gritty texture and panoramic backdrop to western films. So it's no surprise that the animals and plants of the region also became symbols of the wild American West. Yucca plants, saguaro cacti, mesquite trees, tarantulas, scorpions, and Gila monsters populated the American West and the Western. To be a Westerner, or fan of the west, one should know something about the living things one might encounter in his travels to the West or while reading a good western novel. First, one needs to know that there are four major deserts of the Southwest, each with a very different and fascinating landscape. All have been used as settings for westerns.

COME TO VAN HORN, TEXAS, THE CLIMATE IS SO HEALTHY WE HAD TO SHOOT A MAN TO START A GRAVEYARD.

1910 Advertisement In Eastern Newspaper

Dancing with the Devils!
4 DESERTS OF THE WEST

"This country is—and must remain—uninhabited forever."
—Captain R. B. Marcy speaking of the
Texas panhandle in 1849.

The great deserts of the United States, located between the Sierra Nevadas to the west and the Rocky Mountains to the east, are hot, dry, fragile—and beautiful.

1. The Great Basin. This desert includes most of Nevada and overlaps into the surrounding states of Oregon, Idaho and Utah. The *Great Salt Lake* is on the eastern edge of this desert. It's considered a cold desert because of its northern location (elevation 4,000 feet and higher) and the fact that its only moisture comes from melting snow. You won't find many forms of cacti, agaves, and yuccas—just low shrubs like sagebrush, saltbush and grasses. The *Painted Deserts* of southern Utah and Northern Arizona are part of the Great Basin. Many westerns have been shot around *Moab, Utah* and in *Monument Valley*. Director John Ford, made *Monument Valley* known around the world.

The colorful red limestone spires of Monument Valley, Arizona (dk)

The hot and austere Death Valley National Park, California (dk)

2. The Mojave Desert. This desert extends over southern Nevada and parts of southern California, covering 54,000 square miles, with elevations running under 3,000 feet and including *Death Valley* whose lowest point is 282 feet *below* sea level. This desert is cold in winter, very very hot in summer, and always dry and barren—and there are few cacti. What plant life there is, grows low to the ground. Summer temperatures regularly approach 120°F. Average rainfall is less than 6 inches a year; Las Vegas gets only 4 inches, *Death Valley*, less that 2. The *Joshua Tree* is found on the southern edge of this desert and grows nowhere else in the world. The *Joshua Tree National Monument*, found just over the hills from Los Angeles, was used as a setting in many old western movies and TV series' like *Hondo*.

Used frequently in early westerns: Joshua Tree National Monument, California (dk)

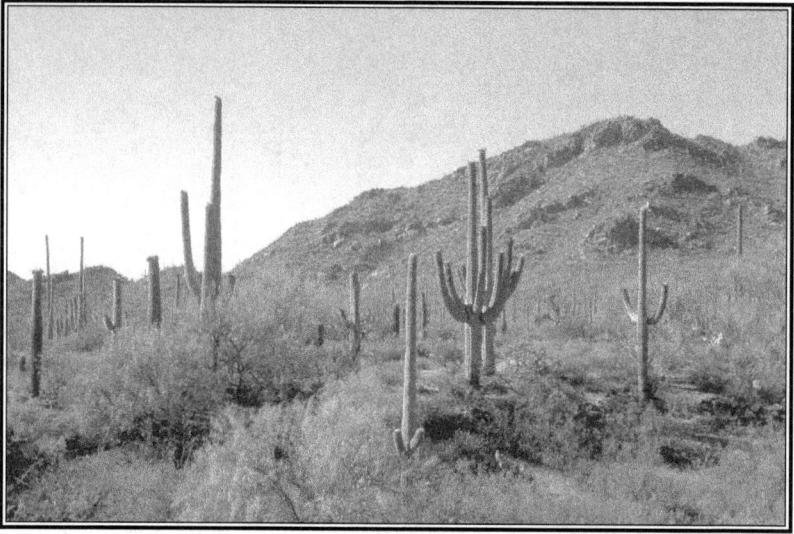

A visual feast of desert cacti: the Sonoran Desert, Tucson, Arizona (dk)

3. The Sonoran Desert. This 106,000 square mile desert stretches over the southern half of Arizona, a piece of California, and covers much of Baja California and into western Mexico. It has a great diversity of plant species making it the most visually interesting desert region, and thus has drawn many western-film productions. It is divided into two sub-desert categories:

The Colorado Desert. The western part of the Sonoran Desert has low elevation, high temperatures and very low rainfall which occurs only in winter. This desert covers the Southern tip of California and reaches east to Phoenix, Arizona. The historic town of Yuma is included in this area. It has sparse vegetation and few cacti. The *Beavertail Cactus, Ocotillo* and *Teddybear Cholla* are found here.

The Arizona Desert. The eastern part of the Sonoran Desert, it reaches from east of Phoenix down to Tucson and into Mexico. High temperatures in both summer and winter create a spectacular desert that has been seen in numerous movies shot around Tucson. It has a large variety of cacti including the tall yuccas and the majestic saguaros, the trademark of the Sonoran Desert. The *Oregon Pipe Cactus National Monument* is in this desert.

4. The Chihuahuan Desert. Mostly in Mexico, this desert extends up into the southern third of New Mexico and the western tip of Texas and along the *Rio Grande River* from El Paso to Del Rio. It has a moderately high elevation with 7 to 12 inches of rain in the summer. It is the largest desert in North America, occupying 175,000 square miles and averaging 3,000 to 5,000 feet in elevation. Nights often get down below freezing for at least 100 days a year. *Creosote Bush, Soaptree Yucca,* and *Tree Cholla* are the most common vegetation. A few westerns have been shot in the *Big Bend* area of Texas like the epic *Giant,* and *Two Rode Together, Bad Girls, There will be Blood,* "Rio Diablo" starring Kenny Rodgers, and The Coen brothers' *No Country for Old Men.* To outsiders, it is this area that most represents the impression of what Texas must be like. In reality, Texas is mostly the southern edge of the great plains with some hill country covered in scrub oak thrown in and some dark-green piney woods found in the eastern most part of Texas. Between San Antonio and the eastern edge of the Chihuahaun is a transition area of *mesquite* trees where *Alamo Village* in Brackettville, Texas has lensed many westerns, the most famous being John Wayne's *The Alamo* shot in 1960.

An unexpected place at the foot of the plains: Big Bend National Park, Texas (dk)

Gullywashers and Dryspells
WESTERN WEATHER LORE

"Sometimes we have the seasons in their regular order, and then again we have winter all the summer, and summer all winter. It's mighty regular about not raining, though.
—Mark Twain on Virginia City, Nevada, 1865

All over the West you hear this response to outsiders, "If you don't like the weather, just wait a minute." Weather that suddenly changes dramatically isn't unusual in the American West, what with mountains, plains, and deserts all woven together. It's no wonder that blizzards, drought, heat, dust storms, tornadoes, and "frog stranglers" have spawned a host of tall tales. A *hyperbole* is exaggeration for effect, and for the westerner it was easy to spin an imaginative yarn, to "tell a windy." Here are a few classic examples from the West.

THE WIND (The Blue Whistlers)

1. **"The wind is so strong in Nebraska**, a crow bar has to be used as a wind gauge; if it only bends and doesn't break, it's still safe to go outside."

2. **"In North Dakota** a flock of snow geese have, on more than one occasion, been seen suspended in the sky from daylight to dusk, unable to gain an inch against the headwind."

3. **There ain't nothin'** betwixt that wind and the North Pole, but a two-stran' bobwar fence—and it's down!"

4. **In Montana**, the barbs on the bob-war fences all point East."

5. **Windy** as a room full of politicians after a dinner of cabbage and beans.

5. **It was so windy in Texas** one day in October, that a hen setting against the wind laid the same egg five times."

6. **It's as windy outside** as Uncle John's tall tales."

THE COLD (The Cow Skinners)

1. **"In Wyoming**, lakes have frozen so fast that frogs are left to spend the winter with their heads stuck out of the ice."

2. **"The Canadian winds** can be so strong and swift that birds are turned to ice in mid-flight, then fall to the ground and shatter on impact."

3. **A cowboy passed a farmer on the road** who was skinning one of his two mules. "What happened?" asked the drifter. "He died of heat stroke," was the farmer's reply. The drifter gave his condolences and continued on his way to a nearby town to pick up some supplies. On his way back, he passed the same farmer again, but this time he was skinning the other mule. "Why, what happened to your other mule, farmer?" The farmer replied disconcertingly, "It froze to death."

Mountain Landscape, 1895, oil painting by Albert Bierstadt. DECA

Sunrise, Yosemite Valley, c1870, oil painting by Albert Bierstadt. DECA

4. **"It was so cold** the cows gave icicles and the polar bears went huntin' for cover."

5. "Today's colder'n a well digger's behind."
    "Even colder'n a well chain in December."
    "But god, it's colder'n a witch's teat in a brass bra."
    "Naw, it's colder'n a mother-in-law's kiss, and that's cold."

6. **"It was so cold** that winter, that I once found my thirsty draft horse with his lips stuck to the well pump."

7. **"On one fine Indian summer day**, I seen a whole flock o' geese land on a pond to get a drink o' water. A hard freeze a-come on quickly while they was a-takin' their nourishment. When they flew off, they took the pond with 'em! Pulled up into the air, the whole dang pond—the lake had frozen to their feet!"

8. **"It's so cold** it would freeze the balls off a brass monkey." Folk-lore has it that a triangular brass plate with indentations was used on early sailing ships to hold the iron balls used in the cannon. When the weather got extremely cold, the contraction of the plate would cause them to roll off the monkey and about the ship.

THE HEAT (The Scorchers)

1. It's so damn hot that if a man was to die and go to hell, you can bet he'd be writin' home for a couple of blankets.

2. Compared to southern Arizona in the summertime, hell is like an icebox.

3. It's so darn hot that it takes me two hours to blow a cup of coffee cool.

4. It's hot as the hinges of hell, and that's hot.

5. It's hot 'nough to burn a horny toad to a crisp.

6. It's hot as a two-dollar pistol (a cheap pistol that overheats when fired).

7. It was so hot this summer, we had to feed the chickens crushed ice to keep 'em from a-layin' hard-boiled eggs.

8. It's so hot in these here parts that when chicks hatch they come out of their shells already cooked.

9. Why it's so blasted hot, the shade of a bobwar fence don't help none neither.

10. It's so hot in Arizona, the birds have to use potholders to pull worms out of the ground.

11. It's hotter than a goat's behind in a pepper patch.

THE SNOW (The Blizzards)

1. **"A westbound freight train** had apparently disappeared in a blizzard somewhere west of Denver when the eastbound freight arrived in Denver claiming to have never passed it. It turns out the westbound train had completely left the ice-encrusted rails near Granby, Colorado and skidded most of a mile down a frozen road that led into the main street of a town. A mile of track had to be built to get the train back on the main line."

THE DRYNESS (Parched)

1. It's so dry in Terlingua, Texas that the residents have to put stamps on their letters with paper clips!

2. It's so dry here in Bisbee, Arizona that the bushes follow the dogs around. I swear it on my mother's grave.

3. There ain't a-been enough rain to wet the whistle of a screech owl.

4. It's dryer'n a grasshopper on a hot griddle.

5. Why, it's so dry, you've got to prime yo'self to spit!

6. Dryer'n the dust in a mummy's pocket.

7. It's been so dry that riled skunks expel only odorless dusting powder!

8. "A scorpion is just a lobster that has lived in Arizona a long time." —Dick Wick Hall, *The Salome Sun*.

9. It's so dry, the trees are whistling for the dogs.

10. Another month without rain and we'll have a herd of jerky on the roof.

11. "I wish it would rain," prayed one Arizonian, "not so much for me, cuz I've seen it, but for my 7-year-old son."

12. It's so dry, the birds is a-buildin' their nests outta bobwar.

13. It's so dry, the tumbleweeds are a-huntin' for dogs.

14. It's so dry, the cows is a-givin' powdered milk!

15. Dry as a powder house.

16. "Everything dries; wagons dry, men dry, chickens dry. There is no juice left in anything, living or dead, by the close of summer. Officers and soldiers are supposed to walk about creaking; mules, it is said, can only bray at midnight; and I have heard it hinted that the carcasses of cattle rattle inside their hides."
   —J. Ross Browne, 1869.

The Grand Canyon, 1913, oil painting by Thomas Moran. DECA

THE RAIN (Fence Lifters)

1. It has rained so much this week that I had to dive down to grease the windmill.

2. It's wet enough to bog a snipe.

3. It's been rainin' so much this week, the ducks have been seen carryin' umbrellas.

4. The range has got boggy 'nough to bog a buzzard's shadow.

5. "Do you remember the year Vinegaroon had an annual rainfall of twelve inches?" "Sure, pard, I was there that day."

6. Whether you call it a *frog strangler, gully washer,* or *fence lifter,* you're looking plumb wet clean to the bone.

THE TORNADOES (Twisters)

Tornadoes in Kansas have been known to suck fish out of ponds, drive wheat straws through glass windows, pluck chickens clean without taking the chickens, and remove carpets from living rooms without ever moving the furniture.

A nursery full of babies was sucked out of a nursery, only to be found miles away still bedded down in their cribs.

In a major hurricane in Tupelo, Mississippi that killed 235 people, residents said a room that was a kitchen, was blown, intact, to the town of Mooresville seven miles away, and that the tornado sucked the feathers off Tupelo chickens.

Yosemite National Park, California (dk)

THE SAND (The Dry Storms)

Two cowboys rode out of El Paso after a sandstorm and stopped to pick up a hat sitting on a sand dune. Lifting the hat, they found a man's head under it. One of the cowboys brushed the sand from the poor devil's face, wherein he opened his eyes and spoke: "Get a shovel, I'm horseback."

A Thorny Proposition
8 CACTI OF THE AMERICAN WEST

*"We seemed to have reached the acme of
barrenness and desolation."*
—Horace Greeley, 1859

Because of their strange shapes, sharp spines, and showy flowers, cacti are beautiful and frightening at the same time. It is the hostile land they have had to inhabit for thousands of years that has made them this way. This section describes some of the most common cactus seen in American westerns.

1. The Saguaro. (*carnegiea gigantea, genus cereus*). Pronounced *sah-wah'-ro*, it's the largest of cacti. Up to 40 feet tall, they look like skinny round-headed people with upward held arms. Fluted like Greek columns, the thick, spiny stems (8" to 24" in diameter) sit erect with twisted branches and small white flowers. Found in southern Arizona and the southeast edge of California, they grow very slowly, living as long as 200 years. If you see one that still doesn't have any arms it is still less than 50 years old. The pulp of the fruit is a favorite of the Papago

All cactus photos by the author

Indians for making jelly and wine. The seeds can be ground into butter and the woody ribs can be used to build shelters.

2. The Cholla. (*genus opuntia*). Pronounced *"cola,"* it's a small, spiny, leafless tree or bush with jointed branches (*spines*) that are cylindrical in shape and have thousands of projecting needles (*sheath*) that give a fuzzy appearance when backlighted by the sun (in fact, one variety is called the *Teddy Bear;* its golden or silvery glow makes it look cuddly, but its hooked barbs will easily embed themselves if you touch it, requiring pliers to remove.

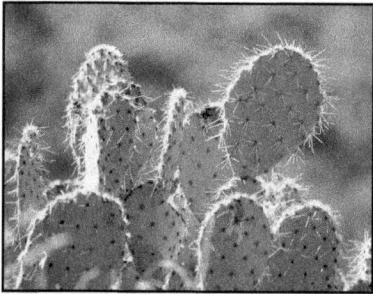

3. Prickly Pear. (*genus opuntia*). A low mound of flat, bluish-green branches (commonly called *pads,* they look like beaver's tails) grow out from each other and have on their surface, clusters of needles called *spines* or fine barbed hairs called *glochids* that are hard to remove from your skin. Colorful flowers and edible fruits grow from the pads in springtime. The pads can be cooked and eaten as a vegetable. They are a nuisance to livestock who get the spiny pads stuck to their noses while trying to graze. If the pads are burned to remove the thorns they can be fed to livestock during dry spells.

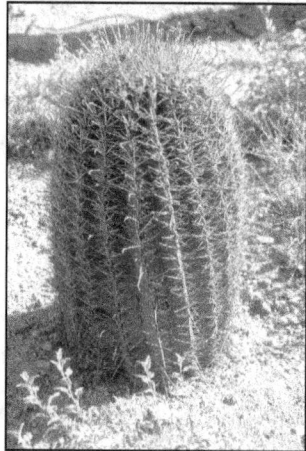

4. The Barrel. (*genus ferocactus* and *echinicactus*). One large stem, 1 to 1-1/2 feet in diameter, shaped like a barrel with prominent vertical ribs and stout hooked spines, they stand 3 to 10 feet in height. On some varieties the spines curve back like a fishhook and indeed were used by Indians for fishing. Flowers are found at the top of the plant in August or September, an unusual time for other cacti. They're found in Southern California and south-central Arizona.

5. Ocotillo. (*fouquiera splendens*). Pronounced "*ock-uh-tee-oh*" it's a funnel-shaped plant with many woody, unbranched, straight stems which have no leaves most of the year. In the spring, there's a tight cluster of red flowers at the tip of each branch. Leaves appear only after a rain and wither away as soon as the soil dries. Early settlers (and even some present residents) made fences and corrals out of this plant. The *ocotillo* is planted in a row where a fence is needed, and grows to form a strong fence-like structure. It is found from west Texas to southern California.

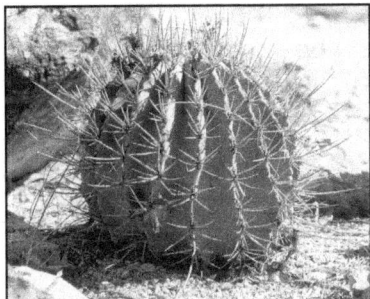

6. The Pincushion. (*genus coryphantha & escobaria*).Round like a ball with protuberances (*tubercles*) covering the core (*areole*) and ending in a cluster of translucent white spines giving many of the varieties a soft "snowball" look. Blooms are large and usually yellow.

7. The Hedgehog. (*genus echinocereus*). This genus includes a variety of differing species, but many have long spines, short stems and are always ribbed.

8. Oregon Pipe Cactus. (*stenocereus thurberi*). This large cactus is similar to the *Saguaro*, except that it has no central stem, but instead many branches curving upward from a central point. The branches are fluted and have constricted rings like joints in a finger. They can grow up to 20 feet high. If you see this cactus in a western, you can bet it wasn't shot in the United States; it's common in western Mexico. The only place in the U.S. is along the Arizona-Mexico border in the *Oregon Pipe Cactus National Monument*.

Saddle Burrs & Thistle Thorns
9 TREES & BRUSHES of the WEST

"You have two stars in western films:
the man and the location."
—Budd Boetticher.

An arid western landscape with a carpet of sand and the heavens as a roof is never completely devoid of plant life. Green, and not-so-green, things dot the floor giving this grand room color, texture, and life-saving shade to small creatures. Even a cowboy and his horse might find a sliver of cooling shade under a lone Joshua Tree. A few of the trees and brushy plants made legendary by the western are listed below.

Photos by the author

1. The Yucca. (*Yucca*). Found in the Sonoran and Chihuahaun desert, it's a palm-like thicket-forming shrub or small tree with a short trunk and crooked branches. It has 1 to 2-1/2 foot-long yellow-green grass-like leaves which are stiff and sword-shaped, all radiating out from a central point at the top of each trunk. The Indians made good use of the Yucca: the flowers and "bananas" were eaten, the seeds ground into flour, the leaves shredded for fibers to make baskets, mats, sandals, and needles, and the roots could be made into soap. Some Yuccas grow large enough to be called "trees" and include the *Aloe, Soaptree and Joshua.*

2. Joshua-tree. (*Tycca brevifolia*). Found in the Mojave Desert, it's a small grotesque looking evergreen (the largest of the Yuccas at 15 to 30 feet) with narrow dagger-like leaves clustered at the ends of many widely-forking, very stout branches. It was named by Mormon pioneers who thought its shape resembled a person praying with uplifted arms.

3. The Mesquite Tree. Two varieties, the *Honey* (*Prosopis glandulosa*) and *Screwbean* (*Prosopis Pubescens*) are found in Texas and the southwest on range grasslands, sandy plains, and in desert transition areas. Requiring very little water and looking like it needs much more. It's a small spiny, deciduous tree with thorns and tiny yellow-green leaves on paired leaf stalks. The *Honey* has a narrow bean-like pod and the *Screwbean* pod looks like the rattler of a snake. Its fruit is full of grape sugar that cattle will feed on if they can't get anything else. From the Spanish word *mezquite* meaning "cattleman treat them like weeds and eradicate them."

4. Big Sagebrush. (*Artemisia tridentata*). The most common Great Basin Desert shrub, it has many branches of grayish-green, strongly aromatic leaves, usually growing to six feet. A variety of animals will eat the brush, and it will make a hot fire quickly.

5. Creosote Bush. (*Larrea mexicana*). A bush found in the alkaline soils of the Southwest which excretes a resinous liquid that was once used to relieve rheumatism. Animals know better and won't eat the bush.

6. Desert Sage. (*Salvia dorrii*). This is the plant Zane Grey wrote about in his western novel *Riders of the Purple Sage* and Charles Russell put them in many of his paintings. It is a broad bush, 8" to 32" high, with many rigid, spine-tipped branches with silvery

leaves and blue-violet flowers. They are found east of the Cascade Mountains and the Sierra Nevadas, from Washington to southern California including Idaho, Utah and Arizona.

7. Tumbleweed (The Russian Thistle, "Salsolakali"). The romanticized tumbling tumbleweed rolling through a ghost town, sauntering past the feet of your mount, is actually the skeleton of a succulent bright green plant that breaks away from its roots when dry and is taken by the wind to scatter its seeds. The skeletons of this species are caught in fence rows along the highways of American deserts. These skeletons can be compressed and burned like fire logs. And, by the way, this scurrilous plant—a western icon—is not native to America. It didn't exist in the American West before the 1880's. It was accidentally brought to North America around 1885 as seeds in a shipment of Russian wheat. So if you see tumbling tumbleweeds in a pre-1880 western setting, well, there goes authenticity. Ranchers hate the "critter" because it readily grows on disturbed soil, and the dryer the soil is, the better it grows.

8. Locoweed. (*Asstragalus*). A small plant with purple or white flowers. It is poisonous to cattle, and legend has it that it will drive them crazy.

9. Peyote. (*Lophophosra williamsii*). Pronounced *pay-oat-e*. A desert plant that lays flat on the ground (looking a bit like a "cowpie.") It is gray and spineless with several pink flowers. Cut and dried "buttons" of peyote, when chewed, produce color hallucinations and are important in certain Indian religious ceremonies. A drink made from it is called *mescal*. (Peyote is illegal to manufacture, buy, possess, or distribute [sell, trade or give] without a DEA license.)

Rodents, Reptiles, & Rabbits
8 DESERT COMPANIONS

"[Gila monsters] never let go—do they Howard—once they grab on to you. They cut 'em in two—the head'll still hang on 'till sundown, I hear. By that time the victim doesn't usually care 'cause he's dead anyway."
—The Treasure of the Sierra Madre, 1949.

A breeze swirls across the dry valley, stirring up red dust devils. It's blistering hot and deathly quiet, but the desert is teeming with life. Tiny living things scurry this way and that. Most are harmless to humans, but some are downright deadly. These animals and insects are hardy souls indeed, having learned to survive in the harsh conditions of the American deserts. Some of these creatures were made famous by western literature and films.

1. The Gila Monster. (*Heloderma suspectum*). It is one of only two American venomous lizards, the other being the *Mexican Beaded Lizard*. The *Gila* is found in southern Nevada and Arizona. This relatively large venomous lizard (1-1/2 to 2 feet in length) can change colors to blend in with its surroundings. Its body is marked with irregular patterns and blotches of black and yellow or orange and pink with black bands extending onto its blunt tail. It lumbers around slowly and awkwardly at dusk and at night looking for birds, small animals, and eggs. Bites from this scary looking creature are rarely fatal to humans. The poison helps to subdue large prey by flowing into the open wound as the lizard munches on its victim!

2. The Desert Tarantula. (*Aphonopelma chalcodes*). The "wolf spider" crawling slowly up the inside of a trouser leg or along the back of a man's neck will send shivers up anyone's spine. This large and hairy, brownish-black arachnid (2 to 2-1/2" long), is found in the desert soils of Arizona, New Mexico, and Southern

California. Hiding by day in abandoned holes, it waits until evening to venture out in search of a mate or food (like insects, lizards, and small animals). It doesn't spin a web, relying on its speed to catch its prey. Tales are told that it can spring at its prey from as far away as six feet. Luckily, it's no more poisonous than a bee. Cowboys used to throw a pair of them into a hat so they would fight each other and bet on which would be the winner.

3. The Giant Desert Hairy Scorpion. (*Hadrurus arizonensis*). Crawling quietly under your bedcovers as you sleep, make a move and you're stung! This frightful anthropod of the southwest is 5-1/2" long with pale-yellow segmented appendages with a black "body." Venom in the scorpion's stinger is used to subdue struggling prey and for self-defense. Scorpions are nocturnal and so are preyed upon by owls and bats. A similar scorpion is the dreaded *Sculptured Centruroides* which is about 2-1/2" long, dark brown to tan, and is extremely poisonous to man. It is found only in Arizona. The scorpions in the American Southwest rarely have a fatal sting to humans, but in Mexico, many scorpions with deadly poisons are present. Don't pick up a rock with your bare hands.

4. The Giant Vinegarone. (*Mastigoproctus giganteus*). Brown to black, about 3" long, this formidable-looking whip scorpion is found in the Southwest and was given its name because it emits a fluid with a vinegary odor when disturbed. It's found under logs and rotting wood and debris, and *indoors*, in humid dark corners! Fortunately, its not poisonous. It is seldom seen because it hides by day and hunts insects by night. The Texas border town that Judge Roy Bean renamed *Langtry* when he became judge and jury was originally named *Vinegarone* for the scorpion that populated the area.

Rattlesnake, South Texas (dk)

5. The Rattlesnake. (*Genera Sistrurus* and *Crotalus*). A heavy-bodied poisonous snake (1-1/2 to 7 feet in length) with a diamond-shaped pattern of blotches along its back and a rattle on its tail that's used to warn threatening predators. It is aggressive and dangerous and will stand its ground, rattling and then striking at an enemy from a coiled position. There are several varieties of rattlesnake found in the arid, dry prairies and deserts of the Southwest. Some are smaller and less aggressive than others. Colors vary. During the day they're often hidden in brush, cactus patches, and rocky areas. They feed on lizards, birds and small animals (like rabbits and ground squirrels). The *Western Diamondback* (*Crotalus atrox*), the biggest of the rattlesnakes, is gray or light brown in color with a large head sharply distinct from the neck, and a row of light-bordered hexagonal blotches along the length of its back. The tail is encircled with broad black and white rings. They can live as much as 26 years and their venom can be fatal. In the summer, they like to stay out of the sun, coming out in the evenings and at night to hunt for prey. On cold winter days they come out in the open to warm themselves. The term "sidewinder" refers to a species of rattlesnake (*Crotalus cerastes*) with a large head and a prominent triangular projection over each eye that looks like a horn. It is brownish or gray with less defined diamond-shaped blotches on its back. It is found in sandy areas in the far southwest (eastern California, southern Nevada, and Arizona) and gets its name by moving quickly over shifting sands by "sidewinding." The snake makes use of static friction to keep from slipping when crossing soft sandy areas. If you've seen one of these snakes in action you'll know why a man of treacherous character might be called a "sidewinder."

6. The Jackrabbit. (*Lepus californicus*). The *Blacktail and White-tailed Jackrabbit* with its very long ears and long back legs is common all over the West. They have a buffy-gray or sandy body peppered with black with a white underbelly so they can blend in with their arid environment. They can make huge leaps very quickly at any sign of trouble. Their habitat is the open prairies and arid regions of the central and western United States. They are able to handle the extreme desert temperatures. During the day they stay out of the heat by nesting in the underbrush, then

Jackrabbit, West Texas (dk)

> *"The jackass rabbit . . . is well named. He is just like any other rabbit, except that he is from one third to twice as large, has longer legs in proportion to his size, and has the most preposterous ears that were ever mounted on any creature but a 'jackass'."* —Mark Twain, *Roughing It.*

in late afternoon they come out to eat green vegetation, alfalfa, and dried plants in winter. A great survivor, the jackrabbit can, during periods of drought, open up some varieties of cacti to get at the water. The *Antelope Jackrabbit (Lepus alleni)* has longer ears and longer back legs and has white hair that is visible on its sides. It is found only in southern Arizona and New Mexico. The long ears work as a body-cooling system in hot weather.

7. The Turkey Vulture. (*Cathartes aura*). Often seen sitting on a fence post or a lone dead tree, the Turkey Vulture is a scavenger, not a predator, feasting only on dead animals. One of America's largest birds—with a wingspan of six feet—the Turkey Vulture is brown-black in color with a featherless red head. The wings are broad, the tail short, and the bird seems to have a hard time taking to flight. The *Black Vulture (Coragyps atratus)*, found only in Texas and the southeast, is smaller and has a gray head and black plumage with whitish wing tips visible during flight. Vultures are often incorrectly called *buzzards*, a term originally applied to hawks in the Old World. Two bony vultures sitting in a dead tree in a barren desert, one says to the other, "Patience my ass, I'm going to kill something!"

8. The Hawk. Soaring high over the arid desert, its harsh eerie scream echoing off the canyon walls, the hawk is seldom actually *seen* in western films, but you can bet every foley will add the call of this shrieking bird to the soundtrack. In the *Red-tailed Hawk (Buteo Jamaicensis)*, the top plumage is dark brown, the breast pale with brown streaks. It is found not only in the desert, but also prairies and brush country. It is able to cover long distances to find its prey of rodents, reptiles, and rabbits. The *Ferruginous Hawk (Buteo regalis)* is found only in the western United States. A reddish-brown with white breast, they eat prairie dogs, ground squirrels, lizards, crickets, and birds.

Bison, Birds, and Bears
MOUNTAIN & PRAIRIE LIFE

"Oh, bury me not on the lone prairie,
Where the coyotes howl and the wind blows free.
In a narrow grave just six by three.
Oh, bury me not on the lone prairie."
—old cowboy ballad

A breeze whistles through the white-trunked aspens, making the shivering leaves sound like a babbling brook. A light snow peppers the yellow, orange, and light-green autumn leaves with speckles of bright white baby powder. A white-striped chipmunk dashes across the fresh snow and disappears into his lair of rotting limbs. This is the high mountains of the American West where several animals have made their way into western lore.

1. The Grizzly Bear. (*Ursus horribilis*). Standing up to 8 feet on its hind legs and weighing in at 300 to 900 pounds (6 to 7 feet long, four feet tall when on all fours), it's a ferocious creature to reckon with if encountered. It normally avoids humans and eats berries, grub worms, roots, small animals, and fish. Brown or black in color, its white-tipped hair gives it a grizzled appearance. It also has a distinct hump on its shoulders. The now famous "Bart" (*Legends of the Fall, The Edge, The Bear*) is a grizzly bear. Not to be confused with the *Black Bear* which is also either brown and black in color, but with no hump, 200-500 pounds, and only two to three feet tall at the shoulders. Found in the Rocky Mountains all the way from Alaska to Colorado. Its a good tree climber and never passes up a tree with a bee hive, being extremely fond of honey. Look above you when walking through the woods. How do you scare off unseen bears? Make noise as you walk by wearing little bells on your ankles. How do you know if bears are nearby? Just look for bear dung. But how do you recognize bear remains? The dung will contain little bells! You see, the Grizzly has become legendary because of the tall tales spun about their "thirst for blood." Native Americans prized the bear not only for its meat, but for its skin to make robes and shelter, and the claws and teeth for ornaments.

2. The Coyote. (*Canis latrans*). A coyote howling at the moon in the dead of night will put a chill racing up anyone's spine. It's found all over the United States, but mostly in the West; 3-1/2 to 4-1/2 feet long, grizzled yellowish-gray or reddish in color, weighing as much as 50 pounds, with short hair like a dog. The coyote has a pointy nose and a bushy tail that is held down even when running. This cunning scavenger feeds on carrion and smaller animals like rabbits, mice, and ground squirrels, but will also eat berries and worms. He could kill a sheep if he was hungry enough. The coyote can jump as much as 14 feet high and cruise at 25-30 mph, sprinting up to 40 mph for short distances. Unlike the endangered wolf, the coyote continues to multiply out of control. As their natural environment disappears, they still survive. Mark Twain in *Roughing It*, aptly defined the coyote this way: "The coyote is a long, slim, sick, and sorry-looking skeleton, with a gray wolf-skin stretched over it, a tolerably bushy tail that forever sags down with a despairing expression of abandonment and misery, a sly and evil eye, and a long, sharp face, with a slightly lifted lip and exposed teeth. He has a general slinking expression all over. The coyote is a living, breathing allegory of Want." The Westerner called the coyote a "Prairie Wolf" for good reason.

3. The Wolf. (*Canis lycanon*). Larger that the coyote (weighting 60 to 120 pounds and about six feet long) this creature is rarely found in the United States anymore, but is still found in heavily forested areas of Canada. Unlike the coyote, the wolf has a broader face and runs with its tail horizontal. This animal hunts in packs, chasing down deer and caribou—sometimes driving them off cliffs. Like the coyote, it howls day or night. In the winter, a wolf would be drawn into the warm camps of humans where they would eat boots and saddle leather. When nearing starvation, the Grey Wolf, a more cunning and dangerous animal, becomes very vicious and will attack cattle and horses. In the Old West, wolf pelts were sent

East for clothing, robes, mats, and fur hats. "Two Socks" in *Dances with Wolves* was a Grey Wolf.

4. The Striped Skunk. (*Mephitis mephitis*). This little nocturnal "stinker" (someplaces called a "polecat") is about the size of a house cat with long black, silky soft hair, bushy tail, and a broad white stripe along each side which meets in a "V" over the shoulder. It waddles when it walks and seems oblivious to its surroundings with not a care in the world. When a skunk is threatened, it sprays a pungent liquid from its anal scent glands; a scent that will linger for days afterward—many bath scrubbings will be required. The skunk eats insects, grubs, eggs, berries, amphibians, small animals and its favorite: caterpillars and hen's eggs. The *Hog-nosed Skunk*, found only in the southern half of Arizona, New Mexico and Texas, has solid white on his back from head to tail. Cowboys of the Old West called any skunk they came upon as "nice kitty."

5. The Prairie Dog. (*Cynomys ludovicianus*). Known by westerners as "the barking squirrel," because its high pitch "yelp" sounds a bit like a small dog. This cute little critter, weighing up to 3 pounds, is about a foot long, has yellowish-brown hair, a short tail, small rounded ears, and large eyes. They burrow homes into the soil, building acres of prairie dog "towns" protected by sentries who sit upright on their hind legs and bark at any sign of danger. They're active by day, their diet consisting mostly of grass. Ranchers don't like them because livestock can break their legs in the prairie dog holes, and farmers found that the little critters love to eat their crops. Their predators include snakes who like their "digs" and move in, and ferrets, badgers, and coyotes. Lewis and Clark gave this critter its name during their 1803 expedition across the Northwest (they also named 1,500 other animals.)

6. The Buffalo. (*Bison bison*). Once the staple and livelihood of the American Plains Indian, the Buffalo has become a part of American West lore. It's a very large awkward-looking animal weighing as much as 2,000 pounds. It has a massive head with short black curving horns and a large hump on the shoulders. The dark-brown hair is long and shaggy on the forelegs and shoulders. Buffalo traveled in large herds, grazing on the grasses of the plains. Buffalo were an integral part of Plains Indian culture, providing

Molting buffalo at Yellowstone Park, Wyoming (dk)

everything they needed: hides for tents and clothing, horns for utensils and decoration, hair for making rope and belts, and meat that could be "jerked" for later eating. (Jerked beef is strips of meat dried in the sun or in the smoke of a fire.) Buffalo could run up to 35 or 40 miles per hour which meant a man on horseback couldn't keep up and had to make his kill in the first few hundred yards. Herds once reached all the way to the Rio Grande. In the millions, they looked like a large black mass covering the horizon. Anglo hide hunting, and a federal policy encouraging the elimination of the buffalo in order to starve out the Indian, nearly exterminated the creature by the 1880's. Various individuals and groups have been trying to revitalize and increase the size of existing herds, to save them from extinction.

7. The Beaver. (*Castor canadensis*). The animal responsible for the early exploration of the American West. Just a very big mischievous rodent (from 2 to 12 feet long, 30 to 60 pounds) with brown fur and a large black paddle-shaped tail. This critter has webbed feet, sharp, orange-colored front teeth, tiny ears and small eyes. It feeds on the leaves, bark and twigs of trees like willow and aspen. The beaver is found in ponds, lakes, and slow-moving streams throughout most of North America where it builds lodges of mud-caulked logs, log dams, and gnaws down full-size trees (The dam creates a water barrier to keep intruders out of his lodge). Beavers can fell a tree as fast as a woodsman with an axe. He uses his flat tail for swimming and for slapping the water as a warning signal. To catch beaver, a mountain man had to place heavy traps in the middle of creeks, staked to hold them in place; a job that was not any fun, especially in winter. The beaver was significant to the early exploration and settlement of the Far West. They were in demand because of the beaver-hat fashions in Europe and the East at the time. You can say the beaver created the Mountain Man, and *The Hudson's Bay Company* nearly trapped them into non-existence. Only the SILK hat in the 1830's saved the last of the beavers, and ended the reign of the Mountain Man.

8. The Bald Eagle. America's national bird, worshipped by Native Americans for centuries, its a large dark-brown bird with white head, hooked yellow bill and white tail. It is normally found around rivers, lakes, and coastal areas where it feeds on fish. This grand bird nearly became extinct, but is now gaining in numbers.

9. The Cougar. (*Panthera concolor*) The westerner feared this ferocious predator. It would attack calves, sheep, deer, and even horses. It had a tawny brownish-yellow coat without any spots or stripes. With a long, slender body and long tail, it was also know as a panther, puma, catamount or mountain lion.

The feared Cougar, Wikimedia Commons

A Ballad
HELL IN TEXAS

—Anonymous

1. The devil in Hades we're told was chained,
And there for a thousand years remained.
He did not grumble nor did he groan,
But determined to make a hell of his own
Where he could torture the souls of men
Without being chained in that poisoned pen.

2. So he asked the Lord if he had on hand
Anything left when he made the land.
The Lord said, "Yes, I have lots on hand,
But I left it down on the Rio Grande."

3. So the Devil went down and looked at the stuff,
And said if it comes as a gift he'd be stuck
For after examining it carefully and well,
He found it was too dry for hell.

4. So in order to get it off'n his hands
The Lord promised the Devil to water the land,
For he had some water, or rather some dregs,
That smelled just like a case of bad eggs.

The rocky Texas Big Bend area (dk)

Windmill in the Texas Panhandle (dk)

5. So the deal was made and the deed was given
And the Lord went back to his home in Heaven.
"Now," says the Devil, "I have all that's needed
To make a good Hell," and thus he succeeded.

6. He put thorns on the cactus and horns on the toads
And scattered tarantulas along the road.
He gave spiral springs to the bronco steed
And a thousand legs to the centipede.

7. And all will be Mavericks unless they bore
Thorns and scratches and bites by the score.
The sand burrs prevail and so do the ants,
And those who sit down need half soles on their pants.

8. Oh, the wild boar roams the black chaparral,
It's a hell of a place he's got for Hell.

9. The red pepper grows on the banks of the brooks,
The Mexicans use them in all that they cook.
Just dine with the Mexican, you'll be sure to shout
From Hell on the inside as well as the out.

> # "If I owned Texas and Hell, I would rent out Texas and live in Hell."
> —General Philip Sheridan, Fort Clark, Texas 1855.

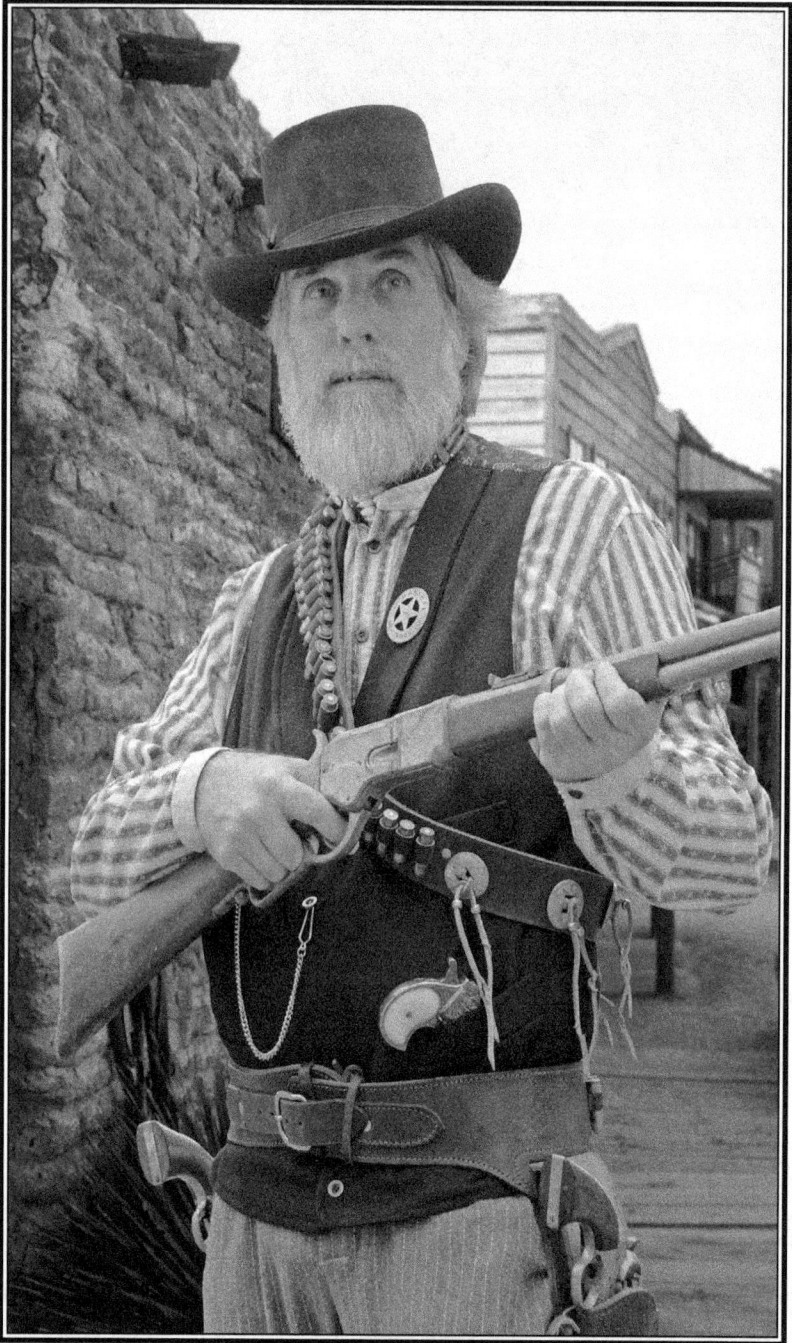

Michael Murray as Marshal Seth Masters, photo and costume by the author

Tin Stars and Ten Galón Hats
THE LAWMEN

"You've been a lawman all your life."
"Yeah, yeah, all my life. It's a great life. You risk your skin
catching killers and then juries turn them loose so they can
come back and shoot at you again. If you're honest, you're poor
your whole life. And in the end you wind up dying all alone on
some dirty street. For what? For nothing. For a tin star."
—Gary Cooper, *High Noon,* 1952

The men of the west who picked up the tin badge and placed it over their heart and swore to uphold the law, were men who made their own law. A gun was their judge and jury, and that's why they got the job in the first place. They were good with their six-shooter and that's what was needed to challenge the bad element. Citizens wanted a respectable place to live and work; crime only hindered the town's potential for success. First there was vigilantism—the citizens had to get rid of the criminal element themselves by what ever means at hand: they might sneak into a criminal's cabin at night, hang him in the barn, and leave a note pinned on his shirt warning anyone outside the "law" that they would get the same justice. Later, when a man good with a gun could be found to do the dirty work for the townspeople, he got the job.

In the real West, the job of town marshal wasn't only about keeping the bad elements out of town, it also acquired many mundane duties like collecting taxes, running off mangy dogs, and inspecting outhouses—the same job as today's city governments.

FIREARMS

ARE PROHIBITED

IN THE

CITY LIMITS

OF

TOMSTONE

—BY ORDER OF THE MARSHAL

Wyatt Earp

Fill Your Hand
FAMOUS LAWMEN OF THE WEST

"All power is inherent in the people, and all free
governments are formed upon their authority."
—Sam Houston proposal for the Texas constitution, 1833.

Twelve men who "wore them low," but pinned on a badge when it suited them, executing, with their guns, the laws of a town's city council. If weapons were prohibited inside the city limits, then they would have to do some "disarmin'."

1. Bill Tilghman (1854-1924).
2. Charlie Siringo (1855-1928).
3. Dallas Stoudenmire (1845-1882).
4. Tom Rynning (1866-1941).
5. Elfego Baca (1865-1945).
6. Sam Sixkiller (1842-1886).
7. Bass Reeves (1838-1910).
8. Tom Smith ((1830-1870).
9. Pat Garrett (1850-1908).
10. Wild Bill Hickok (1837-1876).
11. Bat Masterson (1852-1921) and brothers Ed and James.
12. Wyatt Earp (1843-1929) and brothers Morgan and Virgil.

A Classic Legendary Story:

The Mayor of Sweetwater had wired the Texas Rangers for help to put down a riot. Ranger Headquarters assured the Mayor they would be on the next train. When the train finally arrived, only one Ranger stepped off! The panic-stricken Mayor of Sweetwater demanded, "Why is there only one of you?" And the Ranger calmly answered, "Well, you ain't got but one mob have you?"

John Russell as Marshal Dan Troop, and Peter Brown as Deputy Johnny McKay in the TV
series *The Lawman*, 1958-1962, Warner Brothers Television (author's collection)

QUOTE: **"Give us one thousand Rangers** and we will be
responsible for the defense of our frontier. Texas does not want
regular troops. Withdraw them if you please."
—Sam Houston, 1858"

DUTIES OF THE TOWN MARSHAL

A LEGALLY SWORN IN MARSHAL WILL COLLECT $25 A MONTH IN WAGES
IN RETURN FOR PERFORMANCE OF THE DUTIES ASSIGNED BELOW:

ALL CURRENT WANTED POSTERS MUST BE KEPT POSTED AT THE OFFICE.

ALL LAWBREAKERS MUST BE TRACKED DOWN AND APPREHENDED.
SWEARING-IN TOWNSPEOPLE AS TEMPORARY DEPUTIES IS AUTHORIZED.

THE MARSHAL IS RESPONSIBLE FOR MAINTAINING THE COUNTY JAIL
AND SEEING TO IT THAT TOWN DRUNKS ARE NOT
KEPT LOCKED UP MORE THAN ONE NIGHT AT A TIME.

IT'S THE DUTY OF THE MARSHAL TO SERVE ALL COURT ORDERS TO THE
LAWLESS NO MATTER THE CONSEQUENCES OR POSSIBLE BODILY HARM.

THE MARSHAL SHALL KEEP STREETS CLEAR OF LITTER,
INCLUDING DRUNKS AND SHEEPHERDERS.

THE MARSHAL'S DUTIES INCLUDE MAINTAINING THE COUNTY DOG POUND
AND ERADICATING PRAIRIE DOG TOWNS.

AS THE OFFICIAL FIRE & HEALTH INSPECTOR, THE MARSHAL WILL
SEE TO IT THAT ALL HOTEL MATTRESSES ARE AIRED OUT ONCE A MONTH.

AS THE SANITATION COMMISSIONER, THE MARSHAL WILL
INSPECT ALL OUTHOUSES ON A REGULAR BASIS AND
SUPERVISE NEW DIGGINGS.

AS TAX COLLECTOR, THE MARSHAL WILL COLLECT LICENSE FEES FOR
SALOONS, HOUSES OF PROSTITUTION, AND OWNERS OF PET DOGS.

THE MARSHALL IS AUTHORIZED BY THE MAYOR TO COLLECT COUNTY
TAXES ON A REGULAR BASIS, BUT CANNOT KEEP MORE THAN 5% OF THE
TAKE. HE MAY SELL THE PROPERTY OF TAX DELINQUENTS.

THE MARSHALL WILL OVERSEE ALL HANGINGS AUTHORIZED BY THE JUDGE
AND HE WILL ENFORCE ALL CITY AND COUNTY ORDINANCES.

- CLARENCE TIDWATER, MAYOR, WAGON WHEEL GAP, 1883

Humorous similitude of Old West broadside created by the author

Eaves Ranch, Santa Fe, New Mexico (dk)

The Tin Star
THE PASSING OF WISDOM

The following quotes come from the 1957 movie *The Tin Star* with Henry Fonda as the bounty hunter ex-lawman who is obliged to pass his wisdom to a tenderfoot sheriff played by Anthony Perkins, a man so green and naive that in his new job as sheriff he is sure to get himself killed.

1. "You lack confidence . . . to have confidence you gotta keep a cool head. Don't take any chances you don't have to, but wait, and end the fight with one shot. It's that time you wait, that split second that means the difference between missing a man and killing him."

2. "Take that split second and pull the trigger once, that's what counts, that first shot. Point dead center, and the fight's over."

3. "Learn what to stay out of. If you gotta step into a fight make sure you're the better man."

4. "Study men. Paste this in your hat: a gun's only a tool—you can master a gun if you got the knack. It's harder to learn men."

5. "As long as you're wearing that badge, you gotta walk up, tell him to throw 'em up, and then watch which way his hands move. If they go up, you got yourself a prisoner. If they go down, he's dead—or you are. A decent man doesn't want to kill, but if you're gonna shoot, you shoot to kill."

He Always Gets His Man
THE TEXAS RANGERS

"The Texas Ranger can ride like a Mexican,
trail like an Indian, shoot like a Tennesseean,
and fight like the very Devil."
—John S. Ford, 1846.

A **special breed of lawman** flourished in the Southwest beyond the reaches of city and county governments, beyond the reaches of civilization—along the Mexican border of Arizona, New Mexico, and Texas. Here, the Law had to travel great distances on horseback. They had to ride hard and shoot straight. And they had to administer their own form of frontier justice.

Formed as "ranging companies" in 1823 to fight renegade Indians (the worst of which were the Comanches), the Texas Rangers had no uniform and there was a very limited central control over the men in the field. It could be said that Stephen F. Austin was the first to establish the Texas Rangers when he assigned 25 men to protect the settlers against Indian attacks. On November 3, 1835, the Texas Rangers were formally organized into three companies of 56 men each (just four months before the legendary battle of the Alamo. They were paid $1.25 a day, but had to provide their own horses, weapons, and munitions. Armed with a strong sense of pride for their new country, they kept cattle rustlers, highwaymen and bank robbers "on the run," the likes of which included the infamous Sam Bass and John Wesley Hardin.

One of the first groups to use Samuel Colt's new revolving pistols was, of course, the *Texas Rangers,* who had tremendous success against the Indians with this new handgun, making the Indian's primitive bows and arrows almost useless. Texas Ranger *Samuel Hamilton Walker* made suggestions for improvements to Sam Colt's 1836 pistol which resulted in the Colt Walker in 1847, a "quicker-firing, easier loading, and more dependable" sidearm. The Rangers were off and running.

JOHN COFFEE HAYS   **BIGFOOT WALLACE**

SAMUEL WALKER   **BEN McCULLOCH**

Hi-Yo Silver!
6 Legendary Texas Rangers

*"NAME OF OFFENDER: Bill Jones; OFFENSE: Stealing
Cattle; DISPOSITION: Mean as hell. Had to kill him."*
—First Ranger Report, August 10, 1876.

The Texas Rangers developed legendary status as they campaigned against the pillaging Comanches, repelled the invasion from Mexico in 1842, fought in the Mexican-American War of 1845, and then told the stories of their adventures, which led to books written about them.

1) **William A.A. "Bigfoot" Wallace** (1817-1899). Got his nickname because he was once mis-identified as an Indian named "Big Foot" who had broken into a settler's home and left 14-inch footprints behind. They thought they might be Wallace's big feet, but his turned out to be only 12-inches, but the name stuck.

2) **John Coffee "Jack" Hays** (1817-1883). A Lipan Indian gave him the name "Brave-Too-Much" because of his leadership as a courageous "let's go-get-'em" rallying figure.

3) **Benjamin McCulloch** (1811-1862). Fought at San Jacinto, later died in a Civil War Battle at Pea Ridge, Arkansas.

4) **Samuel H. Walker** (1817-1847). With 15 other Rangers, he held off 80 Comanches, killing 50; two "five-shot repeating pistols" made the difference. He died at 30 without heirs.

5) **John S. "Rip" Ford** (1815-1897). His nickname resulted from one of his assigned duties, the sending of death notices to the families of Rangers killed in the Mexican War.

6) **"Texas" John Slaughter** (1841-1922). A compulsive poker player—who got into more than a few gunfights at the poker table—carried a double-barreled, sawed-off shotgun as an "equalizer." Late in life, he lived in a ranch house that was located over the U.S.–Mexico border, half the house in Mexico, half in the U.S. This was on his San Bernardino Ranch in Douglas, Arizona where he died. It is now a museum.

Members of the Frontier Battalion, a company of the Texas Rangers, c1885
(Library of Congress Prints and Photographs Division)

A Match Game
5 Legendary Texas Rangers

Match the Texas Ranger with a fact about him.

1. Ben McCulloch

2. John "Coffee" Hays

3. "Bigfoot" Wallace

4. John Slaughter

5. Samuel Walker

a. Founded the city of Oakland, Calif.

b. Walt Disney produced a TV series about him in 1958-1960.

c. A good friend of David Crockett; a bout of measles kept him from going with Crockett to the Alamo.

d. He drew a gray bean in the famous "Black-Bean Incident" and avoided execution by a firing squad.

e. Colonel Samuel Colt named a .44-caliber black-powder revolver after him, he helped design it.

ANS: 1-c, 2-a, 3-d, 4-b, 5-e.

A Ballad
THE TEXAS RANGER
Traditional

The music of a sixteenth-century Irish lament was used for this Texas folk song.

Come all ye Texas Rangers, wherever you may be;
I'll tell you of some troubles that happened unto me;
My name is nothing extra; to you I will not tell;
But here's to all good Rangers, I'm sure I wish you well.

'Twas at the age of sixteen I joined a Ranger band;
We marched from San Antonio down to the Rio Grande,
And there our Captain told us—perhaps he thought it right—
"Before we reach the River, I'm sure we'll have a fight."

Before we reached the River, our Captain gave command,
"To arms, to arms, he shouted, "and by your pony stand!"
I saw the smoke a-rising, it seemed to reach the sky,
And then, the thought it struck me—my time had come to die.

I saw the Injuns coming, I heard them give a yell;
My feelings at that moment, no mortal tongue can tell;
I saw their glittering lances, their arrows 'round me hailed,
My heart it sank within me, my courage almost failed.

I thought of my old mother, in tears to me did say:
"To you they are all strangers, with me you'd better stay."
I thought her weak and childish, and that she did not know,
For I was bent on roaming, and I was bound to go.

And all of us were wounded, our noble captain slain;
The sun was shining sadly across the bloody plain,
Sixteen as brave a Rangers as ever rode the West
Were buried by their comrades with arrows in their chests.

Perhaps you have a mother, likewise a sister too;
Perhaps you have a sweetheart who'll weep and mourn for you—
If this should be your portion and you are bound to roam,
I tell you from experience, you'd better stay at home.

Commandancy of the Alamo —

Bexar, Feby. 24, 1836

To the People of Texas & All

Americans in the World —

Fellow Citizens & compatriots —

I am besieged, by a thousand or more of the Mexicans under Santa Anna — I have sustained a continual bombardment & cannonade for 24 hours & have not lost a man — The enemy has demanded a surrender at discretion, otherwise, the garrison are to be put to the sword, if the fort is taken — I have answered the demand with a cannon shot, & our flag still waves proudly from the walls — I shall never surrender or retreat. Then, I call on you in the name of Liberty, of patriotism & everything dear to the American character, to come to our aid, with all dispatch — The enemy is receiving reinforcements daily & will no doubt increase to three or four thousand in four or five days. If this call is neglected, I am determined to sustain myself as long as possible & die like a soldier who never forgets what is due to his own honor & that of his country— Victory or Death.

William Barret Travis,
Lt. Col. Comdt.

TRAVIS' LETTER FROM THE ALAMO BECAME A SYMBOL OF COURAGE

A Multiple-Choice Quiz
THE BATTLE OF THE ALAMO

"I give thanks for the time and the place . . . a time to live and a place
to die. That's all any man gets. No more, no less."
—Hank Worden, *The Alamo*, 1960

The Battle of the Alamo is a story of adventurous men who made a stand for freedom knowing full well they would have to fight to the death. It is a story that will in all probability last for many hundreds of years. Most of what we western fans know about the battle is garnered from the movies which have gone out of their way to intertwine fiction with fact. Thus, we offer this quiz to enlighten and entertain. The next time you watch an "Alamo" movie you'll be able to recognize historical fact from the writer's "poetic license."

Prelude. Fearing that the Americans would outnumber Mexicans in Texas and seize control, the Mexican government—led by Anastacio Bustamante—passed a law in 1830 that provided for the military occupation of Texas and decreed an absolute end to all American immigration. But that didn't stop the flow of determined new settlers to the fertile lands of Texas.

Texas was a mix of Tejanos (native Texans) and newly arrived Anglo Americans without common interests or traditions. This led to indecision and political infighting in the provincial government of Texas. They were divided on the question of whether they should establish a self-governing state under the liberal Mexican Constitution of 1824 or attempt outright independence, establishing their own republic. When the new President of Mexico, the flamboyant General Antonio López de Santa Anna, dissolved the Mexican congress and declared himself a dictator, the first option gradually eroded. Half-a-dozen battles with the Mexican Army had already been fought before the famous Battle of the Alamo, including the rout of General Cos' troops out of San Antonio in December 1835.

At the time of the Alamo battle the mission was in ruins; the church dome and towers had caved in leaving no roof—the stone wall the only thing still standing. In front of the mission was a 12-foot-high wall that surrounded about three acres in a rectangle measuring 250 by 450 feet. Adjacent to the mission was a two-story building called the "Long Barracks" and on the south wall was a long one-story building known as the "Low Barracks." To the right of the mission was a 75-foot opening where there was no wall at all. In January of 1836, General Lopez de Santa Anna led an army of more than 4,000 soldiers on a march toward San Antonio to quell the rebellion. As he marched, a Texas lawyer named Green Jameson fortified the mission compound with raised earthen cannon placements and closed the 75-foot opening with a wall of upright timbers backed with earth. Crumbling stone walls were repaired and weak points reinforced with log supports. About 20 cannons were already sitting in the compound, left there after General Cos' rout in December. On word of Santa Anna's approach on February 23, 1836, a small force of volunteers retreated to safety behind the Alamo's fortified walls.

THE QUESTIONS
CIRCLE YOUR BEST GUESS
(Answers After Each Question)

1. The Alamo was originally:
A. A saloon and opera house.
B. A military fort.
C. An old Spanish mission.
D. A Mexican trading post.
1-C. *The Alamo was an old Spanish mission established in 1718 by Franciscan Friars.*

2. What was the name of the original mission?
A. Mission San Jose y San Miguel de Aguayo.

B. Mission San Juan Capistrano.
C. Mission San Antonio de Valero.
D. Mission San Francisco de la Espada.

2-C. *San Antonio de Valero was the first of five missions founded in San Antonio to Christianize and educate area Indians. The structure that stands today was begun about 1755. All of the missions listed in the question were, and still are, in San Antonio. Another mission, Nuestra Senora de la Purisima Concepcion, is also in San Antonio. They're worth a visit if you're in town.*

The Alamo chapel, build for John Wayne's *Alamo* at Alamo Village, Brackettville,Texas

3. How many Texians attempted to defend the Alamo against the roughly 4,000 Mexican troops?

A. 79 men.
B. 189 men.
C. 276 men.
D. 400 men.

3-B. 189 men are known to have defended the Alamo. There may have been more. Fewer than 20 of them were citizens of Texas. They had come from many U. S. states with the hope of making their fortunes in this new country. The offer of free land grants brought many men to Texas. Bowie came with about 100 men, Travis 25 to 32, and 32 men came from Gonzales; far too few men to defend such a large compound.

4. The Alamo got its name from:

A. A popular saloon in the nearby town of San Antonio de Bexar called "The Alamo."
B. A new kind of ammunition using aluminum found at the site and given the brand name "Alamo."
C. A Spanish military unit which occupied the mission in the early 1800's and was from the village of El Alamo in Coachila, Mexico.
D. A nearby grove of cottonwood trees (*álamos* in Spanish).

4-C&D. Both answers, "C" and "D" have been found in source material, but who can say that one of the other suggestions isn't true? History is always being rewritten as new facts emerge.

5. Who commanded the Texians in the Alamo?

A. Davy Crockett.
B. Juan Seguin.
C. William Barret Travis.
D. Jim Bowie.

5-C. TRAVIS *had been elected as garrison Commander when Col. James Neill left the mission because of illness in the family. Travis and Bowie agreed to joint command of the Alamo*

from February 14th until the 24th. Bowie was Commander of the Texas volunteers and Travis commanded the regulars. The duel command led to some conflict, but during the last days of the battle Bowie was so sick from pneumonia he relinquished his command to Travis. Before the war, 26-year-old Lt. Colonel Travis was a lawyer from Alabama practicing in San Felipe, Texas. He had brought 25 volunteers to the Alamo including Juan Sequin. DAVY CROCKETT was a 49-year-old marksman (he carried "Old Betsy"), hunter, and U.S. Congressman from Tennessee who had already achieved folk hero status. He brought to the Alamo a dozen sharpshooters he called the "Tennessee Mounted Volunteers." JIM BOWIE, a sugar plantation owner and state legislator from Louisiana, had made his fortune in slave-smuggling and land speculation. He was legendary as a knife fighter and designed his own "Bowie knife" in 1830 to "stab like a dagger, slice like a razor and chop like a cleaver." He came to*

THE LONE STAR FLAG

Tin Stars and Ten Galón Hats

COME AND TAKE IT FLAG

San Antonio in 1828—in search of land and silver—and married the daughter of the Governor of Coahuila & Texas giving him a place in Mexican Society. CAPT. JUAN NEPOMUCENA SEGUIN was a Texas-born Mexican liberal committed to the Texas cause. He was political chief of the San Antonio district and used his influence on behalf of the Americans who wanted more self-government. He was captain of the cavalry in the Texas army and was fighting in the Alamo until he was sent to Gonzales to plead for help. He fought with Houston in the Battle of San Jacinto, was a senator in the new republic and mayor of San Antonio before being run out of Texas in 1842 by new American settlers who called him a traitor. He was then forced to fight for Santa Anna, finally able to return to his beloved Texas in 1848.

6. Who led the Mexican Army against the rebellious Texans at the Alamo?
A. General Martín Perfecto de Cós.

B. General Antonio López de Santa Anna.
C. General Joaquin Ramirez y Sesma.
D. General José Urrea.

6-B. *General Santa Anna personally led the Army. Dressed in bright, gaudy, decorated uniforms with a hat cocked sideways, he fancied himself as the "Napoleon of the West," a name he used after stopping the*

BURNET NAVY FLAG

Spanish invasion of Mexico in 1829. The Texians supported him when he overthrew Bustamante's government and was elected Mexico's president in 1833. But then he declared himself dictator in 1835, throwing out all the Federalist laws. General Cós was Santa Anna's brother-in-law, in charge of eastern providences of Mexico including Texas. At the time of the battle, General Urrea was bringing 400 troops up from Mexico to take Goliad.

7. Did Colonel Travis actually draw a line in the dirt for his men to cross if they chose to stay and fight?
A. Yes.
B. No.

7-B. *No. An 1870's painting of the Alamo incident shows Travis drawing a line in the dirt with his sword, with two men on cots and the rest of the men cheering. But this was probably an early romanticizing of the event that may have actually been based on another documented incident in December of 1835. When Ben Milam had recruited volunteers*

for a force of Texians to take back San Antonio from Gen. Cós' army by drawing a line in the dust and shouting "Who will follow old Ben Milam?"

8. What kind of arms did the Alamo defenders have?
A. Flintlock muskets.
B. Percussion-lock muzzle loaders.
C. Percussion "cap and ball" pistols.
D. Winchester repeating rifles.

8-A&B. *Only muzzleloading flintlocks and percussion locks existed by the time of the Alamo battle, the same firearms used in the Revolutionary War. The percussion lock muzzleloader, know as the "Kentucky rifle," could fire only one shot at a time. It would take about thirty seconds to reload, a long time when an enemy is approaching. Black powder had to be poured into the barrel and a lead ball with a greasy patch rammed in with a steel rod. Then, a firing cap had to be placed on a nipple under the hammer. Maximum range was about 200 yards if you*

GOLIAD LIBERTY FLAG

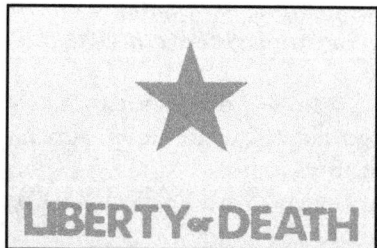

were a good marksman and the Texians were. The Mexicans were still using smooth-bore muskets which were far less accurate and even slower to load.

9. Movies and television have portrayed Davy Crockett to be many different ages at the battle of the Alamo. How old was he really?

A. 28.   C. 49.

B. 37.   D. 55.

9-C. *At 49, Davy Crockett, "King of the Wild Frontier," was one of the oldest men at the Alamo. A man named Robert Moore was 55, but the ages started as young as 18. Jim Bowie was 40. The defenders covered a whole range of ages and backgrounds, a true cross section of Texas and the U.S. Men had come from as far as Pennsylvania and New York. There were men from England, Ireland, and Germany. There were nine Tejanos and two Anglo native Texicans who died at the Alamo. There would have been more, but the men of Mexican descent were the ones sent out to carry messages because they spoke Spanish and knew the countryside.*

10. Why did Travis not get reinforcements even after repeated requests for help?

A. Colonel James Fannin, a weak and indecisive leader, decided to keep his 400 men at Goliad in case of Mexican attack and he thought it not wise to lead his men to the Alamo.

B. Even though Sam Houston was technically the commander-in-chief of the Texas Army, he had no control over commanders in the field.

C. The Texas Army was disorganized and still had no single leadership; a Constitutional government was concurrently being drafted at Washington-On-The-Brazos.

D. All of the above.

10-D. *All of these reasons. Only 32 men from Gonzales, led by George Kimbell responded*

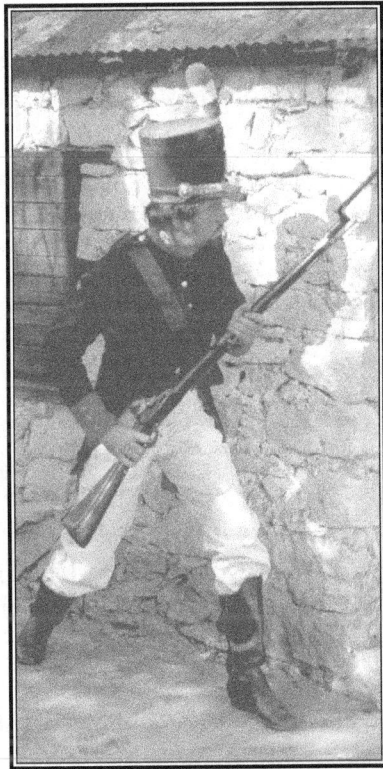

The author as Infantryman Juan Castillo, photo by Glynda Smith

Don Hunk '86

11. On Friday March 5, when Travis realized that no reinforcements would come, he gave the men the option to surrender, try to escape, or fight to the end. Any man was free to leave if he chose. And one man did decide to leave the Alamo. Who was he?

A. Louis Rose.

B. Erastus "Deaf" Smith.

C. John Baugh.

D. Jim Bowie.

11-A. *Louis Rose, a veteran of the Napoleonic wars and a soldier of fortune, had ridden in with Jim Bowie. "Deaf" Smith was not at the Alamo. Smith was Sam Houston's Chief Scout, famous for his heroic deeds during the war. Capt. John Baugh was second in command at the Alamo.*

12. For how long was the Alamo under siege?

A. Six days.

B. Eleven days.

C. Thirteen days.

D. Twenty-six days.

12-C. *The siege lasted thirteen days from February 23 to March 6. For the first week,*

to Travis' cry for help. Even if Travis had gotten support from the rest of the Texas (volunteer) Army, the Alamo most likely would have still fallen, leaving few men to fight Santa Anna in his campaign to remove all American settlers—and history might have been very different.

FIRST REPUBLIC FLAG

the Alamo was sporadically bombarded by Mexican cannon fire, the cannons moving closer each night under the cover of darkness. The Texians worked constantly to shore up the stone walls. Travis had his men fire their 18-pounder every morning at dawn to signal Santa Anna of their intention not to surrender. By March 4th Mexican cannon placements were within 200 yards of the compound causing extensive damage to the stone walls. But Mexican soldiers that close were fair game to Texian sharpshooters. The cannons fell silent on the night of the 5th allowing the exhausted defenders of the Alamo to rest and reflect.

13. On what day did the final assault on the Alamo take place?

A. March 2, 1836.
B. March 6, 1836.
C. April 21, 1836.
D. February 19, 1846.

13-B. *On March 6, 1836, the final attack began at about 5:00 am*

just before daybreak and lasted just 90 minutes. It was a Sunday morning when a Mexican bugler blew the Degüello, the signal used for death in the bullring. An army of 2,600 charged the mission that morning. Infantry with wooden ladders attempted to rush the compound and scale the walls. They were repelled. A second surge was again turned away. Eventually Mexican Infantry got next to the walls where Texan cannon fire and sharp shooters couldn't get at them. They broke through a temporary fortification and poured into the compound. Fighting hand-to-hand, tooth and nail, knife and rifle butt—

1824 CONSTITUTION FLAG

but losing ground—the Texians retreated to the Long Barracks. The Alamo cannons were turned to shoot into the plaza killing many more Mexicans. But within minutes, the Long Barracks and the mission were taken, the Texians dead. Susannah Dickerson and other women and children huddled in the mission. It was now 6:30 and all ordnance fell silent. *(March 2nd was the day the Texas Declaration of Independence was signed; April 21, the Battle of San Jacinto and Feb. 19, 1846, the day Texas joined the Union.)*

14. Jim Bowie has been seen in many movies laying deathly sick on his cot as he heroically died fighting off Mexican soldiers with their bayonets. Did this really happen?
A. Yes.
B. No.

14-B. *No. Jim Bowie lay helpless on a cot in a small room on the south side of the Alamo compound. According to his*

surviving sister-in-law, the Mexicans *"tossed Bowie's body on their bayonets until his blood covered their clothes and dyed them red."*

15. Did any Texians survive the attack on the Alamo?
A. Yes.
B. No.

15-A. *Yes, there were about a dozen non-combatant survivors including Col. Travis' slave "Joe," several Hispanic women and children, a San Antonian named Guerrero who managed to persuade the Mexicans that he had been held prisoner, and Susannah Dickerson (aged 22), the only Anglo, (and her 15 month old daughter Angelina). She was the wife of blacksmith Almeron Dickinson, commander of the Alamo's battery of cannons. They were the only Anglo-American family within the compound. Susannah was chosen by Santa Anna to carry the news of the defeat and warn the Texans of the consequences of further resistance. Three to five other defenders may have survived the final assault only to be executed by a firing squad.*

16. Which statement is NOT true?
A. Eight Mexican soldiers were killed for every defender of the Alamo.
B. The Texians killed approximately 1,500 men of the Mexican force.

C. After the battle, Santa Anna ordered the bodies of the Texians to be buried.

D. The Texians killed fully a third of the Mexican attacking force.

16-C. *A, B and D all are the same statistic, just presented differently. Santa Anna ordered the Texian bodies burned in a huge bonfire*

1845 UNITED STATES FLAG

using wood gathered from the surrounding forests. He wanted to make a point. (Roughly 1,500 dead Mexican troops were buried or thrown into the river. Many had been shot in the back by their own troops as wave after wave charged the mission.)

17. Why did so many men from all walks of life and from many American states come to the Alamo knowing they would have to fight a large Mexican force? Which one is NOT true?

A. They had a strong conviction for liberty and felt they could free Texas from the tyranny of Santa Anna.

B. The Texas government offered large tracts of free land to any man who helped stop Santa Anna in San Antonio.

C. A free Texas was worth fighting for, its fertile lands and potential would assure them of good fortune.

D. Strategically speaking, they felt this was the place to fight and stop Santa Anna, fully expecting support from the rest of the Texas Army.

17-B. *Travis chose to try to stop Santa Anna here rather "than to suffer a war of devastation to rage in our settlements." Educated, ambitious and industrious men came to this new land in the hopes of making a good living, but they knew they couldn't succeed under a dictatorship; they had to have free enterprise to be successful.*

18. How did the Texian's defeat at the Alamo help Texas win the war? Which one is NOT true?

A. Texians now understood that Santa Anna would not accept a compromise, they had to win their freedom or die in the attempt.

B. The United States announced they would send U.S. troops to help Texas.

C. The brave stand at the Alamo against tyranny and for freedom was heard around the world and won sympathy for the Texas cause.

D. Texians were outraged at Santa Anna's treatment of the defenders and wanted revenge.

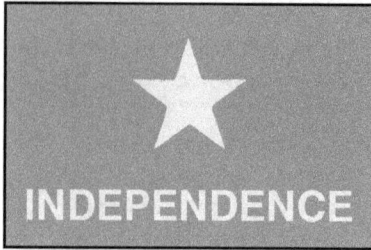

WILLIAM SCOTT FLAG

18-B. *Only "B" is not true. The U.S. didn't help Texas until the Mexican war in 1846. The Alamo defenders had indeed achieved "victory in death" and made their place in history and folklore, symbolizing the spirit of freedom and the continuing fight to prevent oppression by those in power.*

19. What flag was flying over the Alamo during the battle?

A. The "stars and stripes" of the United States.

B. The Mexican Constitutional Flag of 1824 (red, white & green stripes with the number "1824").

C. The Lone Star flag (red and white with star on blue b.g.).

D. The "Come And Take It" flag (showing a cannon).

19-B. *It was the Mexican Constitutional Flag of 1824 representing the democratic government of Mexico that existed before General Santa Anna declared himself dictator. 1824 was the year Texas was* established as a state of Mexico. The "Come and Take It" flag—a cannon barrel and star on a white bedsheet—was raised over the town of Gonzales when word came that Lt. Francisco Castaneda intended to take back the cannon that had been loaned to the town. The first battle in Texas' war for independence resulted.

In conclusion. On April 21, six weeks after the Alamo defeat, Texians got their revenge on the Mexican army. At the Battle of San Jacinto, Sam Houston led 800 ragtag Texians—yelling "Remember the Alamo! Remember Goliad!"—into Santa Anna's encampment defeating 1,250 men in a battle that lasted just 18 minutes. 600 Mexican soldiers were killed and the rest captured, including the General. Only nine Texians lost their lives. Even though Santa Anna failed to squash the Texas revolution, he continued to hold various offices in the Mexican government until 1853 when his authoritarian government was overthrown. He died a powerless pauper in Mexico City in 1876. On March 2, 1836, while the battle at the Alamo was raging, the Texas Declaration of Indepen-

CAPTAIN DODSON FLAG

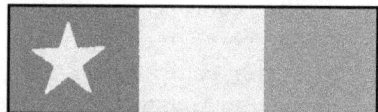

dence was signed by 59 Texians at Washington-on-the-Brazos, creating the Republic of Texas. The first words in the declaration read: *"When a government has ceased to protect the lives, liberty, and property of the people, from whom its legitimate powers are derived, and for the advancement of whose happiness it was instituted; and so far from being a guarantee for their inestimable and inalienable rights, becomes an instrument in the hands of evil rulers for their oppression..."*

Wayne Connors as Poncho Vega (dk)

SAN ANTONIO de VALERO

TIDBIT: The Mexican Army band at the Battle of the Alamo played *Degüello*, the "fire and death call" to signal Santa Anna's "give no quarter," plan to destroy all and take no prisoners. It was Demitri Tiomkin who scored the haunting "Degüello" for Howard Hawk's film *Rio Bravo* (1959) starring John Wayne. The next year Wayne hired Tiomkin and Paul Francis Weber to compose "The Green Leaves of Summer" for *The Alamo* (1960). The "Ballad of the Alamo" sung by Marty Robbins, which became a hit pop tune and which turned up on the soundtrack albums of the film, was never actually used in the movie.

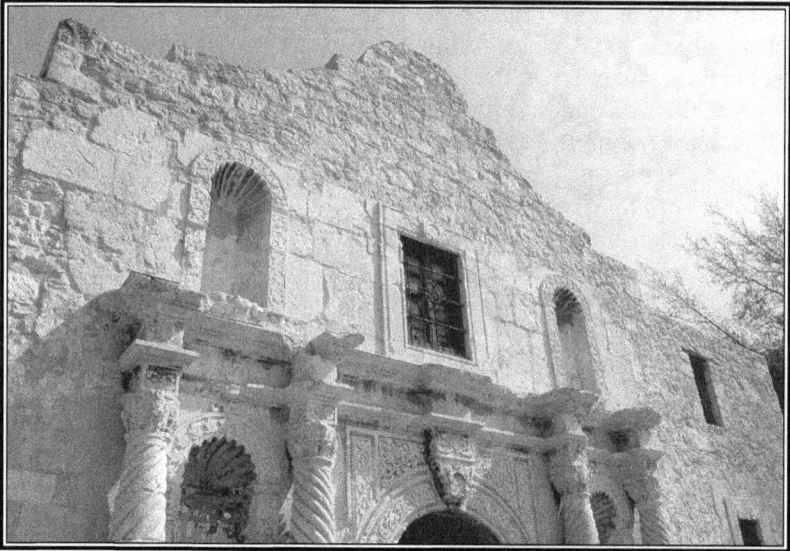

The Alamo chapel as it looks today, San Antonio, Texas (dk)

Originally named *Missión San Antonio de Valero,* the Alamo served for 70 years as the home to missionaries and their Indian converts. Today, it is Texas' No. 1 tourist destination with 2.5 million visitors every year.

A Match Game
5 ALAMO MOVIES

Match the Alamo films with the actor who played DAVY CROCKETT.

1. *The Alamo* (1960).
2. *The Last Command* (1955).
3. "Two For Texas" (1998).
4. "Davy Crockett: King of the Wild Frontier" (1955).
5. "The Alamo: Thirteen Days to Glory" (1987).
6. *The Alamo* (2004).

a. Arthur Hunnicutt
b. Fess Parker
c. John Wayne
d. Crockett not in movie
e. Billy Bob Thornton
f. Brian Keith

ANS: 1-c, 2-a, 3-d, 4-b, 5-f, 6-e.

A Ballad
THE MEN OF THE ALAMO
(aka: The Texans Took A Stand)
By Don Kirk, March 2000

A **true story of courage**—and a willingness to die for freedom—took place in an old abandoned Spanish mission in San Antonio, Texas. The heroism of 189 men willing to die in defense of liberty would enshrine that mission. The siege lasted thirteen days coming to an end on the sixth of March, 1836.

1. By now you've heard the story, of men who did not flee,
Of courageous men who died so Texans could be free.
They wanted for their fam'ly, their friends, and next of kin,
Prosperity and freedom, a chance to start again.

2. The nights were frigid during the spring of thirty-six,
And so, few men did busy themselves with politics.
They had some stock to tend to, and cabins they to mend,
A-tryin' best they might, to keep out that cold March wind.

3. At Washington-On-The-Brazos, a town of no import,
'Twas common men who huddled, around a stove of sorts,
A-jawin' in a manner, was heard across the town,
And what they would decide on, it soon would get aroun'.

4. "The self-proclaimed dictator, Gen'ral Santa Anna,
His terror over Texas, must it be our last hurrah?"
"Declare our, independence?" the questions they would ask,
To make a break with Mex'co, would be a daunting task.

5. They signed a constitution, a shout "Well done!" was heard,
Independence from Mexico, became the final word.
A free republic Texas, was soon to be a-born,
The men of the Alamo—we all were soon to mourn.

John Wayne as Davy Crockett in *The Alamo*, 1960, Batjac Productions (author's collection)

Tin Stars and Ten Galón Hats

6. Presidio la Bahia stood in a quiet glen,
There waited Colonel Fannin's four-hundred fifty men.
But Fannin chose not to march his men to San Antone,
The men of the Alamo—they all would be alone.

7. In San Antone de Bexar, there stood an old mission,
It lay in ruins a-crumblin'; it weren't no garrison.
There in the shadows waited, one-hundred fifty men,
Will Travis, Jimmy Bowie, and Crockett in buckskin.

8. Knives sharp and flintlocks loaded, prepared to take a stand,
The men of the Alamo, from all across this land.
Fur trappers, farmers, doctors—and lawyers of acclaim,
And men that couldn't read a word, or even mark their name.

9. Plumed hat and gaudy outfit, he thought himself the best,
The flamboyant and pompous, "Napoleon of the West."
Ol' Santa Anna bent he, on taking back his land,
To San Antone a-marchin', across the Rio Grande.

10. The interlopin' Anglos, he meant to send to Hell,
Ol' Santa Anna marchin', rebellion he would quell.
The trumpets blared a warnin', and fear was in the air.
Four-thousand men a-marchin', to San Antone de Bexar.

11. The strike of Santa Anna, no way could they withstand,
So General Sam Houston, thus issued this command:
"Abandon your position, you men are in a fix!
The men of the Alamo, are one to twenty-six."

12. For them to stay and fight on, would mean for certain death,
To leave the Alamo, meant liberty's last breath.
The men, they charged their flintlocks, a choosing they to stay,
The men of the Alamo, they did begin to pray.

13. He fired his eighteen-pounder, Will Travis did each day,
A-makin' clear as crystal, of what he had to say:
"No way shall we surrender, it's victory or death!
You bet we'll fight for freedom, to our last and final breath."

14. The mission flew the colors, of eighteen twenty-four,
It stood for Democracy, of which they wished restored.
Thus sent by Colonel Travis, a grave communiqué:
He asked for reinforcements, and they should not delay.

15. In the town of Gonzales, the cry for help was heard:
And thirty-two courageous, left home without a word.
They dropped their plows an' aprons, they left their wives behin',
The men of the Alamo, one-hundred-eighty-nine.

16. For twelve days neverending, they took the cannonade,
Keepin' four-thousand soldiers, beyond the palisade.
Each night they shored the walls of the lonely garrison,
Each night moved Santa Anna, his cannon closer in.

17. On the Fifth, Colonel Travis, he called his men all out:
He said, "There won't be any, reinforcements hereabout.
"You can all try an' sneak out, or fight 'til crack of doom."
For the men of the Alamo, daisies were not in bloom.

18. "And so, what will it be, boys?" Will Travis did pronounce,
"All men die, it's what we do 'afore we go that counts."
"'Tis no muddlement," said they, "we're all avowed to stay!"
The men of the Alamo—they all began to pray.

19. 'Twas dusk, and soon the cannon lay silent 'neath the moon,
And the *Degüello* played on, "no pris'ners" said the tune.
No sleep that soulful nighttide, they knew it was their last,
For liberty in Texas, they would have to stand fast.

20. The trumpets fell to silence, as morningtide did spring.
The sixth of March upon them, the birds began to sing,
A "BOOM" broke the morning tranquil, and startled birds they fled.
The men of the Alamo—they would real soon be dead.

21. A-charging on the compound, were twenty-six hundred men,
A-climbing timber ladders, the walls they wanted to win.
But they were driven backward, and away a-still again,
But finally the soldiers, they had a-broken in.

22. And bayonets were slashin', the Texans overran,
The Alamo defenders, they fought to the last man.
Their bodies bled a blood red, and then no more was said,
The men of the Alamo—they all were dead.

23. And just five days 'afore this—and they would never know—
That independence had been, declared from Mexico.
They would never know, a Republic was born,
The men of the Alamo—we all were soon to mourn.

24. The Alamo defenders, their stand for liberty,
Would give Gen'ral Sam Houston, the time to raise an army.
Santa Anna would be defeated at San Jacinto, boys!
His tail betwixt his legs, and sent home without his toys.

25. They didn't die for money, or honors on a flute,
They fought for liberty, and not for land or loot.
Remember the Alamo, as one they took a stand,
The Texans won your freedom—I hope you understand.

A REPUBLIC

In the words of John Wayne in *The Alamo*, 1960:

"Republic. I like the sound of the word. It means people can live free, talk free, go or come, buy or sell, be drunk or sober; however they choose. Some words give you a feeling. 'Republic' is one of those words that makes me tight in the throat. The same tightness a man gets when his baby takes his first step or his first baby shaves and makes his first sound like a man. Some words can give you a feeling that'll make your heart warm. Republic is one of those words."

Step Up To The Bar
JUDGE ROY BEAN

Vinegaroons scamper about on the Chihuahuan desert floor of West Texas, and just down the hill through the last remaining street of Langtry, is the meandering Rio Grande. The southern transcontinental railroad brought exuberant life to this area for a short moment in time.And with it came lawlessness in a tent city teeming with thousands of railroad workers that dictated the need for law and order—and a judge with an iron hand.Thankfully, Roy Bean filled the bill, though his method of dispensing justice—using a pistol and out-of-date law book—would make any legal mind turn over in his grave.

Judge Roy Bean in his later years
(Wikimedia Commons)

Judge Roy Bean, the youngest of three brothers, was a scoundrel from his earliest days; probably right out of his mother's womb. Born into a poor Kentucky family in 1825, he left for New Orleans at age 16 and was run out of town only to find himself in San Antonio where his brother Sam was a teamster hauling freight to Mexico. In 1848, they opened a trading post together and Roy promptly shot a Mexican desperado who threatened to kill a gringo. Any gringo. But Roy was to be first in line. Mexican authorities came after him so both brothers went north and then on to San Diego to live with their brother Joshua.There, handsome Bean, popular with the ladies, got into a quarrel with another suitor by the name of Collins who challenged Bean to a pistol shooting match on horseback. Collins told Bean he could pick the targets. Bean said they

Judge Roy Bean holding court at the Jersey Lilly, ca. 1900
(U.S. National Archives and Records Administration)

should shoot at each other! On February 24, 1852, the duel commenced and Collins was wounded in the right arm. Both men were then charged with assault with intent to murder and jailed. The ladies were crestfallen and visited him every day, bringing him gifts of flowers, wine, cigars, and their finest home cooking. But the final gift to Bean was some fine Mexican tamales—corn shucks filled with knives. Bean used the knives to chisel a hole through the adobe wall of his cell and make his escape— just two months after the iron door was slammed shut.

Roy Bean made his way to San Grabriel, where his brother Joshua now owned a saloon, and took a job as bartender, but seven months later, his brother was murdered and Bean inherited the saloon.

In 1854, Bean was courting a nice young lady who was kidnapped one evening and taken away and forced to marry a Mexican officer. Bean tracked them down and challenged the groom to a duel. Bean was faster and killed the officer. But it's never that easy to kill a man, and six of the officer's friends grabbed Bean and put him on a horse and pulled a noose over his head. The other end was tied to a tree branch. The men left Bean there, not wanting to actually witness the dirty deed, but the horse just stood there quietly. The officer's bride cut the rope and saved Bean, but he had a permanent rope burn on his neck and a permanent stiff neck. Bean left California and went to New Mexico to live with his brother Sam, now a respectable sheriff.

In 1862, during the American Civil War, the Texas army invaded New Mexico, but the army was repelled and retreated to San Antonio. Bean hooked up with the retreating army after "borrowing" traveling money from his brother's safe. With this experience, Roy became a blockade runner for the remainder of the war, hauling cotton from San Antonio to British ships docked off the coast of Matamoros, and then returning with supplies needed for the war.

Bean chose to stay in San Antonio after the war and ran a hauling business. He tried to run a business selling firewood, but he was found to be using a neighbor's timber. He then tried to run a diary operation, but was soon caught watering down the milk. He then tried his hand as a butcher, but again—the rogue that he was—he was caught rustling cattle from other area ranchers.

Somehow escaping the noose a second time, he married a pretty eighteen-year-old named Virginia Chavez. This was in 1866. Less than a year later Bean was arrested for aggravated assault on his wife, but continued to live and fight with her and have four children together. They lived in a "poverty-stricken Mexican slum called Beanville." Bean opened a saloon in Beanville that quickly became very profitable, and by the late 1870's several railroad companies were building lines west to California. Tent cities for the railroad workers would spring up at the head of the new construction and Bean could see the dollar signs. But

Adobe ruins at the hot and bone-dry Langtry next to the Rio Grande
where the most common creature scurrying around is the poisonous vinegaroon (dk)

Bean needed a grubstake for traveling money and a few kegs of beer. A neighboring store owner solved his problem by offering him $900 for his saloon and all his possessions, except his wife—Bean had already separated from Virginia and would soon divorce her. It was a good price; the store owner wanted the unscrupulous Bean out of town. Bean left all behind—including his children—purchased a tent, some supplies to sell, and ten 55-gallon barrels of cheap "rotgut" whiskey.

In the hot dry air of the spring of 1882, Bean had a well-established saloon near the Pecos River of West Texas in a tent city he named "Vinegaroon" after the large vicious scorpions that populated the area. 8,000 railroad workers were within twenty miles of his watering hole, but with these rowdy men came lawbreaking, and the nearest court was in Fort Stockton, 200 miles north. On August 2, 1882 the Texas Rangers set up a judicial district based in Vinegaroon and Bean was appointed Justice of the Peace for the newly established Pecos County Precinct 6.

Thus, Bean's tent saloon became a courtroom when needed. He declared himself the "Law West of the Pecos" and used one law book as a reference: the 1879 edition of the "Revised Statues of Texas." Any other law books that came his way, he would use as firewood. Bean dispensed his own form of justice. He did not tolerate hung juries or appeals to his rulings. And he chose his jurors from his best customers, expecting them to each buy a drink at every court recess, and there were plenty of those. He became known for his absurd and bizarre rulings, one of which was the case of an Irishman named Paddy O'Rourke who shot a Chinese track worker. An angry mob of his fellow Irish brethren surrounded the court tent, 200 strong, and threatened to lynch Judge Bean if O'Rourke was not freed forthwith. The man was clearly guilty, with many cousins of the chinaman testifying to the dirty deed, so Judge Bean turned to his 1879 law book and flipped through it looking hard for the appropriate case law. Soon, he found the legal definition that said "homicide was the killing of a human being," but for the life of him, he couldn't find a law against killing a chinaman. Bean promptly dismissed the case.

In 1882, Bean followed the railroad construction west, putting down stakes at Strawbridge, but a competing saloon owner spiked Bean's whiskey kegs with kerosene, sending Bean's customers to the competition and forcing him to move again to Eagle's Nest, twenty miles west of the Pecos River. More problems: the original owner of this property had sold a section of land to the railroad on the condition that no part of it be sold or leased to the wanton Roy Bean. But, as luck would have it, Irishman O'Rourke, the man he had acquitted years earlier, told Bean he could use the railroad right-of-way because it was not covered by the contract. For the next twenty years, Bean squatted on land that he actually had no legal right to claim and built himself a substantial saloon of lumber (a rare commodity in West Texas) and named it the *Jersey Lilly* in honor of Miss Lillie Langtry. Bean continued with his duties as Judge of District 6, but without a jail, all cases were settled with a fine. None of the court fines of money, horses, cows, or chickens was sent to the state. In most cases, the fine matched the amount the guilty party had in his pockets! In his entire career as Judge, Bean only sentenced two men to hang, and one of them escaped. Horse thieves were always let go if the horses were returned. As a Judge, he presided over weddings, collecting five dollars for each one and always ended the ceremony with "and may God have mercy on your souls." And, of course, to grant a divorce, he charged *ten* dollars.

In 1896, Judge Roy Bean organized a world championship boxing match between Bob Fitzsimmons and Peter Maher on an island in the middle of the Rio Grande, located there because boxing matches were illegal in Texas. Even though the fight lasted only one minute and 35 seconds, the resulting sports stories spread his fame throughout the United States. He died on March 16, 1903 of natural causes—if you call heavy drinking natural—and was buried in Del Rio, Texas, fifty miles east of Langtry. Langtry is now just a couple of buildings and a few ghostly adobe ruins, but Bean's original saloon is still standing at the Judge Roy Bean Visitor Center in Langtry.

"The Jersey Lilly" saloon, Langtry, Texas (dk). The saloon still sits next to the Rio Grande just off Hwy 90 eight miles west of the Pecos River. It is managed by the Texas Highway Department as a museum and is a great watering hole for passers-by.

The Southwest is an arid, desolate place where even the cacti have to struggle to survive.
The fact that some men also survive there, is a testament to their grit (dk).

JUDGE BEAN IN THE MOVIES

Some **Classic Quotes by Paul Newman** as **Judge Roy Bean** in the movie *The Life and Times of Judge Roy Bean*, 1972:

"The last time that bear ate a lawyer, he had the runs for thirty-three days."

"Ordinarily, I'd take you in my court and try you and hang you. But if you've got money for whiskey, I guess we can dispense with those proceedings."

Bean apologizing to the Marshal's wives: "I understand you have taken exception to my calling you whores. I'm sorry. I apologize. I ask you to note that I did not call you callous-ass strumpets, fornicatresses, or low-born gutter sluts. But I did say "whores." No escaping that. And for that slip of the tongue, I apologize."

"Oh, is that you, ma?" asked the little porcupine
as he backed into a cactus.

The author as "Float" Gibson in search of the Mother Lode, photo by Jo M. Hames

Gold Dust, Greed, and Gunpowder

Gold Dust, Greed, and Gunpowder
THE MINERS

"Gold don't carry any curse with it. It all depends on whether or not the guy who finds it is a right guy. The way I see it, gold can be as much of a blessing as a curse."
—Humphry Bogart, *Treasure of the Sierra Madre*, 1947

The discovery of gold at Sutter's Mill changed America. John Augustus Sutter, a profiteer with many get-rich schemes, managed to convince Mexican authorities in California that he was a Mexican (he was actually Swiss) and was granted 50,000 acres in the Sacramento Valley of California. With money from investors, he built Sutter's Fort—a walled-in hacienda—and raised cattle and horses, planted wheat and established vineyards. After the Mexican War—his business succeeding, dream realized—he began in 1848 to build two mills along the American River to grind his wheat into flower. But as luck would have it, James Marshal, the foreman of his construction crew, saw something shiny in the river. Lo and behold, it was Gold! John Sutter wanted the discovery kept secret until he could get legal title to the land, but word got out and the land was overrun with thousands of 49er gold seekers who destroyed hillsides, dammed up creeks, and stripped the land of all its resources. That was the end of his dream; the heartbroken Sutter went back east and died a pauper in 1880.

Trivia Question: Name three westerns that focus on the search for gold.
ANS: *Treasure of the Sierra Madre* (1948) Humphrey Bogart.
Mackenna's Gold (1969) Gregory Peck.
California Gold Rush (1985) Robert Hays.
"Where the Hell's That Gold?" (1990) Willie Nelson.
City Slickers II: Curly Bill's Gold (1994) Billy Crystal.

'Dillon Examiner', 20 September 1939
10 MINER'S COMMANDMENTS

"When the legend becomes fact, print the legend."
—The Man Who Shot Liberty Valance, 1962.

It is unknown whether this list of "laws" was written in jest, or is a serious comment on miner law, but it is true that the gold seekers found themselves so far from the established lawmakers and law enforcers of the East, that they had to script their own law to deal with the unique problems encountered in a mining district. Here then is one document of rules for the miner:

FIRST COMMANDMENT: Thou shalt have no other claim than one.

SECOND COMMANDMENT: Thou shalt not make thyself any false claims or any likeness to a mean man, by jumping one; for I, a miner, am a just man and I will visit the miners round about and they will judge thee; and when they shall decide thou wilt take thy pick thy pan thy shovel and thy blankets and with all thou hast thou shalt depart to seek other diggings but thou shalt find none.

THIRD COMMANDMENT: Thou shalt not go prospecting before thy claim gives out. Neither shalt thou take thy money, or gold dust, or thy good name to the gaming table for monte, twenty-one, roulette, faro, lunsquent, and poker will prove thee that the more thou puttest down the less thou shalt take up and when thou thinkest of thy wife and children thou shalt hold thyself guiltless though insane.

FOURTH COMMANDMENT: Thou shalt keep the Sabbath day holy and shall do no work other than cooking the pork and beans for the week's supply, getting in firewood and doing the week's wash and baking the week's supply of bread.

SIXTH COMMANDMENT: Thou shalt not drink mint juleps nor sherry cobblers through a straw nor gurgle from a bottle the raw materials nor take it from a decanter; for while thou are swallowing down thy purse and the coat from thy back thou art burning the coat off thy stomach.

SEVENTH COMMANDMENT: Thou shalt not grow discouraged and think of going home before thou hast made thy pile because thou hast not struck a lead, nor found a rich crevice nor sunk a shaft upon a rich pocket, lest in going home thou shalt leave a job paying four dollars a day to take, ashamed, a job back East at 50 cents a day; and serve thee right. Thou knowest that by staying here thou mightest strike a lead and make 50 dollars a day and keep thy self-respect and when thou goest home thou shalt have enough to make thyself and others happy.

EIGHTH COMMANDMENT: Thou shalt not steal the dust or the tools of another miner, for he will surely find out what thou hast done and will call together his fellow miners and they, unless the law hinders them, will hang thee or give thee fifty lashes, or shave thy head or brand thy cheek with an "R" like a horse, to be read by all men.

NINTH COMMANDMENT: Thou shalt tell no false tales about good diggins in the mountains, to benefit a friend who may have mules, blankets, or provisions and tools that he wishes to sell lest thy neighbor, deceived by thee into making the trip shall one day return through the snow with naught left but his rifle, contents of which he shall present to you in a manner that shall cause thee to fall down and die like a dog.

TENTH COMMANDMENT: Remember thy wife and children that are in the East and be true to them in thought, word and deed. Avoid the temptation to become a squaw-man and to people this country with half-breeds, for while there is naught to be said against these boys and girls as individuals, the fact remains that they will give the Indians the benefit of their white training and thus make the redskins more dangerous to the white man.

(Note that there is no "Fifth Commandment." It can only be assumed the writer considered the Bible's Fifth Commandment "thou shalt not kill," was good enough as it stood.)

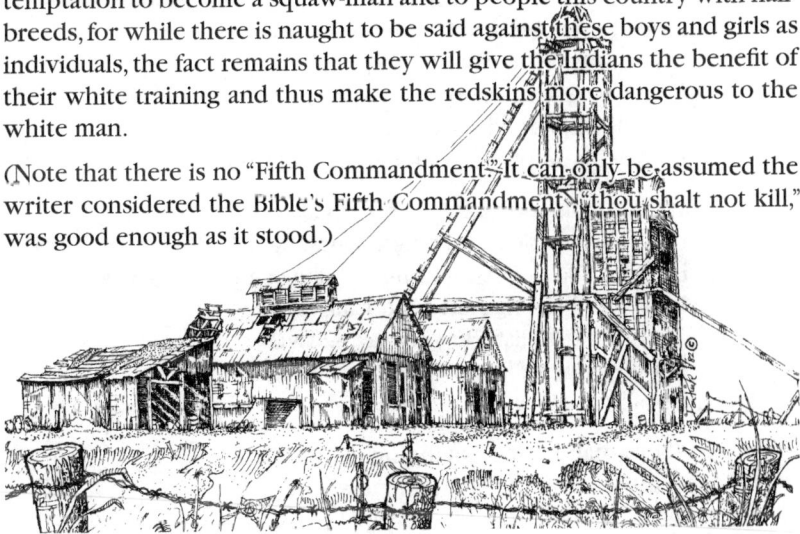

A Mining Poem
CONSTANT FEAR
By Don Kirk

Free verse inspired by an article in "The Miners" of the *The Old West* Series of Time-Life books that expresses what it was like to work deep in a mine in the Comstock diggings around Virginia City, Nevada in the 1860's.

I board the tiny iron cage for my second shift,
And the mine's steam-driven hoist
Lowers me swiftly to fifteen-hundred feet—
The bell sounds and the elevator jerks to a stop.
Flickering candles and tin lamps light my weary way.
With lunch pail in hand, I follow the narrow-gauge tracks
Down a mile of tunnels shored up by heavy, vital timbers.

Sweat pours from my tired, wrinkled brow,
My body drenched with salty sweat;
The temperature a-sweltering one hundred or more.
Bared to the waist, 'tis my white marbled body
Glistening in the cavern candlelight.
I wear tattered underpants cut back to the knees,
And old shoes and a wore-out hat; 'tis all I wear
In the dark depths of that damned 'ol Comstock.

Staring at the dull, bluish-gray silver ore,
I take up my pick, and take my first swing;
Hot chips leap forth searing me like campfire embers,
And from blasting holes and rock crevasses,
Gushes forth blistering-hot groundwater,
But the cool air forced in from the surface,
Does little to relieve the sultriness of this Turkish bath.

A long, half hour of swinging my pick,
And then a short, half-hour's rest.
A few quenching pints of water,

And cooling ice to swirl in my mouth.
Then another half-hour swinging my pick.

The walls of this man-made cavern sparkle like diamonds,
But the silver I chip, glistens not,
'Tis just the iron and copper pyrite that mesmerizes—
Oh, but I must not linger. I must not stop.
I must swing my pick and my sledgehammer,
I must push an ore car and shovel rock as the boss commands;
As another soul is always a-waitin' to take my place
At four dollar an hour.

I must stay sharp to survive my shift
So that I can blow my wages on the devil's drinkin'—
And the company of those fine young ladies a-waitin' above.
I must stay sharp to make it back to Mother Earth's sunlight,
For a misstep and fall
Into one-hundred-sixty-degree groundwater
Would leave my skin a-sliding off my bones like
Chicken a-boiling on a hot stove.
I must stay sharp.
A ricocheting fall through the square sets
Would leave me as just so many body parts to be
Scraped up with a ten-cent shovel—
Little pieces of me to be rolled into canvas,
And hoisted to the surface with a rusty-ole' grapplin' hook.

And yet the possibility of a sudden cave-in
Unsettles me so much more,
As I can do nothing to prevent that unspeakable horror;
'Tis only the superintendent can uphold the engineer's say,
And if the timber framing is not built just so,
The clay deposits a-swellin' on exposure to the ouside air
Could push the timbers to a dooming failure.

When I sit down to eat my mid-shift meal,
I can see in the shadows of the mine,
The gleaming eyes of the tunnel rats a-waitin',
A-waitin' for the food scraps I leave behin'.
The groaning and creaking of the timbers,
'Tis a first warning of a cave-in,
Along with those forever-feasting rats,
Who will suddenly scurry madly about—
'Tis the only warning I shall have.

Just enough to make my heart skip a beat,
For me to take hopeless heed of my inevitable end.

And then there is fire,
The horrible inferno of a sudden burst of flame from
A blacksmith's forge or a carelessly attended candle.
Without warning,
A flickering candle might set a timber ablaze,
Or ignite a pocket of explosive gas.
And I'd never again,
See the sweet smiles of the pretty ladies on "D" Street, or
Enjoy the fellowship of the raucous men at Marty Muldoon's.
Or maybe, just maybe,
There'd be a-blasting charge go off a'fore twas ready,
Or a miner's tools a-tumbling down a mine shaft to
Whack me senseless one last time.
Or just maybe,
Flood waters will pour into the diggin's
To drown me with all those other damned wretched rats.
Without warning. Yes, without warning—
I strike the rock with my pick.

Everyone wanted in on the action.
Actual issued shares of mining stock. Worthless now. Author's collection.

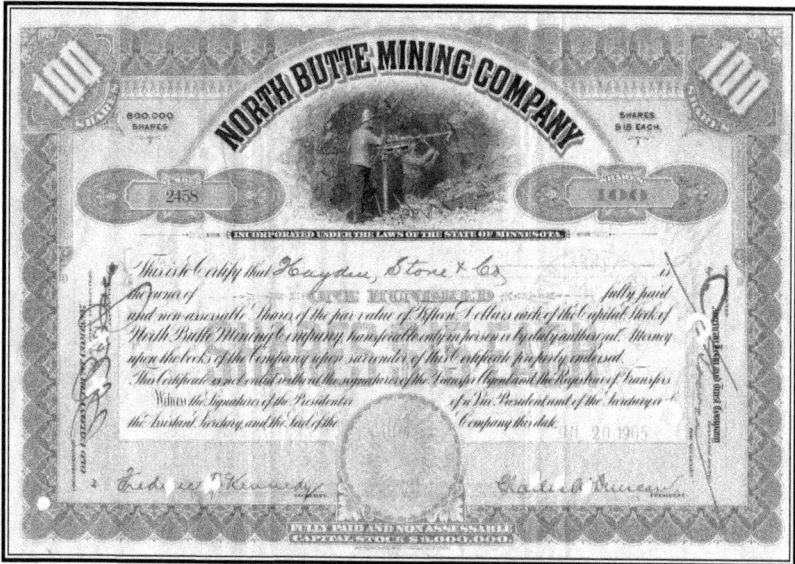

TRICKS TO SALTING A MINE

One way to salt a mine—to make a played-out mine look as if it's the next "mother lode,"—was to use "The Gun That Won the West": the shotgun! Instead of buckshot, a shotgun would be loaded with gold dust and a sucker then easily found. But to fool non-believers who insisted on seeing more of a claim, the hornswaggler would blast out the face of a tunnel of the prospective buyer's choosing, and the victim would find, sure enough, beautiful flakes of gold. How was this done? The dynamite sticks were pre-laced with gold dust by the salter; the explosion would embed a convincing amount of gold into the rock. One wary chinaman was bamboozled when this classic con was executed: on being shown the mine by a seller carrying a shotgun for protection, the chinaman was allowed to pick the spot to dig for gold. Before he grabbed his pick, the seller suddenly shot at a deadly snake flopping about in front of the chinaman. The chinaman graciously thanked the seller for saving his life. The Chinaman indeed found gold, but unbeknownst to him, a hiding cohort had thrown the snake into the scene, creating the excuse for the conman to fire his shotgun loaded with gold dust. Another common trick: A passing drunkard would stagger up to a pile of ore samples pulled from the mine, would trip and break his whiskey bottle on the pile and wander off. Finding gold, the sucker would buy the claim, not aware that the "drunk" was cold sober when he shattered his bottle filled with gold salts.

21 MINING TOWNS OF THE WEST

Bisbee, AZ	Goldfield, NV	Rawhide, NV
Bodie, CA	Helena, MT	South Pass, WY
Butte, MT	Hermosa, NM	Telluride, CO
Central City, CO	Leadville, CO	Terlingua, TX
Chloride, AZ	Moscow, ID	Tonopah, NV
Cripple Creek, CO	Ophir, UT	Tombstone, AZ
Coer d'Alene, ID	Orogrande, NM	Virginia City, NV

Say What?
33 WORDS OF THE MINER

The discovery of gold and silver in the American West made a significant contribution to it's rapid settlement. As in any profession, special terminology is needed to define the materials and operations of placer and hard-rock mining. Just a few are defined here.

1. Adit. The horizontal opening in a hillside that provides access to the vertical shaft of a mine and by which water and ore can be hauled out.

2. Assay. To determine the metal content of a mineral or ore.

3. Bonanza. Spanish term for good luck or prosperity; a rich vein or pocket of ore or anything which yields a large income.

4. Claim Jumper. One who illegally takes possession of another man's homestead or mine claim from the prior and rightful owner.

5. Color. Those tiny particles of gold that appear after shaking out a gold pan.

6. Cradle. Screened rocker used to wash gold from dirt and gravel.

7. Cribbing. Heavy-timbered crate-like construction used to support structures on sloping

Timber cribbing, Victor, Colorado (dk)

sites or to line a shaft to prevent cave-ins.

8. Diggings. The area being dug up in search of gold or silver, usually along the banks of a creek.

9. Dredge. A mechanical or hydraulic device used to dig up creek and river beds to find gold. The gravel is fed into sluices to separate the color (photo at right).

10. El Dorado. A place in the West where gold was found, or said to be.

11. Eureka. A Greek word meaning "I have found it." The excla-

Flume, Leadville, Colorado (dk)

mation was allegedly used by Archimedes when he discovered a way to determine the purity of gold. The word became the miners outcry of joy when they found gold. Many mining towns of the West now bear that name.

12. Flume. In placer mining, an inclined box made of wood and supported by a trestle, for conveying water to a site to wash gravel.

13. Fool's Gold. A bright yellow-orange metal called iron pyrite that looks like gold to the uninitiated, but is worthless. It is hard and brittle, not soft and malleable like gold. If the metal turns darker when wetted, it's not gold!

14. Forty-niner. The name given to a man who went West to hunt for gold in California.

15. Grubstake. To provide a miner with food and supplies in exchange for a portion of the findings of his prospecting.

16. Hard-rock Mining. Mining where drilling and blasting is required to break up the rock to get at the valuable ore.

17. Headframe. A metal or timber frame with a large pulley at the top which is situated over a mine shaft and allows the cage containing men and materials to be hoisted up out of the ground. Also called a *gallows*.

18. Hoist Shack. The building behind the *headframe* which houses the hoist winch and power source.

Dredge, Sumpter Valley, Oregon (dk)

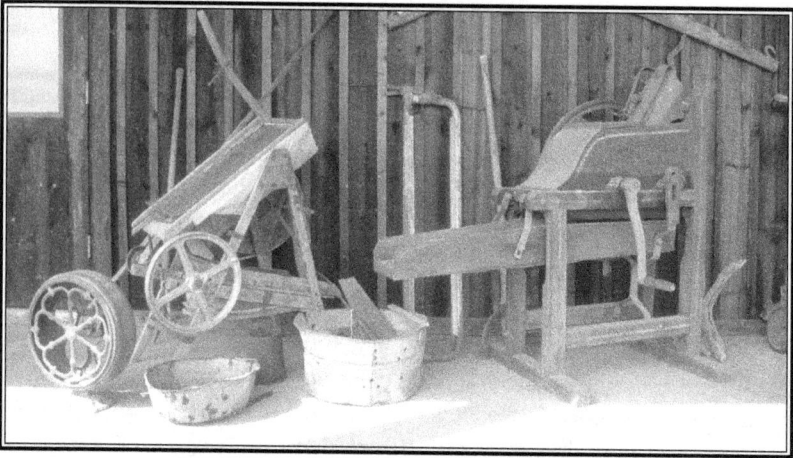

Cradles at Robson's Arizona Mining World, Aguila, Arizona (dk)

19. Hydraulic Mining. The use of a high pressure nozzle to spray a powerful stream of water at gravel along a creek bed to force it into a flume to shake out gold.

20. Lode. A fissure filled with ore-bearing matter. The *mother lode* was said to be the biggest and original source of all the other rich deposits.

21. Long Tom. A long (12 to 20 foot) trough that widens at the lower end and can shake out a lot more gold than the smaller *cradle.*

22. Mining District. A designated area, and given a name, where a concentration of mining activities can be found.

23. Ore Car. A cart on four wheels made of wood or metal that sits on a narrow track; used for moving ore out of a mine.

24. Pay Dirt. Dirt rich in precious minerals. "Hitting pay dirt": turning dirt into money.

25. Panning. To use a gold pan (similar to a pie tin) to separate gold from the sand or gravel at the bottom of creeks and rivers.

26. Placer Mining. The mining of active streambeds or glacial deposits of gravel or sand containing heavy ore minerals such as gold, platinum, etc. which have been eroded from their original bedrock and concentrated as

Hoist Winch, Victor, Colorado (dk)

Ore Car, Victor, Colorado (dk)

fine particles or flakes that can be washed out with a miner's pan.

27. Rocker. A wooden box like a *cradle,* but with a sheet-metal bottom perforated with small holes that prevent the gold nuggets from falling through. To capture small grains of gold, mercury on a metal plate would bond to the gold and could be heated later to separate it.

28. Salting a Mine. Planting gold or silver ore in a worthless mine to attract unwary investors. Shavings from a gold watch could be packed into a shotgun shell and fired into a wall.

29. Shaft. A vertical (or slanted) tunnel giving access to underground mining operations.

30. Sluice Box. A wooden trough through which gold-bearing gravel is washed to separate the gold from the gravel. Gravel is shoveled into the box which has ridges that catch the heavier gold particles as a stream of water runs across it.

31. Stamp Mill. A mechanical device that uses large weights on a camshaft to crush ore in order to get at the valuable minerals. It was usually powered by steam engines or waterwheels (below).

32. Tailing. Waste or refuse in various processes of milling, mining, distilling, etc. It can be seen as huge piles of rust-colored or gray gravel in front of old mine shafts. In the 1980's when the price of gold went up, these tailings were "re-worked." When gold went over $1,000 an ounce, surface mining operations ripped off entire mountain tops.

33. Timbering. The wooden supports and braces used to "shore up" or stabilize mine tunnels and underground workings.

Stamp Mill, Fairplay, Colorado (dk)

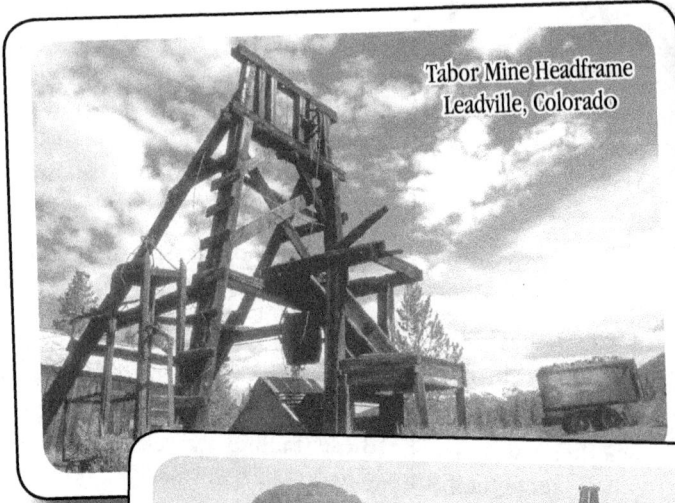
Tabor Mine Headframe
Leadville, Colorado

Photo
Album:
Of
Hard-
rock
Mining
(dk)

Vulture Gold Mine, Wickenburg, Arizona

Mining District, South Park, Wyoming

Mining Operation near Maysville, Colorado

Ore Bin, Tonopah, Nevada

Large Ore Bin, Tonopah, Nevada

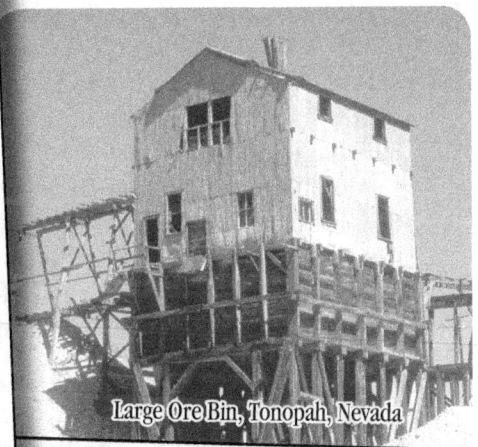

Argo Gold Mine and Mill, Idaho Springs, Colorado

THE LOST DUTCHMAN MINE

In the sixteenth-century, Spaniards mined gold and silver from hundreds of mines and then moved it by pack train to Mexico City. This territory, it turned out, was sacred Indian land with limited food resources and the large Spanish armies soon overstayed their welcome and the Indians sent them packing. The Spaniards had hoped to return (but never did), and legend has it, to hide their precious discoveries, they covered the entrances to their mines. A Mexican citizen named *Miguel Peralta* operated several gold mines in Sonora and Arizona and in the 1840's, on hearing of the impending Treaty of Guadalupe Hidalgo—the treaty that would grant the northern part of Mexico to the United States—he hoped he could find the Spaniards' gold and extract as much of it as possible. With an expedition train of 400 men, he located several mines and loaded up what gold he could—all the while fighting marauding Indians. What he couldn't carry, he hid near the mines, and this is some of the gold still being looked for today.

The most famous of the lost mines, the Lost Dutchman, is in the rugged Superstition Mountains east of Phoenix, Arizona. *Jacob Waltz,* a Prussian immigrant, was headed for the California gold fields when in 1870— legend has it—he saved the life of *Don Miguel Peralta II* in a cantina fight in Arizpe, Mexico. Peralta gave Waltz a map of a gold mine his grandfather had discovered in the Superstition Mountains. Waltz and a partner found the mine and recovered $60,000 in gold ore before Apache Indians attacked and killed the partner. Waltz left after covering the entrance to find another partner to help, but he never returned, dying in Phoenix in 1891. Left with conflicting information about trails and landmarks, treasure hunters are still looking for the Lost Dutchman.

Independence Mine, Victor, Colorado, 1980 (dk)

A Match Game
10 MINER'S SLANG WORDS

Match the miner's slang term with its meaning.

1.	Widow Maker	**a.**	Hoisting bucket.
2.	Granny Bar	**b.**	A water wheel.
3.	Kibble	**c.**	Work area at end of a tunnel.
4.	Hurdy-Girdy	**d.**	A fellow miner.
5.	Wife	**e.**	An ore thief.
6.	Powder Hand	**f.**	A horizontally drilled hole.
7.	Shovel Stiff	**g.**	A large crowbar.
8.	High Grader	**h.**	Worker who handles explosives.
9.	Gopher Hole	**i.**	Drill used for excavating.
10.	Bridal Chamber	**j.**	Man who works a shovel.

ANS: 1-i, 2-g, 3-a, 4-b, 5-d, 6-h, 7-j, 8-e, 9-f, 10-c.

A Mining Poem
THE CAVE-IN
By Don Kirk, September 2010

Free verse based on Frank Crampton's true story of a cave-in outlined in *The Miners*, The Old West Series of Time-Life books. Crampton was a hard-rock miner who was there and lived to tell the tale.

The sharp sounds of snapping timbers
And then a low-pitched overwhelming rumble
That wants to swallow your soul.
Sand sifts through the fissures above,
Then silence.

And "Swoosh!"
A violent rush of thunderous air.
Carbide lamps are blown out and darkness descends.
"A cave-in!" screams a miner.
Men are trapped. No place to run.
Their only exit to the world of the living,
Now blocked.
Tons of the Mother Lode has plugged the tunnel.

Blackness.

Then a calming kind of fear;
The panic of reality not yet realized.
The stale air full of blasting smoke, choking dust,
And the funk of wet timber.
There's plenty of potable water,
But only one lunch pail of Cornish pastie,
And but a few hours of hope-filled candlelight.

As they wait for help to come,
The men fashion crude violins
From powder cases and shoelaces,
And a flute from a rusty piece of pipe.
They stumble through songs like, "I've seen the Elephant,"
And "Only a Miner Killed."

They can hear the far-off rumblings of the rescue party,
But frequent blasts that reverberate in their tiny tomb
Tell them it will take weeks to cut through
The hard rock they know so well.

They know
That water dripping incessantly
Into their claustrophobic coffin
Will surely drown them like rats
Long before rescuers could ever arrive.

Boom!
A loud concussion blows out their candles
As if a spirit of the afterlife has arrived,
And their soggy matches are found to be useless.
Darkness has returned.
Absolute darkness.
They cannot see their hands in front of their faces;
They cannot see their comrade's places.

And then comes the maddening sound of ticking watches,
Growing louder, and louder, engulfing their senses,
Louder, and louder,
Like Poe's beating heart, everlasting.
'Tis maddening, oh, so maddening!
"Enough!" they scream aloud.
Everyone surrenders their prized pocket watch
And drops it into a pool of blistering hot water.

The sweltering heat is stifling;
They rid themselves of their water-soaked clothing,
And sit there, just sit there,
Knees to their chests, teeth chattering,
Muscles sore and weak, jaws aching.

They are no longer singing or playing their crude violins.

They are just sitting in the silence of darkness.
No sense of time, only of place:
Purgatory in all its horrifying glory.
Then bam! Bam!
BANG!
A shriek of pain is heard,
In the darkness, a man is falling, falling, falling—

Bouncing off the timbers.
Down, down, down he goes.
A long, very long, very loud scream.
And then silence.

A deadly silence.
A broken mind.
One of the miners could take it no more.

Days more pass.
And then,
A rush of chilling air.
And a man distant shouting, "Cover your eyes!"
"We're over here!" scream they all.
"How many of you?"
"All but one."

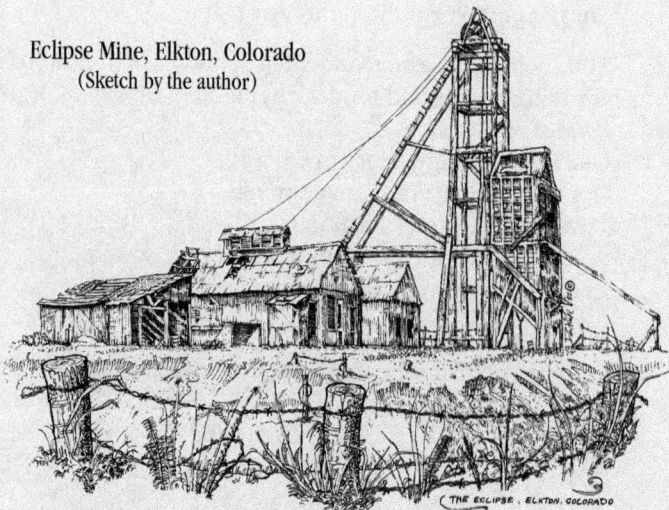

Eclipse Mine, Elkton, Colorado
(Sketch by the author)

12 ACTUAL MINING TOWN NAMES

Coyote Diggings	Grisley Flats	Mad Mule Gulch
Bedbug	Poker Flat	Murderer's Bar
Whiskey Diggins	You Bet	Last Chance
Shirt Tail Canyon	Chinatown	Delerium Trimmings

A Match Game
8 MINING CLAIMS

Match the date and discoverer of important gold or silver finds to the location that is now famous.

1. Discovered January 1848 by James Marshal.
2. Discovered July1858 by Green Russell & Sam Bates.
3. June 1859 by Peter O'Riley & Patrick McLaughlin.
4. Discovered in 1874.
5. Discovered in 1875 by Michael Hickey.
6. Discovered in 1875 by John Fallon.
7. Discovered in June 1877 by Ed Schieffelin.
8. Discovered August 1896 by Skookum Jim Mason and party.

a. The Comstock Lode, Virginia City, Nevada (silver & gold).
b. (Black Hills Gold Rush), Deadwood, Dakota Territory.
c. Sutter's Mill (California Gold Rush), Coloma, California.
d. Butte, Montana, (silver & copper).*
e. Bonanza/Rabbit Creek (The Klondike Gold Rush), Dawson City, Yukon Territory.
f. Cherry Creek Diggings (Pike's Peak Gold Rush), Denver, Colorado.
g. Tombstone, Arizona Territory (silver).**
h. Marshall Basin, Telluride, Colorado (gold).

ANS: 1-c, 2-f, 3-a, 4-b, 5-d, 6-h, 7-g, 8-e.

*When Michael Hickey discovered silver in **Butte**, he found little of it to make it a profitable enterprise, and sold his Anaconda mine for $70,000 in 1881. The worthless "red metal" he found among the silver had just been a nuisance. It wasn't until electricity created a new market for copper wire that the huge mountain of copper made the new owners very rich. By 1892, the Anaconda had become the greatest single copper producer in the world.

The town of **Tombstone got its name when Ed Schieffelin, a prospector, was warned by a passing soldier that the only rock he would find in these dry hills was a tombstone, his, because of the very unfriendly Apache. When Ed hit pay dirt, he gave his mining claim the name "Tombstone."

THE SOURDOUGH

How did the prospector acquire the slang name "sourdough?" A miner valued highly his bread starter (made from flour, water, and yeast*). Without it bread was flat like hardtack and there would be no flapjacks and biscuits. So the miner kept the starter close to his body in a pouch or pot hung around his neck or tucked into his long johns to keep the yeast alive (yeast is dormant in cold weather). The result was a "miner you could smell coming from a mile away!"

*Yeast exists in the air and comes from alcohol, vinegar or berries.

An 1880s Miner's Poem
ONLY A MINER KILLED
By John Wallace Crawford

This song came about after an incident on the day the ostentatious mining king, Commodore Vanderbilt, died (January 4, 1877) and the newspapers were giving full coverage of the deceased multi-millionaire when, at the same time, a wagon rolled quietly down the main street of Virginia City with an unknown dead miner draped in a dirty canvas (a poor man's funeral procession). When the driver was asked by an onlooker what was the matter, the reply was "Oh, it's only a miner killed." The Virginia City Chronicle reported this incident and published the following verses that later, it is believed, Crawford turned into a song.

1. Only a miner killed—oh! is that all?
One of the timbers caved, great was the fall,
Crushing another one shaped like his God.
Only a miner lad—under the sod.

2. Only a miner killed, just one more dead.
Who will provide for them—who'll earn their bread?—
Wife and little ones: pity them, God,
Their earthly father is under the sod.

3. Only a miner killed, dead on the spot,
Poor hearts are breaking in yonder lone cot.
He died at his post, a hero as brave
As any who sleeps in a marble top grave.

4. Only a miner killed! God, if thou wilt,
Just introduce him to Vanderbilt,
Who, with his millions, if he is there,
Can't buy one interest—even one share.

5. Only a miner, bury him quick;
Just write his name on a piece of a stick.
Though humble and plain be the poor miner's grave
Beyond, all are equal, the master and slave.

21 EXISTING MINES AND MINING MUSEUMS

MINES
Victor Mining District, Cripple Creek, AZ
Vulture Gold Mine, Wickenburg, AZ
Mollie Kathleen Gold Mine, Cripple Creek, CO
The Queen Copper Mine, Bisbee, AZ
Argo Gold Mill, Idaho Springs, CO
Hundred Gold Mine, Silverton, CO
Bachelor-Syracuse Mine, Ouray, CO
Blue Bell Mine, Eureka, UT
Maude Munroe Mine, Bodie, CA
The Standard Mill, Bodie, CA
Sunnyside Mine and Mill, Silverton, CO
Edger Mine, Idaho Springs, CO
Phoenix Mine, Idaho Springs, CO

MUSEUMS
Tonapah Mining Museum, Tonapah, NV
District Mining Museum, Cripple Creek, CO
Robson's Arizona Mining World, Aguila, AZ
Old Coal Mine Museum, Madrid, NM
Arizona Mining and Mineral Museum, Phoenix, AZ
Jerome State Historic Park, Jerome, AZ
New Mexico Museum of Mining, Grants, NM
Western Museum of Mining and Industry, Colorado Springs, CO
Ore-Bucket Tramway, Pioche, NV.

Just a fact: Mining was probably the most abusive use of land in the history of the world. Waterways were polluted with the heavy metals mined from deep within the bowels of the earth and the landscape stripped of all vegetation, causing horrendous erosion. The trees were cut into huge timbers to shore up mine tunnels and the cord wood was used to fuel the stoves and huge steam engines needed to raise men and ore. The contaminated ground water was dumped into the rivers to be drunk by townspeople downstream.

A Ballad
THE DREARY BLACK HILLS
TRADITIONAL

From the Black Hills of Dakota, we find this 1874 gold-rush ballad. General George Custer spread the word back East that there was "gold in them thar hills," and the Easterners "came a-runnin,'" but the U.S. government had made a treaty with the Sioux guaranteeing their sacred lands would be protected from encroachment by white settlers. But the interlopers looking for gold, quickly overran the hills, and that eventually led to the fall of Custer's Seventh Cavalry, and the fall of many women and children at Wounded Knee. It turns out there was not much gold there; an officer of the Northern Pacific Railroad in cahoots with Custer, started the gold rush just to stimulate railroad business!

1. Kind friends won't you listen to my horrible tale,
I'm an object of pity and I'm feelin' quite stale,
I gave up my job selling Wright's Patent Pills,
To go hunting for gold in the dreary Black Hills.
CHORUS
Don't go away, stay to home if you can,
Stay away from that city—they call it Cheyenne,
Where Chief Crazy Horse and old Sittin' Bull,
They'll lift up your scalps in the dreary Black Hills.

2. As I went out ridin' one morning in May,
I spied old Kit Carson— he was ridin' away,
He was riding out west with Buffalo Bill,
Gone to huntin' the gold in the dreary Black Hills.

3. The roundhouse at Cheyenne is filled every night,
With loafers and bummers of most every plight,
On their backs is no clothes, in their pockets no bills,
Each day they keep startin' for the dreary Black Hills.

4. When I got to Cheyenne no gold could I find,
I thought of the lunch route that I'd left behind,

Through rain, hail, and snow—froze plumb to the gills,
They called me the orphan of the dreary Black Hills.

5. I wish that the man that started this sell,
Was captive, and Crazy Horse had him in hell,
But there's no use moanin' or swearin' like pitch,
'Cause the man who'd stay here is a son of a bitch.

6. And so, my kind friends, this advice I'll unfold,
Don't go to them Black Hills a-diggin' for gold,
For the railroad speculators, their pockets you'll fill,
From takin' that trip to the dreary Black Hills.

THE TOMMYKNOCKERS

They lived deep in hard-rock mines and were at times helpful, but also meted out the worst of luck. Brought to the West by Cornishmen—experienced miners from Cornwall, England—these Leprechaun-like creatures would make tapping sounds in the mines to tell the miners where the rich ore lay. Some men feared the knocks they heard were the spirits of men trying to dig their way out of a cave-in, but most felt the mischievous Tommyknockers would always warn the men of coming disasters, giving them time to escape. So food was left behind for the little critters, and pity the poor man who didn't. The Tommyknockers were pranksters, blowing out candles, dropping rocks on men's heads, and hiding the miner's tools. These jokesters are still frolicking in the mines today, and miners still listen for their tapping sounds, and leave food scraps behind.

North To Alaska
By Johnny Horton

Country music singer Johnny Horton (1925-1960) recorded this "historical ballad" for John Wayne's 1960 hit film *North to Alaska*.

Way up north (North to Alaska)
Way up north (North to Alaska)
North to Alaska, you go North, the rush is on.
North to Alaska, I go North, the rush is on.

Big Sam left Seattle in the year of ninety-two,
With George Pratt, his partner, and brother Billy, too.
They crossed the Yukon river and found the Bonanza gold,
Below that old White Mountain, just a little southeast of Nome.

Sam crossed the majestic mountains to the valley far below.
He talked to his team of huskies as he mushed on through the snow,
With the northern lights a-running wild in the land of the midnight sun.
Yes, Sam McCord was a mighty man in the year of nineteen-one.

CHORUS
Where the river is winding,
Big nuggets they're finding.
North to Alaska,
To go north, the rush is on.

George turned to Sam with his gold in his hand,
Said: "Sam, you're a-lookin' at a lonely, lonely man.
I'd trade all the gold that's buried in this land
For one small band of gold to place on sweet little Jenny's hand.

'Cause a man needs a woman to love him all the time.
Remember, Sam, a true love is so hard to find.
I'd build for my Jenny, a honeymoon home,
Below that old White Mountain,
Just a little southeast of Nome."

CHORUS
North to Alaska,
To go north, the rush is on.
Way up north (North to Alaska)

Law books and a saxaphone (dk)

Guitar, Songbook, and Chewin' Tobaccie

Guitar, Songbook, and Chewin' Tobaccie
MORE WESTERN BALLADS

"Popular cowboy songs generated innumerable variations and verses as different singers forgot, altered, or added to the lyrics."
— Richard W. Slatta, The Cowboy Encyclopedia

Cowboys on the range, herding cattle many miles by day, would graze them quietly at night. The cows had to be kept calm to reduce the chances of a stampede. A thunderstorm or wolf yelp could mean the loss of their prized beef on the hoof. Cowhands found that singing to the doggies would calm their fears and possibly prevent a catastrophe.

A ballad is a song or poem that tells a story in short stanzas and simple words, and uses repetition and refrain. Perfect for the cowboy on the range. Most old ballads are of unknown authorship and have been handed down orally—across many generations—usually with additions and changes that make them more interesting and quaint. Close adherence to the rules of poetry was never a concern of the cowboy. If it sounded good and he could add a few "da-da's" to make the rhythm work, then so be it.

I included ballads throughout the book, but this chapter has a few I thought appropriate to this book, but wouldn't fit elsewhere.

Photo of the author by Glynda Smith

A Ballad
HOME ON THE RANGE
By Dr. Brewster Higley

We all know the first verse and the chorus, but who knows the rest of this famous cowboy ballad? Few people know where the song actually came from. The ballad was first published in 1873 as a poem called "Western Home" written by a Kansas physician by the name of Brewster Higley. Dan Kelly, a friend and Civil War veteran, put the poem to music. (Note: In the ballad, "zephyrs" are soft, gentle breezes, and a "curlew" is a brownish wading bird with a long bill that curves downward, similar to a sandpiper.)

Oh, give me a home where the buffalo roam,
Where the deer and the antelope play.
Where seldom is heard a discouraging word,
And the skies are not cloudy all day.

Home, home on the range,
Where the deer and the antelope play.
Where seldom is heard a discouraging word,
And the skies are not cloudy all day.

Where the air is so pure and the zephyrs so free,
And the breezes so balmy and light.
Then I would not exchange my home on the range,
For all of your cities so bright.

The red man was pressed from his part of the West,
And he's likely no more to return,
To the banks of Red River, where seldom, if ever,
Their flickering campfires burn.

How often at night when the heavens are bright,
With the light from the glittering stars.
Here I stood there amazed, and asked as I gazed,
If their glory exceeds that of ours.

I love the wild flowers in this dear land of ours,
And the curlew I love to hear scream.
I love the wild rocks and the antelope flocks,
That graze on the mountain tops green.

Oh give me a land where the bright diamond sand,
Flows leisurely down the stream.
Where the graceful white swan goes sliding along,
Like a maid in a heavenly dream.

A Ballad

GOVERNMENT CLAIM

Traditional

How happy I am on my government claim
Where I've nothing to lose and nothing to gain.
Nothing to eat and nothing to wear
Nothing from nothing is honest and square.

But here I am stuck, and here I must stay
My money's all gone and I can't get away.
There's nothing will make a man hard and profane
Like starving to death on my government claim.

But hurrah for Lane County—the land of the free
The home of the grasshopper, bedbug and flea.
I'll sing loud her praises and boast loud her fame
While starving to death on my government claim.

"...and we came on a set of bright human bones sitting in the arroyo. We stood looking at that skeleton. It was clean. I had to think what an indecency it is that leaves only the bones to tell what a man has been."
—Blue, "Welcome to Hard Times," 1960 by E.L. Doctorow

A Ballad
THE GOL-DARNED WHEEL
— Anonymous

Nothing stops a cowboy, not a sand storm, swollen river, snow blizzard, or bucking bronc, but some unknown cowboy finally met his match and wrote this ballad. It's about his first attempt at riding a newfangled contraption called the "wheel" [the bicycle]. Note the descriptive, early mid-western speech in this poem.

I can ride the wildest bronco in the wild and woolly West,
I can rake him, I can break him, let him do his level best.
I can handle any cattle ever wore a coat of hair,
And I've had a lively tussle with a tarnal grizzly bear.

I can rope and throw a longhorn of the wildest Texas brand,
And at Injun disagreements I can take a leading hand.
But I finally met my master, and he really made me squeal,
When the boys got me a-straddle of that gol-darned wheel.

It was a tenderfoot who brought it while he was on his way,
From this land of freedom out to San Francisco Bay.
He tied it at the ranch house to get outside a meal,
Never thinkin' we would monkey with his gol-darned wheel.

There was Old Arizona and there was Jack McGill,
They said I'd been a-braggin' way too much about my skill.
They said I'd find myself against a different kind of deal,
If I would get a-straddle of that gol-darned wheel.

Such a slam against my talent made me madder than a mink,
And I swore that I would ride it for amusement or for chink,
That it was just a plaything for the kids and such about,
And they'd have their ideas shattered if they'd lead the critter out.

They held it while I mounted and I gave the word to go.
The shove they gave to start me warn't unreasonably slow,
But I never split a cussword and I never give a squeal,
I was buildin' reputation on that gol-darned wheel.

Holy Moses and the Prophets, how we split the Texas air,
And the wind it make whip-crackers of my same old canthy hair.
And I sorta comprehended as down the hill we went,
There was bound to be a smash-up that I couldn't well prevent.

Oh, how them punchers bawled, "Stay with her, Uncle Bill!
Stick your spurs in her, you sucker! Turn her muzzle up the hill!"
But I never made an answer, I just let the cusses squeal,
I was building reputation on that gol-darned wheel.

The grade was mighty sloping from the ranch down to the creek,
And I went a-gallyflutin' like a crazy lighting streak,
Just a-whizzing and a-dartin', first this way and then that,
The darned contrivance wobbling like the flying of a bat.

I pulled up on the handles, but I couldn't check it up,
I yanked and sawed and hollered, but the darn thing wouldn't stop.
And then a sort of meechin' in my brain began to steal,
That the Devil had a mortgage on that gol-darned wheel.

I've a sort of dim and hazy remembrance of the stop,
With the world a-goin' round and the stars all tangled up.
Then there came an intermission that lasted 'till I found,
I was lying at the bunkhouse with the boys all gathered round.

And a doctor was a-sewing on the skin where it was ripped,
And Old Arizona whispered, "Well, old boy, I guess you're whipped."
I said that "I am busted from sombrero down to heel."
He grinned and said, "You ort to see that gol-darned wheel!"

BICYCLE TRIVIA: The first verifiable claim for a practical bicycle belongs to Baron von Karl Drais of German in 1817. He called it the "running machine" since it had no gears or pedals, it was a steerable two-wheeler you sat on and pushed with your feet by walking fast. It was also called the "velocipede" or "dandy horse." Pedals and cranks weren't added until the 1860's on a very large front wheel.

A Ballad
ME AND OLD SAL
By Don Kirk, December 2000

This quote from a Random House dictionary, "**Ballad, 1.** a simple narrative poem of popular origin, composed in short stanzas, often of a romantic nature and adapted for singing." This poem is a four-lined ballad of rhymed couplets commonly used by poets of the nineteenth century. This form was frequently used by the American cowboy. It's a story about a cowboy and his horse.

1. She rode like the wind, smooth and soft,
    Turned on a dime, and galloped aloft.
    A true friend, loyal and fast, this was my horse, Old Sal.
    I'm going to see the elephant, it was good-by to my gal.

2. I packed up my bags and booted up my Winchester;
    I threw up my saddle, said good-by to my sister.
    A change 'o clothes and a bottle of Red Dynamite,
    A bedroll and yellow slicker, I cinched them down tight.

3. Up on Old Sal, it's Pike's Peak or Bust!
    Rowels to the flanks, leavin' our past in the dust.
    Makin's and vittles, a guitar lashed to my saddle,
    I yelled to my horse, and said, "we must not daddle."

4. Off we went, by golly, tame the West we shall!
    Bedroll and tincup, me and Old Sal.
    Prairie winds were furious, the thunderstorms were wet,
    But the Injuns were right peaceful—peaceful on a bet.

5. Old Sal reared on her hinds, there was lightin' and hail.
    My ten-galón hat to the wind, I had to bail.
    Dark was settin' in, the ground was soggy wet,
    But she came 'round, Old Sal, a-sauntering back.

6. She eyed me in pleasure; I looked foolish mired in the muck.
    I reached for my Stetson, but my boots were stuck.
    Flat on my face I dearly did fall,
    My pride buried deep in the Muddy Arkansas.

7. Lumbering forward, Old Sal begged for my attention;
    Clinched in her pearly-white teeth was my battered Stetson.
    Hand on the horn and foot in the stirrup,
    Drenched and without grace, I pulled myself up.

8. **I had my Stetson and I had my best pal.**
    I had my guitar, it was just me and Old Sal.
    Flashes of lightin', wind a-frightnin', the plains was eerie.
    Shadows jumped all-around, on this rain-soaked prairie.

9. Blanketed in snow, I was now in a blizzard;
    I sorely needed some food in my gizzard.
    Beef jerky, corn dodgers, and a bag 'o oats for Old Sal.
    She wondered why—oh why—had we left the cozy corral.

10. By morning the storm was clearin'; the air was fresh and clean,
    Old Sal stopped to graze and I took a drink from my canteen.
    In the distance, I could see the Rockies all a-blaze,
    Beckoning, beckoning, beckoning through the blue haze.

11. The wind-swept grassy plains, I was soon to leave behind;
    Determined and hopeful about gold I was soon to find.
    White-capped and silent, Pike's Peak stood a-standin' tall.
    Mustering, commanding, calling: GOLD for us all!

12. I needed a grubstake a-fore I scaled them hills:
    A tin pan, rock hammer, and little-liver pills.
    I needed a pair of canvas ducks—and sugar for Old Sal.
    That was all I needed—to strike it rich and boost my morale.

13. Here was a crick—the clear water a-movin' slow,
    Figurin', calculatin', watchin' its ebb and flow.
    This was a good spot to try my hand at placer minin'.
    To Old Sal I said, "With a little luck we'll be dinin'."

14. I kneeled on my haunches, and dug into the river's san'.
    I swirled the crystal-clear water in my shiny new pan.
    I could see a glint of sparklin' yellow flecks,
    I could see bright gold, even without my specks.

15. I reared up in glee, we had hit the Mother Lode.
    My heart was pounding; I was about to explode.
    Old Sal looked on, perplexed and unsettled by such goin's on.
    I told her she'd be in oats before the summer was gone.

    I had my Stetson and I had my best pal,
    I had my guitar, it was just me and Old Sal.

A Ballad
WHEN JONNNY COMES MARCHING HOME
By Louis Lambert

1. When Johnny comes marching home again,
Hurrah, Hurrah,
We'll give him a hearty welcome then,
Hurah, Hurrah,
The men will cheer, the boys will shout,
The ladies, they will all turn out,
And we'll all feel gay,
When Johnny comes marching home.

2. The old church bell will peal with joy,
Hurrah, Hurrah,
To welcome home our darling boy,
Hurrah, Hurrah;
The village lads and lassies say,
With roses they will strew the way,
And we'll all feel gay,
When Johnny comes marching home.

3. Get ready for the Jubilee,
Hurrah, Hurrah,
We'll give the hero three times three,
Hurrah, Hurrah,
The laurel wreath is ready now,
To place up on his loyal brow,
And we'll all feel gay,
When Johnny comes marching home.

4. Let love and friendship on that day,
Hurrah, Hurrah,
Their choicest treasures then display,
Hurrah, Hurrah,
And let each one perform some part,
To fill with joy the warrior's heart,
And we'll all feel gay,
When Johnny comes marching home.

A Ballad: DIXIE

Traditional by D. D. Emmett

I wish I was in de land ob cotton,
Olt times dar am not forgotten,
Look away! Look away! Look away! Dixie Land.
In Dixie Land whar I was born in,
Early on one frosty mornin'.
Look away! Look away! Look away! Dixie Land.

Den I wish I was in Dixie, Hoo-ray! Hoo-ray!
In Dixie Land, I'll take my stand,
To lib and die in Dixie;
Away, away, Away down south in Dixie.
Away, away, Away down south in Dixie.

Old Missus marry "Will-de-weaber,"
Willium was a gay deceaber;
Look away! Look away! Look away! Dixieland.
But when he put his arm around 'er,
He smiled as fierce as a 'forty pounder.
Look away! Look away! Look away! Dixieland.

His face was sharp as a butcher's cleaber,
But dat did not seem to greab'er;
Look away! Look away! Look away! Dixieland.
Old Missus acted de foolish part,
And died for a man dat broke her heart.
Look away! Look away! Look away! Dixieland.

Now here's a health to de next old Missus,
And all de gals dat what to kiss us;
Look away! Look away! Look away! Dixieland.
But if you want to drive 'way sorrow,
Come and hear dis song tomorrow.
Look away! Look away! Look away! Dixieland.

Dar's buckwheat cakes an' Ingen' batter,
Makes you fat, or a little fatter;
Look a-way! Look a-way! Look a-way! Dixie Land.
Den hoe it down an' scratch your grabble.
To Dixie Land I'm bound to trabble.
Look a-way! Look a-way! Look a-way! Dixie Land.

SEEING THE ELEPHANT
By D. G. Robinson

1. When I left the States for gold
Everything I had was sold:
A stove and bed, a fat old sow
Sixteen chickens and a cow

CHORUS:
So leave, you miners, leave, oh, leave, you miners, leave,
Take my advice, kill off your lice, or else go up to the mountains;
Oh, no, lots of dust, I'm going to the city to get on a "bust."
Oh, no, lots of dust, I'm going to the city to get on a "bust."

2. Off I started, Yankee-like,
I soon fell in with a lot from Pike;
The next was, "Damn you, back, wo-haw,"
A right smart chance from Arkansaw

3. On the Platte we couldn't agree,
Because I had the di-a-ree;
We were split up, I made a break,
With one old mule for the Great Salt Lake.

4. The Mormon girls were fat as hogs,
The chief production, cats and dogs;
Some had ten wives, others none,
Thirty-six had Brigham Young.

5. The damn fool, like all the rest,
Supposed the thirty-six the best;
He soon found out his virgin dears
Had all been Mormons thirteen years.

6. Being brave, I cut and carved,
On the desert nearly starved;
My old mule laid down and died,
I had no blanket, took his hide.

7. The poor coyotes stole my meat,
Then I had nought but bread to eat;
It was not long till that gave out,
Then how I cursed the Truckee route!

To the California forty-niners, no expression defined the gold rush more than the words "seeing the elephant." Those planning to travel west exclaimed with frenzied joy that they were "going to see the elephant." Those eventually giving up and heading home would claim they had only seen the "elephant's tracks" and even that was viewing way too much of the animal.

The expression harks back to the days when circus troupes first began to tour America with elephants. The story goes that a farmer heard that a circus with an elephant was coming to town.........

8. On I traveled through the pines,
At last I found the northern mines;
I stole a dog, got whipt like hell,
Then away I went to Marysville.

9. There I filled the town with lice,
And robbed the Chinese of their rice;
The people say, "You've got the itch,
Leave here, you lousy son of a bitch."

10. Because I would not pay my bill,
They kicked me out of Downieville;
I stole a mule and lost the trail
And then fetched up in Hangtown jail.

11. Canvas roof and paper walls,
Twenty horse-thieves in the stalls;
I did as I had done before,
Coyoted out from 'neath the floor.

12. I robbed a nigger of a dollar,
And bought unguent to grease my collar;
I tried a pint, not one had gone,
Then it beat the devil how I daubed it on.

13. I mined a while, got lean and lank,
And lastly stole a monte-bank;
Went to the city, got a gambler's name
And lost my bank at the thimble game.

14. I fell in love with a California girl;
Here eyes were gray, her hair did curl;
Her nose turned up to get rid of her chin—
Says she, "You're a miner, you can't come in."

15. When the elephant I had seen,
I'm damned if I thought I was green;
And others say, both night and morn,
they saw him coming round the Horn.

16. If I should make another raise,
In New York sure I'll spend my days;
I'll be a merchant, buy a saw,
So, good-bye, mines and Panama.

.....He had never seen one so he loaded up his wagon with vegetables for the market and headed into town. There, sure enough, the circus parade was lead by a big, grey pachyderm. The farmer was elated, finally he had seen the creature he had heard about. But his horses were not impressed and bolted in abject terror. The farmer's wagon flipped over spilling the vegetables. As the sodbuster watched his crop crushed under the march of the circus parade, he said, "By dang, it don't matter, for I have seen the elephant!"

To the gold seekers—and everone else heading west—the elephant symbolized the high monetary cost and likely misfortunes of a westward trek to California in hopes of making a new life. Like seeing an exotic animal, it would be an experience unequaled—an adventure of a lifetime.

FACING THE TRUTH

The author as cowhand Buck Cross, photo by Jo M. Hames

Howdy Pardner

Howdy Pardner
WESTERN WORDS AND PHRASES

*"Humor is the great thing, the saving thing. The minute
it crops up, all our irritations and resentments slip
away and a sunny spirit takes their place."*
—Mark Twain

The language of the Westerner was colorful and practical, and it was influenced by many nationalities all vying for a new life in the West. Sadly, many of the regionalisms are disappearing, the mass media replacing them with nationally approved slang and phraseology. It's thanks to chroniclers like Ramon Adams, Peter Watts, J. Frank Dobie, and Walter Prescott Webb that some of our marvelous West has been preserved for our children. Here then is a fun taste of the way it sounded on the western frontier of America.

A Match Game
6 ACTION WORDS

Match the verbs commonly used in the West with their meaning.

1. dicker	a. swindle
2. chisel	b. walk un-hurriedly
3. git	c. carry
4. eyeball	d. meddle
5. tote	e. leave
6. amble	f. negotiate

ANS: 1-f, 2-a, 3-e, 4-d, 5-c, 6-b.

Ranch windmill in eastern New Mexico (dk)

Howdy Pardner

Well, don't that steal grandma's drawers!
WESTERN COLLOQUIALISMS

When a tenderfoot hears this range vernacular—distinctive, picturesque, and pungent—he is as surprised as a dog with his first porcupine. After he recovers from the shock of such unconventional English, the more he listens the more refreshing it becomes, because, like a fifth ace in a poker deck, it is so unexpected.
—Ramon F. Adams

S imile and exaggeration made for a colorful language that was descriptive, imaginative, witty, and uncluttered by proper grammar. In this chapter, we've got a few humorous examples divided into different categories.

CHARACTER ATTRIBUTES:

TRUSTWORTHINESS

"I wouldn't trust him as far as I can throw an elephant agin' a strong wind."
"I wouldn't dare sleep next to him with my mouth open if I had a gold tooth."
"He's got sand; he'll do to ride the river with."
"He's straight as a wagon tongue."

WATCHFUL

"You'll never find him settin' on his gun hand."

COURAGEOUS

"He's got 'nough guts to fill a smokehouse."
"Gritty as fish eggs rolled in sand."
"He's got more guts than ya' kin <u>hang</u> on a fence."

Professor Finfeather (GS)

COWARDICE

"It'd take only a few o' them lightin' bugs to scare him to running 'til his tongue hung out a foot and forty inches."

"As yellow as mustard without the bite."

DEVIOUS

"Crooked as a dog's hind legs."
"Crooked as a barrel full of fishhooks."
"He's lower'n a snake's belt buckle."
"Crooked as a snake in a cactus patch."
"Low-down as a snake in a wagon track."

STUBBORN

"Stubborn as a government mule."

DRUNKENNESS

"He's so drunk he couldn't hit the ground with his hat in three throws."
"He's wearing calluses on his elbows."
"It looks like somebody stole his rudder."
"He thought he had a twin brother when he looked in the bar mirror."

ROWDY

"He raised hell and put a chunk under it."
"He'd fight you 'til hell freezes over and then skate with you on the ice."

HUNGRY

"I'm hungrier'n a woodpecker with a headache."
"I'm so hungry I could eat the south end of a northbound nanny goat."
"I'm so hungry I could eat a sow and nine pigs and then chase the boar a half-mile."

WORTHLESS

"He wouldn't walk a mile to see a piss ant eat
a bale of hay."
"He ain't fit to shoot at when ya' want to
unload your shotgun."
"He's not worth the sweat on a water bag."
"Worthless as a four-card flush."
"Worthless as teats on a bore hog."

USELESS

"As useless as settin' a milk bucket under a bull."
"As useless as takin' a chicken to Sunday School."

LAZY

"That boy's so lazy he follows the shade around the barn."
"Lazy as a hound dog in the sun."
"He was born tired and never got rested."
"He's a good old dog, but he don't like to hunt."
"He's so lazy he has to lean against a building to spit."

UNWANTED

"He's as welcome as a polecat [skunk] at a picnic."
"He's as popular as the tax collector."
"He's as welcome as a rattler in a prairie dog town."
"He's so unwanted, folks go around him like he
was a Louisiana swamp."

LYING

"He's such a bad liar, he has to hire somebody to call his dogs.

TIDBIT: That old western term "Howdy"—basically a contraction of "How do you do?"—did not actually originate in the West. It had already been around in the rural areas of the East sounding something like "How de do?"

HAPPY

"Grinnin' like a possum eatin'
a yellow jacket."
"Happy as a toad frog
under a drippin' water pump."
"He's grinnin' like a weasel peekin'
in a henhouse door."

BUSY

"Busy as a one-legged man at
an ass-kicking contest."
"Busier'n a Kansas City stockyard."
"Busy as a one-eyed dog
in a smokehouse."
"Busy as a one-armed paper-hanger."

Jonnie "Ivory" Tickler
(Glynda Smith photo)

NERVOUS

"Nervous as a long-tailed cat in a room full of rockers."
"Nervous as a dog dreaming of catching a rabbit."
"His heart is beatin' like a frog's in a dog's mouth."
"So nervous she could thread a sewing machine with it running."

PHYSICAL ATTRIBUTES:

TALL

"He's so tall he can't tell when his feet are cold."
"He's so tall he has to wear short stirrups to save his boot soles."
"She's so tall she can hunt geese with a rake."

SHORT

"He's so short he'd have to borrow a ladder to
kick a grasshopper on the ankle."
"He couldn't brag without a box to stand on."
"So short he couldn't see over a sway-backed burro."
"He's so short he could wear a top hat and walk
under a snake's belly."

FAT

"Add 'nother twenty pounds and she could join a side show."
"He ain't overweight, just a foot too short."

THIN

"He looks like he's just walking around to save funeral expenses."
"He's so thin he has to stand in the same place
twice to cast a shadow."
"He's so thin he has to dodge around in the shower to get wet!"
"The man's so skinny he can take a bath in a shotgun barrel."

SMART

"He lived in the desert so long he knows all the
lizards by their front names."
"He's smart as a bunkhouse rat."
"He don't use up all of his kindlin' getting his fire started."

DUMB

"He couldn't teach a settin' hen
to cluck!"
"He ain't got sense'nough to
spit downwind."
"He ain't got nutin' under his hat
but hair."
"He couldn't track a fat squaw
through a snowdrift."

BIG

"He's as wide as a barn door and
long as a wagon track."
"He's as big as a twenty-mule-team
freight wagon."

Marshal Boss (Jo Hames photo)

SMALL

"She was no bigger'n a bar o' soap after a week's wash."

PRETTY

"She's as pretty as a speckled puppy under a red wagon."
"She's as purty as a hand full of queens."
"She's pretty as a basket full of poker chips."
"She's as pretty to look at as four aces."
"She's as pretty as a mess o' possum livers a-sizzling in hot fat."

HANDSOME

"He's all dressed up like a sore toe."
"He's dressed up like he come out of a mail order catalog."
"He's trim and neat as a new buggy."

UGLY

"She's so ugly she has to sneak up on a dipper to get a drink of water."
"He's like something the cat drug in and the dog wouldn't eat."
"He's as ugly as a stump full of spiders."
"She's so ugly and her teeth are so bucked, she could eat corn on the cob through a picket fence."

Bad Bob (Jo M.Hames photo)

"He had a face that would sour buttermilk."
"She's ugly as a mud fence."
"The man looks like he's been chewing tobacco and spittin' in the wind."
"She's got everything a feller could want: muscles and a mustache."
""She's a might bowlegged; she has to get up outta bed of a night to turn over."
"She's ugly clean to the bone."

MISCELLANEOUS OTHERS:

"He's as ANGRY as a rooster in an empty henhouse."

"He's as NOISY as a restless mule in a tin barn."

"HOPELESS as a grasshopper in a henhouse."

QUICK as a duck on a June Bug."

DISHONEST: "He'll steal a dead fly from a blind spider."

"He's got as much of a CHANCE as a grasshopper in an anthill."

ASKING FOR TROUBLE: "Grabbin' the brandin' iron by the hot end."

STUPID: If you was ta put his brains in a bumblebee,
he would fly backwards.

"His hogs is so POOR, it takes six of 'em to make a shadow."

IT'S A FACT: "You can chisel it in granite."

"He's grinnin' like a jackass that has done ate a prickly pear cactus."

He'd been in the desert so long,
that he knew all the lizards by their first name."

"I'll be kicked to death by grasshoppers if ain't the TRUTH!"

Well if that ain't a FACT, God's a possum.

A Match Game
6 WESTERN WORDS

1. hoe-down	a. chicks
2. loblolly	b. tall tale
3. windy	c. dance
4. crick	d. mail-order catalog
5. peeps	e. mud puddle
6. wishbook	f. creek

ANS: 1-c, 2-e, 3-b, 4-f, 5-a, 6-d.

Has A Loose Cinch
42 DAFT, DEMENTED & DUMB

*"If gunpowder were brains, you wouldn't
have enough to blow your hat off."*
—Bonanza, TV series.

From out West, here's a few "turns of a phrase" for the person considered a tad mentally unbalanced or just plain not too bright.

IF HE'S CRAZY AS A LOON:

1. "He's soft between the head handles."
2. **"He don't have all his eggs in one basket."**
3. "Crazier'n a locoed bedbug."
4. **"His cinch is loose."**
5. "Crazy as a lizard with a sunstroke."
6. **"He's snapped a link in his trace chain."**
7. "Crazy as popcorn on a hot skillet."
8. **"He's a little shy in the hat size."**
9. "I reckon the heat's addled his think box."
10. **"He's got nothing under his hat but hair."**
11. "His bag of marbles has a hole in it."
12. **"The desert air has parched his brain."**
13. "He's odd as a three-dollar bill."
14. **"The sun has boiled his brains."**
15. "His cheese has slipped off his cracker."
16. **"Somethimes I think he's not too tightly wrapped."**
17. "I think his spool is unwinding."
18. **"He's tetched in the head."**
19. "The man is one sandwich short a picnic."
20. **"He's off his mental reservation."**

IF HE'S JUST PLAIN STUPID:

21. "He's so dumb he couldn't teach a hen to cluck."
22. **"He ain't got the brains of a grasshopper."**
23. "He's been out in the sun too long."
24. **"That boy couldn't sell hacksaw blades in a hoosegow."**
25. "He don't know horse dung from wild honey."
26. **"He couldn't drive a nail into a snowbank."**
27. "He musta been in the cellar when they handed out brains."
28. **"He'd walk into a river so he could drink standin' up."**
29. "That boy couldn't track an elephant in ten feet o' snow."
30. **"He ain't got sense 'nough to spit downwind."**
31. "He's so dumb, he can't tell a skunk from a housecat."
32. **"He has an I.Q. about three points above a rock."**
33. "His recollectin' was as dim as the old buffalo trails."
34. **"He's dumb as a box of rocks."**
35. "If he had an idea, it would bust his head open."
36. **"When the lord poured in his brains someone must of jerked on his arm."**
37. "His brain cavity wouldn't make a drinkin' cup for a canary bird."
38. **"His head is so hollow he has to talk with his hands to keep away from the echo."**

Clarence "Slick" McFarley (GS)

39. "If you bored a hole in his head you wouldn't find 'nough brains to grease a skillet."
40. **"That boy don't know diddley squat."**
41. "He's so dumb, he couldn't pour water out of a boot with a hole in the toe and directions on the heel!"
42. **"The boy is three pickles shy of a barrel."**

Two-Bits & Tinhorns
50 WESTERN WORDS GLOSSARY

"Powerful, healthy language always starts in the so-called lower strata of society. When the educated man controls language, it loses its rich taste, its contact with the earth, its very means of renewal!"
—Peter Watts, A Dictionary of the Old West, 1977

The immigrants from Europe, the Mexican population of the Southwest, and the Native Americans all contributed to the language of the Old West. The Spanish greatly influenced the cattle and horse industry. The Indians left names to identify the land and the Whites put their European stamp on it. As a result, many words are pure Frontier American.

1. Arkansas Toothpick. A large knife with a long tapering blade that comes to a point. Like a dagger. Also called a "frog sticker."

2. Badlands. There were numerous regions in the West that were called "badlands" because they were useless for farming and ranching. They were arid, often treeless, rocky lands eroded by wind and water into buttes and mesas. A good example are the badlands east of the Black Hills of the Dakotas.

3. Bite the Bullet. To "stick to one's guns"; to stand firm. Before the invention of metal cartridges, a paper cartridge had to be bit off on the end so the powder and ball could be poured into the end of the rifle barrel. If a soldier did that, it obviously meant he wasn't going to retreat, thus its meaning.

4. Broadside. A large sheet of paper printed on one side with an advertisement or political message and tacked to buildings and fences.

5. Buckskin. The soft skin of a buck antelope or deer used for shirts and leggings.

6. Buffalo a Town. To take over a town by riding through the streets firing revolvers.

7. Buffalo Chips. Dried out buffalo manure. On the plains, where there was little wood to be had, the settlers used the buffalo chip for fuel to fire their stoves and fireplaces. Also called "prairie coal."

8. Bull Durham. A popular brand of smoking tobacco that came in a soft cotton pouch with a label pasted to it on which was a drawing of a bull. It can still be purchased today in the same packaging. The cowboy had to also carry papers to roll the tobacco in. He carried his "makings" to "build a smoke."

9. Bullwhacker. The driver of a freight wagon pulled by oxen. He usually did not ride, but walked alongside the team. He used a 20-foot-long *rawhide* bullwhip to direct and move his team.

10. Bushwhack. To ambush or shoot someone from behind. A no-no in the Code of the West. The word probably derived from early riverboat men who moved their boats in shallow water or in small confining streams by pulling the boat forward by grabbing tree branches at the bow and then walking to the stern. See *dry-gulch*.

11. Catercorner. Diagonally across a square. From the French *quadra* for "four" and the British slang word *cater* for the act of throwing a "four" on a die which has four dots forming a square.

12. Clipper Ship. Used to take Easterners around the Horn of South America to the gold fields of California and Australia (1848-50). It had a long narrow hull and a high, sharp bow built and rigged for fast sailing. The name came from the phrase "it moved at a good clip." It could outrun any other sailing vessel. Early versions were used as blockade runners in the war of 1812 and as African slave ships. The speed record set by the *Flying Cloud* in 1854 (New York to California via Cape Horn in 89 days) wasn't broken until 1989 by a yacht with advanced sailing technology.

13. Daguerreotype. An early photographic process invented by French painter L.M. Daguerre (1789-1851), by which pictures were produced on plates of chemically treated metal or glass.

14. Double Eagle. A US minted gold coin worth $20. It had an Eagle design on each side. It is no longer in circulation. At the time, state banks also issued their own coins and paper money.

15. Draw. A gully, usually dry, that leads into a larger canyon.

16. Drover. The man hired by a rancher to drive his cattle to market. He would be in charge of hiring a "trail boss" and additional "hands."

17. Drummer. A traveling salesman who brought samples of his wares from eastern factories.

18. Dry-gulch. To take by surprise. To shoot from a hidden position at an unsuspecting person. See *bushwhack*.

19. Flatlander. A mountain man's term for anyone not experienced with life in the mountains.

20. Granger. In the Northwest, a derogatory word for homesteaders (farmers or settlers). In the Southwest they called them "nesters." And cowboys used the term "sodbusters" for these squatters because they broke sod.

21. Green River Knife. A high quality knife manufactured in Deerfield Massachusetts (near the Green River) by John Russell, beginning in 1832. Used by the Mountain Men for hunting, butchering, and fighting, it had the trademark initials "GR" stamped on the blade. The name became synonymous with quality.

22. G.T.T. The letters stood for "Gone To Texas" and can be found in the records of lawmen, indicating that a wanted man could not be found—the "books closed on him," case closed. Why? Because Texas was often where a man running from the law would "high tail it" to, where there was little law, a good place to make a new start. Families moving to Texas sometimes marked the front door of their abandoned home in the East with this mark.

23. Haggle. To argue about terms or pricing, hard bargaining.

24. Halfbreed. A derogatory term for a person of both Indian and European descent.

25. Handbill. A small printed sheet of paper bearing an announcement to be passed out by hand.

26. Heeled. Armed with a weapon.

27. Hell Bent for Leather. To go all out, do or die. The phrase came from Maine's 1840 Governor's race where Edward Kent's motto was "Hell-bent for Edward Kent."

28. Hornswoggled. To be cheated, outsmarted, or made a fool of.

29. Hundred and Sixty. 160 acres, a quarter section. The amount of farm land allowed to be registered by an individual under the homesteading laws. A "section" was 640 acres or one square mile.

30. Lasso. To throw a rope over something. From the Portuguese *laso* meaning "snare." Mexican vacarros brought the word to the United States.

31. Line Rider. A cowboy who rides the range rounding up stray stock, checking watering holes, the condition of fencing, and generally overseeing the grazing lands for his employer.

In the winter, he has a tougher job, tending to sick and weak animals, breaking up frozen ponds, and rounding up drifting cattle. He rides alone, cooks alone, and sleeps alone, with only his horse to talk to. A *Fence Rider's* job is to repair fences, continually riding along fence lines and to make repairs, sometimes traveling by wagon so he can carry extra barbed-wire, fence posts and post-hole diggers.

32. Loot. Goods stolen or taken by force. The word came to America from India in the 1850's from the Hindu word *lut* meaning booty or plunder.

33. Malpais. From the Spanish work *mal* meaning bad and *pais* meaning country. It is bad country, rugged, usually volcanic. Clint Eastwood named his movie production company *Malpais*.

34. Muckety-Muck. Mock title of dignity for a boastful or ostentatious person. Probably from the Chinook Indian word *macamuc*.

35. Muleskinner. Not a man who skins mules, but a man who drives a wagon pulled by mules using a long whip to control the team.

36. Parfleche. A cleaned, dehaired and dried buffalo hide or a carrying case made of buffalo hide used in the Northwest during the fur trapping era.

37. Pilgrim. A word now associated with John Wayne who first used it in the movie *The Man Who Shot Liberty Valance*, it means lacking experience in the ways of the West—a greenhorn.

38. Possibles Bag. A term originally used by the mountain men, and later adopted by the cowmen, for a leather or cloth bag on a shoulder strap used to carry personal property—everything one would possibly need. Contents would include such things as a knife, flint & striker for making a fire, gun cleaning and reloading supplies, ammunition, tobacco, cooking utensils, clothing, and extra food.

39. Rawhide. The untanned or only partially tanned hide of a steer or cow.

40. Rendezvous. An annual gathering of fur trappers, Indians, and anyone wishing to trade goods for fur pelts. The first rendezvous (sponsored by the Ashley Co.) occurred in 1825 at Henry's Fork on the Green River in Wyoming. The gathering became a celebration—often the only time a mountain man would see another human being—as men spent their profits on gambling, drinking, and supplies for the trip back into the mountains. By the 1840's rendezvous' were over, replaced by permanent trading posts. In the remote areas, Indians were becoming hostile and the buffalo was replacing beaver as a source of profits. Today, in the Northwest, there are popular reenactments of this event.

41. Sarsaparilla. A carbonated drink, its flavor derived from the dried roots of a plant called the *sarsaparilla* which has fragrant roots and toothed, heart shaped-leaves. The drink tastes a lot like root beer.

42. Seeing the Elephant. To see the world for the first time. To learn about life the hard way. Gold miners traveling West found that searching for Gold was not as easy as they first thought.

43. Side-Wheeler. A steamboat with two paddlewheels, one on each side. Each paddlewheel had its own engine with a separate engineer to operate each.

44. Slicker. A long, yellow oilskin raincoat, cut up in the back so it could be worn while riding a horse. It was also called a "Fish" because of the manufacturer's trademark stamped on the coat.

45. Stern-Wheeler. A steamboat with the paddle wheel in the rear. Like the side-wheeler, it had two engines, but they were coupled to the same shaft by a crank at each end.

46. Tinhorn. A person who is a fake. Cheap and flashy. Originally this word referred to the gamblers who ran a *chuck-a-luck* game. The dice were thrown from a small tin container shaped like a horn. Those who lost at the game referred to the operator who "took" their money as the "tinhorn gambler" and the name stuck for any crooked gambler.

47. Tintype. A positive photograph taken directly on a sensitized plate of enameled tin or iron.

48. Two Bits. Twenty five cents; a bit is an amount equal to 12-1/2 cents.

49. Windage. The lateral adjustment made to the rear sight of a rifle to compensate for the wind. How much to adjust it was determined by watching the movement of trees and shrubs.

50. Yahoo. Pronounced "yay-hoo." A fool; a stupid or thoughtless, or crude, mannerless person. This derogatory word came from Jonathan Swift's *Gulliver's Travels* written in 1726 in which there is a degraded race of humanoid people called "Yahoos."

> **TIDBIT:** In the 19th–century Frontier West, you didn't *carry* anything, you PACKED it. You "packed" a gun. In the wild country of the West, you had to pack everything you wanted to move and load it onto man or beast, pack mule, or pack train. Thus "packed" instead of "carried" came into general use.

Bears, Hatbands, & Fiddles
COMMON WESTERN PHRASES

The **westerner** used colorful, descriptive language. Did your dad or grandmother use any of these terms?

1. **A man who has "sand."** A man with grit and courage. (Grit was defined as a rough, hard man.)
2. **A "salty" horse or character.** A mean horse or man with vim and vigor, but not necessarily a pleasant disposition.
3. **Being on a "high lonesome."** A cowboy who goes on a spirited drinking bout or noisy frolic all by himself.
4. **Cut for sign.** To look for the trail of a man or beast. The trail is "discovered" by *cutting across* a trail of footprints, broken bushes, trampled grass, snapped twigs, or animal droppings.
5. **Draw a bead.** To take aim. The foresight of a firearm is a "bead."
6. **Fiddle on that.** Not worth taking the time to do, a bad idea.
7. **Get the drop on someone.** Means to have the advantage, having a gun in your hand when your opponent doesn't have one in his.
8. **Going off half-cocked.** Attempting something without being fully prepared or mentally ready. A half-cocked six-shooter cannot be fired. The middle position of the hammer is used for loading.
9. **Gonna clean his plow.** To defeat a man, to "whip him."
10. **Half-baked.** A plan that hasn't been completely thought out.
11. **Loaded for bear.** Fully armed, ready for trouble. To prepare to shoot a bear, one loaded his musket with as much gunpowder as he could.
12. **Tight as Dick's hatband.** Very tight indeed. It originated with the very unpopular and derided King Richard Cromwell who surely felt discomfort wearing the crown, which lasted only nine months.
13. **Two whoops and a holler.** Just a short distance, yelling distance. And "not worth two whoops and a holler" is not worth doing.
14. **Up to Snuff.** Capable, competent. From powdered snuff used by the English that had a stimulating effect making one feel "sharp of mind."
15. The **whole kit and caboodle.** The whole lot, everything. Probably from Britain, "kit" or "kith" was a soldier's bag of personal things, and "bootle" was a collection of things or friends.

650

Balloons, Barges, & Battens
28 WORDS OF THE BUILDER

The choice of architectural styles in the West was made by men who wanted to bring a more citified eastern look to their raw frontier towns. They copied details from the new Victorian-era architecture popular in the East. But they found these designs needed to be adapted to the needs of the West and so a new architecture was born: the false-fronted buildings that have now become a symbol of the American West.

1. Adobe. A sun-dried brick made of mud and straw approximately 18 inches long and 5 to 8 inches wide. Mud is put into wood molds, which, after setting up, are stacked in slanting rows to shed rains while they are curing in the sun. The bricks are then stacked to form walls and then plastered over with more mud to shed water.

2. Balloon Framing. A method of construction where small dimensional lumber runs vertically from sill to eaves, and horizontal siding can be nailed to it allowing great flexibility in design. A development that greatly promoted the growth of towns in the West.

3. Balustrade. A row of turned or rectangular posts joined by a rail, serving as an enclosure for balconies, staircases, terraces, etc.

4. Bargeboard. A wide board, usually ornate, attached along the rake of a gabled roof. Common in Tudor and Gothic architecture.

5. Board-And-Batten. Vertical plank siding with joints covered by narrow wood strips.

6. Bracket. A non-structural triangular carving, usually of fanciful form, used under a cornice.

7. Chinking. A material, like plaster, used to fill the spaces between the logs of a cabin.

8. Clapboard. Board siding laid horizontally, the top board overlapping the lower. Used vertically, the boards are butted together.

9. Column. A vertical, cylindrically-shaped, structural support with a base, shaft and capitol.

10. Cornice. A decoratively treated horizontal molding at the edge of a roof.

11. Cupola. A small dome or similar structure surrounded by windows and placed on the roof.

12. Dog Trot or Dog Run. Many early log cabins were built with an opening across the middle of the house to aid in ventilation and provide a covered place for outdoor activities. A one-room cabin was built initially and a second was added later with a space in between which was then also covered.

13. Dormer. A small *gabled* window projecting from a sloping roof.

14. Facade. The exterior face of a building.

15. Fenestration. The arrangement of windows in a building.

16. Gable. The triangular upper portion of a wall at the end of a pitched roof.

17. Gingerbread. Fancy wood carvings on furniture, front porches, along *gables*, etc. applied to *Victorian* houses.

18. Lintel. A horizontal beam of wood, stone, or steel that bridges the top of window or door opening to support the load above.

19. Mansard Roof. A roof with two slopes on each of the four sides, the lower steeper than the upper.

20. Pediment. Triangular *gable* above a door or window.

21. Pilaster. Rectangular column projecting from a wall and appearing to be part of the wall.

22. Placita. In New Mexico, a courtyard encircled by the wings of a house or by several houses.

23. Quoining. Heavy blocks, generally of stone, or of wood cut to imitate stone, used at each corner of a building to reinforce masonry walls, or in wood or brick as a decorative feature.

24. Stucco. Plaster or cement used as a coating or low-relief on ceilings. Also plaster applied to entire *facades* and carved to simulate stone.

25. Victorian. Characteristic of the time when Victoria was Queen of England (1837-1901).

26. Viga. A log with the bark peeled off and used as a ceiling beam. Usually seen protruding through the outside walls of southwestern adobe buildings.

27. Wainscot. Wood paneling applied to the lower part of an interior wall.

28. Widow's Walk. A balustraded lookout on a residential rooftop.

The beginning of the author's "old west" costume collection in the 1980's (photo by Michael Jay Smith)

Ditties and Dofunnies
MORE ODDS AND ENDS

"Creating stuff creates more stuff. It seems to expand like the universe of Einstein—it comes back on itself."
—Author unknown

"You got that right."
—Don Kirk

In this chapter you'll find pigeonholed, those odds and ends, bits and pieces, and bibs and bobs of miscellany that wouldn't fit neatly or respectably in any other chapter of this book. The seaman put his personals in his ditty box and today's gentleman still puts his toiletries in a leather ditty bag. The cowboy of the Old West referred to his collected trinkets as "dofunnies," those things not much use to anyone but himself. Maybe some of the things that follow can be of use to you.

When one collects, even the walls aren't safe. (dk)

An Outhouse By Any Other Name
THE OUTHOUSE

In **the outhouse,** one could solve the world's problems. It was where my father did so much of his thinking. If you couldn't afford toilet paper, you used a sales catalog like the "Monkey Wards," or fruit wrappers or corn cobs, though, he says, these would fill up the hole pretty rapidly. A cup of lime was poured into the hole every week or so to reduce the odor. Holes were usually only about five feet deep and had to be routinely cleaned out with a shovel. This "night soil" could be used for fertilizer. The outhouse was sometimes built with an opening in the back so the chickens could clean it out. But maggots and flies carried diseases, so screen wire was often used on the vent stack and any openings in the little house.

A two-story Outhouse, Silver City, Idaho... Don't ask. (dk)

22 NAMES FOR THE OUTHOUSE

Some loving names for that little building sitting out back.

1. Chick Sales*
2. Privy
3. The Library
4. Out The Back
5. Backhouse
6. Closet
7. Biffie
8. Klondike
9. Jake
10. The Necessary
11. Willie
12. The Office
13. Convenience
14. John or Johnny
15. The Reading Room
16. W. C. (Water Closet)
17. Little House
18. Stool Closet
19. Donnicker
20. Post Office

* **Charles "Chick" Sale**, a stage actor and comedian, wrote a humorous booklet of outhouse advice for rural families called "The Specialist" in 1929. Inspired by a carpenter friend who built outhouses, the book was so popular across the country that Chick's name became synonymous with the "multi-holer" outhouse.

In the 1930's, **"tailor-made Johns"** made by the Works Progress Administration were built using a concrete slab and pit with tin construction, airtight seat lids, and screened ventilators.

His and Hers, Fairplay, Colorado (dk)

1 OUTHOUSE STORY

When toilet tissue was first invented, one privy user wrote *Sears, Roebuck and Co.* for a roll of this new stuff only to get a return letter asking for the catalog number before the order could be processed. The potential customer shot off another letter with this response: "If I had the catalog, I wouldn't need the toilet paper!"

6 QUOTES FROM OLD CODGERS WHO LIVED IT

1. "The thin black & white pages of a sales catalog were favored over the stiffer colored pages. When the mail-order catalogs began using slick paper in the 1930's it was the end of their use in The Reading Room."

Silver City, Idaho (dk)

2. "My dad would use three red corncobs and then a white one to see if he needed another red one."

3. "We kept a broom, a fly swatter, and a long pole for knocking down wasps in the outhouse. We also built a box to hold our corn cobs, and had a cord nailed to the wall to hang the Sears catalog."

4. "To make the seat warmer, my dad used to cut the tops out of fancy ladies hats and nail the brims around the privy holes."

5. "We would plant Wisteria outside the privy which gives off a nice sweet aroma."

6. "As youngsters we had a nail in the outhouse where we put pages of things we wanted, torn from the "Monkey Wards" catalog, in the hope our parents would buy them for Christmas."

13 CRITTERS FOUND IN THE PRIVY

A trip to the outhouse was always fraught with danger, especially at night. You never knew what you might meet up with when you entered the reading room. These were common nuisances:

1. Horse Flies	5. Wasps	8. Mud Daubers	11. Bats
2. Chickens	6. Skunks	9. Bees	12. Lizards
3. Rats	7. Lizards	10. Scorpions	13. Snakes
4. Spiders			

...and all while in a compromising position.

"Outbacks" still in use, St. Elmo, Colorado (dk)

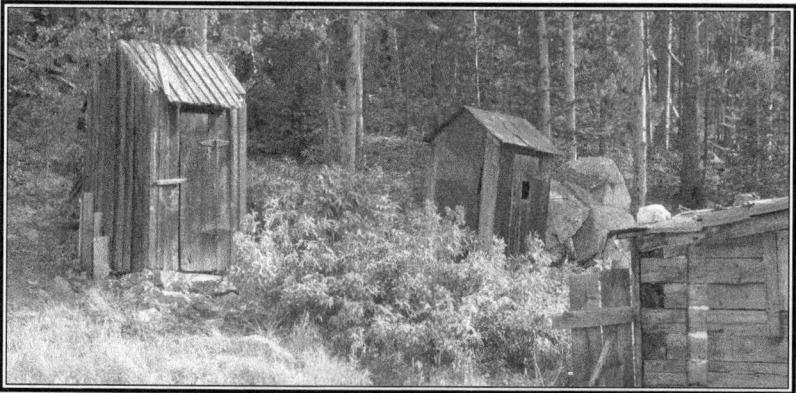

Monday Is Wash Day
13 STEPS FOR DOING FAMILY WASH

A **mother scribbled this recipe** out for her daughter when she became a new bride. Source and date unknown, the spelling left as the original.

1. Bild a fire in back yard to heet the kettle of rainwater.

2. Set tub so smoke won't blow in eyes if the wind is pert.

3. Shave one hole cake lie soap in biling water.

4. Sort things, make three piles, 1 white pile, 1 pile cullords, 1 pile work britches and rags.

5. Stur flour in cold water to smooth, then thin down with biling water.

6. Rub dirty spots on board, scrub hard, then bile—just rench and starch.

7. Take white things out of kettle with broom stick handle, then rench, blew and starch.

8. Spred the towels on grass.

9. Hang old rags on fence.

10. Pore rench water on flowerbeds.

11. Scrub porch with hot soapy water.

12. Turn tubs upside down.

13. Go put on clean dress—smooth hair with side combs—brew cup of tee—set and rest and rock a spell, and count blessings.

1 Recipe For Sore Throat

Lemon Juice (one lemon)
Glycerine (two tablespoons)
Honey (six ounces)

24 WESTERN ICONS

What images remind you of the American West? The following have become symbols of that era.

Wagon Wheel	Cowboy Boots	Windmill
Six-gun	Barbed Wire	Longhorn Cattle
Cowboy Hat	The Stagecoach	Boot Spurs
Saddlebags	A Gun Rig	Western Saddle
Horseshoe	Poker Hand	Covered Wagon
Monument Valley	Spittoon	Saloon Doors
The Marshal's Badge	Branding Iron	Tumbleweed
The Horse	The Bison	Indian Arrows

And towns like "Dodge City," "Santa Fe" and "Denver."

13 CLICHéS OF THE WESTERN

1. End of the trail.
2. Gone west.
3. Crossed the Great Divide.
4. Hell bent for leather.
5. Back in the saddle again.
6. "We'll give 'em a fair trial and then we'll hang 'em."
   —Richard Dillon, *Western Quotations.*
7. "Head 'em up. Move 'em out." —*Rawhide* TV series.
8. "A man's gotta do what a man's gotta do."
   —Alan Ladd in *Shane.*
9. Gunfighter gives a wannabe advice when using a gun.
10. At end of movie, hero rides off into the sunset.
11. Hero rides off *without* the heroine.
12. Every hero has a sidekick.
13. A cowboy sings to his horse.

Gone Fishing
14 SIGNS OF THE TIMES

*"Where satisfaction is not given
money will be refunded."*
—John "Doc" Holliday, dentist, Dodge City

Humor in the Old West can be found in the oddest of places. The hand-painted signs on a proprietor's place of business was one such place. Here then is a sampling of actual signs found in the Old West.

GO WEST. GO WEST.
GO TO KANSAS, COLORADO.
FREE HOMES.
—Kansas Pacific Railroad, 1870

CLANCY'S BARBERSHOP
EARS WASHED WITHOUT EXTRA CHARGE

DON'T SHOOT THE PIANIST
HE'S DOING HIS DAMNDEST

DOGS AND INDIANS NOT ALLOWED
—Butte, Montana

Open SATURDAY-SUNDAY 10 A.M.-5 P.M., Usually.
SOMETIMES THURSDAY-FRIDAY, NOT ALWAYS.

OPEN
WHEN I GET HERE

CLOSED
WHEN I LEAVE

NOTICE
ALL FIREARMS ARE EXPECTED TO BE DEPOSITED WITH THE PROPRIETOR
—Wyatt Earp, Marshal
Dodge City, Kansas

Gone To Milk My Cow
Be Back In Half An Hour

30 Miles To Water
20 Miles To Wood
10 Inches To Hell
Gone Back East
To Wife's Family

Gone To Bury My Wife
Be Back in 15 Minutes

G.T.T.
(Gone To Texas)

CLOSED
Gone To Hanging

SHUT

WANTED
Young skinny, wiry
fellows not over
eighteen. Must be
expert riders willing
to risk death daily.
Orphans preferred.
—Pony Express, 1860

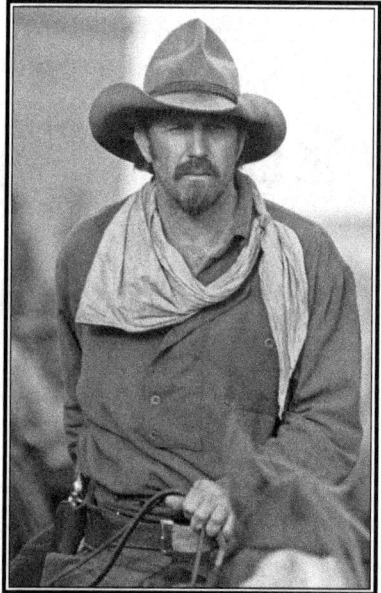

Kevin Costner in *Open Range*,
Touchstone Pictures (Author's collection)

Wagons Ho!
30 TYPES OF WAGONS

"It is not a pleasant, but it is an interesting trip. The condition of one man's running stages to make money, while another seeks to ride in them for pleasure, are not in harmony to produce comfort. Coaches will be overloaded, it will rain, the dust will drive, baggage will be left to the storms, passengers will get sick, rations will give out . . ."
—Demas Barnes, *From the Atlantic to the Pacific, Overland*, 1866.

Just as there are many types of trucks designed for special cargo, the four-wheeled wagon of the nineteenth century came in many custom designs. Wagons were built strong and sturdy for a country that had no paved roads, but they left passengers with a rough, uncomfortable ride—but it sure beat walking.

Baggage Wagon. Used to haul baggage and freight to and from the railroad station. With two horses it could carry up to 3,000 pounds. It had high slatted boards or stakes, depending on the type of load.

Buckboard. A light-weight wagon with a spring seat and flat bed for light cargo. Handy to carry tools for fence building or farm work, or for a trip to town for seeds and flour.

Chuckwagon. A covered wagon with a "chuck box" added to the rear for holding the cook's utensils and condiments. The open door of the chuck box became a

Chuckwagon, Johnson City, Texas (dk)

table for preparing the food. The bed of the wagon carried the cowboy's bedrolls (see page 18).

Civil War Cannon & Limber. A 12-pounder cannon sits centered on the axle of a two-wheeled carriage that for travel was hooked to the "limber" which had two more wheels and carried just enough ammo to get the gun into action. It took four or six horses to pull it.

Concord Coach. A heavy-duty passenger coach, the first built in Concord, New Hampshire by the *Abbot-Downing Company* in 1827. It was so successful that many other manufacturers followed suit. The body of the coach rocked on leather straps—not to comfort the passengers—but to act as shock absorbers to ben-

efit the teams. It was designed to carry nine passengers inside (three sat on a lower center bench) and more on top. 18 to 20 "poor bastards" were sometimes loaded onto the carriage. 6 to 8 horses, harnessed in pairs, were required to pull it. Leather "boots" on the front and rear carried baggage. The coach had an arched roof with a railing around the outer edge for holding extra baggage. It weighted about 2,500 pounds empty. Concords cost $1,500 to build, a princely sum at that time.Averaging about 8 miles per hour, and changing horses every 15 miles, a trip could be made to California in about three weeks for a cost of $200 per person.

Conestoga Wagon. Built in Pennsylvania's Conestoga Valley, it was 10 to 12 feet tall with an arched body, lower in the center to prevent the load from shifting to the ends of the wagon. The canvas top also curved downward in the middle like a saddle with the wooden hoops angled toward the center of the wagon. The sides of the wagon flared outward. The box was 16 feet long, 4 feet wide and 4 feet high; it weighed as much as 4,000 pounds and could carry up to 4 tons of freight. It had very large and wide rear wheels and much smaller front ones. The underbody was always painted blue, and the upper woodwork was painted bright red. It had no seat for the driver, instead, he rode one of the six to eight draft horses or walked alongside. Used from the mid-17th century to the mid 18th century, it could carry up to 8,000 pounds of freight.

Covered Wagon. A canvas tarp is draped and tied down over wooden hoops stuck in brackets on the sideboards. A water barrel, supplies, and tools would be strapped to the sides for long journeys westward. Called "prairie schooners," these wagons were first used by the pioneers in the 1830's to trek west. Smaller and lighter than the *Conestoga*, it was built of maple, oak and hickory with iron tires, axles and connecting rods. It could carry about 2,500 pounds of cargo, had no springs, and wasn't intended for passengers—they had to walk. It was pulled by oxen or mules for up to 15 or 20 miles in a day. Pioneers usually started off on their trek west with their wagons overloaded with their prized furniture and personal belongings, but they quickly realized they would never make it to Oregon and California this way and wound up dumping the unnecessary furniture along the trail.

Drummer's Wagon. The "drummer" or traveling salesman carried sample goods manufactured in the East from town to town trying to get orders from local merchants. Cloth, scissors, tinware, brooms, cooking stoves— everything "pigeonholed" in drawers, cabinets, barrels, and strapped on the sides. The wagons were brightly painted.

All wagon photos by the author (dk)

to twenty mules or oxen. They could carry about ten tons of goods each.

Farm Wagon. Designed for every kind of hauling job on the farm; the removable wagon box could carry hay, corn, potatoes, and hogs.

Fuel Wagon. Large wagon with sides slanting outward and having a dumping mechanism to quickly unload wood for stoves. Common in the Northwest.

Freight Wagon. A large wagon with high sides and pulled by ten

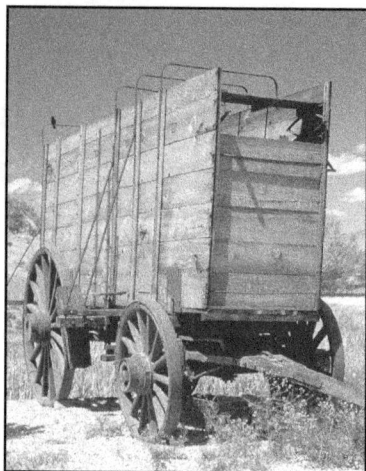

The Hearse. A fancy wagon, painted black and silver, with a flat top supported by Greek columns between which is plate glass and curtains to hide the coffin. Carriage lanterns are attached to each side of the drivers seat.

The Hook-And-Ladder. Besides a number of ladders in different lengths, this wagon also carried

Hose Wagon

shovels, fire axes, battering rams, nets, rope, and the like. It was usually painted red.

Hose Wagon. A fire department's wagon for carrying water hose and several firemen. The canvas hose was folded in the bed of the wagon with one fireman riding on each side between the wheels, two riding on the rear "running-board" and two on the front seat, one driving. It was painted red and highly decorated with gold scrollwork.

Ice Wagon. An enclosed wagon with a canvas tarp on the rear for carrying 100 to 300 pound blocks of ice to businesses and farmers for their newfangled kitchen ice-boxes. At each location the ice would be cut to the size the customer needed and then weighed on a scale hanging on the back of the wagon to determine the cost.

Logging Cart. This two-wheeled wagon with large wheels was pulled over the top of a log and a winch used to pull the log up. It was then pulled by a single horse.

Lumber Wagon. Used in the Northwest to haul board lumber from the sawmill. Pulled by four or six horses, the driver rode up high on the front in a body design called the "California Body." With sideboards, it could be used to haul all manner of things.

Sketch by the author of an ice wagon at Old Tucson Studios, Tucson, Arizona

Medicine Wagon. For the traveling patent-medicine man hawking his miracle cures and celebrated remedies. It's an enclosed wagon for carrying his goods and served as his living quarters. Exquisitely decorated with carving and paneling, the sides were a big colorful billboard to advertise his wares. The back of the wagon opens up to form a stage for live entertainment to draw in the crowds before his sales pitch.

Milk Wagon. A one horse enclosed wagon with doors on the sides for door-to-door delivery of milk; the wagon was kept cool with blocks of ice.

Physician's Phaeton. The wagon doctors used to make house calls. Pulled by a single horse, it had a black canopy with side windows, a high-backed cushioned seat and drawers underneath to store instruments and medications.

Red River Cart. A two-wheeled cart with three sides built without nails or iron and pulled by an ox, mule or cow. It was used in the late 18th century along the Red River for hauling furs.

Sheepherder's Wagon. A covered wagon with bed, kitchen table, and cooking stove (pipe sticking from the roof); the home of a sheeperder.

Sprinkler Wagon. A large wooden vessel on heavy running gear and outfitted with a sprinkler system on the rear, it was used to keep the dust down on town streets.

Stage Wagon. Also called a "mud wagon," (see page 167) it was a small, light-weight passenger coach that could carry 10 to 12 passengers, half as many passengers as the *Concord*, but it could move faster. The passenger compartment was open making for a colder, dustier ride, having only a canvas curtain that could be lowered in front of the window. It was pulled by six horses, the teams replaced every twelve miles at "way stations." Common

in the southwest where it was usually pulled by mules (for that reason mud wagon stage lines were often called the "Jackass Express"), it could handle roads too rough or muddy for the heavier *Concord*. Its center of gravity was lower to the ground, making it harder to turn over than the *Concord*.

Surrey, Canopy-Top. For taking the family on a Sunday drive or to visit the neighbors. Name taken from a cart used in the County of Surrey, England.

Top Buggy. A light-weight carriage for one or two passengers, for business or pleasure.

Jailer's Wagon. Cowboys called it a "tumbleweed wagon. (see page 108). A wagon outfitted with seats and iron jailbars to collect prisoners from around the territory and bring them to trial in a city with a judge, like *Judge Parker's Court* in Fort Smith.

Water Wagon. A round wooden tank of wood stakes would be strapped horizontally on the running gear with ribbons of iron so the wagon could be used to haul water to arid sites.

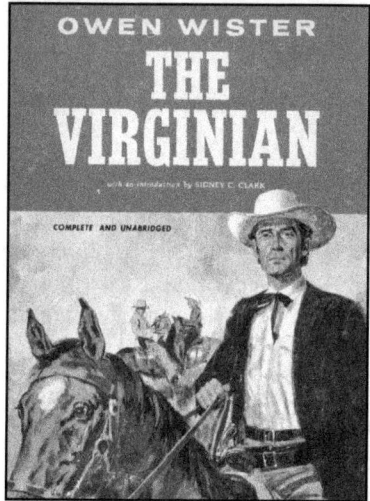

OWEN WISTER

THE VIRGINIAN

A Match Game
4 WRITER'S PEN NAMES

Match these famous western writers with their pen names.

1.	Frederick Schiller Faust	a.	Mark Twain
2.	Edward Zane Carroll Judson	b.	Max Brand
3.	Samuel Langhorne Clemens	c.	Luke Short
4.	Frederick Dilley Glidden	d.	Ned Buntline

ANS: 1-b, 2-d, 3-a, 4-c.

When You Call Me That Smile
59 GREAT WESTERN BOOKS

*"Action, action, action is the thing. So long as you keep your
hero jumping through fiery hoops on every page, you're all right.
The basic formula I use is simple: good man turns bad, bad man
turns good. Of course, there has to be a woman, but not much of
one. A good horse is much more important."*
—Max Brand (western writer)

The western plays well on celluloid. It has a natural grandeur that a book of text can't quite convey about the west, but most of the great westerns came from novels, from the written word. Movies, unfortunately, become associated with the actors and director even though many people made creative contributions to the finished product, and the most important member is usually the first to be forgotten: the novelist who wrote the original story. You can thank writers for romanticizing the West, creating heroes, and making symbols of things that weren't even a part of the West. Max Brand (Frederick Faust) produced 179 books over a period of twenty years making him the "King of the pulps." Zane Grey wrote 54 novels about the American West. Louis L'Amour, at the time of his death, had in print 89 novels and 14 short story collections. Following is a list of some of the great works of western fiction and non-fiction:

YOU CAN'T GO WRONG WITH ANY OF THESE BOOKS

Bar-20 (1911)......................................Clarence Edward Mulford
(1883-1956.)
Betty Zane (1903)..................................Zane Grey (1872-1939)
The Big Sky (1947)................................A.B. Guthrie (1901-1991)
Black Elk Speaks (1932).........................John G. Neihardt (1881-1973)
Bugles in the Afternoon (9143)................Ernest Haycox (1899-1950)
Bury My Heart at Wounded Knee (1970).Dee Brown (1908-2002)
TheCall of the Wild (1903)......................Jack London (1876-1916)
Cheyenne Autumn (1953).......................Mari Sandoz (1896-1966)
The Colonel's Daughter; Or..(1890)..........Capt. Charles King
Conagher (1968)....................................Louis L'Amour (1908-1988)
The Cowboys (1971)...............................William Dale Jennings
(1917-2000)
Dances With Wolves (1988).....................Michael Blake (1945-)
The Daybreakers (1960)..........................Louis L'Amour (1908-1988)
The Day the Cowboys Quit (1971).........Elmer Kelton (1926-2009)
Destry Rides Again (1930).......................Max Brand (1892-1944)
Flint (1960)..Louis L'Amour (1908-1988)
From Where the Sun Now Stands (1962).Will Henry (1912-1991)
The Great Plains (1931)..........................Walter Prescott Webb
(1888-1963)
The Hell Bent Kid (1957).......................Charles O. Locke (1908-1975)
Hombre (1961)......................................Elmore Leonard (1925-)
Hondo (1953)..Louis L'Amour (1908-1988)
Indian Boyhood (1902)..........................Charles A. Eastman (1858-1939)
The Last of the Mohicans (1826).............James Fenimore Cooper
(1789-1851)
Jubal Troop (1939)................................Paul I.Wellman (1895-1966)
The Life of Buffalo Bill...........................William F. Cody (1846-1917)
Lonesome Dove (1985)...........................Larry McMurtry (1936-)
Little Big Man (1964).............................Thomas Berger (1924-)
The Log of a Cowboy (1903)...................Andy Adams (1859-1935)
Lone Star:A History of Texas and.............T.R. Fehrenbach (1925-)
The Long Rifle (1935).............................Stewart E.White (1873-1946)
The Luck of Roaring Camp (1868)...........Bret Harte (1836-1902)
Monte Walsh (1963)...............................Jack Schaefer (1907-1991)
The Oregon Trail (1847).........................Francis Parkman (1823-1893)
The Ox Bow Incident (1940)...................Walter Van Tillburg Clark
(1909-1971)

Paseó Por Aquí .... Eugene Manlove Rhodes
                                       (1869-1934)
Riders of the Purple Sage (1912) .... Zane Grey (1872-1939)
Ride the Man Down (1942) .... Luke Short (1908-1975)
Road to Socorro .... Charles O. Locke (1908-1975)
Roughing It (1872) .... Mark Twain (1835-1910)
Sackett (1961) .... Louis L'Amour (1908-1988)
The Sea of Grass (1937) .... Conrad Richter (1890-1968)
The Searchers (1956) .... Alan Le May (1899-1964)
The Shadow Riders (1982) .... Louis L'Amour (1908-1988)
Shane (1949) .... Jack Schaefer (1907-1991)
Son of the Morning Star (1985) .... Evan S. Connell (1924-)
Stay Away, Joe (1953) .... Dan Cushman (1909-2001)
The Spell of the Yukon (1907) .... Robert Service (1874-1958)
The Squaw Killer (1983) .... Will Henry (1912-1991)
The Time It Never Rained (1973) .... Elmer Kelton (1926-2009)
True Grit (1968) .... Charles Portis (1933-)
The Unforgiven (1957) .... Alan Le May (1899-1964)
Untamed (1919) .... Max Brand ((1892-1944)
Valdez is Coming (1970) .... Elmore Leonard (1925-)
Vengeance Valley (1949) .... Luke Short (1908-1975)
The Virginian (1902) .... Owen Wister (1860-1938)
The Way to Rainy Mountain (1969) .... N. Scott Momaday (1934-)
White Fang (1906) .... Jack London (1876-1916)
The Wolf and the Buffalo (1980) .... Elmer Kelton (1926-2009)
The Wonderful Country (1952) .... Tom Lea (1907-2001)

A Match Game
4 MORE WRITER'S PEN NAMES

Match these famous western writers with their pen names.

1. Peter B. Germano	a.	B.M. Bower
2. Michael Newton	b.	Jackson Cole
3. Bertha "Muzzy" Sinclair	c.	James Reasoner
4. L.J. Washburn	d.	Lyle Brandt

ANS: 1-b, 2-d, 3-a, 4-c.

Penmanship
6 WESTERN WRITERS

The creators of the mythical pulp West produced imagery that was always the same: guns, horses, saloons, and a sprawling, wide-open West where the heroes were required to protect the heroine and fight the villains to the end. Here are six of the great western writers:

1. **JAMES FENIMORE COOPER** (1789-1851). *The Leather Stocking Tales*—the adventures of frontiersman "Natty Bumppo" and Indian sidekick "Chingachgook." The series included *The Pioneers* (1823), *The Last of the Mohicans* (1826), *The Prairie* (1824), *The Pathfinder* (1840), and *The Deer Slayer* (1841).

2. **ZANE GREY** (1872-1939). Born Pearl Zane Gray, he read pulp fiction, as a child. As an adult he wrote romanticized western novels. His first western novel: *The Last of the Plainsman*(1908), and his first published novel: *The Heritage of the Desert* (1909). His stories were about rugged individualism and the healing powers of the desert. Other important novels: *Riders of the Purple Sage* (1912), one of the best western novels ever written, *Wildfire* (1917), *Knights of the Range* (1939), and *The Trail Driver* (1936). He wrote 56 books on the west and 46 were made into movies! The "Zane Grey Western Theatre" (1956-1961) brought his works to television.

3. **LOUIS L'AMOUR** (1908-1988). Born Louis Dearborn LaMoore, he wrote ranch romances to become the

673

"Diamond Dick, Jr.'s Mysterious Diagram," in No. 191 of this Library.

Wild Bill's Last Trail.

By NED BUNTLINE.

most prolific western pulp writer of all time. He wrote four Hopalong Cassidy books under the name "Tex Burns." His first paperback: *Westward the Tide* (1950). 30 of his books were made into movies. The John Wayne film *Hondo* (1953)—from one of his short stories—brought him fame *after* writing a best seller based on the *Hondo* screenplay.

4. NED BUNTLINE (1823-1886). Born Edward Zane Carrol Judson. In May of 1844, he published "Ned Buntline's Magazine." In 1869, after meeting Buffalo Bill Cody, Buntline made him the hero of four dime novels and a stage play. Because of their success, other "penny dreadful" writers quickly followed suit. Buntline wrote over 500 dime novels, becoming the leading western pulp writer of the day.

5. MAX BRAND (1892-1944). Born Frederich Schiller Faust. He sold his first western in 1917 and quickly became "The "King of the Pulps." He penned more than 500 books

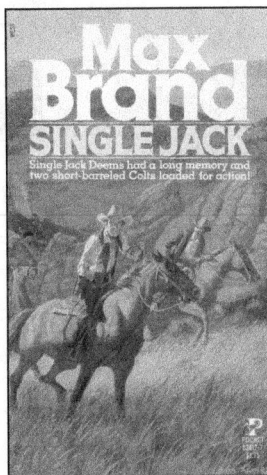

Max Brand

SINGLE JACK

Single Jack Deems had a long memory and two short-barreled Colts loaded for action!

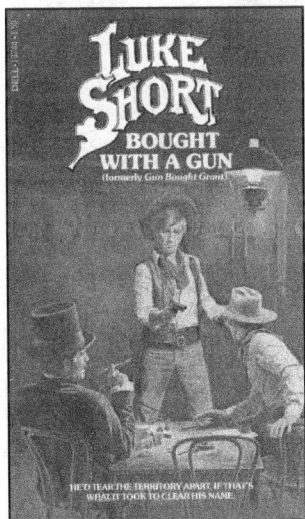

LUKE SHORT

BOUGHT WITH A GUN

(formerly Gun Bought Grant)

HE'D TEAR THE TERRITORY APART, IF THAT'S WHAT IT TOOK TO CLEAR HIS NAME.

under many pseudonyms and genres. Seven books were made into films, including the hit *Destry Rides Again* (1932 and 1939).

6. LUKE SHORT (1908-1975). Born Frederick Dilley Glidden. His first novel: *The Feud at Single Shot* (1935).

9 DIME NOVEL HEROES

One-hundred plus years ago, the dime novel—fictional stories about Wild West heroes—were found under every boy's bed. These novels were instrumental in establishing a western folklore that would forever blur our view of the real West. Some of those dime novel heroes were:

1. Deadwood Dick
2. Calamity Jane
3. Denver Dan
4. Sierra Sam
5. The James Boys
6. Texas Jack
7. Kit Carson
8. Wild Bill Hickok
9. California Joe

ERASTUS BEADLE

Though not the first to publish inexpensive paperback novels about the West, Beadle was the first to issue them in a continuing series and publish them in large quantities. They were books for the masses and the public loved them. Begun in 1860, they sold for 10 cents a copy, and the name "dime novels" was born.

Kit Carson, Jr., the Crack Shot of the West.
A WILD LIFE ROMANCE, BY "BUCKSKIN SAM."

Saddle Up, Turn on the Reading Light
92 Louis L'Amour Novels

*"A book is less important for what it says than for
what it makes you think."*
—Louis L'Amour

Born in 1908, Louis L'Amour penned over 100
fictional "Frontier Stories" along with historical fiction
and non-fiction titles about the American West. Listed here
are only the novels he wrote. Which were made into movies?

Westward the Tide (UK1950, US '76)
The Riders of High Rock (1951)
The Rustlers of West Fork (1951)
The Trail to Seven Pines (1951)
Trouble Shooter (1952)
Hondo (1953)
Showdown at Yellow Butte ('53)
Crossfire Trail (1954)
Heller with a Gun (1954)
Kilkenny (1954)
Utah Blaine (1954)
Guns of the Timberlands (1955)
To Tame a Land (1955)
The Burning Hills (1956)
Silver Canyon (1956)
Last Stand at Papago Wells (1957)
Sitka (1957)
The Tall Stranger (1957)
Radigan (1958)
The First Fast Draw (1959)
Taggart (1959)
The Daybreakers (1960)
Flint (1960)
Sackett (1961)
High Lonesome (1962)

Killoe (1962)
Lando (1962)
Shalako (1962)
Catlow (1963)
Dark Canyon (1963)
Fallon (1963)
How the West Was Won (1963)
Hanging Woman Creek (1964)
Mojave Crossing (1964)
The High Graders (1965)
The Key-Lock Man (1965)
Kiowa Trail (1965)
The Sackett Brand (1965)
The Broken Gun (1966)
Kid Rodelo (1966)
Kilrone (1966)
Mustang Man (1966)
Matagorda (1967)
The Sky-Liners (1967)
Chancy (1968)
Conagher (1968)
Down the Long Hills (1968)
The Empty Land (1969)
The Lonely Men (1969)
Galloway (1970)

The Man Called Noon (1970)
Reilly's Luck (1970)
Brionne (1971)
The Ferguson Rife (1971)
North to the Rails (1971)
Tucker (1971)
Under the Sweetwater Rim (1971)
Callaghen (1972)
Ride the Dark Trail (1972)
The Man from Skibbereen (1973)
The Quick and the Dead (1973)
Treasure Mountain (1973)
The Californios (1974)
Sackett's Land (1974)
Man From the Broken Hills (1975)
Over on the Dry Side (1975)
Rivers West (1975)
The Rider of Lost Creek (1976)
To the Far Blue Mountains (1976)
Where the Long Grass Blows (1976)
Borden Chantry (1977)

Bendigo Shafter (1978)
Fair Blows the Wind (1978)
The Mountain Valley War (1978)
The Iron Marshal (1979)
The Proving Trail (1979)
Lonely on the Mountain (1980)
The Warrior's Path (1980)
Comstock Lode (1981)
Milo Talon (1981)
The Cherokee Trail (1982)
The Shadow Riders (1982)
The Lonesome Gods (1983)
Ride the River (1983)
Son of a Wanted Man (1984)
The Walking Drum (1984)
Jubal Sackett (1985)
Passin' Through (1985)
Last of the Breed (1986)
West of Pilot Range (1986)
A Trail to the West (1986)
The Haunted Mesa (1987)

Louis L'Amour also penned a series of Sackett, Talon, Chantry, Kilkenny, and Hopalong Cassidy books. He also published numerous collections of western short stories. Many of his stories were made into movies. Louis L'Amour said this: "One day I was speeding along at the typewriter, and my daughter—who was a child at the time—asked me, "Daddy, why are you writing so fast?" And I replied, "Because I want to see how the story turns out."

A LITTLE LOUIE L'AMOUR LORE

TRIVIA: Louis L'Amour's family name was "LaMoore," but he changed it to L'Amour, French for "The Love." Born in Jamestown, North Dakota, he left home at 15 and traveled the west taking odd jobs until he settled in Los Angeles and then shipped out as a merchant seaman until WWII when he served in the U.S. Army. He wrote for pulp fiction magazines until the 1950's when his novels began to sell. His first published work was a poem entitled "The Chap Worth While." The screen rights to "The Gift of Cochcise," a 1952 story in *Colliers*, was bought by John Wayne who quickly turned it into the movie *Hondo*. The rest is history.

33 Elmer Kelton Books

"Dad gave me every chance to learn to be a cowboy. I was probably the greatest failure of his life. I was always better at talking about it, and writing about it, than I ever was at doing it."
—Elmer Kelton

The over 40 western novels of Elmer Kelton were far less in number than Louis L'Amour's, but they had a realism and authenticity about ranch life with character driven stories without gunplay that Louis couldn't match. Kelton was born and raised on several different ranches in West Texas, got a degree in Journalism at the University of Texas in Austin and, after serving in the war, became the farm-and-ranch editor of the *San Angelo Standard Times*, then the editor of *Sheep and Goat Raiser Magazine* and the *Livestock Weekly*, retiring in 1990. All the while, he was writing novels that won more Spur Awards from the Western Writers of America than any other western author, even Louis L'Amour. Kelton won seven! And he was awarded four Western Heritage awards from the National Cowboy Hall of Fame. In 1995, the Western Writers of America voted him "the greatest western writer of all time." He died in San Angelo in 2009. Below is a partial list of his novels. The ones marked with a star won the Spur Award.

Hot Iron (1956)	The Man Who Rode Midnight (1988)
Barbed Wire (1957)	Honor at Daybreak (1991)
Buffalo Wagons (1957)*	Slaughter (1992)*
Shadow of a Star (1958)	The Far Canyon (1994)*
Donovan (1961)	The Pumpkin Rollers (1996)
The Day the Cowboys Quit(1971)*	Cloudy in the West (1997)
Wagontongue (1972)	Way of the Coyote (2001)*
The Time it Never Rained (1973)*	Jericho's Road (2004)
The Good Old Boys (1979)	Six Bits a Day (2005)
The Wolf and the Buffalo (1980)	Ranger's Law:A Lone Star Saga(2006)
Eye of the Hawk (1981)*	The Rebels: Sons of Texas (2007)
Dark Thicket (1985)	Texas Sunrise (2008)

His "Texas Ranger" series of novels: The Buckskin Line, Badger Boy, The Way of the Coyote, Ranger's Trail, Texas Vendetta, Jericho's Road, Hard Trail to Follow, Other Men's Horses, and Texas Standoff.

The Covered Wagon of the Great Western Migration. 1886 in Loup Valley, Nebraska.
(Wikimedia Commons)

A Match Game
4 NOVEL STORIES

Match the short synopsis of a western novel with the name of that book.

1. A historical saga that follows ex-Texas Rangers as they drive their cattle from the Rio Grande to Montana.
2. A mysterious gunman rides into the poor farmstead of Joe Starrett and is invited to stay, but must pick up his guns and fight the men who are trying to take Joe's farm.
3. Two drifters, Art Croft and Gil Carter, are drawn into a posse determined to find and lynch the murderer of a local man, only to end badly with the death of three innocent men.
4. During a 1950's West Texas drought, Charlie Flagg tries desperately to save his ranch, but refuses to accept federal aid, choosing to make his own way.

a. *The Ox-Bow Incident* by Walter Van Tillburg Clark.
b. *Shane* by Jack Schaefer.
c. *Lonesome Dove* by Larry McMurtry.
d. *The Time It Never Rained* by Elmer Kelton.

ANS: 1-c, 2-b, 3-a, 4-d.

John Wayne as Will Andersen in *The Cowboys*, Sanford Productions

The Tagline for *Stagecoach* (1939) was "Danger holds the reins as the devil cracks the whip! Desperate men! Frontier women! Rising above their pasts in a West corrupted by violence and gun-fire!"

Writing Trivia: Earnest Haycox wrote "Stage to Lordsburg" which became John Ford's 1939's *Stagecoach*, the motion picture that won two Oscars and launched John Wayne's career. He also wrote "Trouble Shooter" that became Cecil B. DeMille's Oscar-nominated 1939 classic *Union Pacific*. It was good year for Haycox.

A Match Game
4 NOVELISTS IN HOLLYWOOD

Match the western authors with the novels they wrote that were made into movies.

1. Jack Schaefer
2. Alan Le May
3. Henry Wilson Allen
4. A.B. Guthrie, Jr.

a. The Searchers & The Unforgiven
b. The Way West & The Big Sky
c. Shane & Monte Walsh
d. Mackenna's Gold & I, Tom Horn

ANS: 1-c, 2-a, 3-d, 4-b

TRIVIA: *Four Faces West,* a 1948 film starring Joel McCrea was based on the novel "Paseó por Aquí" by Eugene Manlove Rhodes.

What novel by Elmer Kelton was made into a movie about West Texas ranching and was directed by Tommy Lee Jones? Ans: *The Good Old Boys* (1995).

L'Amour Trivia: "During the 1960's, L'Amour intended to build a working town typical of those of the nineteenth-century Western frontier, with buildings with false fronts situated in rows on either side of an unpaved main street and flanked by wide boardwalks before which, at various intervals, were watering troughs and hitching posts. The town, to be named *Shalako* after the protagonist of one of L'Amour's novels, was to have featured shops and other businesses that were typical of such towns: a barber shop, a hotel, a dry goods store, one or more saloons, a church, a one-room schoolhouse, etc. It would have offered itself as a filming location for Hollywood motion pictures concerning the Wild West. However, funding for the project fell through, and *Shalako* was never built." —source unknown

---

Please heed the following rules:
8 MOVING PICTURE PALACE
LANTERN SLIDES

This is the text of **actual early lantern slides** that were projected before or after the silent movie was run in order to remind patrons of proper behavior in the theatre. They were penned by hand and often had additional scrollwork and an illustration or two.

Gentlemen
will please refrain from
Smoking, Spitting
or using
Profane Language
During the Performance.

LADIES
WITHOUT ESCORTS
Cordially Invited

Somebody's Baby is Crying
IS IT YOURS?

NEXT WEEK
THIS THEATRE WILL HAVE
TALKING PICTURES!
TALENTED ACTORS and ACTRESSES
WILL BE BEHIND THE SCREEN.

Our Theatre is
Ventilated
and
Disinfected
EVERY DAY.

Don't Spit On the floor-
Remember the Johnstown Flood.

When leaving this theatre
Please Turn The Seat Up.

GOOD NIGHT

Happy Trails and Western Tales
A FAREWELL

The trail is the thing, not the end of the trail. Travel too fast and you miss all you are traveling for.
—Louis L'Amour

Well, **I'm near the bottom of my brown**, water-stained cardboard box that was full of scraps of paper torn from ringed notebooks, Post-It-Notes, and numerous little white note cards scribbled with barely readable hen scratches. And after trying to organize this information into many dog-eared manila folders, I find some areas of the American West are poorly represented, but I also realize that there is no end to what can be culled from the mass of literature that exists about the American West, and so I hope that this little book whets your appetite and inspires you to go do some serious research about the authentic Old West. I intentionally mixed the folklore, the legend, and the movies of popular culture, with a taste of real American history to show how it has merged into one perception of the West that made America the most unique democracy ever created on this planet.

There are thousands of books—hundreds of thousands—on the subject, but I hope that's not the only place the West is left. The historic places and physical artifacts must also be preserved. I can only hope that in our fast-paced urban society we retain those values that made the people of the great western expansion such an awesome people. The frontier is gone; there is no bringing it back, but honor, integrity, and "a day's pay for a day's work," need not also be lost. The exploration of new frontiers needs not come to a grinding halt. The wondrous oceans and the mysterious outer space are still out there... ready to be settled with laser guns.

A Ballad
THE COWBOY'S LAMENT
(aka "The Streets of Laredo")

Grab your guitar. Here's the lyrics of this popular western song, sung by the cowboy as he rode the range in the late nineteenth century. The original was written by Francis Henry Maynard in 1876 in the legendary town of Dodge City, Kansas. It is still a favorite among cowboys and westerners. The song was based on an old Irish ballad about a soldier's death and burial.

1. As I walked out in the streets of Laredo,
As I walked out in Laredo one day,
I spied a young cowboy wrapped up in white linen,
Wrapped up in white linen and cold as the clay.

2. "Oh, beat the drum slowly and play the fife lowly,
Play the dead march as you carry me along.
Take me to the green valley and lay the sod o'er me,
For I'm a young cowboy and I know I done wrong."

3. "I see by your outfit that you are a cowboy,"
These words he did say as I boldly walked by.
Come sit down beside me and hear my sad story;
I'm shot in the breast and I know I must die."

4. "My friends and relations they live in the Nation;
They know not where their dear boy has gone.
I first came to Texas and hired to a ranchman,
Oh, I'm a young cowboy and I know I've done wrong."

5. "Twas once in the saddle I used to go dashing;
It was once in the saddle I used to go gay.
First to the dram house and then to the card house,
Got shot in the breast and I'm dying today."

6. "Get six jolly cowboys to carry my coffin;
Get six pretty maidens to bear up my pall.
Put bunches of roses all over my coffin,
Put roses to deaden the clods as they fall."

7. "Go gather around you a group of young cowboys,
And tell them the story of this, my sad fate.
Tell one and the other, before they go further,
To stop their wild roving before it's too late."

8. "Go bring me a cup, a cup of cold water,
To cool my parched lips," the young cowboy said.
Before I returned, the spirit had left him
And gone to his Maker, the cowboy was dead.

9. We beat the drum slowly and played the fife lowly,
And bitterly wept as we bore him along.
For we all loved our comrade, so brave, young, and handsome,
We all loved our comrade although he'd done wrong.

A FAREWELL FROM TOM MIX
By Tom Mix

May you brand your largest calf crop,
May your range grass never fail,
May your water holes stay open,
May you ride an easy trail.

May you never reach for leather,
Nor your saddle horse go lame;
May you drop your loop on critters
With your old unerring aim.

May your stack of chips grow taller,
May your shootin' e'er stay true.
May good luck plumb snow you under—
Is always my wish for you.

A GOOD LUCK RHYME
—Anonymous

May your horse never stumble,
Your spurs never rust,
Your guts never grumble,
and your cinch never bust!

May your boots never pinch,
Your crops never fail,
While you eat lots of beans
and stay out of jail!

A GOOD LUCK DITTY
—Unknown

May neither drouth nor rain nor blizzard
Disturb the joy-juice in your gizzard.
And may you camp where wind won't hit you,
Where snakes won't bite, and bears won't git you!

ROY ROGER'S FAREWELL
By Dale Evans
(Theme song from the 1951 *Roy Rogers Show*)

**Happy trails to you
Keep smiling until then
Happy trails to you
Till we meet again.**

Roy Rogers Productions (author's collection)

"Happy Trails!" from Roy, Dale and Gabby

Roy Rogers Trivia: Born name: Leonard Slye. When Leonard needed a stage name, he chose the name of his childhood dentist: Roy Rogers. His nickname: "King of the Cowboys." His horse's name: Trigger. His horse also had a nickname: "Smartest Horse in the Movies." Roy got his horse in 1938 and rode him in every film after that! His dog's name: Bullet. Roy's theme song was "Happy Trails" and it was written by his third wife Dale Evans (1947 to 1998, the year Roy died.) Probably Roy's most famous quote: "When I die, just skin me out and put me up on old Trigger and I'll be happy." Roy didn't get his wish.

About The Author
DONALD K. KIRK

"If we fail to remember our beginnings—the Frontier West—we will fail to be the men we could be; we will fail to be the great America we once were."
—Don Kirk

DON KIRK **grew up watching westerns** on a small black-and-white television set, but it wasn't until he was asked to be the cinematographer on an 8mm movie at college (he had the only movie camera), did he realize he was hooked on the Old West. The next year, he wrote and directed a seventy minute, silent, slapstick western in Super-8! As soon as he graduated from college with a degree in architecture, he and his brother Doug loaded provisions into a red Volkswagen Beetle and made their first journey west to California, shooting film all along the way. Seeing the Old Tucson movie set made an indelible impression on Don. It wasn't long afterwards that he conceived an elaborate plan for a Western Town and Old West Resort. Since then his interest in the American West has grown by leaps and bounds.

After a short tour of duty in the military, Don's interest in the REAL American West blossomed, and he began to collect period antiques, western history books, movie posters, and western costumes—anything western. He managed a Wild West gunfight acting troupe and later participated in living history reenactment groups. As time passed, he gained more than ten years experience in film and motion picture production, six years of practical building experience, and years of dabbling with pen & ink drawing, his subjects, of course, western towns, artifacts, and steam railroads.

Don traveled the western states for twenty years documenting, through still photography, the rapidly disappearing remnants of that unique era in World history known fondly as the Old West.

Because his interest was also in period architecture, he has built an enormous slide file of false-fronted Victorian buildings, wagons, schools, churches, mine complexes and any remaining architecture he could find still standing from the nineteenth century.

He has dreamed of the perfect "Western Town" for over 30 years and believes that it could be much more than a theme park. It could be a historical look into a very unique part of our past, a period that is getting farther and farther removed from the present with a loss of not only memories, but the values of the people that settled the frontier and gave us what we have today. Redrock Canyon Territory, as he calls it, would be the largest open-air museum ever built, containing several western towns on over a thousand acres of classic western scenery. It would be a unique mix of services and activity, all catering to the buff, historian, and general public who want to learn and revel in the legend of our American West.

The author as Prospector "Crusty" Corrigan
(Michael Jay Smith photography)

Lawyer's bookcase stuffed with books about the American West (dk)

Who Wrote It First?
SELECTED BIBLIOGRAPHY

*For one who reads, there is no limit to the number of
lives that may be lived, for fiction, biography, and history offer an inexhaustible number of lives in many
parts of the world, in all periods of time.*
—Louis L'Amour

Hundreds of thousands of books have been written
about the Old West. Serious attempts at revealing the
real American West to flights of fantasy about the
legendary Wild West fill the book shelves of America.
The West is the history of America when it was a democracy (not
a republic) with each pocket of settlers making their own laws to
meet their needs. Without books (and museums) we cannot pass
on our history. A very tiny sampling of books about the American
West from the author's collection is included here.

Silverado starring Kevin Costner, Scott Glenn, Kevin Kline, and Danny Glover.

Columbia Pictures and Delphi II Productions (author's collection)

GENERAL HISTORY

Brash, Sarah, editor. *The American Story: Settling the West.* Alexandria, Virginia:Time-Life Books, 1996.

Chrisman, Harry E. *1001 Most-Asked Questions About the American West.* Athens, Ohio: Swallow Press/Ohio University Press, 1982.

Clegg, Charles and Beebe, Lucius. *The American West:The Pictorial Epic of a Continent.* New York: Bonanza Books, 1955.

Conlan, Robert, editor. *The Wild West: Companion Volume to the Television Miniseries.* New York:Warner Books, 1993.

Crutchfield, James A. *Legends of the Wild West.* Lincolnwood, Illinois: Publications International, 1995.

Davis, Robert Murray, editor. Owen Wister's West: Selected Articles. Albuquerque: University of New Mexico Press, 1987.

Davis, William C. The American Frontier: Pioneers, Settlers & Cowboys 1800-1899. New York: Smithmark Publications, 1992.

Demlinger, Sandor. *Stagecoach: Rare Views of the Old West, 1849-1915.* Atglen, Pennsylvania: Schiffer Publishing Ltd., 2005.

Edward S. Barnard, editor. Story of the Great American West. Pleasantville, New York:The Reader's Digest Association, 1977.

Foster-Harris. *The Look of the Old West.* New York:The Viking Press, 1955.

Grafton, John. *The American West in the Nineteenth Century.* Dover Publications, 1992.

Jones, Constance. *Trailblazers:The Men and Woman Who Forged the West.* New York: Friedman/Fairfax Publishers, 1995.

Knowles, Thomas W., Lansdale, Joe R., editors. *The West That Was.* New York:Wings Books, 1993.

Laut, Agnes C. *The Conquest of Our Western Empire.* New York: Robert M. McBride & Company, 1927.

Lavender, David. *The Great West.* Boston: Houghton Mifflin Company, 2000.

McLoughlin, Denis. *Wild and Wooley:An Encyclopedia of the Old West.* New York: Barnes & Noble, 1996.

Peters, Arthur King. *Seven Trails.* N.Y.:Abbeville Publishing Group, 1996.

Phillips, David R., editor. *The West:An American Experience.* Chicago: Henry Regnery Company, 1973.

Reedstrom, Ernest L. *Scrapbook of the American West.* Caldwell, Idaho: Caxton Printers Ltd., 1991.

Robarts, Brooks. *Historic America:The Southwest.* San Diego, California: Thunder Bay Press, 2002.

Smithwick, Noah. *The Evolution of a State: Or Recollections of Old Texas Days.* Austin: University of Texas Press, 1983. 1900 reprint.

Utley, Robert, editor. *Encyclopedia of the American West.* New York: Random House, 1997.

Viola, Herman J. *Exploring the West.* Wash. D. C.: Smithsonian Institution, 1987.
Walker, Paul Robert. *Trail of the Wild West.* National Geographic Society, 1997.
Ward, Geoffrey C. *The West.* New York: Little, Brown and Company, 1999.
Ward, Geoffrey C. *The West:An Illustrated History.* New York: Little, Brown and Company, 1996.
West, Elliott. *The Way to the West: Essays on the Central Plains.* Albuquerque, University of New Mexico Press, 1995.
Woodward, Meredith Bain. *Land of Dreams:A History in Photographs of the British Columbia Interior.* Canmore,Alberta:Altitude Publishing, Canada Ltd., 1993.
Yenne, Bill, editor. *The Opening of the American West: In Early Photographs and Prints.* New York: Barnes & Noble, 1997.

I. COWBOYS AND THEIR COWPONIES

Adams, Ramon F. *Western Words:A Dictionary of the Range, Cow-camp and Trail.* Norman: University of Oklahoma Press, 1944.
Adams, Ramon F. *Cowboy Lingo: A Dictionary of the Slack-Jaw Words and Whangdoodle Ways of the American West.* New York: Houghton Mifflin Co., 2000. Originally published in 1936.
Alstad, Ken. *Savvy Sayin's: Lean & Meaty One-Liners.* Tucson, Arizona: Ken Alstad Company.
Back, Joe. *Horses, Hitches & Rocky Trails:The Packer's Bible.* Boulder, Colorado: Johnson Books, 1987.
Ball, Robert W.D. and Vebell, Ed. *Cowboy Collectibles and Western Memorabilia.* Chester, Pennsylvania: Schiffer Publishing Ltd., 1991.
Cusic, Don. *Cowboys and the Wild West:An A-Z Guide From The Chisholm Trail To The Silver Screen.* New York: Facts On File, Inc., 1994.
Davis, Mollie E. *The Wire Cutters.* College Station:Texas A&M University Press, 1997. Originally published in 1899.
Dobie, J. Frank. *Cow People.* Boston: Little Brown and Co., 1964.
Forbis, William H. and the editors of the Time-Life Books. *The Cowboys* (the Old West series).Alexandria,Virginia:Time-Life Books, 1978.
Freeman, Criswell, editor. *The Book of Cowboy Wisdom.* Nashville,Tennessee: Walnut Grove Press, 1997.
Friedman, Michael. *Cowboy Culture:The Last Frontier of American Antiques.* West Chester, Pennsylvania: Schiffer Publishing Ltd., 1992.
Hanauer, Elsie V. *The Horse Owner's Concise Guide.* North Hollywood, California: Melvin Powers Wilshire Book Company, 1969.
Hedgpeth, Don. *Traildust: Cowboys, Cattle and Country, the Art of James Reynolds.* Shelton, Connecticut: Greenwich Workshop Press, 1997.
Hughes, Stella. *Bacon and Beans: Ranch-Country Recipes.* Colorado Springs, Colorado:Western Horseman, 1990.
Hendrickson, Robert. *Happy Trails: A Dictionary of Western Expressions.* New York: Facts On File, Inc., 1994.

Jones, Dave. *The Western Horse:Advice and Training.* Norman: University of Oklahoma Press, 1991.

Mackin, Bill. *Cowboy and Gunfighter Collectibles:A Photographic Encyclopedia With Price Guide and Makers Index.* Missoula, Montana: Mountain Press Publishing Company, 1989.

Marshal, Howard W. and Ahlborn, Richard E. *Bucharoos in Paradise: Cowboy Life in Northern Nevada.* Lincoln: U. of Nebraska Press, 1981.

Pavia, Audrey. *Horses for Dummies.* Foster City, California: IDG Books Worldwide, Inc., 1999.

Potter, Edgar R. "Frosty". *Cowboy Slang.* Phoenix: Golden West Publishers, 1986.

Potter, Edger R. *Cowboy Slang.* Phoenix: Golden West Publishers, 1993.

Reynolds, William and Rand, Richard. *The Cowboy Hat Book.* Salt Lake City: Gibbs-Smith Publisher, 1995.

Santee, Ross. *Cowboy.* Lincoln: University of Nebraska Press, 1977.

Seidman, Laurence Ivan. *Once in the Saddle:The Cowboy's Frontier 1866-1896.* New York: Facts On File, 1991.

Slatta, Richard W. *Cowboys of the Americas.* New Haven, Connecticut:Yale University Press, 1990.

Slatta, Richard W. *The Cowboy Encyclopedia.* New York:W.W. Norton & Company, 1994.

Slatta, Richard W. *Cowboy:The Illustrated History.* New York: Sterling, 2006.

Strictland, Charlene. *The Basics of Western Riding.* Pownal,Vermont: Story Publication, 1998.

Tanner, Ogden and the editors of the Time-Life Books. *The Ranchers* (the Old West series).Alexanderia,Virginia:Time-Life Books, 1977.

Ward, Fay E. *The Cowboy at Work.* Mineola, N.Y.: Dover Publications, 2003.

West, John O. *Cowboy Folk Humor: Life and Laughter in the American West.* Little Rock,Arkansas:August House/Little Rock Publishers, 1990.

Watts, Peter. *A Dictionary of the Old West.* New York:Alfred A. Knopf, 1977.

XIT: Being a New and Original Exploration, in Art and Words, Into the Life and Times of the American Cowboy. Birmingham: Oxmoor House, 1975.

II. THE GUNFIGHTERS

Blake, James Carlos. *The Pistoleer:A Novel of John Wesley Hardin.* New York: Berkley Publishing Group, 1995.

Cunningham, Eugene. *Triggernometry:A Gallery of Gunfighters.* New York: Barnes & Nobel, 1976.

Faulk, Odie B. *Tombstone: Myth and Reality.* New York: Oxford University Press, 1972.

Hardin, John Wesley. *The Life of John Wesley Hardin From the Original Manuscript:As Written of Himself.* Seguin,Texas: Smith & Moore, 1896.

Horan, James D. *The Gunfighters:Accounts by Eyewitnesses and the Gunfighters Themselves.* Avenel, New York: Gramercy Books, 1994.

Masterson, W.B. (Bat). *Famous Gunfighters of the Western Frontier:Wyatt Earp, Doc Holliday, Luke Short and Others.* Mineola, New York: Dover Publications, 2009.

May, Robin. *Gunfighters.* Greenwich, Connecticut: Bison Books, 1983.

McCarty, Lea F. *The Gunfighters.* Berkeley, California: Mike Roberts Color Reproductions, 1959.

McGivern, Ed. *Ed McGivern's Book of Fast and Fancy Revolver Shooting.* Chicago: Follett Paublishing Company, 1975.

McNab, Chris, editor. *Gunfighters:The Outlaws and Their Weapons.* San Diego, California:Thunder Bay Press, 2005.

Metz, Leon Claire. *The Shooters:A Gallery of Notorious Gunmen from the American West.* New York: Berkeley Books, 1976.

Myers, John. *Doc Holliday.* Lincoln: University of Nebraska Press, 1973.

O'Neal, Bill. *Encyclopedia of Western Gunfighters.* Norman: University of Oklahoma Press, 1979.

Rattenbury, Richard C. *Packing Iron: Gunleather of the Frontier West.* Millwood, New York: Zon International Publishing Company, 1993.

Rosa, Joseph G. and May, Robin. *Gun Law:A Study of Violence in the Wild West.* Chicago: Contemporary Books, Inc., 1977.

Rosa, Joseph G. *Age of the Gunfighter: Men and Weapons on the Frontier 1840-1900.* Norman: University of Oklahoma Press, 1993.

Toepperwein, Herman. *Showdown:Western Gunfighters in Moments of Truth.* Austin,Texas: Madrona Press, 1974.

Trachtman, Paul, and the editors of Time-Life Books. *The Gunfighters.* (the Old West series).Alexandria,Virginia:Time-Life Books, 1974.

Trimble, Marshall. *Arizona Highways:The Law of the Gun* (Wild West series). Phoenix,Arizona:Arizona Department of Transportation, 1997.

Turner, George. *George Turner's Book of Gunfighters.* Amarillo,Texas: Baxter Lane Co., 1972.

Waters, Frank. *The Earp Brothers of Tombstone.* Lincoln: University of Nebraska Press, 1976.

III. BADMEN ON BOOTHILL

Duff, Charles. *A Handbook on Hanging.* London:The Journeyman Press, 1981.

Madigan, Paul J. *Institution Rules & Regulations: United States Penitentiary, Alcatraz, California.* San Francisco: Golden Gate National Parks Association, 1983.

The Sweet Smell of Sagebrush:A Prisoner's Diary 1903-1912. Rawlins, Wyoming: Friends of the Old Penitentiary in Association with the Old Penitentiary Joint Powers Board, 1990.

Trafzer, Cliff E. and George, Steve. *Prison Centennial 1876-1976:A Pictorial History of the Arizona Territorial Prison at Yuma.* Yuma,Arizona: Rio Colorado Press, 1980.

IV. WEAPONS OF THE WEST

Clancy, Lica. *Guns of the Wild West.* Philadelphia: Running Press Book Publishers, 2005.

Davis, Williams C. *Frontier Skills: The Tactics and Weapons That Won the American West.* Guilford, Connecticut: The Lyons Press, 2003.

Edsall, James. *Firearms And Their Successors.* Union City, Tennessee: Pioneer Press, 1974.

Edsall, James. *The Revolver Rifles.* Union City, Tennessee: Pioneer Press, 1974.

Edsall, James. *The Story of Firearm Ignition.* Union City, Tennessee: Pioneer Press, 1974.

Guns And The Gunfighters. New York: Bonanza Books, 1982.

Harris, Ron. *All About Cowboy Action Shooting.* Accokeek, Maryland: Stoeger Publishing Company, 2001.

McAulay, John D. *Carbines of the Civil War: 1861-1865,* Union City Tennessee: Pioneer Press, 1981.

Myatt, Major F. *The Illustrated Encyclopedia of 19th Century Firearms.* New York: Crescent Books, 1994.

Rosa, Joseph G. *Guns of the American West.* New York: Crown Publishers, Inc., 1985.

Rules for the Management of the Springfield Rifle, Carbine, Caliber .45. Government Printing Office, Washington, 1898.

Sights West: Selections From The Winchester Museum Collection. Cody, Wyoming: Buffalo Bill Historical Center, 1976.

Venner, Dominique. *Frontier Pistols and Revolvers.* Edison, New Jersey: Chartwell Books, 1996

Wexler, Bruce. *John Wayne's Wild West: An Illustrated History of Cowboys, Gunfighters, Weapons, and Equipment.* New York: Skyhorse Publishing, 2010.

Wilson, R.L. *The Peacemakers: Arms and Adventure in the American West.* Edison, New Jersey: Chartwell Books, 1992.

V. THE OUTLAWS

Adams, Ramon F. *Six-guns and Saddle Leather: A Bibliography of Books and Pamphlets of Western Outlaws and Gunmen.* Mineola, New York: Dover Publications, 1998.

Albano, Bob. *Arizona Highways: Days of Destiny.* Phoenix, Arizona: Department of Transportation, 1996.

Alexander, Kent. *Heroes of the Wild West.* New York: Mallard Press, 1992.

Baker, Pearl. *The Wild Bunch at Robbers Roost.* Lincoln, Nebraska: University of Nebraska Press, 1989.

Bell, Bob Boze. *The Illustrated Life and Times of Doc Holliday.* Phoenix, Arizona:TriStar-Boze Publications, 1995.

Bell, Bob Boze. *The Illustrated Life and Times of Wyatt Earp.* Phoenix, Arizona:TriStar-Boze Publications, 1995.

Bell, Bob Boze. *The Illustrated Life and Times of Billy The Kid.* Phoenix, Arizona:TriStar-Boze Publications, 1996.

Breihan, Carl. W. *Lawmen and Robbers.* Caldwell, Idaho:The Claxton Printers, LTD, 1986.

Convis, Charles L. *Outlaw Tales of Nevada:True Stories of Nevada's Most Famous Robbers, Rustlers, and Bandits.* Helena, Montana:Two Dot, Globe Pequot Press, 2006.

Crutchfield, James A., O'Neal, Bill, Walker, Dale L. *Legends of the Wild West.* Lincolnwood, Illinois: Publications International, 1995.

Emmett, Chris. *Shanghai Pierce:A Fair Likeness.* Norman: University of Oklahoma Press, 1953.

Erbsen Wayne. *Outlaw Ballads, Legends & Lore.* Asheville, North Carolina: Native Ground Music, 1996.

Farrell, Robert J. *Arizona Highways:Manhunts and Massacres* (Wild West series). Phoenix:Arizona Department of Transportation, 1997.

Franke, Paul. *They Plowed Up Hell in Old Cochise!* Douglas, Arizona: Douglas Climate Club, 1974.

Hanes, Colonel Bailey *C. Bill Doolin Outlaw O.T.* Norman: University of Oklahoma Press, 1968.

Jackson, Joseph Henry. *Bad Company.* Lincoln, Nebraska: University of Nebraska Press, 1977.

Jessen, Ken. *Colorado Gunsmoke:True Stories of Outlaws and Lawmen on the Colorado Frontier.* Loveland, Colorado: J.V. Publications, 1986.

Kelly, Charles. *The Outlaw Trail:A History of Butch Cassidy and His Wild Bunch.* New York: Konecky & Konecky, 1959.

Michalowski, Kevin. *The Gun Digest Book of Cowboy Action Shooting: Gear, Guns, Tactics.* Iola, Wisconsin: KP Books, 2005.

Miller, Ronald Dean. *Shady Ladies of the West.* Tucson, Arizona:Westernlore Press, 1985.

Outlaws and Owlhoots in the Old West. Denver, Colorado: Colorado Fever Publications and Colorado Historical Institute for Children, 1988.

Outlaws & Lawmen of the Wild West. Mesa, Arizona:Terrell Publishing Co., 1997.

Patterson, Richard. *Historical Atlas of the Outlaw West.* Boulder, Colorado: Johnson Books, 1991.

Rascals & Rogues of Long Ago. Maynard, Massachusetts: Chandler Press, 1989.

Simmons, Marc. *When Six-Guns Ruled: Outlaw Tales of the Southwest.* Santa Fe, New Mexico:Ancient City Press, 1990.

Sonnichsen, C.L. *Roy Bean:Law West of the Pecos.* Lincoln: University of Nebraska Press, 1991.

The Life and Tragic Death of Jesse James:The Western Desperado. Austin,Texas: The Steck Company, 1996.

Triplett, Frank. *The Life, Times and Treacherous Death of Jesse James.* New York: Konecky & Konecky, 1970.

Walker, Herb. *Butch Cassidy:The Congenial Desperado.* Amarillo,Texas: Baxter Lane Company, 1975.

Wilson, Gary A. *Honky-Tonk Town:Havre, Montana's Lawless Era.* Helena, Montana:Two Dot, Globe Pequot Press, 2006.

VI. WESTERN MOVIE TRIVIA

Black, Bill. *Roy Rogers and the Silver Screen Cowboys.* Longwood, Florida:AC Comics and Paragon Publications, 1997.

Cowboy Movie Posters. Bruce Hershenson, P.O. Box 874,West Plains, Missouri, 65775.

Everson, William K. *The Hollywood Western.* New York: Carol Publishing Group, 1992.

Fagen, Herb. *The Encyclopedia of Westerns.* NewYork: Facts On File, Inc., 2003.

Fenin, George N. and Everson, William K. *The Western: From Silents to Cinema.* New York: Bonanza Books.

George-Warren, Holly. *Cowboy: How Hollywood Invented the Wild West.* Pleasantville, New York:The Reader's Digest Association, Inc.

McCoy, Tim and McCoy, Ronald. *Tim McCoy Remembers the West:An Autobiography.* Lincoln: University of Nebraska Press, 1988.

Phillips, Robert. *Silver Screen Cowboys.* Salt Lake City, Utah: Gibbs-Smith Publisher, 1993.

Rothel, David. *Those Great Cowboy Sidekicks.* Waynesville, North Carolina: Woy Publications, 1984.

VII. WESTERNS AND THEIR STARS

Garfield, Brian. *Western Films:A Complete Guide.* New York: Rawson Associates, 1982.

George-Warren, Holly. *Cowboy: How Hollywood Invented the Wild West.* Pleasantville New York:The Reader's Digest Association, Inc., 2002.

Hamilton, John R. *Thunder in the Dust: Classic Images of Western Movies.* New York: Stewart,Tabori & Chang, 1987.

Hershenson, Bruce, editor. *Texas at the Movies.* West Plains, Misouri: Bruce Hershenson, 2005.

Matthews, Leonard. *History of Western Movies.* London: Deans International Publishing, 1984.

Place, J.A. *The Western Films of John Ford.* Secaucus, N.J.: Citadel Press, 1974.

Rothel, David. *An Ambush of Ghosts:A Personal Guide to Favorite Western Film Locations.* Madison, North Carolina: Empire Publishing, 1990.

Schickel, Richard. *Clint Eastwood:A Biography by Richard Schickel.* New York:Alfred A. Knopf, 1996.

Wagner, Rob L. *The Duke: A Life in Pictures.* New York: Michael Friedman Publishing Group, 2001.
Zmijewsky, Boris & Pfeiffer, Lee. *The Films of Clint Eastwood.* Secaucus, New Jersey: Citadel Press, 1982.

VIII. THE CODE OF THE WEST

Ducan, John E. *Manners and Morals of Long Ago.* Maynard, Massachusetts: Chandler Press, 1993.
Hill, Thomas E. *The Essential Handbook of Victorian Etiquette.* San Mateo, California: Bluewood Books, 38 South B Street, 1994.

IX. GAMBLERS AND THEIR GAMES

Bethard, Wayne. *Lotions, Potions, and Deadly Elixirs: Frontier Medicine in America.* Lanham, Maryland: Roberts Rinehart Books, 2004.
DeArmnent, Robert K. *Knights of the Green Cloth: The Saga of the Frontier Gamblers.* Norman: University of Oklahoma Press, 1982.
Findlay, John M. *People of Chance: Gambling in American Society From Jamestown to Las Vegas.* New York: Oxford University Press, 1986.
Hicks, Jim and the editors of Time-Life Books. *The Gamblers* (the Old West series). Alexandria, Virginia: Time-Life Books, 1978.
Rosa, Joseph G. and Koop, Waldo E. *Rowdy Joe Lowe: Gambler With a Gun.* Norman: University of Oklahoma Press, 1989.

X. THE WESTERN SALOON

Barlow, Ronald S. *The Vanishing American Barber Shop: An Illustrated History of Tonsorial Art, 1860-1960.* El Cajon, California: Windmill Publishing Company, 1993.
Brown, Robert. *Saloons of the American West.* Silverton, Colorado: Sundance Publications, Ltd., 1978.
Dary, David. *Seeking Pleasure in the Old West.* Lawrence, Kansas: University Press of Kansas, 1995.
Erdoes, Richard. *Saloons of the Old West.* New York: Gramercy Books, 1997.
Karolevitz, Robert F. *Doctors of the Old West: A Pictorial History of Medicine on the Frontier.* New York: Bonanza Books, 1967.
Stratton, Owen Tully. *Medicine Man.* Norman: U. of Oklahoma Press, 1989.
West, Elliott. *The Saloon on the Rocky Mountain Mining Frontier.* Lincoln: University of Nebraska Press, 1979.

XI. AN OLD WEST CHRONOLOGY

Bowman, John S., editor. *The World Almanac of the American West.* New York: Pharos Books, 1986.

Bowman, John S., editor. *The American West Year by Year.* New York: Cresent Books, 1995.

Boyd, Eva Jolene. *That Old Overland Stagecoaching.* Plano, Texas: Republic of Texas Press/Wordware Publishing, 1993.

Clegg, Charles & Beebe, Lucius. *U.S. West: The Saga of Wells Fargo.* New York: Bonanza Books, 1969.

Flanagan, Mike. *The Old West: Day By Day.* New York: Facts On File, Inc., 1995.

Fodor, Eugene and Fisher, Robert C., editors. *Fodor's Old West: A Practical Guide to Where the West Was Won.* New York: David McKay Company, 1976.

Hooker, William Francis. *The Bullwhacker: Adventures of a Frontier Freighter.* Lincoln: University of Nebraska Press, 1988.

Klose, Nelson. *A Concise Study Guide to the American Frontier.* Lincoln: University of Nebraska Press, 1964.

Laut, Agnes C. *The Conquest of Our Western Empire.* New York: Robert M. McBride & Company, 1927.

Marcy, Randolph B. *The Prairie Traveler.* Old Saybrook, Connecticut: Applewood Books/Globe Pequot Press, reprint from 1859.

McLoughlin, Denis. *Wild & Woolly: An Encyclopedia of the Old West.* New York: Doubleday & Company, Inc., 1975.

Morgan, Dale L. *Rand McNally's Pioneer Atlas of the American West.* Chicago: Rand McNally & Company, 1969.

Nevin, David and the editors of Time-Life Books. *The Expressmen* (the Old West series). New York: Time-Life Books, 1976.

Parkman, Francis. *The Oregon Trail.* Lincoln: University of Nebraska Press, 1994.

Ridge, Martin. *Rand McNally Atlas of American Frontiers.* Chicago, Illinois: Rand McNally, 1993.

Schwantes, Carlos Armaldo. *Long Day's Journey: The Steamboat & Stagecoach Era in the Northern West.* Seattle: University of Washington Press, 1999.

Seetle, Raymond W. and Settle, Mary Lund. *Saddles & Spurs: The Pony Express Saga.* Lincoln: University of Nebraska Press, 1972.

Spring, Agnes Wright. *The Cheyenne and Black Hills Stage and Express Routes.* Lincoln: University of Nebraska Press, 1967.

Strahorn, Carrie Adell. *Fifteen Thousand Miles by Stage: Volume I: 1877-1880.* Lincoln: University of Nebraska Press, 1988.

Weiser, Kathy. *The Great American Bars and Saloons.* Edison, New Jersey: Chartwell Books, Inc., 2006.

Wither, Oscar Osburn. *The Transportation Frontier: Trans-Mississippi West, 1865-1890.* New York: Holt, Rinehart and Winston, 1964.

XII. THE CAVALRY

Barthe, Joe De. *The Life and Adventures of Frank Grouard.* (Classics of the Old West series).Alexandria Virginia:Time-Life Books, 1982.
Dorsey, Stephen R. *American Military Belts and Related Equipments.* Union City,Tennessee: Pioneer Press, 1984.
Graham, Colonel W.A. *The Story of the Little Big Horn.* Lincoln: University of Nebraska Press, 1988.
Hutchins, James S. *Horse Equipment & Cavalry Accoutrements.*Tucson, Arizona:Westernlore Press, 1984.
Katcher, Philip. *U.S. Cavalry on the Plains: 1850-90.* (Men-At-Arms series) London: Osprey Publishing, 1985.
Katcher, Philip. *The Mexican-American War: 1846-1848.* (Men-At-Arms series). London: Osprey Publishing, 1989.
Luecke, Barbara K. *Feeding the Frontier Army: 1775-1865.* Eagan, Minnesota: Grenadier Publications, 1990.
Nevin, David, and the editors of Time-Life Books. *The Soldiers* (The Old West series). New York, 1973.
Overfield II, Lloyd J. *The Little Big Horn, 1876.*
Pegler, Martin. *US Cavalryman 1865-1890:Weapons-Armour-Tactics.* (Osprey Warrior Series #4). London: Reed Consumer Books Ltd., 1993.
Ramsey-Palmer, Paige. *Young Troopers: Stories Of Army Children On The Frontier.* Tucson: Southwest Parks And Monuments Association, 1997.
Reynolds, Lindor. *Forts & Battlefields of the Old West.* New York: BDD Promotional Book Company, 1991.
Rickey, Jr., Don. *Forty Miles a Day on Beans and Hay:The Enlisted Soldier Fighting the Indian Wars.* Norman, Oklahoma: U. of Oklahoma Press, 1963.
Steele, James W. *Frontier Army Sketches.* Albuquerque, New Mexico: University of New Mexico Press, 1969.
Summerhayes, Martha. *Vanished Arizona:Recollections of the Army Life of a New England Woman.* Lincoln: University of Nebraska Press, 1979.
Urwin, Gregory J.W. *The United States Cavalry:An Illustrated History.* New York: Blandford Press, 1983.
Utley, Robert M. *If These Walls Could Speak: Historic Forts of Texas.* Austin, Texas: University of Texas Press, 1985.

XIII: THE INDIAN NATIONS

Blaisdell, Bob. *Great Speeches by Native Americans.* Mineola, New York: Dover Publications, 2000.
Brown, Dee. *Bury My Heart At Wounded Knee:An Indian History of the American West.* New York: Holt, Rinehart & Winston, 1970.

Brown, Epes Joseph and Steltenkamp, Michael. *The Sacred Pipe: Black Elk's Account of the Seven Rites & Black Elk, Holy Man of the Oclala.* New York: MJF Books, 1953.

Bulon, Ernie. *Navajo Taboos.* Gallup, N.M.: Buffalo Medicine Books, 1991.

Capps, Benjamin and the editors of Time-Life Books. *The Great Chiefs.* (the Old West series). Alexandria, Virginia: Time-Life Books, 1977.

Capps, Benjamin and the editors of Time-Life Books. *The Indians* (the Old West series). Alexandria, Virginia: Time-Life Books, 1979.

Cassidy Jr., James J., editor. *Through Indian Eyes: The Untold Story of Native American Peoples.* Pleasantville, N.Y.: The Reader's Digest Association, 1995.

Cunningham, Keith. *American Indians: Folk Tales & Legends.* Hertfordshire, England: Wordsworth Editions Limited, 2001.

Curtis, Edwards. *The North American Indian.* Los Angeles: Taschen, GmbH, 2005.

Debo, Angie. *Geronimo: The Man, His Time, His Place.* Norman: University of Oklahoma Press, 1989.

Edmonds, Margot and Clark, Ellae. *Voices of the Winds: Native American Legends.* New York: Facts On File, 1989.

Goodchild, Peter. *Survival Skills of the North American Indians.* Chicago: Chicago Review Press, 1984.

Hardin, Terri. *Legends & Lore of The American Indian.* New York: Barnes & Noble, 1993.

Hillerman, Tony. *The Great Taos Bank Robbery and Other Indian Country Affairs.* Albuquerque, New Mexico: University of New Mexico Press, 1991.

Hook, Jason. *The American Plains Indians.* (Osprey Men-At-Arms series). London: Osprey Publishing, 1985.

Hook, Jason. *The Apaches.* (Osprey Men-At-Arms series). London: Osprey Publishing, 1987.

Hungary Wolf, Adolph. *Traditional Dress: Knowledge and Methods of Old-Time Clothings.* Summertown, Tennessee: Book Publishing Company, 1990.

Hunt, W. Ben. *The Complete How-to Book of Indiancraft.* New York: MacMillan Publishing Co., 1973.

The Indian Texans. San Antonio, Texas: The University of Texas Institute of Texan Cultures, 1989.

Jahoda, Gloria. *The Trail of Tears: The Story of the American Indian Removals, 1813-1855.* New York: Wings Books, 1995.

Jones, Douglas C. *Arrest Sitting Bull.* New York: Charles Scribner's Son, 1977.

Josephy, Jr., Alvin M. *The Indian Heritage of America.* Boston: Houghton Mifflin Company, 1991.

Kelly, Fanny. *Narrative of My Captivity Among the Sioux Indians.* New York: Konecky & Konecky, 1990.

Künstler, Mort. *Mort Künstler's Old West: Indians.* Nashville: Rutledge Hill Press, 1998.

Orchard, William C. *Beads and Beadwork of the American Indian.* New York: Museum of the American Indian and Heye Foundation, 1975.

Reedstrom: E. Lisle. *Apache Wars: An Illustrated Battle History.* New York: Barnes & Noble Books, 1995.

Shultz, J.W. *My Life as an Indian.* New York: Fawcett Columbine, 1881.

Smith, Carter, editor. *Native Americans of the West: A Sourcebook On The American West.* Brookfield, Connecticut: The Millbrook Press, 1992.

Smith, Monte. *Traditional Indian Crafts.* Ogden, Utah: Eagle's View Publishing Company, 1986.

Atwood, Mary Dean. Spirit Healing: *Native American Magic & Medicine.* New York: Sterling Publishing Co., 1991.

Stoutenburgh, John, Jr. *Dictionary of the American Indian.* New York: Random House, 1990.

Taylor, Colin F., editor. *The Native Americans: The Indigenous People of North America.* New York: Smithmark Publications, 1991.

Taylor, Colin F., editor. *The Plains Indians: A Cultural and Historical View of the North American Plains Tribes of the Pre-reservation Period.* New York: Cresent Books, 1994.

Thom, Laine, editor. *Becoming Brave: The Path to Native American Manhood.* San Francisco: Chronicle Books, 1992.

Tomkins, William. *Indian Sign Language.* New York: Dover Publications, 1969.

Waldman, Carl. *Encyclopedia of Native American Tribes, Third Edition.* New York: Infobase Publishing, 2006.

West, Elliott. *The Way to the West: Essays on the Central Plains.* Albuquerque: University of New Mexico Press, 1995.

White, Jon Manchip. *Everyday Life of the North American Indian.* New York: Indian Head Books, 1979.

Woodhead, Henry and the editors of Time-Life Books. *The First Americans* (the American Indian series). Alexandria, Virginia: Time-Life Books, 1992.

Woodhead, Henry and the editors of Time-Life Books. *The Spirit World* (the American Indian series). Alexandria, Virginia: Time-Life Books, 1992.

Woodhead, Henry and the editors of Time-Life Books. *The Buffalo Hunters.* (the American Indian series). Alexandria, Virginia: Time-Life Books, 1993.

Woodhead, Henry and the editors of Time-Life Books. *Realm of the Iroquois.* (the American Indian series). Alexandria, Virginia: Time-Life Books, 1992.

XIV. THE TELEVISION WESTERN

Jackson, Ronald. *Classic TV Westerns.* New York: Citadel Press Book, Carol Publishing Group, 1994.

Milch, David. *Deadwood: Stories of the Black Hills.* New York: Charles Melcher, 2006.

Summers, Neil. *The First Official TV Western Book.* Vienna, West Virginia: Old West Shop Publishing, 1987.

Summers, Neil. *The Official TV Western Book Volume II.* Vienna, West Virginia: Old West Shop Publishing, 1989.

Summers, Neil. *The Official TV Western Book Volume III.* Vienna, West Virginia: Old West Shop Publishing, 1991.

Summers, Neil. *The Official TV Western Book Volume IV.* Vienna, West Virginia: Old West Shop Publishing, 1992.

Summers, Neil. *The Unsung Heroes.* Vienna, West Virginia: The Old West Shop Publishing, 1996.

XV. THE WESTERN RAILROAD

Abdill, George B. *Rails West.* New York: Bonanza Books, 1960.

Adams, Kramer A. *Logging Railroads of the West.* N.Y.: Bonanza Books, 1961.

Alexander, Edwin P. *Down At the Depot:American Railroad Stations From 1831 to 1920.* New York: Bramhall House, 1970.

Alexander, Edwin P. *Iron Horses:American Locomotives 1829-1900.* New York: Bonanza Books, 1941.

Beebe, Lucius and Clegg, Charles. *The Age of Steam.* New York: Promontory Press, 1990.

Beebe, Lucius and Clegg, Charles. *The Trains We Rode.* New York: Promontory Press, 1990.

Brown, Dee. *Hear That Lonesome Whistle Blow: Railroads in the West.* New York: Simon & Schuster, 1977.

Botkin, B.A. and Harlow, Alvin F. *A Treasury of Railroad Folklore.* New York: Bonanza Books, 1989.

Brown, Dee. *Hear That Lonesome Whistle Blow: Railroads in the West.* New York: Simon & Schuster, 1994.

Cahill, Marie and Debolski, Tom. *North American Steam:A Photographic History.* New York: Crescent Books, 1991.

Chappell, Gordon and Hauck, Cornelius W. *Narrow Gauge Transcontinental:Through Gunnison Country and Black Canyon Revisited.* Golden Colorado: Colorado Railroad Historical Foundation, 1971.

DeNevi, Don. *Western Train Robberies.* Millbrae, California: Celestial Arts, 1976.

Ellis, Hamilton C. *The Lore of the Train.* New York: Crescent Books, 1987.

Erbsen, Wayne. *Singing Rails: Railroadin' Songs, Jokes & Stories.* Asheville, North Carolina: Native Ground Music, 1997.

Erbsen, Wayne. *Railroad Fever: Songs, Jokes and Train Lore.* North Carolina: Native Ground Music, 1998.

Feitz, Leland. *Cripple Creek Railroads:The Rail Systems of the Gold Camp.* Colorado Springs, Colorado: Little London Press, 1991.

Fisher, Kay. *A Baggage Car With Lace Curtains.* Colfax, CA: B&K Fisher, 1986.

Harter, Jim. *World Railroads of the Nineteenth Century:A Pictorial History in Victorian Emgravings.* Baltimore: John Hopkins University Press, 2005.

Hughes, Timothy, editor. *Trans-Continential Excursion: 1870.* Boston Board of Trade. Williamsport, Pennsylvania: Hughes, 1981.

Jensen, Oliver. *The American Heritage History of Railroads in America.* New York: Bonanza Books, 1975.

Jensen, Larry. *The Movie Railroads.* Burbank, CA: Darwin Publications, 1981.

Krause, John and Grenard, Ross. *Colorado Memories of the Narrow Gauge Circle.* Newton, New Jersey: Carstens Publications, 1988.

Lone, Carl. *Journeys By Rail.* New York: Mallard Press, 1992.

Lyle, Katie Letcher. *Scalded to Death by the Steam.* Chapel Hill, North Carolina: Algonquin Books, 1988.

Myrick, David F. *New Mexico's Railroads: A Historical Survey.* Albuquerque: University of New Mexico Press, 1993.

Nordhoff, Charles. *C.P.R.R.: The Central Pacific Railroad.* Golden, Colorado: Outbooks, 1976.

Ogburn, Charlton. *Railroads: The Great American Adventure.* The National Geographic Society, 1977.

Patterson, Richard. *The Train Robbery Era: An Encyclopedic History.* Boulder, Colorado: Pruett Publishing Company, 1991.

Phillips, Lance. *Yonder Comes the Train: The Story of The Iron Horse And Some of The Roads It Travelled.* New York: Galahad Books, 1986.

Polkinghorn, R.S. *Pino Grande: Logging Railroads of the Michigan-California Lumber Co.* Glendale, California: Trans-Anglo Books, 1984.

Porter, Horace. *Railway Passenger Travel: 1825-1880.* Maynard Mass.: Chandler Press, 1987.

Rae, William Fraser. *Westward by Rail: The New Route to the East.* New York: Indian Head Books, 1993.

Reed, Robert C. *Train Wrecks: A Pictorial History of Accidents on the Main Line.* New York: Bonanza Books, 1968.

Solomon, Brian. *Trains of the Old West.* New York: Michael Friedman Publishing Group, 1998.

Thompson, Ian. *Narrow Gauge Railroading.* Cortez, Colorado: William and Merrie Winkler, 1984.

Wheeler, Keith. *The Railroads.* Alexandria, Virginia: Time-Life Books (Old West Series), 1973.

Wood, John V. *Railroads Through The Coeur d'Alenes.* Caldwell, Idaho: Caxton Printers Ltd., 1983.

Yenne, Bill. *The Romance & Folklore of North America's Railroads.* New York: Smith Mark Publications, 1994.

Zauner, Phyllis. *The Train Whistle's Echo: Story of the Western Railroad Era.* Tahoe Paradise, California: Zanel Publications, 1981.

XVI. WESTERN PLACE NAMES

Cheney, Roberta Carkeek. *Names on the Faces of Montana.* Missoula, Montana: Mountain Press Publishing Company, 1983.

Stewart, George R. *A Concise Dictionary of American Place-Names.* New York: Oxford University Press, 1970.

Tarpley, Fred. *1001 Texas Place Names.* Austin: University of Texas Press, 1980.

Urbanek, Mae. *Wyoming Place Names.* Missoula, Montana: Mountain Press Publishing Company, 1988.

XVII. THE WESTERN LANDSCAPE

Fischer, Pierre C. *70 Common Cacti of the Southwest.* Tucson, Arizona: Southwest Parks and Monuments Association, 1989.

MacMahon, James A. *Deserts* (Audubon Society Nature Guides). New York: Alfred A. Knopf, 1990.

Murray, John A. *Cactus Country: An Illustrated Guide.* Boulder, Colorado: Roberts Rinehart Publishers, 1996.

Prescott, Jerome, editor. *The Unspoiled West: The Western Landscape As Seen By Its Greatest Photographers.* New York: Smithmark Publishers, 1994.

Woodall, Ronald and Watkins, T.H. *Taken by the Wind: Vanishing Architecture of the West.* New York: Little, Brown And Company, 1977.

XVIII. THE LAWMEN

Binkley, William C. *The Texas Revolution.* Austin, Texas: The Texas State Historical Association, 1979.

Cox, Mike. *Texas Ranger Tales. Stories That Need Telling.* Plano, Texas: Republic of Texas Press/Woodware Publishing, 1997.

Hardin, Stephen. *The Texas Rangers* (the Elite series). London: Osprey Publishing Ltd., 1991.

Haythornthwaite, Philip. *The Alamo and the War of Texas Indepencence 1835-36* (Osprey Men-At-Arms series). London: Osprey Publishing, 1986.

Harrigan, Stephen. *The Gates of the Alamo.* New York: Alfred A. Knopf, 2000.

Lind, Michael. *The Alamo: An Epic.* New York: Houghton Mifflin Company, 1997.

Long, Jeff. *Duel of Eagles: The Mexican and U.S. Fight for the Alamo.* New York: William Morrow and Company, 1990.

MacKay, James. *Allan Pinkerton: The First Private Eye.* Edison, New Jersey: Castle Books, 2007.

Nelson, George. *The Alamo: An Illustrated History.* Dry Frio Canyon, Texas: Aldine Press, 1998.

Peña, José Enrique de la. *With Santa Anna in Texas: Narrative of the Revolution.* College Station, Texas: Texas A&M University Press, 1975.

Reid, Stuart. *The Texas Army 1835-1846.* Osprey Men-at-Arms Series. Elms Court, United Kingdom: Osprey Publishing Ltd, 2003.

Robinson III, Charles M. *American Frontier Lawmen, 1850-1930.* New York: Osprey Publishing Ltd., 2005.

Robinson III, Charles M. *The Men Who Wear the Star.* New York: The Modern Library, 2001.

Shirley, Glenn. *Law West Of Fort Smith.* Lincoln: U. of Nebraska Press, 1968.

Siringo, Charles A. *A Cowboy Detective: A True Story of Twenty-Two Years With a World-Famous Detective Agency.* Lincoln: University of Nebraska Press, 1988 (1912 reprint).

Tinkle, Lon. *The Alamo.* New York: McGraw-Hill Book Company, 1958.
Thompson, Frank. *Alamo Movies.* East Berlin, PA: Old Mill Books, 1991.

IXX. THE MINERS

Bancroft, Caroline. *Colorado's Lost Gold Mines and Buried Treasure.*
Boulder, Colorado: Johnson Books, 1995.
Bancroft, Caroline. *Tabor's Matchless Mine and Lusty Leadville.* Boulder
Colorado: Johnson Books, 1990.
Bancroft, Caroline. *Unique Ghost Towns and Mountain Spots.* Boulder,
Colorado: Johnson Books, 1990.
Bond Jr., Marshall. *Gold Hunter: The Adventures of Marshall Bond.*
Albuquerque: University of New Mexico Press, 1969.
Bird, Allan G. *Bordellos of Blair Street: The Story of Silverton, Colorado's
Notorious Red Light District.* Pierson, Michigan: Advertising, Publications &
Consultants, 1993.
Bolotin, Norman. *A Klondike Scrapbook: Ordinary People, Extraordinary
Times.* San Francisco: Chronicle Books, 1987.
Buys, Christian J. *A Quick History of Leadville.* Montrose, Colorado: Western
Reflections Publishing Company, 2004.
Clifford, Howard. *The Skagway Story.* Anchorage: Northwest Books, 1990.
Carr, Stephen L. *The Historical Guide to Utah Ghost Towns, Third Edition,
1990.* Salt lake City, Utah: Western Epics, 1972.
Cohen, Stan. *The Streets Were Paved With Gold: A Pictorial History of the
Klondike Gold Rush 1896-1899.* Missoula, Montana: Pictorial Histories
Publishing Co., 1977.
Conlin, Joseph R. *Bacon, Beans and Galantines: Food and Foodways on the
Western Mining Frontier.* Reno, Nevada: University of Nebraska Press, 1986.
Cunningham, Chet. *Cripple Creek Bonanza.* Plano, Texas: Republic of Texas
Press, 1996.
Feitz, Leland. *Victor: Colorado's City of Mines.* Colorado Springs, Colorado:
Little London Press, 1969.
DeJauregui, Ruth E. *Ghost Towns.* New York: Crescent Books, 1998.
Downs, Art. Wagon *Road North: Saga of the Cariboo Gold Rush.* Surrey, B.C.:
Heritage House Publishing Company Ltd.
Feitz, Leland. *Cripple Creek!: A Quick History of the World's Greatest Gold
Camp.* Colorado Springs, Colorado: Little London Press, 1979.
Feitz, Leland. *Victor: Colorado's City of Mines.* Colorado Springs, Colorado:
Little London Press, 1969.
Frady, Steven R. *Red Shirts and Leather Helmets: Volunteer Fire Fighting in
the Comstock Lode.* Reno Nevada: University of Nevada Press, 1984.
Graves, F. Lee. *Bannack: Cradle of Montana.* Helena, Montana: Montana
Magazine, American & World Geographic Publishing: 1991.
Grimstad, Bill. *The Last Gold Rush: A Pictorial History of the Cripple Creek
& Victor Gold Mining District.* Victor, Colorado: Pollux Press, 1983.

Harris, Lorraine. *Barkerville, The Town That Gold Built.* Surrey, B.C.: Hancock House Publishers LTD., 1984.

Jameson, W.C. *Buried Treasures of the American Southwest: Legends of Lost Mines, Hidden Payrolls and Spanish Gold.* Little Rock, Arkansas: August House, 1989.

Johnson, Robert Neil. *Southwestern Ghost Town Atlas.* Susanville, California: Cy Johnson & Son, 1968.

Johnson, William Weber and the editors of Time-Life Books. *The Forty-Niners* (the Old West series). New York: Time-Life Books, 1974.

Kamphausen, Dana Dunbar. *The Central City Story.* Idaho Springs, Colorado: The Dana Company, 1976.

Lawliss, Chuck. *Ghost Towns, Gamblers and Gold.* N.Y.: Gallery Books, 1985.

Lee, Mable Barbee. *Cripple Creek Days.* Lincoln: University of Nebraska Press, 1984.

Leisk, Alan E. *The Tommy Knockers.* New York: Carlton Press, 1987.

Marryat, Frank. *Mountains and Molehills* (Classics of the Old West series). Alexandria, Virginia: Time-Life Books, 1982.

Margo, Elizabeth. *Women of the Gold Rush.* N.Y.: Indian Head Books, 1992.

McDonald, Douglas. *Bodie: Boomtown-Goldtown! The Last of California's Old-Time Mining Camps.* Las Vegas: Nevada Publications, 1988.

McDonald, Douglas. *Virginia City and the Silver Region of the Comstock Lode.* Las Vegas: Nevada Publications, 1982.

Miller, Donald C. *Ghost Towns of Montana.* Boulder, Colorado: Pruett Publishing Company, 1981.

Paher, Stanley W. *Nevada Ghost Towns & Mining Camps.* Las Vegas, Nevada: Nevada Publications, 1999.

Ragsdale, Kenneth Baxter. *Quicksilver: Terlingua and the Chisos Mining Company.* College Station, Texas: Texas A&M University Press, 1976.

Sievert, Ken & Sievert Ellen. *Virginia City and Alder Gulch.* Helena, MT: Montana Magazine and American & World Geographic Publishing, 1993.

Stoehr, Eric C. *Bonanza Victorian: Architecture and Society in Colorado Mining Towns.* Albuquerque: University of New Mexico Press, 1975.

Turnbull, Elsie G. *Ghost Towns and Drowned Towns of West Kootenay.* Surrey, B.C.: Heritage House Publishing Company Ltd., 2001.

Varney, Philip. *New Mexico's Best Ghost Towns.* University of New Mexico Press, Albuquerque, New Mexico, 1981.

Voynick, Stephen M. *Leadville: A Miner's Epic.* Missoula, Montana: Mounatain Press Publishing Company, 1992.

Wallace, Robert and the editors of Time-Life Books. *The Miners* (the Old West series). New York: Time-Life Books, 1976.

Weis, Norman D. *Ghost Towns Of The Northwest.* Caldwell, Idaho: The Caxton Printers, Ltd., 1993.

Wrisley, Kristin. *The Mother Lode: A Celebration of California's Gold Country.* San Francisco: Chronicle Books, 1999.

XX. WESTERN BALLADS

Crawford, Richard, intro. *The Civil War Songbook: Complete Original Sheet Music for 37 Songs.* New York: Dover Publications, 1977.

Edwards, Don. *Classic Cowboy Songs.* Salt Lake City: Gibbs-Smith, 1994.

Erbsen, Wayne. *Outlaw Ballads, Legends and Lore.* Asheville, North Carolina: Native Ground Music, 1996.

Erbsen, Wayne. *Railroad Fever: Songs, Jokes and Train Lore.* North Carolina: Native Ground Music, 1998.

Erbsen, Wayne. *Humorous Cowboy Poetry: A Knee-Slappin' Gathering.* Salt Lake City: Gibbs-Smith Publisher, 1995.

Silber, Irwin. *Songs of the Great American West.* New York: Dover Publications, 1995.

XXI. WESTERN WORDS AND PHRASES

Adams, Ramon F. *A Dictionary of the American West.* Norman: University of Oklahoma Press, 1968.

Black, Donald Chain. *Handy as Hip Pockets on a Hog: The Colorful Language of the American Southwest.* Dallas: Taylor Publishing Company, 1989.

Chariton, Wallace O. *This Dog'll Hunt.* Plano, Texas: Wordware Publishing, Inc., 1989.

Chariton, Wallace O. *That Cat Won't Flush.* Plano, Texas: Wordware Publishing, Inc., 1991.

Dobie, J. Frank. *Tales of Old-Time Texas.* Boston: Little, Brown and Co., 1955.

Funk, Charles E. *A Hog On Ice.* New York: Harper Colophon Books, 1985.

Funk, Charles E. *Thereby Hangs A Tale.* New York: Perennial Library, 1985.

Funk, Charles E. *Heavens to Betsy!* New York: Perennial Library, 1986.

Funk, Charles E. *Horsefeathers & Other Curious Words.* New York: Perennial Library, 1986.

Mathews, Mitford M., editor. *A Dictionary of Americanisms.* Chicago: University of Chicago Press, 1951.

Slatta, Richard. *The Cowboy Encyclopedia.* New York: W.W. Norton & Company, 1994.

Wilder, Roy Jr. *You All Spoken Here.* New York: Viking Penguin Inc, 1984.

XXII. ODDS AND ENDS

Barlow, Ronald S. *The Vanishing American Outhouse.* El Cajon, California: Windmill Publishing Company, 1985.

Hale, Leon. *Texas Outback.* Austin,Texas: Madrona Press, 1973.
Fannin, Angela Farris and Fannin, Jerry W. *Johnnies, Biffies, Outhouses, Etc.* Burnet,Texas: Eakin Press, 1980.
Jakes, John, editor. *A Century of Great Western Stories:An Anthology of Western Fiction.* New York:Tom Doherty Associates, 2000.
L'Amour, Angelique, editor. *A Trail of Memories:The Quotations of L'Amour.* New York: Bantam Books, 1988.
L'Amour, Louis. *The Collected Short Stories of Louis L'Amour:The Frontier Stories:Volume Two.* New York: Random House, Inc., 2004.
McCutcheon, Marc. *Everyday Life in the 1800's:A Guide for Writers, Students & Historians.* Cincinnati, Ohio:Writer's Digest Books, 1993.
Randisi, Robert, editor. *Boot Hill:An Anthology of the West.* New York:Tom Doherty Associates, LLC, 2003.
Wheeler, Richard S., editor. *The Best of Spur Award-Winning Authors.* New York: New American Library, 2000.

THE MYTH OF THE WEST & ANALYSIS

Knowles, Thomas W., and Lansdale, Joe R. *Wild West Show!* New York: Wings Books, 1994.
Kreyche, Gerald F. *Visions of the American West.* Lexington, Kentucky: University Press of Kentucky, 1989.
O'Neil, Paul and the editors of Time-Life Books. *The End and the Myth* (the Old West series).Alexandria,Virginia:Time-LIfe Books, 1979.
Steiner, Stan. *The Waning of the West.* New York: St. Martin's Press, 1989.
Turner, Frederick Jackson. *History, Frontier and Section:Three Essays by Frederick Jackson Turner.* Albuquerque: University of New Mexico Press, 1993 (reprint).
Turner, Frederick. *Of Chiles, Cacti, and Fighting Cocks:Notes on the American West.* New York: Henry Hold and Company, 1996.
Webb, Walter Prescott. *The Great Frontier.* Lincoln, Nebraska: University of Nebraska Press, 1986.
White, Richard and Limerick, Patricia Nelson. *The Frontier in American Culture.* Berkeley, California: University of California Press, 1994.

WESTERN ART & WESTERN CARTOONS

Aldrich, Lanning, editor. *The Western Art of Charles M. Russell.* New York: Ballantine Books/Randon House, 1975.
Best of the West (series of books). Longwood, Florida:AC Comics/Paragon Publications, 1999.
Bruce, Chris, *Myth of the West.* Seattle,Washington: Henry Art Gallery, University of Washington, 1990.
Charlier, Jean-Michel and Giraud, Jean "Moebius." *Blueberry 1: Chihuahua Pearl.* New York: Epic Comics, 1991. (Other volumes available)
Cromwell J. and Ruffner, *Desperadoes:Volume One.* North Hampton, MA: Tundra Publishing LTD, 1992.
Easter, Deborah, editor. *Myth of the West.* Seattle,Washington: University of Washington, 1990.

Erwin, A.W. *Hooves & Horns* (four volumes). Graham,Texas: Hooves & Horns Cowtoons, 1994.

Ewers, John C. *Artists of the Old West.* Garden City, New York: Doubleday & Company, 1973.

Jackson, Jack. *Lost Cause:The True Story of Famed Texas Gunslinger John Wesley Hardin.* North Hampton, Massachusetts: Kitchen Sink Press, 1998.

Grafton, John. *The American West in the Nineteenth Century: 225 Illustrations from "Harper's Weekly" and Other Contemporary Sources.* New York: Dover Publications, 1992.

Kelton, Elmer. *The Art of Frank C. McCarthy.* New York:William Morrow and Company, 1992.

Kelton, Elmer. *The Art of James Bama.* Trumbull, Connecticut:The Greenwich Workshop, 1993.

Kubert, Jo & Infantino, Carmine. *Jesse James: Classic Western Collection.* Somerset, New Jersey:Vanguard Productions, 2001.

Künstler, Mort. *Mort Künstler's Old West Cowboys.* Nashville,Tennessee: Rutledge Hill Press, 1998.

Paintings & Sketches by Charles M. Russell. Terrell Publishing Company, 1993.

Lynde, Stan. *Rick O'Shay, Hipshot, and Me.* Billings, Montana: Cottonwood Graphics, 1990. (Other books of his art are available, including "Partners", "Ladigo","Rick O'Shay:The Dailies" and "A Month of Sundays—The Best of Rick O'Shay and Hipshot".)

McCaulley, Bud. *McCaulley Did It.* Amarillo,Texas:Trafton & Autry, Printers, 1971.

Read-Miller, Cynthia, intro. *Main Street, U.S.A. in Early Photographs.* New York: Dover Publications, 1988..

Reed, Walt, editor. *The Western Art of Harold Von Schmidt.* New York: Peacock Press/Bantam Books, 1976.

Reid, Ace. *Ace Reid and the Cowpokes Cartoon.* Austin,Texas: University of Texas Press, 1999.

Reynolds, Patrick M. *Illustrated Texas Lore* (series of books).Willow Street, Pennsylvania:The Red Rose Studio, 1989.

Ryan, T.K. *Presenting the Best of Tumbleweeds.* Boca Raton, Florida: Cool Hand Communications, 1993.

Storz, Frank, editor. *The Western Paintings of Frank C. McCarthy.* New York: Ballantine Books, 1976.

Turner, George. *George Turner's Book of American Indians:True Tales of Great Warriors.* Amarillo,Texas: Baxter Lane, 1998.

Vatine, Oliver and Clément, Alain. *Trio Grande:Adios Palomita.* North Hampton, Massachusetts:Tundra Publishing Ltd., 1993.

Whalen, John. *How the West Was Really Won! The Big Book of the Weird Wild West.* New York: Paradox Press, 1998.

Willoughby, Jim. *Cowboy Country Cartoons:A Cartoon Excursion Through the Whimsical West of Jim Willoughby.* Phoenix,Arizona: Golden West Publishers, 1988.

Wister, Owen. *The Illustrations of Frederic Remington.* New York: Crown Publishers, 1970.

XII. Being a New and Original Exploration, in Art and Words, Into the Life and Times of the American Cowboy. Birmingham, Alabama: Oxmoor House, 1975.

COOKBOOKS

Hanson, James A. and Wilson, Kathryn J. *The Buckskinner's Cook Book.* Chadron, Nebraska: The Fur Press, 1979.

Hughes, Stella. *Bacon and Beans: Ranch-Country Recipes.* Colorado Springs, Colorado: Western Horseman, 1990.

Leslie, Eliza. *Seventy-Five Recipes for Pastry, Cakes and Sweetmeats.* Chester, Connecticut: Applewood Books/Globe Pequot Press, 1828.

Medley, Wild Wes. *Original Cowboy Cookbook: Recipes from 1840's.* Hurricane, West Virginia: Wes Medley-Original Western Publications, 1989.

Rodgers, Rick. *Mississippi Memories: Classic American Cooking from the Heartland to the Louisiana Bayou.* New York: Hearst Books, 1994.

Simmons, Amelia. *The First American Cookbook: A Facsimilie of "American Cookery" By Amelia Simmons.* New York: Dover Publications, Inc., 1984.

Sloat, Caroline, editor. *Old Sturbridge Village CookBook: Authentic Early American Recipes for the Modern Kitchen.* Old Saybrook, Connecticut: The Globe Pequot Press, 1984.

PROFESSIONS & MEMOIRS

Batman, Richard. *James Pattie's West: The Dream and the Reality.* Norman: University of Oklahoma Press, 1984.

Bealer, Alex W. *The Art of Blacksmithing.* Edison, New Jersey: Castle Books/Book Sales, 1995.

Brown Dee. *Wonderous Times on the Frontier.* N.Y.: Harper Perennial, 1992.

Carter, Robert A. *Buffalo Billl Cody: The Man Behind the Legend.* New York: John Wiley & Sons, Inc., 2000.

Cody, William F. *The Life of Buffalo Bill.* Alexandria, Virginia: Time-Life Books, 1982. Orig. Pub. 1879.

Conrad, Howard L. *"Uncle Dick" Wooton* (Classics of the Old West series). Alexandria, Virginia: Time-Life Books, 1980. Orig. Pub. 1890.

Cook, James H. *50 Years on the Old Frontier.* Norman: University of Oklahoma Press, 1980. Orig. Pub. 1923.

Dary, David. *Entrepreneurs of the Old West.* Lincoln: University of Nebraska Press, 1986.

Dary, David. *Red Blood and Black Ink: Journalism in the Old West.* New York: Alfred A. Knopf, 1998.

Delano, A. *Life on the Plains and At the Diggings* (Classics of the Old West series). Alexandria, Virginia: Time-Life Books, 1981. Orig. Pub. 1854.

Dellenbaugh, Fredericks. *The Romance of the Colorado River* (Classics of the West series). Alexandria, Virginia: Time-Life Books, 1982. Orig. Pub 1902.

Drago, Harry Sinclair. *The Steamboaters: From the Early Side-Wheelers to the Big Packets.* New York: Bramhall House, 1968.

Hopkins, Virginia. *Pioneers of the Old West.* New York: Bonanza Books, 1988.

Laycock, George. *The Mountain Men.* Danbury, Connecticut: Outdoor Life Books, 1988.

Larkin, Jack. *The Reshaping of Everyday Life: 1790-1840.* New York: Harper & Row, 1988.

Lavender, David. *One Man's West.* Lincoln: University of Nebraska Press, 1977.

Luchetti, Cathy. *Under God's Spell: Frontier Evangelists, 1772-1915.* San Diego, California: Harcourt Brace Jovanovich, 1989.

Parkhill, Forbes. *The Wildest of the West.* N.Y.: Henry Holt and Company, 1951.

Samuel, Ray; Huber, Leonard V. and Ogden, Warren C. *Tales of the Mississippi.* Gretna, Louisiana: Pelican Publishing Company, 1981.

Sandoz, Mari. *The Beaver Men.* Lincoln, Nebraska: University of Nebraska Press, 1978. Orig. Pub. 1964.

Sandoz, Mari. *Old Jules: Portrait of a Pioneer.* New York: MJF Books, 1963. Orig Pub. 1935.

The Scouts (the Old West series). Alexandria, Virginia: Time-Life Books, 1978.

Shirley, Glen, editor. *Buckskin Joe: A Memoir by Edward Jonathan Hoyt.* Lincoln: University of Nebraska Press, 1966. Orig. pub. 1955.

Victor, Frances Fuller. *The River of the West: The Adventures of Joe Meek, Volume One: The Mountain* Years. Missoula, Montana: Mountain Press Publishing Company, 1983. Orig. Pub. 1870.

Victor, Francis Fuller. *The River of the West: The Adventures of Joe Meek, Volume Two: The Oregon Years.* Missoula, Montana: Mountain Press Publishing Company, 1985. Orig. Pub. 1870.

Watson, Aldrena. *The Blacksmith: Ironworker and Farrier.* New York: W.W. Norton & Company, 1990.

Wheeler, Keith and the editors of Time-Life Books. *The Chroniclers* (the Old West series). Alexandria, Virginia: Time-Life Books, 1976.

Williams, Richard L. and the editors of Time-Life Books. *The Loggers* (the Old West series). Alexandria, Virginia: Time-Life Books, 1977.

Wilson, R.L. & Martin, Greg. *Buffalo Bill's Wild West: An American Legend.* New York: Random House, 1998.

FOLKLORE

Ault, Phillip H. *The Home Book of Western Humor.* New York: Dodd, Mead & Company, 1967.

Brown, Lois, editor. *Tales of the Wild West.* New York: National Cowboy Hall of Fame/Random House, 1993.

Carmony, Neil B., and Brown, David E., editors. *Tough Times in Rough Places: Personal Narratives of Adventure, Death, and Survival on the Western Frontier.* Salt Lake City, Utah: The University of Utah Press, 2001.

Dobie, J. Frank. *Tales of Old-Time Texas.* Edison, New Jersey: Castle Books, 1955.

Howard, Robert E. *The Riot at Bucksnort and Other Western Tales.* Lincoln, Nebraska: University of Nebraska Press, 2005.

Howard Robert E. *The End of the Trail Western Stories.* Lincoln: University of Nebraska Press, 2005.

Laver, Charles D. *Tales of Arizona Territory.* Phoenix, Arizona: Golden West Publishers, 1990.

Meyers, John Myers. *The Westerners: A Roundup of Pioneer Reminiscences.* Lincoln: University of Nebraska Press, 1997.

Munn Debra D. *Big Sky Ghosts: Eerie True Tales of Montana: Volume One.* Pruett Publishing Company, Boulder, Colorado, 1993.

Parkhill, Forbes. *The Wildest of the West.* N.Y.: Henry Holt And Company, 1951.

Pronzini, Bill and Greenberg, Martin H. *Great Tales of the West.* New York: Galahad Books, 1982.

Smithwick, Noah. *The Evolution of a State or Recollections of Old Texas Days.* Austin. Texas: University of Texas Press, 1983.

Trimble, Marshal. *In Old Arizona: True Tales of the Wild Frontier!* Phoenix, Arizona: Golden West Publications, 1985.

Trimble, Marshal: *The Law of the Gun.* Phoenix, Arizona: Arizona Department of Transportation, 1997.

Water Trails West by The Western Writers of America. Garden City, New York: Doubleday & Company, Inc, 1978.

MISCELLANEOUS

The Afro-American Texans. San Antonio, Texas: University of Texas Institute of Texan Cultures, 1994.

Beard, Daniel. *The American Boy's Handy Book.* Mineola, New York: Dover Publications, Inc., 2003.

Black, Naomi. *Dude Ranches of the American West.* Lexington, Mass.: The Stephen Green Press, 1988.

Buffalo Bill and the Wild West. Brooklyn, New York: Brooklyn Museum, 1981.

Bowen, John. *Legendary Towns of the Old West.* New York: M&M Books, 1990.

Bullis, Don. *The Old West Trivia Book.* Baldwin Park, California: Gem Guides Book Company, 1993.

Daniels, George G. and the editors of Time-Life Books. *The Canadians* (the Old West series). Alexandria, Virginia: Time-Life Books, 1977.

Dary, David. *Entrepreneurs of the Old West.* New York: Alfred A. Knopf, 1986.

Dillon, Richard, editor. *Western Quotations: Famous Words From the American West.* Temple, Arizona: Four Peaks Press, 1993.

Enss, Chris. *How The West Was Worn: Bustles and Buckskins On The Wild Frontier.* Guilford, Connecticut: Globe Pequot Press, 2006.

Fischer, Christiane, editor. *Let Them Speak For Themselves: Women in the American West, 1849-1900.* New York: E.P. Dutton, 1978.

Grimm, Brothers. *Household Stories by the Brothers Grimm.* Mineola, New York: Dover Publications, Inc., 1963.

Horn, Huston and the editors of Time-Life Books. *The Pioneers* (the Old West series). Alexandria, Virginia: Time-Life Books, 1979.

Kalman, Bobbie. *Historic Communities: 19th Century Clothing.* New York: Crabtree Publishing Company, 1993.

Katz, William Loren. *The Black West.* New York: Simon & Schuster, 1996.

Luchetti, Cathy and Carol Olwell. *Women of the West.* New York: The Library of the American West/Orion Books, 1982.

O'Neil, Paul and the editors of Time-Life Books. *The Frontiersmen* (the Old West series). Alexandria, Virginia: Time-Life Books, 1977.

Powell, F.E. *Windmills and Wind Motors.* Lindsay Publications, Inc., Bradley, Illinois, 1985.

Reedstrom, E. Lisle. *Authentic Costumes & Characters of the Wild West.* New York: Sterling Publishing Co., 1986.

Reiter, Joan Swallow and the editors of Time-Life Books. *The Women* (the Old West series). Alexandria, Virginia: Time-Life Books, 1978.

The Spanish West (the Old West series). Alexandria: Time-Life Books, 1976.

Victorian Fashions & Costumes From Harper's Bazzar: 1867-1898. New York: Dover Publications, 1974.

Wexler, Bruce. *The Wild West Catalog.* Philadelphia: Running Press, 2008.

Starring John Wayne as Sheriff John T. Chance, Dean Martin as Dude, and Ricky Nelson as Colorado

Publicity still for *Rio Bravo*, Armanda Productions (author's collection)

Where To Find it?
INDEX OF CATEGORIES

"If there were no valleys of sadness and death,
we could never really appreciate the sunshine of
happiness on the mountain top."
—Roy Rogers

Well, finally, the index at the end of the book. Why not put it at the beginning? Is it easier for a right-handed person to use his left hand to thumb to the back of the book, or vice versa? But would the index be a boring, dull "chapter" to have at the *beginning* of the book? This book, as a compilation of miscellaneous information initially meant to be browsed, can then be used as a reference by referring to this index. But a comprehensive index with all the names and places mentioned in this book would be almost as long as the book itself, so this is a minimal list of "categories" to help you find what you want.

Where Can You Find It?

Thank you
Photo and Art Credits

*"He was so big that when he stood up,
his chair stood up with him."*
—Charles Marquis Warren speaking of Raymond Burr.

Most of the art and photographs in this book were created by the author, but grateful acknowledgment is made to all those who have granted permission to reprint copyrighted material. Every reasonable effort has been made to locate the copyright holders for these images. The publishers would be pleased to receive information that would allow them to rectify any omissions in future printings.

Kris Ford photos, pages 44, 142.
C.R. Nowell photo, page 716.
Dover Electronic Clip Art: 120 Great paintings of the American West, 2008, pages 18, 390, 441, 451, 452, 453, 454, 533, 534, 537.
Dover Electronic Clip Art: Cowboy and Western Cuts, 1998, used behind text.
Dover Electronic Clip Art: Horses, 2003, used behind text.
Glynda Smith Photography, pages 302, 338, 410, 575, 621, 638, 639, 640, 643.
Jo Hames Photos, pages 212, 594, 632.
Library of Congress Prints and Photographs Division, pages 26, 27, 42, 43, 132, 167, 174, 177, 337, 379, 383, 388, 396, 398, 400, 407, 427, 428, 455, 566.
Michael Jay Smith Photography, pages 67-71, 141, 143, 412, 652, 689.
National Archives and Records Administration, page 589.
Wikimedia Commons, pages 78, 155-157, 159, 171, 553.

Argosy Pictures, page 390.
Armanda Productions, page 715.
Arness Productions, page 328, 459.

Batjac Productions, page 584.
Bruce Landsbury Productions, page 474.
Campanile Productions, page 223.
Cinergi Pictures Entertainment, page 193.
Columbia Pictures, pages 260, 691.
De Passe Entertainment, page 222.
Fly "A" Productions, pages 264, 289.
Frontier Productions, page 469.
Hopalong Cassidy Productions, page 288.
John Ford productions, page 201.
Malpaso Company, page 229.
National Broadcasting Company, page 462.
MGM Television, page 474.
Paramount Pictures, pages 178, 183, 187, 211, 214, 226, 237, 238, 253.
Revue Studios, page 478.
Roy Rogers Productions, page 687.
Sanford Productions, pages 36, 679.
Stanley Cramer Productions, page 196.
TIG productions, page 435.
Touchstone Pictures, page 660.
United Artists, pages 181, 411.
Universal International Pictures, page 233.
Walt Disney Productions, pages 457, 467.
Warner Brothers, pages 189, 560, 564, 474.
Wyatt Earp Enterprises, 467.
ZIF Television Productions, page 469.

REV4

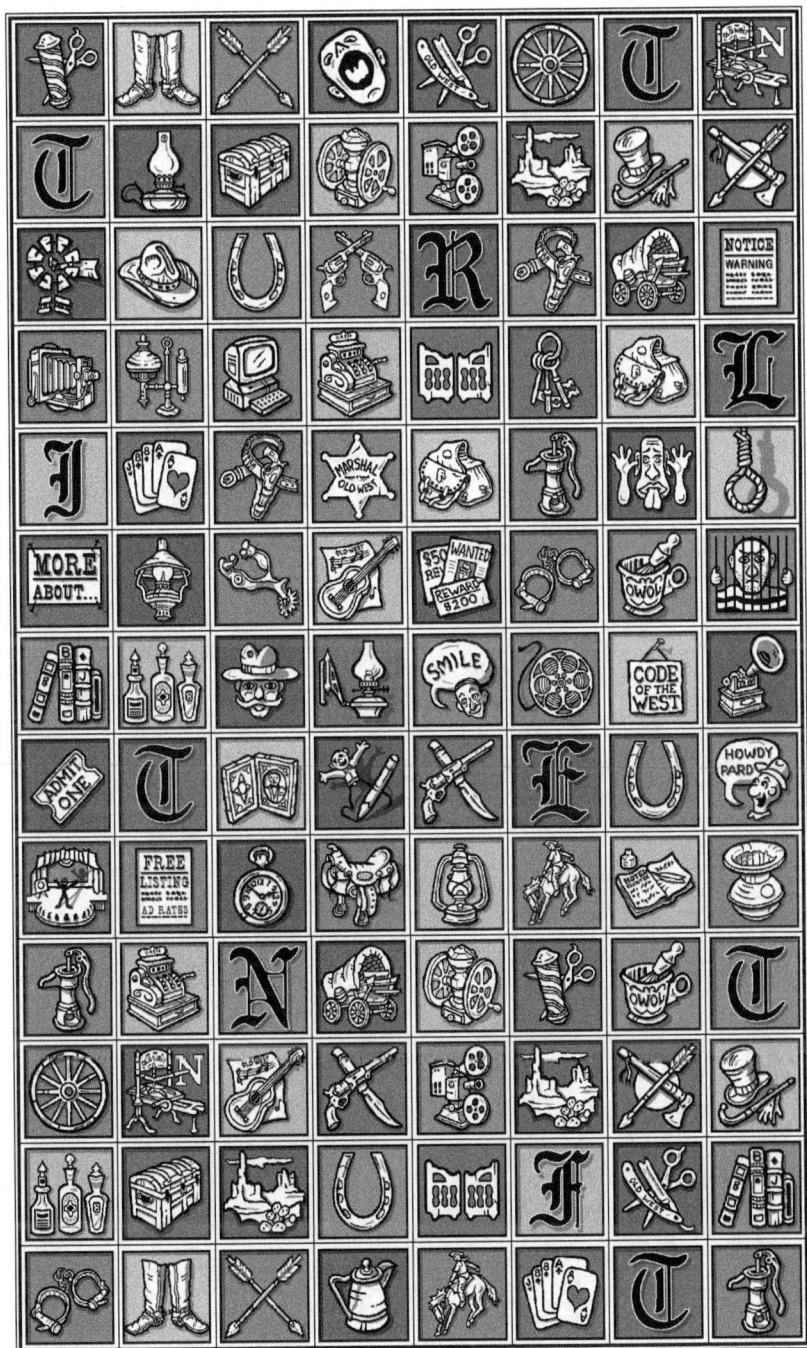

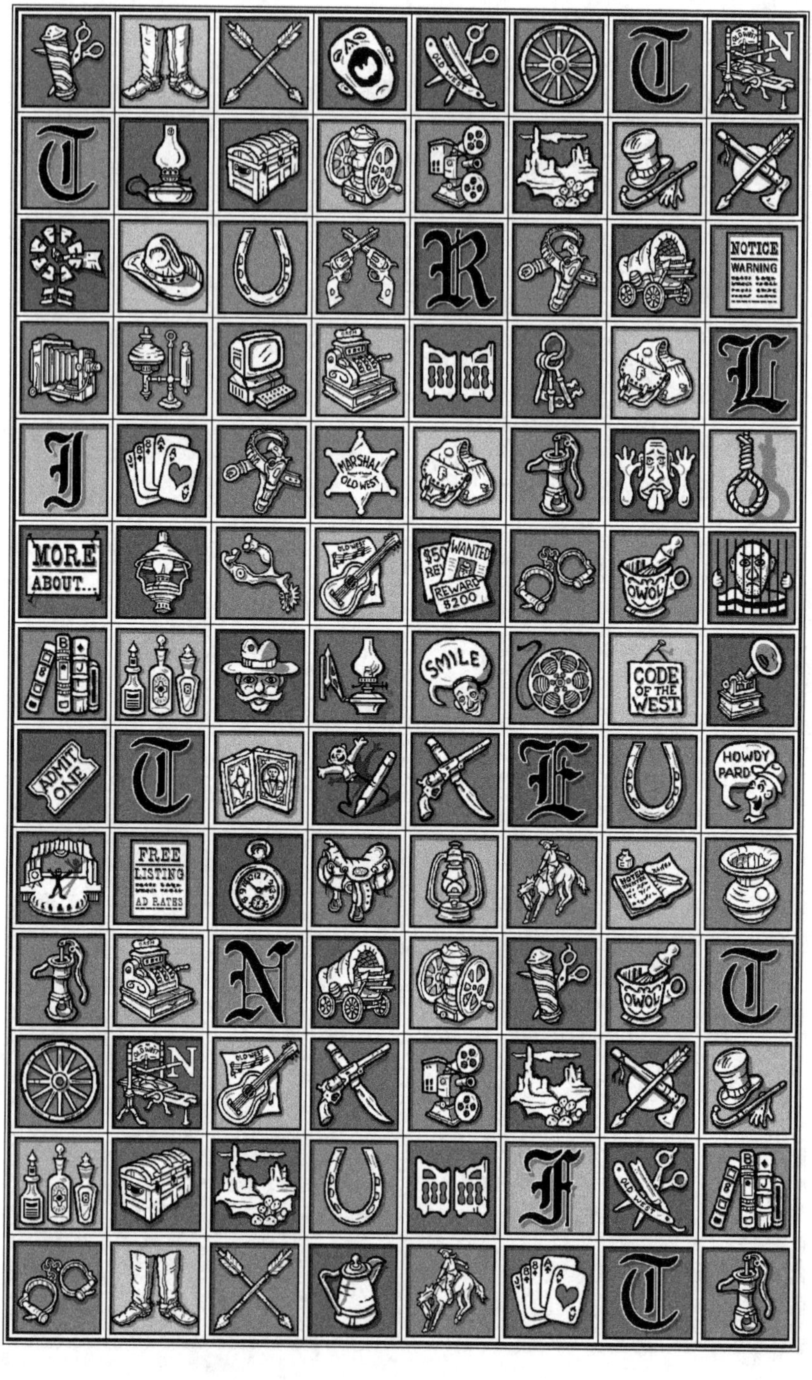
NOTICE
WARNING
MARSHAL
OLD WEST
MORE ABOUT...
WANTED
REWARD
$200
SMILE
CODE OF THE WEST
ADMIT ONE
HOWDY PARD
FREE LISTING
AD RATES

CPSIA information can be obtained
at www.ICGtesting.com
Printed in the USA
BVHW040900020419

544361BV00007B/29/P

9 780965 434119